War of Loyalties

By Schuyler McConkey

McConkey Press

Cover design by Damonza.

Published by McConkey Press

Printed in the United States of America

ISBN: 978-0-6929705-4-6

To Carrie-Grace
You were a faithful listening ear so many times.
This book belongs to you with all my love.

Chapters

Part One

Part Two

Part One

Chapter One
A Question of Duty

London, England – March 1917

Doctor Jaeryn Graham stepped out of his cab in front of a shop specializing in window glass exports. Devoid of aesthetic interest, but solid in its way. Inside, a radio droned out the latest war news and propaganda posters plastered the walls with bloodthirsty red slogans. Samples of frames and various types of glass lined the walls, displayed in well-ordered cabinets.

A young man in waistcoat and shirtsleeves sat behind a reception desk, keeping up the fiction of a clerk ready to show his wares. Only a select few knew the shop had a different purpose.

On his way through to the back hall, Jaeryn tipped a wink at the clerk. "How's business?"

The youth nodded in response. "Oh, just fine, doctor. Mr.

1

Ryson's waiting to see you. He thinks you're late."

"Let him, then. It's not easy to get from Folkestone to London with the train delays."

The doctor's jaw had a steely look about it as he entered Samuel Ryson's office. Closing the door behind him, he clenched one of his hands as the familiar breath of fear ghosted through him.

"Ah, Graham. I've been expecting you." His gray-haired supervisor motioned him to a seat. "I expect you are sufficiently recovered from your last escapade, hmm?"

"Completely." Jaeryn flexed his fingers at the mention of what he had just accomplished. They were straight and unblemished, except for two—and those two, crooked as they were, caused a proud lifting of his chin as if he would gladly have them over the eight whole ones.

Ryson grunted his approval. "You never take much time to get back on your feet. Did you establish contact with the agents in Folkestone?"

"I did. Our disgust was mutual."

"None of that. Once they know you weren't part of the Irish revolt, they'll come around to respect you. Were you able to purchase the medical practices?"

"Both of them, just as you wanted."

"Excellent. With two medical routes, you should have sufficient access to the people you'll need to know. Besides, it would look strange if you only had one, with your colleagues rushing off to the front. As it is, you might get some persecution, being a fit man and not enlisting."

Jaeryn made no effort to disguise his indifference. "There's not much anyone can do about it. No English bureaucrat can force an Irishman to enlist. It's the law."

"You do your countrymen no favors with such remarks." Ryson's eyes glared in frosty displeasure. He threw a quick glance at the door, making sure it was locked, then pulled a map out of a desk drawer and pointed to the lower portion of it. "Your practices are in Folkestone. Have you been able to establish a connection with Mr.

Emmerson in the northern area of town yet?"

"The MP? He was one of my first patients. He's dying. His heart won't hold out until summer."

"I heard. At the beginning of the war, he was a consultant for our War Cabinet. In January of this year, we audited his correspondence and found a letter asking if he had distributed code identities to certain unidentified contacts in Folkestone. Such a measure was neither initiated nor cleared by our office."

Jaeryn listened intently. "So you are assuming it could be a private venture?"

"We fear so. At the same time, we intercepted a list of troop observations put in a compromised drop location and headed overseas. Folkestone's location, with troop stations and overseas shipping so nearby, makes it a perfect observatory town for German spies. It would be a prime location from which to betray British interests. With major offensives in France being discussed, we can't afford to have insiders leaking troop information to the Germans ahead of time."

"So you want me to watch for signs of counter-intelligence?" Jaeryn pulled out a notebook and wrote down several details that he wished to take extra care to remember. Ryson hesitated when the Irishman put pen to paper, but he relaxed again as he saw that the words were not English, but Irish.

"Precisely. Find those code identities Emmerson spoke of and determine who they belong to. We think he may be growing a cell of agents for his own purposes. You will be in charge of discovering whether that is the case."

Jaeryn nodded his assent. "Anything more before I go?"

"Yes. We're writing to America for an assistant for you."

Jaeryn snapped his notebook shut. "I thought you said you trusted me. And why America?"

Ryson shook his head. "It's not the trust. The young man's father has connections in London and wants a career for his son in British Intelligence. He assured us it would be worth our while. His son has a talent for languages and could possibly give us a new foreign agent in time. Here's a picture."

Jaeryn took the photo and inspected it. The new agent was younger than he, if appearances were a good judge. The blue eyes and wavy brown hair could not have produced a sharper contrast to his own dark hair and slim form. Intelligent and definitely not Irish. He studied the details until they were burned in his memory. If this new development was what he thought it was, he was going to need every ounce of information he could get.

"What's his name?"

"Doctor Benjamin Dorroll. He'll be going by Dailey here." Ryson locked the picture back in the file cabinet behind his desk. "His father specifically requested that we place him with you."

Only a flicker of Jaeryn's eyelashes showed his surprise. "Did he? Why me?"

"Mr. Dorroll's reasons were not divulged to me by our superiors. He's an influential war consultant, and he was told to write to his son and offer the position. The service can't afford to lose a link to a person that could be a worthwhile asset."

"Curious."

"It is." Ryson lowered his voice, and Jaeryn leaned forward. "We're tracking his correspondence. Nothing so far. Whatever his reason for wanting his son to work with you, he won't say what it is. But he has enough influence with the War Office to make them acquiesce. I find the whole thing quite strange."

"Why?"

"I only knew of one son: an army captain, Edmond Dorroll. He's done well for himself in the war. This other son I had never heard of until his father requested the position for him. I cannot find any evidence that Benjamin Dorroll has been in England for some time. And I find it strange that Matthew Dorroll would want the position for the younger son instead of the older."

"Curious." The word lilted, long and drawn-out, and Jaeryn smiled again to himself. "Do you think Matthew Dorroll has some unknown interest in Folkestone?"

Ryson's angular face remained impassive. "Perhaps. Try to find out what his interest was in our placing his son with you specifically. We can't be too cautious. If Benjamin Dorroll accepts, you'll see him in May."

"Excellent, I'll be on the lookout for him." Jaeryn took the file folder and stepped to the door to unlock it.

"Graham." With the door unlocked, Ryson sank his voice to a mere whisper. "Much depends on this mission, and there are aspects of which I cannot yet speak. You have not failed us yet. Don't let this be the first time."

A golden glimmer sparkled in Jaeryn's eyes, and the flash of his white teeth appeared again. "I do not fear failure. I play to win."

And with that, he left by the back entrance. Instead of going straight home as he had originally planned, he walked a few blocks to execute a private commission of his own. He wanted to add a personal bodyguard to his operations as well as this new man—a bodyguard that he could choose himself. Just this morning, a death threat had been slipped through his mail slot. He suspected he was not entirely welcome in Folkestone. But if he told Ryson about it, Ryson would want to know why, and that would never do.

Once at the post office, Jaeryn scrawled out his message and handed it over to the plain-featured, red-headed girl running the telegraph. She wrinkled her nose as she tried to decipher his black smudge, then gave up and asked him to read it to her.

"Sorry," Jaeryn apologized. "It says: *Need help. Bit of a risk, but I'll make it worth your while. Meet me in Dover. J.*"

With his message sent, Jaeryn assessed the street for anyone who might be watching him. Satisfied that all was clear, he set off at a brisk pace toward Paddington Station. The dense London smog dimmed the streetlights to a dusty glow, and he was glad. It reduced his visibility to anyone attempting to observe his movements.

A member of parliament starting up a possible spy ring in Folkestone. Well, that was a step up from his other assignments.

Jaeryn rubbed his hands together. With six years of dedicated work to his credit, it was about time he got more trust.

And he wasn't about to hand his position to a replacement, either. After this last mission, he deserved his superior's trust. An Irishman didn't go through hell for nothing, especially for an Englishman.

* * *

Richmond, Virginia – April 1917

April 20th, 1917

Benjamin,

Far be it from me to force you into something you dislike, but I am grateful you are consenting to acknowledge your British heritage. I am pleased to hear that you applied yourself so steadily in school, for your French and German, as well as your Latin, will certainly be vital to your advancement. Your practitioner's degree will be of great benefit also, as many towns are short of medical help. Patriotic, indeed, to fill two posts of need for your mother country at the same time.

You may bring your wife and sister, of course. Your superiors will not place you in dangerous work, nor will you hold an official intelligence position until after you have completed your first assignment. You will be in a low-key setting, suited to your abilities, and therefore a family establishment will offer you even better concealment than if you came alone. I need not remind you that your wife should know little of your activities and nothing at all if you can manage it. Perhaps your duty to assist your native England will be enough to satisfy her, though I would not presume to offer you advice.

I have enclosed a cheque for the cost of your membership exam, which you are to take as soon as you reach England, and your registration for legal medical practice. Upon your successful completion of these tasks, you may report to the enclosed address to receive your first assignment. I myself will not be involved in your work; I merely requested the position for you. But if you feel inclined to write and tell me how your work progresses, I will receive your reports with interest.

* * *

When Mrs. O'Sean offered to spend the day helping them pack up, Ben jumped at the chance. She was an old friend, and it would be his last opportunity to see her before he set sail for England.

"I think we're almost finished, lad," the older woman said, as the afternoon drew to a close. "We're going to miss you, traipsing off to England like this."

"I wouldn't leave you if I could help it," Ben said, looking wistfully around the little sitting room, plucked bare of most of its furnishings. "I'll be back soon. Just a short assignment to oblige my father, and then I'm coming straight home."

She leaned over and patted his shoulder as she had countless times when he was small. "You don't sound too eager to go."

"Not especially," he admitted. "After I accepted, I heard more about Atlantic crossings."

A tight, worried silence stretched between them. "They haven't been safe for a long time," she said. "And now that America's in the war, they're even more dangerous. Didn't you know before?"

"I never cared." He drove the final nails in a box Mrs. O'Sean had handed to him. "I never had reason to. I worked at the clinic, and Charlotte worked at the hospital, and we were just starting to think about a family of our own. None of that over there mattered."

"You think it's safe to bring Charlotte with you, then?"

Ben stacked the box with the others, each filled with the things he and Charlotte had decided to leave behind. "No. I would have missed her terribly, but I wasn't fond of risking the crossing. We argued about it."

She smiled. "It looks like you didn't win that one."

He laughed in return. "She has a charming determination when she wants something. I'm picking up my sister tonight, too. Mother wants me to take Pearl off her hands, so I'm bringing her with us."

"How nice," Mrs. O'Sean said brightly. "Then you'll both be able to see your father."

His hand reached for the letter in his jacket pocket. The paper, covered with his father's decisive script, was ragged now. He had read it again and again—at breakfast, driving to see patients, waiting for Charlotte to get ready for bed—until the wear and tear of the handling had turned it so fragile he didn't dare to do more than carry it with him. But for all the readings, there was still one thing in it he couldn't find, and that worried him.

"Pearlie's never met him. That was enough to persuade her—" He broke off there. It had been enough to persuade her to a change of name and a new way of life. But neither of those things were permissible to speak of. "I don't think she realizes the actual danger of living in England, closer to the front."

Mrs. O'Sean stood with her hands on her hips, surveying the scattered odds and ends left to be wrapped in newspaper. "Why did you take it into your head to want an English practice, laddie? You don't like change."

His flaxen-haired young wife, clad in a linen skirt and coral shirtwaist, peeped around the doorframe and joined the conversation. "He tells me he's only doing his duty by my relatives." Her eyes sparkled, for Charlotte had none of his reservations about the move. "I have cousins in Folkestone—well, second cousins from my father. But really, he's going more because his father told him to." She glanced demurely at Ben and broke into her light, sweet laugh as he opened his mouth involuntarily to defend himself.

He remembered his decision as if he had made it that morning instead of one short month ago. His day at the clinic had started off routinely, with the low chatter of patients waiting for their turns. He still remembered his exultation when Doctor Randall offered to contract him as an official assistant, since his internship was drawing to a close—his eager acceptance—the bitter disappointment that followed. Everything came to a shocked standstill when the afternoon nurse burst in with a paper containing the declaration of war. Then he

8

came home to find the letter from his father on the kitchen table. He and Charlotte had talked it over the following night and well into the next morning. But as he finished the letter, a tug to see the father he had never known had made the decision before logic could decide.

"I never wanted to go to England," Ben said. "But I couldn't get seeing him out of my head. Just once. He's never asked for me until now."

Mrs. O'Sean nodded in approval. "A good choice. If you've prayed about it, and the good Lord told you that's where he wants you, then that's where you should go."

One bookshelf remained in the front room ready to dismantle. She removed Ben's medical books and put them in a storage box while he and Charlotte finished taking down the pictures. "I almost wish I was going with you," Mrs. O'Sean said, running a cloth over a dusty cover. "My oldest two are working in England, about as near the front as you can get. I haven't seen either of them since you headed off to college."

Ben brightened at the possibility of someone to remind him of friends back home. "I'll look them up. Where are they?"

Mrs. O'Sean looked doubtful. "Erin's in Dover. Turlough moves about so much, I don't know where you could find him. I always have my heart in my throat in between letters, hoping he hasn't gone to the trenches yet." She shook her head in fond sadness. "Not a church-going, respectable lad like you. I doubt you'd get on with him." She laid the last book safely in its box. "Well, I should go home before my menfolk get off work." Handing her borrowed apron to Charlotte, she reached out and hugged her good-bye. "Take care of your man in England, lass. Write me when you get settled." Her hands, worn and calloused from years of scrubbing clothes, patted his own as she let him go.

Charlotte opened the curtains so they could see her down the street. They knelt on the sofa and watched until she turned the corner. "I'm sure you'll miss her, darling." Charlotte drew the curtains closed again and looked around the bare walls of the dismantled room. "I think we're finished packing, thanks to her."

"I'm glad she came," Ben replied. He cast around for something to take his mind off the parting. The empty room reminded him too much of all that he had given up in the last week. "We have time for a soda before we pick up Pearlie, if you like."

Charlotte slipped her arms around his waist. "That sounds splendid. Give me five minutes to write my cousins. I want to mail the letter while we're out so it gets to them before our arrival."

He rubbed her shoulders to ease away the tiredness. "Remember to sign off with the surname they gave us, *ma chérie*. These relatives of yours don't know your married name, do they?"

"No. It's been years since I corresponded." A hesitant frown crept between Charlotte's pretty eyebrows—the first he had seen from her that day.

She'd promised not to ask for specifics, though even now that promise grieved him. Secrets were never wise between a husband and wife, and soon his whole career and half of his life would be concealed from her. Now, with steamer berths secured and departure less than four days away, second thoughts were rather pointless. Still, he couldn't resist trying the worn-out thread one last time. "I don't want to risk you on this trip. If you stayed with your parents—"

She looked up at him and rested her hands lightly on his shoulders. "I'm not going to leave you. You'll need me where we are going."

Holding her warmth, he drank in the sparkle from her eyes that life had never had cause to dull. His chest tightened at the thought of losing it. "There will be secrets between us. You will hate them. We're just a channel away from France and the battlefields, and you will see things that I never wanted you to see. War might touch you, and I couldn't bear that."

"I am a nurse, and I am strong enough. Besides, I would rather have you keep secrets to my face than write them in a letter. And we're not going to die on the crossing."

"How do you know that?"

She drew away from him and crossed her arms in defiance. "I have absolutely no intention of dying until after we have children."

As soon as the words left her mouth, she tilted her head, eyes dancing. He swallowed back mingled amusement and exasperation. "I wasn't aware the Germans took their orders from you."

She gave him a playful smile. "You see? I am an asset after all." Then she hugged him close. "It's only a detour. We will go, and then we will come home and make our life together the way we always wanted."

Charlotte left to write her letter and he stood in the empty room alone. What was it he had sworn to himself when war broke out between England and Germany three years ago? That he was not English and would have nothing to do with the war. He had kept his word. He had finished school, married Charlotte, and completed his residency year in Richmond, just as he had wanted to. But along with seeing his father, this new opportunity meant a higher income—and his creditors weren't getting any easier to ask extended deadlines from.

Benjamin Dorroll's mother, a southern belle of old colonial stock, had married a British seaman at twenty years of age. Two little boys and many disagreements later, she returned to America, disillusioned, penniless, and pregnant with a little girl. Matthew Dorroll had agreed to take Edmond. She took her younger son. Since neither felt confident of being able to procure a divorce, they left it at that. Life continued for the next nineteen years, with Ben thinking little of his European heritage and caring even less until the letter came from his father.

It mattered little, in the end, where he chose to place his allegiance. After America's declaration of war, defending one country meant defending the other. But no matter how many times he tried to comfort himself with that thought, Ben knew, deep down, that it did matter.

Ever since his four-year-old eyes had watched the dark waves of the Atlantic separate him from the Liverpool pier, Great Britain had carried the stigma of being the country that put him out, and America had become the land that took him in. Supporting one seemed a desertion of the other. His hand reached towards his pocket and almost involuntarily pulled out his father's letter again. Ben searched the lines for the one thing he hadn't been able to find—one sign that his father was eager to see him again. There was none. He sighed and tucked the ragged paper back in his pocket again.

* * *

London, England – May 22, 1917

Nothing had happened to take the responsibility of the decision out of his hands: neither the opinions of others before he left, nor the Atlantic crossing—which, while it kept them pinned to the rail scanning for signs of enemy engagement, turned out to be surprisingly non-eventful. Now here he was, a bewildered foreigner and freshly-registered medical assistant, standing in front of a window glass export company on a cool morning at the end of May. The name on the business card his father had sent him read "Samuel Ryson." Ben clutched the strip of pasteboard as if it would infuse some confidence in him when the time came to meet the man.

He found the door unlocked, so he walked in and looked about him. A young clerk threw aside some papers and came to greet him, pulling down his shirt sleeves as he did so. "Excuse me, sir. You were looking for…?"

"Samuel Ryson," Ben said. His voice dropped down even lower at the next sentence. "I don't have an appointment."

"And your name is…?"

"Doctor Benjamin Dailey." It had taken him a while to get used to saying the alias. He had practiced it in the evenings with Charlotte and his sister so they could grow accustomed to it. Now the hesitation before he spoke was barely perceptible, even to a keen observer.

The young man gave a quick nod. "Of course. I'm Jeremy. Let me tell him that you are here. I'll be back in a tick." Jeremy stepped into a side hallway, not easily visible from the street, and returned quickly. "If you'll follow me, doctor."

Then Jeremy led him down the hall and opened the first door on his right. "Doctor Dailey, Mr. Ryson."

As soon as Ben entered the office, a grave-faced man behind the desk gestured him to a seat. Ben took it, gripping his hands together so their ceaseless movement would not betray his nervousness.

"I am pleased that you have arrived on time." The man's gray eyes were keen but not as welcoming as Jeremy's. "Your father was most insistent on recommending you. We intend to help you, Doctor Dorroll, but we don't intend to risk our interests, you'll understand."

"I understand perfectly, sir." Ben took a few quick glances around the room before making himself completely comfortable. The small, windowless apartment smelled of stale air and old cigars. It had just enough space for a large oak desk and one bookshelf filled with record books. The desk held a large mass of newspapers, a typewriter, a fountain pen, and a cigar box full of pencils, as well as a telephone. Clearly the office of a man of many affairs.

"The paycheck is what you're probably most interested in. I know your kind." Ryson drew a white envelope out of one of the desk drawers and held it out. "This is an advance on your first month's wages. It should give you enough to cover lodging and preliminary expenses. You won't make much money from your medical work, but I'll let Doctor Graham fill you in on that."

Ben tucked the envelope in his jacket, relieved that he would now have enough to set up housekeeping when they arrived in Folkestone. "I'm obliged."

Ryson slipped on a pair of spectacles and pulled out a file folder. "It's not a gift. You'll be earning it, or you'll be returning it. I assume you were told that you'd be working with a doctor in Folkestone?"

"Yes, sir. That's all I know about him."

Ryson selected a strip of pasteboard from the file folder and handed it to Ben. "There's his card. His name is Jaeryn Graham, and he has longtime connections to the Home Section of the Secret Service Bureau. He's twenty-eight and Irish to boot, but he's loyal for all their madcap ways. Graham will inform you of the medical practice laws once you are there. What you see of private British concerns you will keep strictly confidential. We have a large weight on our shoulders in this work."

Ben nodded. "I understand."

"No, you don't." Ryson's cold gray eyes never ceased from their appraisal of him. "No one your age can possibly understand the responsibility of knowledge."

He drew himself up and corrected Ryson quietly but firmly. "I have had enough responsibility in my life to be used to the weight of it, sir."

Ryson stared at him for a long moment, and his confidence withered under the gaze. "Whether you take full responsibility or not, your actions and knowledge will always put the people you are about to work with in some form of jeopardy. Please bear it in mind. Now an end to that." He closed the folder he held with a crisp snap and put it away. "We've also run your medical credentials by our General Medical Council and gotten the proper credentials issued for you to practice medicine here in our country. Please take them with you. You will need them straightaway. Any questions?"

Ben shook his head.

"Excellent." Samuel Ryson opened a drawer and took out eight sovereigns, which he gave to Ben. They felt cold and hard and...off. Ben rubbed his finger softly over the insignia, then looked them over until he found a discrepancy in their makeup. A slight smile crossed his face at his success. A tiny hole, the size of a pin-prick, which no one would ever suspect unless they knew what they were looking for. Using two fingers and his thumb, he twisted the coin's top face one way and its bottom the opposite. The sovereign came open, and a small piece of paper fell out.

Ryson nodded, pleased when Ben found the catch. "Graham

never could figure out how they worked. You'll use those well, I trust. They're for passing messages when you need to be discreet. They're properly weighted, so you'll never be able to tell the difference from a real sovereign." He opened another drawer. "This case is for you as well. Do you know how to use a firearm?"

Ben took the wooden box. It looked like a letter desk with carved detailing on the lid. Inside, a Webley revolver rested on a velvet casing.

Ben's throat felt dry as he weighed the pistol in his palm, then carefully laid it back in the box. "I've used a pistol before."

The dull finish on the black barrel looked sinister, as if it were eager to snuff out the life of anyone remotely resembling a Hun sympathizer. "Do you think I'll need it?" he asked.

Ryson looked up over the frame of his glasses. "I don't like that question. It implies a hesitant spirit that will not be of service to you."

"I've been trained to save lives," Ben said. "I would hope any doctor would be hesitant to kill."

"Some lives are not worth saving. If you ever came to the point at which it was necessary to sacrifice one man's life in order to protect our troops overseas, then yes, doctor, you would need it. Are you prepared to give that kind of loyalty?"

Ben sat with his hands clasped tight together, searching his soul for the answer. At last he raised his head. "I have only ever had one kind of loyalty, and that is to the right thing. If integrity can be of service to you, then I will give all I have of it."

Something flickered through Ryson's eyes so quickly that he almost missed it. Ben couldn't tell quite what it was. Ryson reached over to shut the box and said, "Then Great Britain will thank you for it. I suggest you leave now, doctor. If you hurry, you'll have time to catch the last train to Folkestone tonight."

"I'd like to go tomorrow, if it's all the same to you. I want to see my father while I'm London." Now that the initial business meeting was over, he could taste the excitement as the words left his mouth. From the time he had stepped onto the pier at Liverpool, and as he had stared out the train window with the wheels clacking away the distance mile after mile, he had savored the hope set before him.

Ryson's face grew even more dour. "Is this pressing?"

"Yes."

"Very well. If you must."

Ben found breath enough to brave the man's displeasure and make one more request. "I wondered if you knew his telephone number? I don't have it."

"Jeremy has it. You may use the phone at his desk."

* * *

Ben stood before the telephone with the piece of paper Jeremy had given him tightly clenched in his palm. He reached out and picked up the black telephone receiver. As soon as the operator spoke, he looked down at the paper and slowly read out the connection, number by number. Then he stood in the silence, waiting.

A tired mid-day whiteness shone through the western window. The dusty floorboards creaked under his feet as he shifted. Jeremy's pencil tapping sounded as loud as gunfire. He took a quick breath.

"Matthew Dorroll."

All of a sudden, he realized he had never planned what he would say. So he said the first thing that came to his tongue. "I'm your son calling. I—I've arrived in London."

There was a long silence at the other end. Then his father said, "Ah."

Ben's hand slipped on the receiver, and he switched hands to dry the sweat on his jacket. "I've finished—that is—I wondered if I could see you tonight. Before I leave London."

He almost thought he had lost the connection, his father took so long to reply. "I'm afraid—unfortunately you find me involved rather heavily in convoy arrangements for Atlantic crossings. Another time might be more convenient."

16

"I could come tomorrow morning," Ben said hopefully. "The Folkestone train doesn't leave until ten."

"It may be wise to delay a meeting until after you have completed your assignment. Would you object to a brief postponement?"

Ben's hand clenched at his side, crushing the paper with the telephone number. "Would you mind telling me why?"

His father's voice was business-like. "Your primary purpose in coming to England is to advance the war effort. My primary purpose is the same."

"I thought you wanted to meet. That's why I came. I thought—"

His father cut him off with hurried words. "I would rather not see you until this assignment is completed. As soon as it is, you will be my son, and you may call me again." He paused briefly, and his voice softened. "I think that's a fair arrangement, after all this time. Don't you?"

Something like actual pain shot through Ben's chest. "Yes. Yes, of course, if you want it that way."

He looked at the receiver in a daze. The white sunlight had disappeared from the window. Jeremy's pencil tapping had stopped. The young man at the desk had a sympathetic look on his face, and Ben could not bear to see it. He blindly shoved the receiver back on the hook and walked out the door.

Chapter Two
First Warning

"Paper, mister. Get your newspaper here. Two pennies for the *Times*. Want a paper, sir?"

Ben glanced at the war headlines and shook his head. At the moment, finding lodging and getting settled was all he cared about.

"Are you all right, Pearl?" he said, gripping her elbow as he steered her through the crowd at the station. He shifted the handle of her bag so it wouldn't cut into his fingers and made haste for the platform awning that would shelter her from the rain.

"Yes, I'm all right," she replied, brushing away her honey-blonde curls, turned dark from the wet.

He noticed the slight tremble in her chin that she had never been good at hiding and turned her so she was facing him. "I don't believe you."

She laughed and brushed her hand across her eyes. "It's what you've always said. I'm just taking after my older brother."

Ben patted her shoulder. "I wouldn't if I were you. What is it? New places overwhelming?"

"I thought we would meet our father while we were in London."

"We'll see him soon enough. I had to come to Folkestone as soon as possible, on particular business. Right now we have the local doctor to meet, and then we'll find a place where you can rest."

After looking back to make sure Charlotte was safely off the train, Ben hailed a cab. One disengaged from the traffic and pulled close to the platform, casting up mud from its wheels. He showed the driver the card with Doctor Graham's name on it. The man tugged at his cap with a grin and said, "Right. Doctor Graham's it is, sir."

Ben doubted that he was supposed to take Charlotte and Pearl with him, but neither woman wanted to be left on her own in this new place. They sat in silence as the cab rattled past the shops. The buildings were tall enough to block the sky. Rain poured down, turning the cobbles slick and streaming down storefront windows, blurring the wares on display inside. When the driver stopped at a two-story brick house, Ben motioned his wife and sister to stay and knocked on the doctor's front door.

Almost instantly a man's voice called, "It isn't locked. Come right inside." But before Ben could get the door for himself, it flew open, revealing a young man with a welcoming smile.

"I'm Ben Dailey, come to see Jaeryn Graham." Once successfully through the introduction, Ben felt his pulse settle down again to a regular rate.

"Pleased to meet you." The thick lilt in the doctor's words made his sentence hard to follow. Dark curly hair almost reached Graham's collar in the back, and his green eyes with their concentrated gaze took him in as if they could read him to the soul. "Come out of the wet. I just tore myself away for dinner. I only have a half hour, but we can get started now and talk more this evening." Jaeryn glanced past Ben and saw Charlotte and Pearl waiting in the cab. "Oh. I didn't know you brought family with you."

"My wife and sister. They're dependent on me for support." His words tumbled out defensively, and he could have cursed himself for not sounding more conciliatory. But it was too late to change them.

"No need to worry. Welcome to Folkestone, ladies," Jaeryn

called. He hurried down the steps and offered them a hand down from the cab. Charlotte returned the doctor's offered handshake with her gentle firmness, but Pearlie shrank back under Jaeryn's observation. When the doctor turned to go inside, Ben felt her hand slip around his arm.

"Right this way, please." Jaeryn led them down a dark, wood-paneled hall to a room with a mail slot in the door. As they entered, Ben gladly recognized the scent of disinfectant and gloves. He had missed it in the last two months and finding a piece of familiarity in an unfamiliar place put him more at ease.

"I see patients here in the consulting room," Jaeryn explained. "People drop their cards through the slot when the door's closed to tell me they're here. Just across the way is the waiting room if you ever come when I'm in the middle of a private appointment." Across the hall a quiet murmur sounded of patients waiting to see him. "I've brought in another desk for you, but I haven't divided up the patient roster yet. Are you registered?"

"Yes. London took care of that before I arrived." Ryson had given him documents with his false identity to make it official, even down to a second degree that he could hang next to Jaeryn's in the office.

"Excellent. We'll set you up right away. Can I see your degree?"

"It's packed away in the trunks." Ben let go of Pearl's hand with a reassuring squeeze and dug through his pocket. "But I have my passport."

"That'll do." Ben handed it over, and after a quick glance, Jaeryn handed it back to him with a nod of approval. "Looks to be in order. I hear you can speak French."

"*Un petit peu.*" A glow of pride ran through him.

Jaeryn chuckled. "Good. I can't speak a word of it, and communicating with the Belgian refugees has been no end of a nuisance. As soon as you're set up and registered, I'll turn most of them over to you."

"I am a trained nurse as well if it would be helpful to you,"

Charlotte offered. "And I hope it will. I would love to be of use here."

A look of decided pleasure lit Jaeryn's face at the news. "I see you'll be more of an asset than I expected. Excellent; we'll discuss that in due course. Rest assured, there are plenty of places in town that could use your help if I can't." He flicked the curtain aside and glanced out the window. "The rain's let off a little. If you have no objection, doctor, I'm going to take you for a short tour of the high street and fill you in on some details. It won't take long. Sorry to have to walk, but we can't take a cab with any privacy."

"I don't mind." Ben smiled wryly. He had walked everywhere in college, and he was quite hardened to long distances and ghastly weather. Probably even more than Graham, though the man looked slim enough to be active.

"My kitchen is at your disposal while you wait, ladies," Jaeryn said. "You'll find plenty of tea. Everything's shop-bought, so it should be pleasant enough. Come along, Dailey."

Ben paused, digging in his pockets for money to give Charlotte for the cab, but she waved him away. "Don't worry about the trunks. I'll make the arrangements."

Jaeryn locked up the consulting room but left the front door open for any patients who might come in while he was out. Then he led the way down Tontine Street. Shops, most of them two stories with shopkeepers' living quarters on top, lined the narrow street. Women and children, their arms full of packages, walked in and out of the shops doing their marketing. The close row of buildings offered them more shelter from the elements than the train station platform, but a steady flurry of drops made most people walk with hats pulled down, collars turned up, and coats well-buttoned against the wet.

"We get quite a bit of inclement weather here," Jaeryn remarked, speaking up so he could be heard above a shrill woman scolding her rag-tag offspring. "Do you have a place to put up?"

The street narrowed, and Ben motioned Jaeryn to go first through the crush. "Nowhere, yet. Ryson told me to ask you where I should stay."

"You won't have much selection, I'm afraid. I'd suggest that you ask the postmistress about lodgings; she'll know which spots might be open." Jaeryn's long legs carried him with a rapid stride. "By the way, people are keen to catch spies here. They like to think they're all professional informants. Try not to act out of the common way, or they'll be sure to suspect you. And don't bring me any tales about flashing lights or curtains being used as signals—those tricks are too old and well known to be of any real use, and the police are sick of false rumors."

"I'll try not to." They split for a moment to go around two soldiers, out walking with sweethearts, who blocked their way. When they were abreast again, Ben snatched a sideways glance at Jaeryn and found the Irishman staring back at him.

Jaeryn broke his gaze, but his eyes sparkled in anything but penitence. "Just sizing you up. I hope you don't mind. You're a brave man to want to work with me."

The Webley Ben had slipped in his pocket on the train still felt unnatural against his side. After his talk with Ryson, Jaeryn's hint confirmed his suspicion that the work wouldn't be as mundane as his father had described. "Not particularly. I'm just helping you collect information and pass it on, right? There's nothing requiring bravery in that."

"Entry-level agents field that kind of work. I'm talented enough to receive more interesting assignments." The raindrops came further apart now, so Jaeryn pushed back his hat and shook off the wet. "I'm surprised they sent you here, actually, with your experience level."

Ben forced himself to keep an even tone. "I'll do my best to catch on."

The doctor whispered a couple of words under his breath that didn't sound quite English before he replied. "You'll have to if you want to make a success of yourself. I've worked with six assistants before, and the inexperienced ones lived to regret it."

Ben hoped he wasn't the sacrificial seventh. "Why aren't they working with you now?"

"One of them took it into his head he could do more for the war effort. He died at the Somme last year. An absolute waste." Jaeryn frowned, and his fingers clenched the cuff of his coat sleeve. "I'm not sure it would be helpful for you to know about the others. But if you have any ideas of partial commitment, now would be the time to back out."

Jaeryn stopped abruptly to hear his reply. Horses whickered as they waited for their owners, and the occasional blare of an automobile horn, combined with the swirl of chatter, created a din that made Ben wish for Jaeryn's quiet consulting room again. But the cacophony of noise did not disguise his delayed response. After the silence had stretched out to an uncomfortable length, Jaeryn said, "Well?"

"I came expecting to stay," Ben said.

Jaeryn gave a quick nod as he resumed his walk. "And your wife and sister? Do they want to stay?"

"Even if they didn't, I'm not about to send them back. One Atlantic crossing was enough."

"Well, I hope they don't mind the danger, being so near the coast." Jaeryn let the subject drop and pointed out the various shops as they passed. "Stokes' greengrocers should be able to supply all your grocery needs. We also have a confectioner's, and if you go in for that sort of thing, the Brewery Tap serves up a nice pint, I've been told."

"I'm not—I don't go in for that sort of thing," Ben said tentatively, wondering what Jaeryn would think of him. He rather expected to be ridiculed by the slim, young man who carried himself with such a confident air.

"Pity. If you did we could have turned it to good use. There's the butcher; you'll have to get your order in early if you want a nice joint of meat with the war demands. Plumber, newspaper, and fruit shop finish the lot." Jaeryn pointed out a clock tower crowned with spiky turrets rising above the other buildings further down the street. "I attend Tontine Congregational on Sunday mornings; you're welcome to join us if you like. And I nearly forgot: Ann Meikle runs the post office for all your needs along that line." Jaeryn's lips tightened as he gestured to the building he had overlooked. "A Scottish woman, and a shrewd one, you'll find. She's one of us."

Ben noticed the dislike in his tone. "Is something wrong with her?"

"You're quick on the uptake, aren't you?" Though Jaeryn's cheerfulness never diminished, Ben could sense the tension underneath it. "I'd rather not prejudice you with my opinions and let you form your own. She's the town's angel for helping at the soldier canteens. But she has the poor taste to dislike Irishmen." He winked.

Silence fell between them as they reached the corner by Tontine Congregational Church, and Jaeryn raised his arm for a cab. "Don't talk about our work while we're driving," he murmured. "Radnor Park, please, cabby."

The cabby dropped them two blocks away at Jaeryn's request, and after telling him to wait for them, Jaeryn led Ben past a small pond. "This is Radnor Park. You'll need to know it well." He pointed across the pond where a building cropped up above the trees. "That's the Royal Victoria Hospital. You'll also know that well, I'm sure. This way."

There were a few scattered people out in spite of the inclement weather, and Jaeryn avoided them, skirting the edge of the pond where boys knelt, letting loose toy boats. He took Ben down some steps to a tree-lined walk further away from the people and held up a finger for silence, watching to make sure they were alone. Then he pointed to the stone wall lining the steps. "If you start at the bottom and count thirteen stones over, you'll find you can pry up the thirteenth with a knife and a good strong pull." He knelt down and pulled a knife from his pocket, suiting the action to the word. Behind the stone, there was a little hollow in the earth with a small, padlocked box hidden away. Jaeryn pulled it out and handed it to him. "It's the very best combination lock; I'll give the combination to you when we get back. Ryson's messenger picks up our communiqués there and takes them to London. This drop will be your responsibility to check." He twisted the padlock through the combination, and as the lid popped open, it revealed a small envelope folded inside. "There. Now let's get out of here, before somebody comes." He replaced everything as he had found it until even the keenest eye couldn't have told they were there. Then he ran up the steps, looking at the envelope as he went. "Hullo. How odd. This is for you."

Ben took it and looked at the hand on the outside. It was one he didn't recognize. He slid a thumb under the flap corner to open it, but Jaeryn laid a hand on his arm. "We may be observed. Listen to the rest of this quickly before we get back to the cab: there are two drop points in Folkestone. This is the most convenient because it's nearest to the hospital. We only use the second drop point if the Radnor Park location is compromised beyond recall. If ever something happens to me, or your communication is of a time-sensitive nature, look up the address for Mr. Emmerson in the patient roster and give it to his butler, Peters. Can you remember that?"

"I never forget things."

"Grand. Just grand." The words were lightly spoken, but Ben caught an undercurrent of something else that made him uneasy as Jaeryn climbed into the cab and ordered the driver to return them to the clinic.

As soon as they were inside the consulting room, Jaeryn pulled the window curtains tighter together and said, "Let's have a look at the letter, then."

Ben took it out again, ran his thumb along the flap, and pulled a thin, half-folded card out of the torn envelope.

He'll have my throat for this if I sign off, so take an anonymous tip as welcome and beware that skellum Irishman, Jaeryn Graham. He's not one of us. You're better off going back where you came from. War and hate and dark business isn't the kind of life you'll be looking for.

"Well?" Jaeryn held out his hand. "Let me see it."

Ben frowned at it, reading over the lines again. "I don't think I'm supposed to show it to you."

"Of course you're supposed to show it to me. You don't think you can come fresh into this work and keep secrets, do you?"

"No. But there's a particular reason—" He held the letter for a moment, thinking. "What if I put it in the drop and sent it to London? I could ask them what to do."

Jaeryn withdrew his hand and the frown lines faded around his brow. "If you want to waste precious time, I suppose you must. But do it now. They generally come to pick it up before dark."

"I'll need the combination for the lock, then."

"Right." Jaeryn reached into his desk drawer and extracted a piece of paper. "Here is the combination for the lock at Radnor Park. You'll need to commit it to memory before you leave."

Ben glanced at the list of numbers and handed it back. The frown appeared again between Jaeryn's brows. "Are you not interested in remembering them?"

He waved a hand apologetically. "I have them down."

"Oh, I see." Jaeryn's tone of annoyance faded. "You are quick at the remembering, then. One last thing before you go. The other agents in town aren't fond of me and may want to meet you when I'm not around. When we meet a new agent, we work the word 'Channel' into one of our opening sentences as a password, so we know you're one of us. You're to respond with the countersign 'Eanswythe.'"

The phone rang, interrupting him. Jaeryn picked it up. "Graham.... Yes. I'll come right away." He put down the phone and began grabbing medicines. "Patient with heart failure. Call me with the nearest number I can reach you at as soon as you're settled. And don't forget to put that message in the drop."

Ben thought he heard Jaeryn mutter, as he sprinted through the door, "I hope he's dead this time." But it seemed like such an odd thing to say that he frowned, shook his head, and went off to find Charlotte and Pearl.

Chapter Three
First Secrets

"Is he gone yet, Peters?" Jaeryn asked as Mr. Emmerson's butler let him into the estate house. Peters led him at a fast clip through the marble-floored entrance hall and up a winding staircase to the second story.

"Not yet, sir. He seems to be more stable now." Peters quickened his pace down the hushed, red-carpeted hall towards his master's bedroom. "We found him on the stairs to the third story where he collapsed. He hasn't tried to go up there in several months. It must have been too much for him."

Jaeryn sped up to keep abreast with him. "Has he said anything? Dropped any hints that could help us?"

"Nothing at all, sir. He seems to be quite in his right mind."

"Blast."

Peters opened the door for him, and he hurried to the four poster bed where the old man lay.

"I'm right here, Mr. Emmerson." Jaeryn felt the man's pulse and reached for the first medication to slow down the rapid heartbeat. Dropping it carefully on the old man's tongue, he helped him swallow and guided him back to the pillow again. He reached for the collar buttons to loosen them, but Peters stopped him. "Mr. Emmerson was most distressed when I tried to do that earlier, sir."

"He needs air." Jaeryn watched the chest rise and fall, laboring for breath, and reached for the buttons, undoing them with a swift twist. Mr. Emmerson's fingers twitched on the bed, but he couldn't gather breath enough to protest. Then Jaeryn grabbed the morphine from his bag. It was a pity to have to give it to him, but it couldn't be helped. He pulled out the stopper and poured a dose.

As he raised the man's head for the second medication, a thin cord of black ribbon slipped into view at the collar's opening. Jaeryn's fingers itched to pull it out, but he resisted the urge and laid his patient back down again.

For the next half hour, he thought the man was going to slip over the edge. The breath fluttered in and out, seeming almost gone on occasion. But the pain gradually lessened, and as the foxglove took effect, the heart rhythm slowly steadied. It was maddening to see him hang on to life so tenaciously, but as Jaeryn watched and waited, he spent the time plotting how he could turn this to good account. As soon as Mr. Emmerson was steady enough and had fallen asleep, Jaeryn beckoned for Peters who was sitting in the corner waiting to be called.

"Absolute rest. Keep him in bed and as quiet and comfortable as you can. While he's quiet, you'll have free rein of the house to keep searching for anything that may be to our benefit. If he has any legal affairs left to be attended to, I think he should consider them. This is the second time this month."

"Of course, sir. I'll make sure those details are seen to."

Jaeryn looked down at the sleeping man on the bed. Mr. Emmerson was sleeping deeply enough not to notice if anyone touched him. He tugged out the black ribbon and found a silver key hanging on the end of it.

"Peters, do you know what this key is for?" he whispered.

"No, sir. I've never seen it prior to this."

"It must be important to him if he didn't want you to see it." Jaeryn gently lifted the sleeping man's head just enough to slip the key out from around his neck. "Do you think it's the one we've been looking for?"

Peters looked doubtful. "It looks too small to be a door key, sir."

Jaeryn untied the ribbon and slipped the key off it. "Perhaps, but perhaps not. I'll have Fenton make a copy and you can look into it."

Peters took the ribbon Jaeryn handed him with a faint air of consternation. "He might miss it, sir, when he wakes up."

Jaeryn looked undecidedly at the key. Then he pulled out his own key ring and slipped one off. "I'll make an exchange, so he won't notice. It can be a guarantee, until I return it." He gave the substitute key to Peters and pocketed the other one. "Right. If that's all, Peters, I think I'll let you go. Keep an eye on him, and let me know if anything changes. He can't hold out much longer."

He hurried down the stairs, glancing at his watch as he went. It was almost five o' clock—time for the evening drop box collection. This had taken him longer than he thought. He slipped into the car Peters had ordered brought round for him, breathless with his haste.

"Radnor Park, please, driver. And hurry."

* * *

When Ben left Jaeryn's clinic, he ignored the cabby lingering at the end of the street. It was the same driver, and he didn't think the same driver ought to be used twice for the same location if he wanted to avoid attracting attention. He walked to the corner of Tontine and Dover where he found another, and gave the man directions back to Radnor Park. Then he pulled out the paper and looked it over again. Someone wanted him gone, and someone mistrusted Jaeryn—that much was obvious. Moreover, the letter writer was not the only one who wanted him gone. Jaeryn's veiled warnings about danger hadn't been meant for reassurance, or he missed his guess.

Ben reached for a pencil and copied down the message before

flipping to a fresh page and dictating a note for London. Well, whoever disliked him would just have to stand it. He wasn't about to go home until his father had agreed to see him.

After completing the errand to his satisfaction, he returned to Jaeryn's kitchen and found Charlotte and Pearl still there with the trunks stacked around their feet. They hadn't taken Jaeryn's offer of eating anything, but Pearlie seemed less pale than before, though her blue eyes were heavy with the fatigue of travel. When he appeared, she stood with alacrity and pinned her gray picture hat on again.

"Do you want to wait here while I run down to the post office?" he asked. "The rain has let up, but it's still wet out."

Charlotte brushed the wrinkles out of her skirt and shook her head. "I'm tired of sitting. Let's stay together."

Ben offered an arm to each of them and took them out the same way Jaeryn had led him only a few moments before. As soon as they were out of the house, Charlotte looked up at him. "What do you think of Doctor Graham? Will you like working here?"

"I'm inclined to think he isn't thrilled to see us here."

"He might have been busy, darling. Don't give him the impression you don't like him," Charlotte said.

Ben sighed. "I wouldn't be surprised if he thought that already."

She slipped her arm out of his and held his hand instead, attempting to comfort him. "Well, it's not too late to show him otherwise. England isn't as bad as you anticipated so far. Folkestone seems like a pleasant town, and so does the man you'll be working under."

"We had all those things in Richmond. The only thing I came for, to meet my father, hasn't happened. The rest of it didn't matter." That smarted most. He wouldn't care about the upheavals in the least if only he was acknowledged as his father's son. The voice of rejection still rang in his ears underneath the torrent of new information he was taking in.

"Why didn't we see him while we were in London?" Pearl asked.

Ben looked down at her. She was so grown up now. Fifteen years ago she had been the pretty, blonde-haired sister he had carried up to bed at night and comforted to sleep when she was scared. When he left for college seven years ago, she had been thirteen and so shy she would only talk to him. Now he wondered who she actually was under the calm, submissive exterior. She had barely spoken a word since he picked her up from his childhood home. "I had to come here first to get settled," he said. "But not to worry. I'm sure he'll see us soon."

"Besides," Charlotte said, "he doesn't even know we've arrived."

Ben kept silent. Charlotte stiffened and opened her lips to speak, but they reached the post office just then and he pushed open the door to prevent her. The doorbell tinkled as they entered, and a hunched woman with reddish-brown pulled straight back hurried up to the counter.

"What can we do for ye, laddie?" She tapped her blunt fingers in a cheerful staccato on the counter, but her tone remained business-like, in keeping with the orderly rows of mail slots behind her.

Ben reviewed the cover story that Ryson had arranged with him and plunged in. "I've just arrived from America. I'm the new assistant to your doctor."

"Which doctor would ye be referring to?"

"Jaeryn Graham." Ben detected a shadow on the woman's face after he mentioned Graham. Evidently the dislike was mutual. "He told me you might know of houses for rent near the main part of town."

Mrs. Meikle shook her head. "Nothing near town, but ye gang out to the downs, right on the cliff about two miles. The road ends, and you'll see two wee stone cottages overlooking the Channel. Mrs. Goodwin lives there, and she's looking to rent one of them. It's lonely, but a grand view."

Ben hoped a cab driver would be able to interpret her vague directions. "Thank you very much."

A little ringing sound caused her to lift a finger and hurry over to the telegram apparatus. After writing down the message transmitted

31

by a series of rapid clicks, she returned. Her combination of small eyes and blunt nose resembled the expression of a baby sparrow. "Why haven't ye enlisted?" she demanded. "Are ye afraid?"

"No." He winced at the accusation. "I had other circumstances that kept me from serving in arms."

Her face softened in pity. "My son's dead over there. Lost him at Mesopotamia. Thousands of lives wasted all because someone in London didn't have the sense to know when they were in over their heads."

"I'm sorry." Ben felt sweat trickling down his neck and resisted the urge to run his finger around his collar. "I didn't meet their physical requirements, but fortunately I have the talents to serve my country in other ways. Doctoring is sorely needed."

"Well, you Americans took long enough about coming to help." She gave him a reproving look out of her beady little eyes. "Why didn't ye come sooner?"

It was his accent that wasn't helping. Not to mention his vague replies. He had never told falsehoods before, but if he was forced to start now, at least he ought to make them sound genuine. Swallowing down his distaste for it, Ben tried again. "I'm British, actually, but I grew up in America. As soon as I finished medical school, I came back to help with the war effort."

The woman eyed him in curiosity. "Well, you'll have plenty to do in Folkestone." She paused for a moment, then asked, "Were ye wishing any stamps, doctor—"

"Dailey," Ben said hastily. "No, thank you. I merely wished to inquire after lodgings." He turned to go, but before he reached the door, the woman called after him again.

"Ye never asked my name, laddie. If ye're to stay here a while, ye might want to know."

He tensed, angry with himself for his clumsiness. Charlotte opened her mouth to rescue him, but he answered before she had a chance to speak. "I apologize, Mrs. Meikle. I heard it beforehand and neglected to inquire."

The woman smiled. "No matter." Then her smile faded. "Take a piece of advice, laddie. Gang to a quiet place and work out your cover. It's a good thing I'm on the British side, or you'd be dead before yer mission's scarce begun. Yer muckle green to be sent ferreting out spies."

Ben could only hope that Pearlie didn't understand half the words the postmistress was saying, though he couldn't hope to be so lucky with Charlotte. He managed to make a civil goodbye before exiting the place as quickly as he could.

When he gave the direction "Mrs. Goodwin" to the cab driver, the man set off without need of further guidance. Evidently she was well enough known to be a common landmark. As they left the close-packed buildings behind them, Ben allowed himself to relax for the first time that day. Pearl inched closer to him on the seat, slipped off her hat, and laid her head against his shoulder. "I'm glad we're going to be near the coast. I liked being near it at home."

"Remember when I used to take you there? On Sunday afternoons?"

"Yes." She smiled at the memory. "And we'd lay on the beach until we were dry enough to go home. I still went there after you left. It made things better, somehow."

"I'm glad I was worth missing."

He grinned at Charlotte's sputtered protest. The shops and dwellings gradually vanished, giving way to a deserted coastline as they neared the Channel. A line of low hills appeared through the cloud cover, and their muted, restful green dazzled the city-weary Americans with an aura of peace. Though it was impossible to see France due to the haze, the stony gray cliffs dropping off to the Channel were more than enough to content them. As Charlotte opened the door, they heard the water roar above the purring of the cab.

"Road ends here, governor," said the driver. "You see that cottage, about a hundred yards down, facing the Channel? Right there's Mrs. Goodwin's, and the one farther beyond is empty."

Ben asked the man to wait until they were sure of their lodgings and beckoned for Charlotte and Pearl to come with him. Furious barking sounded as they approached the cottage, and the door rattled open before they even had a chance to knock. A petite lady looked out. She had lacy wrinkles covering her cheeks and a soft cloud of white hair. The barking grew louder as a brindled dog tried to strain free from her hand on his collar. He snapped and growled, his muscled shoulders rippling under his fur as he fought to get to them.

"Quiet, Nimrod." She pulled him back by his collar. "Go and lie down." He bared his teeth at them and whined before he followed her pointing finger. There was a sofa in the room behind her, and he curled up next to it, leaning his head on his paws and keeping an alert watch out of his dark eyes.

"He's a guard dog. Helps me sleep at nights, here alone." She looked at them inquiringly. "What can I do for you today?"

Ben cleared his throat. "I'm Doctor Dailey, newly arrived from America, and this is my sister, Pearl, and my wife, Charlotte. We're looking for lodgings, and Mrs. Meikle recommended your cottage. We were hoping you would be willing to rent it to us."

Mrs. Goodwin opened the door wider. "Come in," she said, "and sit down. You must be tired."

They took the chairs at her pine table, scoured until it was almost white. A wood stove stood against one wall, throwing out a pleasant warmth, and Mrs. Goodwin set out a plate of scones and a saucer of jam.

"I'm glad you've come," she said. "The committee came round and said I didn't have enough people in my cottage and I needed to be lodging more. I don't think it will fit more than three, but they were satisfied with that number for the present. Lodging is scarce; they need all they can get nearer town for the soldiers. I have two lodgers in the cottage already, but I gave them notice that they're to move out as soon as you sign the papers."

Ben drew back at that. "I wouldn't want to trouble them. I can find another place, I'm sure. Do you know…?"

"I'll be glad to be rid of them, doctor. You'll be doing me a favor if you take the place. Come and look at it now if you like."

She led them outside, Nimrod giving them a parting growl as they left, and took them along a path of trodden grass to the other cottage. One of her lodgers stood lounging against the door—a small, dark-eyed fellow with his arms crossed over his chest. He scowled when he caught sight of them. When they went inside, the other lodger stood up from the sofa: a tall, lean man with an unkempt crop of dark hair, whom Mrs. Goodwin addressed as Christopher and asked to step outside.

The cottage was much smaller than their home back in Richmond. A combined living area and kitchen comprised half of it, with large windows that faced the sea. Two bedrooms, each of equal size, took up the rest. The floor in the kitchen and hallway was of flagstone, but the bedroom floors appeared somewhat newer, covered with clean pine. There were simple bedsteads and nightstands in the bedrooms and an icebox and stove in the kitchen. And that was all.

"There are pots and pans and dishes," Mrs. Goodwin offered. "Also extra sheets and linens. Electricity was just installed, and we pump in water from the well. There's only a fireplace in the main room, but hot water bottles will keep you warm on cool nights. I'll give it to you for six shillings a week if you want it."

"Thank you, I think that's satisfac—"

Charlotte's fingers pressed into his arm, interrupting him, and a little pucker appeared between her eyes. "If you will give us one moment, please," she said to Mrs. Goodwin.

"If you like." The old lady shut the door and left them in the empty room. As soon as she was gone, Charlotte shook her head. "Darling, surely we can find a better place than this."

"I'm sorry it's not as good as—"

"No, it's not that." She pointed to the lights. "Something doesn't seem right to me. Why would a tiny cottage like this have electricity? It's too far out and too expensive to be wired with the rest of the town. No committee would ever approve it."

Ben shrugged. "It's convenient."

"It's not natural." Her blue eyes took on a darker hue. "Besides, it's next door to any activity that might happen in the Channel. For heaven's sake, it's closer to France than Folkestone is. Pearl and I will be alone for most of the day and probably half the night as well. That happened while you were interning, and I have no doubt it will happen here. If we're left to fend for ourselves, I want to know this place is safe, especially because—"

"Because what?"

"You know what." She lowered her voice. "Because of the entire reason we're here."

He berated himself for not finding a place for them to wait while he met with Graham. "What do you want me to do? The postmistress said there were no other availabilities. You're probably safer out of town than in it—planes want major damage, not deserted little cottages."

Her eyes pleaded with him, and Ben tried to soothe away her fears. "I'll be here as much as I can at night. That dog would warn you if anyone was coming during the day, and I'll get another Webley. I don't think you'll need it, but it is worth it if it helps you feel safer."

Charlotte bit her lip and looked down at the rough flagstone floor. "You won't be home. I know you won't be."

"I'm sorry, *ma chérie*," he said. "But we've used up our savings, and we can't afford the hotels. I don't have credit in town yet to borrow money. I'm sure she wouldn't offer it if…" Ben trailed off. He didn't know that Mrs. Goodwin was trustworthy any more than he knew about the rest of the people he had met that day. "One night won't hurt. I promise I'll ask tomorrow, and if anything better turns up, I'll engage it instead."

"Very well." Charlotte look to Pearl, who had stepped aside to the window during their conversation. "What do you say, Pearlie? You have just as much right to speak as either of us."

Pearl shivered. "I hate that dog. It looked like it wanted to eat us."

Ben laughed. "It's not a pet. It's meant to keep people away."

She gave a resigned lift of her shoulders. "I can settle anywhere, as long as it's soon."

"Good, then. I'll tell the woman we're agreed."

It might be a strange cottage, but it did have the benefit of being far from prying neighbors. Ben pushed his doubts away and left them to find Mrs. Goodwin. There would be time to investigate the matter later after a good night's sleep.

As soon as he told her they were agreeable to being her tenants, the brown-eyed fellow named Hugh, still leaning against the side of the cottage, cursed under his breath.

Ben threw a glance over his shoulder. "I'm sorry. I don't want to make you leave."

"Never mind him, doctor," Mrs. Goodwin interrupted. "This place is rightfully yours. He has plenty of friends he can put up with." She spoke to Hugh. "You start getting your things out."

Ben gave her the first week's rent, signing the contract at her kitchen table, then hurried back. One of the fellows must have invited Pearlie to take a seat on the sofa, and she had removed her hat and her gray fitted jacket. As Ben entered, Hugh brushed past him with a worn leather satchel and left without a word.

"I'm sorry to inconvenience you," Ben said.

Christopher looked up from the bundle of trash he was collecting. "It don't matter; I'm used to it." He winked at Pearlie. "Looking for someone to go out with sometime?"

"She isn't," Ben interceded. "Why don't we leave you to collect your things? I'm sure you don't need us underfoot."

The man shrugged. "As you like. But you're not bothering me."

While Ben paid the cab driver and collected the luggage, Pearl stood near him, gazing out over the Channel and breathing in the salty sea air. After the cab had left, she spoke so low that he almost missed it. "Ben?"

"Hmm?"

Now that they were alone, a touch of eagerness lit up her face. "It feels like home—with you here."

"Does it?" Ben touched her cheek and brushed back a strand of curls from her face as if she were six instead of twenty. "I'm sorry you had to be alone so long. I was a terrible hand at writing letters. I hoped you'd find a fellow to marry you and get you out of that place."

She looked altogether too solemn for a girl her age—like she had forgotten how to smile, except when one ghosted back by accident. "I've never wanted a fellow, really. I already have you."

"I think you can find better than that. Stay with the luggage a moment, will you?"

He left her and followed Charlotte, who had wandered further toward the cliffs to look at the waves and the evening sunlight. "Are you sure you're all right with this place?"

Charlotte nodded, but he wasn't convinced.

"I'm sorry it's not as comfortable as the house we had in Richmond."

"Don't worry about that, darling."

"You seem unhappy," Ben persisted.

"It isn't the cottage, really. It was something you mentioned earlier." She looked down for a moment. "Why didn't you tell me that you had talked to your father?"

"I would have, but it didn't matter much." Charlotte raised her eyebrows, and Ben shrugged. After a year of marriage, he ought to have known better. "Or rather, because it mattered too much. I planned to tell you about it soon."

"What did he say?"

"He said now was not a good time to meet. That I was to wait until this was done."

"But darling, he might have a good reason," Charlotte said, seeming eager to persuade him. "It might not be because he doesn't want to see you."

"He made it quite clear he wasn't interested in speaking to me. He didn't ask about Pearlie, either." Ben glanced at Pearl, standing alone by the luggage, and then out to the Channel, and his jaw clenched. "I should have gone to war like my brother, Edmond. If this is all some kind of revenge for not enlisting at the beginning—"

"Then I might have lost you just after we met. I couldn't have borne that." Her face sobered. "What are you going to do now?"

He clenched his hands without realizing it. "I am going to finish this. I don't know why he wants it done so much, but when it is over, he'll have no choice but to see me."

Charlotte stepped forward and straightened out his fingers, twining hers firmly through them to keep them from closing again. "Promise me you'll tell me sooner next time," she said.

Ben drew his hand out of hers—gently, so as not to push her away. "I think you're just beginning to realize, *ma chèrie*, how much I won't be able to tell you while we stay here."

Chapter Four
Hell on Earth

The sound of the waves from the Channel was a ceaseless roar that greeted Ben as he opened the door the next morning. He hurried out to look before heading into town. A cool breeze filled the air with its salty tang, and the sky showed mother-of-pearl and pink in the sunrise. Thick mist hovered over the water, hinting at rain. Far above him, the gulls circled back and forth on the wind currents, calling to each other with shrill mews. Ben breathed it in, content to soak in the calm and leave the world behind. It soothed the nervousness that he felt at starting his first day and almost made him anticipate the return to clinic work with pleasure.

In spite of the haze, he could see patrol boats out on the water that looked as small as children's toys, prowling back and forth on the lookout for enemy activity. The sight was well worth paying for, and had the cottage not given cause for concern, he would have been content to live in it just for the view. Growing up, he had loved his family's visits to the shore, and in spite of his seasickness on the voyage in April, he considered it a small price to pay for two weeks on the Atlantic. The sea, even with its occasional mercurial instability and the constancy of its ever-changing nature, filled a deep longing in his fractured and insecure life.

A door slammed behind him, and Ben turned to see Mrs. Goodwin waving to him. "I'm going to town, doctor," she called, "to do the washing for my clients. Are you going the same direction?"

He smiled. "Yes. We could walk together if you like."

"I don't mind a young arm for support if it's convenient." Ben promptly offered his to her, and Mrs. Goodwin slipped a soft, wrinkled hand around it.

"Did your other renters find a place to stay the night?" he asked, as they set off on their way.

"A friend offered to put them up. Don't worry about them, doctor. They weren't paying rent here. I was hoping they'd get drafted and I could see the back of them." The old lady's worn-out apron brushed comfortably against him as they walked. "When I heard you were coming, I wanted you to have it. You'll find it quiet since it's so far out, and you seem like folks who like quiet."

How had she known he was coming? She hadn't said the password, had she? Jaeryn hadn't mentioned telling anyone about his arrival, and only the Irishman and Ann Meikle had met him officially so far. "Who told you we were coming?"

"Our postmistress had said Doctor Graham expected a new assistant soon, and since there were no other lodgings available, I told her I would open my place for you."

"I see." Mrs. Goodwin's explanation only served to increase Ben's reservations. Ann Meikle hadn't mentioned hearing of him beforehand—unless her remark about working out his cover was due to prior knowledge of his coming. "We were surprised to find electricity so far out of town," he said.

He kept a sharp lookout for hesitation on her part, but Mrs. Goodwin did not seem ill at ease in the least. "Oh, it's worth it. I wouldn't want to be left with only candles, especially living by myself most of the time. I asked for it to be put in last autumn before the weather turned bad."

The road branched off in two separate directions, and Mrs. Goodwin let go of his arm. "Here's where we part ways, doctor. I have my work, and you're bound for Doctor Graham's, I imagine."

"Yes, ma'am." Ben tipped his hat. "A pleasant day to you." He pursued the rest of the way alone, turning over what he had learned in his mind as his right hand fingered the ragged edge of the letter that he still carried in his jacket pocket.

The blue sky of Wednesday morning had turned to a gentle drizzle by the afternoon, and it made a peaceful accompaniment to the business at Jaeryn's clinic. Ben spent the day assisting— meeting the people he would be taking care of, handling certain appointments at Jaeryn's request, and generally familiarizing himself with the Irishman's methods of conducting business.

Jaeryn kept his records meticulously organized, and Ben had no trouble finding the files he needed. In fact, the Irishman's organization had taken on the form of an obsession, for even when Jaeryn's back was turned he spoke up immediately if Ben returned an item to the wrong place. It didn't take long for Ben to get used to Jaeryn's preferences, even if the meticulousness amused him, and soon he was arranging everything to the doctor's satisfaction.

"What's your phone number?" Jaeryn asked, in between one patient and another. "I wanted to call you last night and couldn't."

Ben looked up from a new medicine he was examining, one that he hadn't used in the States. "I don't have a telephone. We rented a cottage at Copt Point, and they don't have them installed there."

Jaeryn's brow furrowed at that. "Copt Point is a lonely spot. Wouldn't you rather put up in my guest room so you can be—"

Ben shook his head. "Thank you, but I'm sure we can manage if you don't mind a little inconvenience. It's only until we find something better."

"As you wish. Since you came with your wife and sister, I can't blame you for preferring your own place." Jaeryn glanced at the appointment book and paused. "I'll have you take this patient. He's a returned private and speaks mostly French. His lungs got burned by the gas in February, and he just recovered partial sight a few days ago. His face was destroyed by a bullet. He's healed, but he travelled with bandages to hide the extent of the injuries."

Jaeryn put down the cost next to the appointment and wrote Ben's name on the man's record as the primary physician. "I hope you don't mind the effects of war. But it is part of living here."

He left to call the man in, and Ben took a deep breath, gathering himself for what he was about to see. But nothing could quite prepare him for the real thing as he welcomed the man and tried to set him at ease. A mass of bandages covered the entire left side of the man's face and mouth. Ben pulled on a pair of gloves, bracing himself with the familiar scent of latex and antiseptic. "Right. I just need to examine your eyes and see how you're progressing, and we'll work from there."

He was about to unpeel the first layer of bandage when the man laid a hand on his wrist. "They haven't let me—see—myself." Ben stooped closer to try to decipher the muffled rasping. "I'd like to—see—mirror."

Ben glanced at Jaeryn, but he was working at his own desk and made no move to interfere. He laid a gentle hand on the man's wrist and removed it from his own. "Let's have a look first, and then we can talk about it, shall we?" Working with deft precision, he unpeeled the bandages one by one. As he removed them, he could have wept at what he saw. They weren't needed for healing anymore, but he understood why the man hadn't been able to stop wearing them yet. The whole left half of the man's face was gone from what it had been, with ridges of skin and fading red scars. He knew at a glance the man had lost his sight for good in left eye. The mouth was practically gone. The other eye, clear and bright and blue, shone out from the wreckage with a mournful expression in its depths.

After he had asked a few questions, he reached for fresh bandages to cover the scars. The man shifted in his chair. "Mirror."

"I think it'd be better to wait a bit until you've healed more.

Perhaps a week or two."

"No." The word came out in an anguished rattle, and the private half rose from his chair.

"It's up to him," Jaeryn said without turning around. "He can have a mirror if he wants it."

Not seeing a mirror, Ben grasped the handle of one of Jaeryn's bottom desk drawers to see if he kept it there. Before he could get it open, Jaeryn's hand shot out and seized his wrist. "Only personal items in there. If you're looking for a mirror, it's in the tall cabinet." Though Jaeryn said the words casually enough, the tense grip belied them. Ben found the mirror and heard the rattle of a key as Jaeryn locked the drawer. He turned around just in time to see which key it was before he brought the mirror and reluctantly gave it to the private.

The man closed his good eye and held the mirror in his lap for a long moment. Then he brought the mirror to his face and opened it. He drew in an unsteady breath, and something wet trickled down the side of his nose as he took at what remained of who he was. "They're"—he gasped for breath—"wasting us out there."

A chill of silence spread through the room like a cancerous blight. Ben groped for anything to say that wouldn't sound trite in the face of such loss. But nothing came. And so he stood in respectful silence until the man handed back the mirror without a word.

By the time the private was freshly bandaged and ready to leave, Ben had found the words he was looking for. It was a habit of his, searching for just the right phrase with the same care he liked to search for the right cure. He laid a hand on the man's arm as he opened the door for him. "You have a hard road ahead of you. It probably looks darker than you expected right now. But you can make it through this recovery and build a new life for yourself."

The blue eye, dimmed with the knowledge of what it had just taken in, gave no sign of hearing. The man made his way down the passage with a defeated shuffle and closed the door with a weak click behind him.

"All right?" Jaeryn asked, when he returned.

"Well enough." Ben threw the gloves away and found the antiseptic jar. "What did he mean about being wasted?"

"It was a gas attack in March gone wrong. The Canadians tried to send it off and it came back on them in the trenches. Poor fellow was blind from it until recently. According to London, the whole campaign was supposed to be a grand accomplishment. Great advances against the Germans. Liars."

As Ben took a seat at his desk, Jaeryn swiveled his leather chair to face him. "Ryson tells me you finished your medical residency not long ago."

"Yes."

"Apologies for being inquisitive, but would you mind telling me your age? You must be older than I expected, with a family establishment already set up."

People always thought he was older than he was, and Ben couldn't really blame them. "I'm twenty-four."

"In return, I'm twenty-seven." Jaeryn's ever-present smile flashed out again, grating on Ben's nerves. The supply of insincere geniality appeared to be inexhaustible. "Ryson told me you were a British citizen," Jaeryn continued, "but your accent belies that report."

"I was born in England." Reluctance to tell the entire story caused him to settle on a partial admission, though he revealed as little as he could get away with. "My mother was American, and I took after her."

"And do you have any other family? I know from Ryson that your father lives in London."

"He does, in Kensington." Ben took one of the mugs and helped himself to the sugar. "Other than that, it's just my sister." Something kept him from mentioning Edmond's name. "Do you have any family?"

Jaeryn shook his head. "I don't have relatives nearby, and I don't keep hired help. For one thing, I'm a bachelor and prefer my solitude. For another, I don't want anyone looking through my papers. Mrs.

Goodwin comes to take the laundry and tidy up once a week, but that's all." He grinned. "So what kept you in America all this time? Are you the prodigal son banished from grace?"

Ben tried to keep his voice pleasant, though the teasing question raked at a hidden sore. "I don't think my relations with my father would interest you or have bearing on our work here."

"A politely worded invitation for me to mind my own business." Jaeryn chuckled. "Fair enough." He stood up and went to the door, checking to make sure the hall was empty. Then he came back and slid a piece of paper from under the patient book. It was the same note Ben had placed in the drop the day before to send to London. "While we're here, I wanted to warn you about a mistake you made yesterday. You received a note about me, questioning my trustworthiness, which that blasted Ann Meikle wrote. It's utter nonsense. But if it had been true, you as much as told me what you were going to do with it. I was able to collect it after you left it there. That kind of error won't get you far in secret intelligence."

Ben looked down at the paper, his mouth open in angry protest. "You told me what to do with it. I had no reason not to trust you."

"Doesn't matter. It won't be me every time that will bait you like that."

What could he say? Jaeryn was right enough that he had been careless. He clamped down the protest and took the paper from the desk. "Thank you for the reminder not to trust you."

"You're welcome." Jaeryn gave him the smile that somehow was not quite a smile again. "See that you remember it."

* * *

Jaeryn released him early that evening, and after stopping to pick up some things for Charlotte, Ben went straight to Copt Point to see how the ladies had fared. Charlotte met him at the door, safe and sound and in good spirits, and her eyes brightened when she saw him coming.

His own spirits rose at her eager look of welcome. "Hello, *ma chérie.*"

"Hello." As soon as Ben reached her, he slipped his arm around her waist and kissed her until she laughed and pushed him away. "You look tired," she said. "Was something hard today?"

"There was a man with gas burns. It made me think of Edmond."

Charlotte leaned her head on his chest and rubbed his back in a gentle, soothing motion. "Where is Edmond now?"

"I never knew. I haven't heard from him since I left England as a child." He handed her the parcels he was carrying. "I got the groceries you wanted."

She looked down at the envelope in his hand. "Did you get a letter? I didn't think you would hear from anyone so soon."

Ben glanced at the address, and his lips tightened. "Mother. I told her to write care of Ry—someone who could forward the letter on from London."

"Ah, what does she say?"

"Didn't read it." He tossed it on the table. "I'll send her the money she wants tomorrow."

"Darling, that's not a nice way to talk about her," Charlotte protested.

Ben stopped where he stood. "I—I didn't mean it that way. I don't mind sending her money. It's just inconvenient with that creditors wanting last month's money, and I still haven't told them where we are yet—"

"You only just got here. You couldn't tell them sooner." She patted his arm as she passed him. "Speaking of letters, I'm going to write to my parents. Am I allowed to mail it with my real name?" The corners of her eyes creased in laughter. "They'll want to know what I've done with you if I put Dailey on the envelope."

Ben hung up his jacket and stretched out on the sofa to relax. "Yes. But give the letter to me, and don't ever mail one from the post office." Jaeryn had told him to put his letters in the Radnor Park drop to be picked up and mailed from London. As far as letters coming

47

into Folkestone, Ann Meikle was the soul of discretion, or so they hoped.

Charlotte pulled out the letter box and set it on the table. "You should write your brother. Maybe he could help us see your father again."

"I wouldn't know where to send it," he said, his eyes already closed.

"Well, you ought to have enough connections by now for someone to help you."

"Maybe." Opening his eyes, he sat up and reached for a sheet of paper. He had some correspondence of his own to attend to. He was positively hungry to hear home news again, and the sooner he wrote to Mrs. O'Sean, the sooner he could expect a reply.

* * *

Charlotte lay beside him, breathing peacefully as they slept for the second night in their new house. She had fallen asleep nestled into his side with her hand on his chest, and Ben lay quite still, taking care not to wake her.

She was a point of security in a swirling vortex of bills and complications and broken memories. She had been that way in college—drawing him out of himself and inviting him to her home for Sunday dinners, where her parents made him welcome for her sake. Ben still wasn't sure what she saw in him, but she was the first woman besides Mrs. O'Sean who had offered him help instead of asking for it, and she was the first woman from whom he had accepted it. She had soft skin and a smile that was gentle or bright by turns, and she always carried herself with her head held high and a ready word for everyone she met. After a few months of friendship at medical school, he had loved her too much to graduate and go his way without her.

In spite of her reassuring warmth at his side, Ben lay awake, thinking. The explanation Mrs. Goodwin had given about Ann

48

Meikle's knowing of their coming didn't convince him. With the way things stood between the doctor and the postmistress, he doubted Jaeryn would have mentioned him. But Mrs. Goodwin might be telling the truth. After all, when he met Mrs. Meikle she had as good as told him to his face that he was an agent. But neither woman had used the password Jaeryn mentioned, so he didn't dare initiate contact—yet.

A small sound startled him, and Ben strained his ears to identify what it was. When silence followed, he turned over and tried to go to sleep, but after a few moments of fruitless effort, he gave in and decided to investigate. He peered out the window into a dark night, so dark that he could not see to the cliffs. A slight breeze drifted over his hand, and he realized with misgiving that the window was cracked open. After securing the shutters, he slipped on his boots and grabbed his revolver. Pearlie lay peacefully asleep when he peeked in her room, and her window was closed and untampered with. A circle around the cottage showed him nothing except some flattened grass under the windowsill. But as he examined the window, Ben glimpsed something caught in the shutter, and pulling it out, found that it was a scrap of paper with writing on it.

Go home. This isn't the place for you.

He looked up. Mrs. Goodwin's house showed dark and silent. Whoever it was had left the message and gone.

He went back to bed and tried to sleep, but his mind would not let go of the warning. It was written in a different hand than the message in the Radnor Park drop. That made three people who didn't want him here.

And then he remembered that Nimrod hadn't barked.

* * *

From a medical perspective, Jaeryn Graham found his new

assistant entirely satisfactory. The young man kept to himself and didn't try much to put patients at their ease by talking, but the genuine interest he took in each one had a soothing effect without many words. In his gentle touch was the desire to relieve pain, and more, to alleviate the distress of mind that pain often brought.

From an agent's perspective, Ben Dailey left a little to be desired. But as far as he was concerned, that, too, was just the way he wanted. Dailey hadn't been crafty enough to dissemble about the note, and he hadn't mentioned his brother, which made two black marks against him if he ever needed to be removed. But that wasn't enough. If Dailey was London's favorite, Jaeryn wanted more incriminating evidence to balance in the scales against him.

After Ben left for the evening, Jaeryn dashed off a note and placed it in a private drop box, one that he had not alerted his new acquaintance to. The following morning, on the twenty-fifth of May, he received a reply and left Ben to look after the clinic, deceiving him with the pleasant fiction that he was attending to a patient call.

Jaeryn set off at a rapid pace for the Brewery Tap, ducking as he entered the low doorway, and made straight for a table near the back. The barmaid brought back his order for a half-pint of best bitter and a cup of tea, and he sat with the untouched cups a few minutes before the other man arrived.

"You needed some help, doctor?" the spy purred, declining to shake hands.

Jaeryn leaned his elbows on the table, taking care to avoid the grease spots that spattered its surface. "Yes. I have a key for you to take to a locksmith. I want a copy made. And Fenton—make sure you don't do it in Folkestone."

Fenton took the key and gave it a close scrutiny before tucking it in his pocket. "Of course, doctor."

"I assume word's gotten around about Dailey coming to town," Jaeryn said.

"It did. A new man picked by London. Ann Meikle was less than pleased."

"For once she and I have something in common. I'd like to see him returned to wherever he came from. Your assignment is to find something that would disqualify him from continuing here."

Fenton studied his buffed fingernails as he tilted his head and considered. Jaeryn knew by the man's dour face that he didn't think the proposal was wise, but the right amount of money always overcame any little difficulties. Jaeryn fingered the crisp, ten-pound note agreed upon beforehand as payment for the meeting. Evidently the sight of it argued his cause well.

"I'll do it," Fenton said. "As long as you keep my connection confidential. I have no intention of involving myself in your feuds." He held out his hand for the money, and Jaeryn gave it to him. "Did you want arrangements to get rid of him, or just to scare him off?"

Jaeryn's eyelids narrowed in disgust. "The latter. You know very well I've never asked you to kill anyone."

"One never knows how far you'll go." Fenton took a long draught of the beer. "By the way, this will cost you extra—since it's for private interests, instead of those of the British Empire."

"It is for the British Empire. I know nothing about this fellow and have no reason to trust him yet. A man in my position has to be careful."

Fenton smirked. "A man in your position."

"A man falsely suspected of being an Irish sympathizer. I don't want to be unjustly replaced after years of hard work." Jaeryn stirred sugar into his tea. It was cold by now, merely a conventional cover for the conversation; and there was nothing he hated so much as cold tea. "Watch who contacts Dailey and whom he contacts. I also want any information you can give me about his father's interest in Folkestone. Tell me about prior visits here. Any friends. Find out about the other son. If you can get Mrs. Meikle to give you copies of any letters, I'll pay extra, but I doubt you can do it."

"She doesn't dislike me as much as she dislikes you."

Jaeryn looked down at his crooked fingers. His jaw tightened at the sight of them. "You have the time and the capability to go places that I am not able to, so I leave him in your hands."

Fenton inclined his head as a gracious acceptance of the compliment.

"And," Jaeryn continued sternly, "if you cross me for your own interests, I shall collect the necessary information to have you prosecuted for past misdemeanors."

The middle-aged agent glanced at his watch and rose from the table. Straightening his cufflinks, he brushed a speck of dust from his dark sleeve and placed his pay in an inside pocket. He did not offer his hand in farewell. No doubt it seemed too incriminating a thing to do.

Jaeryn left shortly after Fenton did, making his way through tables filled with men having a peaceful drink. He squinted at the bright sunlight as he reentered the street and set off back home. He was taking a risk, setting a spy on a fellow agent, but the level of fracture their unit had undergone made it imperative that he remove the competition. As long as Fenton remained discreet, it shouldn't be a problem. Dailey could find another career back home, and if he had to enlist, England would have one less man to interfere in matters that didn't belong to him. And with that, Jaeryn dismissed his qualms of conscience.

The boom of guns startled him as he walked down the street. He glanced up at the sky and saw it was empty. The noise probably came from the recruits practicing at the Shorncliffe camp. He still forgot where it came from once in a while. He saw Dailey's wife and sister standing further down the street, discussing something together, and as the boom sounded again, they too startled and looked about for the cause of it. Jaeryn chuckled to himself. They would grow accustomed to it soon enough.

* * *

As Ben knelt to wipe down the examining chair with antiseptic, he heard the click of the door latch and knew Jaeryn had returned. He would show Jaeryn the mysterious note now that their day's work was done and see what could be done about different lodgings.

The windows stood open to air out the clinic, and the evening sunshine streamed in, blowing the curtains aside. Jaeryn entered the room and went straight to the appointment book to see what had happened in his absence. "Hello, Dailey. Did everything carry on all right?"

"Yes, I finished with the patients." Ben stood up and sealed the cleaning solution, taking care to put it back on the correct shelf. "I have a question for you."

"Anything you like." Jaeryn snapped the book shut and gave him his full attention.

"I found this last night." He took out the small card of paper with the message on it and handed it over. Jaeryn smiled as he read it, and Ben felt a flicker of surprise.

"I've gotten the same writing before, not long after I arrived here." Jaeryn handed it back. "I'm not sure who sends them, but they obviously want to probe and see why you're here. Something must have happened to alert them to you specifically. The best course of action is to keep alert without giving them reason to think you're more than you say. We don't want German sympathizers discovering who the agents are here."

"Not much chance of that, since I don't know either." He waited in pointed silence, but Jaeryn didn't pick up the hint. "The dog that Mrs. Goodwin keeps didn't bark. He's chained up outside at night. It must have been someone he knew."

Jaeryn looked pleased. "That's observant of you. See if you can find out how long she's had the dog and who it might be familiar with, and we'll proceed from there." He opened the medicine cabinet and shoved an envelope under his record books. "You do have a firearm, don't you, if you need it?"

Ben pointed to the revolver lying on a shelf where patients couldn't see it. "I do, but my wife would still prefer being closer to town. Ann Meikle said she didn't think there were any housing options other than Copt Point, so I'm not sure what to do."

Jaeryn seemed preoccupied during the last sentence. "Do you hear a plane?" he asked abruptly.

"No." Ben stared at him in astonishment.

"Maybe it was just my imagination. Well, you could always come here if you like. It would please the overzealous committee women. They've wanted me to take in lodgers for ages, but they couldn't press the point because I split my house with the clinic."

Ben wasn't sure sharing a house with Jaeryn Graham would be an improvement on Copt Point. "Thank you, but I don't—"

Jaeryn frowned and held up his hand for silence. He cocked his head to listen again. "Are you sure you don't hear a plane?"

Ben strained to hear the thrum of an engine above the clatter and clang of the market. "No, I—" Then he too caught a faint droning, followed by a muffled rumble. The hair rose on his arms, though he could not have said why.

"That's odd." Jaeryn walked over to the window and peered out. "It must be the recruits practicing at the camp." The crease between his brows deepened. "I suppose the plane is one of ours, isn't it?"

Ben felt a sudden urge to run. "I don't know."

Perhaps it was a premonition of dread that fell over them, or merely the mesmerizing stillness. Whatever the cause, they stood motionless, counting the rumblings to themselves. The silence lasted one moment, perhaps two. It was broken by a massive boom.

A rain of glass shattered from the windowpanes. Jaeryn cried out as the shards landed full in his face. A second boom sounded, and shrieks pierced the bright evening. Ben's heart thudded in panic. But the thought of Jaeryn dying in front of him quickened him to action. Pushing through the shaking world, he ducked as books tumbled off the shelves and medical tools clattered to the floor. He managed to pull Jaeryn away from the window before a third crash shook the ground and threw them to the floor. Blood ran down Jaeryn's face, but in spite of the agony, his eyes flashed with excitement. He crawled under the desk to protect himself from more flying glass. Ben made haste to follow his example. Before he reached it, something sharp hit the back of his head, and then—nothing.

* * *

When he woke up, he couldn't remember at first where he was. On the floor. In a strange room. After a long moment of silence, Ben sat up and looked about him. Then he remembered. The crescendo of noise had turned him half deaf, and he sat dazed in the aftermath, listening to a low ringing sound. A strange orange glow flickered on the windows, but he didn't have any idea what it meant. It was Jaeryn who brought him back to a sense of reality. He caught sight of the Irishman rocking back and forth with his hands clenched. Most of the contents from his shelves lay in chaos around him.

"The pane of glass shattered in my face. Do something, for mercy's sake." Jaeryn grimaced as he spoke, and the blood still trickled in rivulets down his face. Ben scrambled up and set to work searching through the wreckage for the things he would need.

It took him a long time to find a pair of tweezers. The shouts and screams sounded continuously, and Jaeryn was anxious to finish and get outdoors to help. Ben picked out the largest pieces of glass and washed away as many of the others as he could, observing more than one flinch on the part of the man under his hands.

"You need sutures," he murmured, laying down the tweezers and rummaging for a needle and suture equipment.

Jaeryn pressed his shirtsleeve to the cut, staining the white cuff with a fresh surge of blood. "We don't have time for that. There are people waiting. Leave it, and I'll come back later."

When, at length, they were able to enter the street, neither of them was prepared for the scene that met their gaze. Smoke poured in billows from several of the buildings. What they could see gave them a fair idea of what they couldn't. The shops all along Tontine lay in heaps of crumbled ruin. The Brewery Tap, Stoke's grocery, Mrs. Meikle's post office, and the newsagent's—none of them were untouched. Mangled bodies lay amidst the rubble. And churning inside Ben was the bitter anguish that there was no way he could gather up all this ruin and find a way to mend it without leaving someone hurt.

Already medical workers and rescue teams from the training camp moved about, lifting dead and wounded women to makeshift ambulances. The largest fire raged in the remains of the grocery across the street. A team of men worked frantically, pouring sand to try to smother it. One of them, a lean, muscular fellow whose red hair was streaked black with soot, held the position closest to the fire and worked with a will, but he paused to wave as Jaeryn came out of the clinic.

Jaeryn waved back and shouted urgently, "Tell me where most of the casualties are."

"Bouverie Road, doc," the man yelled. "This place is the worst, but they'll need help there, too."

"I'm going to Bouverie," Jaeryn said, snatching up a bicycle he kept leaning against the house. "I know where it is; you stay and help wherever you can." The latter words were flung over his shoulder to Ben as he pedaled away.

"Come quick," the red-headed fellow called. "I got a woman who needs a doctor bad."

Ben ran—slipped—steadied himself and picked a hasty path through the wreckage, not wanting to know what he was stepping on.

The woman's face was blackened with smoke. Her whole dress was stained with blood, torn open. She clung to him in panic, trusting him to somehow turn a nightmare to day again. "Help me. Help me."

He couldn't help her. He saw at a glance it was only a matter of time. "I'll do what I can. Let go so I can use my hands."

"I'm so thirsty. Give me water. Help me. Please help me."

"Water would kill you. Please let go."

"Do you think I'd mind?" She screamed it in his face, leaving him shaken. It was the last thing she ever did. Her eyes closed shut, and she fell limp. The red-headed man looked on, appalled.

"I'm sorry—"

Just then, Ben heard a little, high-pitched moan. Shifting the woman's body to the side, he exposed a pink, flowered dress and a dark-haired girl, her face all clenched in pain. When he felt her neck, no answering pulse met his fingertips.

"No!" An anguished wail sounded from behind him, and a young man dropped down beside him, scooping up the little girl in his arms. "No. Mitze, no." He looked to Ben. "Do something."

The one phrase he hated most in all the world was the only one he could say. "There's nothing I can do."

"She's not dead. She can't be dead." The young man held her limp body close, rocking her back and forth.

This must be what hell is like. The smoke from little flickers of flame stained the bright sky, stinging Ben's eyes with the acrid fumes. He left the man and the little girl behind and started a few feet from Jaeryn's doorstep. All through that long night he worked with others to put broken bodies back together or prepare those irretrievably broken to be taken to the morgue. Tears gathered and threatened to spill over. By a mighty effort he brushed them back and managed to subdue his outward reaction to an expression of dull horror. Some of the dead were unrecognizable. He noticed he was trembling, and then realized he had never stopped since the first crash.

"Are you hurt?" A gruff voice pierced through the horror. He looked up and saw a short, agile, gray-haired man bending over him.

"No, help someone else." He looked down at his clothes. The shirt that had once been white was red; so were the pants and jacket. No wonder they thought he was one of the wounded. He was out of bandages. The clinic was out of them too. Suture equipment—not even a hospital would have enough.

After what felt like an eternity of hours, when they had to carry lanterns and flashlights to see their work, Jaeryn returned and offered him a glass of water. Even in the dim glow of a flashlight, the Irishman's face looked pinched with pain, but at least his scratches were scabbed over. "Are you all right?" he murmured, forcing Ben to turn his gaze away from the wreckage.

Ben didn't answer the question. "The grocer just found his son. He's dead. Only fourteen years old."

Jaeryn ran his fingers through his hair, then jerked them out and looked regretfully at the blood on them. "We've all grown too comfortable with the noise from the camp practice. People won't be complacent for a long time, that's certain. Most of the dead are women." He scrutinized Ben's face. "You look done up."

Nausea rose up in his throat. "I'm fine."

"I—I'm sorry this happened so soon after your arrival." Jaeryn gently thumped his shoulder, then left to resume his work. Much, much later, when the darkness lightened to gray dawn and the streets were empty of the bodies, they found each other again.

"The Victoria Hospital's full," Jaeryn said, "and they're taking the rest of the injured to Shorncliffe. You've done good work yourself." He clapped him on the shoulder again, a rough offer of comfort. "I think we've done all we can for now. Why don't you go home and rest up for a few hours? We'll have plenty of patients in the morning to keep us busy."

Through the fog in his mind, Ben recalled the broken windows and chaotic mess on Jaeryn's floors. "Do you need a place to sleep?" he asked.

"If you have a spare room, I'd be grateful." Jaeryn looked at the volunteers. The red-headed fellow was still scrubbing up blood in the streets. "Hell on earth, this. One minute people are shopping, and the next—"

Ben stirred and nodded. Charlotte and Pearl were going home as soon as he could save up for tickets. He had no intention of putting the two people he most loved in more danger.

Jaeryn nudged him, and he looked up to see a constable waving.

"Excuse me, Doctor Dailey?" a bobby yelled over the people who were gathered around him clamoring for help. "There's a young woman waiting over on Dover Road who says she's your wife. She needs to speak to you. I believe it's urgent, sir."

Chapter Five
Completely Confidential

"What's the matter?" Ben called back, hurrying through the crowd as best he could. The blood pooling in the street stained his shoes, and more of it splashed on his pant cuffs by the time he reached the man. Jaeryn followed at a discreet distance, ready to help if needed, but far enough away so as not to overhear.

"I told her this was no sight for a woman," the constable said. "She's waiting at the corner of Tontine and Dover. You'd best see what she wants; it might be something to do with today's attack. If I can help, you be sure to call, and I'll come."

Ben left Jaeryn to his own devices and hurried off. He caught sight of Charlotte in a crowd of women, and she detached herself from the group and came to meet him. Her hair had fallen out of its twist, and her face appeared drawn and tinged with gray in the dawn light.

"Are you all right?" he asked, taking her hands in his. His heart beat faster, and he could see that she was only keeping control of her tears by a great effort.

"We were on Tontine when the bomb dropped," Charlotte said hurriedly.

"No." Ben gripped her hands so tight that she flinched and he realized he had hurt her. "Are you all right? Where is Pearl?"

"I'm not hurt. I've looked everywhere for her. I left her in the drapers' shop while I ran another errand, and the bombers circled over before I returned. They came near to where I was, but not near enough to hurt me." Her gaze flickered down to the ground, and she brought it slowly up to his face again, as if in her remorse she found it hard to face him. "I tried to find Pearl as soon as it was over, but a policeman made me go to the hospital to inquire, and it took hours to get in and search. She isn't there. I've looked all night—"

Dread tightened around his heart. "God have mercy. We must find her."

"I would never have left her if I had any idea what was about to happen. We'll find her, Ben, I know we'll find her..." Charlotte's voice trailed off, and she swallowed hard.

"It wasn't your fault." Ben squeezed her hands and let go. "I'll talk to the constable and see what he advises. Stay right here until I come back."

The constable's advice made Ben cringe at the thought of what he was about to undergo. After directing Charlotte to wait at the Victoria Hospital and make more inquiries about where the patients might have been taken, he remembered Jaeryn and hurried back to their former meeting place. Jaeryn stood exactly where he had left him, in front of the ruined grocery.

"My sister. She was on Tontine when the bomb dropped," Ben said. Jaeryn gave an exclamation of concern. "I don't know where she is, and Charlotte's turned the Victoria Hospital inside out. I'm going to the morgue."

"I'm so sorry. Do you want me to come with you?" Jaeryn looked more than ready to help and stood expectantly, waiting for the plan of action.

"No." Ben realized his hands were clenched and opened them

slowly, drying the sticky sweat off on his jacket. "There's no need for both of us to see it. I'll come back if I find her and tell you what happened. Unless you would rather go on to our cottage and rest now."

"No, not at all." Jaeryn's face settled into grim lines in spite of his sympathetic tone. "I'll wait at my house. Please call if I can be of any assistance."

The constable directed Ben to the morgue and gave him a note to move him up in the crowd. He jogged through the streets, avoiding civilians, closing his ears to the screams of bereaved still kneeling in shock where they had received their news, trying to avoid the gore smeared over the sidewalks. There were dozens waiting outside the morgue to be let in for the painful duty of identifying people they knew. Ben gave his note to the Coroner's Officer, Mr. Chadwick, who immediately led him through the large, echoing room to where the remains were laid out. The place was oppressively hot, but well-lit, with sheets draped over the bodies. "I've never seen a sight like it," Chadwick said. "Prepare yourself for a shock. Not all of them are—well—whole."

"I know. I helped remove the bodies from the streets," Ben said, feeling another wave of grief pass over him. *Oh God, have pity and let her not be here*, he entreated. It might be too late to send Pearl to a safer place now. He would never forgive himself if it was.

"Who are you looking for, doctor?" Mr. Chadwick asked, waiting to pull back the first sheet. "There's no need to see more than you have to."

Ben took a deep breath. "My little sister. She's twenty years old and blonde with blue eyes, and she's small."

"We've mostly young women. We'll see if we can find her, but I certainly hope she's not here."

They looked together, and sometimes Ben was able to shake his head immediately, but other times he had to look more closely to find something—anything—to know that it was not Pearl. Most of the dead were horribly maimed, and a dreadful ringing in his ears from the apprehension drowned out the quiet hush of their resting place. He caught his breath more than once at the sight of honey-blonde tresses, and time after time let it out again when they proved to be someone else's. Something inside him wrenched in anguish as he scanned the bodies of little children and young women—even a few women that turned out to be elderly upon examination. At length, he shuddered and turned away. "She's not here."

Mr. Chadwick pulled the sheet over the last body. "I'll call you if another comes through that might be yours, doctor. Where can I reach you?"

"Jaeryn Graham, on Tontine. He'll take a message for me. I'm his assistant."

"Very good, sir. I hope you find her alive and well."

Ben reentered the street and looked about him. After the grueling horror of the night, the houses still looked the same. Most grieving people had now taken their tears elsewhere, but the line to the morgue stretched around the block. Here and there a man or woman stood with the uplifted chin, the stoic face, still clinging to a shred of hope. And though the hope might later be dashed, at least they had those last few seconds of not knowing before the surety of good-bye. There were more people needing help than were there to offer comfort, and he himself might need that same comfort soon. But perhaps it wouldn't come to that. The hospital at Shorncliffe would be the next logical place to look. He must search there and keep praying.

As Ben crossed the street, he was so absorbed in making plans that he nearly collided with a lean, red-headed man walking the opposite way. "Hey, mister. You look like you're on a mission," the man greeted, his cheerful tone rather out of place in the grief that surrounded him. "Can I help you out?"

"I doubt it." Ben stepped aside for the man to pass, impatient at the delay. "Excuse me for getting in your way."

"Are you looking for someone? I've been volunteering and might know where to find them. There's always a chance I could save you an hour or two." The stranger grinned and thrust his hands in his pockets, confident of his powers of service. It was then that Ben recognized him as the same worker who had helped put out the fires earlier. His face and arms were stained black, and they were blistered and raw from the heat, but his spirits seemed undaunted for all he had been through.

Ben gave up trying to avoid the man's questions. "My sister went missing. She was on Tontine during the bombing, and we haven't found her in the Victoria Hospital or the morgue. I'm going to Shorncliffe next to see if she was taken there."

"What's she look like?"

"Blonde. Blue eyes. Small." Ben tried to slip past, but the man stepped in the same direction and blocked his way.

"I've got one of those," he said eagerly. "Found her in the streets and sent her down to wait in a church. I promised to come back for her. What's your sister's name?"

"Pearl Dailey."

"That's her, then."

A mighty relief surged through Ben at the words. "Oh, thank God. Please, tell me where you took her." The man nodded and set off back the way he had come.

"Was she all right?" Ben asked, dreading what the answer might be.

"I found her in a faint and brought her to the hospital where the docs checked her out. She wasn't in much pain, and she seemed all right," the man reassured him. "She said a brick struck her in the chest and threw her to the ground, so it's probably just bruising or something of that sort. I told her I would help her find her folks as soon as the streets were cleared, and I've gone to look in on her every hour or so. She fell asleep for a while." A three-days' growth of beard adorned the man's face, and he presented a grizzled expression on the whole. Pearlie had probably been more frightened by her rescuer than the drop itself.

"Thank you so much for looking after her." Ben quickened his pace, and the man grinned at the effect his good news had. "I don't know what we would have done if you hadn't come by," Ben said, not wanting to seem rude in spite of his haste.

"It was a pleasure. She's a pretty little acushla."

"Yes." Something about the man's voice sounded different. He had been trying to work it out while they talked, and couldn't quite lay his finger on it.

The accent was American—that was it. He had heard so much British lately, not to mention French, that his own way of speech sounded foreign. But the man's accent wasn't entirely American either. Here and there a hint of something else sounded in the vowels.

Ben pointed to one of the side streets. "Let's take a detour before we go to the church. My wife is waiting for me at the Victoria Hospital, and I want to relieve her fears as soon as possible."

They found Charlotte sitting on a bench in the Victoria Hospital waiting room, and as quickly as he could, Ben told her the whole story. She thanked the man earnestly, and he brought them to the door of the church before leaving them.

Pearl lay in a pew amidst the chatter of workers resting from their labors. She looked up as the church door opened, her face streaked with tears. As soon as she saw who it was, she cried again, this time with relief. Charlotte held her close to comfort her, and Ben kissed her forehead—something unusual for him. "Thank God you're all right, Pearlie You're safe now. It's over."

"I thought *you* weren't all right." Her face, hot and flushed, quivered as she tried to force herself to be tranquil again. "I didn't know what I would do without you. I'm so glad you're not dead."

He patted her nervous fingers, which clung to his coat sleeve. "I'm sorry it took me so long to find you. I'll hire a cab as quickly as possible so we can go home."

It took him a while, but at length he was able to find a cab, and he ordered the man to take them home. The cold morning light washed over the Channel as they walked up the path to the cottage. The slate-colored waves roared ceaselessly against the cliffs as if all was as it should be. He unlocked the door and Charlotte offered to put on a kettle for tea, but Pearl wanted to lie down before taking any. Ben went to bed as soon as he undressed, barely noticing when Charlotte joined him. For a few precious hours, the Tontine tragedy and all its horrors faded into oblivion.

* * *

Jaeryn was in his own bed early the next morning when he woke to the ringing of his doorbell and rolled over with a groan. At least the person had the courtesy to enter legally. They certainly didn't have to. He had examined his windows earlier that morning, and not a single pane of glass remained unbroken, leaving the premises ready and waiting for any thief who wanted easy pickings. He was so exhausted that he had been content to simply shake the glass out of his sheets and leave repairs for later, but he couldn't leave them that way another night.

Muttering over the inconvenience of his profession, Jaeryn pulled on a gray knitted sweater and hurried down the stairs. "Hello?" he said, throwing open the door and running both hands through his hair in an attempt to straighten it. At the sight of the man who stood there, he let his manner shift from kindness to exasperation. "Have you no idea what happened last night? Some of us are still out there."

"You aren't, doctor," Fenton replied, pushing him aside and entering the consulting room. After taking the precaution of pulling the curtains closer together, the spy took an envelope out of his jacket pocket and laid it on Jaeryn's desk. "Besides, you look like you were sleeping, and not long ago at that." He shook his head reproachfully. "I've been working for you. I do wish you would show more appreciation for my efforts."

"Oh, I appreciate them. I appreciate them fully," Jaeryn snarled. "Now get on with it and get out. I would think even you could find a small dose of empathy for the tragedy we've undergone."

"It's not worth my while."

Jaeryn caught his breath, then hid his anger by taking up the envelope. "What's this?"

Fenton's mouth was set in a self-satisfied manner with a hint of malice lurking around the corners. "The keys you wanted copied and the first installment of information you requested on Benjamin Dailey. I've tracked down his father, Matthew Dorroll, in London. Matthew Dorroll is a retired private investigator for Scotland Yard. Lives alone, and according to the kitchen maid, who proved to be a valuable source of information, he hasn't left London since 1914. His youngest son graduated from Johns Hopkins and married Charlotte King a year ago. A poor decision, to start a family so soon. Ann says he's gotten letters from a private credit establishment in Virginia. Apparently he borrowed a substantial amount and they want to know where he is."

"Do they? Send them a letter informing them, won't you? Make sure they can't trace it back to you. I don't want Dailey finding out we had something to do with it."

"I will not." Fenton shook his head. "You can write yourself. London would not be pleased if I sent something like that."

Jaeryn scowled. "I could make you regret some of your past actions if you don't cooperate."

Fenton seemed unperturbed by the threat. "You asked for my services, didn't you? I give them my own way or not at all."

"You're a nuisance," Jaeryn groaned, returning to the present. "But being pressed for money as well as seeing the effects of war ought to be enough to get rid of him. I gave him a gas burn patient yesterday, and the bomb drop might send him home if nothing else does. It was ugly out there."

"You are ruthless, aren't you?" Fenton's drooping features upturned in a smirk.

"When I need to be. I'm holding off on agency work as much as possible in the meantime. If I can manage to send him home by the end of the month, the less he knows the better."

Fenton took out a notebook and turned over the pages with his thumb. "As another item of business, I had a message from Peters last night. He said to tell you the key didn't work. I'm not sure exactly what he meant by it, but I assume he was referring to the duplicate I made for him yesterday."

Jaeryn slammed the desk with his fist. "Blast. Did he say anything else?"

"That was all." Fenton glanced out the window. "I believe that's Dailey coming now."

"So soon?" Jaeryn scrambled for a bank note in his wallet and shoved it towards him. "Get out before he sees you."

Fenton looked at the note, and something like a smile hovered over his mouth as Jaeryn hurried him down the passage to the back door. Just before he left, he held up the slip of paper, and Jaeryn saw in dismay that he'd given the man a twenty-pound note. "Actually, I think I was mistaken. It must have been someone else. But I do appreciate the extra income. Good day to you, doctor."

* * *

Ben was on his way again by seven, for when he awoke the thought occurred to him that he had forgotten to check the drop at Radnor Park the previous night. The park was deserted at this time of morning, especially after the events of the day before. He found the box hidden just as Jaeryn had directed and made sure it was empty. Then he replaced it and continued on to the clinic.

Before he could knock, Jaeryn pulled back the consulting room curtains and poked his head through the open window. A strong smell of antiseptic drifted out. "Good morning. The door's not locked."

Ben entered the study and paused in amazement. Jaeryn had swept up the glass and replaced the books and other articles on their shelves. Aside from the empty window frame showing where the glass should have been, the room appeared just as it had the previous morning. "You've been busy."

67

Jaeryn leaned the broom in a corner and brushed his hands together. "A little better, eh? Ready for patients again, and I have a man coming to replace the glass later this morning. We get priority because we're medical workers. How is your sister today?"

"We took her home, and she went to bed. I left this morning before she had woken." Jaeryn had been kind, and he didn't want him to think he didn't appreciate it. "Thank you for asking."

"Well, I hope she suffers no serious effects from yesterday." Jaeryn took a pile of unwanted papers from his desk and dumped them in the trash. "Let's divide up the routes, shall we?" He pulled out a map and the patient lists. "I have two medical practices, one that I bought for myself. That's this list here." He pushed one of the papers forward. "The other list is the route I keep for another doctor who's serving at the front. Doctors didn't want to go to the front back in '14 because they would lose their practices, so the rule is I keep it for Winfield while he's gone and we split the profits."

Ben took up Winfield's patient list and scanned through it, hardly seeing the names. By all rights he should be looking over a list of his own right now instead of sitting here.

"His patients are more on the northern side of town," Jaeryn said. "I think it makes best sense for you to take over his patients, and I'll keep building up my own practice while we both manage the clinic."

Ben realized after a moment of silence that Jaeryn was waiting for him to answer. "I'm sorry," he apologized. "I was preoccupied."

"So I noticed." Jaeryn didn't seem upset and picked up again from the beginning. "If we make a division like that, Mr. Emmerson is on your route. His estate and King's were under Winfield's jurisdiction, but if you don't mind, I'd like to keep Emmerson under my watch. I expect his heart to give out soon, and I want to hold as much authority as possible with the staff when the time comes to make our move."

"Certainly. You have the best right since you were here first." Ben put the Emmerson address on Jaeryn's roster. He had volunteered to write the list of names so he could read it afterward, for Jaeryn's handwriting was very nearly illegible. "I would like to take the King estate if you don't mind."

Jaeryn looked curious. "Why?"

"My wife has some connection to the family. Cousins or something, a couple of times removed." At Jaeryn's look of alarm, Ben quickly added, "They don't know me. I shouldn't have any trouble."

"Oh? Well, that could come in useful. Why didn't you tell me sooner?"

"We have been a little busy until now."

Jaeryn raised an eyebrow at that but let the remark pass without comment. "Then the King estate is yours, though I doubt you'll have much cause to go out on his account. If he needs you at all, he'll probably call you for one of his servants or his son. That boy has a habit of getting into scrapes."

This first news of King's son piqued Ben's interest. "Does he? I would have contacted Colonel King today if it hadn't been for the bomb drop. What sort of man is he?"

"You'll have an opportunity to meet him in a couple of weeks if you don't mind waiting." Jaeryn rummaged through his desk drawers and pulled out an envelope, from which he extracted an engraved invitation card. "This came in the morning's post. Colonel King is hosting a dinner on the seventh of June and invited me to attend along with a guest of my choosing. I'm sure he would have delayed it after yesterday's events if he could have, but he can't take back the invitations now. You can come with me and tell me what you think of him. We didn't like his friendship with the former German ambassador before the war broke out. They were quite often in each other's company. He hasn't given any sign of questionable activities, but after we detected treasonous correspondence from his rival in Parliament, Mr. Emmerson, we put King under surveillance too."

Ben took up the card and examined the scrolls and elegant script. "It would be the perfect opportunity to observe his loyalties."

"Grand. I'll give you an introduction, and we'll get you started in

Folkestone society as a proper British gentleman."

A proper British gentleman. All his aims, up until now, had been for something entirely different. Back in Richmond was a little house, now in someone else's hands, and Mrs. O'Sean's loving counsel, and no reason to hide things from Charlotte. He missed all that, and though Jaeryn hadn't intended it, the Irishman's jest made him more homesick than ever.

* * *

All the townsfolk wore mourning clothes and grieved for those lost in the Tontine tragedy. A pall of grief settled over the clinic as patients waiting to be seen talked in low voices, more than one through scattered tears. Six days after the incident, on Saturday, the second of June, Jaeryn closed up the clinic for an hour in order attend the memorial service, and Ben returned to Copt Point to bring Charlotte back to town. While she was dressing, he went to find Pearl.

She was standing outside near the scrub of bushes that grew along the cliff's edge. When he came up beside her, she didn't say a word. "All right, Pearlie?" he asked. "You've barely spoken since—last week."

His little sister leaned her face into his shoulder and he felt hot tears soaking into his shirt. "It was so wrong. How could they do that?"

God help her, it was still better than France. They had a home left. They had a town left. There were still fields greening over in the springtime, unscarred by trenches and mass graves. "I don't know why. I don't think we common people do. We're just—all caught up in the wars that have been created for us."

He waited until the quiet, gasping sobs had quieted and gave her his handkerchief to wipe her face with. Her blue eyes were set wide apart with a nervous gaze that kept her from looking people in the face for long, and soft tendrils of blonde curls hung loosely over her shoulders, for she didn't pin them up like Charlotte. She looked rather pretty, now that he thought about it, with her small, arched brows and delicate chin. He hadn't stopped to notice properly since coming to England.

Pearl took the handkerchief and sniffed. "Why are we here? This war doesn't belong to us."

"We're here to see our father."

"We haven't seen him."

"He won't let us—that is, not yet. He wants me to finish something first. I can't tell you what it is, but as soon as it's done, we'll go straight to London."

"He doesn't love us, then," she said in a flat, dull voice. "If he did, he would let us come."

"He couldn't help loving you," Ben said soothingly. "He just has to see you first. I'll make sure it happens." He cupped her chin in his hand and raised her heart-shaped face to his. "Have I ever let you down before?"

"No," she said in a small voice.

A note of hesitation at the beginning of her response stung him like a dart. Ben realized with a pang of guilt that he had hardly spoken to her since taking her back under his protection. Small wonder they had grown apart during his absence and marriage. He shifted uncomfortably, unable to find words to address the wound between them. "We're about to leave for a church service. Do you want to go with us?"

Her face crumpled again with grief. "I want to stay home. I can't bear to go."

Ben sighed and acquiesced. "Mistress Goodwin will be next door. She's going to the service tomorrow, so you can stay if you like."

He was reluctant to leave her, but there was no more time if he didn't want to make Charlotte late. A short walk took the two of them to the parish church, and when they entered through the doors, Jaeryn waved them over to join him in his pew. He was dressed in sober black, his dark, wavy hair still damp from trying to comb it

71

down. "I don't mind the sympathy, but I could do without the patriotism," Jaeryn said, speaking low. "It's all cant, in the end."

It wasn't until later that Ben understood what he meant. Distinguished men, from a marquess representing the King to the Archbishop of Canterbury himself, came to attend the service. Over the words of patriotism and commendation for the soldiers at the front, Jaeryn leaned over and whispered in his ear. "We're not proud of the politicians that sent them in over their heads, are we?" Ben said nothing, but a tiny part of his soul couldn't help agreeing.

After the service was complete and the congregation stood to file out, Ben scanned the audience for anyone he might know. Mrs. Meikle nodded to him as he caught sight of her. He joined her as the stream of people filed toward the doors, and Jaeryn watched him go, making no effort to disguise his disapproval.

"Good afternoon, Mrs. Meikle," Ben said. "I'm glad you weren't hurt last week."

Mrs. Meikle turned around, and when she saw who was speaking, her homely face brightened considerably. "And ye too, laddie. The streets surely took to shaking, didn't they?"

"Yes. Were you on Tontine when the Germans flew over?" he asked.

"No. I had locked up and gone home. The poor folk, losing all their loved ones like that. But our post office is up and running again. A man came in three days afterward to look over my place, and the damage wasn't too bad. Besides, we had the good fortune not to lose any letters." Mrs. Meikle cocked her head with mock reproof in her dull brown eyes. "I haven't seen ye for ages. Ye should come by and visit me sometimes."

Ben could barely suppress a smile at her talk, but he managed to hide his amusement. "I'll try. A doctor leads a busy life, and I rarely have time for visiting."

"I ken. Is this yer pretty wife?" Mrs. Meikle patted Charlotte's arm with her black-gloved hand. Charlotte offered a tentative smile and looked to Ben for an introduction.

"My wife, Charlotte. Charlotte, this is the postmistress, Mrs. Meikle." Ben glanced behind him as he made the introduction and found Jaeryn was no longer close at his elbow. The Irish doctor stood in a side aisle, deep in conversation with a man in a plain black suit and French cuffs who held a paper in his hand. Mrs. Meikle's talk fell empty on Ben's ears, for he wondered what they were speaking about. Jaeryn held out a banknote, and after receiving it, the man disappeared into the crowd.

At that moment, Ben felt a pressure on his arm and found Charlotte trying to attract his attention back to Mrs. Meikle.

"I thought I might see ye here, laddie, and brought a letter that came in for ye." Mrs. Meikle handed him an envelope, and he glanced at the writing. It wasn't in a hand he recognized, and the top corner held no return address.

"The real letter's inside," she said in a low voice. Ben opened it and smiled when he found a letter from Mrs. O'Sean, mailed to his London address and forwarded on.

"Thank you, Mrs. Meikle," he said, shoving it into his jacket pocket. "I'm obliged to you."

Jaeryn came up then and gave a frosty nod to Mrs. Meikle, who returned one of her own with the same degree of coolness. "Dailey, don't forget that you're in charge of the calls tonight," Jaeryn said. "I have some errands to run, so I suggest you drop Mrs. Dailey off home as soon as possible and come back to the clinic."

"Ye're in an awful rush, aren't ye, doctor?" the postmistress said sweetly.

"Yes, ma'am. I like to keep busy," the Irishman replied.

"And a good resolution too, so long as a body keeps busy with honest work."

"Certainly." Jaeryn touched his hat brim in farewell.

Their little group broke up after that, but Ben suspected, as he set off home with Charlotte, that the words exchanged between the doctor and the postmistress held a deeper meaning than they wished to let on.

* * *

Jaeryn didn't return from his errands before dark that night, so Ben drew the curtains as the dusky shadows lengthened on the opposite storefronts. Mrs. Goodwin had warned him of the consequences if folks left their shades up, and he didn't want to incur the stiff fine that came from leaving the lights visible to the street. Not to mention that extra light might help the Germans wreak more havoc, and this town had already seen enough grief.

"Do you have a moment, doctor?"

The voice behind him caused Ben to start. Leaning against the doorframe stood a man who looked surprisingly respectable to be breaking in. Ben recognized him as the same man he had seen with Jaeryn after the memorial service. His dark brown hair, parted to one side and smoothly combed, had begun to recede on his forehead, and his eyes were keen and blue. Aside from a few wrinkles around his mouth and eyes, he looked quite handsome in his black suit. And he must have the means to gratify good taste, for he wore diamond cuff links with his French cuffs.

"Who are you?" Ben demanded. Charlotte had the Webley back at Copt Point. He probably wasn't supposed to leave it with her, but he that was the best way to keep her protected for the present until he got a spare one. Ben snuck a furtive glance at Jaeryn's shelves for a firearm, but Jaeryn hadn't left any lying about in case of need. He circled over, putting himself between the desk and the intruder to gain a line of defense and be nearer to the telephone. "How did you get in?"

The man offered no threat, only smiled and held out his hands palms up as if in token of his peaceful intentions. "My name is Fenton. Jaeryn Graham and I work together. Pleased to meet you, sir, and welcome to Folkestone. You're the new agent, aren't you?"

Ben caught himself before he replied in the affirmative. Jaeryn hadn't mentioned anyone matching this man's description. "I have no idea what you're talking about. You're invading a private residence, and if you don't leave—"

"Oh, come, doctor, no need to deny the truth. It's common knowledge. We're all in this together, and you were bound to meet other agents eventually." Fenton sidled closer. "The Channel's not a peaceful place at present, is it?"

Most times in life he was shorter than other men, but this fellow he was on a level with, and Ben felt a small satisfaction at being even. The password didn't escape his notice, and he gave the countersign in return. "No. But Eanswythe is quiet enough, I think you'll find."

"Very good, doctor," Fenton said, offering the compliment as if he was amazed to find him worthy of one. "I see London isn't wasting our time after all. I've come to introduce myself and deliver a commission from London. By the way, what's your agent number? For writing about you in future?"

"I don't know. I don't have one."

"Jaeryn Graham didn't give you one, I'll be bound. He doesn't want you here, doctor."

"Why wouldn't he?"

"Heaven only knows why the Irish take things into their heads." Fenton took a paper out of his pocket. "This came for you tonight. An assignment for you alone, and it's entirely confidential. The note I received enclosed says Jaeryn Graham is not to know anything about our exchange." He held it out. "Open the letter and tell me you understand the directions before I leave."

Ben snapped the red, official-looking seal. Inside, he found a message in a shaky, wandering hand, along with a smaller sealed paper and a key.

Go to the Emmerson estate at half past eleven o'clock and knock on the back door. The butler will let you in without question. Take the key to the library on the ground level and unlock the second desk drawer. Take out the false back and put the folded note inside the compartment. Lock the drawer again, leave by the library window without speaking to anyone, and put the key and this note in the

Radnor Park drop on the seventh of June at five in the afternoon. Do not fail in this.

Ben glanced at the clock. The hands showed quarter past now. He took a deep breath. He had never entered anyone's house without their knowledge, and when he married, he had been able to look his wife in the eyes and assure her he had never told a lie before. Now that the order stared him in the face, it revolted him. He should have stopped to think about all this intelligence business properly instead of rushing off to London. After this he would be left with a smudged personal record, all for the chance of seeing a man who wanted to take advantage of him and wouldn't even tell him why.

"What's wrong, doctor?" Fenton sidled closer to try to get a glimpse of the paper, but Ben crumpled it tight, crushing his reluctance into the creases.

"Just—giving up some things. I've read it, and I understand."

"Good luck, then." Fenton tipped his fedora, and his departure made no more sound than his arrival. Ben called a cab and pulled out the list of Jaeryn's patients, scanning feverishly through the list for Mr. Emmerson's name. He found the address just where it ought to be—they were all alphabetized—and crammed the papers in his hat as a cab arrived at the door. Opening his wallet, Ben frowned at the dwindling change. He would have to find something besides cabs for transportation if he wanted enough to spare for his creditors. They would start breathing down his neck as soon as they received the letter with his address. "The Emmerson house, please, cabby. Drop me off at the end of the drive. And hurry," he added.

He kept the papers tucked away, wishing he had not left the Webley at home now when he needed it most. He could fall back on his fists, and he wasn't afraid to use them, but he hadn't resorted to force in a long time, and he wasn't about to if he could help it.

The cabby dropped him at the end of a long gravel drive. Ben paid him and watched the vehicle leave before tracing his cautious way up to the house. A light shone in the second story, but the front

76

of the house was dark, shut up for the night. He kept beneath the trees lining the avenue until he reached the side wing. The rooms were dark here, too, and Ben drew a breath of relief as he quietly crunched past them, making as little noise as possible.

The back was not so deserted. A light shone out behind the curtains of the window next to the back door. He watched it for a moment, unsure of what it signaled, and reached for his watch to check the time. It still lacked three minutes until the half hour. Crouching down, out of sight to the window, Ben waited until the second hands ticked their way to eleven thirty. Then he went to the door and gave a soft knock.

Nothing happened, and gathering himself, he knocked louder. The light in the room lessened. A moment later, he heard the bolts rattle. The person who opened the door was a gray-haired gentleman, devoid of jacket and vest and obviously preparing to retire for the night. "Come in, sir. The library is this way."

The man, whom he assumed must be the butler, held a lamp shaded in his hand. It cast long shadows on the white walls and oak wainscoting, eating up the distance between them and the door to the main part of the house. Ben kept his hand on the key in his pocket as the butler pushed open a door and crossed the marbled entrance to another long hallway. This one was richer, with paintings and carpeting and dimmed lights. The butler pushed open the first door and handed him the lamp. "This is the library, sir. I'll leave you to yourself. If you'll turn down the light before departing, I would appreciate the favor."

"Right." Ben took the lamp and waited for him to leave, but the older man hesitated, a look of concern on his face.

"Is Jaeryn Graham aware you're here, sir?"

"No. He's not to know about it."

"I see, sir. Goodnight."

The man closed the door, and Ben stood alone. Shadows concealing countless books towered beyond his small circle of light, but he didn't have time to explore them all now. Crossing to the desk, he pulled out the key and inserted it into the lock before he had time to care—before all the revulsion of prying into another man's affairs could send him fleeing. A hasty rattle and pull opened it, and he tapped towards the back, listening for a hollow sound. The drawer was shallow enough, and as his fingers brushed along the back edge, they encountered a small lever, which he pulled towards him. The false back came away. The compartment was empty. He put the smaller, sealed note inside and fitted the catch again.

There was no undoing it now, whatever he had done. His actions could have laid a trap to bring a man to prison or even a death sentence for all he knew. Whatever this led to would be on his hands. And he might never find out what happened—that was the injustice of it all.

"You'd better be worth it," he muttered in the dark.

A tall, floor-to-ceiling window looked out on the lawn. After blowing out the lamp, Ben unlocked the window and stepped through, closing it softly behind him.

Chapter Six
Slip in Judgment

At dawn on the seventh of June, Ben woke to the earth shaking.

His heart jolted into terror, and he nudged Charlotte hard by the shoulder. "Get up. Something's the matter. We have to get out of the house." He had just enough time to glimpse her expression of fear before he slammed out of bed into his shoes. The ground continued to tremble as he ran to Pearl's room and pounded on the door. "Pearlie, wake up. Get out. It isn't safe here."

He hurried out the front door and looked up at the sky for signs of aircraft. There was none—no humming, no warning drone of bombers waiting to loose death. Mistress Goodwin appeared in her doorway holding Nimrod by the collar. Her face looked old and gray in the morning light as she, too, scanned the sky, just beginning to yawn itself awake. She crossed the grass toward him. "What is it, doctor?"

"I don't know," he said. "I don't understand what just happened."

Later that morning, Jaeryn, too, had no idea as they opened the clinic and started the day. "I think it must have been France," he said, as he made himself a hasty breakfast while the two of them got ready. "We're close enough to the Channel to feel disturbance from the front. But we'll find out tonight. Colonel King's gatherings always have information that the average man doesn't."

Ben opened his desk drawer and slipped inside the key and the letter that he had been ordered to put in the Radnor Park drop. He had almost forgotten them due to the worry of the morning. Jaeryn eyed him as he locked the drawer up. "Got something private?"

He hated this lying. "No. Why should I?"

Jaeryn picked up his empty plate. "Oh, just paranoid, I suppose. Carry on, Dailey, and try not to worry about what's going on in France too much. Our focus is here."

* * *

Jaeryn put away the patient files and locked up the desk drawers at half past five to give them both time to get ready for Colonel King's dinner. "Dailey, I know it's late, but there's one more call to finish up just five minutes from here, and it won't take you long. If you'd finish it before we leave, I'd be grateful."

His assistant's face brightened with more than his usual alacrity. "I'd be glad to."

Jaeryn waited until Ben was gone before turning the key in the consulting room door. Finding another spare key on his ring, he inserted it into Ben's desk to unlock the top drawer. It was empty.

"Blast," Jaeryn whispered, staring at the wood, which stared unhelpfully back at him. "He must have taken it with him." He glanced at the clock and used the phone to dial the Emmerson estate.

"What can I do for you, sir?"

"Peters? Send Fenton down to check the Radnor Park drop. I'm at King's tonight. I want to be informed right away if he finds something."

"Very good, sir."

There was nothing more to be done about it. Jaeryn hurried to his room, where his suit hung ready-pressed, and growled his way into evening dress at his small washroom mirror. He heard the click of the downstairs door as he straightened his necktie and peeked out to see which way Ben would go when he came in. But Ben came straight up the stairs instead of stopping at the consulting room like he expected, and Jaeryn ducked back into his room before he could be seen.

Once they were on their way in a borrowed car, Jaeryn issued Ben a stream of instructions on proper etiquette, too preoccupied to notice the slight smile on the other's face as he spoke.

"Does the colonel have a wife?" Ben asked when Jaeryn had made an end of the subject.

"Did," Jaeryn said, driving as fast as he dared to make up for lost time. "Two of them, actually. His first wife died during King's campaign in India, and he married again—a woman much younger than himself who supplied him with an heir. King was forty-eight when his son was born, and now the lad's sixteen—and a handful, according to my sources. Outlandish name, too."

Ben didn't seem particularly interested in King's son. "What happened to the second wife? My wife met her several years ago, and remembers her as a kind woman."

"Dead as well." Jaeryn rounded a curve in the road with caution and then sped up again. "They lived abroad at the time, but I never learned the whole story. Some people hint at a scandal, but my sources haven't found any proofs to substantiate it. The boy was twelve when his mother died, and he's never really gotten over it. He has an incredible talent for music, and King's grooming him for government service. He's ready to begin studying at Cambridge next year."

"A bright mind, then," Ben said.

Jaeryn thought he detected a hint of enthusiasm in the quickening of his voice. "In some areas, but I doubt he'll go far. You won't meet him tonight unless by accident; this is an adult occasion. Although, since you're a distant relation, you may get a glimpse of him after all."

When they arrived at the large Edwardian mansion, Jaeryn led the way up the sweeping stone entryway and nodded to the butler who opened the door for them. Ben omitted the nod, which made Jaeryn remember that it wasn't necessary as they handed over their hats and coats to the footmen who stood waiting on the guests. He caught sight of Ben darting little glances here and there to take in everything around him: the other guests; the grand, red-carpeted staircase; and numerous arched doorways leading off into other rooms. The American would do well for himself if he was given half a chance. Observation made up more than half of their work, and success often depended on good recall of details.

There were three men left in front of them when Jaeryn felt a light tap on his shoulder. He turned to find a servant holding a message on a silver tray, and he picked it up, discreetly working it open in the palm of his hand while King was occupied with the last man in line.

The fifth window in the main drawing room in five minutes. Vital. P

Jaeryn slipped the paper into his wallet just before King turned to them. Their host stood tall in his black dinner dress. That, coupled with his thick gray eyebrows and white hair, gave him an imposing air, and Jaeryn hoped it wouldn't be too off-putting on his new assistant's first time out.

"Doctor Dailey, sir," Jaeryn said. "My new assistant."

He held his breath as King looked down at the young newcomer. Any man probed by that experience keenness couldn't help suffering a slight tremor. King maintained the air of a smooth and civil host as he did it, but the sense of appraisal was thinly disguised. Ben didn't appear fazed in the least. It must have been his upbringing, Jaeryn thought indulgently. He was too American to know when to be nervous.

"A pleasure to meet you, Doctor Dailey," King said. "I believe I heard your name recently, but I don't remember where."

Ben inclined his head in greeting, then stood straight and composed with the same self-assurance he might have used with an old acquaintance. "My wife wrote your son a few weeks ago to tell him we were moving to England. I'm married to the former Charlotte King."

"Ah, yes, I recall reading her letter. My son was pleased to receive it. Did you bring Mrs. Dailey with you, doctor?" King looked expectantly down the line of men and women, but Ben shook his head.

"I'm afraid not. I came as Jaeryn Graham's guest."

"If I had known, I would have sent you an invitation of your own," King said. "That shall be remedied in future. Come, doctor; since you're new to Folkestone, I shall introduce you to some of my friends."

Jaeryn watched Ben go with an uneasy feeling and hoped that he wouldn't say anything imprudent. He stood alone, idling his way down the room towards his destination, rather daunted by the tall, white columns between each window and the clusters of high-backed, velvet-cushioned chairs, not to mention the loud laughter from the other guests. Was their host showing more attention than necessary to a distant relation? No one had been able to determine which side King was on in this European affair, and it was possible he was an ally. Ryson hadn't revealed their intelligence efforts to the colonel, but it would be foolish to believe he was entirely unaware of the activity going on in Folkestone.

After looking closely to make sure he was unobserved, Jaeryn sidled closer to the fifth windowsill and stood with his back to it. A slight catch of breeze drifted over his hand; Peters had already worked it open.

"Peters?" he whispered.

"Sir, the Radnor Park drop was checked as you asked. Dailey was given an assignment without your knowledge that took place at the Emmerson estate four nights ago. It was confirmed that the assignment supposedly came from London, but I have direct proofs of it being planted there by our adversaries. He—"

Jaeryn cut him off with a gesture as one of King's guests, a short, stout man with white hair, made his way towards him. He wiped the expression of concern off his face and shook hands with genial welcome.

"A good job about this morning, wasn't it?" the man said.

"Right," Jaeryn said. "A very good job." He crossed his gloved fingers behind his back in hopes the man would go away. Inside, his mind whirled. Dailey had gotten a false assignment and accomplished it. The fool. London would have a fine mess on their hands when they learned the Folkestone ring was given away by their precious recruit's blunder.

"I noticed it, of course. Must have rousted more than one person out of their beds. Absolutely destroyed the Germans and gave us the advantage in the next offensive. We can net them up at our leisure." The man chuckled as if it was the gladdest thing he had ever heard of.

Jaeryn understood exactly why some men were strangled. "Quite."

"Lloyd George is doing a good job of it at present. It was a dreadful inconvenience, getting the right man for the position, but it paid off in the end. Don't you think so?"

"I can't say that I do." He said it absent-mindedly, until the offended expression on the man's face brought him to in a moment of frozen horror.

"Really, doctor?" the man said. "How extraordinary."

Jaeryn grabbed at the chance to extricate himself. "I'm afraid I must entirely disagree. Now, if you will excuse me." He folded his arms across his chest and planted himself where he stood, radiating defiance.

The man started at him in open-mouthed disapproval. "Well—well, I suppose you can't expect the Irish to be too knowledgeable about that sort of thing," he muttered, before going off to inflict himself on another one of his cronies.

"Get on with it, Peters," Jaeryn whispered.

"Yes, sir. After looking at the communication, Fenton placed it back in the drop and waited to see what would come of it. A young man with dark hair, formerly lodging in the cottage of Mrs. Goodwin, opened and took the contents. He is now at the Star Inn, having a drink. I left Fenton to watch him and drove straight here."

"Right. Get Dailey and meet me outside. I don't care how you get him, but he must be gotten immediately, and King mustn't suspect."

Jaeryn wasted no time finding King's butler, still taking coats at the entrance. It was a toss-up whether he ought to slip away quietly or to take the obvious approach, but if he was missed while he was gone, he didn't want to raise King's suspicions. "Stafford, I'm terribly sorry, but I've been called away. I should be back before dinner is announced."

"Of course, Doctor Graham." Stafford gestured one of the servants to go and fetch his car around for him, and Jaeryn waited with an outward show of unconcern and an inward seething of anxiety until Ben joined him on the steps with a worried expression.

"Peters said someone had been shot. What's happening?"

"No one's been shot." Jaeryn hurried down the steps as the servant pulled up his car. "You've been an idiot." He waited until they were both inside before he said, "What in the name of spy craft possessed you to execute an anonymous order from London? If we're not dead before tonight, I won't have you to thank, that's certain."

Ben stilled in the seat next to him. "I don't understand," he said in a small, hard voice.

"Someone fabricated orders and sent them to you. If we don't hurry, they'll have enough information to expose us to Emmerson's henchmen. We have to silence them."

* * *

It was all a lie, that letter. And he had done it for his father's sake. If his father ever found out, he would laugh and probably say it was no more than he expected. A thread of fear worried through his

85

thoughts as Jaeryn drove along a winding hollow of back roads Ben hadn't discovered on his own yet. He wanted to ask who they were going to silence and how it was going to happen, but he didn't dare. He just sat and wound his fingers in and out, in and out, until Jaeryn pulled a revolver out of his pocket and handed it to him. "We're almost there. Make sure this is ready."

Ben's mouth went dry. "What are you doing to do with it?"

Jaeryn reached out for him to hand it back. "Never mind. I see I'd better take care of it. Now follow orders to the letter if you want to go back home again."

They pulled up at a little white-painted, two-story inn. The sun was waning in its strength as Jaeryn parked the car. He slammed the door, gesturing for Ben to wait, and disappeared inside. When he came back, his face had a shadowed, set cast to it. "Fenton will bring him out in a moment. I want you to help him get the man into the back seat as quickly as possible, and then we're going to drive away. Make sure it doesn't appear violent."

Ben kept his hands clenched and his eyes on the front door of the inn. His wish—knowing what would be the result of putting the paper in the library—was about to come true, and now he would do anything to take it back again.

The door opened, and a man, unsteady on his feet, was propelled through it by the fedora-decked agent Ben had met four days before. Stumbling alongside was the same man who had asked his sister for a date on their first evening in town. Reluctantly, Ben got out and helped steady them just as Christopher was about to tip too far.

Fenton gave him a brief nod and spoke to Jaeryn. "It took nine shots, but he can't spell his own name now." Ben looked at him, horrified until he realized it was the whiskey and not the gun.

Christopher grinned at him as he slumped into the back seat. "Want a drink with me?"

Jaeryn looked about them to make sure there were no observers. "Let's go. Good work, Fenton. Get in the back seat, Dailey, and help search him."

Ben looked at Christopher, but there was no answering recognition in the drunken laugh that met his gaze. "Jaeryn—"

"Get in before someone sees us."

The sheer command of Jaeryn's voice propelled him. As the car pulled down the road, further away from Folkestone and closer to London, Fenton rifled through one of Christopher's jacket pockets and Ben reached into the other. It didn't take long. The left pocket of his trousers held the letter and the key that Ben had placed in the drop only a few hours before. Fenton took it from him and handed it up to Jaeryn. "It's safe. He was never able to deliver it."

Jaeryn pocketed the evidence without taking his eyes from the road. "I'm thinking I know how this happened. Emmerson must have caught wind of the missing key and suspected me of taking it. He probably learned about Dailey being in town and laid a trap, thinking he could unmask both of us at once."

A moment of silence followed, and the only sound was the crunch of road under the tires and the wind in the trees as the sun turned from evening peak to downward glow. "He can't go home," Jaeryn said.

It was the last word that broke him. Home—someone was not going home tonight, and all because he had obeyed orders that he thought had been official. "Jaeryn, you can't do this."

"We haven't got a choice, Dailey. It's part of being an agent." Jaeryn stopped by the side of the road and parked the car where empty fields with long grass and scrub bushes stretched out. He got out, and Ben sat unmoving, horrified, while Fenton opened the car door.

"Hold him down a moment," Jaeryn ordered. Ben made no move to touch him, so Fenton held the drowsing man down by both shoulders while Jaeryn hit him under the chin. Christopher slumped unconscious.

Jaeryn looked at the helpless figure. For the briefest second, his tight control slipped and his face creased with pain. "Sorry, old fellow. Wouldn't do it if I had any other choice." He gave Ben a long look, and the hardness he had shown hitherto softened. "Stay here, Dailey."

Ben stayed, the world turning to a numb swirl of gray. The car seat bounced as the weight left it and Jaeryn and Fenton shifted the man out. But there was no sound. Just the wind in the trees, and the shuffle of footsteps, and a long, painful stretch of silence. His soul screamed with the pain of it until the footsteps shuffled back again and someone touched his shoulder.

"He's gone." Dimly, through the haze, he recognized Jaeryn's voice. "It was painless. Fenton's contacting another agent to take care of it. All trace of this will disappear by night."

Ben's numbed brain began to find words. "You could have shipped him off to the front. You could have had him arrested. This wasn't *necessary.*"

"I couldn't. He was about to expose you, and through you, all the rest of us. We'll have tickets forged to Liverpool and one of our agents can plant a story about him. It'll look like he skipped out, and all of us will be safe. It's a blessing we caught him before he reached Emmerson." Jaeryn looked concerned. "I know it seemed ruthless. But I have to ask you to give me the benefit of the doubt. Now pull yourself together, Dailey. We have a dinner to attend, and I can't have you exposing us."

Something iron entered his soul at that. Jaeryn had been an agent long enough not to do things needlessly, and he probably understood best why he had done what he did. What had happened had needed to happen. But that did not mean he ever had to like it, and if Jaeryn could go straight to the next thing without showing grief, then he would never know that anyone else had cause to struggle.

Ben lifted his chin, hiding all trace of horror or sorrow, though the faintest edge of accusation seeped through in spite of his efforts. "I can handle it."

"Good fellow." Jaeryn clapped him on the shoulder as Ben got out of the back seat to shift to the front. "You'll make an agent after all."

Under the shining light of the gold chandeliers, Jaeryn blinked away the weariness and fought to muster up the easy smile that was expected of him. Normally, he spent the evening counting the hours until leaving. Tonight, he wanted to disappear into the grounds and make peace with what he had done. But making peace wasn't an option.

The long dinner table stretched out resplendent with a white linen tablecloth, cut-glass goblets, gold-edged dinner service, and serving dishes heaped with pyramids of plums and strawberries. Waiters moved about proffering wine and lighting extra candles in wall sconces. Colonel King's collations lacked nothing and breathed easy elegance in spite of the inconvenience of the war shortage. Few possessed the indelicacy to drop dark hints about the source of the abundance, although those who graced the occasions felt no compunction at joking about a secret supply. Men from London, men from Dover, men from Ramsgate, and certain illustrious citizens of Folkestone were invited to these social occasions, and it was a handy way to pick up private, up-to-date information about the front and the government—both for England and for England's enemies.

Jaeryn was placed next to his assistant during dinner, but Ben refused to speak to him except when he was forced, and he was obliged to spend most of his time conversing with the lady seated on his other side. To everyone else, Ben carried on effortlessly, and Jaeryn hardly believed his ears when he caught wind of Ben discussing America with an MP as if he had not just seen a man die. It must be anger—some men found hidden resources when they were forced to it, resources they didn't have otherwise. Hopefully it would last him the whole evening.

After dinner, Jaeryn wandered through a side door into a back hall. He couldn't stand the company any longer. His own revulsion over what he had had to do was setting in, and if he had to endure another trivial conversation, he feared he would collapse under the strain of it.

Opening the first door he came to, he found himself in a little sitting room with all the guests' coats laid out on a table in the corner. King's butler, Stafford, a short, agile, gray-haired man, stood with a tan ulster in his hand.

Stafford turned when Jaeryn's shadow blocked the doorway. "Can I bring you something, sir?" he asked gravely.

Jaeryn kept an offhand tone, though it took an effort. "No, thank you, Stafford. I'm quite comfortable and in need of nothing except a moment's privacy."

"Very good, sir." The gray-haired butler replaced the coat and left Jaeryn alone. More out of curiosity than anything, Jaeryn picked up the overcoat to see whose it was and found a thin leather billfold inside. It looked innocent enough, but he picked it up and opened it. Inside he found a five-pound note, well-worn and creased, and a brand-new picture passport with the name Nathan Speyer. At the name, a thrill jolted through him. He had heard it when he first came to Folkestone, tossed about as gossip from one man to the next. "The best friend of King's son," one young MP had said. "He'll do well for himself in the war." At the time, he had sent Fenton for a full dossier, keeping Ryson in the dark about his actions. If King and Ryson were interested in Nathan Speyer, then there would be power, and he wasn't about to lose a trump card if he could pick it up.

Jaeryn replaced the passport and the money exactly as he had found them and slipped the wallet in his pocket as he drifted back into the overheated drawing-room. Everything was so polished and shining that his likeness reflected back at him from the wood floor. Wandering to and fro, Jaeryn listened to the gossip about the delay in American involvement in the war, putting in occasional questions when they were expected of him and trying to appear agreeable. With a sense of relief, he saw Ben disengage himself from conversation with a tall man with gray-streaked hair and make his way toward him. Jaeryn excused himself from his latest conversation and sauntered to a place along the wall free of observers.

"Who were you speaking with?" he asked.

Ben didn't appear too keen to see him. "A secretary of the War Office named Allan Evesham."

Jaeryn watched the man make his way with kingly bearing through the crowd. "I've seen him here once or twice. He's a London official who comes down every six months or so. He and King used to be friends until the war, but with the suspicion surrounding King, Evesham doesn't come much."

No trace of a smile crossed his assistant's face. "He said he was stopping here on a return trip from France. The quaking this morning was a blast at Messines. It's the greatest victory they've had for months."

So that was what the old diplomat earlier had been blathering on about. "What else did he say?"

"He said it made him hope."

Jaeryn sighed and cast about for something else to talk about. A quartet of musicians with their stringed instruments provided the soft background accompaniment of Boccherini's Minuet, highlighting the monotony of the affair. He waved off a waiter approaching with a tray of coffee. "King seems to like you, from all appearances."

No reply.

"Did King introduce you to that fellow over there?" He gestured discreetly to a young man with straight dark hair, almost too young to be in such a crowd, who stood chatting with another couple.

Ben followed the gesture with his eyes. "Yes. Nathan Speyer. I didn't catch anything beyond his name."

Jaeryn edged away from the group of men nearing them and motioned Ben to follow. "Nathan Speyer may be of interest to us. King dropped a hint to a Parliament acquaintance of his recently, and one of my informants picked it up. Quite confidentially, you understand. Apparently, King and Ryson partnered to groom this young protégé for a rather delicate position, or so I gather. I'd like to collect more specific facts. Can you introduce me, do you think?"

91

"I will," Ben said sternly, "but he just lost his sister in the bomb drop last month, and if you have any pity, you'll leave him out of your scheming."

They worked their way around the room until they reached Nathan Speyer. When Ben made the introduction, Jaeryn pulled out the worn leather wallet. "I'm glad we were introduced, Mr. Speyer, for I have something that I believe is yours. I found this wallet just a short time ago in the coat room. Pardon the intrusion, but I had to find out who it belonged to."

Nathan took it and pulled out the passport inside. "I'm much obliged, doctor. I didn't realize it was missing." A hint of amusement crossed his face. "If you were in the coat room, I suspect you were the lost-looking fellow I saw wandering about just now."

Jaeryn bowed in acquiescence. "I'm afraid you've discovered my reticence for politics."

Nathan chuckled. "I can't blame you. This is my first occasion, and I'd rather be upstairs with his son, Starlin."

"You must be new to Folkestone, then?"

"I came from Dover originally and transferred here to be King's secretary when my father went to the front. I was taking care of my mother and sister until they both died in the bomb drop."

"My condolences." Jaeryn groaned inwardly. He couldn't bring himself to pry into the life of a man who had undergone so much loss recently, valuable connection or not.

"Thank you, doctor. A pleasure to meet you."

Nathan nodded and moved off, leaving the two of them alone again. As soon as he was out of earshot, Jaeryn turned to Ben. "He's King's secretary. He would know something if anyone does. Dailey, your wife is King's cousin, you said?"

Ben's jaw tightened. "Yes."

"Well, see if you can strike up a better acquaintance with the King family. Get into their inner circle. I'll let you handle this angle from here on out. Report back as you find information." He waited for Ben to reply, and when none came, he frowned. "Did you hear me?"

"I heard."

Ben turned his back on him and strode off, and Jaeryn looked around the room. King was nowhere in sight, and Dailey wasn't about to be pleasant company. He would just have to return to counting the hours again until he could leave.

* * *

Charlotte was in bed when Jaeryn dropped him off at half past eleven. Ben slipped in beside her. A lonely, crying thing inside him ached, but he was not sure what it was. He lay face-down in the pillow, rigid, unmoving, willing the sight of Christopher's drunken grin to erase from his memory forever. Something hot and wet slipped out, and before he realized quite what was happening, he stifled a shivering breath. Charlotte wrapped her arm around him and helped him sit up. She held him close, smelling of jasmine and home—everything that he wanted in the middle of a desert of things that he very much didn't.

"Did someone die today, darling?" she whispered.

She always had an uncanny sense when he had lost a patient. She had little idea what kind of loss this was. "He was young. He shouldn't have died. It was unjust."

Charlotte snuggled closer, rubbing her hand back and forth across his shoulders, trying to bring ease to them. "Not everyone can heal. It isn't your fault."

"He wasn't sick. Or hurt. And I didn't want it to happen." Ben shut his mouth on the anger before it betrayed him into saying more. "I should have prevented it."

"Darling, you can't—" She stopped, and he could tell in the silence that she was thinking. "It wasn't a patient, was it?" she asked.

"No. And it was all because I made a mistake. Something went wrong, and I was tricked. We all were. There was no other way to keep everyone safe, Jaeryn said." Frustration edged his voice. "I don't think I belong here. I'm lost in this kind of work, and he isn't helping."

Her voice was low and fierce, though the fierceness was not for him, he knew. "You are strong and brave and kind. And you did what you thought you were supposed to do. If he does not want you here, then we will face him and show him that twenty years of bravery are too strong to be undone by three weeks of war."

The crying thing inside him lessened, like a small animal still licking its wounds but no longer dying. "I heard tonight that the British started an offensive at Messines this morning, and it went well. If it keeps going well, it might be what they need to win the war. We could go home soon."

She ran her soft fingers along his cheek, and a smile slowly kindled on her lips. "We will go home soon. And until we do, I will be your home, my love."

* * *

Dailey said nothing as he wished him goodnight. Jaeryn sighed as the car pulled away, leaving Ben standing in the night, faced away, shoulders rigid. It would be a long time before he regained the man's trust. He had never wanted something like this to scare an unwanted assistant back to America, but he doubted Dailey would be staying much longer now.

Jaeryn drove to the clinic and found the lights on and an old friend waiting for him. Everyone else knew him as the red-headed fellow who had put out the fires on Tontine, but Jaeryn knew him better than that. "Terry."

"Hey, doc. Got that errand taken care of for you."

Jaeryn undid his necktie and took off his dinner jacket. "Sometimes I think London forgets how hard that kind of decision is."

"You did right, doc. You were as gentle as you could be." Terry perched himself on the edge of the desk. "I gave the dead fellow a salute for the burial—kind of made up for not warning him, I figured. How'd Dailey take it?"

Jaeryn leaned his chin on his hands. "I think he'll hate me forever now. He doesn't—doesn't understand that sort of thing. He's never had to see it before."

Terry pulled out a lighter. Jaeryn frowned at him, and he shoved it back in his pocket. "Well, most people probably don't realize this exists, I guess," said Terry. "It's war."

Jaeryn shrugged in reply, and a moment of silence fell between them. Then Jaeryn said, "If you came for something to eat, Mrs. Goodwin restocked the kitchen today."

Terry's hand snuck back to his pocket again and fiddled with the lighter inside. "No, I was going to stop by to ask you a favor, but then after earlier, I figured you'd want someone to chat with, too."

"My Irish priest." Jaeryn smiled in spite of himself.

Terry laughed. "I'm not a priest."

Jaeryn tried to rub the weariness out of his face. "So what's the favor?"

"I just want you to check up on a new friend of mine. No rush, but she should be seen in the next couple of days. She's new to town. Just came in from Dover, and I helped her settle in today. She doesn't know a soul here, and she needs some taking care of."

"Dailey's taken over Winfield's route, but if you want me, I can come instead."

Terry shrugged. "Either way, doc. I just want someone good to look in on her."

"He's quite capable." Habit drove Jaeryn to find a pencil and paper. "Give me her name and address, and I'll have him stop by on Monday. What's her condition?"

"Alisa Dorroll. Out on Newnham Lane, in the two-story farmhouse with the overgrown drive. She'll tell him about herself."

"Very well. I'll send him to check on her."

"Grand. I'll say good night, doc. Don't beat yourself up. You had to watch out for all of us."

Not until Jaeryn saw Terry out the front door did the full meaning of the lady's name strike him. Alisa Dorroll. She couldn't be related to his new assistant—probably just a strange twist of happenstance. But if it wasn't happenstance, Ben Dailey had the most right to see her.

He climbed up the stairs to his room and rifled through the fresh laundry to find his comforting string of beads underneath. They were worn and fragile, and fourteen years of loving use had smoothed them to a shine that no finish could have done on its own. There was only one way to end a night like this with any kind of peace. And that was to end it, as he had ended every night for the last seven years, in prayers.

* * *

On Friday morning, the day after King's dinner, Ben took the list of assigned house calls Jaeryn handed to him. The last one brought him to a halt. Alisa Dorroll. When he looked up, he caught Jaeryn glancing sideways in his direction, and anger flared in his chest. Ben folded the list and shoved it in his bag without comment. "I'm thinking I need better transportation arrangements for some of these calls if you want me to be back sooner. The cab is too expensive for the outlying ones."

"Right." Jaeryn busied himself with his own list. "I could lend you the bicycle I used to use, unless you want to set yourself up with a horse."

"I'll take the bicycle." He pulled out medications he would need and put them in his bag. "The last woman on my list is new. Do you know what she wants?"

He caught Jaeryn sneaking another sideways glance his way. "I don't. I heard she was new in town and might need help."

"I'll see her for myself, then." Ben shouldered his bag and reached for his Homburg as he headed out. If Alisa Dorroll was related to him—and he hardly dared hope she wasn't—she had a right to know his connection to her. Or maybe not. After all, his object in Folkestone didn't concern her. If she were not related to him, then it would be foolish to give his real name away. She might tell someone else by accident, and gossip spread fast if what he heard on patient calls was any indication.

He put off her visit as long as possible while he wrestled over what to do, and he even considered riding home to discuss the matter with Charlotte. But in the end, he decided to find out who the lady was before telling anyone about it, and three o' clock found him bicycling down a shady back lane in Folkestone's farming district to meet her.

Jaeryn had scrawled the house numbers so close together that it was hard to distinguish between them, but at length, Ben thought he had the right place. The white, two-story house sat well back on the property, and a gnarled oak sheltered it from the view of the road. A weathered stone barn stood a few paces beyond it to the southwest, and in the fenced-off paddock a Percheron horse dozed in the shade, its tail flicking now and then to brush the flies off its back. One or two fields on the property looked planted and cultivated, but on the whole this swath of land, hinting at former wealth, lay fallow.

The entire place lay hushed and deserted. The driveway was empty of any means of transportation, and no chickens or other livestock made the usual clamor he heard passing other Folkestone farms. Aside from the horse and a disheveled gray tabby kitten lying on the front step, he didn't see any signs of life. Ben almost hoped there weren't any as he walked up the overgrown drive and knocked at the side door. Receiving no answer, he persisted louder, and after a continued silence he tried the doorknob to see if it was locked.

"What do you want?" A stern young woman's voice startled him, and Ben peered through the window, but he could not see past the blue-checked curtains.

"We received a phone call from this place asking for medical assistance. I'm Doctor Jaeryn Graham's new assisting physician, Doctor Benjamin Dailey," he said, trying to sound reassuring.

"No one needs help here." In spite of the words, the woman's voice choked a little.

"Please," he entreated, "I promise, I come in peace. I will not hurt you."

Ben waited in silence for a moment, but she didn't come, and he turned to go, disappointed at his failure. When he reached the bottom step, he heard the door latch click and turned around. A small woman stood before him in a man's work shirt and trousers. As soon as he saw her, his heart went out in pity at her plight. Both of the garments were entirely too large, but neither of them disguised the fact that she was carrying a child—and due to deliver soon, if his guess was correct. Her dark brown hair was pinned up loosely, and her mouth had a frightened, tired expression to it. Ben offered his hand slowly, so as not to startle her. "I'm Doctor Dailey. Can I help you?"

Her blue eyes were big, expressionless, and empty of vitality. "No one's ill," she said weakly. "I mean, no one needs a doctor yet, at least." Her eyes took on a cornered look.

"Are you sure? If you aren't able to afford medical services, I won't charge you. But you should get some help if you really need it."

"I…I…" Her voice trembled, and she stopped.

Looking more carefully at her, Ben decided that she was older then she appeared. Though she barely reached five feet in height, faint lines showed on her forehead; and while her face was soft, it didn't hold the softness of juvenility. Then he noticed the thin gold band on her ring finger. He pointed to it. "Is your husband over in France? I have a brother there as well."

"I don't know." Her chin trembled, and she began to cry like the child she resembled. "I just received a letter this morning. He's very ill, and he might be…dead soon." The last words were whispered, as if by speaking them she might comprehend what they meant.

Ben re-ascended the stairs and led her into the house. Making their way to the kitchen, he escorted her to a chair and urged her to sit down. "Can you tell me your name, Mrs.—" A tear dripped down her face, and she ducked her head to hide it, but another came faster, and another, and her small shoulders shook with the sorrow she could not hold back. Ben sat patiently and looked away until her sobs silenced. When she finished, her lips parted.

"Go on," he said encouragingly. "This is a time of war, and wars make it necessary for us to share what we otherwise would not. I promise I will be discreet."

The young woman wiped her eyes with the backs of her hands. "I don't know what to do. His baby will come soon, and I don't have anyone to help when I'm ready. I was living with an aunt in Dover until recently, but I can't anymore, so I came here. It's a family house. It's mine now." She looked up at him to see if he understood, and Ben smiled at her.

"Of course. Do you have any idea when your due date is?"

She shook her head. "No. I've never had a baby before. But soon, I think."

"We'll get you the help you need. I'll come by in the next couple of days and bring a woman I trust to tell you all you need to know. It would be nice to know your name."

"Alisa," she said. "Alisa Dorroll."

It didn't take much effort to love her trustful frailty, and Ben wanted nothing more than to be able to smooth over her difficulties for her. "May I ask when you last heard from your husband, and what his name is?"

"I haven't heard from him in a long time—even before he was ill." Her red-rimmed eyes held a wistful expression. "And now he might be gone without me even knowing. His name is Edmond Dorroll."

Ben felt as if a cold hand had reached out and slapped his face. It was his brother after all, and his brother was dying. "When did he last write?"

"I received a letter the first week of March. He came here on leave in October, and we married then. He asked me to marry him before he enlisted, but I was too young, and we had to wait. I only had him one week before he had to leave. And he's only written once since then." Another tear trickled down Alisa's face and she wiped it away, trying to keep from crying again.

"I see." Ben barely formed the words, but by an effort, he managed to make them sound natural. "I will come back to help you more. I promise. Will you be all right for a couple of days?"

"Of course. I've been alone since my husband left." Alisa pushed back her chair to see him to the door. "Thank you for coming," she said earnestly.

Ben motioned her not to get up. "I'll show myself out. Don't worry anymore. I will take...see that you are taken care of. If you think you are going into labor before I come back, call the Tontine clinic right away and ask for myself or Doctor Jaeryn Graham. God bless you, Mrs. Dorroll. Keep your courage up."

As soon as the door closed behind him, Ben leaned against the frame and took a long, slow breath. He missed Mrs. O'Sean. If she lived closer, a visit to her kitchen might be timely about now.

* * *

If he had hopes of finding time to fit a sister-in-law into the new puzzle of things, Jaeryn dashed them as soon as he came back to the clinic. The rest of the house calls had taken him past dinner time, and Jaeryn met him in the hall as he opened the door. "Dailey, I'm glad you came by. I wanted to catch you before you went home."

Ben shifted his bag off his shoulder and pulled out the medications to put back. "What is it?"

"The Radnor Park drop was completely compromised yesterday. I had Fenton set up a new one at the St. Eanswythe church. It's in the graveyard next to the tombstone of a Rebecca Rogers. You can't miss it." He pulled out a sheet of paper and offered it. "Here's the new combination."

Ben glanced at it and then crumpled it. "I'll remember it."

"Good. The other thing was, we headed off trouble last night, but it doesn't bode well for the future. Until we know for sure that we weren't compromised, you should keep a close eye on your own security and that of your wife and sister as well. All communications that purport to be from London must be discussed together from here on out. Someone knew how to infiltrate our drop." Jaeryn rubbed a hand over his face, but the concern could not be wiped away. "If we can't find out how the leak happened, our Folkestone ring could be the entry point that lets German traitors into the British Secret Service."

Ben took up his medical bag to empty it. "I'll take extra precautions after this."

He put the medications back as Jaeryn crossed his arms and stood watching him. "I know you don't like the decision I made yesterday, but it's part of secret intelligence. If you want to progress, you'll have to get used to it."

He clenched his teeth as he turned the bottles so the labels faced front. "I don't think murdering someone is the kind of thing I want to get used to."

"You say it like I wanted to do it. How did you expect to lead in intelligence if you aren't prepared for hard decisions?"

"Lead?" Ben threw him a confused glance. "I'm sorry, I'm not sure what you mean."

"You're here to work up to a leadership position, aren't you? What are you interested in? Collecting intelligence data? Deciphering messages? Handling a spy ring of your own? You'll be well-suited abroad with your talent for foreign languages."

"I'm only here to help you finish this, and then I plan to return to America," Ben said quietly.

Jaeryn stood with his mouth open in frozen shock before recollecting himself. "I was under the impression you wanted a career in intelligence. That's what Ryson told me."

"No, I only came for one assignment. As soon as it's finished, I'm going home to set up a practice."

Surprise effectively silenced any further questions Jaeryn might want to ask. He looked rather dumbfounded, but Ben could see his green eyes processing their conversation as fast as the slim white fingers snatched up prescription papers. Jaeryn scrawled something across the first page, then tossed down his pencil and looked up. "I thought you came as a replacement. They despise the Irish here. I thought—"

Ben pressed his lips together in a thin line. So all this time Jaeryn had thought he was someone to be frightened and sent home. "I'm not going to replace you."

"No offense. Now that I know, I'll make sure you get a square deal for whatever it was you came for. I'll—" The phone rang and Jaeryn picked it up. "Graham…He's dead? You're sure? …We'll come now." He clattered down the receiver. "That was Peters. Emmerson is dead, finally."

Ben's heart picked up a faster beat. "What did he die of?"

"Heart failure. Died in his sleep a few minutes ago." Jaeryn opened drawers and pulled things out of cupboards with an air of suppressed excitement. "I've waited since the beginning of the year for this moment. Peters agreed to let us in for a few hours to look through the old man's papers. We won't have a better chance, as the executor of his will comes tomorrow."

"I'll call Charlotte and tell her I won't be—" Ben stopped when he remembered that Charlotte had no phone to answer him. Well, she wasn't likely to worry if he returned late; he had been late a couple of times already without incident. Though he did wish, after what Jaeryn had said, that he had left more than a second Webley with her.

"You'll have time to go home and tell her if you like," Jaeryn said. "We'll leave separately so we have a better chance of avoiding detection. I have two house calls I wasn't able to get to. You'll take one, I'll take the other, and that way if anyone's tailing our movements we should be able to shake them. Ask if you can leave by the back door when you go. If I give you Emmerson's address, do you think you can find it on your own?"

"Certainly." Ben took out the appointment book he kept and wrote down the street names Jaeryn gave him to help him in the right direction. He didn't recognize all of them, but he felt pretty sure he could manage without trouble. "What do you hope to find while we're there?"

"What I need, and have been trying to find for two months, is any sort of written communication with agent identification numbers as signatures. Since April, not one agent identification code has come to my attention. If we could get just one number, that would give us a chance to try to infiltrate their communications. Emmerson may have copies somewhere in his home. We may also find other letters of particular importance as well. They'll very likely all be coded, so we'll copy anything that looks useful and send it by message to London for deciphering. We have until dawn to look, but Emmerson's library is extensive, and we'll have none too much time." Jaeryn stood up and put the dishes in the sink to wash later. "Ready for your first real try at some espionage work?" he asked cheerily.

Ben tried to make his enthusiasm match Jaeryn's. "Of course."

Jaeryn glanced at his watch. "The time is seven at present, and we should be in Emmerson's library by half past eight. You are armed and loaded, I hope?"

"Always. And I found another Webley to leave with Charlotte."

"That's wise. I find it remarkable that you were familiar with the use of firearms before you came here." Ben didn't offer any explanation, and Jaeryn did not press further. They each collected the supplies they would need in relative silence and left in haste by the back door.

Even with the bicycle Jaeryn had loaned him, Ben had little enough time to stop by Copt Point. After telling Charlotte he would not be home until the next morning, he started on his other errand, which took him to the Lower Sandgate Road along the Channel. Jaeryn hadn't given him a hard assignment—merely a routine follow-up on a little Belgian boy whose cast he had removed two weeks before. When he finished, Ben left as instructed by the back door and pedaled through town in a northerly direction.

Soon the misting drops plastered his hair to his forehead. His tires slipped on the wet cobbles, and he had to weave around puddles the rain was fast increasing, while keeping a sharp lookout for anyone who might be observing him. But he didn't see a soul besides ordinary pedestrians. Once he passed through town, his way took him along dirt roads filled with ruts that he had a hard time avoiding in the darkness. Trees stretched out dripping branches under the charcoal mass of clouds, and gusts of wind rippled the thick fields of wheat. A fitting night to spend in a house of death.

At a quarter after eight, Ben turned up the wet gravel drive. Jaeryn silently joined him, and they kept to the shadows until they passed the front gate. Jaeryn pressed the bell next to the front double doors, and a butler in neat black opened them.

"Hello, Peters. How are you this evening?" Jaeryn asked, handing him their coats and wiping the water from his boots.

The gray-haired, slightly heavy-set butler looked like the epitome of British integrity. Ben could see at a glance why Jaeryn trusted him. "Quite well, thank you, sir," Peters said, taking their hats and placing them on a hat stand with gold hooks. "The servants are out of the way, and I have drinks set out in the library, as well as a fire. I will lock up here once you have everything you need."

"Very good." Jaeryn rummaged in his bag and pulled out a pen and paper. "You search the upstairs rooms and bring us any important papers you find. We'll start in the library. I trust you opened the safe for us?"

"Yes, sir," Peters said. "The first bookcase is in slight disarray, as my late employer kept his safe behind the bottom shelf."

"Excellent. Keep someone on watch in case we are interrupted. Where's Emmerson's will? I should like to look at it."

"His lawyer has it, sir. He will be bringing it down from London sometime in the course of the morning."

Jaeryn frowned. "Of all the luck. Well, we'll have to do without it. All right, we don't have time to waste." He walked across the dark parquet floor and pushed open the double doors opposite the front entrance, issuing instructions as he went. "Let's fill out the death certificate first. I need both of you to witness it. Then we'll see what Emmerson has hidden away. Anything else I should know before we begin, Peters?"

"No, sir."

"Very well. Upstairs then, shall we?"

Jaeryn seemed to know his way about the rich, old-fashioned mansion quite well. He crossed the high-ceilinged hall to an imposing spiral staircase and ran up the polished steps as if they were his own. Ben caught a glimpse of gold-framed paintings and mahogany side tables as they hurried along the upstairs hall, but he didn't catch much before Jaeryn turned off to another wing and opened a door.

He was quite ready for the presence of death that met them; after all, he had seen it many times before. An old man with thinning white hair, wrinkled skin, and a shrunken frame lay with the embroidered bedspread pulled up to his chest. His face looked stern even after life no longer animated it, especially his thin-lipped mouth. Ben watched as Jaeryn leaned over the great four-poster bed and examined the body once again for any signs of life. There were none. Within short order, Jaeryn had filled out the certificate and checked it over, after which he handed it to Ben to sign, and then to Peters.

When they had finished, Jaeryn asked, "Peters, have you found what that key we copied was used for yet?"

"No, sir. There are a great many locks to try in this house, and it hasn't fit any yet. I just finished the first floor this week."

Jaeryn sighed. "Keep trying while we work in the library. This may be our last night undisturbed here, so we mustn't waste it. Come along, Dailey."

Then they all filed out and their work commenced in earnest.

Chapter Seven
Mr. Emmerson's Library

The heavy aura of ages past and ages future hung over Ben as he entered Mr. Emmerson's library. Thousands of hard-bound volumes lined the wall, and the shelves were so lofty that he estimated the ceiling at twelve feet or more in height. It smelled of dust and ink and wood polish, and that, coupled with the heavy silence, gave off a comfortable invitation for visitors to sit down and take their ease. Worn leather armchairs, old-fashioned desks, reading stands, and a large globe filled the floor space, while a rolling ladder stood at one end of the room allowing access to the higher shelves. Ben saw Jaeryn take a deep breath, almost one of sheer bewilderment, and glance at the clock. The hands pointed to quarter-to-nine. Half an hour gone since they arrived, just in looking over the old man's body.

An elegant table stood in the center of the room, with tea things laid out to help them keep alert. Next to the tea tray lay a huge, leather-bound book. Ben walked over and opened the cover. It cracked with age, and flakes of paper from the spine came off on his hand. Inside, in cramped penmanship, he found a complete list of every book and its placement.

"This ought to help," he said to Jaeryn, who had finished taking a survey of the room and now came over to where he stood.

Jaeryn flipped through the pages to give them a cursory examination. When he saw the extent of the collection, his accent sounded heavier, and his forehead creased in anxiety. "I hope we don't have to look through the books. That would be a beastly business. But if we exhaust the other possibilities without finding anything helpful, we'll begin on them. I don't think it will come to that, though. Emmerson's intercepted letters gave hints of his underhand activities, so he must have other incriminating evidence that isn't too deeply hidden."

"What do you want me to look for?" Ben asked.

Jaeryn closed the huge ledger with a dull thump. "Any letters in German or French or English that purport to have some connection to his German affiliations. Any scraps of paper that look like innocent gibberish. Any written indication of whom he intended to leave his house to. He must have left some directions for his successor besides what he wrote in his will."

Ben still wasn't quite sure, but Jaeryn seemed confident, and he hoped the process would prove fruitful. "Why didn't Peters look into this before now? We don't have much time, and we're not familiar with Emmerson's habits like he is."

Jaeryn gave a short, sharp laugh. "Whoever said he didn't look into it? Don't worry about Peters; he's one of ours. It's not always possible to look for something without detection under your employer's nose. Now, you take the safe, and I'll run through these desk drawers. Be as quick as you can, and put everything back exactly where you find it."

Just as Peters had said, the first bookcase was pulled out to give access to the wall safe. Ben knelt down on the rich Persian rug, unlocked the safe with the key Peters had laid out beside it, and removed the papers. He then stacked them so he would know exactly where to return them when he finished. It still gave him an odd feeling, looking through someone else's affairs without their permission. He wouldn't want someone doing the same to him. But Jaeryn didn't look in the mood to be argued with, and he didn't dare protest. There were certificates of stocks and bonds, signed receipts of investments, land purchases, and ledgers of the estate's income by year. Those he laid to the side. The safe contained no mementos, no record of a family life, and no old photographs from past generations of Emmersons tucked away for safekeeping. Indeed, it was as if the old man lived void of relationships except for his political work. But that political work seemed deeply important to him. Emmerson kept detailed diaries of the bills he worked to pass in Parliament, with all the correspondence relating to them in a separate file for each bill.

Once he emptied the safe, Ben pried around the edges to test whether or not a false back hid another compartment. That effort proved fruitless, so he returned the safe to its hiding place and moved the bookshelf back against the wall, keeping out one letter that he wanted to examine in greater detail.

The formidable grandfather clock read half past nine. Ben took a seat in one of the easy chairs and laid the letter out on the tea table. It was a short note written to Emmerson in January, a notice for the disseverment of a joint bank account in Germany, signed "C——." Ben read the letter over for some time but found nothing else to indicate that the message contained a double meaning. Puzzled, he glanced over at Jaeryn, who sat frozen in concentration as he read through a stack of his own.

Clearing his throat to attract Jaeryn's attention, Ben laid down the letter in front of him. "What do you make of that?" he asked.

The doctor squinted slightly as Ben pointed out the sentence noting the manufacturer's location. "Germany. Written at the turn of the century. Put it in a pile for us to keep, and we'll forward it on to London."

Ben took back the sheet of stationery as if it burned his fingers to touch. "The letter is legally the property of Emmerson's heir, unless the will says otherwise."

"You're not going to stick at that now, are you? After all, I don't mean to throw it back in your face, but you've already shown that you don't mind some deception. As unfortunate as it is, taking evidence is part of our vocation." Jaeryn dismissed the matter with a wave of his hand and returned to his own perusals.

Ben put the letter down again. "No. I want to know there's a better way. This is stealing unless you have a more appealing name for it. I didn't steal in what I did."

Jaeryn's voice tensed with impatience. "I would prefer to discuss the ethics of our methods at a more convenient place. For now, this is what we know, and this is what we're acting on. I'll take the moral responsibility for it. And I won't even make you carry what we take if you would object to doing so." He placed a stack of papers back in one of the desk drawers, taking care to make sure they looked the same. Then he glanced at the clock, whose hands were rapidly creeping forward, and again at his companion, and his expression softened. "You ask questions that I do not know the answers to. I wish I did. For now, we lie so that others may tell the truth. If we come to a better understanding of it, then we will reconsider when that time comes."

"You think that since I didn't refuse to keep a secret for your spy, I should have no reason to draw back now." Ben twisted the envelope to the letter in his hands until Jaeryn pulled it away. "But I had a code of integrity before I came here, and breaking it that time was not an easy decision to make."

"Was your decision to involve yourself in this work an easy one?"

Jaeryn's green eyes held just a hint too much interest, and Ben backed away a step. "No. Do you want Peters to have any help upstairs?"

"Not right now." Jaeryn stretched his cramped muscles and poured a mug of tea, taking it over to the window for a quick break. "He has plenty of help. We aren't the only people here tonight. I'd rather not have you go upstairs at present, as his assistants aren't people you should meet."

Ben went to another clerestory window and looked out. Bright stars winked in chilly indifference on the old house and all the secrets he and Jaeryn were trying to wrest from it. The lawn sloped gently down to a small lakelet, with trees gathered about its edge and a stone bridge crossing over to the other side. The depths looked cool and unruffled. On the far edge, a small pavilion offered shelter to wanderers enjoying the shrubberies. But there had been no one to enjoy them for a long time now. Just a shriveled old man, plotting the overthrow of his native England until death halted his labors. Perhaps the next owner would be more worthy of the beauty and turn it to good instead of evil.

"We must get to work again," Ben said. He felt tired after a busy day, and he knew Jaeryn wanted just as much to go home and call it a night, but they wouldn't have another chance to make such a thorough search.

Jaeryn nodded and set his mug of tea down on the windowsill, its steam rising up like a little frosty breath. "Try the ledger. I'm still going through the desk. So far I've only found old invitation cards and inconsequential records."

Ben turned back to the dim old shelves and shuddered. "Let's hope we don't have to start in on the books."

"We'll come to them if we must. I'm hoping the ledger yields something, so we don't have to think about that."

Jaeryn continued rummaging, and Ben flipped through the list of books, scanning for any odd markings that would indicate a section to be checked. During the long silence, he lost count of time and didn't hear the heavy ticking of the clock until a low groan of impatience from Jaeryn broke his concentration and he glanced up. "What's the matter?"

Jaeryn had taken his jacket off, exposing a leather shoulder holster to view, and his hair was disheveled from his explorations under the desk. "I wish Emmerson hadn't sent the will to his lawyer. Why would he keep it in London, unless he had something to hide?"

"I don't know." Ben turned back to the ledger. The stack of pages he had gone through appeared discouragingly thin next to the number of pages yet to be examined. "I hardly see the point of this."

"You wouldn't," Jaeryn snapped. "We must start somewhere and use the time we have. You've already given us one clue, and we may unearth something else." The Irishman stood up to survey the rows of books again. Even his courage seemed to fail him at the prospect. He went over to the bell pull. "Peters is guiding a search team upstairs to go through all the beds and furniture. I'll ring for him and ask if he's found anything."

Jaeryn rang, and Peters answered with a promptness that surprised both of them. Unlike the two doctors, he looked quite fresh and energetic, as if he were about to host a dinner party for expected guests.

"Well?" Jaeryn asked. "Anything to report?"

The gray-haired butler stood tall, pleased with himself but careful not to let his excitement overcome his reserve. "We are about to take a closer look at something, sir, which may interest you. It is the empty room."

"I thought we had the wrong key," Jaeryn said.

"We did at the time, sir, but that has since been remedied. I would have mentioned it before, but you preferred that we search the second floor before going up to the third. We just finished that, and I thought you might wish to examine this one for yourself."

"What does it have in it?" Jaeryn shut the desk drawer and made preparation to follow him.

"A map, sir. A map of the world, to be exact. I think you'll find it worth your time."

Jaeryn led the way out of the library and raced up the stairs, with Ben following behind and Peters bringing up the rear.

"Use the servants' stair, gentlemen. At the end of the east hall," Peters called after them.

In spite of attempting to match Jaeryn's speed, Ben took a keen interest in all that they passed. He could not help but notice the heavy curtains drawn close to shut out the night, deep red carpets covering the floor, and red-painted walls lined with ornately-framed portraits of Emmerson's ancestors. Ben could not help but wonder if they would have rolled in their graves at discovering their recently deceased progeny's pro-German loyalties.

Just as Jaeryn set foot on the servants' stair, the doorbell sounded, and they halted to listen. "Who would that be?" Jaeryn asked, reaching toward his shoulder holster for the Webley.

Peters looked just as mystified. "I couldn't say, doctor. Shall I answer it?"

"Yes, yes, it wouldn't be wise to ignore it. Give me the keys to the room we're heading for. We'll listen from the top of the stairs, and if we need to, we'll hide in one of the bedrooms. Don't let the caller up to the second floor if you can help it. Otherwise, signal your men first so they can leave by the back entrance."

Peters obeyed and gave them the keys. "The last room in the upstairs hall, sir. But the caller will be suspicious of the lights."

"Can't be helped," Jaeryn said. "Make up something. Tell them Emmerson's dead, and the doctor just—no, don't bring my name into it."

The bell rang again, and Peters started down the stairs with Jaeryn whispering directions over the railing. "I've reconsidered. Tell them you called the doctor and he's taking care of the last formalities now. I'll warn the others to leave."

Peters nodded and continued down the stairs.

Jaeryn turned back, and a twinkle leaped into his eyes at Ben's ill-concealed disgust. "Take the keys. Go upstairs and see what you can find. I'll follow as soon as our guest is gone. Now hurry, and don't look behind you."

Ben heard a muffled curse or two from voices other than Jaeryn's as he began his ascent of the servants' stair to the third floor. But he obeyed orders and did not look back. He locked the stairway door as soon as he had passed through it and hurried up another flight to a long hall, almost identical to the one beneath. Once he reached the last room, he hastily tried the knob and found it fastened. A small brass skeleton key, almost lost amidst the others, proved to be the right one. After unlocking the door, Ben secured it behind him and took in his surroundings.

This room proved to be quite as ornate as the rest of the house. Electric lights stood on the mantelpiece. Peters must have lit the chandelier in preparation for their visit, for that and the wall sconces cast long shadows across the blue wallpaper. Landscapes of foreign estates lined the walls, and marble pillars supported the fireplace at the head of the room, while blue and gold carpet with fleurs-de-lis at the corners accentuated the elegance. But he found he had not yet seen the half of it, for as he tilted his head back to look at the chandelier, he saw the ceiling. Elaborate crown molding of braided chains and wreaths of carved flowers covered its entire surface, and Ben caught his breath at the splendor.

In spite of the grandeur, the room seemed to have no purpose. Where the other rooms held a bed and a dressing table or a sofa and bookshelves, this one had only a row of gold and cream-cushioned chairs, pushed off to one side. The only other signs of useful activity were a couple of small tables, also removed to one side.

At length, Ben recollected his object in coming and glanced about for the maps Peters had mentioned. One wasn't hard to find: a map of the world, lifted down from the wall—the largest one he had ever seen. Ben knelt in front of it to examine it more closely. There was nothing worth noting that he could see. But it was obviously there for a reason, and its presence, coupled with the room's evident lack of purpose, gave ample cause for further investigation.

Turning it over, Ben drew out his pocket knife and carefully cut the mounting free. What he found under the backing caused him to whistle softly, for underneath the first map lay hidden a second and much smaller one, detailing the Folkestone streets.

The door opened, and Ben grabbed for the Webley in his jacket pocket.

"Never mind." Jaeryn panted heavily from running up the flights of stairs. "It's only me; Peters gave me another set of keys to get in here."

Ben returned the pistol to his pocket. "Who was at the door?"

"King." Jaeryn knelt down next to him, his green eyes shining from the chandelier's glow. "Heard a report about Emmerson's death and wanted it substantiated. He didn't stay long. Probably would have come up if Emmerson were still living, but once he heard I was with the dear departed, he didn't consider it necessary to linger. Odd hours to come and crow over a rival. You'd think he would have some respect, especially in his line of work."

Ben frowned in agreement. "It is odd. Were King and Emmerson friends?"

"Hardly. They have been enemies for a long time in the House and would debate for hours on insignificant details just to inconvenience each other. With all the time I've spent studying their careers, I don't recall one single bill they agreed on. When Asquith was replaced, King fought to keep him in, but Emmerson thought he was incompetent. Getting Lloyd George in was the last thing he did before his heath failed." Jaeryn, too, looked around the room and raised his eyebrows at the grandness.

"It could have been a blind for the public to keep them from suspecting a partnership," Ben said, though he doubted the words as he spoke them.

Jaeryn gave a short chuckle. "I would suspect not. Emmerson was a Liberal, and King kept to the Conservative side of the debates out of spite, though he made an exception for Asquith. Now, let's see what we have here." He looked at the maps in front of them.

Ben turned his attention back to the larger map and examined it again, but it proved no more illuminating than before. "There may be something here, but I don't see it. Not a marking or a note."

Jaeryn looked, but though he searched long, he had no better success than his associate. "I wonder why Emmerson kept the room locked. Let's have Peters up, and maybe he can give us an indication of where to look next."

Peters had nothing to offer about the maps themselves, but when Ben inquired, he did tell him how he had managed to procure access to the room. "Mr. Emmerson always kept this room locked, sir. He shut it up fourteen years ago and ordered it never to be tampered with. Plenty of the servants gossiped about it, you may be sure, but we never saw him use it, and I never bothered about it until recently. Three Decembers ago, Ryson contacted me about the suspicions surrounding my employer. It was hardly the time for the customary trust of a master and servant, so I took the liberty of looking for a way to get in without his knowledge. It took me a long time to find the key. Doctor Graham thought he found it a few weeks ago, but when I tried it, I found he was mistaken. I found the actual key this evening."

"And how did you manage that?" Ben asked coolly.

Peters stood with his hands clasped behind his back, a one-man incarnation of the old order class system. "Well, sir, three years' work culminated in success this evening. One of our men was looking in a third floor bedroom and found a locked wooden writing box in the armoire. It had not been used for some time, and upon trying the key that Doctor Graham discovered two weeks ago, it fitted exactly. Another key was inside the box. I took the key and found it fit the lock for this room." Peters sought encouragement from Jaeryn's expression and found complete approbation there. "But I didn't see anything out of the ordinary besides the map. I thought perhaps you might discover more."

"Did the men go through this room yet?" Jaeryn inquired.

"Not yet. They were just beginning on this floor when Colonel King called."

Jaeryn got up from the floor. "We'll take these maps down to the library and have them search here now. They're waiting out near the back door; I barely had time to send them off before you let King in. Come along, Dailey, and we'll return to our post. Bring the world map, if you please, and I'll take the other."

Back in the library, Jaeryn shoved the forgotten tea tray to one side and spread the maps out on the table. The two of them had looked for several minutes before Ben spotted anything out of the ordinary. "Emmerson used tacks in the world map to mark certain locations."

Jaeryn's eyes followed to where he pointed. "I don't see them."

"Well, the holes are there all the same. Look."

Jaeryn leaned closer and tilted the map toward the light. After a second fruitless attempt, he sighed and pulled out a pair of wire-rimmed glasses that Ben had never seen before. Once he put them on it took a good deal of squinting and more than one protest, but after procuring two lights to set directly beside the map, Ben at length got Jaeryn to agree with him.

They rang for Peters and asked him to bring a box of tacks and a corkboard so they could mark the locations Emmerson deemed significant. Jaeryn scribbled down the locations on a pad of paper as they worked. "Berlin," he muttered. "Bamberg. London. Dover. Folkestone. Dublin. The Channel. France."

There wasn't room for both of them in that part of the world, so Ben moved over to the United States. Tracing his finger over Baltimore, he felt a rough hole where a tack had been placed. He took one out of the box Peters had given them and pushed it down into the cork, then paid close attention as he scanned the eastern seaboard. Another tack hole appeared in the capital of Virginia.

"This is odd. Why would Emmerson mark where my mother lives?"

Jaeryn glanced at it, and then at him, and Ben realized he had admitted more than he intended to.

"Perhaps because your mother lives there?" Jaeryn shifted to hide the way his mouth quivered at the corners. "But I doubt he knew that, as the necessary precautions to hide your identity have been taken. Unless, of course, your mother is someone of special interest."

"She isn't," Ben said quickly. "But I find it odd…London, Richmond, Balt—"

Jaeryn interrupted. "You needn't tell me the exact locations of all your personal connections if you don't wish to."

"I know. But they marked where I lived, and where my mother

lived, and…and I have London connections as well." Ben wound his fingers nervously in and out of one another as he made the admission.

"Easily explained, perhaps," Jaeryn said. "The Baltimore pin may be for you, but I doubt Emmerson did it himself. It's been a couple of months since he was in good enough health to climb a flight of stairs. London contains many important men, not the least of which is—well, our supervisor. Folkestone we would expect them to mark. Richmond may be a puzzle that we have yet to discover the meaning to. Besides, you're not enough of a spoke in the wheel for them to mark your family, yet."

"You're the last man I would expect to overlook the obvious." Ben picked up a tack and toyed with it. "Besides, Emmerson probably marked where you came from as well."

Jaeryn grinned. "I didn't find anything. I think we've finished with this map for the present, so you can set it in front of the shelves over there. What time is it?"

Ben glanced at the grandfather clock. "Half-past one."

"Ring for Peters and tell him to bring something to eat, then." Jaeryn rubbed his face and yawned. "If I'm going to stay up all hours, I'd like to be in comfort while I do it. Besides, I have a question for him."

Peters brought in a tray of strong coffee and sandwiches, as well as something Jaeryn's investigators had unearthed on the third floor. "We found what we believe to be the original pins for the map, sir. Two boxes of them, one plain and one with numbers." The butler poured the gold thumbtacks out on the table. There were twelve with numbers painted on their heads and ten plain. Jaeryn pointed to the map of the world, and Ben silently marked the locations with the plain pins Emmerson had used. That left the numbered pins in Jaeryn's hand. His forehead creased in thought.

"Do you recall any occasion when Emmerson used the room, Peters?"

"No, sir. I never saw him go into it."

"Very well. You can leave us now, and I'll call you again when I need you. Thank you." As soon as Peters left, Jaeryn returned to the map of Folkestone and ran his fingers over it, searching for more pin holes. He found two on Tontine, one at Emmerson's estate, and the rest he threw down next to it.

"There isn't one at Copt Point," he said. "That confirms that Emmerson must not have used the maps since your arrival. I think an agent of his must have helped him mark Baltimore, with his state of health. It is possible someone told him you were coming. If that's the case, then I'm afraid they must have your real name as well." Jaeryn checked over his list to make sure he had written all the locations down before he pulled out the pins. "Well, we've done all we can for tonight. Doubtless we've missed something, but I'll have to come back to examine the maps again anyway. Lay this key over by the letter, will you?"

Ben didn't offer to take it. "I'd rather you did. I'll replace the maps in the frame. I'm the one who took them out, after all."

"Leaving the dirty work to others, I see." Jaeryn obliged. "Have it your way for tonight, and we'll revisit the question later. A favor in return, if you will." He drew off his glasses and put them away. "I'd rather you didn't mention I used those. Ryson doesn't know, and I prefer to keep them to myself."

Ben smiled at the secrecy. "Why? There's nothing wrong with glasses."

"Never admit you have a weakness if you can help it," Jaeryn said tersely.

A soft knock sounded on the library door, and Ben called, "Come in."

"We just found something else, gentlemen." Peters held an object in his hand that looked like a partial deck of playing cards. "You'll wish to copy these, I'm sure. Several of them were hidden in the chairs, slipped between the cushion and the seat back, and some were behind a panel over the mantlepiece."

The three of them huddled close together, and the dark-paneled walls gave the light a sober hue as Peters flipped over the cards. There were twelve cards that matched the numbered thumbtacks. Mr. Emmerson's signature appeared on all of them, and below his name was a five-number code, a different one for each card.

"Thank heaven," Jaeryn breathed. "This is what I wanted to find. Copy them all down, Dailey; there's something in French on each one above Emmerson's signature. We can leave as soon as we conceal the traces of our having been here, and we'll take the information back to the clinic so you can translate the French for me there. Set the rest of the house to rights, Peters, and we'll clean up the library. You can send the others home."

"Yes, sir. Directly."

At two o' clock they walked out the front door, and Peters locked it behind them. They found their two bicycles and wound their way back to the clinic in the dark, hoping that no one would catch them and turn them in for suspicious activity.

"There were twelve cards, but I only saw eight chairs in the room," Ben whispered later, as Jaeryn fumbled with the key to unlock his front door.

Jaeryn paused in astonishment. "I didn't notice that. What caused you to spot it?"

"Nothing." Ben shrugged. "I'm supposed to notice little things, that's all. Peters said he got some of the cards from over the mantlepiece, so that must be where Emmerson kept the extras. I wonder if Peters remembered where he got each one from."

"I hope so. I'll have to check with him on that." Jaeryn seemed astonished at his level of perception and rather gratified as well, and Ben felt a glow of satisfaction at having done something to please him.

Definitely a strange evening, he reflected, as he rode home on the bicycle. Visions of the empty, gold-enameled room on the third floor filled his mind as he pedaled rather sleepily over the road to Copt Point. He thought of the pile of notes and the key locked in Jaeryn's desk. Someday they were going to have a discussion about that. He had lied several times now, but he wasn't about to steal to advance the British cause. They were asking enough from him as it was.

There was no light on in either cottage, and Ben was relieved to find everything safe and as it should be. Pearlie lay fast asleep, and Charlotte, nestled comfortably in their bed, stirred when he came in and woke when he came to bed. She was used to unplanned absences after a year of marriage to a medical man, but he didn't like to test her too often.

His last conscious thought was the remembrance that he must tell her about Alisa as soon as possible.

Chapter Eight
An Honest Lie

Ben barely had time to snatch a few hours' sleep before the alarm beeped him awake again. He reached over and turned the clock off, then saw Charlotte wide awake and smiling at him. Reaching over, he sleepily stroked her hair. "Good morning, love. I need your help today if you have the time."

Charlotte pulled herself up on one elbow and yawned. "I'm busy today. Since you and Doctor Graham haven't called for me yet, I went to the maternity home yesterday and volunteered my services."

"I'm glad. You're probably bored here."

"Not until recently. I had housekeeping to set up. Pearl doesn't want to come with me, but I'm going to make her. I can't leave her here all day."

Ben shoved aside the blankets and sat up. "That would be wise. Jaeryn said yesterday we'd better keep an eye out after what happened. He doesn't think the Germans have any concrete proof of our involvement, but I'd rather you stay close to town."

"I will." She slipped out of bed and took up a brush in front of the small mirror he had hung above the nightstand. "What was it you wanted me for?"

"I attended a patient yesterday that you need to know about. Someone called Thursday evening about a woman who needed help, and Jaeryn assigned her to me. Her name is Alisa Dorroll, and I visited her yesterday afternoon." He saw her hand pause mid-brush. "She tells me she is Edmond's wife and expecting her first child."

Charlotte gave an exclamation of surprise. "How did she—"

Ben shook his head and said, "I don't know any details yet, but needless to say, I'll ask her as soon as possible. She's here alone, and she said Edmond was wounded over in France. She has about one month left until her baby is born, possibly sooner if my guess is correct." He slipped into a clean shirt and trousers and reached for the shaving kit. "I'm going back today. She would feel more comfortable with a woman there to prepare her. I don't think she has the faintest idea what she's gotten into."

"Does she know who we are?"

"I didn't tell her. It wouldn't be wise right now. Something that happened the other night put us in more jeopardy than we were, and I don't want to risk it for her sake."

A faint frown creased Charlotte's brow as she gathered up strands of hair to braid. "I understand that you need to keep your identity a secret, but you had no idea you would find your brother's wife here. You owe it to her to tell her who you are."

"I'm sorry." His palms turned damp with sweat at her disapproval. "I wish she could know. But when I agreed to come here, I promised to take on the identity I was given, and I must be true to my word. Other men's lives as well as mine—and even yours and Pearl's—are affected by my secrecy. Under the circumstances, it's an honest lie."

Charlotte wound the flaxen braid around her head, slipping in pins to keep it in place. "You promised me when we came here that whatever secrets you had to keep, you would remain honest, upright, and God-fearing. God-fearing they may be, and upright I have no doubt, but you have just told me that they are not honest. If they were, you would be able to tell her the truth."

"Please come." He shoved away the guilt and teased, "I'm not sure Jaeryn Graham would have the same amount of soothing influence."

She stifled a laugh. "I'll come. The poor thing. That's the least I can do for her, and no more than our duty with Edmond gone."

Ben went out and knocked on Pearl's room, and at her soft call to enter, peeked in around the door. "Good morning. Are you coming in with us today?"

Pearlie sat on the side of her bed, her blonde ringlets half-down around her shoulders, as she coiled it up into a low, loose twist at the back. "I would rather stay here. It doesn't bother me to be alone. I'm used to it."

Ben raised his eyebrows. "Why would you want to be alone? There aren't any books. There's no one to talk to."

Pearlie lifted her chin, a smile hovering on her lips. "You know nothing about housework. There's always something to be done."

Ben watched her as she straightened her bed and took up an apron. "You can stay today if you like. We'll talk tonight about a better option in future. You can work at the maternity homes or in the soldier canteens volunteering, but you can't stay here all the time." Charlotte appeared in starched collar and cuffs, her leather handbag over her arm, and he snatched a kiss from her. "Don't leave yet, *ma chérie*. We'll walk into town together. I'll make the appointment with Mrs. Dorroll for five."

* * *

All day Saturday, the two doctors kept a strict watch on each other to make sure their weariness didn't affect the quality of their care. Jaeryn looked hollow-eyed, and Ben felt as if he could sleep for two days straight, but they managed to make clear judgments in spite of it. In his spare moments, Ben copied down a list of the card numbers to send to London and translated the French above

Emmerson's signature into English. The French was merely a confidentiality commitment and didn't give them any information, but the numbers themselves Jaeryn felt quite sure were agent identification codes. If so, they were an invaluable find. When they matched the numbers with names, they would know for sure which agents Emmerson had turned, as well as the identities of the people in town who had been German agents from the beginning. Simple in theory, but not in practice. Jaeryn planned to put all the papers in a bundle and take them down to the St. Eanswythe drop after dark for London officials to look through. After that, they would have to wait for the information to be processed and returned before they could proceed.

At five, when Charlotte had finished volunteering for the day, Ben met her at the maternity home. He had a bicycle from Jaeryn, and she managed to persuade one of the nurses to let her borrow the bicycle that the errand boy used as long as she promised to return it by dark. So together they set out in the direction of Newnham Lane and the farming district.

Alisa Dorroll opened the door almost immediately upon their knock. She turned pink with shame when she caught sight of Charlotte and stepped back a little behind the door. Charlotte held out her arms and offered her a warm hug.

"I'm the doctor's wife come to see you," she said. "Please don't feel embarrassed. There's nothing wrong with needing help. I'm a nurse, and we're here to see what we can do for you."

They examined her in the tiny bedroom off the kitchen. Charlotte's presence eased her while he examined her and asked her questions, answering the ones she asked him. When he had finished and Charlotte had helped her fasten her dress again, they returned to the kitchen and he slid into a seat opposite her at the table. "I think you're quite all right, Mrs. Dorroll. I don't see anything to be concerned about with you or the baby."

She still couldn't bring herself to look him in the face. "I'm glad."

He nodded to Charlotte, and she picked up from him. "We

wondered if you would be willing to talk about your husband, so we can help you."

Alisa Dorroll bit her lip, and he felt her body tense, even though she sat on the opposite side of the table. "What do you want to know?"

"Well, how you met and when you were informed he was ill. Anything at all you could tell us about him," Charlotte said.

Alisa brushed back a strand of dark brown hair and laid her two hands softly around her middle before she began. "I met him in Dover two years ago. I had been hired to help at a party, and he talked to me there. He said he was on leave from the front, and he'd just been promoted. I tried not to talk to him more than was right, but he kept coming back, and he was so kind and brave and gentlemanly. I hadn't met anyone like him before. I was a post girl during the week, and after the party he asked me to go out with him. But he kept me out late one night and the post master was angry, so I promised not to see him again. I thought he would forget all about me. Then he came back last October and said that he loved me and he had enough money to marry me so I wouldn't have to work anymore. We married then in case we wouldn't have another chance." Alisa stopped to keep from breaking down, and Charlotte reached out and gently rubbed her shoulder until she continued on. "When he left, he told me he would write first, but no letter reached me until March. I thought he sounded disturbed, so I wrote back and tried to cheer him up. Just last week, the day before you came, I received a letter from a friend of his who found my name in Edmond's belongings. He thought I should know that Edmond hadn't written because he was in critical condition. Gas poisoning, I believe he called it. But I don't know what that is, or how serious it might be. Do you know what it means?"

Ben glanced at Charlotte, and in his mind's eye flashed the anguished face of the man he had seen on his first day at Jaeryn's clinic. "It can be severe," he said hesitantly.

Alisa watched his expression, and a troubled fear crept into her

125

eyes. "Do you think he won't recover?"

Ben fingered his wristwatch as he tried to decide how much to tell her. "Many cases do recover, Mrs. Dorroll, but it depends on the seriousness of the burns. It would be premature to say, as I don't know the extent of his injuries."

"If he recovers, will he be able to come home and rest for a while?"

"For your husband's sake, I hope not." His heart went out to her, but Ben thought it better to prepare her for the truth. "If he comes back to England it will be because his eyes or lungs have been severely affected and he is no longer fit for service."

Alisa sat for a few moments biting her bottom lip. She drew herself up and closed her eyes tight for a moment to keep back tears. "He told me if I had a boy to name him Matthew."

After the baby's grandfather. Ben assumed she didn't know Matthew Dorroll personally, for she didn't talk as if she did, and he didn't dare ask. "We'll see that you lack for nothing, whatever happens. I must take Charlotte home before it gets too late, but before I go, what provision did your husband leave you? If you need anything at all, I would be glad to supply it."

The little flicker of hope that Ben saw in Alisa's eyes when they first arrived died away, leaving them as sad and empty as before. She gently rubbed her belly with both hands. "I am well provided for. I want for nothing, and I have someone bring my supplies to me every week."

"Very well, then," Ben said. "If you give me your number, I'll call in a couple of days. Do you have any hired help for the housework?"

Alisa shook her head. "I don't know anyone here, and I haven't made inquiries yet."

"I can find someone to help," Charlotte reassured her, "both before you deliver your baby and after. And I'll come as well. We'll take good care of you, darling."

They said goodbye soon after, and as they pedaled the return route to Copt Point, Ben caught Charlotte watching him as if she

126

wanted to read his thoughts. At length, he broke the silence. "How could he leave her like that, newly married, without friends, and with no help to speak of? Not only that, but he's left her with a child to care for, and she's nearer sixteen than eighteen in her knowledge of the world. And now he may be dead, which leaves her a widow. Or he'll be disabled for life, which isn't much better."

Her skirt gave a loud snap from the wind against the tires. "Now will you tell her who you really are?"

The faint gnawing of regret that had haunted him since learning about Edmond's marriage returned full force. "Not yet. Perhaps someday soon I will be free to do so. But in the meantime, I'll watch over her, and between us we'll try to keep her safe and happy."

When they returned to Copt Point, the smoke they expected to see wasn't curling up from the chimney. The cottage lay shuttered up, and when he knocked, Pearlie didn't answer. Nimrod set up a furious barking from the other cottage, and they heard a sharp, muffled command from Mrs. Goodwin. Ben knocked again. As the silence lengthened, he and Charlotte exchanged worried glances. He took out the spare key and unlocked the door.

Inside, the rooms were dark and deserted. The floors had been swept clean, the beds made up, and the stovetop scrubbed. Ben found a white square of stationary on the table.

I took the Webley and I've gone to London. I'll be back in time for supper.

He gave an angry exclamation. "Of all the foolish notions. She doesn't know how to use a Webley."

Charlotte put her hand to her mouth as he let the paper fall to the table. "What are you going to do?"

Ben picked up his own Webley and slipped his wallet into his coat. "I'm going to London."

"She might be on her way home already. You'd be better off checking the train times and meeting the next one at the station." Charlotte hurried over to the drawer which held a few of their

127

valuables and pulled out a time sheet.

Ben took it from her and scanned down the list. "There's one due in fifteen minutes. If I hurry, I'll have time to catch it."

"I'll come with you."

He held out a hand to stop her as he headed towards the door. "No. Stay here. I'll have a hard enough time catching it as it is. If I have to go to London, I'll leave a message with Jaeryn for you."

He reached the station with two minutes to spare. The whistle blew in the distance as he leaned his bicycle against the side of the station and took up a place at the platform. The train pulled to a stop with a puff of steam, and passengers hurried out. Ben looked from face to face as business men and soldiers hurried down the steps past him. He stepped forward when he saw a woman, but another man moved forward to take her arm, and he realized she had dark hair. One car emptied, and he paced down the platform to the next one. And in the middle of the line of passengers, there Pearl stood, dressed in her gray traveling suit and picture hat. She clutched a leather handbag and darted little glances back and forth across the platform as another man came up behind her. Ben recognized Hugh, Mistress Goodwin's former lodger. He spoke in her ear, and Pearl shook her head as she hurried down the steps. Hugh hurried down after her, but before he could take her arm, Ben came up. Pearlie's eyes widened when she saw him.

"Thank you for your offer of assistance," Ben said. "I'll take her home." He dismissed Hugh with a nod and walked with Pearlie until they were out of earshot. "What did he want? Did you go to London with him? You should have told me what you were about."

She kept her eyes downcast. "I didn't see him until the train home. He sat near me, but I didn't like him. If I had told you, you wouldn't have let me go, and you wouldn't have gone yourself, either."

He hurried her through the crowd, gripping her elbow. "Why did you leave? You know better than to travel alone. There could have been an air raid. Someone could have taken you."

Pearl slipped her elbow from his grasp. "I was safe."

He glanced back, but Hugh had disappeared in the crowd. Why had she gone in the first place? A swirl of reasons cascaded through his mind, but they were all unlike her. And then he knew. "You went to see our father, didn't you?"

She didn't nod, just looked straight ahead with her chin set firm and her eyes stormy.

"Did he see you?" Ben persisted.

She did not answer, and after a moment of silence her chin trembled, and a soft, sobbing gasp escaped her lips. "For all the good it did, I could have stayed in Virginia, in the house I loved with the things that were familiar. I wouldn't have had to see all those dead people." She walked faster, and he picked up his pace to keep up with her. "I don't think anyone would miss me if I was gone."

"Wait." Ben reached out and grabbed her arm, forcing her to stop. She looked down, the brim of her gray picture hat hiding her face, but he tipped her chin up and forced her to meet his eyes. "That's utter nonsense. I would miss you. Ever since you were old enough to miss me when I went to school, and wait for me to come home. You were my one good thing all those years."

She finally lifted her gaze to his face. "But now you have Charlotte. And I have no one. Even Mother hasn't written me since I came here."

He searched her eyes, troubled, trying to read what was underneath the sudden outpouring of hurt. "You could make friends. I hope we'll be going home soon, but there's no reason in the world why you couldn't meet people here."

Pearlie clenched the strap of her handbag. Her eyes looked defeated as she drew in a defiant breath. "I am twenty years old, and I am not volunteering at the maternity home. I am old enough to choose."

He traced a hand down her arm. "What can I do? I want you to be happy here, but I have to keep you safe. Tell me what you want."

Her breath drew slower as she calmed down, and her little white-gloved fingers twisted in and out of one another. "I want…I want a place that feels like home. A place where I can sweep the floors and put the washing on the line and polish the windows, and love it every day. When you were gone I didn't have anyone to love, but I could always love home." Her breath caught and choked. "I want to *be* loved. I want to see my father."

Ben thought of Alisa, just come, alone, and desperately in need of help. Perhaps there was a way to fulfill two claims of duty after all. He took Pearl's hand this time instead of her elbow, and she didn't feel as tense under his touch. "Maybe I can give that to you after all. I was going to tell you, only you ran away before I came home for supper. Charlotte and I went to see Alisa Dorroll today. She has about a month until her baby comes, and she doesn't have friends here. We mustn't tell her who we are. It wouldn't be safe for her. But if you came as a friend, then you would have an old house full of memory to care for, and I know she couldn't help but love you. It would be your own place, to make a life for yourself for however long we're here. Would you like that?"

She thought for a long moment as they took up their walk again towards the line of cabs. Then she nodded. "I would like to try it."

"Grand." He squeezed her fingers. "I'll have to teach you how to actually use a Webley, just to be on the safe side. And mind, you're not to breathe a word about our relation to her."

"I can keep secrets." She glanced up at him sideways.

Ben smiled wryly. "You've proven that. Let's go home for supper."

* * *

After supper, he showed Pearl the Webley while Charlotte wiped and dried the dishes. Pearlie listened carefully, and when he took her out and set up a target along the shore, she did well for a first try— well enough to give him confidence that she could use it to good purpose if she was hard-pressed, and even better if she practiced.

When they were done, he put the Webley in the case Ryson had given him and presented it to her. Her eyes shone as she took it with careful hands and disappeared into her room. When she was gone, Charlotte brought out the stationary box to write to her parents, and he pulled out a sheet of his own.

"Is she all right?" Charlotte spoke low so Pearl wouldn't hear as she put the kettle on for tea. She reached up for one of the china tea cups she had managed to bring all the way from Virginia.

"She's all right. She agreed to go to Alisa's. I think she might be happier on her own for a while."

Charlotte's brow furrowed, but she didn't comment further. She took some letters from her apron pocket and placed them on the table next to him. "I heard from my parents today."

He pulled out an ink pen and the half-full ink bottle. "Are they well?"

"Yes. We also got letters about the May and June payments we haven't made yet. The creditor was upset."

He paused from dipping the pen in the ink. "That's odd. I sent them a letter with our address, but it wouldn't have had time to get to them by now. I wonder how they found us." Sighing, he leaned his chin in his hand. "I have a half-dead brother and a homesick sister and more bills to pay than money with which to pay them. Just grand."

"Maybe they sent a letter to your mother and she told them."

He shrugged and pulled out a blank sheet of paper. There was no sound but the scratching of pen on paper and Charlotte's low hum now and then as she sat thinking about what she wanted to say.

June 15th, 1917

Dear Mrs. O'Sean,

Since arriving in England less than a month ago, I feel as if I've left behind me not only everything I knew, but also everything I was. This place is so different. There are soldiers marching down to the harbor to go off to war every day and reports posted weekly at the town hall of those who became casualties and are not coming back. Our whole lives revolve around the foreign conflict. I keep up with the war reports through my patients, for they talk about the latest bulletins when I call on them. Everyone's talk, extra pennies, and time are spent working to help our men succeed. Since I have neither the funds nor the spare time after medical work to give to the causes, I live on the outer fringe of things. Every other day some committee or other comes to the clinic asking for money, and every other day Jaeryn Graham gives them enough to make them dance with gratitude. When they turn to me, I am forced to decline. I wish I could offer something to help as well.

Charlotte is well, and so is Pearl. I'm going to have my wife work with Doctor Graham and I soon, but Jaeryn asked me to wait until he and I were better acquainted, so for now she keeps busy volunteering at the maternity wards, by her own request. She loves telling me about the mothers and babies when she comes home, and I pick up from stray comments that they, too, love her presence.

Charlotte has made friends among the other nurses, but Pearlie hasn't made any new acquaintances. I think my sister is quite content with her own company. Pearl pleaded with me not to make her volunteer at the kitchens for the soldiers like the other girls her age, and I won't require it. Some people might think I ought to because she's a grown woman and could do a great deal of good. But she is in a strange place, with strange people, and I want to give her time to adjust. She acts as timid around Charlotte and I as she does towards new people she meets in town. I hope we can gain some of her trust soon so we can help her feel more at ease.

I haven't seen my father yet. I want to see him, but I am afraid to attempt it. I don't know what he's like, and living in the hope of reconciliation seems better than knowing for sure that it won't happen. But yesterday I just discovered a sister-in-law who lives here. She doesn't know that I am related to her. I was caught between two difficulties, and deceiving her was the only way out. I probably shouldn't be telling you this much, but I hope they will let my letter through, for I must tell someone. She told me that my brother is missing somewhere in France, poisoned by the Germans, or perhaps even dead. I have to write my father when I'm done here to tell him. Perhaps he'll answer this time.

I don't get to church anymore. The doctor I work for has me take calls on Sundays, and I am left to my own devices. Charlotte wants me to go with her, and I want to attend as well, but it can't be helped for the present.

132

Sometimes I wonder whether I was right in coming to England in the first place. Whether I ought to have taken the position simply because I knew I must take something and my father wanted me to do it. You asked us if we prayed about it before we went, and we did—but I worry that I made up my mind beforehand and so suited God's answer accordingly. And I don't know how to get out of the commitment. I wish I could see you to get some advice. I have lied so many times in the course of my work that I have lost count, and the man I work with sees it all as part of some game we are playing for the glory of it.

Perhaps some men are called to this work, but I do not seem to be one of them. I hope God will show some kind of mercy for my ignorance—some mercy that both provides a way out and lets me satisfy my father at the same time.

I enjoyed receiving your letter a couple of weeks ago, and hope you continue to do well. I haven't heard from Mother, so please write and tell me all the news from home and your family. You had another son, as I recall, who was old enough to enlist if he wished to. I hope he manages to come through without a scratch if he is already at the front. Keep Edmond in your prayers, for if he's still alive, he'll need them.

Yours Truly,
Benjamin Dorroll

When his sheet was filled and his name signed, he rifled through the stationary box for envelopes. At the bottom of the stack was another half-started letter. Ben picked up the scrap of paper and glanced at the first lines.

Dear Father,
I miss you. I came all the way from America to see you. Why do you insist on waiting? What more time do we need?

He felt a stab of guilt at the invasion of Pearlie's privacy, but his eyes tore on through the sentences in spite of it.

I've never seen you in my life before, and you never replied to the letter I sent you. What have I done? I am tired of being taken from place to place, and looked after, and told nothing. I am not a little girl anymore....

The sentence trailed off there, unfinished. Ben set the paper back underneath the others and looked at his own letter, penned so carefully to avoid all traces of what was really going on. He would have to finish his work here soon if the British couldn't finish their part in the war first. His little sister was aching for home.

Chapter Nine
In Which Terry Finds His Acushla

"Something's on your mind, isn't it?"

Jaeryn's voice startled him, and Ben realized he was standing motionless in front of the shelves, one hand clenched at his side. Confound the fellow. Observation was all very well up to a point, but inconsiderate when practiced too skillfully. "I'm not keeping anything from you that you should know," he said, turning back to making a list of the medications they needed to order.

Jaeryn rolled his eyes. "Good grief, Dailey, I don't go around every moment expecting you to stab me in the back. I'm here to help you out."

"I'm sorry, I didn't mean to accuse you." Ben tried to calm the nervousness that nearly choked him and steadied his voice for what he was about to ask. "The fact is, I'm short of cash just now, and I don't have credit at any of the stores. I wondered if you would be kind enough to loan me some money."

Immediately, Jaeryn pulled out his pocketbook. "Sure. Are you out?"

"I've been out," he admitted.

"And no doubt your cupboard's empty. I know you. Here." The Irishman extracted a stack of banknotes and tossed them over. "Pay it back when you're able."

Ben shook his head and didn't offer to touch them. "You don't have to give me all that. I only need enough to get me through the month."

"Take it." Jaeryn folded up the pocketbook and crossed his arms, refusing to take the money back. "You might need it. I know Winfield's practice doesn't pay much, and you have a family to support. Don't hesitate to ask again if you need more."

"I'm obliged to you."

Jaeryn looked as if he was about to speak, then hesitated, and said, "You don't have to tell me if you prefer not, but have you ever asked someone for money before?"

Ben turned so Jaeryn could not see his embarrassment. "Never. I've always paid my own way until now, except for private credit loans to cover my education." But he could not keep the catch out of his words as he replied.

"Well, then," Jaeryn said, and the soft lilt he used to calm worried patients sounded in his voice. "I'm honored to be of service to you."

He disappeared, and Ben was glad of the chance to find his equilibrium again in the empty room. The clock pointed to half past the hour. The patient lists were ready for the day. Today was Tuesday, the twelfth of June, and he had finally worked up the courage after three days to ask for the money that Charlotte was worrying about. Pearlie would go to Alisa Dorroll's today, and it would just be Charlotte and him left at Copt Point, like it had been in Richmond.

Jaeryn returned with a steaming mug cradled in both hands. "I've been trying to puzzle out how Emmerson might have suspected your involvement. I'm sure he was the one who set up the library plan after I took his key. Your landlady hasn't given you cause for concern, has she? Could she have told him?"

"No, not—" Ben remembered her suspicious mention of Ann Meikle the first morning they walked into town together. "Yes, I suppose she has. She gave me reason to think that she knew I was coming to England before I arrived. Someone told her about us, and she turned out her other renters so we could take her extra cottage. She was quite particular that we should have it."

Jaeryn paused just as he was about to drink his tea. "Good heavens, and you actually rented the place?"

Ben felt a flash of annoyance. "I didn't know anywhere else to go. Besides, she seemed harmless enough, and she's done nothing to cause concern since. She never interferes with us."

Jaeryn's voice had an edge to it when he replied, though he kept it smooth and civil. "Did Mrs. Goodwin mention the person who told her you were coming?"

"Ann Meikle," Ben said reluctantly.

A malicious spark rose in Jaeryn's eyes at her name. "I wouldn't put it past that woman to interfere. I never told her about you ahead of time. And I wouldn't put it past either of them to gossip about you. It would be better if you had a telephone. I'll see what I can arrange, and if I must, I'll pay for it to be put in myself."

"Wouldn't Ryson cover an expense like that?" Ben wondered what it must be like to pay for everything as if money were no object. He had no idea, and probably never would.

"No, he won't. I'll take care of it." Jaeryn set his jaw against further protest. "Your knowledge of languages alone is too valuable for me to lose you. Whoever is offering threats won't bother you if they think you're a respectable citizen after all. They'll drop off after a while."

"You sound as though you speak from experience."

Jaeryn reached down, opened one of his lower desk drawers, and pulled out a cardboard box. He pulled off the top to reveal the inside full of letters. He handed it over, and Ben took out a few of them to see what they were. Every paper contained a death threat, crude in tone and written in different hands, and one, in particular, caught his attention. He had seen that kind of notebook paper before. The same type of paper that he had found tucked in his shutters with a warning to go home.

You can't escape justice by hiding here. If the authorities in London won't hang you for an Irish lawbreaker, then we'll take matters into our own hands.

Ben looked up. "These are terrible."

Jaeryn shrugged, and the tension in his face changed to a look of pride. "No, they aren't. I count them as some of my most valuable possessions. I have no qualms about admitting my nationality to anyone."

"I don't see why they think your nationality would be sufficient cause to kill you," Ben said, thumbing through the other threats, most of which were of the same ilk.

Jaeryn rubbed his face with his hands, and lines of stress crisscrossed his forehead again. "It was because of the revolt in Ireland last year—a whole rag-tag group of men fought to get their independence from the British government and got hung for it. It's still a sore spot with some. A nightmare of an Easter for anyone with Irish blood, and even though I had no part in it, the agents here have little respect for me or my authority now."

"I see." Ben leaned forward and asked, "What if they try to follow through?"

"I have no intention of dying, but if I'm killed, I expect Ryson would consider promoting you to my position."

Ben dropped the letters into the box, shoved it back, and shook his head. "I don't want your position."

Jaeryn broke out into a quiet chuckle. "I wouldn't mind keeping it myself." He grinned, covered the box and locked it up the drawer again. "I'm going to open the front door for patients. I'll be right back."

When he returned, he wasn't alone. Pearl came a few steps behind him, carrying her valise. "I've finished my shopping," she said, "and I paid a cabby to bring the trunk here."

"I didn't expect you so soon. I have a call to make that's rather pressing." Ben glanced at his watch and then at Jaeryn. "Can she wait in your kitchen for a half hour?"

"I can take her myself, if it's all the same to you. I have the time this morning."

Ben glanced at Pearlie and a silent interchange of question and answer passed between them. He sighed and acquiesced. "If you don't mind."

"Come. I'll take you in the motorcar. It's not mine, but I rent it, and it's safe enough."

* * *

Jaeryn picked up Pearl's trunk and led the way out. After stowing it in the back, he motioned for her to get in first, and she slid through the driver's door into the passenger's side. He started the car and got in beside her. "Are you liking Folkestone, Miss Dailey?"

"I don't mind it. We like seeing the Channel every day."

"Were you near the sea before?"

"We were close to the Atlantic. At least, when I was very little. Then we moved further away, and I missed it. I always liked being near the ocean."

Jaeryn adjusted the throttle and picked up speed. "You should go down to the Leas. Have you been there yet?"

She shook her head.

"There are lifts down to the shore, and it's a pleasant walk. I've seen the view several times. It was the worst when the Belgians came. I was in Folkestone back in 1915 for a brief jaunt, and they came in boats, just fleeing over. Wounded and terrified, and..." He trailed off and glanced at her. "I'm sorry. It was terrible. I was a doctor, so I helped. You're fortunate not to be a Belgian woman."

She sat silent, her hands folded in her lap, and he wondered if he had gone too far. Her brow had clouded at the word fortunate. Maybe she wasn't after all. Blast Dailey for not telling him anything.

He found himself at the end of Newnham Lane and watched the

house numbers as they passed by. It was a white farmhouse, and Pearlie pointed to the number as they drew parallel to the driveway.

Jaeryn didn't know what he had expected, but the man walking along the edge of the driveway took him completely by surprise.

"Terry. I didn't expect to see you out of bed at this time of morning."

"Oh, Emmerson told me to look after Mrs. Dorroll, so I come around every day and do odd jobs for her. The house needs fixing—it's been empty for a while." Terry caught sight of Jaeryn's blonde passenger then, and his eyes lit up. He offered a hand over the side of the car and engulfed hers in a hearty shake. "I've seen you before. Are you the doctor's sister, or an elf come down from Ireland for a visit?"

She drew her hand back from his touch. "I am Pearl Dailey."

Terry hefted her trunk out of the back and set it on the ground. "Do you mind if I call you Acushla instead? You look like an Acushla."

Pearl hesitated. "I…don't…"

"Stick with Miss Dailey, Terry." Jaeryn slid out and handed her out of the motorcar. "I can take your trunk in if you like."

"I got it." Terry reached for it hastily and picked it up again. "Have you met Mrs. Dorroll yet?"

Pearl shook her head. "No. My brother came to see her last week."

"I'll introduce you, then." He glanced over his shoulder at Jaeryn. "Be right back."

Jaeryn muttered under his breath and stayed by the car, wishing he could think of a reason to go with them. Terry opened the door without knocking, and Jaeryn heard him call someone inside the house. The door slammed closed behind them.

He didn't think it ought to take more than five minutes to deposit a trunk. Ten at most, counting an introduction and Terry's chief weakness—talking. But when a quarter of an hour passed without sign of his return, Jaeryn gave up waiting and knocked peremptorily on the side door.

"Right there," Terry called. Jaeryn heard the scrape of wood on stone and suspected the trunk hadn't made it up the stairs yet after all. He waited, tapping his fingers in an impatient staccato on the porch railing until Terry's voice returned. "I'll see you tomorrow, Miss Acushla."

He opened the screen door and Jaeryn shook his head at him.

"What?" Terry looked like he'd been caught in the cookie jar. "She said I could call her that."

Jaeryn raised an eyebrow. "Did she."

"Well. She didn't say no, exactly."

"I'll do you a favor and forget to tell her brother. Want a ride home? I can't stay long, and it looks like we have some catching up to do."

"Gotta feed the horse first. We can talk in the barn if you want." Terry tugged on a pair of high boots he'd left on the steps and led the way across the overgrown drive towards the stone shed. Jaeryn waited until they were out of earshot from the house. He glanced back once and saw a blonde head peeping through a part in the kitchen curtains. "When did all this start? You didn't tell me you had an odd job."

"Oh, Peters assigned it to me on Monday. Apparently old Emmerson had a niece or something he wanted to take care of while her husband was at the front. Peters told me to come by and make sure she had everything she wants and bring the shopping deliveries."

Jaeryn followed Terry into the darkened stable. "Emmerson assigned you a job, and you didn't tell me about it?"

Terry rubbed the Percheron's nose as he passed by to grab a sack of feed. "Well, she only arrived two days ago. I brought her on the train. Doc, have you seen her? She doesn't even come up to my shoulder, and a spy would make her faint away. She doesn't have anything to do with this."

"Anything about Emmerson has something to do with this. Besides, after she came to town Dailey went to see her. Less than two days after that, his sister shows up at the house to take care of her. He's not a Dailey, and I'll guarantee he found out she was related to

Emmerson. Who is she married to?"

Terry poured the feed into the horse's feed box. "Edmond Dorroll. Army captain."

Jaeryn snapped his fingers. "That's his older brother."

"Is it?"

"Mind you don't tell anyone. Did Miss Dailey mention anything about being related to her?"

Terry shook his head. "Not that I could tell, but I wasn't looking for it."

Jaeryn stepped out of the way as Terry reached for a pitchfork. "So…some of the Dorrolls are connected to Emmerson. I'd like to know why."

"What do you know about the new doc?"

"Nothing that he's told me. I think he likes it that way. Fenton's found a little, but now that we know this, I think I'll send him looking for more. The father gets his son a position—the son came all the way from America—the sister-in-law shows up with a connection to Emmerson, and Dailey obviously didn't care to mention it to me." Another thought struck him. "If she's a niece, does that mean she could inherit?"

Terry shrugged. "I don't know. Peters hasn't heard who the heir is yet."

"See what you can find out, then. The leak in our communications didn't happen until Dailey came to town. And he was the one who leaked it." Jaeryn slapped him on the shoulder. "Well done, Terry. This could prove useful after all."

* * *

When Jaeryn got back to the clinic, Dailey was still gone. He pulled out a sheet of stationary and a pencil. Tapping the pencil against his lips as he leaned back in his chair, he thought of Ryson and what would be the best angle from which to appeal to him.

We've encountered a leak in communications and I am concerned for our safety. I have people depending on me who have families to go home to. A mistake of Dailey's caused the leak. If it was intentional, I'll see him hang for it. But there's no evidence yet to support that, and I'm concerned that if the leak exposed us, he and his family could be targeted. First blood has been shed, and they will not let it go unpunished. I have leads to follow up which I won't write here for reasons of safety. But we need extra security in the meantime. Someone to watch and make sure there is no one tracking us in days to come. I could use the extra man power.

He signed his name and folded it up, sealing it tight. This one he wouldn't risk in the St. Eanswythe drop. He would take it straight to his own, the one on the Leas. And while he was at it, he would go to the Radnor Park drop and make sure no one had left anything in it before Fenton sent the word around that it wasn't to be used any more. The London messengers had ceased checking it. If anything had been left there, it would be waiting for the first person to come its way.

When he parked his car and got out, he realized Radnor Park was more crowded than usual. A group of soldiers stood on the green, responding to shouted orders with stern salute. Jaeryn paused a few feet away from a group of youngsters watching in rapt attention and watched with them. The man shouting at the soldiers had the Irish brogue. Jaeryn knew the lilt as well as he knew his own voice—the rhythm and lift of the vowels that garnered him the hate of his fellow agents. It was unfair, he thought, as anger lit a flame in his chest, that an Irishman was only respected when he went off to the front, enslaved to British wars and British demands. They were blind, that lot of young fellows standing on the green. Not Irish enough to fight for their own freedom, absorbed by free will into an Empire that would grind them into the mill of its own ambition.

"Doctor. I didn't expect to see ye here."

Jaeryn turned and saw Mrs. Meikle's hunched figure a few feet away. "I didn't expect to see you either. Who's at the post office?"

"I don't usually answer to regular folk," she said sweetly, "but there's a post boy minding it while I'm gone. I step out every dinner time to see the soldiers here at work. It gives me a bit of fresh air and the children are grand to watch." She glanced at the soldiers as they saluted and were told to stand at ease. "It's good to see an Irishman working, isn't it? I wonder if they'll be off to help the boys in France."

Jaeryn crossed his arms and frowned. "Oh, I'm sure they'll be shipped off wherever the slaughter is highest. The Irish usually are."

"I'll debate that with ye if ye'll give me a ride back to the post office."

"Sorry. I'm busy."

"Too busy to help an old woman? Surely it wouldn't take you long."

His gaze narrowed. "Too busy to help a perfectly capable Scotchwoman, you mean. I have things to attend to, Mrs. Meikle."

"Ye'd do well to make an effort at maintaining good relations with your colleagues." Her brogue twisted the last word into hopeless incomprehension. "Besides, Fenton's stopping by tonight, and he'd like to see ye."

"Tell him I'm at the clinic." Jaeryn set off toward the steps leading down to the drop point and called over his shoulder, "Good evening, Mrs. Meikle."

He went down the steps with a sauntering pace, pausing for a long time at the bottom as he pretended to look at the small waterfall pooling in the stones. A few feet away the stone hiding the drop box looked as undisturbed as it always did. When he was convinced the coast was clear, he pulled out his knife and counted the stones, then pried up the right one. The black box inside was still locked, and he flew through the combination. Inside, a little twist of paper was thrust into the bottom. Jaeryn pulled it out and smoothed it over his knee. What he saw made his brow furrow in confusion.

It was a typewritten list of numbers, some of them denominations of hundreds, some of them thousands, with dates next to each one from the past week and names of the hotels along the Leas. Attached to it was a scrawl he recognized as Mrs. Meikle's: *Thought you might want to know about this.*

His lips tightened, and he shoved the box back again. Finally, he had caught that woman at her own game.

* * *

"Doctor, you can't jump to conclusions over a single piece of evidence." Fenton leaned on his elbows on Jaeryn's desk as Ben peered over his shoulder. The square of paper lay spread out between the three of them.

"Give me one good reason why I shouldn't have her arrested." Jaeryn jabbed his finger down on the sheet of paper. "One good reason. This is her writing after all."

Fenton shook his head. "It didn't have to be her that wrote it. The sheet is typewritten. She told me about it this evening. She found it in an envelope going through the mail to France."

"She knew the drop was compromised. Even so, I'm surprised even she would think it was safe to send something through it when we might still look there. It's a pity she'll be thrown over by such an amateur mistake."

Amusement twitched at the corners of Fenton's lips. "She didn't know the drop was compromised, doctor. I told her tonight before you called me to come here."

"What do you think it is?" Ben asked. "Some kind of code she made up?"

Fenton spared him a glance. "She'd call both of you daft skellums for thinking it was her. She didn't sign off with a number that matches any of the numbers you found in Emmerson's library, so you can't trace it to the other side for sure. You can't jump to conclusions just because she hates you being Irish."

Jaeryn's fingers half-clenched. "I'm not jumping to conclusions, and she'll be leaving with the bobbies before the night is over."

Ben was ignoring them, tracing his finger down the column of dates, hotels, and numbers. Then he looked up, dawning realization over his face. "It's a list of soldiers. It must be. You said you were watching them out at Radnor Park today. Whoever wrote this is sending their division strengths off to France along with the hotels they're staying at."

Jaeryn paused mid-rant and looked down. He traced his own finger down the list, fitting the pieces together in his mind. "I believe you're right, Dailey. Which compounds her wrongdoing."

Fenton covered his mouth with his hand and gave a delicate cough. "She's sent things to London before. She and I have an— arrangement. We've used it on occasion before this if we have something private that Ryson needs to be aware of and that we don't want all the Folkestone agents to see."

"Then the two of you are a pair of fools together," Jaeryn said. "I'm supposed to see everything that goes through to London. How can I get an accurate picture of what's going on in Folkestone if I don't have all the evidence? Even if she wasn't the one who made the lists, she still kept evidence from me. I'll write to Ryson and have her dismissed."

"Doctor, she's been with the British Secret Service as long as you have. An Irishman suspected of being a revolting rebel can't pit his opinion against a staunch Scottish postmistress. Ryson won't take it without clear evidence."

Jaeryn slammed his hand down on the desk. "*I wasn't in the revolt.* How many times must I tell you before you believe me?"

Ben looked up from the paper, a faint line of annoyance across his brow. "What is it you dislike about Ann Meikle so much? You've never said."

Fenton sighed. "Back in April he intercepted a note she wrote to Ryson saying he took trips to Calais involved with the Irish revolts. Suggested he be carted off to jail with the rest of the rebels." He shook his head at Jaeryn, frowning. "They've been at each other's throats ever since. I think they're wasting time, trying to prove each other traitors."

"I won't have to waste any more time," Jaeryn said. "It's true."

"Doctor, there is absolutely no evidence that she wrote this list. No bobby's going to arrest her when it's your word against hers. For now, you're better off watching for another slip. If she's against you, she'll make a mistake again sooner or later. You would be a fool to cut the thread that could lead you back to other German agents. Leave Ann Meikle alone."

"It's only sense to wait," Ben said, taking the list and locking it away.

Jaeryn swallowed back his anger and managed to avoid shooting Dailey a disgusted look. "Fine. Keep using a compromised drop and let her keep sending soldier lists. If battles are lost because information falls into the wrong hands, it's both of your responsibilities."

Fenton straightened and tugged down his coat sleeves. "I think I'll still be able to sleep at night," he said dryly.

* * *

The evening of Sunday, the seventeenth of June was to be Charlotte's last at the cottage until after Alisa's baby was born. Alisa had agreed to have Charlotte stay with her as well as Pearl once they explained that they couldn't be reached by telephone if she needed help. They were glad she proved easy to persuade. They knew it couldn't be long now, and they owed it to her not to leave her in Jaeryn's hands, for if she ever found out their relationship, she would surely be hurt and puzzled that her own family had left her to the care of a stranger.

After washing up the supper dishes that evening, Ben asked Charlotte to find a sweater and come out with him for a stroll along the cliffs. She had never seen the Channel from the edge at night, for he was cautious and didn't want her walking without him after dark. But this would be their last chance for a few weeks, so she held his hand and they stood together, listening to the crash of the surf on the rocks below.

"Will you mind living in the country for a bit, sweetheart?" he asked.

"It's a little less remote than here." Charlotte looked up at him, and her lips turned up rather mischievously as she replied. "I'll enjoy having people nearby at night, and your brother's little woman seems like sweet company. I wish she knew who we really were," she ended with a sigh.

They had been over that before, several times. He didn't know what to tell her. So they dropped into silence, and the only things around them were the rhythmic waves, the scent of her jasmine perfume, and the taste of salt in the air.

"Darling," Charlotte said, after a moment's pause, "I have been wondering about something, and I am curious as to how you would answer it."

"Ask away." Ben closed his eyes and pulled her closer to him.

"You've not mentioned Edmond since Alisa told us about him getting hurt."

He opened his eyes again and looked down at her in surprise. "Is that a problem?"

She shrugged. "It does seem strange that it doesn't—hurt you more."

"It's not that it doesn't grieve me," Ben said slowly. "I don't know him well enough for it to affect me personally. We're more like distant cousins than brothers, when it comes down to it."

"I see."

A cold, hard wind gusted around him, and he shivered beneath his cardigan. "Alisa let me read his last letter to her, and he's done well for himself. It almost makes me wish I had known him."

"Did you tell your father about him?" Charlotte asked.

"I wrote and told him about the gas poisoning, but not about Alisa. She's Edmond's secret, and not mine to tell. I also inquired where I can direct a letter to Edmond, so if my father writes back, I'll try to get in touch."

A light drop of rain fell on Charlotte's collar, leaving a water mark in its wake. Ben moved to go inside, but she held him back to watch as a gray mist blew over the surface of the water, swirling it about into little eddies and currents. Another raindrop joined the first, and then a third, icy to the touch, but she didn't seem to care, and he didn't mind waiting for her to drink it in.

"I must go and pack, darling," Charlotte said at length, squeezing his hand and entwining her fingers. Her tone held a wistful note, and she made no haste to leave.

Ben's hand crept to her hair pins, as it always did they were alone together. Her flaxen waves loosed from their tight constraints, and the wind caught them, swirling her hair about her slender figure. "Nervous about leaving?" he asked, and a supreme contentment coursed through him at the soft lightness around his fingers.

Charlotte leaned her head on his shoulder. "Not for myself," she replied. "But I'll miss you dreadfully."

"We've been apart before, you know, and survived it. Besides, we'll see each other quite often."

"But somehow this is different. I don't know if you'll be safe here, all alone at night."

Ben kissed the top of her head. "God keeps us both safe as long as he likes, and there's no use fretting about it. *Je t'aime, ma chèrie.* Don't worry about me. Call Doctor Graham if anything's urgent, and he'll take a message for me. I'll use his phone in the evenings to call to you."

As they reached the front door, Ben saw Mrs. Goodwin looking out her window, and he waved in greeting before shutting out the escalating storm.

* * *

Twenty-four hours later, Jaeryn returned home from a patient call and opened his front door to find a little square of paper lying on the

149

carpet. Someone had pushed it through the mail slot while he was out. He picked it up.

Even if the government lets the Irish go free, some of us aren't going to let it happen forever. Justice never miscarries.

What Irish? Jaeryn dropped the paper as his heart picked up a beat, turning to an excited patter in his chest. Where was the newspaper? He hadn't had time to look at it for days. He tore through the mail on the side table, dropping some of it to the floor in his haste to get at the folded pages of newsprint. Flinging open the sheet, he found the headline in one of the columns.

Amnesty. For all of the Irish rebels. All the men who had been kept in prison since the revolt. Jaeryn breathed out a long sigh. If the British had given amnesty, then there was nothing left for people to hold against him. London would have no more reason to replace him with even the most competent of foreigners.

The thought of his assistant made Jaeryn glance at the clock. Dailey was due back in a few moments from his last call, and he wanted to check for a reply from Ryson in case it required discussion before they parted ways for the night.

He drove out to the Leas, found a place to park his car, and sauntered nonchalantly along the circular promenade overlooking the Channel. The general vicinity would be deserted during the supper hour. Most of the hotels along the walk held soldiers bound for France, offering them one last taste of comfort before they left for the front. But right now the soldiers were inside. The only living people observing him were the guards in front of the hotels who kept away intruders.

He left the Leas walk behind and kept heading towards the pier. The wind whipped at the edges of his coat as he stepped onto the pier planking and counted to seven, then knelt down and felt underneath the edge. The dark waters crashed below with a hollow echo. A square little box met his touch, and he pulled it up, twisting off the lid. Inside, he found the message from London he had been waiting for. He tore it open.

Extra men not possible at this time. Caution and alertness should be all that is necessary to maintain security. If Dailey's security is not maintained, we have other agents in Folkestone to carry on. If Dailey is compromised, we will remove him from his position and return him to America.

Jaeryn crunched the paper in his fist and scrambled to his feet again, muttering under his breath. He could read between the lines as well as anyone. Ryson simply didn't care.

When he showed Dailey the note, Ben took the paper from him and scanned through the lines, dropping his bag absentmindedly on his desk as he did so. Since King's dinner, Ben had never revealed much emotion, but Jaeryn thought he detected a faint shadow on his assistant's face after he finished the note.

"I always thought you were important to London," Jaeryn said.

"I never got that impression." Ben gestured to the letter with a grimace. "Even if I had, that doesn't sound to me as though I'm terribly important."

"I won't allow it," Jaeryn said with some heat. "Just because they think they have enough agents if you're knocked off; it isn't fair."

"Tell that to the soldiers at the Somme. It wasn't fair for them, either." Ben's face sobered even more. "Do you think we're just faceless pawns to them? Dispensable, in the grand scheme of things? I'd rather not die for someone who doesn't even care."

Jaeryn smiled in spite of himself. "Most men prefer not to."

"No, I didn't mean that. It isn't the dying. I don't really care about that. It's just, I'd rather not die here. Like this. I don't think I could die now and say it was for something noble, or even average good."

Jaeryn eyed him as he emptied the bag and pulled out the antiseptic. "Defending your country is a good cause."

"It isn't my country. I'm just here…" Ben trailed off. He turned

151

on the warm tap water to begin the process of cleaning his instruments.

"Here?" Jaeryn prompted him.

"I'm just here to do what England says is the right thing until I can go home and do what I know is the right thing."

Jaeryn's face tightened into grim lines. "If you are the man I think you are, I don't want you to die either. Don't worry, Dailey. London can easily dispense with us, but I take care of men on my side better than that."

* * *

Ben walked slowly through town on his way home to Copt Point. He couldn't help peeking through the windows of the lighted houses as he passed, watching the families sitting at their dinner tables, chatting together. He missed Charlotte's company, and though he had rarely spent evenings with her even back in Richmond, the thought that there would be no chance of seeing her tonight took the eager expectation out of going home. The bed would be lonely without her comforting presence. Earlier that morning, Jaeryn had offered the use of his telephone to reach her, but when Ben called, he didn't chat for long. He hoped Jaeryn wouldn't listen in, but he wasn't quite sure, and he couldn't talk at his ease with the doctor close by. So he had only made sure that Charlotte was doing well and then said goodbye.

The sky darkened as he turned onto the deserted stretch of road leading to Copt Point. Now he was quite alone as far as houses went. Every now and then a crunch of gravel met his ears, and he kept his hand hovering near the pocket that held his Webley. He endured it as long as he could, then, taking his courage in both hands, whirled about to look behind him. The road stretched out deserted. There were no trees to hide strangers this close to the cliffs, and he scorned himself for being paranoid. Picking up his pace to a brisk walk, he cut across the grass toward the cottages and took out the key to unlock his door. As he fitted the key in the lock, Mrs. Goodwin's voice stopped him.

"Doctor." She hurried toward him and motioned him to wait. "Before you go in, I'd best tell you. Someone's been here while you were out."

Ben paused with the knob in his hand. "They have?"

The old woman nodded. Though she kept a calm exterior, the ceaseless movement of her hands betrayed her alarm. "I returned from one of my jobs an hour ago and happened to see your curtains open. They haven't been open since your wife left you, so I looked inside, and I could tell someone had broken in and searched through your things. You'd best see for yourself."

Ben opened the door and stared in disbelief at the sight that met his gaze. Whoever had rifled through his things had made a thorough job of it. The windows overlooking the Channel were smashed to bits and the cupboard doors pulled off their hinges. Running into the bedroom, he saw his bed stripped of sheets, the mattress flipped, and every drawer pulled out of his dresser. That window, too, had been vandalized. His clothes lay strewn over the floor, pockets turned inside out and emptied. A gasp of dismay escaped him.

Mrs. Goodwin clucked her tongue and stood with her hands on her hips. "Who would have done such a thing?"

Ben frowned, too preoccupied to answer the question. What had they wanted? What information could he possibly have that neither he nor Jaeryn knew about—information so vital to the German agents that Emmerson's spies wanted it at any cost?

"Thank you, Mrs. Goodwin," he said, hardly paying attention to his words. "I'm sorry the place is such a mess. I'll pay for the windows."

"Are you going back to town to tell the police, doctor?"

He didn't dare stay the night, and he didn't dare leave. If he returned to town he might be waylaid on the road. If he stayed on this deserted stretch of coast, he had no guarantee that the person would not come back again. But on the whole, he had better means of defense in the cottage than on a dark road by himself. "Not yet," he said. "I think I'll stay here until morning. Lock your door and secure the windows. If you feel the slightest bit uneasy, don't hesitate to call. I'll be awake."

Ben shut the door on her protests and checked for the gleam of brass near the breach of his revolver to be sure the chamber was full. Then he opened the door again and stooped to examine the lock. When he found that the intruder hadn't left a scratch, he called after his landlady's retreating figure. "Mrs. Goodwin."

"Yes, sir?" She hurried back.

"Does anyone else have a key to this cottage?" Ben asked.

"Why, no, doctor. Only I do, and I keep it safe around my neck while I'm in town. They didn't use a key to get in, that's certain. They must have come through the window."

He examined the ragged remains of glass, but they offered no clue. "Are you certain there's no other key?"

Mrs. Goodwin's faded blue eyes held nothing but perplexity. "Not that I know of, sir. But I don't own the cottages; I only keep them."

Ben caught his breath at her words. "I thought you told me they were yours."

The old woman twisted her apron in her fingers, and a gust of wind from the Channel blew strands of her white hair across her wrinkled face. "Mine to take care of. Not mine to own. A woman like me would never have the means to buy a house."

"Indeed. Then who owns them?"

"Colonel King, sir."

King. Ben exhaled as he heard the name, stunned at this new revelation. Then one other person had a key at least, for King doubtless kept one. He would want to know that his property had been broken into. Unless he had broken into it himself, in which case he knew already. The irony of discovering that he rented from Charlotte's cousins was swallowed up by the greater problem of whether or not her cousins had played a part in searching through his personal effects. Even if they had not, they might have given the key

154

to the person who did.

"I'll speak to him about it, Mrs. Goodwin. Tomorrow."

Ben closed the door and sat down on the edge of the sofa, taking courage from the heavy weight of the Webley between his fingers. The lights were smashed in too badly to be used, and a chill breeze crept through the open windows, rustling papers and stray objects on the floor. Not wanting to be left without a light, he found a candle that had rolled under the kitchen table and hunted about for a match to light it with. But none turned up in the chaos, and giving up his search, Ben returned to his seat to wait as the June twilight faded away to darkness.

Chapter Ten
Setting the Stakes

The next hour crept away, tedious minutes of sitting at the ready, terrified lest he fall asleep and leave himself vulnerable to an attacker creeping in through the open window. At least Charlotte and Pearl were safe, far on the other side of town. This was no place for women. But then again, if Emmerson's spies knew his habits well enough to time a break-in, then he could hardly comfort himself with the illusion that his wife and sister were free from observation. And they were—he covered his face and groaned aloud—out of his sight and his protection, asleep in a country farmhouse with only a pregnant woman as their companion.

He must think. What was best to be done? If he told the police, they would make inquiries into his habits and reasons for being under threat, which would never do. Besides, if the police were sharp enough to catch the person or persons who had broken in, the intruders would never be caught for their greater crime of being civilian spies. No, calling the police would not do. But on the other hand, if he did not and there was any doubt on the part of the people watching him as to his true identity, his silence on the matter would convince them. They would know he was there to find them out and put an end to them. Perhaps Colonel King would report it and save him the trouble. He must consult with Jaeryn as soon as he had a good chance of reaching town without being waylaid.

By peering closely, Ben could see the hands on his wristwatch. They pointed to half past midnight. He got up to walk about, impatient at the idleness of waiting. If he cut across the downs he might be able to take a roundabout way to Jaeryn's and elude his pursuers, assuming they were still out and watching for him. He could not wait until morning; the torture of the stillness would drive him mad long before then.

Snatching up his jacket, Ben climbed out through the kitchen window as quietly as he could. He shivered as he left the shelter of the house behind him, though he could not tell whether it was from the chill of the night or the terror of being in danger. Crouching down at the corner of the house, he strained his eyes to peer through the darkness. Five minutes passed in uneasy listening until he was sure he could sense no other human presence sharing the same stretch of land.

Slowly, he rose to his feet. He had just stretched to his full height when a muffled shot broke the stillness, and he jerked back. A small arc of fire and smoke traveled up over the Channel. It was a flare and not a gunshot. Someone was signaling, but who or why or where he couldn't make out. Ben crouched down again to look and listen in the dark as best he could. If someone was in the scrub at the cliff edge, they weren't visible. Another rustle caught his ears—this time a prolonged one, as if a small night creature was creeping past him. He could just make out the quivering scrub at the edge of the cliff. Silently, he pulled out his revolver. Then a muffled thud and a groan sounded, and a man shot up amidst the scrub and took off running across the downs.

Ben waited, stunned, as Nimrod broke out into furious barking from inside Mrs. Goodwin's cottage. Someone had fired a signal flare, and another man had attacked the signaler and run away. Glancing out across the water, he watched for the wink of lights, but in the ten seconds he dared to delay, he saw none. He put a hand to the earth to crawl closer to where he thought the victim lay, but before he could move, the victim stood up. The man stumbled slightly, but gradually gained his footing and disappeared over the lip of the cliff into what could only be the madness of a midnight climb down to the rocks of the shore. Ben hesitated. The two men were undoubtedly going in the same direction, trying to cut each other off—one risking the shoreline and the other trusting the speed of the open road—to reach whoever it was that had been signaled. If he could catch them, see who they were signaling, then perhaps he would have something concrete to tell Jaeryn to amend for his first error with Fenton.

There was nothing to do but to follow after. Stripping off his jacket and tucking his gun into his belt, Ben braced himself and set out across the downs toward the road. The man who had taken the road was out of sight ahead of him. All the better for keeping himself concealed. With the faint crunch of gravel on the road underfoot, he picked up his pace. He must run and he must catch him. Upon reaching the road, he pushed himself even faster and shifted his direction west.

It was just him, the object of his pursuit, and the dark of a night in England. It sent the excitement pumping through his veins. For a brief, odd moment, he rather liked the feeling. Then it occurred to him that he hadn't planned what to do if there was someone at the end of this chase. Was he prepared to fight? That thought sent a different type of excitement rushing through his body. This time it was also tinged with fear. He was not sure if he was ready for that sort of thing yet.

On the heels of that thought, he saw a figure on the road before him. The man was far enough away not to know that anyone was following him, but he was still close enough that Ben needed to take precautions. Ben shifted to the grass at the edge of the road, gulped down air, and pushed on.

He followed the man down the Lower Sandgate Road, past the

houses and the tall hedges lining either side. The man never stopped and never looked back. Then, all at once, he took off running as if he had no time to spare and the utmost importance hung on his every step.

He led Ben a merry chase. Once the lack of roadside grass forced Ben to take to the street again, it was impossible to keep quiet, but if his own loud breathing was any indication, he suspected the man he was pursuing wouldn't be able to hear him anyway. A shout followed him when they took a more populated street, but he didn't stop to answer. Once they passed through town and drew closer to the Leas, he knew his suspicion was correct. They were headed to the harbor.

Ben thought his heart would burst before they reached the Folkestone docks. The man ahead of him clattered across the harbor railway tracks, seemingly unwearied by the long chase. In his exhaustion, Ben forgot caution and pushed himself too far. Just as he passed the Custom House, he tripped over an uneven dip in the road. His involuntary cry betrayed him.

The man stopped and whirled around. Through the sweat and weariness, Ben could see enough to recognize that the man was tensed, a gun outstretched in his hand.

"Who are you?"

Ben kept silent and edged closer to the Custom House wall. With a sickening jolt, he realized there wasn't anything to cover him if the man took it in his head to shoot.

"Who are you?" The words grated out, panicked and angry. "Give me the password!"

Then the dull thump of feet on the dock boards sounded. Both of them froze. Ben strained his eyes beyond his assailant and saw a tall shape making its way toward them. For an instant, his attacker turned his head away, and Ben took the opportunity to press into one of the doorway alcoves of the Custom House beside him.

A muffled choke sounded from just ahead. "What are you doing here?"

"*A dhúnmharfóir.*" Ben didn't know what the words meant, but

159

they sounded fierce enough. They were followed by a couple of heavy thuds and a muffled groan cut off in mid-utterance. Ben kept silent, pressed against the brick as his heart thumped urgently in his chest.

A low mutter sounded in the stillness. "German trash."

Ben did not stop to see who it was. He backed away from the Custom House, keeping his gun pointed in the direction of the sound. Two minutes' swift walking brought him to the other side of the harbor rail tracks, nearest the town proper. He turned and set off at a run until he reached the west end of Tontine and paused, panting, in a shop doorway. As soon as he was sure of being undiscovered, he pressed on, running until he could run no more and then slowing to a walk.

There was something odd about two men signaling from Copt Point and then running all the way to the docks to meet their comrade. The victim who had taken the shore route was probably still struggling in the dark. Or he might be injured by now, the uneven ground catching heel or leg and twisting the ligaments mercilessly.

And why, once they reached the docks, was a rescuer there at the exact moment he was discovered? Had he been followed? Surely no one could have known he would end up in that spot when he did not know himself.

The shops on Tontine were dark. Every now and then a blast of guns sounded from the camp. The air raid signals, installed since the raid in May, started up their shrill warning once, but Ben did not pay them any heed. He found Jaeryn's shutters double locked when he reached the clinic. The Irishman hadn't given him a copy of the key.

Ben found a handful of pebbles from the street and tossed them up to the second floor bedroom window. It only took three before he heard the lock rattle, and the front door opened a crack. "Come in," Jaeryn whispered. "Is someone behind you?"

Ben pushed through the door and bolted it as soon as he was inside. "Perhaps. I almost got in a fight a while back."

"With who?" Jaeryn flipped on a flashlight and scrubbed at his face to bring himself fully awake.

Ben's legs trembled from running so far, and he could hardly get breath enough to respond. "Someone was sending out a signal from Copt Point, and I followed them all the way to the docks, but I never did discover what they were after. One of them tried to shoot me when he saw I was following."

He pushed open the consulting room door without being invited. Jaeryn kept a pitcher of water just inside on a small table, and he poured himself a glass and sank down on the edge of the desk with a sigh of relief. The Irishman followed after, pouring out questions with a worried lilt. "They tried to shoot you? Are you hurt?"

He drank deep before replying. "No, I'm not. No thanks to them."

"Who were they?" Jaeryn watched him intently as if by his gaze he could drag the details out of him.

"I don't know. But they had to have been pro-German sympathizers. They also rifled my house. Everything was smashed to bits when I got home this evening."

"Blast." Jaeryn frowned. "I thought it had been long enough, and we were safe from discovery. Now they have a link to our side and we don't have one in return. There wasn't anything they could have found, was there?"

He grinned at the humor of the thought. "Bedding and a few old clothes, but that's about all."

"It's not a matter for jesting," Jaeryn snapped. "Something has happened to bring you to their attention, and after tonight you no longer have the benefit of anonymity."

The relief that Ben had felt at being safe in Jaeryn's study died away and apprehension gripped him again full force. "But I have no papers. Nothing, absolutely nothing that they could want. I doubt they even know for sure I'm involved. This seems to be an act of outright panic on their part."

Jaeryn sat down in his leather swivel chair. "Maybe they were looking for something to prove you were a part of all this, after the incident at Emmerson's library failed. Or perhaps it's not because of what you know, but because of who you are."

The phone rang, startling them both, and Jaeryn picked it up. Ben handed him a paper and pencil to write down the address in case he was wanted for something. Jaeryn grabbed the paper and held the pencil poised, but after a moment he set it down again. "It's not urgent," he said, replacing the receiver on its hook. "Where were we?"

"You said who I am might be a threat to them," Ben said. "I don't see why, when they don't know what I'm here for."

Jaeryn shivered without his dressing gown and crossed his arms over his chest to keep warm. "Our antagonists want to discover our identities just as much as we want theirs, and by all appearances, they've found something that makes them suspect you're a hindrance to their work. At least we haven't set up an identity code for you yet, so they won't know that much. Now," he said briskly, "of course you'll stay here for the night, but we must decide what to do after that. I'll have a telephone installed for you within the week, that's certain."

"Do you think I should stay at all?" A flash of hope rose up in Ben that here, perhaps, he had the release to return to America that he wanted.

Jaeryn paused for a long moment, tapping his fingers together as he thought. Then he looked up. "It's possible they don't know it was you following them. I think they must, but it's a dark night, so there is a slim chance that your identity is still a secret. But it's entirely your choice. In this instance, you are the one playing for the stakes, and you must give your free consent. How high would you like to set them?"

"Set them?" Ben frowned. "I don't understand."

"Well, you can pull out and go home. Or you can stay where you are and play for the pool. There may be more to you than either of us realizes, and I should like to know what it is." Jaeryn smiled. "I admit, I'd be hard pressed to get you a dismissal without better reason than a threat to your life. But I won't force you to gamble more than you wish, so tell me if you want to risk it, and we'll press ahead."

Ben thought for one pleasant moment about pulling out. If he did, he could put the whole nightmare behind him—the lies, the tight finances, the work he detested. If he didn't, there were all the dangers yet to face, and it would only get worse. But then again, if he left he would never find out why his father wanted him to come, and Alisa would have to fend for herself, abandoned for good not only by one brother but by the other as well. And there was another reason.

"I've been thinking…ever since we found the soldier list the other day. And tonight, as I was walking home, I was thinking about that note from Ryson."

Jaeryn picked up a pencil and slid it back and forth between his fingers, watching him in silence.

"I was thinking of all the thousands who have been lost. It's been three years of war now."

The pencil continued sliding back and forth, and Ben watched it, forgetting for a moment how much he distrusted Jaeryn and why. "I have decided that whether or not my original reason for coming to England ever comes to pass, it would be a shame to pull out and let more lists like that slip through to the other side. If their humanity is lost in all the London tactical fights, then I would like to be one person who cares enough to think of them as real people. We've got the chance to take away at least one threat out of the many they'll face." He lifted his chin. "I do not like you or your work. But I will stay."

Jaeryn chuckled. "Good fellow. At this point, you'll have to watch your ways anywhere you go. If someone has been told to harry your steps, we can hardly delude ourselves into thinking that they'll give up finding proof of your involvement so easily. We'll keep you in town until you have a telephone, and then you'd best go back and brave it out. With precautions, of course. How long is your wife gone?"

"I don't know."

Jaeryn's lips twitched. "And you can't guess, of course. Very well, I won't press you. When she comes back, you shouldn't leave her alone at night. I'll take back the night calls when she returns. For now, I think the guest room should be safe enough to sleep in. By the way, you never told me: how did you escape the shooter?"

Ben wondered again at the miracle of the mysterious rescuer. "I think I had some help."

He gave Jaeryn the whole account and suspected, after a pointed question or two about the foreign speech, that Jaeryn knew more of the mystery than he let on. But when Ben asked, Jaeryn refused to hazard any guesses as to the identity of his attacker or the man who had come to his defense.

* * *

"We're not here to help the police," Jaeryn said the next morning when they discussed how best to handle reporting the matter. "Obviously, we want to stay out of trouble, so you'll have to tell them. But reveal nothing of why you're here. For all they know, it was just a random break-in. I wouldn't mention the incident by the Custom House either if I were you."

Ben shook his head. "Mrs. Goodwin must have heard the flare. If I don't say something, she'll wonder about it."

"Confound it." Jaeryn pounded the desk in frustration and winced at the force he had used. "Well, then, you'd best tell them that, too. But mind, you know no reason why anyone would want to rob you; you know nothing of what they're looking for. If they insist, try slanting the blame King's way. That may be of use to us." He set his jaw, and his eyes flashed at Ben's look of distaste. "You can consider that superior's orders, if necessary."

Ben called the King estate as soon as he and Jaeryn finished discussing their course of action. The butler, Stafford, connected him immediately to Colonel King, who received the news with surprise but did not seem overly alarmed.

"Well, doctor, it's a lonely stretch of coast." The colonel's voice was deep and smooth in spite of the early hour. "I have no doubt strange things take place now and then between Copt Point and France. Perhaps you ran into some fracas with the war activity in the Channel. They're working at destroying the mines the Germans have placed there. Haven't you heard the explosions?"

Ben's voice had a cool civility to it when he replied. "I have, but I doubt it has a connection, sir. It seemed to be on a much smaller scale than that."

All the same, he made use of that conjecture when the police met him at the cottage and gave it a thorough search. They took his fingerprints and collected a couple of the objects to take to their lab and test, and he said nothing whatsoever about the chase. They would save that part of the story to send to London.

The police did not find any fingerprints and decided that the intruder must have been wearing gloves. Since nothing was taken, that left them with very little evidence to go on. Though Ben tried not to appear too eager, he was glad to hush it up and let it go for Jaeryn's sake.

Jaeryn did his best to put his pounds and shillings to good use regarding the telephone, and had it merely been a matter of money, he would have encountered no difficulty. But when Ben sounded Mrs. Goodwin on the issue, she said it wasn't her place to decide such a thing and that she would have to speak to Colonel King about it. She came back with an utter refusal on account of the distance from town. Jaeryn then took a cab out to Copt Point to try and persuade her, but without success. In spite of every sensible reason they could think of, she remained unmoved. She was not unkind about it; she even seemed sympathetic with their difficulties, though her sympathy didn't extend to the accepting of a bribe, which Jaeryn attempted when all other avenues failed. She did, however, allow them to put new shutters over the windows and a stronger lock on the door.

The first night back at the cottage, Ben could hardly sleep. He kept the revolver on the nightstand where he could have it within instant reach. It must be in times like these that men took to vices to cope with stress. He wondered what Jaeryn did.

But one night passed to another, and then still another without the incident being renewed. He was plagued by the uneasy thought that perhaps he was worrying for no cause. Perhaps the struggle had ended with a knife thrust between the ribs, and his intruder was dead. But Jaeryn did not think it likely that the rescuer had committed murder, so Ben kept a vigilant outlook as he walked his rounds, and he locked his door securely every evening.

It was a good thing that Jaeryn had lent him more money than he needed. Half of the generous loan went to replace the damaged furniture, though Colonel King paid for the windows and lock. He would have to tell Charlotte about the incident when she returned, but he didn't want her worrying about him in the meantime, and he hoped the passage of time would lessen the concern she might feel when he came back, though he rather doubted it.

Since Alisa was expecting her first, Ben felt confident that Charlotte would be able to phone Jaeryn's office before Alisa actually delivered. They would be able to manage quite well with Pearl's help, but he wanted to be there if he could, and he was glad when, late on the morning of July fourth, Jaeryn had a message waiting for him at the clinic.

"Your wife called to say that Alisa Dorroll is in labor." Jaeryn shot him a sideways glance, and a narrowing of his eyes showed that he would like to ask more but did not dare to.

"Thank you." Ben concealed the rush of pleasure that filled him at the news and acted as if it were a mere everyday occurrence.

"Do you want any help?"

"Not necessary. I've delivered babies before."

"Good, then." Jaeryn turned back to the tools he was cleaning. "Your wife would be helpful here. I recall you mentioning she might be able to work at the clinic when she first came. Do you think she could arrange it if I paid her well for her time?"

Ben saw no reason to refuse. He knew as well as Jaeryn that they could not manage all the smaller things between them, and she would be of more use here than volunteering for the hospital. It would be extra income for them, too, and they needed it. Jaeryn complicated his practice so much by trading services with the poorer patients and paying Doctor Winfield practice dues that the routes couldn't support two incomes. Ben suspected that Jaeryn gave him more than he should, though he couldn't prove it by the books, and he didn't want to ask. Even so, his principal income came from London, and since he now had to split it between two households, he would miss the loan installments this month as well if Charlotte didn't start earning money soon.

"As soon as Alisa no longer needs her help, I'll bring her in," Ben promised.

He called Charlotte back, and she told him that early labor was progressing steadily. She thought he could keep to normal routine until the afternoon, so Ben decided to take care of as many house visits as he could manage in the meantime. At six that evening, Charlotte called again and told him to come. He borrowed Jaeryn's bicycle and followed the familiar way down Tontine Street, which still showed signs of damage from the bombing, and out to the farming district.

Alisa Dorroll's farm stood in the warm glow of a pink summer's evening, peaceful and serene. The warm glow turned to soft dusk, and the soft dusk had merged into inky blackness before they laid her firstborn son beside her and saw her safely resting. As soon as she fell asleep, well cared for and blanched from the pain she had undergone, Ben and Charlotte left Pearl to watch Alisa and the baby while they stepped out onto the back porch for a breath of air. The stars lit up the heavens, and the glow from the moon shone full on their faces. Ben reached out for Charlotte's hand.

"She named him Matthew," he remarked. He wondered what his father would think if he knew his first grandson was named after him. Surely it would please him. Ben hoped Edmond wouldn't wait long to tell, once he knew.

Charlotte smiled, though rather wearily. "The baby didn't cry until you took him, you know. I think he likes his mother better." She laughed at his look of dismay, then sobered and asked, "Are you sorry now that she doesn't know who you are? You can't claim him as your nephew unless she does."

Ben thought of Alisa's big blue eyes clenched shut and the trusting pressure from her hands when she clung to him for strength, her face furrowed in its effort of concentration. "Yes," he admitted. "She's a dear little woman, and it is as if she has adopted us for her family. I wish she knew who we were. But it is too dangerous, and though I am sorry for it, I am glad that she does not know. If she did—"

"What?" Charlotte turned to him, and he saw that she guessed at the trouble he wanted to conceal from her.

"Nothing. But it is safer for her that she does not know. And I trust to God that our relations with her will bring her nothing of harm while we are here."

The crickets chirped, and the smell of new-mown grass gradually diffused the antiseptic from their hands and clothes. Ben suddenly realized how tired he was and how early the morning would come.

"Do you like your nephew?" Charlotte asked.

"Of course, I do." He wrapped his hands around the porch rail and looked out over the carefully tended vegetable garden and the large, empty field beyond. "He's a fine baby and shows every sign of being a healthy one. If something should happen to Edmond, a son will be a great comfort to her. I am glad for her sake that she isn't alone now."

Charlotte's voice, when she replied, sounded quicker and higher than usual. "I like him, too. Ben, I want one of our own."

Ben looked down at her in alarm. "You're not serious, are you? This is hardly the time to be thinking of that."

"When will that time be, then?" She tried to ask the question lightly, but Ben could tell she cared more about his answer than she wanted to show.

He hadn't even considered what meeting Alisa might mean to Charlotte. An eighteen-year-old girl, married only a handful of

168

months, to be a mother already while Charlotte herself had been married over a year. They hadn't discussed children since their decision to come to England. But to start a family now would be nothing short of insanity.

"We won't wait too long," he said. "After all this is over we can think about it some more."

"I'll remind you of that."

Ben thought he saw her lips trembling, though he couldn't quite tell in the darkness.

"Charlotte, are you all right?"

"I…yes." She drew a deep breath and slipped her arm through his. "I'm just tired, that's all. Come, darling. You may as well sleep on the sofa in the parlor, for it's quite late in the evening to bike all the way to Copt Point."

He decided he must have been mistaken.

* * *

Ann Meikle hadn't seen fit to give them any communications from London for quite some time now. Ben expected they would hear back on the evidence from Emmerson's soon, and he came to inquire for mail two or three times a week, but the postmistress never offered anything besides ordinary civilities. A few days after the birth of Alisa's baby, however, Ben saw Mrs. Meikle waving to him as he passed the post office, so he paused his errands to run in and speak to her.

"What is it, ma'am?" he asked, coming up to the counter and taking off his hat to her.

"Afternoon, laddie. I have a pile of mail for ye." She handed two envelopes to him, both addressed in different hands, one with a British stamp and one unstamped. No return address appeared in the top corner of the envelopes. Ben turned them over to see if the addresses were on the backs, and halted in amazement when he recognized his father's penmanship.

"Why, thank you, Mrs. Meikle," he said. "I'm much obliged to you."

She nodded. "And how is the wife doing, laddie?"

"Very well, thank you." Ben was so absorbed in the surprise of hearing from his father that he forgot to say good-bye until he was halfway down the street and it was too late to turn back.

A letter. All the weary waiting faded now that he had a tangible piece of writing in his hands. Here, at last, was the explanation he wanted, the invitation to come to London—the address to reach Edmond. Perhaps, soon, he would see his father for the first time in twenty years, and he had some achievements to show that might prove he was not unworthy of notice.

In spite of the anticipation, however, Ben did not rush to tear it open. Indeed, he held it at arm's length rather as if he were afraid of it. He opened the other letter first—a fat envelope which contained a note from Ann Meikle, directing him to give it to Jaeryn as soon as he could. Ben turned his steps back toward Tontine and opened his father's letter as he walked. The original envelope had been discarded, no doubt censored for security reasons, but the person doing the censoring had perfectly copied Matthew Dorroll's hand in writing the correct alias and his Folkestone address on the new one.

Benjamin,

I did not know about Edmond's injuries until you wrote me. What appalling news, that he should be debilitated for life at such a young age. Please tell me how you heard about him as soon as possible, for I myself have received no news of him since May, and I have connections that you do not. How you found out is inconceivable, unless—but you do not have the sources I have. Please forward me anything you hear from him so I may be sure I get the latest reports. I have enclosed his address on a separate card, though whether he is still in France or receives letters, I do not know. Don't place much hope in contacting him, but if you still wish to attempt it, I will not try to dissuade you.

You asked me if your sister's letters went astray in the post. They did not, but at present, my business is such that I cannot find time to leave London, and I would not wish to inconvenience you by asking you to visit here. No doubt we shall meet before long, but in the meantime, do your best to be industrious with your work and bring it to a successful conclusion. It is a matter of personal honor to me that you show yourself worthy of the confidence I have placed in you.

In your last letter, you mentioned the thought of returning to America, and though I do not wish to order you to do anything you dislike, I must ask you not to leave yet. Your brother is not able to distinguish himself in the war now, and I would like one of my sons at least to prove that our family was not inconsequential in the conflict. If you can find it in your inclinations to humor me a little longer, I would be much obliged.

Yours sincerely,
Matthew Dorroll

Ben read the letter once and then stared at the words until they faded to a blurred outline. The eager anticipation he had felt now drained out of him. He crushed the sheet of paper until his nails cut into his palm.

"You could have written more than that." He raised his hand into the air and made as if to throw it into the street. Instead, he exhaled a deep sigh. "Maybe you had a reason I don't know about."

His face settled into grim lines as if the load he carried felt heavier than before, and he lifted his chin, trying to banish the sense of betrayal that crowded in.

"Hey, mister." Ben looked up and saw a lounger crossing the street, sleeves rolled up to the elbows and a pack of cigarettes in his hand. The man appeared to be talking to him. "Aren't you the doctor's fellow?"

Ben shoved the letters in his pocket so he could shake hands. "His assistant. Dailey. What can I do for you?"

"I met you back when this street was torn up, if you remember," the fellow returned cheerfully. "I'm a friend of someone you helped out. Alisa Dorroll's her name, and I heard you delivered her baby a few days ago."

"I did." As Ben took in the tangled mess of reddish-brown hair and a light growth of beard, a flash of recognition crossed his mind. "I'm sorry, I recall an acquaintance, but I don't know—"

"Your sister. I found her in the bomb drop and kept her all safe at the church until you came to get her. Terry's my name."

"Ah, yes, I recall you now. Thank you again."

"Not necessary." Terry flashed him a grin. "You've been kind to the little woman I look out for, and I'm much obliged to you. Her man's over in France, so she doesn't have any friends. I work at Emmerson's estate, so I see her quite often. He included her in his will."

"Included Alisa Dorroll in his will?" Ben frowned, and then remembered that the question would not be a civil one. "I'm sorry; it's certainly none of my concern. But I am curious, along with several friends of mine: when is the heir coming to claim his inheritance?"

Terry shook his head. "Not right away, from all appearances. There's a steward at the house now, and he's running things until the person chooses to make an appearance. Hasn't told me who the new boss is yet, though."

Jaeryn would like to know that. "If you hear anything more, I would be obliged if you could tell me."

"Sure thing. I must be going, doc, but I'll see you around." Terry set off down the street before stopping and calling over his shoulder, "You have a pretty little acushla for a sister."

"Thank you," Ben said, pleased by the compliment. Terry winked and continued on his way.

Ben smiled at his cheerful demeanor and wondered what kind of position Terry held at the Emmerson estate. Jaeryn might know whether or not he was someone they needed to watch. Then he thought of the bomb drop on Tontine, and Pearl, and realized Terry had called his sister by a love name for the second time.

Chapter Eleven
Starlin King

About a week after Ben's meeting with Terry on Tontine, Mrs. Meikle had another letter for him at the post office. Ben recognized Colonel King's heavy stationary and found it was an invitation for him and Charlotte to come to dinner on Saturday, the twenty-first of July. He took a moment to jot down an acceptance and bought postage to send it off before leaving for another house call.

He finished his last call about nine and Jaeryn took him home because it was late and he didn't want him riding in the dark alone. Ben was glad not to have to walk. This existence required a fair bit of stamina, traversing most of his route on bicycle—quite the contrast to the lazy days in Richmond. Most of his internship he had spent riding in a carriage and running errands. Now everything was different, for though Folkestone wasn't large, the scope of his practice encompassed a much wider and more challenging patient load than before.

When Ben arrived home, he locked and shuttered everything before splashing cold water on his face to keep himself alert while he wrote to his mother. He had already waited too long to reply to her letter from the end of June, and unless he wanted a stern rebuke, he must send the requested funds quickly.

At the beginning of the salutation, his pen ground to a halt, and he put it down and dropped his head in his hands. What could he write? She didn't care how they were doing. She had a new grandson that he couldn't tell her about, and the thought occurred to him that by keeping it concealed he lied to her, too, as well as to his father. There was nothing to say.

Opening up the thin leather wallet, he pulled out the money inside and flipped through the bills. They weren't enough. He could write and tell her the truth, but that thought didn't appeal to him. Ben took up the pen and made a second attempt. Some of the money remaining from Jaeryn's loan, which he kept safely hidden away at the clinic, might satisfy her for another month. He would need to get the currency changed to American, so when he finished the short note, he left the envelope unsealed and put in the pound notes for safekeeping.

After supper the room felt small to him, sitting alone on the sofa with the curtains drawn, waiting to go to bed. It was the time of night when the evening mist twisted itself about the scrub lining the rocky cliff edge, an eerie twilight that sent a man's blood pulsing hot and swift through his veins. Ben walked out the side door and down to the edge where the scrub grew thickest. The light rustling of the wind in the grass made him hearken back to the recent night when he had fled for refuge to town. But there was no one here now. Tonight he was alone and free.

Lights from a fishing boat a mile or so off shore winked, braving the German submarines for an evening's catch. Far to his right, Ben could just make out the haze of the Folkestone pier jutting out from the shore, though he suspected it was more his imagination that formed the shape than the actual object itself. Somewhere out there, beyond his sight, through the fathomless darkness, lay concealed the misty coast of France where Edmond was recovering from his horrid ordeal. And as he stood and watched, a boom of warfare sounded from far, far away.

Perhaps it was mere chance or possibly something more, but just as he reached the edge, he caught sight of something that he had missed when he examined the site of the strange signaling occurrence. The grass grew ankle deep all the way to the cliff edge, and the scrub bushes could have hidden anything until time itself forgot. But something glittering and coppery hung from the edge of one of the bushes, and Ben crouched down to see what had caught his attention. Stamped into the soft dirt and wound about the lowest branch was a strand of rough twine. A slight tug produced another glint of metal and loosened something which caused his mouth to open in astonishment. Ben knew enough of soldier's gear from watching the troops march down to the harbor to recognize the object he held—a set of dog tags. He rubbed the mud off the two copper-colored ovals, but he couldn't make out the raised letters and ran inside to give them a better examination.

Upon taking a closer look, he knew by the black and red stripes on the twine that the dog tags were of German manufacture. He didn't dare wash them before showing them to Jaeryn, but he made a few discoveries all the same. Along with the mud, something more sinister stained the string; blood now dried and darkened on the edge. The twine was not broken or strained in any manner, so it had probably been dropped by accident rather than taken by force. But why right at the cliff edge?

When Ben brought the dog tags round to the clinic the next morning, Jaeryn locked the clinic door in between patients so he could look at them. As soon as the doctor sponged the copper with a damp cloth, he caught his breath. They lay on the table between the two men, an evil gleam shining from them.

"Thank you for bringing these." Jaeryn reached to take them away, but Ben was quicker and covered the dog tags with his hand.

"I want to know why they're important."

He thought Jaeryn intended to refuse him, but at length, he saw signs of relenting and got the information he wanted.

"Perhaps you recall the protégé of King's I mentioned at his dinner we attended back in June," Jaeryn said. "The one that Ryson had plans for. The name on the tags is his name—Nathan Speyer."

The dark-haired young man had seemed so open and honest when they met. Ben drew his brows together in concern. "If he's pro-German, then Ryson is at a severe disadvantage without knowing it."

"Precisely." Jaeryn winced. "Not to mention the fact that King's son and Nathan Speyer are close friends. The two young men go everywhere together; you've probably seen them around town without knowing it. Speyer could be using Starlin to leech vital information for the German side. If this is the case, then I think Ryson should be informed as soon as possible. Either King knows Speyer is pro-German and fully supports the double dealing, or King himself is innocent of treachery, and Speyer is taking advantage of him."

"What exactly does Ryson want from Nathan Speyer?" Ben asked.

Jaeryn put the dog tags into an empty medication tin and locked it in his bottom desk drawer. "You'll have to inquire of the man himself. I don't know. I'm going to write a note and send these express to Ryson. Put them in the St. Eanswythe box as you pass today, and we'll let him deal with it. I have to go to London to report our progress soon; I'll fully brief you on my return. As to whether Nathan was at Copt Point the night you found your place trashed, I couldn't say. We'll start making connections and see if we can find any more proof to substantiate that theory. I wish either of us had more of an acquaintance with him. It would help to no end."

Ben put the tin with the tags in the drop as Jaeryn requested, then decided to instigate an investigation of his own regarding his sister-in-law's connections with Emmerson.

Alisa seemed to be recovering well from her baby's birth. Ben saw no reason for concern, but he stopped by every couple days to check on her and to see his wife and sister. Sometimes he saw Charlotte there and sometimes not, depending on whether she was out volunteering. But today he wanted to see Pearl, and he was pleased to find her alone in the kitchen.

"You look quite at home," he said, dropping a kiss in her hair and tossing his bag down on the counter. "I've come to show you more about the Webley, if you have time."

She was filling the sink with water and swishing soap into it to wash a stack of dishes. "I think you'll find I've improved since last time."

"Oh? Have you been practicing?"

"Quite often. Alisa's friend who helps with the horse didn't want to leave us alone at nights, so he warned the neighbors about the noise and showed me how to use it." She tossed her hair over her aproned shoulder. "He said he hadn't seen anyone catch on so fast."

"You have hidden talents." Ben laughed. "I'm glad. When Charlotte's gone, you're practically alone here. Keep the Webley nearby. I don't think you're in danger, but I sometimes wonder if I should bring you home again instead of leaving you here."

She pulled a cloth out of the kitchen cupboard and submerged the plates in the hot water. "If there is danger then Alisa can't be left to live by herself. I lock up securely, and I'll keep watch."

He protested as she splashed the silverware into the water too. "Yes, but you don't understand—"

Her hands stopped their work, and she met his gaze squarely. "I understand enough. I've never had a friend to love until now. If staying requires learning a different way of looking after myself, I can do it."

Ben bit off his remonstrance and stared at her, for her words showed that she more than merely guessed at what he was doing. "You catch on faster than I thought you would. I'll not pretend with you, then. I came today because I wondered if you could help me with a piece of information. Has Alisa had any visitors or calls? Anyone official looking? Her uncle just died, and I thought she might have heard from someone."

Pearl shook her head as she washed another dish. "No, I don't think so. Here, you can make yourself useful." She handed him the dish and a towel to dry it with as a smile played around her mouth. "Well," she added, "we do see the one man who comes to help with her outdoor work."

"Does he come often?" Ben asked.

A pink flush crept into her cheeks, and she ducked her head down to hide them. "Every afternoon, to take care of the horse. But he doesn't stay long. Sometimes an hour, sometimes two. He delivers Alisa's food orders for her. I offered to do the marketing early on, but she said it wasn't necessary because someone had already taken care of it. A man ordered it done for her—a Mr. Emmerson, I think—or he was, only he died."

"What does she get from Mr. Emmerson? Do you know?"

She took the last dish from him and put it away in the white-painted cupboard. "He gives her an allowance, and he left it in his will that she should continue to have it until his heir comes to possess the estate. Ter—she got a letter from the steward this week, and the current owner wants to continue to make sure she is provided for."

"Perhaps you can do a little investigating for me."

"I think I could."

"Find out what her connection to Emmerson is. It must be something significant, or she wouldn't be getting money from him. If you happen to hear the name of his heir, I would like to know the person's identity. Perhaps Terry can help you?"

Pearl glanced up sideways at him from under her soft lashes. "I'm sure he would be happy to."

* * *

Late in the afternoon on the day of Colonel King's dinner, Jaeryn took the train up to Samuel Ryson's hot, airless headquarters. For security reasons he didn't often meet with Ryson, but after receiving the dog tags, Ryson sent an imperative summons for Graham to come to London immediately.

Jaeryn twisted his fingers together as he listened to the terse commands his supervisor gave him. He hated this windowless room. The lack of escape routes brought back old nightmares of missions gone wrong.

"You'll leave those tags out of your investigations," Ryson ordered. "Your assistant found them, you say?"

"Outside his house." Jaeryn ran his hand along his neck to wipe the sweat from the back of his collar. "Which I hardly think he'll let drop. This is the first substantial clue we've found that indicates who the German sympathizers working for Emmerson might be. Our lives are under threat from them. I understand that Speyer may be part of your political plans, but I can't lose the security of my workers on his account. Is he a German?"

Ryson returned the lid to the medication tin with a loud snap and put it back on his desk with a slam that made the tags rattle. "Of course, he's German," Ryson said. "What would you expect with a name like that? And what's more, he's of vital importance to me."

"More important than Dorroll?" Jaeryn remarked.

The razor-keen features on the man opposite held seasoned indifference, attained from long years of watching agents come and go. "Certainly. Nothing against the fellow, but he's a new recruit, and in a somewhat small position at present."

"Nonetheless, it is enormous and daunting to him. I don't think you realize what you put us through. Your last letter made him think he was someone to be easily sacrificed. Not exactly the way to inspire loyalty." Jaeryn spoke accusingly, and the two men locked eyes in a silent power struggle. In spite of Ryson's superior position, Jaeryn often found it necessary to take a forceful hand in their conversations. He knew he could count on a certain amount of leniency because of his past services, and he had no qualms about using it.

Ryson broke the deadlock first. "Dorroll's father was a talented private investigator in Great Britain after he retired from the navy. The son should be able to take care of himself. Which brings me to another point I wish to speak to you about. He's been there two months now, and I want to make sure we're not wasting our resources. Is Dorroll helpful to your work?"

"I find his services indispensable, sir," Jaeryn spoke the half-truth as assuredly as he dispensed diagnoses to his patients. "In fact, I think his coming is the most fortunate thing you've ever decided on. He's observant, and he frees up my time by helping with the medical work. I can't lay a single charge at anyone's door in Folkestone, but two weeks ago Dorroll forced a crack in someone's confidence. His presence shook them, and they rifled through his house."

Ryson's cold gray eyes flickered with interest. "What? Why?"

"I don't yet know. I hope I can find out before it's too late."

Jaeryn felt the displeasure in the air and wished he had the talent for smooth words with men above him. "I set Fenton to work following a line of investigation on the father's career in intelligence, but he hasn't been as useful as you said he would be." The Irishman scowled as he thought of Fenton, left to his own devices. He was still gone on his alleged business trip, and Jaeryn half-suspected that he had left the continent to dig further into the Dorroll family. "I only hope I can keep Ben Dorroll with me a little longer. He's not keen on being here, and you don't pay him enough to give him an incentive to stay."

Ryson made it clear that Jaeryn had gone too far this time. "I don't recall telling you what your assistant makes, and if he hasn't broached a complaint, then you needn't take up his cause yourself. I hired you to make sure justice is executed on German sympathizers. Leave the social reform to those whom it concerns."

Jaeryn persisted. "A worker deserves fair wages. He has a hazardous position and a family to support. America could be using him, you know. If I were you, I would do more to secure his loyalties. I don't know if he's able to make it completely from paycheck to paycheck, and considering that his life has been endangered by the success of this work, you offer little for what you're asking in return."

"Well." Samuel Ryson rose from behind his desk. "Just remember that Benjamin Dorroll is completely replaceable, as are you. Keep the information coming, and leave the dog tags alone. They're none of your concern. And doctor—the last three troop units out of Folkestone were expected upon their arrival at the front. Their numbers, names, and commanders were known in advance. That is hardly the kind of result we have seen from you in the past."

Jaeryn raised his chin, and his voice tautened in defiance. "I'm working on it."

Ryson gave him a hard look over the rims of his glasses. "Jeremy will see you out. He has a packet with information about the Emmerson estate to send home with you."

Jaeryn was careful to let no rash words fall from his lips as the young clerk let him out the back door. For one thing, anger would hardly help his good standing, and he did not want to jeopardize that. For another, he would make no promises to stay out of Speyer's business. He had every right to investigate and find out what he needed to know. Ryson wasn't the only one with men's lives in his hands.

Jeremy paused at the door. "All right, doctor? You look upset. That knocks you off your game, you know."

"Oh, just dealing with him." Jaeryn gestured back to Ryson. "He made me late for a dinner with Colonel King, and there was a particular young man I wanted to see there."

"Send a telegram. Tell your assistant to talk to him instead." Jeremy shut the door behind him, leaving him in the gathering dusk.

It was both puzzling and intriguing that Speyer seemed so important to authorities in London. At least, Jaeryn told himself, he'd had the foresight to take pictures of the dog tags before sending the evidence on to London. Given his suspicions, they would certainly come in handy.

* * *

Ben sat alone in the clinic, taking patients when they appeared and writing down appointments in the big ledger Jaeryn kept on his desk. Graham's hand was an absolute scrawl. He would have asked for a translation had his mentor been there, but Jaeryn was away in London, so he had to decipher it on his own.

The sky clouded over as he worked diligently on his files, and the clock hands crept on toward six. Misty rain splatted against the clinic window while quiet rumbles of thunder sounded in the distance. Upstairs in the guest room, his suit hung pressed and ready for dinner, and he expected Charlotte any moment.

He paused for a moment at half past six when a boy delivered a telegram from Jaeryn. It informed him that Jaeryn hadn't caught the evening train in time, but wanted Ben to keep to the plan nonetheless. Ben nodded in satisfaction; he rather looked forward to a dinner engagement without the observation of the Irish doctor.

Shortly after the boy left, a light knock sounded on the consulting room door, and he glanced up and saw Charlotte standing there in her gray silk evening dress. He had only seen her wear it once or twice in Richmond, as they didn't often attend fancy dinners together. But tonight, she looked young and proud and happy dressed in her best with a few soft ringlets framing her face and neck. The tiny strand of pearls clasped about her neck and the little pearl drops in her ears were from her parents—he could not yet afford to give her such things.

"What do you think?" she asked, turning so the light enhanced the shimmering folds of embroidery on her skirt.

Ben tilted his head in mock inspection and smiled his approval. "You look absolutely beautiful, sweetheart. Give me twenty minutes, and I'll be ready to take you. Why don't you call a cab while I get dressed, so it's here in time?"

The doorbell sounded and Charlotte's eager smile faded away. She had been disappointed too often of evenings out to hope for better results now. Ben grimaced with annoyance and glanced out the window to see a sleek black Model T in the drive. A man came up to the doorbell and pressed it as hard as he could with one leather-gloved finger, and Ben recognized him as one of King's servants.

"Please come in," Ben called, making haste to open the door. The portly fellow stood on the step, rain spattering his light brown ulster, but made no move to enter.

"Is Doctor Graham in?" he asked.

Charlotte peeked around the study door to hear their conversation. "No," Ben said, "but I'm his assistant, Doctor Dailey. What can I do for you?"

"Colonel King's son was brought home half-drowned." Ben gave an exclamation of shock, and he and Charlotte exchanged surprised glances. "We brought him round all right," the man said hurriedly, "but his father would like a medical opinion. He said you and Doctor Graham were both invited to this evening's dinner, and he ordered me to bring you in the car immediately, sir."

Ben gathered up his suit and medical supplies, and he and Charlotte were ushered into the automobile's back seat. They were shut in a warm shell with raindrops pattering on the roof and a soft, leather-cushioned seat. He could get used to comfort like that pretty quickly if he had the opportunity.

"What happened?" Ben asked as the chauffeur pulled out into the street traffic and set off at a rapid speed for the estate.

"The boy wanders out on his own quite often," replied the gray-haired, gravel-voiced chauffeur. "He doesn't have any restrictions, and for the most part, he manages to stay on his feet. Just shy of an hour ago a group of fishermen brought him home nearly dead. They picked him up just before he went under for good, or so I'm told, sir. He's a young fool, but a kind-hearted scamp for all that."

The servant relapsed into his accustomed aloofness and finished the rest of the drive in silence, pulling up in record time at the front entrance. Ben hurried up the stone steps and pressed the doorbell, leaving Charlotte to follow after as best she could. The butler, Stafford, recognized him immediately and admitted him without question, leading the way up the grand staircase to a room in the west wing. Servants preparing for the evening affair stopped to make way

183

for them as they hurried through the halls. The house was ablaze with light, and Ben heard the musicians tuning their instruments, but he had arrived before the first guests.

Stafford handed him off to one of the maids, who led him into a grand suite furnished in brown leather and navy blue. Boxing gloves, tennis racquets, and various balls cluttered the sitting room, hinting at its owner's active existence. On one table lay a polished papier-mâché violin case and a well-worn portfolio of music.

In the bedroom, several servants were gathered about a large four-poster bed, chafing the figure on it to restore some warmth.

"Hands off," Ben ordered as he entered the room. "That won't help him." He looked down at the lad on the bed, a freckle-faced, sandy-haired boy in his mid-teens, and felt for his pulse. It beat thinly in his wrist, and the cold seemed to have numbed it. When Ben let go, the lad's arm slipped down, slid off the bed, and dangled toward the floor. His chest rose and fell in quick, shallow breathing.

"How cold is the Channel this time of year?" Ben asked, examining the lithe body for any sign of injury.

"Eighteen degrees sir, most likely. We're not in the peak season yet," a manservant offered.

Ben cast up the difference between their system and his and bit his lip when he reached the result. "It's still cold enough for hypothermia. The servant who brought me here said he had already come around."

"Yes, sir; he's awake now if you rouse him enough."

"Then go fetch something hot drink. That ought to bring his temperature up." Ben inserted a thermometer into the boy's mouth. "Bring some more blankets and hot water bottles."

The two maids left and the manservant remained. Charlotte entered at that moment with her silent tread, taking a survey of the situation.

"Is he hurt?" she asked in a low voice, so as not to disturb her cousin.

"I don't think so." Ben gestured her to come nearer. "Just chilled.

Come where he can see you when he wakes up." He asked the young man standing at the foot of the bed, "Are you Starlin's personal help?"

"Yes, sir. I'm George, his valet, sir." The servant looked concerned for his young employer. The house help seemed to take more interest in the boy than his own father did, for King hadn't put in an appearance yet.

Charlotte knelt down and tucked in the warm water bottles as they were handed to her, and the maids heaped on extra blankets. Starlin's arm still hung down toward the floor, but his breathing came stronger and more steadily, and the tiny line of mercury in the thermometer was rising. Ben shook the boy's shoulder to hasten his stirring. "Wake up, Starlin."

The boy's long lashes opened on a pair of large, almond-shaped blue eyes. He blinked when he saw Charlotte and raised himself on one elbow, pushing away the hair that fell across his forehead. "What happened?"

Ben guided him back down again. "Don't rush. But I'd like to ask you that question. I'm the doctor. Someone brought you home nearly drowned, and when you're well enough, you can tell me why."

Starlin yawned. "I'm better now. It was nothing, only a swim."

Ben raised an eyebrow. "Why were you out swimming in the Channel?"

"I'm good at swimming." Starlin's chin jutted out in defiance.

"I see," Ben said. "And does your father commonly allow you to swim in frigid, submarine-infested waters? We are in a war, you know."

"I know." He brightened visibly. "Your troops landed in France less than three weeks ago. I think things are turning around in France. I thought Haig was a fool with his plans, but after he took Messines from the Germans, I think he's all right."

Ben wasn't sure whether to laugh or shake the boy in exasperation. "Never mind London's plans. I want to know why you took your life into your hands in such a rash manner. If no one had

185

been there, you would have caused your father a great amount of heartbreak."

"I don't know what business you have to tell me off, doctor. If my father doesn't object, you have no right to." It hadn't taken Starlin long to recover, for he sat up now in his indignation. "Say, who are you, anyway?"

"The new doctor in town; Doctor Dailey. I'm Jaeryn Graham's assistant."

"Oh, him. I've seen him once or twice." Evidently, the recollection was not a pleasant one. Starlin's gaze traveled to Charlotte and a curious, indefinable expression filled his eyes. "I don't believe we're introduced," he said.

"I'm Charlotte Dailey." She sat back to see how he would take her presence. His face lightened from its set look and softened into something like relief and welcome, but only for a moment. As soon as the expression appeared, the lad locked it away again. "You wrote you were coming."

Charlotte gave him a warm smile. "I did, but I didn't expect to meet you this way. It's good to see you." She stood up and looked ruefully at her skirt, for it had crumpled while she knelt there.

"And he's your husband?" Starlin glanced up at Ben. His eyes were a brighter blue than Charlotte's, and where hers held gentleness, his held only suspicion.

"Indeed he is," Charlotte said. "I hope you'll like him very much."

Starlin gave a quick nod, and Ben sensed a friendlier air toward himself than before. He waited for Starlin to say more, but the boy only clasped his hands together tightly in his lap and stared down at them. Charlotte looked to Ben rather uncertainly, unsure of what she should say next, and Ben returned to the matter at hand.

"Suppose you tell me why you were in the Channel. Is it a habit, or had you taken a dare?"

A flash of defiance crossed Starlin's face. "I do it when I want to. This time I wanted to be rid of someone. We were at the end of the pier, and the Channel was the only way out."

One of the maidservants brought in a cup of hot cocoa and offered it to Starlin, who hugged its comforting warmth close to his chest. Ben waited until she left before speaking again. "You were being threatened?"

Starlin frowned at his persistence. "I don't know. We had a disagreement. I didn't want to talk to him anymore."

Interrogating Starlin King was worse than extracting teeth, and he had done that a few times.

"Who was your friend?" Charlotte asked as Ben took out his watch. He held the boy's wrist as he watched the second hand and noted with satisfaction that the rate was normal.

"His name's Nathan Speyer," Starlin said. "He enlisted yesterday because he turned eighteen. I'm going to enlist when I turn eighteen."

At the mention of Nathan Speyer, Ben started with surprise. Jaeryn had mentioned that they were good friends, but he had forgotten in all the excitement. Nathan couldn't have told Starlin the truth about enlisting the day before, for they had the German dog tags in their possession. No fool would enlist in two armies at once. And if he was enlisted, why wasn't he at the front?

"So you and Nathan had a fight," Ben put in.

"Yes." Starlin didn't seem in the mood to answer many more questions. He looked tired, and the slight pinch in his face showed that he had a headache. "He said I didn't have a right to fake my age, but I don't think he has any right to say so. He jumped in and followed me, but I swim faster, and it didn't take me long to leave him behind."

"He followed you?" Ben felt sick at the new revelation.

"You like repeating me, don't you?"

A knock sounded at the door, and George appeared with a tray of dinner for the boy. None of them took notice.

"Do you know what happened to your friend?" Charlotte asked softly.

"No." Starlin's face quivered for a moment before he managed to smooth it out into blank indifference.

The manservant cleared his throat. "Excuse me, madam, but Nathan Speyer went home. The fisher-folk told the tale in the kitchen. They pulled him out along with my master, but Speyer was quite fit himself."

Ben sighed with relief. Charlotte's young cousin certainly seemed to be a plucky fool when no good was involved. Glancing at a clock on the mantle, he saw that the hands pointed to quarter past seven. The guests would be in the drawing room waiting for dinner to be announced, and he must join them as soon as possible. He dismissed the valet with a nod. Though he felt a strong urge to admonish Starlin, he recognized by the boy's hunched figure that he was suppressing keen anxiety over what had happened, so Ben let it go. "You might have been responsible for killing your friend, but I think you know that already, and I have no doubt that was far from your intention. Did he threaten you?"

In spite of Ben's sympathetic tone, Starlin King folded his arms in token that he was finished with the conversation. "You've asked me enough questions, Doctor Dailey. What passed between him and me was a matter of honor, and it turned out all right. I don't see the point in making a fuss over it."

Ben would have said more, but Charlotte gave him a warning glance, and he restrained his words with an effort. "I only need one thing from you before we leave," he said, forcing himself to keep a calm manner. "I will need Nathan's address so I can check in on him and make sure he's all right."

Starlin complied all too easily. "It's over on Urry Lane, just east of Newnham Lane in an old tavern. After his folks had died he didn't have much money, so he found a place to put up in that no one would want until he could go to the front."

"Very good; we'll leave you to get some rest, then. Try to spend a quiet day tomorrow to recover. I'll stop in again before I leave this evening."

Starlin nodded again. "Yes, sir." He paused awkwardly as if he was at a loss for words. Ben gave him a small smile and nod, and

Starlin seemed to take that as sufficient dismissal, for he flashed a broad grin back and took the tray of dinner his valet proffered.

"Show the doctor to a room," Starlin ordered his valet, "so he can dress for dinner. And get Mrs. Dailey anything she wants." He bobbed his head to Charlotte. "A pleasure to meet you, Mrs. Dailey. I hope you'll come again."

"Please, call me Charlotte," she said kindly. "And you're welcome to come our way any evening you like. We live at Copt Point; we'll be easy to find."

"I know the place; my father owns it," Starlin said nonchalantly, holding his knife and fork poised to eat as soon as they left.

"Does he?" Charlotte's blue eyes held a merry twinkle as she saw Ben flush red at the words. "I'm so pleased you told me. I might not have known otherwise."

George led them to another well-appointed chamber; the suit Ben had brought with him was laid out on the bed, and there were fresh towels and soap in the adjoining bath. Within a short time, Ben had arranged his suit to his own satisfaction and combed his hair into perfect order. Standing in front of the full-length mirror, making sure he looked presentable, he asked, "Charlotte, what do you think of Starlin?"

She sat in an easy chair, leaning her chin on her hand. "He's not a little boy anymore. He was more eager to see me last time I came, but he was only nine then, so that's natural."

As soon as Ben left the mirror, Charlotte stood before it to re-pin a few strands of hair that had escaped. "I wrote him for a couple of years after his mother died, and I think talking about it helped him process the whole affair. But as soon as he left school, he stopped writing, and I entered college then, so I stopped too. I found his letters before we left the States. He mentioned loving music in the most recent one and said his father had promised to buy him a Guarnerius, but that's all I remember. I don't know what he's like now."

They left the bedroom, and Ben offered her his arm at the head of the staircase. "I think he liked you. You might try to smooth out a few of his rough edges if you get the chance."

Charlotte laughed in agreement, and they descended the stairs together and stood for a moment in the doorway of the drawing room, unwilling to attract the attention of the other guests. Waiters moved about setting out trays of coffee and champagne. Most of the guests were oblivious to their presence, but Colonel King noticed and instantly disengaged himself to speak to them.

"Thank you for seeing my son, doctor," King said in greeting. "I must apologize for the inconvenience."

The colonel appeared to hold his political alliances as a matter of higher importance than his heir. Ben felt an intense tug of sympathy for the sullen boy upstairs. "It was nothing. I'm glad I could be of help. Starlin appears to be a strong young man, and I have no doubt will make a complete recovery in a day or two."

Ben introduced Charlotte and endured the round of small talk with quiet civility while Colonel King reacquainted himself with her. All the men and women in the room were strangers; Nathan Speyer had evidently gone home after his ordeal, and Jaeryn was not there to relieve the monotony. Neither was Allan Evesham from London. But Charlotte appeared bright and animated as she chatted with the older gentleman beside her, and her delight resigned him to the evening. It hadn't been a complete waste of time, for they had both made a connection with Starlin, which they might not have otherwise.

Stafford opened the door and announced dinner.

* * *

By waiting as long as they did to come to Great Britain, the Dorrolls had missed the bleak months of the previous year when the populace panicked over short rations and had only six weeks of bread left. The food supply had since stabilized somewhat, but the shortages were not over, nor their far-reaching effects. Some of Ben's patients grumbled about losing their land to the government for food production and about the Women's Land Army taking over the farming. In July, Alisa lost several of her fields for the benefit of the national food supply—though that proved to her benefit as well, as she wasn't in any position to work them herself.

Ben thought, when he first arrived in Folkestone, that people were fed all they needed and store shelves kept well stocked. But as July passed, he began to find that he couldn't buy everything on Charlotte's lists, and the grocer's heavy sigh grew louder every time he stopped in. On the Monday after Colonel King's dinner, as Ben watched the boy in the back unloading shipments, he inquired about them, and the clerk admitted that they were growing smaller due to shortages.

He mentioned it to Mrs. Meikle at the post office. "Food's running out, laddie," she said after she checked for letters in his box and gave him one. "I think it'll be the ration cards soon."

Ben took the letter and glanced at the unfamiliar handwriting. "Ration cards are all very well when people have money, but if prices go up, I fail to see how the cards benefit. The committees won't be able to support every needy family who comes begging for money grants."

The postmistress shook her head, a faded strand of hair falling down on either side of her face. "The ration cards help. If anything they'll spread the food around and make it more even. In the end, it depends on how long the boys have to fight. If they keep at, it we'll all have to tighten our belts for their sakes. France wasn't successful enough in April, and we're needing a bit of success now more than ever."

Ben hadn't stopped to read the telegrams of war news posted at the town hall for the last two weeks. "Success? Has anything happened recently?"

Mrs. Meikle lowered her voice as the bell tinkled, announcing another customer. "Word has it the Russian government split yesterday. All three political parties are like dogs snapping at each other's throats. Soldiers are killing people in the streets. The people

191

don't want war, and the workers are on the verge of a revolt. I don't know what's happened since, but I know there's still a ruckus of some kind."

Ben knew Jaeryn would want to hear the news. He glanced at his watch and saw that he had time to stop by the clinic before the nurses in St. John's Road expected him for his rounds. "I'm surprised you heard so soon."

"It's easy when a body keeps their ears open, with folk coming in and out all day."

"But if the Russian government collapses—"

Mrs. Meikle looked grave. "Then the Germans have more forces to fight our boys." She pressed a sovereign into his hand. "Give that to Jaeryn Graham."

She turned to help her next customer. Ben left the post office and opened his letter without paying much attention to it. If Russia became destabilized, France and Great Britain would lose one of their strongest allies. God only knew what would happen here in England after that. He might look war in the face more closely than he had ever thought possible.

When he looked down, the salutation in the letter drove the Russians temporarily from his mind.

Little Brother,

I was never so surprised in my life as when one of my mates brought your letter and read it to me. Whenever the nurse leaves me alone, I take out my pencil to work on returning the favor. Not that I'm much for letter-writing. It won't be long, for this unlucky gas poisoning has sucked all the strength out of me. I doubt if I shall ever fully get it back again.

I was lucky to pull through, but my face is a mess from a piece of shrapnel and always will be now. I was out of my head for a while, and they wouldn't tell me the damage when I first woke up. I managed to snag a mirror in spite of them and fainted for my pains when I saw myself. I've never looked since, and had I been blessed with the resources, I might have pulled the trigger. They took my gun away, so I am still alive to write to you. I'm done with the fighting. My lungs are damaged about as badly as my face, and I'll never see action again.

How strange that you ended up in Folkestone. I've fond memories of that place, and from what you said in your letter I believe you've discovered why. She's a sweet little woman, and it's good to hear she and the child are both well. I'm glad you found her. Please keep an eye on her as long as you stay in the area. She's rather young and needs a good deal of taking care of.

When they let me out, I won't come home right away. It would be too difficult to face Alisa like that and such a shock for her. I'm not ready. My nerves are shot to pieces—never knew I had any until this. I've almost killed nurses more than once waking up from the nightmares, and I couldn't do that to her. I'll come home when I can stand to. Don't think ill of me.

Edmond Dorroll

Ben shuddered as he finished reading the letter. He could not find it in his heart to blame Edmond for his reluctance, coming back a shell of the man he had been. Give him a few weeks—or a couple of months—and he would return to his wife and be hailed as a war hero for his sacrifice. Until then, he should be given all the time he needed.

Ben stopped at the clinic to give Jaeryn the news about Russia. The Irishman's jaw settled into grim lines. "We'll have to be prepared for anything now. I wish we knew who was sending the lists of soldiers. Any compromise now is a weak point for every agent in Great Britain, not just for Folkestone troops and shipments. We have to strengthen our forces."

"Ann Meikle sent this to you." Ben handed him the sovereign.

Jaeryn twisted it open and read the note inside. He snorted and handed it over. "Read that."

Russia's crumbling, and we need to pull together. I didn't make that list. If you don't start keeping me abreast of facts I have every right to know, I'll stop helping you get information at the post office.

"Fool woman." Jaeryn ripped the paper to shreds. "What happened at King's dinner?"

A few minutes sufficed to relate the incident with Starlin, which Jaeryn found most amusing, and when Ben finished, Jaeryn informed him of the warning Ryson had given him about Speyer.

"You found the dog tags." Jaeryn pulled down a pair of crutches he kept hanging on the wall to take to one of their patients. "Stop by Nathan Speyer's and strike up an acquaintance with him as soon as you can."

"But Ryson told us to leave him alone."

Jaeryn looked over his shoulder, and Ben could not read the expression in his eyes—unless, perhaps, he detected a faint hint of rebellion. "I'm not going to be another wasted soldier. I won't obey orders from London when they put all of us in jeopardy." A slow smile spread over Jaeryn's face. "And you're not going to tell Ryson of my delinquencies, are you?"

No, he was not. But he wished Jaeryn didn't have to be quite so cocksure about it.

Chapter Twelve
Rebel on the Run

Later that evening, Ben walked at a swift pace down Newnham Lane, intending to make an efficient call on Nathan Speyer and then be on his way to other responsibilities. It took longer to reach his destination than he expected. One by one the houses slipped past as he rode down past Alisa's until Urry Lane and Newnham Lane intersected.

Ben turned left and noticed that the aspect changed immediately. The country had its poorer districts just as the city did, and this road appeared destitute compared to the other streets he frequented. The large fields grew only daisies and chicory, with the shacks of houses spaced far apart, as if ashamed to look each other in the face. A quarter of a mile down Urry Lane stood the remnants of an old tavern with half of its windows devoid of glass and a few roof tiles lying in the yard. Indeed, yard seemed a charitable thing to call it, for the knee-high grass looked no different than the rest of the field around. No fence enclosed the property, nor did any sort of path lead up to the door. Yet in spite of that, Ben saw little circles of flattened grass where someone had passed not too long before him. He pounded on the door.

A wary voice called in answer. "Come in."

The door opened, and Ben stood face to face with the slim, dark-haired, fair-skinned young man. In spite of his disheveled appearance and an angry cut on his upper lip, Speyer's expression seemed confident and poised, stern beyond his years, with a faint hint of sadness. Little wonder, after losing his mother and baby sister. He might be German, but he was human, and the sorrow of it must be a heavy burden to bear.

"What do you want?" Nathan asked.

Ben apologized for the intrusion. "I'm sorry to disturb you. I'm looking for Nathan Speyer, and if my guess is correct, you are he."

"I am." Nathan stepped back to allow him through the doorway. "Come in."

The instant Ben stepped into the house, he realized his error. The firm muzzle of a revolver pressed into his side and a steady hand grasped his wrist, twisting it until the water came into his eyes.

"Now," Nathan spoke beside him. "Suppose you tell me why you are actually here."

"Let go, please," Ben said. When Nathan made no move to obey, Ben took one of the thin shoulders in his free hand and dug his fingers into the pressure point of the nerves where he knew it would hurt most. An answering catch of the breath showed that it was not without effect, and he hoped Nathan wouldn't decide to shoot. "Strange that you don't recognize me from Colonel King's dinner in June."

"Did we meet? I don't recall." Nathan loosened his grip a little but kept the revolver steady.

Ben contemplated making an attempt to break free, but he didn't think Nathan was as hostile as he pretended to be, and decided to try peaceful means first.

"I'm Doctor Dailey," he began, but he got no further before both the hand and the revolver withdrew. Ben exhaled softly with the release of the pressure and clasped his hand around his wrist to ease the twinge in it.

"Starlin spoke of you a few hours ago." Nathan laid the revolver back on the side table. "You'll have to excuse my caution, as it's not often an American doctor makes a friendly call at my place. Perhaps you would like to sit down so we can discuss your business in comfort. Not here, though. I never use this room."

He led the way upstairs to a small bedroom with neat furnishings and two chairs. His voice held no hint of a foreign accent, so he must have been English-bred despite his ancestry. "Apologies for being hasty," Nathan said again. "It's the best way to deal with tramps, and a few have entered that door uninvited."

"Did Starlin King hurt you badly yesterday?" The heat, unbearable enough outdoors, only intensified in that closed upstairs room. Ben wanted to take his jacket off, but he knew he wouldn't be staying long and resigned himself to making the best of it.

Nathan eyed him oddly. "Who told you about that?"

"He did. But I would have known you were hurt just by looking at you. I'm a doctor; I'm trained to see those things." Ben smiled. "Besides your bruised lip, you walked rather stiffly; but you weren't limping, which suggests a blow to the abdomen."

"I see." Nathan's hand went instinctively to his left side before he stopped himself.

Ben left off his pretense and went straight to the point. "Did Starlin's disagreement turn more violent than you anticipated?"

"Starlin does not always play by the rules," Nathan replied, with the benevolent look a large dog might have for a puppy trying to bite him.

"Starlin can learn the rules," Ben said. "Let me have a look." Nathan made no protest and unbuttoned his shirt, pointing out an ugly purple bruise on the third rib. Just underneath the bruise, Ben found a shallow cut from a sharp blade, scabbed over and healing.

"It could be a hairline fracture," he said, trying to detect any appearance of swelling. "How did Starlin hit you?"

Nathan watched him feel the rib and made no sign of being in pain. "I believe he used a walking stick."

Ben pointed to the cut. "That never came from a walking stick. Does the boy always take an unfair advantage?"

"He wouldn't do such a thing. I carry my knife in my pocket, and I was careless with it." Nathan looked as if he rather regretted allowing the examination, but he sat still in resignation and didn't try to cover the cut.

It did not appear to be serious, and Ben felt fairly sure the rib had not cracked. He could do nothing for that except leave a few painkillers, but he poured some antiseptic on the cut just above Nathan's upper lip. "Starlin told me you followed him into the Channel," he remarked, returning the antiseptic to his leather bag and sitting down on one of the wooden chairs. "Was your disagreement of a serious nature?"

Nathan shook his head. "I told him about my enlistment, and he confided to me that he meant to forge his birth certificate to enlist himself. He wanted my help, and when I refused to give it to him, he took to the Channel to cool off. He's a headstrong lad. I followed him to see that he stayed safe."

Ben allowed his blue eyes to bore into Nathan's brown ones. "Some fishermen brought him home half-drowned. I don't call that safe."

"I don't mean physical safety," Nathan explained. "I mean safety from the Germans. You don't know it, doctor, but Starlin runs a level of danger he is ignorant of. His father is involved enough in the government to receive advance information about the war, which puts those close to him at risk. The boy's a firebrand and gets into trouble easily, and I agreed to watch him along with my secretarial duties. Helping him to enlist would violate my agreement."

It was as if Nathan wanted to allay his unspoken suspicions. "So Colonel King hired you to protect his son."

Nathan's lip curled at the idea. "I would not accept money for that sort of thing. He pays me to keep his papers in order."

"I see." Ben was inclined to like the young man for his clear, straightforward way of speaking.

Nathan clasped his hands over his knees and kept his gaze down on the worn pine floorboards. "I have exhausted my influence with Starlin. Now I do him more harm than good, so I have determined to leave. It is my duty, to him and to—"

"To what?"

Nathan lifted his chin. "To my country." He rose from his seat. "Thank you for coming, doctor. I enjoyed making your acquaintance, and you brought some relief to my hurts."

Ben left after a few words of farewell and a promise to check back in a few days, for Nathan did little to disguise the fact that he no longer welcomed his company. At least they had made an initial connection, and he had an excuse to come back.

Ben felt sure Nathan Speyer remembered him from their meeting at Colonel King's. Or perhaps Nathan knew him from invading his cottage and rifling through his things. The cut under his ribs could not have been from carelessness; it probably matched the smear of blood on the butcher's twine holding his dog tags together. Yet Ben was inclined to think that the young man wasn't the one responsible for the break-in. Speyer had not been the only person there that night—he might have come for noble purposes but lost his tags in a struggle with an armed opponent.

But the German address on the tags couldn't be explained away easily, and the young man had an interest in Copt Point that he wished to keep concealed. Ben hadn't detected any deception in those dark eyes when Nathan answered his questions—only grief and duty and a stern resolve. The evidence was too condemning to allow appearances to lull him into a false sense of security.

* * *

Four days later, when he stopped by Alisa's during the mid-afternoon, he found Charlotte frowning over a sheet of letter paper in the parlor. "What's the matter?" he asked, smoothing out the lines in her forehead with a gentle hand as he wrapped an arm around her.

"Oh." She gestured to the paper and shoved it away. "I was trying to write to my parents. There isn't anything to write. They asked for newspaper clippings. I don't want to send them."

"I wouldn't want to either. I don't think Russia's going to be with us much longer. It hasn't looked any better these last few days. We've got to win in France if we're going to win. Mrs. Meikle says they've started plans along a battle line in Ypres, and they're gaining ground. You could write to them about that, once it comes out in the papers. She finds out from private sources sooner than she should."

"Messines seems like such a long time ago. I suppose we were naïve to think one victory could be a turning point."

"It doesn't seem like a month already." He saw a steaming teapot on the coffee table, slipped off the towel covering it, and poured a cup. Then he set the fragrant golden drink in front of her. "There." He laid a hand on her hair. "Leave the letter for later."

Charlotte wrapped her hands around the cup. "But it isn't going to be any better later." She took a sip and set the cup down again. "I need money for groceries today. I think I could purchase everything with a pound, if you had it."

He knelt down beside her chair and reached for his wallet. An empty place where he kept the money met his gaze. "Blast. I used it all. Can you wait a day?"

Charlotte looked surprised. "What did you use it on?"

Furniture. Safety. Turning their cottage to rights again. "I used the last of it in a letter to mother this morning."

The wrinkle between Charlotte's brows returned. "Has she ever tried to earn money for her own upkeep? I don't think she's contributed to society in any way since I've known you."

"Not since I was old enough to earn it, and I started young."

"We are in a war. I think she ought to help. I have half a mind to write and tell her so."

He stiffened. "Please don't."

"Just because your father never took care of her doesn't mean you have to be her second husband all your life." She cupped a soft hand under his chin. "When will you see that? I am jealous for all of you. Doctor Graham has a third of you, and your mother has another third. We had moved on to a new life, and then you fell right back into the old one again—trying to make up for your father, wondering when you would ever become his son." Ben stood up, but she grabbed his hand, preventing him from leaving her side. "If you are to belong to someone at all, then I want you to belong to me. You could have a son of your own and start over."

He could never find the words he wanted. They were all locked away somewhere, the words that would tell her the part that mattered belonged to her, and he was sorry for it all—the old family wounds, and the war, and inability to leave things behind. He could only say, "Are you angry with me?"

Charlotte's reassuring grip didn't lesson, but the wrinkle stayed between her brows. "No. But you are bound to a crippling sense of duty, and I want to see you free."

A tap sounded on the door, and they heard Alisa's soft "Hello."

She stood dressed in a light purple shirtwaist that Ben had never seen before, Matthew firmly nestled in one arm. Charlotte turned, her face smoothing out and brightening, and Ben, too, put on a front of cheerfulness. "Hello, Mrs. Dorroll. How is Matthew today?"

She gave him her customary timid smile. "He's growing fast, doctor."

"And how are you?"

"I'm well. Come in, won't you? I have more tea ready, and we were just about to sit down for lunch. Won't you join us?"

Ben couldn't resist after catching sight of the buttery brown scones, pools of cream, sharp cheddar, and real English tea. Alisa pressed him to take a cup and plate and help himself. He complied and enjoyed taking a leisurely lunch with his wife and sister instead of eating in haste between one call and another. Alisa watched him with a quiet glow of pleasure, and when he had done, asked, "Would you do me a service, doctor?"

"Anything," Ben promised, gathering up the remaining crumbs and dusting off his fingers.

"I wondered if you were busy this evening," Alisa said, giving Matthew her finger to suck to soothe him.

Ben thought for a moment. "No—no, I can rearrange my schedule. Would you like me for something?"

She hesitated. "I wondered if you would like to come to dinner. You see, Matthew is one month old today, and we want to celebrate, but we want you to be here, too. And I wondered if you would be willing to carry an invitation to someone else as well."

"Yes, I think I could manage to be here." Alisa and Pearlie exchanged delighted glances, and Ben winked at Charlotte, taking care that they couldn't see him. "And of course I can carry an invitation."

Alisa left her baby with Pearlie while she found a paper to write on, and she returned to give Ben the address of her other guest, who lived in a house on Urry Lane.

"Terry lives with a couple of other men. He's nice, but they aren't." Alisa shuddered as she mentioned the other lodgers. "I hope they won't give you trouble."

"I won't let them. Don't worry about me." Ben was even gladder to spend the evening at Alisa's now, for it would give him a chance to judge how things stood between his sister and her rescuer. If Terry's "acushla" and Pearlie's evident pleasure at his company meant anything, their friendship was certainly progressing at a fast rate, and he wanted to be informed.

Ben put his dishes in the sink and kissed Charlotte before heading down the road that had seemed so wearisome when he called on Nathan four days before. It didn't seem particularly so today. He wondered as he walked what sort of men Alisa's friend had as housemates, and if they turned hostile toward callers without much provocation.

Terry's residence sprawled a mile down Urry Lane in the opposite direction of Nathan Speyer's, but it did not look much better. The two-story farmhouse with shuttered windows stood far back from the road. Paint hung in long peels from the siding, and rusting farm machinery lay abandoned in the yard. If Terry and his friends had an honest livelihood, they must practice it a long distance from their living quarters. They didn't do much for the upkeep of their house, either, for the grass grew knee-high around it.

Ben strode up the brick path and knocked at the door. A tousled red head popped out of an upstairs window. "Hello, mate," it called.

Ben tipped his head back and recognized the man he had met in the street with the cigarettes. "Hello. Can I have a moment of your time?"

"You've got it, doc," the man said cheerfully. "Wait a moment, and I'll come down."

Terry appeared at the front door in less than the allotted time. A three-days' growth of beard and an indomitable grin covered the lower part of his face. He must have tried to comb his thick hair before coming down, but in spite of the attempt, it showed little change for the better. Ben guessed him to be in his mid-thirties, judging by his powerful, well-developed frame and the gray hair or two that sprang up among the red. He had a shirt and trousers on, both none too clean, and he wore no shoes. His nails had black stains under them and his bare feet were filthy. Evidently, his vocation was something to do with the soil, but if he were a farmer he did not make use of the empty fields he lived on. When Terry offered his rough, calloused hand, Ben took it politely, trying to ignore the grime as he did so.

"What can I do for you, neighbor?" Terry asked. "If you want a house, the one next door is empty." He pointed to a ramshackle structure three fields away. "I don't think the owners would object to your borrowing it."

"No, thank you," Ben said hastily. "I have a dinner invitation for tonight from Mrs. Alisa Dorroll. I believe she's a mutual acquaintance of us both."

"Right." The man flashed a grin. "I'll come. I wouldn't want to miss her cooking or your company."

Ben returned the good-humored glance. "You have a silver tongue. And I think I wouldn't be wrong in saying that it's an American one."

"I learned it from my mother, doc. Turlough O'Sean, at your service—but call me Terry, please. Turlough is an odd handle to get hung up over, and much too formal."

O'Sean. The name washed over him like a burst of home. It couldn't be—but it might. Mrs. O'Sean had mentioned a son named Turlough living abroad.

"I think I know your mother." Ben stepped inside and found himself in a trashed entrance. Empty glasses and dirty laundry, cigarette butts and crumpled newspapers were scattered over the sofa and floor, not to mention a revolver and a couple of daggers. "She lives in Richmond, and she said she had a son in England."

"I'm the one." Terry picked up a soda bottle from the side table and uncorked it before offering it to him, but Ben didn't dare drink it and shook his head. "Any friend of mum's is a friend of mine. You said your name is Dailey?" The gray-blue eyes under Terry's thick eyebrows held a bright twinkle.

"Benjamin Dailey. Pleased to meet you," Ben said. "I never expected to find you here."

"Oh, I haven't spent all my time in England. A few months earlier and you would have missed me." Terry looked at the soda bottle and took a swig of it himself.

The slight lilt in the vowels clicked in Ben's mind. "Perhaps you've been spending time in Ireland as well?"

"Only for a year or two." The jovial fellow seemed rather surprised at his guess. "Who taught you to be observant?"

Ben smiled. "I picked up the talent. What brought you from Ireland to Folkestone, if I may ask?"

"Weel," Terry O'Sean drawled, "I've knocked about some, but I jumped in over my head on Easter, 1916."

Ben frowned. "The Irish revolt?"

"That's right." Terry held out his wrist and displayed a Celtic cross tattoo. "Tried for freedom with the Irish Republican Brotherhood. When it failed, England wasn't safe for a while, so I made a quick exit to France, and after a year I came back. Not all the way—just to Folkestone."

"How deep were you involved with the IRB?" Ben asked.

Terry matched him wit to wit. "And what dirty little secret forced you to change names? My mother mentions you now and again in her letters, and you're a Dorroll."

Ben shrugged in acknowledgment of his defeat. "Actually, I didn't come to pry into your life story."

"Thank you." Terry grinned. "There ain't much interesting about me. But you, now—I can tell Alisa tonight that she's acquainted with a sneaky little doctor who has a different name than what he lets on."

The openness panicked him, and Ben took a stronger hand than he had intended. "I'm willing to involve the authorities if you betray me, which I think both you and I would be loath to do. Goodbye."

"No, wait." Terry seized him by his jacket sleeve and held him back. "I was only joking. Let me make it up. Tell me who you are and why you're here. I'm used to evading the law, and maybe I can deal you a good hand." Terry's eyes held nothing but sincerity. *"Nous serons amis,* what?"

Ben relaxed. "I'm not trying to evade the law, but thank you all the same."

"Well, no matter then. Until tonight, and you and I and the womenfolk will have a jolly good time." Terry grinned and slapped him on the back. "Nice to see you again, doc."

"I'm glad to make your acquaintance." Ben nodded in return and offered his hand. "I believe you know my sister better than you know me at present."

"Do I?" Terry's eyes brightened. "You might be right about that."

* * *

Terry waved from the front window as Ben paid the cab driver, and Alisa's happy face peeked out beside him. Ben waved back and went around the side of the house to the kitchen door. The warm, yeasty scent of bread met him as he climbed the three wooden steps, and he saw some of the dinner dished up and waiting—potatoes and fresh bread and a crock of sweet honey on the counter. Pearl stood unfolding a tablecloth and humming a little tune to herself. Her curls were pinned up securely to keep them from her face; she wore one of Alisa's aprons to cover her dress. The door squeaked as it unlatched, and she turned around and saw him.

"Left to do all the work, are you?" Ben teased.

Pearl smiled. "I don't mind. Alisa isn't ready to do this yet, and I kept house for Mother, you know. Go in and join the others; everything will be ready in a minute."

When Ben entered the sitting room, he saw Matthew cuddled in Terry's left arm. A look of sleepy content emanated from the baby's face. Alisa gestured Ben to a seat between Terry and Charlotte on the sofa, and she took one of the rocking chairs.

"Hello, doc," Terry said. "Want to hold him? He'll like you."

Ben had scarcely taken a seat before Terry handed Matthew over. He tensed as the soft, warm bundle was thrust upon him and watched the boy anxiously to see how he would take it. Ben usually managed to think of an excuse whenever Alisa offered to let him hold her son. This time he wished he could have, for Matthew's look of content changed to one of grave concern and a protesting wail rose from his mouth. As soon as the baby burst into tears, Ben lost whatever shreds of confidence he had started with. He sat in misery until Alisa took pity and slipped out to soothe her son.

"You've sure got the touch, haven't you?" asked Terry, with his perpetual grin.

Ben shook his head and frowned when he felt Charlotte shaking with laughter next to him. "I'm a doctor, not a nursery-maid."

Pearlie came in then. Terry nodded and gave her a broad wink. "Hello again, Pearlie."

Ben opened his mouth in protest as he heard Terry use their pet name for her, but he never got the words out. The man meant no disrespect, and it seemed rather harsh to rebuke him. Ben gave Pearl a slight, reassuring nod and plunged into a stream of small talk. Or rather, he pulled the plug that unleashed a stream of joviality from his new acquaintance.

Alisa entered the room amidst a ripple of laughter and invited them into the dining room for an old-fashioned chicken dinner. For once they could eat without thought of tomorrow, which refreshed Ben and Charlotte, for it reminded them of the days just after their marriage when things were easier to come by. Even Pearl seemed to relish it, though she had lived until April with an extravagant mother who liked to indulge good taste.

After dinner, Alisa brewed a pot of tea and rocked Matthew to sleep while Terry pulled out a cigarette to enjoy a smoke. Ben's lips twitched at that, and when Pearl caught sight of his amusement, she hardly dared to meet his gaze. A red flush of embarrassment covered her face, and Terry completed her confusion when he sat down on the end of the sofa beside her, but she didn't say a word or make any move to stop him.

Wondrously, Ben forgot the war and the police investigation and his reasons for being in Folkestone. The four around him shared laughter and stories—mostly Terry's stories—and he was content to sit and listen, not even keeping up his end of the conversation as he felt obligated to do at Colonel King's. Here he did not need to be a wise man of the world or an unprincipled intelligence agent or the head of a family establishment. He was simply his own quiet self, listening to Pearl's bright laughter and Terry's happy chat, and watching Charlotte's crochet hook slip in and out of the white yarn she used to make bandages for the hospital.

His watch showed ten by the time he said goodnight and let himself out the door. Terry didn't seem the least bit disconcerted by the hour. He would doubtless head home as soon as he realized how late it was, and Ben felt comfortable leaving before him.

After listening to see if he could detect any sound of footsteps following him, Ben determined that he was alone and relaxed into a desultory walk toward Tontine. He would go see Jaeryn and tell him about Terry. Jaeryn ought to know about him; there was nothing concrete to prove he had a connection to their work here, but gut instincts weren't safe to ignore, and Terry had given signs that afternoon of being deeper than he let on. Jaeryn was probably getting ready for bed by now if he wasn't on a house call, but he wouldn't be offended at a late visit—besides, he was used to interrupted nights in his medical work.

One of the pubs showed a clandestine light in the back as Ben passed. Doubtless, the landlord wanted to rake in a few more shillings before the constable showed up on his beat. The rest of the town lay abed and asleep, as all honest men were supposed to be, but lights still shone in the crack between Jaeryn's curtains. Ben lifted the brass knocker and tapped softly against the heavy oak door. The click of the latch sounded, and Jaeryn answered him in his dressing gown and slippers. When he saw who his guest was, the Irishman opened it even wider and locked the door behind them.

"Are you all right?" he asked, a worried lilt in his voice.

Ben almost laughed. He must have become quite the figure of dread to Jaeryn if the man thought something had gone wrong just at the sight of him. "Of course; I only stopped in to tell you that I made an acquaintance today that I think might be another lead. His name is Turlough O'Sean."

"Did you?" He wasn't sure, but Jaeryn seemed less than pleased at his news. "What's going on?"

"Terry told me he was a former Irish rebel hiding out here, and he knows my real name from America. I knew his mother. He's fast friends with Alisa Dorroll, and I think he's in love with my sister."

Jaeryn let out a sharp whistle between his teeth. "He must be a fast worker."

Ben knit his eyebrows and a stab of worry shot through him at the insinuation. "Do you know anything about the man? Is he safe to be trusted with her? I know his mother, and he comes from good folk."

"Far be it from me to dictate your friends, Doctor Dailey." Jaeryn's green eyes sparkled impishly. "Or your sister's sweethearts—that's entirely in your hands. But I didn't think you were the sort to take up with runaway Irish rebels. They're rather disreputable folk last time I checked."

"That's too bad. He seemed nice enough." Ben felt a pang of disappointment that the first open and honest man he had met should prove to be unsafe. "But now that I think about it, Turlough O'Sean has enough unaccounted time to be watching the soldiers and collecting troop numbers. Nathan Speyer strikes me as too busy with his position at King's house to have a task of that magnitude, unless King is covering for him. I'm not about to put my sister at risk."

"From what I've heard, he's a kind fellow," Jaeryn said. "He may be a rebel, but that doesn't mean he's a scoundrel. I'll set my agents on his track and see what he might be spending his time on and why he's living here when he'd be safer abroad. It certainly seems worth an inquiry." He undid the latch and opened the front door. "Dailey, I'd like to have you and Charlotte to dinner one night, so I can get to know you both in your unprofessional capacities. We've had a hard run, and it's good to have a break now and then." He peered out into the street. "I forgot it was so late. You shouldn't be out alone. I'll drive you back."

Ben waited in the hall while the other doctor ran upstairs for shoes and regular clothes. Jaeryn was in good humor tonight, and the invitation to dinner had been kind. He almost found himself taking a liking to the dark-haired Irishman. They might have gotten off to a rough start, but they weren't making such a bad job of it now that they had gotten used to each other's ways. They were working together quite well, in fact. And after dinner with Terry and Alisa, it was almost—almost—starting to feel like home here.

Chapter Thirteen
Allies Change Hands

Ben dropped by Jaeryn's house earlier than usual on the sixth of August. He arrived at the clinic and found the front door unlocked. Jaeryn must be awake early for a wonder. The consulting room door, however, was closed, so Ben dropped his card in the slot to let Jaeryn know he had arrived.

Turning to cross the hall to the waiting room, he paused as he heard Fenton's voice from the consulting room.

"—mother is pursuing a serious relationship with a Mr. Creswick of Richmond, Virginia. It might be worth your while to know more about him. She often has him to dinner at her house, and according to the servant I spoke with, things are rapidly progressing further than a friendship. Still, the son is her sole provider."

Ben heard Jaeryn's voice interrupt. "I knew that."

"And has been for a long time," Fenton replied. "Also, word has it that Dorroll wasn't eager to sign up for his current work due to his financial encumbrances."

"Which I also knew."

Ben held his breath to hear Fenton's reply.

"The laundry woman said that Lisette Dorroll left an address with them to forward the money he sends, but she doesn't want any more contact with her son."

"Well, you put your trip to good use. Any word on Dorroll's father?" Jaeryn asked.

Ben made a sudden movement as if to push open the door and surprise them, but he drew his hand back at the last moment and listened again.

"I did discover that Matthew Dorroll often visited Folkestone prior to the war," Fenton said, "but his last visit was in March of 1914. I'm still tracing the reason for that visit, but it parallels the date of his retirement, which was one month after. Ann Meikle read the letter Dorroll sent to his father a couple of weeks back, but she didn't find anything in it. She made a copy for you."

Ben heard the sound of a chair scraping and tiptoed to the waiting room where he could no longer hear the conversation. The study door opened, and then the outer one closed. After Ben heard Jaeryn return to the consulting room, he walked in. Jaeryn looked surprised and appeared to be suppressing some excitement.

"What happened?" Ben asked, acting as if he hadn't overheard the conversation. Jaeryn expression retreated into an air of studied nonchalance as he rifled through his desk drawers. "Oh, nothing. Just something I was thinking over before you came. What brings you here so soon?"

Ben glanced about for Fenton's copy of the letter from his father and caught Jaeryn slipping an envelope under a tray on his desk. A dull burn of fury flamed up within him. He had to say something to buy himself more time while he thought through what had just happened. "I wanted to tell you Charlotte's coming tomorrow. We talked about it last night, and she's ready to help. I encouraged it because she's coming back to Copt Point this afternoon and I don't want to leave her there alone."

"I'm glad to hear it." Jaeryn seemed to have recovered himself completely. He opened the curtains and unlocked the medicine cabinet for their day's work. "Oh, Dailey, I wanted to tell you. When I went to London, Jeremy gave me a report on our findings in Emmerson's library. They analyzed the letter you pulled out of the safe and they're fairly sure it originated in Germany. Ryson suggested we determine whether Ann remembers anything about it. She was postmistress in January. Perhaps you could ask her and see what you can dig up."

"You have more authority with her than I do." Ben went over to his desk and removed the mug of tea and stacks of binders that Jaeryn had left there.

"I don't follow," Jaeryn said, bewildered by his unwillingness. "What's the matter?"

Ben pulled a box of pencils out of his desk drawer and shut it again with a heavy slam. "Nothing. I'll look into it."

An uneasy silence settled between them as Ben took his notebook and jotted down the house calls that Jaeryn had assigned to him. By the conciliatory manner Jaeryn kept up, he must be wondering if his conversation with Fenton had been overheard. Ben wasn't about to give him a hint that he had. Let him sweat longer.

Jaeryn took out his own notebook. "You mentioned you were going to Nathan Speyer's the other day. I haven't heard what happened."

"Did you want to?"

"Of course, I do." Jaeryn kept his gaze averted as he wrote, but he did not seem angry at Ben's evasion.

"Well, it's quite evident the blood we found on the dog tags is his. I found a knife wound on his side when I treated him." Ben dug up Nathan's record in his files and handed it over. "I suspect he got the scratch at Copt Point the night someone broke into my place. He claimed to be recently enlisted in the British army, but he didn't say how much longer he'll be in Folkestone. I think the whole story of his enlistment is a front for leaving the area unquestioned. Whichever army it was supposed to be, it seems like he ought to have reported for duty by now."

Jaeryn nodded. "I want to know why he's leaving. See if you can pick up anything, and don't hesitate to use whatever means necessary. If you like, you can ask Ann to look through his letters for you."

Jaeryn had some kind of cheek to think he would stoop to such tactics. Ben clenched his fists to get a grip on himself. "I'd rather not. Didn't Ryson order us to stay out of it?"

Jaeryn's green eyes remained as placid as a still pool of water. "Leave Ryson to me. Speyer's a liability to us, and I can't take chances. I also have something else for you to do which I doubt you'll like any better. But I would be obliged if you would do it."

"I'm listening."

Jaeryn's frown at his terseness held more concern than anger. "Take the key to the room Emmerson kept locked up and see if Emmerson marked Nathan Speyer on the map. Peters will let you in; the house is so big you shouldn't have any problems, though I doubt the steward keeps a close eye on things. You know how to avoid detection in any case. Don't forget to wear gloves, and it would be best if you went on a Sunday morning. The steward is a dedicated church attendee, or so I've heard. While he's at services, you can work undisturbed. Will you do it?"

Ben sighed. "Of course, if you wish it."

Jaeryn took up his hat and the house key. "I'm going out on calls now, but there is one more thing. If you still have that threatening note you received back in May, I'd like you to bring it in tomorrow. I want to send it on to London and have the handwriting analyzed."

His thoughts jerked from his outrage for a moment, and he shifted uncomfortably at the unexpected request. "Actually, I don't have it. I kept it in my bottom dresser drawer, but last week it wasn't there. I can't think where it would have gone. Why do you want it?"

"You lost it?"

Ben flinched. "I'll find it."

"You can't lose things like that, you know. It's useful evidence in a court of law. And you never did look into possible intruders that wouldn't have set her dog to barking."

"I know. I'm sorry. I've had—a great deal to think on lately." Ben flipped through the empty pages of his appointment book without looking at them. "One piece of paper didn't seem to matter. But of course, there is no room for mistakes in this work."

Jaeryn smiled. "This isn't a game of perfection, really; it's more a matter of taking advantage when the other side slips up. It's all right, Dailey. You'll pull through, and I'll do my best to help you. With all the patients you have to take care of on your route, not to mention your brother ill, I know you've had a lot on your shoulders."

Ben caught his breath. "I never told you my brother was ill."

"Of course you did." Jaeryn frowned in uncertainty.

"Did I? Or did you read it in my letter to my father?"

Jaeryn stood frozen for a long moment. Nothing moved, nothing made a sound to break the awful silence.

"I don't know—I mean—I suppose that's where I heard of him, yes."

Ben stood up and walked over to the tin tray Jaeryn had used to cover the envelope earlier. A quick breath sounded through Jaeryn's teeth when he picked it up and pulled out the letter. Ben spread it out and it lay there between them, a little square of violated trust.

"I thought when I put my letters in the drop to be mailed out they went straight to London." Ben's voice cut through the silence in taut accusation.

"I told Fenton to make sure and check them," Jaeryn admitted.

"Would you like to tell me more of your dealings with Fenton?"

Jaeryn twisted his hat between his hands. "I don't think that would be helpful."

"On the contrary, perhaps it might. A little matter of distrust, perhaps? That day I told you someone followed me—you knew who it was. It was Fenton, wasn't it? But you let me think it was a threat to my life instead."

The outside door rattled to announce their first patient. Jaeryn hastily shut the consulting room door and locked it.

"Not to mention the fact," Ben continued, his voice rising, "that

214

you sent him to Virginia to pry into personal affairs that I had every right to conceal from all of you. Of all the dirty tricks, setting underworld leeches to spying on me is lower than I ever thought you'd sink. Why did you do it?"

The Irishman's jaw clenched at the rebuke. "Don't speak so loud. You were young and stubborn and inexperienced. I had my own interests to protect. I didn't intend to pry at first, and later I had no choice. I apologize."

Ben shook his head. "I don't think that's enough this time. What did you find out?"

"Dorroll, I didn't—it's—" Jaeryn held out his hands entreatingly. "I'm sorry. I didn't know the extent of what Fenton had done until he came this morning. There was nothing you would have disapproved of at the start. He told me your father was a Scotland Yard investigator before the war, and Ryson told me that much himself."

"He was what?" Ben caught himself before he admitted that Jaeryn knew more of his father than he did. "What else?"

Jaeryn sighed and kept his gaze on the floor. "Also that you have had to cut corners close to send money to your mother, and that your father refused to see you when you came to London."

Ben could hardly contain his consternation. "Is that all?"

"Not quite," Jaeryn admitted. "He also told me you worked under disadvantages growing up and had to take loans from a private credit establishment to get an education."

"And?"

"That's all. I swear."

When Ben spoke, his voice, though it sounded calm, had a hard edge to it. "To be quite candid, my private life is none of your blasted business."

Jaeryn threw his hat aside and came a step closer as if he were facing a wrathful tribunal. "Listen to me. I'm sorry for prying, but your brother was related by marriage to one of our main suspects, and I had to be sure you weren't previously connected. Fenton says you're in the clear. Now we have to put this behind us and work together. Every piece of information we learn fits into the solution somehow, and it's evident that both you and your father are pieces we need. We must lay everything on the table so we can consider our options." He watched Ben's withdrawn face to see if his words had been persuasive enough. Thinking to add the last bit needed, he said, "You can't keep your own identity so confidential that we risk losing an important link. Can't you trust—"

At the last word, Ben cut him off. "Stop," he said thickly. "I don't need any more of your patronage. I don't know whether you think of me as a tool to be used at your pleasure or some kind of charity case ready to accept anything you have to offer. But I am neither."

"I never thought—" Jaeryn protested.

"And whatever my father brought me here for, I have no prior knowledge of it and no part in it."

Jaeryn brought his hand down heavily on the desk, and Ben flinched at the crash. "I couldn't take that chance. I knew nothing about you or him. You admitted when you came here that you only had an interest in working on this particular mission, so we couldn't help but suspect you."

Jaeryn's accusation took the protests from his mouth. But the news did not serve to lesson his resentment. Ben pulled out the reply from his father that he kept in his jacket pocket and threw it over. "If you want proof that I'm not personally involved, then read this—if you haven't already."

Jaeryn picked it up and furrowed his brow as he read. When he finished, he looked remorseful over his mistake. His accent sounded heavier when he was agitated. At that moment, his words were nearly unintelligible. "You kept so much to yourself, I thought—I didn't know. What can I do to bring things back to what they were?"

Ben shook his head. "I don't think it's as simple as that."

Jaeryn began to speak and then trailed off into silence. Ben did not care to break it, for he felt that if he did, the fragile glass of his privacy would shatter for good. Jaeryn had penetrated much deeper

216

than he wanted. He had even found out things Ben himself did not know. He watched the dark-haired doctor apprehensively, and when Jaeryn looked up, Ben tensed in anticipation of the next question.

"Tell me, Dorroll," Jaeryn said. "Whatever reason your father had for sending you here, he must have told you something. I promise to be discreet with the information you give me. I think it may have a connection to our work."

Ben walked over to the window to look out on the street. Already the shops were open and doing a brisk day's business. Knots of screaming children played in the gutters, and matrons and housemaids were haggling over the prices of beef and cabbages as if nothing untoward had occurred. Perhaps nothing had. Should he care so much? Just part of the work, Jaeryn would say. Do anything to expose others' secrets, and get used to others doing the same to him. He wasn't the only one Jaeryn was probing for confidential details. Besides, perhaps the doctor saw the mistake for what it was.

Jaeryn walked over and joined him. "We can work together on this," he pleaded. "We must, or we may fail."

Ben kept his gaze on the street. "Did Fenton tell you that I used to live in England?"

"Yes, but only until you were four." Jaeryn nodded. "And then your mother took you back to her family in America."

"What would you do if a man who had ignored you for twenty years asked you to put your life on hold and take up work you hated? Because it was your duty to your country?" Ben's shoulders dropped a little lower as he spoke, and he finally looked up at Jaeryn's face. "And then he would not see you after all, when you came to see him?"

Jaeryn gave a sharp laugh. "I think I would tell him I cared about as much for him as he seemed to care for me and that we would be better off staying apart."

"That's what I thought you would say." Ben settled his expression into a tight reserve again. "Your country has a remarkably small claim upon my loyalties for the kind of sacrifice I'm making."

"Does your father have a connection to our mission?" Jaeryn persisted. "He requested that Ryson place you in Folkestone."

"My father told me he had nothing to do with my placement." Ben returned to his desk and took up the letter from his father. He tore it to shreds, continuing until the scraps of paper were so small they could not be put together again. As the white pieces fluttered down, he came to grips with his shock at Jaeryn's revelation. "I didn't know why he asked for me to come here. I have not seen him or spoken to him since my arrival, and I had to write six times to get this note." He kept his gaze fixed intently on the medical certificates hanging on the opposite wall. He couldn't imagine anything worse than baring his personal life to a man who couldn't respect it enough to leave it alone. "He also told me, as you saw, that my presence is essential to him, and so I have agreed to stay. That, I swear, is all I know. Though in light of what you've just said, I don't doubt he places more significance on my work than he lets on."

Jaeryn laid a hand on his shoulder, but Ben shrugged it off. "Perhaps," the Irishman offered tentatively, "your father has help to offer us if we can persuade him to open up." He put his hands in his pockets and made an attempt at cheerfulness. "Your relations could prove useful. I always felt that you weren't here for nothing."

Ben flushed. "I'm not here simply on my own merits, is that what you mean?"

"Well, hardly." Jaeryn grinned. "I had seven years' experience before I was given this position. But Dailey," he said, turning serious again, "if you really can't bear to stay and you think your father's involvement is something you'd rather not investigate, I'll let you leave."

Ben crushed the scraps of his father's letter in his palm and threw them into the trash. "No. I'll see it through for his sake if for no one else's. I have no choice. You probably know about my brother's military career as well?"

A red tinge of embarrassment crept over Jaeryn's face. "A little— or rather, yes, I do."

"He's done; he'll be physically impaired for the rest of his life. I was the second son, and now more than ever I must do something to bring the family credit."

"And you'll do your father credit, I'm sure," Jaeryn said soothingly. "I'm glad you found out about this business with Fenton, Dorroll. It might have been better to keep the whole affair to myself, but I've wanted to have this conversation with you for some time, and I'm glad for the opportunity for us both to open up."

Ben looked up, and the hot wave of anger flamed within him again at the words. "If you think I'll forget what you've done, then you deceive yourself. It isn't opening up to have all your personal affairs laid open at someone else's choice. Why didn't you bring your questions to me in the beginning?"

"Because I knew you would not answer them." Jaeryn sighed and threw up his hands. "I don't understand why you should be so offended."

"Sending a spy after me was despicable and underhanded."

Jaeryn drew back. "That's rather harsh."

"Furthermore," Ben said, ignoring him, "your criticism of me for keeping the business in Emmerson's library secret from you when you had equal if not worse secrets with Fenton was downright hypocritical."

The Irishman straightened his shoulders and stood tall at the accusation. "Oh, now, I don't think that's fair. You could do damage with the kind of secrets I have the experience to handle. Even in searching you out, I did so with good reason and in an acceptable manner." Jaeryn glanced at his watch. "I have to go; I'm sorry. We'll talk more later. I hope you'll still let Charlotte come tomorrow."

Ben gritted his teeth. "I wouldn't have my wife work in your wretched clinic if it were the last place on earth. And I don't see that there's any more to discuss. After today, I wouldn't be surprised if I felt I had to turn you in for treason along with the rest of them."

Jaeryn froze for a moment, and then he said gently, "I know you don't mean that."

"Yes, I do." Ben lifted his chin. "I'm paid to follow your instructions, but I'm not required to turn over my private concerns to you. Nor is it necessary that we have any other association than that which is required for our work."

Jaeryn drew his dark eyebrows together and his voice hardened. "You're saying that you would like me to stop being so sociable."

"That would be a fair assumption. And as you've seen fit to set a watch upon me, I think it only fair to tell you that the observation will be mutual."

Jaeryn's expression went blank. "What do you mean?"

Ben felt his own face harden into rigid lines. "I believe you're holding back things of your own. One slip and I'll be ready for you."

Jaeryn clenched his hands and looked as if he were about to speak further. Instead, he exited, slammed the front door behind him, and strode out onto Tontine Street without a word.

Ben sat alone, feeling drained and empty. Disbelief over Fenton's words, over Jaeryn's callousness, over his own indignation swirled together and turned his head spinning. Perhaps he had spoken to Jaeryn too hastily. But Jaeryn had only tried to smooth things over, not acknowledge his wrongdoing. Evidently, the doctor had participated in enough unscrupulous lying in his seven years of espionage activity that he no longer cared about it.

The whole sordid mess at home—it had been simply between Pearl and Charlotte and himself, and the Irishman's prying had exposed their privacy shamelessly. Had it been only Jaeryn, the revulsion might not be so strong, but the dreadfulness of the exposure was increased by the fact that he had used such a low means as Fenton to get the knowledge.

"You've been a fool," he told himself savagely. The phone rang, and he picked up the receiver to attend to a patient call.

* * *

When Charlotte returned to Copt Point that afternoon, she

noticed the heavy locks and new furniture immediately.

"You didn't tell me you were threatened," she said when Ben finally confessed about the break-in. Her face showed disapproval and a strong hint of anxiety.

Still seething over the events of the morning, he spoke more roughly than he intended. "It was nothing you should be concerned about."

Charlotte drew herself up at his sternness. "You should have told me sooner. Did the police find out who did it? I want to know—"

"I've told Colonel King and reported the incident to the police, but they didn't pick up a clue as to the person. We've changed the locks and secured the windows, and that's all we're able to do. Beyond that, I'd really rather not discuss the matter." Ben cut her off before she could reply. "I've been safe since it happened and see no reason for concern."

She would not be put aside like a child, nor did she seem daunted by the exasperation in his voice. "What did Doctor Graham say about it? Was anything taken?"

"There was nothing missing," Ben began, but then he broke off. Or perhaps there was. The death threat—the one he hadn't been able to find. Gone without a trace from the dresser drawer where he kept it. But that couldn't have been the only reason for the break-in. Who would tear up his whole cottage for such an insignificant object? Besides, that couldn't explain the shots in the nighttime or the blood on the dog tags. "There was a note missing—a threat. It was nothing. Just a scare tactic someone tried after we arrived. Jaeryn gave me the choice to stick it out or not and tried to install telephones, and then he sent me back."

"How could he let you put yourself in danger like that?"

They stood the length of the table apart from one another. Ben crossed his arms. "I'm dispensable, Charlotte. London made it quite clear that I can be replaced if something happens. I've given them everything, only to find out this morning that not even Jaeryn trusted me. He's been looking into us—dragging up everything. He knows all about home and growing up, and more about my father than I do, and he never told me. It feels like desecration." Slowly, he let his arms fall to his sides again. "I think I could find it in myself to hate him for it."

Charlotte's hands clenched, and her blue eyes flashed with anger. "I know I could find it in myself." Her voice trembled with wrath. "How dare he do it? He ought to have asked you."

"He certainly should have."

"I wish I knew how to help you." Charlotte made an impatient gesture. For one moment the steadfast manner she kept up for him slipped from her grasp, betraying her anxiety, though her fury was more for his enemies than for him.

Ben could not dissolve his irritation easily, but the extent of her anger unnerved him, and he made an effort to speak more gently for her sake. "Never mind. You don't have to bother yourself about him, *ma chérie*. It's not for you to worry about."

Charlotte shook her head. "It is for me to worry about. Everyone thinks they have a claim on you, and they offer nothing in return. Your father wants your career but won't let you see him. Your mother wants your money. London wants your help with the war effort. I don't know what Jaeryn Graham wants from you, but it must be something if he's kept you this long. You may be a dispensable object to them, but to me, you are my husband. I will not let them take and take when we receive nothing in return."

His voice betrayed his anguished frustration. "I don't know what to ask for."

She took a step closer to close the gap between them. "I can think of a hundred things. You could ask for some guarantee of safety. You could ask for your mother to earn some of her own keep and for Jaeryn Graham to respect your personal affairs. And if they will not give it to you, then you can leave."

"But Charlotte, there are men at the front making sacrifices. For their sake I can't refuse—"

Charlotte threw up her hands. "There you are again, thinking some soldiers whom you've never met have a claim on you. All these people have cut you off from the home you fought to make, and I cannot help but hate them for it."

She closed the rest of the distance between them and took both his hands in hers. "You have had enough pain to last you a lifetime. We had dreams together. Why are you giving them up so easily?"

Ben could hardly swallow back the panic that made his heart race even now that her voice had softened. He had seen her outbursts of justice before, against the pain she saw in her work; but it had never been directed against him. "I shouldn't expect London to care about me when I haven't proven myself. As for my mother, she's had pain too. I don't want to cause her more if I can help it. Please try to see."

"I love you for caring. But you are worthy of being cared for in return. I do not want to see you thrown away."

He had already given more time than he had to spare from his afternoon routine, and much as he hated to leave her, he couldn't give any more. Before he returned to town, Ben made sure she had her own Webley and also looked to see if Nimrod was chained at the back of Mistress Goodwin's cottage. In spite of the lack of activity over the last two weeks, he wasn't about to take chances. Then he left Charlotte to her own devices and returned to his work with a nagging remorse over their disagreement troubling his mind as he went.

The route from his last patient call to the cottage at Copt Point would normally have taken a little over an hour. But that night, reluctant to find out if Charlotte was still angry with him, Ben chose a circuitous path through the marketplace, paying little attention to where his wandering took him. He wanted to clear his head. After the events of the morning, he must now work with a man in whom he no longer had confidence. If Jaeryn would lie about something as small as his dealings with Fenton, he could also lie on a much larger scale— the level of his involvement, or even where his loyalties actually were in this whole affair. Yes, he would have to be wary of Jaeryn. And he must also find someone else to work with, for it was vital to have a trustworthy fellow agent in this whole confounded business.

He turned onto Tontine and walked through the heart of Folkestone, which was still healing from the bomb damage in May. The greengrocer's, now rebuilt, had a brand-new coat of paint on the outside. Glass windows shone from new frames, and had he not been there in May, he never would have suspected the bomb drop had happened. Further down the street, a man stood on the front steps of Jaeryn's clinic, waiting for someone. When the man slicked his hand through his hair, Ben recognized the slim, white fingers. At the sight of that familiar action, his resentment cooled off a degree. Jaeryn had seemed genuinely remorseful this morning. Perhaps he had broken trust too hastily with the Irishman. If he walked over, if he said one word of regret or apology, he had no doubt his colleague would willingly pick up where they'd left off.

Before he made up his mind, a whistling heralded the approach of another person, and Jaeryn climbed down his front steps and joined a man who was sauntering up the street. Ben caught his breath as he recognized Terry's red hair.

"Hello, doc," Terry greeted him, waving as soon as Jaeryn caught sight of him.

Jaeryn's white teeth flashed out, and a few smile wrinkles creased the corners of his eyes. "Hello, Terry. What brings you here?"

"Just stopping by." Terry leaned nonchalantly against the brick house and crossed his arms, but he could not keep still, and one of his feet tapped out a rhythm as if to an inner melody in his soul. "I saw a friend of yours this afternoon."

Even from where he stood, Ben could see surprise on Jaeryn's face, and a note of interest crept into the Irishman's voice. "Who?"

"Dorroll. He came by to see his wife."

Ben gritted his teeth at the use of his real name. So Terry broke his word quite easily as well. He strained his ears to hear more, but they went into the house. Eager not to lose any of their conversation, he crossed the street and tried the doorknob. It was locked.

The street lay deserted—hushed and still, all the stores closed up for the night. He could manage a little espionage without being detected. He crept softly under the consulting room window to listen, and good fortune was his, for Jaeryn had cracked it open—heaven only knew why. He heard the rustle of newspaper. "I brought back a French paper last night for you, doc. Doesn't give much more news than we already know, but I can read it to you."

He heard Jaeryn's voice, clipped and precise. "Just tell me what they said."

"It's raining. They fought like fury last week, trying to get Passchendaele so they can cut off German subs leaving port there. The paper's full of all the patriotic jumble, but I couldn't find much worth celebrating. Wish I could have gone to see for myself."

"Don't you dare. It's only been a week. They need time and dry weather."

"You should light a candle to the saints to make it stop raining," Terry said absently.

"Did Dorroll look all right?" he heard Jaeryn ask.

"Seemed rather low in life outlook, now that you mention it," Terry replied.

"I see."

Ben heard the striking of a match and then the penetrating smell of cigarette smoke drifted out. He couldn't help feeling amused. No doubt Jaeryn had weighed the possibility of someone overhearing them against the unpleasantness of the smoke scent infusing the room, and his cat-like tidiness had won out.

Jaeryn's voice sounded in mild reproof. "Those aren't good for you, you know."

"Right." Terry kept smoking as the twilight deepened, and a cricket started up its chirping under the step, right at Ben's feet.

"Does Dorroll trust you, do you think?"

"So-so." The silence hung over them again until Terry said, "He's got a nice little thing for a sister."

"Terry." A note of warning crept into Jaeryn's voice. "She's for someone respectable when she's ready to marry, and now is not the time in any case."

"Ah."

"Would you like to help me?" Jaeryn's lilt sounded much thicker than Terry's, but now that Ben heard them together, he could trace the similarities of speech between them.

"Anything for a friend."

"Dorroll and I had a rather serious disagreement this morning, and I have particular reasons for wanting his trust back. He won't come on his own if he can help it. If you see an opportunity to put in a good word for me, I'd be obliged to you. It's for his own safety as well as our success."

"I'll do it," Terry said. "Mum always liked him, and he seems a nice fellow. Wouldn't want anything to happen to him."

"Thank you, Terry."

Ben slipped around the side of the house so they would not see him when they came out. The front door opened and Terry's heavy tread sounded down the sidewalk, but when Ben listened for the door to close again, it did not. Jaeryn must be sauntering back and forth in the street a while longer. Here was another chance to make up, but, while he wasn't particularly unhappy with Terry, his ire with Jaeryn remained, and he stayed put in the shadows. He would manage perfectly well, he told himself, without this friendship.

He intended to wait until Jaeryn went inside before trying to leave, and he forced himself to keep still when the doctor's footsteps passed uncomfortably near his hiding place.

"Ta bron orm."

The sudden breaking of the silence startled him, and the low talk continued on, rising to the heavens in a kind of melody, though not with any music. Ben looked about to detect its source and was forced to conclude that it came from the Irishman himself. The murmured words stirred passion and wonder and heartbreak all in one—a savage, ancient sort of beauty. Then it died away, and after deliberating for a moment, Jaeryn turned back inside, and Ben pursued his own way homeward, rather breathless with what he had overheard.

Two days passed, and their deadlock proved to be stronger than Jaeryn, by all appearances, had expected. The doctor made no move to speak to him for reasons other than the strictest needs of business, and Ben kept his own counsel. He could not tell whether Jaeryn was angry, afraid, or simply biding his time in the hope that the whole argument would fade away to nothing. They kept conscientiously to their work in spite of the disagreement, neither avoiding nor seeking out contact. Ben told Charlotte that he was not ready for her to begin work at the clinic and she should continue her volunteering in St. John's Road for the present.

Jaeryn was out Wednesday evening when the clinic closed. He had not left a note with a time to expect his return, so Ben picked up the list of house calls he had yet to finish and asked the phone operator to direct medical calls to the Victoria Hospital while he was out.

Before attending to his other calls, Ben stopped by Alisa's to catch Terry. But when he spoke with Pearl at the back door, she told him he had come five minutes too late; Terry had already gone home. After considering the matter, he decided to continue on and visit Terry at the house on Urry Lane. It wouldn't be much out of his way, for he also wanted to check in on Nathan to see how his recovery was progressing. The sooner he put an end to the matter, the better.

When he reached Terry's place, however, his new acquaintance was not the one who answered the door. Ben could hardly conceal his surprise when the door opened and he recognized Mrs. Goodwin's former lodger, Hugh.

"What do you want?" Hugh asked.

"I'm looking for Turlough O'Sean." Ben's hand crept closer to his jacket pocket where he kept his Webley. Hugh saw the movement, and a smirk of contempt twisted his thin lips. "He's not here at present."

Ben put his hand down again with an effort, though he rather doubted the wisdom of it. "When do you expect him back?"

"I don't know. He didn't say." Hugh shut the door before he could speak again.

Ben wasted no time in leaving and turned his steps in the opposite direction toward Nathan's, wondering how Hugh knew Terry.

It didn't take him long to reach the old tavern, and Nathan Speyer was standing at the door when he arrived.

"Hello, doctor," the young man called. "You just missed Starlin. Or did you send him?"

"No." Ben shook his head. "I never told him to come."

"I thought you might have ordered him to give me an apology." Nathan's brown eyes shone in amusement. "This is the first time he's done it, at any rate. No matter. I'm well, if that's what you came for."

"I did, and I'm glad to hear it."

After his first greeting, Nathan's face settled into its usual quiet watchfulness, but he seemed pleased with the visit for all that. "Thank you. I would pay you for your services, but—"

Ben waved a hand in dismissal. "It's no matter. I only came to see if you were healing, and you needn't worry about the money. It was nothing."

"Can I do anything else for you?"

"Not at all. Shall I wish you good luck at the front, or are you here for a while longer?"

"Until the end of August." Nathan shrugged his thin shoulders. "So as you wish."

Ben considered his duty fulfilled with that. "I'll wait, then. I'm sure I'll see you before you leave. Goodnight, Mr. Speyer."

A gunshot tore through the stillness. The two men looked at each other, waiting for another sound to indicate where the first had come from.

"Do you suppose that's Starlin?" Ben said quickly.

A hint of concern appeared on Nathan's face. "I saw a man come down this way while Starlin and I were talking. A red-headed fellow; he rides by on his bicycle every evening, but I'm not acquainted with him. They might have met."

Ben reached for his medical bag. "I'd better see if someone needs help. Would you come with me?"

"Surely." Nathan caught up a revolver from a side table and closed the door. They set out at a rapid clip along the road, scanning to the right and left of them, and Ben was glad he had a companion. Two were better than one. As soon as they reached the road, they saw a distant figure limping toward them. They picked up their pace and recognized Starlin, his hand pressed to his side and a small stream of blood running down his lip. He looked panic-stricken as they came up alongside him.

Ben spoke, "Come sit in the grass for a few moments and tell me where you're hurt."

Starlin's lips opened, then closed, then opened again, and he muttered, "I'll be all right."

"No," Nathan said gravely. "You're in no state to walk home, so you'd best come clean. We thought we heard a shot."

Starlin shot an angry look at his friend. "I'm not shot. I just—I just cracked a rib, I think."

"Let me see." Ben pulled Starlin's coat off, though the lad clutched at it defiantly, and pulled up his sweater and shirt. "Let's take a look at your side." When he touched the skin over the left ribs, Starlin doubled over and gasped and Ben whistled under his breath. "I'll find you a ride home. You can't walk on your own in this state."

Nathan picked up Starlin's coat to help him on with it again. As he did, a silver pistol tumbled out onto the road. The explanation of the loud crack showed on the boy's face as clear as if he had confessed it with words. Ben stooped to pick up the revolver and opened the chamber of the weapon with shaking fingers. One of the bullets was missing. He looked in silent accusation at Starlin, who winced in reply.

"Suppose you tell me—" Ben began.

"I'm sorry," Starlin shrieked, "I'm sorry! I didn't mean to. I just—he was—I didn't listen. He told me to go away, and I didn't see what right he had. We mixed up, and when he cracked my ribs I thought he might kill me, so I pulled the gun out. Somehow it—it—"

Ben took a firm grasp of the boy's shoulders. "You must gain control so I can save the man. All you have to tell me is where." He coaxed. "Where?"

"Just—just down a ways in the grass. You'll see him lying there," Starlin gasped out.

"One of my neighbors has a horse and buggy," Nathan said. "I'll borrow it." He turned on his heel and set off running back the way they had come.

Ben helped Starlin back up to his feet and said, "Starlin, follow Nathan back but don't try to keep up. Nathan, take the revolver and keep it safe. He isn't to be trusted with it."

Then he set off on a dead run. He had raced for life several times in his profession, but never on foot and never for anything so grave. This time he wondered if the victim would be alive when he reached him. It didn't take long for him catch sight of the bicycle tipped crazily on its side, and just beyond it, the crumpled body lying in the grass. Ben fell to his knees beside Terry and hunted through his medical bag for supplies as he talked.

"Turlough. Where are you hurt?"

"Hello, doc. Had a kid—just—" He coughed up some blood.

"Never mind, don't try to talk. Just let me look at you." Blood everywhere. The whole side of his shirt was drenched with it, and the red liquid was fast spreading to the grass underneath him.

"I'm not rightly sure." Terry's voice faded, and Ben saw him growing limp. He grabbed his hand to keep him alert.

"Terry, stay with me; I need your help."

"Doc, listen," Terry said, grasping his wrist with a sudden surge of energy. "I have a sister living in Dover. If I don't make it—"

"You will. Breathe as steadily as you can. I've sent for help."

"Erin—" The next word caught in Terry's throat before he could get it out, and he tried to swallow and catch his breath enough to speak clearly.

Ben found the instrument case in his bag and retrieved a pair of scissors. "Terry, listen to me. Be quiet while I take care of you. Lie still and try to stay with me."

"But Erin—"

"Yes, yes, I'll take care of Erin. Now, I'm going to look for your wound."

Ben talked ceaselessly as he cut away part of Terry's shirt, trying his best to minimize the pain. He had no memory afterward of what he said, nor did it seem to matter, for Terry wasn't paying attention either. Ben found the bullet wound easily enough, and panic rose hot in his throat as he guessed that it must have entered through the lung. He searched hurriedly through his supplies and pulled out gauze to press against it.

"Terry, I'm going to check to see if the bullet went through."

Terry didn't answer. The blood slowly drained from his face, and a clammy sweat broke out on his forehead. Though his heart rate was heightened, his pulse ran sluggish through his wrist, and as he tried to get a breath, he struggled to shift his position.

"Don't move. Try to stay with me," Ben ordered. As he said it, Terry's eyes glazed over and closed. Ben shifted him to his side and noticed a second stain on the back of his shirt. He must get Terry to the Royal Victoria somehow, and soon, if he wished to save him. Ben layered on gauze until the blood could no longer soak through and taped it well to keep it in place. Then the clip of horses' hoofs sounded on the road, and he saw Nathan driving up with the buggy he had promised and Starlin on the front seat beside him.

"Hurry," he ordered as they came alongside. "We're running out of time."

Starlin held the reins. Nathan jumped out and helped him lift Terry into the back seat, and Ben climbed up as well and shoved his jacket under Terry's head. Then Nathan turned the horse and set out at a rapid pace for the Victoria Hospital.

Chapter Fourteen
The Aftermath

They said nothing on the drive. There was nothing to say. Ben laid his watch on his knee and kept checking it to tally how much time they had left before Terry bled too much. It would be a hard pull, but due to the lateness of the evening the traffic was light, and they had a fair chance at an unhindered road to the hospital. Ben bit his lip once or twice as they passed along the rutted country roads and spoke sharply to Nathan after one particularly heavy jolt. Starlin gripped his hands together until the skin stretched white over his knuckles and braced his legs against the footboard to keep from jostling along with the buggy. He looked like he was in more pain than Terry at the moment. The poetic justice of him receiving what he had dealt out to Nathan would have been almost amusing had it not happened under such grave circumstances.

Rutted country roads gave way to the hard-packed streets of the more inhabited sections, and then to rough cobblestones. Ben held Terry steady with firm hands on each shoulder and cringed when he saw the blood soaking through the gauze. They had no time to stop and try to bandage it better, so he put more pressure on it and told

Nathan to drive faster.

It took them all of eight minutes and forty-nine seconds—he had counted every single one of them—before they pulled up at the Royal Victoria's front entrance. Ben ordered Nathan to hold the horse and Starlin to stay exactly where he was. Within twenty seconds he had a stretcher brought out and helped the nurses carry Turlough into an operating room.

The hospital staff prepared the anesthesia as quickly as they could. Just as they had laid Terry down and stripped the rest of his shirt away, he stirred. He looked ghastly with his face tinged gray, and his hands trembled of their own accord. He couldn't open his eyes, and a smile was beyond him, but when Ben took his hand, he felt a faint pressure.

"Hello," Ben whispered. A sting came to his throat as he looked down at the face of one of his best friend's children. He leaned down to catch the faint, slurred words.

"Not...sick."

Ben laughed, though it caught in his throat. "You're a fighter, Terry. Pull through it; we need you."

He saw Terry's lips moving and leaned closer. "Say it again, Terry?"

"Erin."

"I'll take care of her. Set your mind at rest."

"Ja—" Terry choked with the effort of talking.

The surgeon came over, and Terry's eyes widened when he saw the laryngoscope nearing his mouth. After a moment's quick work, with a small struggle on his part, they administered the anesthesia through the tube, and he lay still. After that, they sent Ben away.

Nathan looked up in surprise when Ben reappeared and offered Starlin a hand down. "That didn't take long."

"The nurses are good here," Ben said. Starlin started up the walk toward the hospital entrance, and Ben and Nathan looked after him, but neither man called him back. "I'll look after Starlin and let you know what happens when I have news. Terry will be in surgery for a

233

while if all goes well."

Nathan pulled out Ben's leather medical bag and handed it to him. "Do you think it would help if I stayed?" he asked, motioning to Starlin standing stiff and erect by the door.

Ben shook his head. "I'll take care of him. You can go home, and I'll tell you what happens to him tomorrow."

"Let me know about the other man, too, when you hear, doctor." Nathan clambered up and slapped the reins, and the horse took off back the way they had come.

Starlin looked terrified as they sat down in the waiting room. He tried to cross his arms, but couldn't manage it, and waited in sullen silence for Ben to speak.

"It will be all right, Starlin." Ben patted his shoulder. "I'll ask for a room to patch you up."

A nurse obliged him and gave them a cramped examination room down the back hall. Starlin inched himself onto the chair and unbuttoned his shirt while Ben washed away the traces of blood still on his hands.

"Breathe for me and let me listen to your lungs," he ordered. After listening and probing for a moment, he suspected there were two ribs broken. Terry had hit hard indeed, and under what provocation he could not begin to guess. Ben took out a compression wrap from his bag and bound up the ribs, and Starlin grimaced when he taped it in place.

"I can't breathe."

"You'll be fine." Ben peeled off his rubber gloves and tossed them in the trash. "I'll send you home with some painkillers that ought to help. If you're having more trouble breathing after you go home, tell someone and come straight here."

Starlin buttoned his shirt again. "What's going to happen now?"

Ben tried to break the news as gently as possible, but he knew Starlin would not like it all the same. "Now I am going to call the police."

Fear leaped into the lad's blue eyes. "But it wasn't my fault. I didn't—"

"It's all right," Ben soothed. "I'll phone your father first so we can get this straightened out together. Why not rest in the waiting room while I contact him? There's no one else there, so you'll have it to yourself."

Starlin complied grudgingly.

As soon as he made Starlin comfortable in the waiting room, Ben asked the nurse to alert a constable and have him come take down a report of the incident. After that, Ben used the hospital phone to call Colonel King. When he explained what had happened, Colonel King gave a muffled groan of impatience on the other end. "I don't understand how someone smart enough to enter Cambridge can forget everything he knows about handling firearms safely. I'll come down and hush it up."

Ben didn't try to keep the hardness out of his voice. "I'd rather you came down to do justice, sir. He's injured a friend of mine."

"I don't have time for a court case, doctor. Keep the boy out of trouble until I get there, will you?"

When the constable and Colonel King arrived, Ben sat in an isolated corner until they wanted him. The nurse came in to dim the lights for the night. She left only three on in the waiting room, and shadows shrouded most of the benches, giving the group a measure of privacy. Ben tried to guess what the men were saying by their expressions. Starlin kept up a blank aloofness to hide his fear, and his father was doing most of the talking. Evidently, King was quite confident in his ability to handle the situation.

When the constable finished and walked over to his corner, Ben rose and pulled the pistol out of his pocket. "This is the weapon, sir."

The man waved his hand. "You can give it back to the boy's father. But if you'll tell me exactly what you know about this whole affair, then I can finish my report."

Ben gave him all the information he knew, which was scanty enough, and after a long cross-questioning admitted that he had not been present at the act and could shed no more light on it than

Colonel King. But he could give a medical report, and offered a concise account of Starlin's injuries and what he knew of Terry's. It was lucky for the boy that he had gotten hurt, for that supported his story better than the most passionate of protests.

"So it's one man's word against the other." The constable closed his notebook with a dissatisfied grimace. "Well, King's son claims that it was self-defense, and until the other man can give his side, we'll have to wait and see."

"I trust there will be just reparation, sir," Ben said in return. "No matter the reason, it was a sorry deed, and the boy caused a great deal of suffering by his carelessness."

The constable looked bored with the whole affair. "Until this—what's his name?—Turlough O'Sean is out of surgery, there's nothing we can do. I'll keep in touch."

Ben glowered with disgust at the back of the constable's blue tunic as he walked out, but he controlled himself before anyone saw his expression. In disapproving silence, he handed over the pistol to Colonel King. The man held enough authority to prevent anyone from making an issue of the matter, and unless Terry recovered enough to protest, the battle was already lost.

Colonel King grasped his son's shoulder with one strong hand as he took the gun. His brown orbs looked perfectly composed, but he had the decency to keep the pistol himself instead of handing it back to Starlin. "Thank you for looking out for the boy. I assume there's no reason for him to stay longer?"

Ben stood as straight and tall as he could manage against King's greater height. "No medical reason whatever." Turning to Starlin, he said, "I'll stop by tomorrow evening and look in on you."

He stood by the window and watched the sleek black touring car pull away. It would be a long wait before he heard anything about Terry, and he didn't want to leave Charlotte alone until morning. It was already later than he expected, and he had no way to communicate with her unless he walked to Copt Point. All in all, that seemed the best thing to do to set her mind at rest regarding his whereabouts.

Charlotte was sitting in the kitchen mending his shirt collars when Ben trailed up the path and knocked on the door. "I'm not here to stay," he explained, as soon as she opened it. "But I didn't want to leave you wondering. Starlin King got himself into an accident with Turlough O'Sean, and I have to stay in town until early tomorrow morning. Are you all right to wait here?"

"Of course," Charlotte assented. "But what happened?"

"They mixed up in a fight, and Terry got the worst of it. Pray for him; for both of them. I don't know what's going to happen. I can't manage any better than to leave you here alone tonight. Are you sure you'll be all right?"

"Just a moment." She disappeared into the bedroom and returned with her sweater and handbag. "I'll come with you and wait at the hospital."

Ben opened his mouth in protest. "You'll feel exhausted tomorrow if you stay out all night. It could be hours yet."

"I don't mind." She fastened her hat with one deft push of the pin and draped her sweater over her shoulders. "Let me come, darling. Two are better than one in a long wait, and I couldn't bear to sit here doing nothing and think of them in pain."

By eleven they set out for the Victoria Hospital. Ben kept a firm grip on her elbow and one hand close by his revolver. She was an added vulnerability on this dark stretch of road, and every crunch of gravel under her boots, every one of her quiet breaths from the exertion of the fast walk, set his nerves on edge with worry. He pushed her even faster, and when she suggested slowing down, he made as if he did not hear her. Charlotte stopped.

"What are you afraid of?" she asked.

Ben kept a firm grip on her elbow and propelled her to keep walking. "Nothing. But it's dark, and we're alone, and I want to keep you safe."

Charlotte slipped her hand into her own pocket by her side and laughed up at him. "I think they'd find both of us ready."

Ben put a warning finger on his lips. "Don't laugh. Just keep talking like we have nothing to hide, but not so loud." His throat clenched. "You didn't grow up needing to be handy with a revolver. Heaven help me if your parents find out what you've had to do."

"I would do anything to stay with you. I'm not good at it, but I think I could at least frighten someone if I had to."

"Has anyone been hanging around?"

"No. Mrs. Goodwin's old lodger, Hugh, comes to her house for supper now and then, but he leaves again. I don't think it's unsafe. She walks alone to her laundry clients, and nobody worries her."

"But you're the wife of someone who's involved in more delicate work, and that makes a difference."

Not until the first lights of the town appeared did he relax his caution. Perhaps he should have worried about himself more than Charlotte as far as exhaustion went. As soon as they reached the hospital waiting room benches, a weariness crept over him, and he felt his eyelids drifting shut in spite of his best attempts. "Sitting down was a mistake."

"Or maybe it was sensible." Charlotte offered an inviting, cashmere-clad shoulder. "I'll wake you when they come. Get some rest for tomorrow."

Ben shook his head and sat up even straighter. During the first half hour, he tensed every time a nurse passed through the room, fearing they came to tell him it was too late. He tried to keep awake and even paced back and forth to stay alert, but at length, he slid down on the bench for the last time and only opened his eyes when he felt a hand on his shoulder.

A frightened shriek woke him even further, and he came to, realizing that Charlotte was trying to loosen his grip on the nurse's wrist.

"I'm so sorry," he apologized. "You startled me, that's all."

"It's no matter." The nurse straightened breathlessly and looked at him with wide eyes. "You brought in Turlough O'Sean, didn't you?"

"I did." Ben reached down for his watch and looked at the time in disbelief. "What happened?"

She referred to her file record. "He just came out of surgery, and we're bringing him around from the anesthetic. The bullet did pass through one of his lungs. We had to clean out the fabric shreds since the shot was fired at such close range. We trust we got them all, but there is still the possibility of infection, of course."

Ben smoothed down his hair and stood up to try to make himself more alert. "Did the lung collapse?"

"Yes, sir." The nurse bobbed her head. "We stitched him up and gave him a blood transfusion. I don't expect you'll see a change one way or the other for a few hours. If you want to call in later, the nurse on duty may have more to tell you. Unless you prefer to stay, of course. You're welcome to as long as you like."

"No, thank you." Ben shook his head. "I have my practice to attend to, but I'll come again soon. If something serious happens, please leave a message with Doctor Graham." He turned to Charlotte. "Wait here, *ma chèrie*. I'm going to run an errand, and I'll come right back for you."

It was raining when Ben passed down the slippery cobblestones of the Victoria Hospital walk and made his way toward Tontine. He had no umbrella to keep off the wet, and as he strode through the nighttime darkness, he groaned over the awkwardness of what he was about to do. Jaeryn must be told; there was no way around it.

His watch read quarter to four.

As he climbed the steps to Jaeryn's house, Ben noticed with surprise that the curtains were open and the lights on. Jaeryn opened the door as soon as he reached the top step and flashed him a glance of surprise, followed by hopefulness. Then the Irishman smiled and beckoned him in out of the rain. "You knocked," he said politely.

Ben raised an eyebrow. "Not quite."

"Ah. I must have misheard." When Ben made no move to come inside, Jaeryn invited him again. "Come in."

Ben hung back as Jaeryn laid a hand on his sleeve. "No, I won't take up your time. I just—

"I insist. It's raining outside, and you should dry off. I'll make you a drink; you look awful."

"I've only come for a moment," Ben protested.

"Don't be ridiculous." Jaeryn held the door open, and he stepped in and waited until the Irishman reappeared with a steaming mug of coffee. "Here you are. Careful, it's hot. How have you been managing?"

Ben held the mug tightly to warm his wet hands and felt new life returning to his stiff back and shoulders. "I came to tell you about Turlough O'Sean. He's in the Victoria Hospital with a gunshot wound."

"I'm sorry to hear he's in such a mess. Should I be worried this time?"

"I'm afraid so. He's coming out of anesthesia now."

"Blast." Jaeryn's lips twisted in concern.

They stood in awkward silence while Ben offered a concise account of the surgery results. Jaeryn seemed more exasperated with Starlin King than need be, but in Ben's experience, people were often angrier over accidents than premeditated damage. He watched Jaeryn pace about for a few moments, ranting over it, before he turned to go.

Jaeryn stopped his scolding. "Wait. I'll get you an umbrella."

"I wouldn't want to inconvenience you." Ben handed back the empty coffee mug. "Thank you for taking the trouble."

A slight frown crossed the Irishman's face. "If it were any trouble, I wouldn't offer it." Jaeryn hurried upstairs and came back with an umbrella, which he offered with a swift return to his kind manner. He followed Ben down the hall.

"Thank you for telling me, Dorroll. I know it wasn't easy."

Jaeryn glanced at the window he had crouched under to hear Terry's conversation and Ben, too, looked at it. "Not everyone can command the Irish," he said, as they stood together at the door.

Jaeryn remained imperturbable. "That's true enough. Even the

British haven't been able to."

A slight smile escaped him in spite of himself. "I meant the Irish language."

Jaeryn grinned back. "I thought you were listening that night. You'd best be off before I take your umbrella away."

He shut the door.

* * *

Ben managed to catch some rest and set out again at half past seven to pick up Terry's bicycle. Nathan had promised to retrieve it and leave it at Jaeryn's clinic, but when Ben arrived, Nathan was up and about, so Ben gave him the latest news.

"Well, living through the night is a good sign, right?" Nathan asked. "And I'm glad to hear Starlin managed to avoid hot water. He doesn't need any more, poor chap."

"Is being in hot water a common occurrence for him?" Ben asked as he climbed on the bicycle.

Nathan smiled. "Wherever Starlin goes, trouble usually follows, doctor. He hasn't had an easy time of it, raised in that big house with no mother." The young man stared down at his scuffed brown shoes. "You lose a part of yourself after that."

"I'm sorry." Ben felt rather awkward at Nathan's candor, for he suspected the young man was thinking of his own mother as much as Starlin's. "If you find yourself at a loss—for anything—you can come to us at the clinic."

"Can I?" Nathan looked at him with an inscrutable expression. Silence hung over both of them, tension from secrets almost breaking the surface, but neither of them daring to risk it.

Nathan was young, Ben thought. Perhaps he was in over his head with the Germans. If he wanted a way of escape, it would be a pity if they couldn't give it to him. But still, it wouldn't do to betray themselves.

"Of course." He backtracked, stumbling over himself in his

attempt to erase the previous statement. "I still have a mother, but I think I know what you mean—about missing yourself."

Nathan turned, went inside, and closed the door without a word.

Ben took the bicycle for his own use; it would make it a good deal easier to get around, and he reasoned that since he was attending to Terry's affairs, it was all right. He called at the kitchen door of the Emmerson estate to inform Peters of the accident. After that, he set off to tell Alisa why Terry wasn't coming to take care of the farm work. It was only eight o'clock when he arrived, but the sitting room curtains were open, and Pearlie met him at the door with Matthew in her arms. "Pearlie. I have some bad news I need you to break to Alisa."

A worried frown creased her brows. "What is it?"

"It's about Terry." Ben heard the click of the door latch and glanced behind her to see Alisa peeking through, listening. "He was shot yesterday, accidentally, on the downs north of town. He's in the Victoria Hospital recovering. He underwent surgery last night and is recovering now. That's all I know for the present."

"He didn't come yesterday night. He said he would. I thought— he had left." Pearlie hugged Matthew closer against her chest for comfort.

The door opened all the way, and Alisa came into the room. But instead of turning to comfort her, Pearlie fled to her with a little gasp of anguish, and Alisa wrapped her arms around her. Holding her close, she murmured something too low for Ben to catch.

"Is she going to be all right?" Ben whispered.

Alisa looked at him over Pearlie's golden braid and nodded. She gave him a gentle, sad smile of reassurance. "I'll take care of her. I think she'd rather have just me right now—if you don't mind," she said timidly.

"Of course, if that's what she wants. I promise I'll call as soon as I have news." Ben waited to see if Pearl would turn to him for comfort like she always had before. But she seemed content leaning her head against Alisa's and did not turn when he said goodbye.

Hugh answered the door at Terry's place this time. The thin, lithe fellow was reluctant when he asked for Terry's belongings, but after a great many explanations, Ben managed to secure them and took them home strapped to the back of his bicycle.

Charlotte was awake and ironing her dress for the day when he arrived. She was relieved to see him safe home again. While she made breakfast, Ben examined the lock on Terry's trunk to determine how hard it would be to undo. The handle disintegrated in his hands while he did so, and the lid fell open to reveal a motley collection of belongings. Taking great care to keep things intact, he pulled out a couple of shirts, a handgun, and other clothes and toiletries. At the bottom, he found a pile of papers.

They proved to be letters, all from one Erin Reinhardt *née* O'Sean living in Dover. The earliest ones had the round script of an unpracticed girl, and he could trace their change over time into adult penmanship. The one on top of the stack was blotted and looked to be written in a great hurry. He had promised Terry he would help her, and that meant reading them, for no one else knew what the problem was. Grimly, Ben pulled out three sheets of paper from the latest envelope. She had not even written a salutation, nor could he find a date amidst the scrawl.

Oh, Terry, I don't know how to tell you. What have I done? I never thought that his love for me extended so little that he would leave me now, in my present situation. For the past three years, he has remained content to help the hurt and sick and join the teams of men building bomb shelters. I thought I satisfied him—that his country was forgotten, and he would never return to his homeland. Once or twice he mentioned a passing regret, but with my tears or my kisses, I could always persuade him to stay.

I have deceived you in my letters. I told you that all was well, that I was in good health, and that Ernest continued working for the war effort. None of it is true, and I cannot bear it alone any longer. I cannot tell Mum or Dad, so you are the only person I have left to confide in. You were good and kind to forgive me when I married without your knowledge, and I have no doubt that you will forgive me now.

One night in mid-June, Ernest found a girl to watch Brogan so we could have the house to ourselves. He took me out for dinner and gave me a bouquet of narcissi, and never since our honeymoon had he been as sweet and considerate as he was then. He told me he loved Brogan and me and spoke of his hope that we might have more children soon if I wished it. I loved him so much that I never suspected his real intent. The shame, Terry. I cannot keep from crying as I write. How could he deceive me so? To say those loving things, to pretend he was content with living as I wished, and then to do what he did the following morning—

He woke me early and kissed me. I saw he carried a traveling bag, and he told me he must leave England—that he had finished his work here and his sovereign needed his service. You can imagine my horror—to find out I have been supporting him in his mission to collect information for the German cause. All this time, under the pretense of advancing our side, he has been passing along troop numbers and spying out our defenses. He succeeded all too well, and in spite of my pleadings and promises of secrecy if only he would repent, left to enlist with the Kaiser. He said he would come back for me at the end of the war. And he wanted my prayers—the audacity! I told him I never prayed and I did not believe in God.

That he left me despite my entreaties is what rankles most. To turn traitor to everything he knew I held dear—to leave me the disgrace of the neighborhood— and all in the name of patriotism. He said if I loved him as much as I claimed, I would make an effort to love Germany for his sake. That I would gladly bear disgrace now so I might have the satisfaction of suffering for future good. Future good! My face burns as I think of the embrace he dared to give me. I told him I never wished to see him again, and I would make sure he never saw Brogan either. He laughed. He said I was overwrought and I would come around in time.

I have been forsaken by all who know me, for my plight could not be kept secret, and however unwilling I may be, I am married to a member of one of the most hated countries in Britain. I cannot find anyone who will hire me to work for them. The neighbors have no mercy, and I am ignored—or worse, feared—even in the shops. For what did I sacrifice my life, Terry, if this was to be the result? Must I give up my dreams of love and a happy home? Many girls in our town enjoy the pleasures of motherhood without the sanction of church or government, and they are forgiven. Yet I, who have done everything according to honest law, am disgraced because my child shares his heritage with our enemies. I write 'our' deliberately, for I will never love or honor a spy. Oh, Terry, it wasn't Brogan's fault that he came from a German father, and yet I almost hate him despite it. I have prayed every day that God would take both of us, but He has not done so, nor do I think He will.

You may not tell our parents. I hold you to your promise of secrecy, and that man will not lift a finger of interference. I cannot bring myself to seek a divorce, but I may be driven to it if the distrust of the neighbors lasts much longer. Then— if only I had not borne a child—my parents need never know of the affair. I am not sure what to do. I cannot tell them, nor will I for the present. But Ernest is not coming back, that I can assure you. How blind, how deluded I was to promise my hand to him. It is impossible that a soldier of the Kaiser should be a good man, and I hate to think of all the acts of oppression he will be fighting to support. But I need not support them, whether or not he does. My loyalty is my own to give as I choose, and I will not bestow it on such a bloody cause. He has made his choice, and now I am as a widow—or worse.

Do not hope that I will change my mind, for I have sworn by all I hold dear to abide by my decision. Forgive me for concealing it so long; I wanted to keep it from you for a little while yet, but I am so weary now, I cannot bear it alone any longer. I wish I was dead—I wish he was dead. The fates are too cruel to force me through this. I feel I shall go mad if I do not ease this pain soon, yet I cannot work up the courage. Rest assured that all is at an end between me and that man who called himself my husband. I cannot undo the past nor rectify the future. I must drink my cup. Please don't think badly of me for my cowardice.

His eyes blurred as he folded the sheet and placed it in its envelope. He must find a train to Dover as soon as he could manage it. In a sudden flash Terry's easy grin rose up, and Ben wondered if Erin Reinhardt had ever possessed the same sense of humor. If so, he doubted that she had it still.

He felt a warm hand on his shoulder. "What's the letter?" Charlotte asked.

Ben handed it silently over his shoulder. Her hand kept resting on his shoulder while she read, and he waited in the silence. "Are you going to tell her mother?" Charlotte asked at last.

"Probably. If Terry dies, I'll have more than one thing to tell her." His fingers reached up to meet hers. "I wish we could have kept the war separate from home while we were here."

* * *

When Ben Dorroll set off at a brisk walk down the street after delivering the news about Terry, Jaeryn slumped with relief against the doorframe. It had been close—very close. If the tight-lipped American had come a moment later, he would have seen Fenton marching up the other side of the street to keep an appointment at the clinic. Four in the morning didn't seem an unreasonable hour to hope for privacy, but there were no guarantees.

Jaeryn had contemplated his plans long after they went awry, but after careful consideration, he saw no need to change them. He still wanted to know what the Dorrolls were up to, and Fenton was the best avenue for finding out, even if he did go about it in a disreputable manner. Besides, Jaeryn rather suspected that Ben's threats, though genuine enough in the heat of the moment, were far from becoming a reality. Ben had a great many things on his mind, and extra work during clinic hours would keep him from becoming troublesome. It wouldn't be long, either, before Charlotte came to help. A few days' perplexity on her husband's part about her safety would see her installed as attending nurse quite soon.

Fenton sidled up the steps and slipped into the hall without invitation.

"We were interrupted in our last conversation," Jaeryn said, "but nothing has changed. I don't suspect him of wrong now, but I still want you to tell me anything you can about him."

"Very good, doctor."

"You might have been cleverer about your investigations. I thought I could rely on your skills to be discreet."

"Ben Dailey is a deal more suspicious than most, as I think you would agree."

"You're right about that," Jaeryn mumbled.

Fenton held out a hand in expectation of his payment, but Jaeryn waited a long moment before obliging him. "I have your money," he said at length. "And I'll say this for you, you've earned it. But there won't be any more passages to America for some time to come. I don't wish to use my own income to fund your trips. Do what you can here in Folkestone, or perhaps London will hold more information for you. I've given you five pounds for train fare should you need it. Don't use it for anything else."

Fenton pocketed the money. "Insults never do have the intended effect, so you'd best leave off, doctor."

"Fair enough. But I think you've been paid generously for all you've given. I've had to clean up some of your blunders, and with Dorroll that's no light undertaking. Remember, in the future you're only to collect information that can be legally obtained. I don't want your investigations drawing more of his attention than they've already attracted. There are several people taking an interest in him besides you and me, and he's already in danger as it is."

"I don't take an interest in him," Fenton corrected. "You do."

"I do. Therefore, it would be wise for you to do so as well." Jaeryn restrained himself to merely dropping a hint. "Thank you for coming so early. We may have to do that more than once in future. I'll leave a note in our drop when I want you next."

As soon as the door closed behind Fenton, Jaeryn went into the consulting room to watch him from the window. Fenton carried no umbrella, but Jaeryn didn't feel the same urge to offer one as he had for his colleague. Dorroll would have walked home without it; Fenton paid for a cab and didn't think twice about the matter.

Jaeryn remembered Terry as he closed the curtains and turned the lights off. He would get a couple hours of sleep, then go down to the Victoria Hospital to make inquiries before opening up the clinic.

Chapter Fifteen
Hazards of the Job

Ben took his first spare moment to call on Starlin King. Two days after Terry's accident, when he had finished arranging for one of his patients to care for Alisa's farm work, he skipped lunch and walked to Colonel King's. Considering what Starlin had done and the ensuing police investigation, not to mention his cracked ribs, the boy couldn't be comfortable at the present moment. And he still hadn't explained why he shot Terry in the first place.

"I'm concerned for the boy," Colonel King admitted when the maid showed Ben into the study. "Not only did he get roughed up in that unfortunate fracas, but he seems to have sunk into a depression because of it. He's been sulking in his room all day and wouldn't touch the food I sent up. Refused to see me when I knocked on his door this morning. I'm not sure I can handle any more of his escapades."

"Suppose I talk to him," Ben suggested.

"I would be grateful, doctor. I even considered calling in Revered Carlile, but—well, you know." A cutting amusement lurked in the man's brown eyes. "Starlin isn't keen on interference from evangelicals."

Ben climbed up the massive staircase to Starlin's room. The boy wasn't in the four-poster bed, so Ben peeked into the blue and leather sitting room. The sporting equipment was gone, and Starlin lay on a sofa behind a large folding screen, staring at nothing.

"Hello, King." Ben pulled up a chair without invitation and made himself comfortable. "I thought I'd drop in for a visit."

Starlin's eyes dropped shut to a mere slit, refusing to acknowledge his greeting.

A violin case lay open on the table, though it didn't look as if it had been used since the accident. Ben tried that for a conversation starter. "Charlotte said you liked playing the violin. Is this the Guarnerius you told her you were getting?"

Starlin nodded. A stack of books lay close to hand—psychology, fiction, science—with the unmistakable signs of fingerprints and fraying on the cloth-bound covers. It was well for him that he was intellectual, for it would serve to make his recovery less tedious than it would have been otherwise.

Ben gave up and addressed the cause of hurt in the face before him. "Charlotte said to tell you she would visit as soon as she could. I called at the hospital today, and Terry is still alive. He has a decent chance of recovering with good care, and the Victoria Hospital has the best care to offer."

Still nothing. The eyes were completely closed now.

"Starlin, it wasn't all your fault, so there's no need to torment yourself. Terry may pull through yet. He won't hold it against you. You felt justly threatened for your life, and the shot itself was an accident."

The white lids showed a slit of blue and then closed again. Ben lost a grip on his patience. "I should think you would show a little care for others, young man. Your father is worried about your lack of animation and poor spirits. He said you refused to speak to him this morning."

Starlin shifted impatiently and opened his eyes at last. "No, he isn't worried. He never worries about me. Would you please go, doctor? I'm thinking, and I would like to be alone."

"That's precisely why I came upstairs. I'm going to take a look at you and see that you aren't any worse."

He helped Starlin sit up and loosened his brocaded dressing gown. There was heavy bruising down one side, but that was to be expected, and he didn't show any signs of serious complications. Ben pulled out a bottle of white pills and labeled the dosage on them. "I'm leaving you some painkillers, and you shouldn't drink alcohol while you're on them. Not that you would, but I have to say it."

"I drink what I like." Starlin's blue eyes flashed, eerily similar to Charlotte's when she was angry. "I think I'll pass on the painkillers."

Ben ignored him. "With cracked ribs, you won't have much choice in the matter."

"I don't need them," he protested.

"Then you'll have extra insurance for next time." He helped Starlin tie his dressing gown together and settled back again, putting his hands on his knees. "Starlin, did something happen after your father took you home? Was he angry with you? I can speak with him if you like, and I'm sure he'll be reasonable."

Starlin shook his head. "No. Nothing."

King had gotten some sort of explanation from the boy; there was no doubt about that. The colonel wasn't likely to be open about the facts due to legal reasons, so pressing Starlin was the only option.

Ben tried a different tack. "Would you be willing to talk to me? We want to know why you were in danger, and why Mr. O'Sean wanted to harm you."

"I've told my father all anyone needs to know," Starlin said.

"If you could tell me anything at all that would be helpful. What did he say to you? Had you met him before this?" Ben searched for any sign of giving way, but there was none.

Starlin laid down and gasped at the pain of moving. "I hadn't met him until yesterday. With all thanks for your concern, doctor, I have nothing more to say."

"Well, then, I suppose I will bid you good-bye." Ben rose to go but turned and tried one more time to soften him. Jaeryn wouldn't be happy that he hadn't found out anything. "Starlin, please be careful. I'm here if you need someone to help you."

As he left, he passed a map on the wall above the fireplace that he had never noticed before. It was a large world map with tacks marking the victories on either side of the European conflict. The gold tacks were Britain, and he discovered after a quick observation that the silver ones marked German victories. It was not strange for a boy of Starlin's age to follow the war efforts in such detail, but the fact that the tacks were identical to Emmerson's sent a chill down Ben's spine.

"So you are following the war?" he asked, throwing a glance over his shoulder.

Starlin didn't reply. He had closed his eyes again.

* * *

Dreams haunted him, waking or sleeping. Dreams of childhood, dreams of college life, dreams of the bombing on Tontine. Starlin, the night he almost drowned. Terry, choking on the tracheal tube on the operating table. Again and again he saw Terry's weak grin and the bloody clothes. Over the ghosts of his dreams came the almost daily air raid sirens. He had grown used to ignoring them on his rounds, for he had too many visits on his list to stop for a false warning. But he started up more than once in the night seeking his now all too familiar weapon, and the thought of what he might do in a moment of panic with Charlotte lying next to him made him catch his breath in fear. If he was this afraid when he was with her, he couldn't leave her on her own. He would have to swallow his pride and bring her along to Jaeryn's where she would have some form of protection. That was all there was to it.

Terry was medicated most of the time to keep the pain under control. Ben had gone once to see him, but he was asleep at the time—or at least, not alert enough to open his eyes. The surgeon left the wound open to prevent infection and wrapped it in gauze and bandages until a few days determined how well it was healing.

For a wonder, Ben found himself at home on Saturday morning, free to write Edmond and clean his Webley. Charlotte pulled back the curtains so the view of the Channel could keep them company while they worked. They never tired of watching it. It was the one unchanging feature in their existence, and they clung to that stability. But there was something more than stability: an untamed grandeur that wound about them and gripped their hearts and brought them back to gaze again.

"This feels almost like home now," Charlotte remarked, as she set the flatirons on the stove to heat. "I saw the sea often when I was a child, and it looked just like this."

"Snob," Ben teased, going over by the window so as not to have the gun near her while emptying it. "You were a rich only child. I'm surprised you even considered marrying me. You don't get holidays by the sea now."

"No." She returned a saucy smile. "Now I live by it with someone I love instead."

Charlotte went outside to collect the sheets from the clothesline he had put up for her, and when she returned with a full armload, he brought up the subject of her working at the clinic. "You're still alone too much. If you transferred over to working at Doctor's Graham's, I could take you home at night after I'm finished. Would you like to change?"

She considered a moment, as she spread out a sheet on the kitchen table. "I've always wanted to work with you, but I don't like the thought of working with Doctor Graham."

Ben jabbed a brush into the barrel. "Oh, he'd be polite to you. I don't think you would be at all uncomfortable. Besides, he's out late morning and early afternoon. And I would feel safer having you there. He would let you have his guest room for your own use during the day."

"I don't mind, then." She tilted her head sideways to examine her work. Then she returned one iron to the stove, picked up the other one, and continued on.

He laid down the gun to focus on what he wanted to say. "If you would rather, I could bring Pearl home instead to keep you company. She'll be coming back by the end of the month anyway; a couple of week's difference won't matter, and I'll feel easier about you."

"Alisa seems to like her. I don't mind if she stays there."

"She can't." He shook his head decidedly. "Then she's alone and you're alone, and that's hardly sensible."

Charlotte glanced at him in between smoothing out the creases and gave him one of her knowing looks. "I think you have another reason."

Ben took up the Webley again and cleaned the chambers. "I do. She and Alisa are two innocents between them. The only difference is, Alisa is a married one and Pearl is not. I want her to stay that way for the present. She would be better off at home."

Charlotte shook her head. "A change of location isn't enough to dissuade a lover. You were more persistent than that when you were courting me. Do you think someone is in love with her?"

"I think, based on how distressed she was at the news, that she's at least interested in Turlough O'Sean."

"Oh." Laughter rippled across her face. "Yes, I suppose that's something to consider. He is rather old for her, isn't he?"

Ben frowned. "That's not what I was thinking of."

She tucked away the signs of laughter from her mouth. "I know; I was only jesting. But he isn't visiting her right now, and perhaps a separation will end the attraction."

"I don't think seeing him as a martyr to an imbecilic sixteen-year-old will help matters."

She sighed in agreement. "I suppose. But has she told you she likes him?"

"No," Ben admitted. "But he likes her. And I don't think he would be as familiar with her as he seems to be if she didn't give him

253

some encouragement. I could ask Alisa. I think Pearlie's confided in her more than me now."

"I think it would be much better to ask Pearl herself. Have you seen her since the accident?"

He wiped away the last trace of smudging from the chamber grooves and pulled out the lubricant. "No. I was going to stop by the hospital this afternoon to ask about Terry so I could tell her and Alisa the latest. The nurse said they'll put his stitches in soon, as long as they don't find any sign of infection."

"I'm glad he's on the mend." Charlotte folded up the sheet and placed it on a chair, then spread out the next one. "I would be agreeable to working for you and Doctor Graham. I've wanted to change from volunteering for the maternity wards for some time."

Ben gave her a sideways glance over the Webley. "Oh? I thought you liked doing that."

Charlotte gave a little lift of her shoulders as she switched the irons again. "I did. But a change of scene would do me good. It's work that others can do just as easily as myself, and I don't want to stay there long-term."

He looked at the Webley, shining and clean, with a glimmer of satisfaction. Then he reloaded the bullets into the chambers so the gun was full and ready. "I'll take you in with me on Monday."

He stopped in at the Victoria Hospital at quarter to five that afternoon and found that Terry had been asking for him. The head nurse was on the phone to the clinic in hopes of reaching him, and as soon as she heard he had arrived, she met him in the waiting room and beckoned him to follow her. Terry lay in a bed toward the middle of the men's ward. His eyes were open this time, but his pasty white face showed he wasn't much better.

"Hello, doc," he greeted.

Ben knelt down so they could talk at eye level. "Hello, Terry. How do you feel?"

"I feel like someone used my lungs—for shooting practice—and then thought I'd want them back."

"You can talk at least." Ben smiled, glad to see his spirits were undaunted in spite of the accident.

Terry rolled his eyes. "You're seeing me at a good moment. They doped the pain just before you arrived."

"Are the painkillers helping?"

"Don't feel like it." Terry lay on his right side, and Ben saw someone had kept his face clean-shaven for him. "Just try to look better to—spite 'em."

A nurse walked by to the next bed, and Terry followed her starched figure with a wistful gaze. "Give yourself some time, my friend," Ben said. "It will take a while for you to mend."

Terry lay for a few moments with his eyes closed. When he spoke, his voice was slurred from the medication. "I can't remember."

Ben leaned forward. "Remember what?"

Terry opened his eyes again and frowned, trying to concentrate. "I wanted—to tell you something."

"About me? Or you, perhaps?"

"No. Let me think."

Ben waited and bit his lip to keep from talking. A bell tinkled, summoning help, and he startled alert out of habit, realizing an instant later that it was not for him.

"It was Erin," Terry said at last.

Ben looked back and winced. "I haven't forgotten, Terry. I just haven't had a chance to get away."

"No—no." Terry thumped the sheet in frustration. "Just listen." He waited to make sure Ben would stop, then said, "She needs to know she can trust you. I can't write, but she'll recognize my ring. They found it in my pocket and gave it back to me."

Terry held out his left hand, and Ben caught sight of a thin sparkle that hadn't been there Wednesday evening. He slipped it off and placed it on his own finger for sake-keeping. It flashed a twisted flame of gold and sapphire in the most delicate setting he had ever seen.

"Heirloom, Terry?" he asked casually.

"No," Terry leaned deeper into the cool pillow. "I bought it a long time ago. I'll give it to little Acushla one of these days. Take it to Erin when you see her, and she'll know it's from me."

The gems, polished to perfection, must be worth a pretty penny. Ben slipped the ring off and looked at the inside of the band. There was an engraving on it in Gaelic but it meant nothing to him, for though he knew some foreign languages, he had never studied this one. "What does this say?"

"Always remember."

"Remember what?"

He glanced back at Terry, who was now breathing slowly and steadily. The medication had taken its effect.

* * *

"For you." Jaeryn jerked a thumb toward his desk as soon as he entered, and Ben picked up a brown, box-like structure with a leather handle and a metal knob.

"A camera? What for?"

"It just arrived." Jaeryn showed great pride in the apparatus. "The newest Brownie on the market, and you'll find it useful when you go to Emmerson's tomorrow. During church, remember. I hope you don't mind skipping church once; you can go to the evening service if you like."

"I don't mind." Ben pulled the lever on top to open the lens and looked curiously inside.

"Good. Take pictures of the maps and cards and thumbtacks. Get as many as you can of the room as well. Take a picture of the lock, and if you have an opportunity, one of the safes in the library. Come back afterward and I'll develop the film."

Ben set the camera down on the far corner of his desk so it wouldn't get in the way. "I don't have a key to leave it inside if you're out."

"Oh." Jaeryn considered a moment. "Well, I'll meet you at the evening service. It's not a perfect meeting place, but it will do."

"Is there any harm in giving me a key?" Ben tried the hint, even though he doubted Jaeryn would change his mind.

"Here's a key." Jaeryn grinned, tossing one over. "This is the one for Emmerson's room, the one we—borrowed."

"You know that's not the one I mean." Ben pressed his lips together in a thin line.

The pleasantness faded from Jaeryn's face. "That's the one I mean. I have something else for you to do as well. I know you had the incident with Terry O'Sean come up, but you haven't been to Ann Meikle to ask about the letter yet, and we need that information. Also, when you buy some postage, tell her to keep the change. I want you to give her a note in one of the hollow sovereigns."

Ben unlocked the drawer where he kept his sovereigns and pulled one out. "What do you want the note to say?"

"I've already written it. You'll have to use one of your sovereigns, because I've used all mine and Meikle hasn't given them back yet. You might mention it to her if you think of it. There are three of them." Jaeryn picked up the note to give it to him, but just then the phone rang, and in the preoccupation of answering it he kept the slip of paper clutched in his hand.

It was not a brawny hand like Terry's. Aside from the crooked index and littlest fingers, the fingers were smooth and scarred and unblemished, and they didn't look used to manual labor. Jaeryn must have had a fortunate ride of it up to this point with the trust of the London headquarters and a host of people at his beck and call. No doubt he had earned the privilege. But he had a heavy weight on his shoulders. Lately, Ben had noticed, Jaeryn was starting to lose his ready answers, delaying his replies so long that even his patients remarked on his absence of mind.

Jaeryn clicked down the phone and handed him the paper. "Here you are."

Nathan Speyer has recently come to our attention as a possible suspect with the Emmerson division. Claims to be enlisted in the British army, but we have evidence that he's signed up with the Germans instead. Want information about his background, London connections, and family. Ask Fenton to look as well.

Ben looked up in astonishment. "You don't know he's connected to Emmerson. I don't think Ryson would be pleased with this. And if Mrs. Meikle's not loyal to you anymore, then it hardly seems wise—"

Jaeryn cut him off. "It's wise. Trustworthy or not, Meikle is still responsible for passing on rumors and propaganda we want people to hear and alerting agents to possible threats."

It was evident that Jaeryn wanted him to obey without question, but Ben persisted, desperate for some show of trust. "Why are you passing information on to them if they're suspected of being false?"

"In her position as postmistress, she can inquire quite easily without drawing suspicion. I want my people to be aware. They can search for information about him that I can't," Jaeryn said crisply. "Here's some money for a little enticement around town if you need it for discoveries about Speyer. Use it discreetly, and don't use it to bribe any of our agents. He and Ann Meikle ought to keep you busy for a while. Speaking of which, now that we're discussing Speyer, have you found out any more about him?"

"No, I haven't." Ben gave up and folded Jaeryn's note inside one of his hollow coins.

"Keep looking, then. Find his vulnerable point and use it for all it's worth. You and Meikle are good friends, so you should work quite well with one another."

Ben paused, and his eyes narrowed. "Is that supposed to mean something?"

"No." Jaeryn shot him a warning look, though his tone stayed even. "I have neither the time nor the inclination for a disagreement with you. And while you're at Emmerson's estate tomorrow, see if you can make any headway on his inheritor. Ask Peters if he knows yet."

"You think whoever got his place is involved in this?"

Jaeryn shook his head. "Emmerson may have passed it on to an innocent bystander. He was a wise man and left hardly one incriminating document behind him. I doubt he would want to draw attention to his successor by leaving him his estate."

Ben fastened the two halves of the sovereign together until the match was flawless.

"True."

"Do you think you can remember all that?"

"Without a doubt." As Ben turned to go, Jaeryn opened his top drawer, and Ben looked back involuntarily. Inside was a tall, tapered candle that had never been lit lying on top of a crisp, recent newspaper. "I haven't read an up-to-date paper. Did they say what happened in Belgium?" Ben asked curiously.

Jaeryn looked up. "The *Daily Telegraph* said there was a moon last night. If it can stop raining over there, we might have a chance to make progress."

"I heard men drowned in the mud." Ben shivered at the thought. "I've never wanted to drown."

"You would, though, if it was the right thing to do. I've known you long enough to know that."

Ben didn't respond to the compliment. All of a sudden, he remembered again that despite Jaeryn's warm welcomes, he was not trustworthy.

The next morning, he escorted Charlotte to the church door and, with more than one stab of guilt, apologized for leaving her there. Swinging the Brownie by its handle strap, Ben set off in a roundabout fashion through town, passing under the great arches of the viaduct on Foord Road and weaving through the streets to avoid detection. The streets were deserted of horses and cabs; every decent Christian was in church. He quickened his pace so he could finish his errand before Emmerson's steward returned for dinner.

He might have attempted an anonymous entrance simply to try his prowess, but Jaeryn had informed Peters of his coming, and he had to use the buzzer instead. The gray-haired butler let him in, as dignified and starched in his tweeds as if he were wearing his black suit at an evening assembly. "You want to see upstairs, I presume, sir?" he said, in his hushed, practiced way.

"Yes, please." Ben followed him up the winding marble stairs, unstrapping the camera and preparing it for action as he went along. "When does the steward come back, Peters?"

"At half past one, sir. You have quite a full hour and a half to yourself if you wish to be gone in plenty of time."

"Well, I have no intention of staying that long. Thank you, Peters. I know my way from here, and I'd best go alone. I won't take anything, I promise you."

Peters continued down the hall. "I'm happy to lead the way, sir. You may take whatever you wish; I have Doctor Graham's instructions."

Ben nodded in acquiescence, though he had no intention of availing himself of the permission. "Doctor Graham and I want to know the identity of Emmerson's inheritor. When is the will to be made public?"

"I'm not aware yet, sir. It was a living trust, and therefore does not go through probate. The will is confidential. Emmerson's steward has been in contact with the necessary people, and he has asked that the household help stay if we are willing to do so. Naturally, none of us have left."

"Do you have any ideas?"

"Nothing substantial, sir." Peters fingered the small gold watch chain that stretched across his waistcoat and disappeared into his pocket.

"Very good, then. I shall pass that along. A good day to you, Peters; I'll see myself out the back door."

He ascended the back staircase up to the third floor, traversed the long hall, and unlocked the door. The room was empty as before; there was the same gold molding with fleur-de-lis trim, the same range of chairs standing sentry on either side. He found the large frame leaning against the wall and removed the maps, systematically taking pictures of them with and without the pins inserted. Then he moved on to the rest of the room. When he found any detail he thought might have a bearing on the case, he captured it and hoped it would develop clearly. He'd never used a camera before, but he hadn't thought it necessary to tell Jaeryn. After all, taking a picture seemed a straightforward process once the tricky bit of inserting the film roll was done.

The cards with the identification numbers were gone. Though he searched high and low between the chair cushions and around the mantle, they were nowhere to be found. As he had been instructed, Ben looked at the maps more closely to see if there were any new places marked. Nathan Speyer was represented now, and so was he, a clear dot at Copt Point with a circle around it and a star. Evidently, his presence was a matter of special import, though why that should be he still had no idea. He could not find any more marks in Folkestone and turned back to the world map. There was a second mark now in Richmond, Virginia: two pinholes side by side. Curious, indeed.

A prickling sensation curled up the back of his neck, and he quickly turned on his heels to look behind him. There was nothing. He chided himself for being paranoid and hurriedly replaced the maps in their frame, doing his best to return them exactly as he found them. Something about this room worried at his mind, but he did not know what it was. He paused to look over it, each detail engraved in his memory from the last time he had been there. Not a thread of carpet looked out of place. At length, he shrugged and gave up. Perhaps the sensation came from nervousness. At any rate, he would have the pictures to look over later. With one last baffled glance, he closed the door and locked it behind him.

It was only quarter to one by the time he descended the central staircase. After opening a few doors and finding nothing to interest him, Ben left by the back door and hurried round to the kitchen entrance. It wouldn't do to have any of the servants see him wandering about, but he wanted to speak to Peters again before he left. He gave the cook his request, and Peters met him on the cobblestone walk leading to the stables.

"What can I do for you, doctor?"

"I'm merely curious, that's all," Ben said. "But would you find out for me why Mr. Emmerson chose a living trust for his will? It's not exactly traditional for a man of his property and estates."

Peters, in his dignified way, looked somewhat concerned. He coughed delicately. "Well, sir, I believe it may have resulted from a disagreement with one of his political acquaintances."

"Colonel King, do you mean?"

Peters coughed again, even more delicately. "No, sir."

"Who, then?"

Peters' expression remained inscrutable. "Matthew Dorroll, sir. He was Mr. Emmerson's private investigator for many years until an unfortunate disagreement caused my late employer to break off their relationship. In thinking over the matter of late, I believe that had a part in the secrecy."

Ben started as if he had felt a knife thrust enter him. "What sort of disagreement?"

"I was not informed, sir. It occurred a month before the announcement of war, and Mr. Dorroll never came back. Mr. Emmerson changed his will to a living trust shortly thereafter."

Fresh proof that his father had reason for placing him in Folkestone. The betrayal ripped into him, leaving a jagged shard of misgiving behind. "Thank you, Peters," he said absently. "I believe that will be all. I'm much obliged to you."

* * *

Jaeryn was home Sunday evening when Ben dropped off the camera and was entirely agreeable to having Charlotte begin helping the following day. He agreed not to expose her to their disagreement when she was present, offering everything from the kitchen to the guest room to make her comfortable. She would be on the busiest street in town when they were out, and therefore not likely to be bothered in any way. Altogether Ben liked the new arrangement, even if it did stick in his throat to ask Jaeryn for a favor.

Charlotte came with him Monday morning, and Ben reintroduced her to Jaeryn before leaving for house calls. From the look of Jaeryn's bloodshot eyes, the Irishman had been up most of the night developing pictures, but in spite of that he welcomed Charlotte with charming courtesy and told her he was pleased to start working with her. When Ben left, they were looking over the medical supplies together.

Monday quickly passed into Tuesday, and Tuesday into Wednesday. Ben hadn't seen Alisa, he hadn't seen Terry, and he hadn't seen Nathan, either. He managed to drop the sovereign off at Ann Meikle's in spite of other customers, as well as a letter he had written directing her to communicate with him in future instead of Jaeryn. But he didn't dare inquire about Emmerson's letter. He was making a mess of things, and he knew it; there weren't enough hours in the day to juggle both his patients and his espionage activities. Jaeryn noticed the patient records piling up undocumented, and after receiving a terse suggestion that he might want to attend to it, Ben worked on them in the evenings to get caught up.

On Wednesday evening, a sleek black automobile pulled up to the clinic just as Ben and Charlotte were leaving for home. The chauffeur leaned his head out the window, and Ben recognized him from the month before. "Colonel King sent me to say that Starlin is ill and needs you right away."

Ben motioned for Charlotte to get in first. "It would be helpful if you could come with me."

She slipped into the seat, and he climbed in after her and slammed the door shut.

"How is he ill?" Charlotte asked.

"I was not told, madam. I was simply ordered to go for the doctor."

While they skimmed through town Ben asked Charlotte, "Are you

263

liking the clinic?"

"Mmm," she said, laying her head on his shoulder.

"I like having you there. At least I know where to go when you write the patient lists."

Charlotte's face crinkled in merriment. "I should charge more for having to read Doctor Graham's handwriting."

"We'd be rich." They laughed together, and he realized how long it had been since he had actually laughed about something.

Upon their arrival at the King residence, Ben turned to Charlotte and said, "Wait here until I talk to his father." The footman placed a chair for her in the hallway and led Ben to Colonel King's private study.

"Ah, you're here at last." King offered his hand in greeting.

Ben shook it. "I'm sorry to hear about Starlin, sir. How is he ill?"

"High fever, began this evening. Or at least, he told us about it this evening. I'm not sure the exact time it started. We noticed him coughing, and it caused him too much pain for him to continue hiding it."

Ben made no effort to disguise his skepticism. "Did he hide the fact, or was he unattended?"

"A bit of both, actually."

"I see."

A hint of defense entered King's voice. "You don't understand. He asked most particularly to be left alone, and he's not a lad to be denied. We sent for you as soon as Starlin's man found something to be amiss."

"Certainly, sir. Please wait here while I examine him, and I will come down to tell you what I find."

He left the study and beckoned Charlotte to follow as he ran up the stairs to Starlin's room. George, the valet, nodded to them at the sitting room door. Starlin lay on his bed, strands of long blond hair sticking to his forehead. They entered just as a coughing fit seized him, interspersed with gasps of pain that he could not hold back.

Ben knelt down beside him. "It's going to be all right, Starlin. I'm here to take a look at you."

"Easy for—" Starlin tried to speak, but he could not finish his sentence.

Charlotte guided him up on the pillows so he could get a deep breath. "Don't talk; you'll irritate your coughing."

"You don't—"

"Starlin, be quiet and obey," Ben said firmly. "When you stop coughing enough to drink, I'm going to give you a painkiller." He felt Starlin's forehead. A light sweat dampened it, and his shirt clung clammily to him. Ben waited patiently until Starlin's coughing relaxed, then dug out the heroin and gave him a spoonful to suppress the cough. After he had examined Starlin's throat and ribs, he sat down and looked the lad in the eyes.

"I don't want you talking much, but I have to ask a few questions, so please keep your answers to a minimum. When did you start feeling ill?"

"Off and on, last night," Starlin mumbled.

"And the coughing spasms, did they start this morning?"

"Yes."

Ben looked skeptical. "So you asked to be left alone instead of telling anyone."

Starlin rolled over and pressed his forehead into his hands. "Would you just leave it alone?"

Ben softened his tone. "You'll be all right."

"It hurts too badly."

He must have been feeling sick indeed to admit that. Ben returned with Charlotte down the red-carpeted staircase to Colonel King's study.

"Well?" the father asked.

"Very likely it's pneumonia from the cracked ribs. I've already treated many cases of it, and it's not uncommon at his age. Only time will tell for sure, but from the symptoms he's describing, I think it's more serious he would like to admit."

Colonel King frowned. "I wonder why he didn't want to tell me."

"Yes, well, I would wonder that as well if I were you," Ben returned. "Forgive me for the observation, Colonel, but from Starlin's stray comments, I suspect that you know your son very little, and he trusts you even less."

King betrayed no sign of anger at his frankness, probably because of Charlotte's presence. The gray eyebrows contracted a mere fraction, but the set of his mouth remained as serene as ever. "You are young to be airing such opinions. How do you suggest treating him?"

"I'll do everything I can, but he'll be in considerable pain from his ribs." Ben thought through the options. "For now, I'll give him medication for the pain, and we'll force fluids and dose him with heroin to try to break up his cough. I'll stay here for the next few hours, if you don't mind, and help him out. But if you can spare your chauffeur to take my wife home, I would be grateful."

Charlotte broke in in a low voice. "I may as well stay with you. We can take turns with him, and you can get some rest that way."

Colonel King bowed to her. "My chauffeur is available whenever you wish to leave. Or, if you both prefer to stay, the guest suite closest to Starlin will be made over for your use."

Ben looked at Charlotte, and she nodded in return. "Thank you, sir; that's kind of you, and we'll take the offer of the room. Now, if you'll excuse us, we must return to your son."

Chapter Sixteen
Love Breaks Trust

Starlin groaned as Ben entered his room two evenings later. "Go away."

"I brought you a glass of water and a couple of pills to take." Starlin shook his head, and Ben coaxed him as best he could until a coughing fit did what words could not. Starlin seized the glass and gulped it down so fast that Ben took it away.

"You'll set yourself to coughing again if you aren't careful," he warned.

"I don't care." Starlin sighed and pushed back his hair with a sweaty hand.

Ben set it down on the coffee table and caught sight of a small wineglass half-hidden behind the bottles. "Did you drink anything while I was out?"

"Enough water to fill the Channel."

"I'm sure. Anything else?"

Starlin's blue eyes narrowed and stared up at him with blunt defiance. "Why?"

Ben reached over and picked up the wineglass. "Circumstantial

267

evidence led me to suspect. Why don't you give me an explanation?"

"I'm too tired," Starlin drawled.

"I think not." Ben let the smile fade from his lips and drew his brows together. "Don't lie to me."

"It's none of your business," the lad flashed back.

A heavy silence filled the room, with not even the ticking of a clock to relieve it. Starlin crossed his arms and shifted as best he could on his own. At last, Ben spoke. "If you drink it again, I will ask someone to watch you and make sure you do not. I can't take the chance of you exacerbating your condition even more. I expressly forbade you to take alcohol."

Starlin's mouth clenched with pain as he slid down flat on the pillow. Then he turned his head away and closed his eyes.

They spent the late evening together as normal, but it lacked the semi-comradeship that had existed before the incident. Starlin spoke as little as possible, and after a few attempts at drawing him out, Ben retired into his own thoughts, only coming out of it to give instructions. He noticed Starlin wearying sooner than usual and helped him to bed at half past ten. Charlotte would be waiting for him to take her home.

The room itself seemed to drowse in its nighttime hush as he turned off the last light but one, and Ben took care to make as little noise as possible. Now that he had a moment to look around without being suspected, he wanted to examine the maps more closely. Jaeryn had suggested that he look around at the King estate since he had the opportunity. He loathed the idea, but when Providence—or mere misfortune, he was not sure which—placed the opportunity in his hands, he had no choice but to do as the Irishman had asked.

The frame holding the map detached from the wall without difficulty, and he removed the map and made sure there was not another in the back. The pins looked innocent enough. A different style than Emmerson's, he found, after pulling one out and examining it. There was no pin marking Dublin, and there were none in America at all. All the same, it made him uneasy. Starlin was surely too young to have a hand in this business. But he was rumored to be intelligent above the average, and Ben knew from experience that the boy kept a close mouth when he took a notion not to reveal anything.

Ben replaced the map, biting his lip as the paper crackled in his hand, and searched through the rest of the room. The drawers in the various tables were almost empty, unlike the jumble that most people collected over the span of sixteen years. One contained a wallet which he took out and opened. The inside pocket held six one-pound notes, a ten-pound note, and some small change, but nothing else of consequence. He even opened the violin case to see if Starlin had hidden something under the precious instrument. The strings gave off a soft thrum when he brushed against them, and he pressed his hand on them to still the sound. Nothing appeared there, either.

Then he heard a soft sound in the hall.

Ben reached over and turned off the last lamp, sinking down to the floor in the corner so as not to be at eye level. There was no sound, but he could see a faint light diffuse into the room as a presence passed through the door. His finger brushed the handle of his Webley, and holding his breath, he strained his eyes wide in the darkness. It was a man; he knew that much by the close-cropped silhouette of the head. When the intruder passed by a mirror on the wall, Ben had just enough light from the reflection to catch the shadowy outline of Stafford, clad in a light dressing gown.

Ben bit his lip, trying to quiet his breathing. The butler stooped over something, and then the click of the door latch sounded again and Ben knew he had gone out. After a moment of listening, he crept to the door and peeked out. A glow emanated from the lower level as if a room beneath was brightly lit, and Stafford passed down the stairs.

Ben flipped a light on and checked the time on his wristwatch. The clock hands read ten to midnight.

Nothing had disappeared from the coffee table. He hadn't heard Stafford open a drawer. Starlin's robe lay draped over the sofa, and on a moment of impulse Ben reached inside the pocket. Down at the bottom he felt a sharp edge of paper and pulled it out. It was death threat against Starlin.

A surge of anger swept over him as he read it. With Starlin's lungs in their current condition, smothering—or any other method, for that matter—would take little effort. And no one would be the wiser. He debated whether to return to Copt Point or keep watch for the rest of the night where he was. He must tell the boy's father, or better yet, Starlin himself, to put him on his guard. But either course of action held a terrible risk. Stafford might be acting at King's instigation. If the colonel was innocent and something happened, Ben would be in a sorry mess, but if that was not the case and he revealed his knowledge, King would have the advantage. He would wait to ask Jaeryn and see what was best to be done. Nothing was likely to happen tonight, at least. Ben smoothed the paper out and placed it in his wallet for safekeeping.

Someone was talking in the other room, not even bothering to whisper, and he opened the door to find out whom.

"Starlin?" he whispered.

"Not if all…it. Told him—"

Starlin lay in the big walnut four-poster, the sheets twisted around his body and clinging to him, damp with sweat. His eyes were closed, but his lips moved in a steady muttering of pointless phrases. Ben knelt beside the bed and touched his shoulder. "Starlin, are you all right?"

Eyes bleared with sleep opened on him in puzzled recognition. Ben pulled the boy up on the pillows and inserted a thermometer into his mouth. "I think you're running a fever. I'm going to take your temperature." Starlin's eyes were dull, and when Ben looked at the mercury level, it had risen to one hundred and two. "Here. Lie back down again," he said gently. Starlin obeyed without a murmur, and his eyes drifted shut again. The boy wouldn't remember what had happened the next morning, but Ben knew he could give him some relief. Medication would bring his temperature down, and a cold compress might help—if he was willing to betray his presence to

Stafford. In this instance, surely being a good doctor trumped being a good agent. Ben pulled the bell-rope that rang the servant's hall, and George answered the summons a few moments later in a rumpled shirt and trousers.

Ben issued orders as he pulled out the aspirin. "Wake Colonel King, please, and tell him his son is worse. Then send up ice water and towels. Be quick."

George shook his head. "Colonel King left at ten this evening on business, sir. He won't be back until dinnertime tomorrow."

"Never mind, then." Ben rolled his eyes. "Communication seems to be a commodity of little value in this house."

"Sir," Starlin's valet replied noncommittally and hastened to obey his instructions.

* * *

Ben stayed the rest of the night, for it was morning before Starlin's fever broke. Even then, the lad remained exhausted in his room, and Ben left before breakfast, confident that his patient would sleep most of the day. He stopped by Copt Point to pick Charlotte up and explained his absence to her while helping himself to the coffee and oatmeal kept warm on the back of the stove. She had dark circles under her eyes, and he inwardly berated himself for leaving her without any word from him.

"Darling?" she said, as she waited for him to finish eating. "I have something to tell you."

"Tell away, then." Ben clattered the dishes into the sink and left them for later. In spite of his attempt at cheeriness, he was beginning to dislike people telling him things. Nothing good ever came of it.

"When Doctor Graham was out yesterday, I couldn't find something I needed, so I searched through his drawers. There was a box of death threats there that I couldn't help seeing. I won't speak of it to anyone, but I thought you ought to know that I had seen them."

Ben frowned. It wasn't like Jaeryn to leave the drawer unlocked.

271

"I know of them. Thank you for telling me." He was going to add that she ought not trouble herself over what she had seen, but deciding that the reassurance would be pointless as well as an outright lie, he left it unspoken. He slipped a clean necktie around his collar and folded it in place. "Did you see anything else?"

Charlotte shook her head. "I didn't look much. They were all papers, and I wasn't looking for papers."

"I suppose it's better that you didn't." Ben picked up his bag of supplies. "Are you ready? I'm going to drop you off and then stop by the hospital and see how Terry's doing."

He left her at the clinic door and continued alone through the early morning streets to the Royal Victoria. As he entered the men's ward, he saw Terry sitting up on the edge of the bed, his fingers resting firmly on the head rail. A white-capped young woman moved in haste up the neat rows of beds with a reproving look on her face. Terry was clean-shaven today, though his hair waved as unruly as ever, and in his eyes, Ben read something he had seen before: the look of a strong man cornered, trapped, subjected to a confinement both unfamiliar and unwanted. It must be hard on him, for there was no trace of the cheery grin on his face at the moment.

The nurse reached Terry and laid a hand on his shoulder. "Why don't you lie down again, Mr. O'Sean. What can I do for you?"

Terry gripped the metal headboard to keep himself upright. "I think I'll die if I don't leave this place."

"No, you won't." She freshened up his pillows and patted them invitingly. "You're here to get better, not to die, and you can't get better if you leave now."

In the ten days of his stay, Terry had lost all his color, and after the effort of sitting up, he looked utterly drained. "I'll pay my bills if you'll just let me out of here. Come to think of it, how much is this costing me, anyway?"

"Your expenses are being taken care of by a friend. Now lie down again and try to sleep."

He resisted her efforts to persuade him. "I want to sit up. I've been lying down for days on end."

"No, no." She gave him a pretty smile. "No complaining from a strong man like you."

"Strong?" Terry took hold of her wrist and moved it off his shoulder. "If you really believed that, you'd let me sit up. You'd let me leave. I'll kill myself if you don't let me go, I swear I will."

"Calm down, please." She tried to free her wrist, but he would not let go. "Let go of me and lie down this minute."

Ben hurried forward to help her. "Hello, Terry."

Terry looked up and a smile spread across his face, his grip relaxing long enough for the nurse to extricate herself. Ben nodded to her, and she left Terry in his hands with a grateful look, for she knew both him and Jaeryn by sight.

Ben pulled up a chair and leaned forward, his hands clasped over his knees. "Are you ready to stop being stubborn and lie down again?"

"They just stitched me together this morning." Terry gripped the metal headboard and pulled his legs up into the bed, thumping the pillow as he resumed his old position on his side. Ben couldn't help feeling amused at the resentment on his face.

"Terry, that wasn't a good idea. You could have hurt yourself."

"I think it was." A rush of pleasure swept over Terry's face, and he closed his eyes, savoring the memory. "I haven't felt something hard in days. This is an awful coddle-trap, and I've had enough to last me for the rest of my time. How's Pearlie?"

Ben didn't like to offer much information on that subject, but he couldn't refuse Terry something. "Quite well, thank you. And she was sorry to hear of your accident."

"She was?" The lines around Terry's mouth tightened, and he gripped the edge of his sheet a moment before continuing. "I hope you didn't worry her. I wouldn't want that. How's the kid I mixed it up with?"

Ben saw Terry's left hand reaching toward the place where his wound was and gave him a warning glance. "You prevented him from getting into more mischief, at any rate. He has a couple of cracked ribs to thank you for and pneumonia on top of that. He's been paying for his sins just like you."

"Oh." Terry's voice faded. "I didn't mean to hurt him that much." He paused for a moment, then said, "Do you still have that ring I gave you?"

He caught sight of Terry's other hand, palm upward, the fingers slowly falling from their clenched position. "It's safe. Is something wrong, Terry? You don't look quite yourself."

"Get it back from her after you've shown it to her. I want you to keep it until I—until I— ask for you."

"Until you ask for me? Don't you mean until you ask for the ring?"

"I—I can't see straight."

Ben saw a red trickle staining the white hospital gown. "You're bleeding. I'll go for help."

Terry looked down, and a faint hint of amusement mixed with a healthy dose of anxiety spread across his face. "I guess sitting up was a mistake. Don't call that starched-up little paragon. I'm sorry, I mean—never mind. Tell me good-bye and mention it when you leave."

Just as he stood and was about to hurry off, Terry reached out, groping for a support, and latched on to his sleeve. He muttered that the world was spinning and he wished it would slow down.

"I need help right now," Ben yelled. Several of the patients turned Terry's way, and even those who couldn't turn pricked up their ears. A nurse came to the doorway. "It's Terry, isn't it?" She shook her head half-amusedly, half-impatiently. "I'll get help."

"Hurry," Ben called after her. Terry's eyes were dilated, and in spite of the strong grip of his fingers, Ben saw his eyelids drooping as if they were too heavy to hold up anymore. "Stay awake, Terry." Evidently, Terry didn't hear him, for he paid no regard to the request. His hand loosened its hold just as a doctor and two nurses holding suture equipment pushed Ben out of the way. He only had time to hear "fool" whispered once before he left to give them room for their work.

The carefully-made progress was lost now. He didn't need to be involved in the case to know that. Terry's moment of gratification had been dearly bought, for the window of infection he had passed was now reopened, and the torn tissue would have to re-knit. Likely the surgeon would take out the stitches the nurse had put in and leave it an open wound until it healed better. Hopefully, he would recover as well as the time before.

As he exited the room, Ben heard a reproachful voice and a penitent one mingled and was relieved to know that Terry had come around so quickly. In spite of his exasperation, he could not prevent a twitch of laughter from crossing his lips.

* * *

On his rounds later that morning, Ben stopped to make way for a detachment of soldiers departing Folkestone for France. The sober, perfect ranks cast his mind back to Nathan Speyer's grudging expression of loyalty to his country. He wondered if Nathan had left for the front, but it didn't seem likely, as Starlin hadn't mentioned it. Come to think of it, Nathan hadn't been told of Starlin's illness. Determining to put off a more disagreeable errand at Alisa's, Ben set off on Terry's bicycle for the northeastern portion of the farming district, making good time to Nathan's ramshackle house. In the noon brightness, the house looked even more derelict, and the long grass was already going to seed.

When he knocked, Nathan's voice came from an upstairs window, though his face was not visible from any of them. "What's wanted?"

"It's Dailey."

"I'll be down in a minute. You can come in, doctor."

Ben opened the door and waited near the entrance, adjusting to the dim light after the muted brightness of an English summer sun.

275

Nathan came halfway down the stairs and gave him a quizzical glance from under his dark eyebrows.

"I wanted to know if you had left," Ben said, not bothering with a formal greeting. "I saw soldiers leaving this morning and thought of you."

"I saw them too." Nathan resting his elbows on the stair rail. "I leave from Dover. One more week and then I'll be gone for good."

"Would you like to see Starlin before you go?"

Nathan's eyes brightened at the mention of Starlin's name. "If he would like to see me. He hasn't come around in a while."

"He's been ill with pneumonia."

"I'm sorry he's been sick. It's a rather confining feeling when your time is someone else's, isn't it?"

Ben was taken aback at the rare moment of confidence. "You and I both know." He took care to keep his face empty of expression. "Unlike Starlin."

"Unlike Starlin." Nathan came down the rest of the stairs and crossed his arms, leaning against the bottom post.

It was his last chance to talk to the young man, and Ben decided to take advantage of the opportunity. "Tell me. Starlin never talks about his education, and though I hear he's going to Cambridge this fall, his father hasn't mentioned it. He was taken out of boarding school once upon a time, wasn't he?"

Nathan nodded. "He went to boarding school when he was young, but he wanted to learn faster than they liked, which caused trouble. His father secured a private tutor for him, and he applied himself quite diligently until he finished last summer." The sunlight that managed to filter in between the curtains cast a delicate shade on Nathan's face, washing it out pale between the shadows. "With his temperament, he'll be perfect for Parliament one day. I presume that's what his father intends him for. Until then, he waits."

"That seems a waste of time considering his talents."

Nathan gave a smooth, easy smile. "But it's not our opinion that counts, is it, doctor?"

Ben eyed him, trying to read his meaning. "I suppose not."

Nathan hesitated a moment as if he wanted to say more, but whatever the source of his reluctance, it was too strong for him to overcome. Neither offered to speak until the silence stretched to embarrassment. Ben offered his hand. "I will bid you good-bye then, Mr. Speyer, as I doubt we shall see each other again before you leave. If you would like to visit Starlin, he's available in the evenings."

Nathan gripped his hand heartily. "I am sorry that I am not, then. He's a fine boy, and you're of service to him in more than his health. I am honored to have met you."

When Ben stood outside and saw that he didn't have another patient call for a half hour, he realized there was nothing to do but face what he had been avoiding. Five minutes later, Alisa gave him a seat in her living room and offered him tea. He declined it. Then, without asking, she handed him her little boy, her blue eyes dancing, and sat down in the chair beside him. Matthew sat on his lap with a doubled-up fist crammed into his mouth, staring straight ahead with round, wondering eyes. But he didn't cry.

Alisa smiled. "See? He doesn't dislike you."

Ben eyed him rather warily. "He's a handsome baby, Mrs. Dorroll. You haven't heard anything about your husband, have you?"

"No." Alisa shook her head and twined her fingers together.

"I'm sorry to hear that. I know the waiting must be difficult for you."

"Everyone must wait in these times, doctor. It isn't the waiting, it's the wondering." Her hair hung down her back in a braid today, a bit wispy here and there, and she looked small compared to the troubles she faced.

"Wondering about…?"

"Whether he will decide to return."

"He has every reason to. Surely nothing but new duties or illness could keep him away."

Alisa raised her chin, and her eyes held disapproval that at first he imagined was for him. "I will love him as long as I live, doctor, but he could have written or asked someone to write for him in all this time."

Ben opened his lips, but no words came.

One of Matthew's knitted shoes fell off his foot. Alisa reached down for it and fitted it back on again. "I do not know how I will ever be a father as well as a mother to my baby if Edmond decides not to come back."

Matthew whimpered in response to the raw hurt in her tone, and she rubbed her finger down his chubby arm to soothe him. Ben looked down and pressed his lips together. If Edmond did not come back, then he must make it up to her somehow. "You will be taken care of, Mrs. Dorroll, never fear. I have connections. I will make some inquiries again."

"You are kind, doctor." She smiled faintly.

"I have every reason to be, and I hope to God that what you fear doesn't happen." Ben took a firm hold of Matthew Benjamin and handed him back. "Now, if you don't mind, I would like to speak to Pearl alone for a moment."

Pearl came in with a flush of pleasure on her face, willing and eager, completely unsuspecting of his intentions. She wore a light blue waist with her serviceable brown skirt and looked charming with her honey-blonde curls half covering her shoulders. Her eyes quickly took in his expression, and the smile turned to one of uncertainty. He offered a thin one in return.

"What is it?" she asked, a trace of uneasiness in her tone.

"I've come to tell you something." Ben paused, lips parted, praying desperately for his request not to hurt her as much as he knew it would. "You may think that I have little right to say it, but I must try. You are underage, and it is my duty to protect you."

"What is it?" She stood with her small shoulders erect and braced for she knew not what. Ben steeled himself and plunged in.

"Before Terry was shot he came here every day, and you and he were together a good deal. Those around you, including myself, should have paid more attention. But I am not blind to the fact that you seem to enjoy his company. Is it true that you have feelings for him?"

Her eyes were averted from his face now, and he worried that she had shut her heart to him. He knew her answer by her silence. "You must not love Terry, Pearl. It isn't right that you should."

Pearl's chin quivered, and she looked up at him with a steady, clear gaze. "Why? He's a good man."

"I have no doubt he's perfectly safe as far as good intentions go, but you know that's not enough. No, wait"—as she opened her mouth to interrupt. "I don't expect you to marry a saint. Goodness knows you won't find one. You may be able to offer your love to him one day, but if you have any desire to find happiness for yourself or him, then you must hold back. He's under a political cloud right now, and until you have proof that he's not in trouble with the law, he is dangerous to you." Ben reached out to touch her arm, but she drew back, and he did not force his reassurance upon her. "Do you understand, Pearlie?" He had intended to order her to put all thoughts of Terry out of her head, but brought face to face with her he softened his words. "I ask you to wait, that's all. Will you do that?"

She lifted her chin resolutely and held back her tears. "I don't think you have a right to ask me. But I will—if you wish it."

He almost wished she would protest instead of taking his request like a piece of unwilling property. "Thank you, Pearlie. I'm sorry."

"It's no matter," she lied, with a false brightness that deceived neither of them. "If you'll excuse me, I believe I have a—a headache."

Ben stood alone after she had left. He had brought her to Folkestone and placed her in the way of love. And she had found it and embraced it and treasured life the more for it. Now he had taken love away from her, and he hated himself.

* * *

By August twenty-third, Ben had a spare afternoon to buy a train

279

ticket to Dover and visit Terry's sister. Starlin was well enough to be left alone for a day, so he put Terry's ring on his finger, promised Charlotte that he would be back by evening, and set off.

The tracks traveled south along the Lower Sandgate Road, giving him a view of the beach and pier below as they passed. He saw the Channel only for a moment before the track curved inland again, but a glimpse was enough to catch the warlike strength of a freighter bound for Calais and the silver-sheened waves tumbling into whitecaps. Ben sat for the whole ride by the smudged window, the clack and steam of the train wheels making the perfect accompaniment to the day. The clouds turned to rain after a half hour or so, and a foggy mist shrouded the fields and twisted about the tree trunks, but in the peaceful heat of the train car, it was no less a pleasure than sunshine would have been.

When Ben entered the busy station at the end of his journey, he hailed a cab and pulled out Erin Reinhardt's letter to Terry for directions. The driver took him to a brick townhouse with white-mullioned windows. As Ben knocked on the low black door, a small, dark-haired boy peeped around the edge of Erin's curtains, his nose pressed against the glass.

A light flashed on in the front window and footsteps hastened toward the door. When it opened, he saw a young woman with soft, red-gold hair piled up on her head. Her blue eyes looked as big and alive as Terry's, but where his held a spark of laughter, hers held a shimmer he could not identify. She stood almost tall as he did, but because of her light-boned frame, she seemed much smaller than she was. On seeing a strange man, she almost closed the door before he could speak.

Ben slipped the ring off his finger and held it out. "I am Benjamin Dailey. Terry sent me."

A spark of recognition entered her eyes when she saw the ring, but she kept the door almost closed. "Who are you?" she demanded. There was no trace of an Irish accent in her voice, unlike Terry, and Ben wondered what had made her move away from home.

"I'm a doctor over in Folkestone. Terry asked me to come for him since he couldn't come himself."

Two little hands gripped Erin Reinhardt's leg, crushing the skirt of her light blue housedress. The boy Ben had seen at the window looked up at him from behind the protection of her figure. Erin pulled away, and he crammed three fingers in his mouth for comfort now that his protection was gone. Erin's eyes hardened with suspicion. "I thought Doctor Jaeryn Graham practiced in Folkestone."

Ben nodded. "He does, but I'm his assistant. Terry gave me his ring as an introduction."

She held out her hand, and he placed the sapphire band in it. She turned it around, examining it, and then slipped it on her empty ring finger. "I've been the victim of lies before, doctor."

"I know. I am truly sorry."

"What do you propose to do about it?" Her voice tautened, and a twist of mockery played around her mouth. "You must be an amazing rescuer, or Terry wouldn't have sent you."

He ignored her anger and kept his voice steady and matter-of-fact. "May I come in for a moment?"

She shrugged. "If you wish."

Ben ducked through the doorway. After closing the door, Erin led him to a small, white-painted sitting room. The boy followed and crouched on the rug at his mother's feet.

"Is this your son?" Ben asked.

"Yes. His name is Brogan."

Brogan looked up at him with wide, dark eyes and hair almost inky black. He did not resemble his mother at all in his face or features, and Ben could only guess that the boy bore a striking resemblance to his father.

Ben set down his medical bag. "What kind of assistance did Terry want you to have? Medical or monetary or moral support?"

"I need no medical assistance, and I need no money. I wouldn't take any of his." Erin's expression softened as she mentioned her brother's name. "He only sent you here because I was weak enough to ask for pity. I regretted it after I posted the letter."

He sensed that reasoning would go further with her than comfort. "I haven't known Terry long, Mrs. Reinhardt, but even in our short acquaintance I can see he has an unquenchable love for life."

"Yes." She ground the word out as if she resented it.

"And your child holds that heritage as much as—or more than— he holds the heritage of German cruelty. I think Providence has a way of balancing evil with good in time. Much good can come from Brogan."

"You may believe so, but many would disagree with you."

"Then many are wrong." He took a stronger hand now that his suspicions were confirmed as to the kind of woman he had to reckon with. "The idea that culture and country determine virtue is a misguided one. You should not live under the shame of that ignorant judgment."

Brogan looked from one to the other as if trying to process what his mother and the stranger were talking about, but he did not seem to comprehend the object of their discussion.

Erin looked down at the toddler. "Then I share their ignorant judgment. I believe the Germans are wicked to the core. I took off my wedding ring the moment that man left this house. Since then, I've born the false disgrace along with the true. I am strong enough to take it."

"I would suggest that you return your ring to its usual place. You don't need the added censure of people's misunderstanding. Or, if you prefer, I can make arrangements for you to live in Folkestone, where your story is not known."

"Let people think what they will. I will never wear his ring again."

Ben looked down at the slender band of gold around his own finger and winced at the thought of Charlotte taking hers off as easily as Erin had done. "I think you would be more at ease wearing it."

She shifted impatiently. "You don't understand my situation. Please don't make it more difficult by offering uninformed advice.

You mean well, I know, but I don't think you are fit to judge what would ease my mind."

In the long silence that followed, she waited in triumph for his reply while he struggled for an answer. He could not give one without talking about himself more than he wished to, but neither could he remain silent if he wished to heal an ounce of this young woman's burden. Terry wanted him to try, and that, after all, was why he had come. "I have known the pain of rejection," he said carefully, "but unlike you, I have never known the pain of rejecting others. Someone I knew left me just as your husband left you. That person in my life never wanted to come back, while your husband, from what I understand, loves you with all his heart and soul. Don't throw that love away. Life without it is a lonely thing."

Erin smiled condescendingly. "My husband does not love me. He loves Germany."

Another silence followed, in which she sat with her chin leaning on her hand. Ben watched her bright, dry eyes gazing into space, and realized that hers would be a longer struggle than a few words of persuasion could end.

"Will you come back with me?" he pleaded. "Terry is ill and could use someone to care for him. He was shot two weeks ago, and though he is recovering, he is still in some danger. I will find you a place to stay if you will come."

She shook her head. "No. I will not come."

"Away from this place, perhaps you could look at your situation more clearly—"

"I will not come."

In spite of the news of Terry's accident, she neither cried nor looked remotely worried. Her misfortunes seemed to have drained her sensibility to further trouble. Ben felt a deep pity for the beautiful woman. Terry was so full of life—it seemed strange that someone so closely related to him should not share the same passion. But in spite of his continued persuasions and offers of help, Erin would not listen. She would consider leaving, she conceded, if she could not find work to support herself before the month was out. There was nothing left to do but ask for Terry's ring back and find a cab to take him to the station.

As he boarded the train, the thought occurred to him that perhaps his mother had felt like Erin twenty years ago when she left England.

* * *

Ann Meikle's shop was empty and near closing time when Ben returned from Dover, but he was determined to take care of his long-delayed errand despite the lateness of the hour. There were no customers there, thank heaven. He did not know what she would say to him, and he liked to have her alone lest she throw out one of those odd statements of hers that ruined his presence of mind.

"All right, laddie," she said pleasantly, as the tinkle of the bell announced his presence. "There's two letters for ye." She passed them across the counter, and Ben put them in his coat. "I have some stamps if ye want to lay in a store before the price goes up."

"Not today. I've come to talk to you." He slung his medical bag on the counter and stretched to loosen the tightness in his muscles from sitting in the train all afternoon. "Any news yet about that sovereign I gave you?"

Mrs. Meikle gave a throaty chuckle. "Nothing at all. Even Fenton's not turning up anything about Speyer this time. He's traced the mother, but not the son. She was born and raised in Dover and met her man on his vacation from university. The lad's grandparents are still living over in Cornwall, but they don't know anything out of the ordinary about the lad. They saw his family last Christmas, and Speyer's father got shipped off to the front in January."

Ben felt a tremor of misgiving again at meddling with Speyer against Ryson's orders. At least Jaeryn would be pleased with the information. "That's helpful. Tell Fenton to keep looking, please. We could put anything to use."

"Sure, laddie."

He turned to the more important subject that Jaeryn wanted to know about. "I dropped in tonight because Graham wants to know if you remember a letter. It was in January, and he says you were here then. Do you remember anything coming from Germany for Mr. Emmerson about a bank account? It was dated this year."

A flinty spark entered Ann Meikle's eyes "I've been waiting for ye to ask that question. I might."

Ben leaned his hands on the counter and injected a hint of sternness into his voice. "Suppose you tell me what you remember."

Her eyes lost not a fraction of their mutiny, but, all the same, she managed to produce a measure of honesty. "It came from America, laddie, not Germany. The bank account was German. The letter was American."

"Why didn't you mention it earlier?"

"Some things are only worth mentioning if ye have someone ye can trust." She jabbed her finger into the counter, and he drew back and clenched his hands. "Remember that."

The tinkling of the telegraph bell interrupted them. Ben watched her translate the whirring clicks into words and place the message in an envelope, then lay it aside. She came back, fixing him with her sharp little eyes. "I have something to tell ye. Will ye be secret?"

He felt like he was standing on a city street watching a German bi-plane circle over his head. "Of course."

She pressed her advantage. "And what will ye swear on?"

"I swear on nothing. But I'll give you my word, and until I came here, I had a reputation for honesty."

"Ye mustn't tell yer doctor friend. Promise that, and it's yers." Mrs. Meikle watched the indecision spread over his face and finished her conditions. "I'll not give ye another chance. And if ye don't take it, I have something which could be the end of him here. I don't think ye want to be looking after this job yerself, do ye, laddie?"

"No." If only there was more light in her shop to judge her countenance by.

"What's yer answer, then?"

Ben clenched his hand until he could see the indent of each nail in his palm. "You'll give it to me if you know what is to your benefit," he said at length.

"I'm not such a fool as that. Take it or leave it, laddie. It's your choice. Or if ye'd prefer not to commit yerself, I can give ye a wee peek at it while ye decide."

Ben grasped at the chance. "I'd like to see it, please."

Her gnarled fingers reached into her apron pocket. "And what price would ye be offering?"

"You aren't doing your reputation any favors, Mrs. Meikle. I suggest you turn it over without protest."

She crossed her arms. The trump card had changed hands. "No, laddie. Not without a proper return."

Jaeryn had ordered him not to bribe any agents. But Jaeryn was not here to judge the matter, and of the various compromises presented, this one looked promising. Ben took out a crumpled five-pound note and gave it to her. "That's all I can give you."

"It's sufficient." She pulled out a piece of folded stationary from her pocket. "There, now. Cast your eyes on this. I got it back in May and held it secret until the right moment."

It was a heavy piece of cream letter paper, woven to withstand years of lying in a drawer. But for all its durability there was a slight fuzzy fray along the side, and the corners had lines across them, showing that they had been bent on more than one occasion. The message was written in a strong, spiky black, but there was no date and no salutation.

I have word that I am not long for this world. The new doctor who gave me the verdict tells me that my end will be an unexpected one: perhaps days, perhaps weeks, perhaps months away. We have worked long together, you and I, and you have been a good man for our cause. I will not leave you on your own and am already preparing my replacement. The person I have chosen will direct you with a greater spirit and intelligence than myself, I think. Curb zeal if it threatens to be detrimental. You must supply the steadiness that will be lacking when I am gone.

Keep a careful watch. We are laid by the heels, and I cannot flatter myself that our research will be unimpeded for long. I have never taken the strongest measures possible, for I know from experience that moderation is a better cover than hasty violence. But you may see differently, and you must act according to your lights.

I will meet my end with all the tranquility with which I have lived my life thus far. What my next existence may be I cannot pretend to guess. But if I have one wish left, it is that somehow I may be able to enjoy the full results of the plan I have set in motion. I have already put in a good word for you with my replacement. Be loyal; our cause is a just one, and you will not go unrewarded. Indeed, if I owe anything to anyone, I believe it is to you.

Ben tried to keep it, but Ann Meikle was too quick for him and snatched it away. "No, no. That's not for ye to take home unless you'll agree to break with Jaeryn Graham."

Ben reached out his hand in a powerless plea for her to change her mind. "I have no intention of breaking with him. I'll buy it."

"It's not for sale. You've seen it, and that's all ye're getting, unless you'll see sense and agree that he wrongly accused me."

He knew without a doubt that this was something from Emmerson—it had the same writing as the message asking him to come to the library all those months ago—but without reading through it again, he would not be able to learn from it all he needed to know. Besides, they needed it in their hands as a physical piece of evidence. "How did you find it?"

Ann Meikle smiled sweetly. "That's my secret, laddie. I'm a canny woman, and I'll have ye know that many secrets pass through my hands, including some of yers. So do with yer knowledge what ye like, but that's all ye deserve today, and that's all I'm giving ye."

"I could force it from you."

"Ye could. But you and yer doctor friend would be much better off if ye didn't. Now out. It's time to close up."

"Close up, then, and I'll wait to talk to you."

"If you don't get out of my shop, I'll call the constables on ye, and then ye'll have a fine time explaining that one without making London angry. Jaeryn Graham suspects me wrongly, and I'll not help him anymore."

"You must admit he has good reason."

"He'll regret what he's done. Out." She pushed him to the door and slammed it after him, bolting it with a malicious rattle.

He did not enjoy the prospect of admitting to Jaeryn that he had been wrong about her. This time he did not think Jaeryn would enjoy the knowledge either.

* * *

Charlotte was not in the examining room when he reached the clinic, and when he inquired, Jaeryn told him that she had left for the evening. "She asked me to take her to Alisa Dorroll's." Jaeryn's voice lilted thickly, as it did whenever he felt tired or abstracted, and his mouth had a stern set to it.

"Is something the matter?"

Jaeryn shook his head. "It's nothing. At least, it shouldn't be. Ryson wants you in London. He says he wants you alone, and you should go tomorrow."

"Why?" The muscles in his throat tensed. It didn't seem like Jaeryn to be disturbed over such a small request.

Jaeryn, too, looked uneasy behind the eyes. "That's what you're going to find out. What were you doing today? Charlotte said you were in Dover."

Since Jaeryn couldn't help the situation, Ben determined not to reveal any more of it than he could manage. "I was. Just a business trip; nothing to do with our work here."

"I see." Jaeryn didn't press the point. "I went to Emmerson's while you were gone. I wanted to get fingerprints from the room for future reference. You wouldn't object to me taking yours?"

Ben thought it of little use to protest. He silently inked his fingers and pressed them on the paper Jaeryn offered. Jaeryn scrawled his name at the top—his real name—and laid it aside to dry. He saw Ben's face and looked at it more closely. With a sharp exclamation, he tore off the top and rewrote the alias.

Ben took the scrap and tore it to bits. "What has happened?"

"It's nothing. A fluke incident, I'm sure of it." But Jaeryn's lips parted in indecision, and at length he gave in. "Oh, very well. While I was up in Emmerson's room, I took the maps down to look at them. They've been switched out for new ones. There's not a mark nor a blemish to be found on either of them."

Ben frowned. "Like you say, it could just be a precaution."

They looked at each other, and Jaeryn said, "But it isn't."

"Then evidently they're following our train of thought, and they know what we're doing." He told Jaeryn what had happened at Ann Meikle's, and Jaeryn made him write down as much of the letter as he remembered, which was more than he thought possible but not nearly enough to satisfy either of them.

Ben handed over his efforts after he had dredged his memory for the last detail he could call to mind. "I don't know what possessed her to show it to me."

"Who knows? She's unpredictable at best. Anything could set her off. Maybe she wanted to make us think she was on our side again."

"She did a pretty poor job if she was trying to convince us. We could pretend we believe her."

Jaeryn's eyes narrowed. "I doubt she'd fall for a ploy like that. I'm not about to let her into our confidence again. She had her chance, and she lost it. What do you think the letter means?"

"I think it was written to someone who was close to Emmerson. Not the person who would be taking over leadership, but someone he worked with and trusted. I think he wrote it after you took the key and he knew he had been discovered. I don't know to whom."

"Blast." Jaeryn frowned. "We'd be best off severing connections with Ann Meikle, but try once more to get an explanation about the letter before you do. Offer her any incentive within reason."

After that, Ben didn't think Jaeryn knew that he was in the room anymore. He left the loan payment he had brought with him on Jaeryn's desk for him to find later. Then he went out and hailed a cab to take him to Alisa's.

It was too dark to take Charlotte home by foot, but she was sorry he had to resort to paying for the cab. "It's no matter." Ben ushered her into the back seat, which was pitch black without the headlights on. "We'll be getting next month's money soon, and I have enough until then to spare for one cab ride."

When they reached home, he told her about Pearl and Terry and asked her if he had done right. She could not disagree with him, but the hurt of it showed on both their faces, especially after he told her of Terry's relapse.

It wasn't until he had hung up his coat in preparation for going to bed that Ben felt the envelopes in his pocket. He reached in to find the letters Ann Meikle had given him. The one from Mrs. O'Sean he saved out. The other, from Edmond, he tore into immediately.

Little Brother,

At last my luck is beginning to turn. They've let me out, and I'm in America to find some peace away from the front. I never know where I'm going from one day to the next, but write to me and send your letters to our mother. If I have the strength of mind and she hasn't burned them by the time I come, I'll pick up your replies when I pass through Richmond.

Tell Alisa I think of her. Haven't wrapped my mind around the fact that I'm a father yet, so can't say I think often of the baby, but you needn't mention that. I'm glad to be done with this awful war. The nightmares aren't any better. No doubt I'll pull though in time. I'm sure you think I'm slacking while all the rest of you work to keep the Huns at bay, but I hope you won't look down on me too much. You always were the good one of the family, if I recall correctly.

My train is leaving, and I must post this, so I have no time to tell you of a piece of good fortune that just came my way. But I'll write again, you may be sure of it, as soon as I get the chance.

Edmond

Chapter Seventeen
The Cost of Betrayal

Ben told Charlotte he had to go to London, and he left at seven on August twenty-fourth to catch the morning train. He had not gone far when he caught sight of a dark-headed figure on the road. It was Jaeryn.

Ben wondered what could possibly be more important to him than a few extra minutes of sleep. Whatever had disturbed Jaeryn the night before must be gone, for he looked quite satisfied with the world, and he wore a gray knitted sweater which gave him an air of casual comfort.

"I didn't know you had taken to morning walks before opening the clinic," Ben remarked as they came up with each other.

Jaeryn turned and fell in alongside him. "I wanted to see you before you left." He strolled along with good-humored ease, forcing Ben to relax his pace. "In general, I detest morning walks. I don't know why Ryson wants to see you today, but you have my permission to tell him I have complete faith in your abilities."

"I'm obliged to you."

"No, you aren't." Jaeryn laughed. "But sometimes, Dorroll, you

291

need help beyond your own efforts, and today may be one of those days. You're an eloquent fellow on occasion, and I'm sure the talent will come in good stead with Ryson. Do be agreeable."

Ben wanted to say that he had no intention of being otherwise, but he bit back the words. "Of course."

"Anyway, that wasn't the main thing I came to tell you. Charlotte will be alone at the clinic today if you've no objection; I'm leaving on a short business trip this afternoon, and I won't be back until Monday. But I'll walk her into town so she's not alone. She needn't come back to Copt Point either, if you like. The guest room is available for both of you to use while I'm gone."

"Thank you very much."

A strange look of pleasure spread across Jaeryn's face before he averted his eyes back to the Channel. "I found the money you left last night. You needn't have returned it so soon. I wouldn't want you to be in any difficulty."

"It was no matter. I wondered if you would mind checking in on Starlin today before I come home. I hate to leave him for the entire day."

"Of course. I'd be glad to."

Jaeryn looked eager to continue the conversation, but Ben contented himself with saying "I'm obliged to you" again, rather coolly, and they pursued their way in silence until their roads diverged.

* * *

As Ben waited to board the train to London, he temporarily forgot about Ryson's summons in thinking about his father. He planned to attend to his business and return to Folkestone by evening, but he had recollected the night before that since his father lived in London, it might be his duty after recent developments to attempt seeing him. Now that he had proof of his father's involvement, it would be foolish not to talk to him. He ought at least to try a phone call. Before he boarded the train, Ben decided to send a telegram telling his father where he was and offering to meet him at a café.

He wasn't sure that he wanted to see his father any more. A faint remembrance of a bronzed, brown-haired man standing on the dock while the Liverpool steamer pulled away was all he had from his babyhood. Even that had not been a long glimpse, for his mother had pulled him below deck almost immediately. He didn't even know what his father looked like.

There must have been something he didn't know about to cause the marriage to fall to pieces, and if he was honest with himself, he couldn't really blame Matthew Dorroll for desiring a separate existence from his wife. An old demon ghosted up in his mind: the fear that his father must have wanted a separate existence from him as well. But Ben shoved it aside again as the train pulled to a stop and he got off at Paddington.

Once he was through the crush of luggage, the men calling for porters, and the smell of coal, he found a cabby in a side street and directed him to the neighborhood of Ryson's office. He peered out the finger-smudged window as they rumbled along. London looked terrible because of the bomb drops. Missing buildings, shattered windowpanes, and empty streets combined to give a dismal impression. But in the untouched districts, where he changed cabs to conceal his route, it was as if no time had passed since his arrival in May. If he hadn't had Terry's ring on his finger for safekeeping, he would have been tempted to put the whole spring and summer down as a bad dream.

When Ben entered the window-glass export shop, Jeremy was sitting with his feet on the desk, spinning a paperweight around his finger. He dropped it with a crash and smiled with pleased recognition. "Same appointment as last time, doctor?"

"Yes, thank you."

"Ryson's expecting you, and you can go straight in. Best of luck." Ben almost suspected Jeremy of winking, but decided that it wasn't likely. Though his eyes and the slight quirk of an eyebrow made him look as if he were about to share a good joke, his mouth held an unyielding reserve and warned that any secrets kept within were well guarded.

The hallway was devoid of any decoration whatsoever, nothing but plain wood paneling with three doors to break up the monotony. Ben knocked on Ryson's door and entered, though he did not hear an answer. The bookshelves stood on a different wall than he remembered from his visit in May, and a thicker layer of dust covered them. The clicking of the typewriter resumed after a moment of silence upon his entrance. Ryson finished his sentence and released the sheet of paper, folding it precisely into thirds and inserting it into an envelope.

"Hello, doctor." He removed his glasses, his blue eyes meeting Ben's in a direct gaze. "Take a seat, please, and tell me how you find your work progressing in Folkestone."

Ben sensed a threatening undercurrent in the dour face and weighed his words well before replying. "We're making progress, sir. I think with good time and effort we should bring to light the extent of Emmerson's work. We just unearthed a letter from him, and he says he did indeed choose a replacement. I have pictures of the maps we told you about, which I thought Jaeryn would have sent to you by now——"

Ryson interrupted him. "And the people you're working with; do you find their loyalties true? We suspected more than one desertion when we assigned Doctor Graham to the area, though I haven't received any reports of such since your arrival."

He hardly knew who was involved. Besides Ann Meikle and Peters, Jaeryn kept tightly sealed on who else might be working for their side. "Only two of our number, sir. Peters and Jaeryn. Ann Meikle, we have quite good proof, is not one of us."

"I remember Graham mentioning something of that sort. I trust you don't give her any vital information if she's compromised."

Ben bit his lip. "We tell her some things. But we're careful about it."

Ryson's gaze cut sharp through him. "If I found out otherwise, I might be concerned about the trustworthiness of your methods. And your methods must be absolutely trustworthy for you to continue holding your current position."

"Yes, sir."

"Suppose you explain this to me, then."

Ben took the scrap of paper handed to him and slowly made out the words written on it. He recognized it as the note from Jaeryn that he had passed off to Ann Meikle, and a shiver ran through him. He looked again at the paper and realized that something was not quite right. It took him a moment to identify what it was, for the source was so familiar. Then he saw with a chill of horror that he was not looking at Jaeryn's illegible scrawl, but his own small, precise handwriting.

"Well?" Ryson said sharply. "Perhaps you aren't aware that I ordered you to leave Speyer's concerns alone. Or if you are, you didn't know the extent of the consequences." He laid down the other note that Ben had written to Ann Meikle, ordering her to report her concerns to him instead of Jaeryn. "Giving confidential information to an untrustworthy link further weakens the compromises in our communications, and is strictly against the orders which I gave to Jaeryn Graham. I trust he passed those orders on to you."

"I heard of them, sir." Ben swallowed hard and began weighing his options.

Ryson took the papers back and locked them in his drawer. "Your meddling has done significant damage to my concerns. Why do you think Speyer is involved with Emmerson? Did you unearth proofs?"

Ben wished he could see Jaeryn tossed off the Folkestone Pier for not informing him better of the dynamics between Folkestone and London. "We knew Speyer had to be involved, sir, especially after we found the tags. And we couldn't overlook his possible involvement in Emmerson's work when our lives were under threat. It would have been foolish to ignore him."

He drew back, abashed by the fury in the Ryson's gaze. "I cannot fathom why you thought it permissible to disobey my orders. I could lock you up for your actions. This does warrant your dismissal."

Ben wasn't sure he had understood the words right. "Are you—are you in earnest, sir?"

"Entirely so. I would dismiss anyone of you who meddled with Speyer after my orders, even Doctor Graham himself."

"It was with the best of intentions that this was done," Ben said, trying to buy himself more time. "I don't think it can be detrimental to your purposes. If you give me another chance, I promise it won't happen again. Speyer's leaving in a week, and we can hardly jeopardize his position after that."

Ryson refused to be pacified. "You've already done enough to hinder my plans. His leaving will do nothing to remedy that."

He had to speak twice before he could get the words out. "What does it mean if you dismiss me?"

Ryson slipped on his wire-rimmed glasses and matched his fingers tip to tip. "You were here on trial, but we had no permanent contract with you. I will give you three weeks to wrap up your concerns in Folkestone and leave the area. You may invent whatever story you like to explain your departure. This month's check is the last you will receive from us."

"Yes, sir." Ben felt like his collar was choking him, and he gripped his fingers together to hide their trembling. If he didn't tell the truth now, Jaeryn's part in it would sound like a ridiculous attempt to pass the blame. He tried a partial admission. "Sir—I believe the paper was an attempt to frame both Doctor Graham and myself."

Ryson raised one thin gray eyebrow. "How so?"

He couldn't decide exactly what to say.

"Do you claim that you had no part in the affair?" Ryson continued impatiently.

"It was not an intentional defiance of your orders." His tone sounded more like begging than he liked, and after he spoke, he remembered that Jaeryn, at least, had been quite intentional.

Jaeryn's good-natured soul with his clear green eyes and two crooked fingers rose up before him, and somehow he could not get the truth out. If he told Ryson that the whole affair was Jaeryn's fault, Jaeryn would lose any good opinion he still had of Ben. No; if Jaeryn was to tell Ryson the truth of the matter, he would have to confess it of his own volition. And Jaeryn was more valuable to the investigation than he was.

Ben squared his shoulders and lifted his chin. "I apologize, sir. And I accept your decision."

Ryson handed him the envelope he had filled at the beginning of their meeting. "That's for Graham, to explain the matter to him. You can keep the Webley, but you are to return the hollow ammunition and the coins to him before you go."

"Yes, sir." His throat clenched with the anticipation of what he would have to tell Charlotte. Jaeryn wouldn't know until Monday, as he had no way of reaching him.

He rose to leave. "May I have the letters, sir?"

"You may not. I intend to destroy them."

Ben turned and walked out, ignoring Jeremy's wave from the desk.

What a fool he was. Now he had a wife, a grown sister, and no money to sustain either of them. He could throw himself into the Thames and be done with it, but he would leave many people behind who were depending on him. He laughed grimly. Life clung harder than that to penniless suppliants. Perhaps someone would give him a loan. Jaeryn would, though Ben didn't think either of them would be in the mood for the request after their coming discussion. No, he wasn't about to ask Jaeryn, or his father either.

There was one good thing about the whole mess. He would be able to leave England and go home where he had always wanted to stay in the first place. He had given it a fair try, and his father couldn't blame him for the results. He would go back to Virginia and set up the practice he had planned for so long and leave all the people and problems of Folkestone behind.

Then Terry's grin flashed before his mind's eye, and the idea of a peaceful American practice didn't hold as much charm as it had three months ago.

* * *

Jaeryn kept his word and brought Charlotte to the clinic, giving her all the directions she needed for handling patients in his absence. It was later in the afternoon than he had expected by the time he stopped at Starlin's. When he finished, he had half an hour to spare before his train departed, so he decided to visit Terry. He had only been to see him once since the accident and felt rather remorseful about the neglect.

Jaeryn looked about the men's ward, and it didn't take him long to find the place where Terry lay. The Victoria Hospital owed its fast-healing soldiers to the fellowship of the cheery American. Terry lay with his eyes wide open, his grand love of life showing strong in his smile. His hands played with the white sheets as if loath to hold still.

"How are you?" Jaeryn sat down next to him, glad to see him much improved since Ben's last report.

"I'm not dead yet." A sheen of sweat covered Terry's chin and forehead, but he was alert and energetic enough to talk.

"You'll get better, Terry."

"Sure, I will. I never worried any." Terry grimaced. "That kid sure did enough damage to lay me up for a while, though, and I've been out of my head since you saw me last. They said I got an infection."

Jaeryn leaned his chin on his hand. "You could press charges."

"Or not. He didn't mean anything by it."

"Well, if it's any comfort, Starlin King is still laid up in his room recovering from pneumonia." Jaeryn smiled at Terry's dancing eyes. "You gave him quite a crack to his ribs, and Dailey made a mistake treating it. By the way, Dailey went to Dover last week."

A questioning note crept into Terry's voice. "Oh? What happened?"

"That I couldn't tell you."

"I hope he can help Erin."

"You shouldn't make him deal with your problems." Jaeryn shook his head in good-natured rebuke. "He has enough as it is."

Terry laughed. "Maybe he doesn't need help as much as you think he does."

"Perhaps so." Jaeryn rose and clasped Terry's hand. "But I think he needs more than he's getting."

It was almost uncanny how well Ben and Terry got on together. They were such opposites, yet Terry, in his own lively way, had earned the doctor's trust without really trying. And he, Jaeryn, had not. He had tried everything he could think of without success, and the knowledge irked him.

Jaeryn walked to the train station and handed over the change for a ticket. Benjamin Dorroll had no idea what he was involved in. He was too morally legalistic to make a success of espionage. The American had a deeply-held stubborn streak, and from all appearances, he was far from reaching the end of it. It was in the set lines of his mouth—in the rough calluses on his hands that he must have developed before he decided to take up the life of a general practitioner. Fenton must know where those calluses came from, but Fenton concealed whatever information he chose, helpful or otherwise.

Perhaps Terry was right. He should let go, quit searching for chances, let Dorroll come around in his own good time. But he would try one more serious conversation after Dorroll returned from London. Surely one more wouldn't hurt.

* * *

A slight chill diffused through the air when Ben returned late in the afternoon, coupled with a cool drizzle. He wished he had brought his trench coat instead of his jacket as he cycled through Folkestone's main streets to Colonel King's. He had called Charlotte to let her know he was back from London, and he had a last house call to make. Stafford answered the front door bell with a mildly disapproving air and led Ben to the study when he asked to see the master of the house.

Colonel King rose to shake hands. "I called Jaeryn Graham in today as you told me, doctor. He said he could add nothing to your excellent work. According to his opinion, Starlin seems to be holding his own and will soon be back on his feet. He left a little over an hour ago, so you needn't have come so soon."

"Oh." Ben shied away from the thought of going home so soon. "Well, since I'm here I'll go up and see Starlin before I leave."

"He's in your hands. Did you have a successful trip?"

Ben shrugged. "It went as well as could be expected. My errand was not a pleasurable one."

"I am sorry to hear it." Colonel King said. "Stafford informed me that you bicycled here. You should have called my chauffeur."

"My visit here is strictly professional, and I would not wish to take advantage."

"It is open to you all the same, as is anything else you may require."

Ben thanked him and excused himself to go see Starlin. He entered the sitting room and saw the boy fast asleep on the sofa. Shaking his shoulder gently so as to avoid startling him, Ben pulled up a chair and waited for the first incisive look from the sharp blue eyes. But they remained closed. One minute passed, and the second, and the third, with no response.

"Starlin, wake up." Ben shook him again and grabbed for his pulse. It beat steadily, but the breathing came in an irregular rhythm through Starlin's open lips. When Ben caught the scent of the tea on his breath, he understood what it meant. Someone had taken advantage of his absence. A half-empty cup of tea cowered on the coffee table like a guilty culprit, its tepid contents clouded with milk.

If someone had intended to kill, their plans had gone awry.

Starlin opened his eyes after a great deal of coaxing, but though he sat up and made terse responses, he wasn't fully coherent. As soon as the boy could sit up on his own, Ben helped him to the washroom and handed him a glass of water with ipecac diluted into it. "This is going to hurt, but it will clear your system. Drink as much of it as you can stand."

Starlin obeyed, and the medication didn't take long to make him start vomiting. Whoever had poisoned him had been cruel, Ben thought, a furrow of anger on his brow. No wonder Starlin hadn't drunk all the tea; it must have tasted horrible.

When Starlin finished, he looked up and swore. Ben thought it best not to rebuke him for it. "I'm sorry. You've been drugged, and I don't want it harming you any more than it has. Take it easy for a moment; I'll be back as soon as I can."

He locked all the doors leading into Starlin's room and pocketed the key before descending to the lower level. Colonel King was in a well-lit room with a view of the stone porch, playing a game of billiards. His brown eyes shone fiercely in concentration as if each ball were a living thing and he was their master, striking them into place.

Ben interrupted him in the middle of a shot. "Your son has been given a strong dose of narcotics." King looked up in surprise, and the ball clanked to the side. "I want to know who prepared his tea and who gave it to him."

The colonel leaned his cue in haste against the table. "Good heavens. Is he all right?"

Ben led the way down the hall, talking over his shoulder as he went. "If he had drunk all of the cup I found, it probably would have killed him. That would mean a charge of murder. As it is, it should be a charge of attempted murder."

Colonel King pushed his study door open. "Why did you leave the boy alone in that condition?"

"He's waking up. I'll return to him when you and I have

301

investigated the matter."

At Ben's request, the colonel summoned the kitchen maids into the study. Ben sat in the corner and listened, but not one—whether terrified, concerned, or indifferent—admitted to serving the tea. After a lengthy period of threatening, coaxing, reasoning, and questioning, one kitchen girl admitted to taking the tray up to the sitting room and sank into a fit of hysterics, screaming that she had nothing to do with drugging it. According to her, she had left it on the side table and invited Doctor Graham to take some before he left, but he had declined her offer and gone on his way. They were inclined to believe her. When Colonel King finished, they were no nearer to finding out who had done the deed than they were at the beginning.

After Stafford ushered the maid out and shut the door, Ben turned to King. "How are you going to protect your son, sir?"

King sighed and rubbed his forehead with the tips of his fingers. "Well, he is rather high-strung. I wouldn't put it past him to take it himself."

Ben felt sorry for the boy upstairs, beset by difficulties with no experience to handle them and no one willing to show him the way. "If you suspect him of such a thing, you should try to help him. Starlin has taken a beating, shot someone, almost drowned, and taken or been given a drug overdose all in the short time that I've known him. It's time somebody looked into the cause of it all. He could have died while I was gone this afternoon, and you none the wiser."

"I'll see that the boy stays safe." King stood up, and Ben had to look up to meet his gaze. "If it's necessary to seek the protection of the authorities, then you will be the first to know."

Ben thought it best to show a measure of diplomacy, but he relaxed none of his insistence. "Promise me you'll leave someone you can trust in his room. If it's him doing it, then he shouldn't be left alone. And if it's someone else, another presence could quite possibly deter them. I know there is little use in me taking matters into my own hands. Your influence is too strong for mine. But I will be pursuing my own lines of investigation, with which you cannot interfere."

"You're a brave man, doctor," Colonel King said quietly.

He tilted his chin defiantly. "I'm not easily dissuaded."

King invited him to stay for dinner while he waited to see how Starlin recovered, and Ben accepted the invitation. The servants looked edgy. He couldn't help hesitating before every bite, and he looked askance at the fresh fruit and seasoned delicacies. No one took tea after dinner, but Colonel King took his usual glass of port. Ben excused himself early and spent the evening sitting by the sofa where Starlin slept, thinking over how this latest move might be connected with the investigation. It pointed away from Starlin's involvement, whatever the map meant. Likely Emmerson's replacement had something to do with it. If only they knew who that was.

He wouldn't be able to investigate the matter as he had threatened. In three weeks he wouldn't be here, and even if he told Jaeryn, Starlin would still have to look out for himself. He wanted to find someone to keep a watch over the boy who would not only be trustworthy but politically disinterested.

When Starlin's valet knocked on the door later in the evening, Ben gestured the young man to come in. "You look a likely fellow," he said, hoping it wasn't too awful a deception. "Would you do something for me?"

George set down a silver tray of coffee things. "Anything, sir."

Ben lowered his voice to a conspiratorial whisper. "Keep a watch on young King here, and be discreet about it. If you see any signs of trouble, go straight to the authorities and don't bother to ask his father first. Will you do that?"

George looked doubtful. "That might mean my position, sir."

"Do you know where the former member for Parliament lived? Mr. Emmerson?"

"Yes, sir." The valet nodded.

"Well, then, if that were to happen, go there and ask for Peters. Tell him I sent you for work, and he'll see that you get it."

George tapped his chin in consideration. "All right then, sir." He stood ramrod-stiff and brought his heels together in imitation of the recruits at Shorncliffe. "I'll do it."

Ben reached in his jacket for his wallet, then pulled his hand out again empty. It wouldn't do to bribe him. "Thank you very much. You won't regret it, and I'll make sure you don't go unrewarded." He had no idea how he would keep that promise, but he would find some way to see it through.

Starlin woke up at that moment and looked in wonderment at him. "What's the matter?"

"You've been out awhile." Ben touched his forehead and was glad the skin felt cool and normal. The sleepy blue eyes tried to take him in, but they couldn't seem to focus right away. "Take it easy. You have plenty of time."

Starlin hid a yawn with the back of his hand. "What time is it?"

Ben smiled. "It's nine in the evening. I came here this afternoon, but you were out then, and have been ever since."

His eyes widened in shock. "I feel like I have a hangover."

"Yes, well, you would be able to judge that comparison, wouldn't you?"

Apparently, his tired brain didn't register the hint, for he made no response to it. "I didn't like the other doctor who came today."

"Why?" Ben poured out a cup from the coffee tray and handed it to him, and Starlin pulled himself up to take it.

"He knows too much about people." The lad drank deep, grimacing at the lack of cream and sugar.

"Doctor Graham can't help it, Starlin. It's just a sixth sense. Now, I have something to tell you."

He told Starlin about the drugged tea, the investigation with no results, and the possibility of danger. Starlin's eyes held a faint glimmer as Ben asked, "Do you know why anyone would want to do this?"

He shook his head, but there was hesitation in his manner.

Ben raised his eyebrows. "You need to tell me the truth."

"You can't make me," Starlin taunted.

"It doesn't benefit you to hide it. You're still sick, and it wouldn't take much to put you out of the way right now."

Starlin shook his head again, but there was a hint of fear on his face. "I'll watch my back, then. And that's all I have to say about it."

Ben gave him a meaning glance. "You did a fine job of that today, didn't you? It was a good thing I came."

But Starlin could not be persuaded to tell him any more, and he had to content himself with trying again another time.

An undefined premonition teased him on the walk back to Jaeryn's house, as if his mind knew something it would not put into words. There was something he was missing about this whole business: a piece to the puzzle which should be obvious, but which he was not remembering.

As soon as he arrived, Charlotte gave him a list of calls requiring immediate attention, and he headed out again. By the time he finished them, it was near midnight. She was asleep when he returned, curled up on his side of the bed as she often was when she missed him. He didn't want to disturb her. He hesitated outside Jaeryn's room, then shook his head and settled for the living room sofa.

The dark green velour felt cold and unyielding. He realized how little he thought of his cottage as home, how little he thought of Jaeryn's clinic as home, how un-at-home he had felt ever since coming to Folkestone. If he could have one wish granted, he would ask for a steady life in the country he loved and evenings spent with his wife. Perhaps through being given the sack here his wish would be granted.

As he pulled off his shoes, the teasing thought that had bothered him all evening finally took shape in his mind. Jaeryn Graham had been the only known visitor to Starlin's room the day before. It was around the time Jaeryn left that Starlin drank the tea, and Jaeryn could have bribed a servant to lace it with the drug if he wasn't able to do it himself. Whatever drug it was, he would have unquestioned access to it, and no one would have thought twice if he had ordered it given to the boy. Calculating the time it took to walk to the King estate, Jaeryn must have left Folkestone half an hour before his own train arrived from London. They had just missed each other at the station.

If this was true, then Ben had just sacrificed his own position to keep a clever swindler in his place. Come to think of it, the Irishman never really spoke of his loyalty for England. He had only mentioned it twice: the morning after the bomb drop and during the Ypres uneasiness in July. Perhaps Jaeryn was more qualified, but if his loyalties were not sincere, then Ben had just given Folkestone the easiest win the Huns would ever have.

Treachery that held an entire secret intelligence force in its grip took a well-informed mind, inexhaustible influence, and large amounts of money. It could be a millionaire, a politician, an army veteran—someone who held numerous threads, and whom no one would ever suspect.

A doctor fit that description perfectly.

The misgiving gnawed at Ben's mind after he turned off the light and courted the sleep that refused to come. At length, the ringing of the telephone granted him a momentary distraction, and he went out on a house call to the west side of town—one of Jaeryn's patients whom he had never met before.

When he returned, his watch read almost seven in the morning. Charlotte lay awake on the guest bed with her head pillowed on her arm. Her blue eyes held a sleepy look—just like Starlin's, only much nicer. Ben entered, and she smiled in greeting and drew herself up on her elbow, her white chiffon nightgown slipping down over her left shoulder. Ben took off his jacket and climbed up on the bed beside her. "You look nice this morning."

She wrinkled her nose at him and smoothed down the flaxen hair that was tumbling out of her braid. "I do not." Then she cuddled up next to him, her warmth soft and inviting. "How was your trip to London yesterday?"

"It went well—" He cursed himself for trying yet again to lie to her. "Actually not. It was difficult."

"Oh?" She shivered and pulled her nightgown up over her shoulder. "Did you see your father?"

"No. I never heard back from him." It was just as well. He owed it to Jaeryn to tell him first, which he couldn't do until he returned. "I'll write to him when I get the chance. You must prepare yourself—something is happening, and I don't know what it will mean for us."

Her face fell, and she clasped her hands around her knees. "How long will it be before you can tell me?"

"Early this week, if I can manage it. I will as soon as I can. It's not life-threatening, *ma chèrie*. It's just—" He got up and slipped on his shoes, unwilling to stay any longer. "It's just that some men lose out."

He settled for tea instead of breakfast and made it strong, with double portions of sugar, to wake himself up. As soon as the morning hours at the clinic were over, Ben locked the door and set off at a swift pace on Terry's bicycle in the direction of Starlin King's. He wanted to see him again and get more information than he had been able to the night before.

Starlin rose as Ben entered, a bit unsteady on his feet but showing remarkable improvement considering the previous day's drug caper. His wet hair lay slicked back, curling slightly at the tips and coming down to his dressing gown collar.

"You're looking better," Ben said.

Starlin nodded jauntily and reseated himself. "Did you find out what I was doped with?"

"It was chloral hydrate. You're lucky. You could have died." Starlin looked more relaxed than usual, so Ben took a seat beside him on the sofa.

Starlin shrugged. "I didn't. I'm going to dress for the day."

"You can if you like, as long as you don't overdo it."

The lad ran his fingers through his hair, and a few drops fell to the collar of his nightshirt. "I'm not going to stick around here much longer. I'm going to leave as soon as I get my automobile."

"Tell me more."

"Nope."

Ben sighed, gearing up for a struggle with Starlin's logic. "How will you support yourself? Living costs money."

Starlin motioned for him to wait there and made his way toward a table on the other side of the room. After a long search through the drawers, he returned with a leather wallet in his hand. He sank exhausted onto the sofa and dropped it in Ben's lap.

"Still want to dress for the day?" Ben opened the wallet and found the worn pound notes he had seen when he searched it several weeks before. "Why did you show me this?"

"It's my allowance."

Ben tossed the wallet on the coffee table. "It might pay for petrol."

Starlin's eyes flashed. He folded his arms and fixed his gaze on the carpet.

"You can't enlist. You don't know a trade," Ben reasoned.

"I have no reason to stay."

"You have no reason to leave."

Ben thought it best not to press for more information and left by the back door to avoid the rest of the household. He did not feel able to face the boy's father just yet.

It was after he reached home that he remembered the letter from Mrs. O'Sean that Ann Meikle had given him. He reached in his pocket to see if it was still there. Sure enough, he found it crushed under his notebook and a bottle of aspirin, crinkled but otherwise none the worse for wear. Thank heaven. It was better that he was reading it now; some home news would be a welcome relief after all the horrible surprises of the last couple of days.

He opened it and read with disbelieving eyes of the last disaster he could have dreamed possible.

Dear Ben,

Your mother came by yesterday and said she was done with my services as laundry lady. She's getting her own maid and won't need to hire out the work anymore. I'm so sorry, lad. It must be a shock to have her marry again after all these years. From what I can gather, she's glad you're away while she makes the arrangements. Perhaps you are too. It may not be so bad. Give yourself some time to get used to it before you make up your mind to hate the man. He's not your father, but I know good will come of it in spite of it not being what you had hoped.

I haven't heard from you lately. Write soon and tell me how you're doing. Sending love and prayers from home.

Mrs. O'Sean

Married. A sickening twist of anger gripped him hard. There had never been a divorce. Perhaps Mrs. O'Sean didn't know, but Lisette Dorroll was as bound by law as she had been twenty years ago. And her prospective partner either didn't know or didn't care. No wonder she was glad he was away.

He was the only one with the ability to break it up—and not only the ability, but the duty. That meant going back—confrontations—accusations. Everything he had worked to avoid for the last twenty years. A heavy burden fell on his spirit, and he resumed his walk slowly. He must leave as soon as he could get a free berth. There wouldn't be time to make arrangements for Alisa to go with them. That meant he would have to leave someone behind to take care of her while he was gone.

A vision rose before him of what Charlotte's face would look like when he told her the choice they had to make. Fear boiled up and choked him, a living, breathing force that he had no more strength to grapple with.

* * *

Jaeryn hadn't telegraphed ahead to let him know what time he was coming home on Monday. Ben hadn't really expected him to; there was no reason for it. But, all the same, he had hoped for some advance warning before he had to reveal what had happened with Ryson. With every click of the door Monday morning, he tensed and expected the Irishman to enter. Time and again it proved to be a patient, and after a while the sharp expectancy settled to a dull ache.

In the end, he didn't even hear Jaeryn arrive. He just looked up and saw the man standing there, observing him, as full of breezy good nature as if he was freshly returned from a holiday. Jaeryn wore the same gray cardigan as the previous Tuesday morning when he had come to Copt Point, and he had a newsboy cap tucked under his arm.

"Afternoon." Jaeryn tossed his jacket on the examining table and sat down in his leather chair. "I locked the door so we could talk."

"Splendid." Ben couldn't keep the tight edge from his voice. "Charlotte's at home this afternoon."

"Oh?" Jaeryn pulled the ledger over and examined it. "Why?"

"I asked her to go."

"What happened?"

He did not answer directly. When it came down to it, he wasn't keen on telling Jaeryn what had gone wrong. "I wish you had left Speyer alone. We weren't supposed to have anything to do with him."

Jaeryn flinched. "Scruples getting in the way again?" His tone was light, but a hard note crept in behind the words.

"No. Nothing of that sort." Ben twisted the pen between his fingers until he caught Jaeryn watching him and threw it down. "Starlin King was drugged just after you left him on Tuesday. He could have died." He hadn't meant to say that either, and he hoped madly that his suspicions weren't too obvious.

As he glanced sideways at Jaeryn, the Irishman tensed and pushed his chair away. The open cheeriness shifted in an instant to a wave of anger that outstripped everything Ben had seen from him thus far—a white heat that burned cool and calculating and ruthless in its rage.

"I do wish, Dorroll, that you'd make some kind of effort to be civil. You may detest me, but you needn't be so open about it. I'm not going about poisoning people, if that's what you're implying."

"I don't see what I've done to make you accuse me of incivility." Ben gripped his self-control desperately. "If I've caused you offense, then I'm sorry for it."

A faint spark shot up in Jaeryn's eyes. "No, you aren't. You're never sorry, and you're never obliged for anything. I like you, I really do, but if you would stop being a self-sufficient little demigod, you might find your life considerably easier. Exactly how low do you think I am?"

"Never mind. What did you want to talk about?"

"Oh, don't be thick," Jaeryn snapped. "The reason for Ryson calling you to London, that's what."

Ben glared at him. "He found the note you sent to Ann Meikle."

Jaeryn's lips moved quickly and silently in something Ben suspected it was well he didn't say out loud. "What did he say?"

"He was upset and made it clear he didn't want anyone meddling with Speyer. In fact, your note was enough to warrant a dismissal."

The color drained from Jaeryn's face. "So he sent you back to tell me."

"No." He had been thinking about what he would say for a long time, rehearsing it over and over and over again. He was ready. "It was in my handwriting, so Ryson dismissed me. You are free to stay."

Jaeryn sat speechless.

"Do you realize," Ben said, in a voice that was hardly audible, "this is the first thing I've ever failed at?"

That was enough to bring back Jaeryn's words. "Why, you arrogant little—"

Ben interrupted him. "No. You don't understand. I mean that some people don't have the option of failing. You have that choice, and you probably always will, but I've never had it."

"I don't know what you're talking about." Jaeryn closed his eyes as if trying to collect his patience. "Nor," he added, opening them again, "do I have any idea—why didn't you tell the truth? I would have thought you would be happy to see me kicked to the gutter."

His soul revolted at the injustice. "There's no need to be abusive. I've lied—again—to help you. Your position is secure, and I have less than three weeks to leave England. I don't see why you're not more pleased."

Jaeryn got up and paced back and forth, his boots treading loud over the wooden floorboards. "Whatever is happening, I have no idea what it means. But I do know one thing: my life was a deal easier before you showed up on my doorstep. Try again, and give it to me straight. What exactly passed between you and Ryson?"

Ben took a deep breath and began again. "Ann Meikle sent your note to Ryson. Only it wasn't your note she turned in. She forged another copy in my handwriting. That, coupled with the real note I gave her, made it look as if I was the one who instigated the rumor. Ryson doesn't want Speyer meddled with. I think his work must be more vital than ours."

Jaeryn stopped his pacing, outraged dignity in the rigid lines of his shoulders. "That was a fool thing to do under your present difficulties. You'll never provide for a family if you look out for other peoples' interests first."

"I was forced," Ben muttered.

The spite was graven on Jaeryn's face as if in cold marble. "You chose."

A thick silence bridged the gap between them. Jaeryn drummed his fingers on the desk. A small smile played over his face, but the angry glint remained in his eyes. Ben's attempt at patience was slipping through his grasp. "As you like. I'm not going to argue."

Jaeryn took to pacing again. "Perhaps we're looking at this too hastily. I'll run up to London and explain the truth of the matter. It may require a bit of persuading, but Ryson will take you back."

"You would get dismissed by admitting your own guilt. I'd have to take your place. If you have any pity, I would rather you didn't."

"You're pleading for pity." Jaeryn gave a ringing laugh. "That's something new. Were you jumping at an easy opportunity to get away? Most men would want a way out that wasn't ignominious, but so far you've never fit any mold I tried to place you in."

Ben gritted his teeth. "Your insults are childish."

The Irishman raised his eyebrows and shrugged. "I've been accused of many things before, but childishness is not one of them. Perhaps—"

"What exactly do you have against me? Something has changed your good opinion of me, and I wish to know what it is."

Jaeryn waved his inquiry away. "Oh, we needn't bring up past grievances. Mind, I'm not going to accept your charity without some return."

Ben pressed his lips together. "And be well rid of me. You may as well say the rest of it."

"I'd offer to help you find a different position," Jaeryn said, ignoring him. "But I wouldn't want to insult you."

"You've already done enough of that."

"You can't keep the practice. I'll have to look out for a new medical assistant as well as for help with our other work, which is a fearful inconvenience."

Ben stood up and jerked open a drawer, pulling out the medical tools he owned and piling them on his desk. "I hope you find a better one on both accounts than I have been."

"There's little doubt of that." Jaeryn spoke under his breath, but Ben heard the words, and tightened his face into a blank mask.

"I will send you the necessary information by post to wrap up my side of the medical work. You have said quite enough, sir."

Jaeryn did not reply, though Ben waited long for a response.

He swept the last of his things into his black leather bag. At the door, he glanced over his shoulder. "I'm not coming back. You can make what explanation you like to your patients. Say I've enlisted or died, or anything else you like. I won't be here to contradict you."

Jaeryn's green eyes looked him over for a moment. The Irishman swung about on one booted heel and shoved his hands in his pockets. "Get out."

Ben took one last look at the man whose meddling had caused him so much misery. Then he closed the door of the Tontine clinic and set off toward Copt Point. Whatever kind of enigma Jaeryn Graham was, it had only deepened in the last hour. He doubted he would ever unravel it. And at the moment, he had no desire to do so.

Chapter Eighteen
Partings

Rage and shame gripped Ben as he tramped blindly away from Jaeryn's. He took the back streets to avoid people, only encountering the occasional soldier with a sweetheart who was too engrossed to notice him. Minutes slipped past one by one, dulling the burning sting into a hopeless ache that was almost worse than anger ever could be.

The wind whistled through the trees as he walked further and further from home, unwilling to tell Charlotte what had happened. His hair ruffled in the breeze, and a swirl of thoughts about what he could have done better ran through his head with a swiftness that left him dazed.

He had less than three weeks to leave England. Less than three weeks to explain to everyone he knew why he was moving on and to his father why his work had fallen through. And it stuck in his throat to accept the help Jaeryn had offered, though he was hardly in a position to refuse.

It was past sunset when he turned toward Copt Point. A pearly sliver of the moon looked down on him as the sky darkened from twilight to blackness. The Channel whipped and roared. He passed the cottages and stood at the edge of the rocky slope. The salt air wet and puckered his lips. There must be a madness that blew from this narrow strip of water that attracted men to it. Himself—Starlin—Nathan Speyer—the fishermen who risked life and liberty to earn a scanty income under the nose of the Germans. He stood there fighting with the despair, then turned with sinking heart back toward the cottage and the inevitable conversation with Charlotte.

The door slammed shut behind him from the pressure of the wind. Charlotte, sitting at the table, looked up startled at his entrance. She set down her fork and reached up her face for a kiss. "You're home. Have you eaten?"

"I'm fine, thank you. I have something to tell you."

She kept her gaze fixed on him as he pulled off his coat and sat down opposite her. He reached out and sought her hand, and he didn't know until she told him afterward how hard he hurt her when he gripped it.

"My work here has finished rather unexpectedly. As of now, I have no means to provide for us."

"Oh my." Her voice trailed off, and her eyes widened with astonishment.

That was one of the things he liked about Charlotte: she didn't go into hysterics over a shock. Perhaps it was her training as a nurse that had developed the steadiness in her character—or a year and a half of living as a doctor's wife. He knew she was afraid, but she struggled just as hard as he did to put a good face on it.

"What does that mean? Did you just find out?"

Ben traced a finger along the knife scars on the tabletop. "No. I found out Friday, but I wasn't at liberty to tell you until Doctor Graham came back. I have been instructed to leave Folkestone."

"Why?" She shifted, and he knew she wanted him to look her in the eyes. "Where are we going?"

"Back to America, to set up a practice if I can." He rushed on to forestall the objections she might make. "Doubtless many people would counsel me to stay here and see what I could do in England or

315

even Scotland, but I have no connections or means of recommendation here."

A note of fear registered in her voice. "Will you have to enlist?"

"It is one of my options. I can't wait long for work to turn up." Ben braced himself for what he was about to tell her. "I can't stay long in any case, sweetheart. I just got a letter from home."

As he unfolded Mrs. O'Sean's letter and laid it in front of her, she watched him as if she were in a nightmare, wanting him to wake her up. Even more concern dawned on her face when she read the news. "She can't be getting married. I thought you told me she was still married to your father."

"She is. I must go back and put a stop to it. And…Charlotte…I need you to stay and take care of Alisa while I am gone."

"No."

"Alisa needs someone to take care of her, and I have no one but you to rely on." His chest tightened at the stunned disbelief dawning in her face. "I need you."

"No." A tremor ran through her slim body. "It would be much more sensible to take us all with you. This place is dangerous, even more dangerous than an Atlantic crossing would ever be, and I'm sure Alisa would be willing to leave—"

The heat in the fireplace behind him made the room almost unbearable. Or so he told himself. "You will be safe as soon as I am gone. Charlotte, I have no choice. It's a legal matter that my mother is trying to circumvent in my absence. For the man's sake, as well as for hers, I must expose her as soon as possible."

"I don't want you to leave us," she pleaded.

He tried to ease her panic. "You know people here."

"But you won't be here. Pearlie has Alisa to be friends with, and I just have—" She gripped her hands tight together, and her voice went flat. "I just have you."

"But Alisa is here in Folkestone," he said, "and we have a duty to her until Edmond returns. Pearlie couldn't take care of Alisa alone."

Her face crumpled at the finality of his decision. She put her hands over her mouth, and her shoulders shook as a silent rush of tears swept over her. Ben sat twisting his hands together while she gasped and tried to recover her composure. They had seldom parted before, and though he knew she would not refuse him in the end, the tearing asunder ached.

He did not know exactly what to do, but he stood up all the same and pulled her chair back, putting a hand under her elbow. "Come sit with me, sweetheart." He drew her to the sofa and waited until the heavy, choking sobs settled down to a softer weeping, rubbing the back of her hand with his thumb. "I'm sorry."

"It's all right." Her lids were heavy, and she shivered and caught her breath. "I understand. It was just a moment."

He pulled out a worn linen handkerchief and offered it to her. "I've considered asking Alisa to board you as well as Pearlie if you like. Then you wouldn't have to manage rent and landlords. That would ease some of the burden, wouldn't it?"

Charlotte struggled to find her words, and he waited until she could speak again.

"Tell me what you're thinking," he said, noting the reticence in her face.

"I'm sorry. But if you had no objection, I should like to tell her who we really are before we ask her to board us. I wouldn't feel right keeping it from her."

"She's had enough hard partings in her life. If she doesn't know until afterward, it might hurt her less."

"That isn't right. Why don't you tell her now?"

"It would be better for me."

They sat on the sofa together, content to allow the silence to mend the grief. The baby flames flickered purple and green from the twisted driftwood and let off a loud pop now and then as they caught on a knot. Smoldering crumbs of ash flew out and caught in the black grate. Ben looked down at the flaxen head leaning against his shoulder. "I'm sorry I can't do better for you."

Her wet cheeks shone in the firelight, and she passed the back of her hand over them to dry them. "How long do you have before you must leave?"

"Less than three weeks."

"I miss you already." Her voice was mellow from crying, and she tucked her hand under his arm and melded into his side until he could feel the loose waves of her hair against his face. "I know you're doing the best you can for us. It's just hard to be strong sometimes."

"It is a curse, being strong." His voice went rough, and he swallowed back the sting of sadness. "But it is our cross, and we must carry it."

* * *

Tontine Street, Folkestone
August 28th, 1917
I am informed by R— that your tickets are being held at his office for you to collect on your way west. We have secured first-class passage on the H.M.S.
Drake, *departing from Liverpool on the tenth of September.*

Please leave a record of all the names and addresses of the people you've been treating. Don't make a fool of yourself inventing elaborate stories. Tell them you're being transferred and that will be sufficient.
Jaeryn Graham

Ben folded the paper carefully as he walked away from Alisa's. They had certainly made quick work of the situation. Jaeryn must have left a message in the drop Friday night to be taken to London, and whoever his henchmen were, they had obeyed his orders to the letter.

Alisa had readily agreed to his request for Pearl and Charlotte to board with her. She had been reluctant to let Pearl go home in the first place, and now that she no longer had to face a separation, she was willing to do him any favor in her power. She was only sorry that he was leaving himself, and asked several times, in all innocence, what had brought about such an unexpected change. He did not know what to tell her. In light of Jaeryn's note, he was glad he had kept his explanation brief, merely saying that some business had called him home to Virginia. What made it worse was that she told him Edmond had family in Virginia, and he did not have the courage to tell her the truth. He might see Edmond soon. Perhaps Ben could tell him about Alisa and mend the gap between them. The thought of being carelessly called "little brother" in person was a source of comfort to which he clung.

Rain from the night before had laid the dust down nicely on the tree-lined stretch of road that ran past Alisa's place. The great maples had touches of orange and crimson about their leaves, and a silvery nip of frost gave the air a chill breath. A squirrel skittered across the road and up an oak tree, sending a shower of nuts cracking off the bark and branches. He had time to notice it, for a wonder. Summer was waning now, so silently that he almost hadn't marked the turning of the season.

He soon realized that he was not the only one on the road. Ahead of him walked a man with a small bag slung over his shoulder and a larger one in his hand, evidently planning to travel quite a distance. Ben could hardly blame him. Anyone would be well served to leave Folkestone as soon as they could manage it.

It wasn't until the sun's rays shifted out of his eyes that he recognized the dark hair as Nathan Speyer's. Nathan walked at a brisk pace, yet there was a tense set and a slight stoop to his shoulders. His training must be complete, and he was off to Dover to take up the work so vital to men in London. He was too young. Eighteen or so, from what Starlin had said.

Nathan shifted the strap of his bag from one shoulder to the other, unaware that he was being observed. Ben did not call out to stop him. His present position was due to his former meddling, and he had no inclination to strain the situation further. Best let Speyer pursue his way unquestioned, and perhaps he would still find good success in his endeavors.

He had nothing to do now. With the rift between him and Jaeryn, he and Charlotte had no new calls on patients, only a few recurring visits that he would finish the following week and Starlin, whom he would keep as long as he could. He didn't enjoy the thought of Jaeryn taking over Starlin's medical care. They would make a pair of enemies, the two of them, and in his anger, Starlin was likely to commit any number of reckless acts that would only be compounded by the lecturing Jaeryn would certainly give.

He would be left to his own devices until the tenth of September. Thirteen days remaining, and he would give Charlotte as much of them as he could.

Though it was no longer his responsibility, Ben walked to St. Eanswythe's after he saw Speyer and made his way through the graves to Rebecca Rogers's tombstone. Technically he was disobeying orders by unlocking it, and this would be the last time he took the risk. There was never anything there. But a premonition teased him as he worked through the combination, and he was hardly surprised to see a flutter of white fall to the ground when he tipped it over. Nor was he surprised to find his own name on it.

I have something of consequence to tell you. Be at The Star Inn, eight o' clock sharp this evening and secure a corner table. F.

He felt he had no choice but to obey. The smoky pub with its crowd of drinkers repulsed him—some taking a Saturday evening pint in all respectability, others settling in for their customary late-night carousal. But at eight o'clock, according to instructions, he chose a table for two near the back and waited for Fenton to appear.

It didn't take long. The man slipped into the booth at quarter after the hour smelling of French cologne, his diamond cuff links winking under the lights. Fenton smiled a small, cat-like smile at Ben's disgust and stated his business without preamble.

"I hear you are going to America, doctor."

Ben made no attempt to be civil. "What business is that of yours?"

"None." Fenton leaned his elbows on the table, matching his fingers tip to tip. "But it's the business of those I'm working for. I have something to tell you that's for your benefit if you care to listen—"

"Be quick, then. I don't have all evening."

"—and for the right incentive. Yes, you do. You have free evenings for weeks to come."

Ben gritted his teeth. "Don't make me throttle you."

Fenton smirked. "You don't have it in you. Now, do you have any incentive to offer me?"

"None. You can keep your dirty information or do whatever you want with it, but I'm not going to support you selling secrets."

"Well, then, I'll give you the information at no cost."

Ben looked at the man with open skepticism. "I thought you were cleverer at lying that that."

"It's not a lie." Fenton signaled the brown-haired young woman passing their table for drinks. "Take it or leave it as you wish."

They locked eyes until Ben surrendered under his glance. "Very well. Out with it."

"One of our British contact points lives in Baltimore. His name is Alex York, and he'll be helpful to you." Fenton laid down a business card with the man's address and phone number.

Ben took it up. "I remember the name. He sent us our passports to come here. What about him?"

The woman returned carrying two tankards of beer and set one before each of them. Fenton waited until she was well away before replying. "I traveled to Virginia shortly after you arrived in Folkestone, at Jaeryn Graham's request. If you keep your eyes open when you return to your mother's, you may be able to find something that will benefit our work here. York will give you any help you need while you're there."

Ben pushed the mug away, though he would have preferred to hurl it in Fenton's face. "Jaeryn's work is no longer mine."

"Perhaps not. But he'll never be in Virginia, and it's up to you whether or not he'll get the information he needs."

He sighed in resignation. "What am I supposed to look for?"

Fenton reached for his unwanted glass of beer and took a long draught of the golden brew. "Your mother has strange friends, doctor. I think you would do well to find out why they have an interest in her."

"Is it my understanding," Ben said, in ominous quietness, "that you brought me to a pub to give me mere insinuations?"

Fenton held up both hands, palm out as if to protest his innocence. "Well, that's what you're trained in, isn't it? You have the ability to follow up on what I've given you. Otherwise, I wouldn't have given it."

He rose from the polished wooden chair, and Ben reached out to stop him. "No. Wait. Tell me more."

The deep-set eyes twinkled at his discomfiture. "That's all, doctor. You haven't given me an incentive for premium information."

He watched Fenton shoulder his way through the crowds of men and disappear through the entry.

When he returned to Copt Point, the light was on in Mrs. Goodwin's kitchen. In spite of the lateness of the hour, he knocked on her door. The knob rattled, and she opened it, the lamp from her kitchen table casting her figure into shadow.

Ben took off his hat to her. "I've come to give you this month's rent. I apologize for the tardiness."

"It's no matter." She let him inside and left the door open while he pulled out the money from his wallet.

He handed it to her and took a deep breath. "I also wanted to tell you something. I'm returning to America in a few weeks on transfer. We are grateful that you let us use this place, but my wife and sister need lodgings closer to town, so I wish to give notice."

Mrs. Goodwin looked surprised but out of politeness made no inquiries, for which he was thankful. "It was at your disposal as long as you needed it, doctor. When will you be leaving?"

"The tenth."

"Then God bless you, and all success to your work." The old woman touched his jacket sleeve with her wrinkled hand. "You seem a kind person and a good man, and I am pleased to have met you."

Her words were the only soothing ones he had heard in the last two days. "Thank you,

Mrs. Goodwin. I'm much obliged to you."

* * *

Starlin had made enough improvement to be miserable in his state of indolence by the Saturday before Ben's departure. Too well to sleep all day and too weak to be active, the boy lay on the sofa flipping through books he had read numerous times before. A pile of Dickens lay on the coffee table, and he kept the Guarnerius near at hand as well. Ben could never prevail upon him to play, but Colonel King had mentioned in passing that the boy would resume lessons as soon as he felt well enough.

Coming for the last visit before he turned Starlin over to Jaeryn's tender mercies, Ben paused at the sight of his patient's anguished face.

"What is it?" he asked kindly.

"I'm bored to tears lying around here." Starlin crumpled the latest *Times* between his hands and scowled. "I wish I had my automobile."

"You couldn't drive it if you did have it. You're not strong enough yet."

"I know, I know. You don't have to rub it in." He clasped his hands behind his head and voiced the doleful protest that he had repeated often in the last days. "I don't see why you have to go away."

Ben knelt down and opened his bag of instruments. "Yes, well, I wouldn't expect you to."

He had met with Colonel King, explaining his departure and recommending Jaeryn to take over Starlin's medical care. King inquired whether he planned to return, and to avoid arousing suspicion, Ben said he thought it likely. Until it was safe for Charlotte and Pearl to cross the Atlantic, no one would question his absence. After a while, he would drift away from most people's consciousness, and when the war was over, he would make amends to the others. Terry wouldn't be fooled by an indefinite absence, and he owed it to Alisa to come back in time. He would let Jaeryn deal with his patients. He had never been an official practicing doctor anyway; he was merely a medical assistant to circumnavigate the wartime laws.

"You'll be gone when I get my automobile," Starlin remarked.

Ben held the stethoscope to Starlin's chest to listen to his breathing. It was much better than it had been a couple of weeks ago. "I'll be sorry to miss it. When is the happy day?"

"A month from now. October sixteenth."

"Well, I wish you all success."

Starlin buttoned his shirt again. "Not much chance of that."

"Why ever not?" Ben folded up the stethoscope and returned it to his bag, making a note on the boy's medical record.

"I don't know how to drive, and my father says he won't break his neck showing me how."

He tapped his pencil against his chin and thought for a moment. "Can't you hire someone to show you?"

Starlin's eyes brightened. "I hadn't thought of that."

"Now, while I'm away, Doctor Graham will come once or twice to make sure you're back on your feet."

"Oh, spare me, please."

Ben paused his writing to give him a reproving glance. "Watch your tongue, young man. You've made a good recovery after all you've been through. The longer you stay away from the alcohol, the less you'll need to see him."

Starlin picked up his violin and placed it under his chin, testing the strings with his bow. "Cabernet Sauvignon is good. Besides, you'll be away, so you'll never know, will you?"

It was the first time he had caught genuine amusement on Starlin's face, even if it was only the barest smirk. Ben was pleased

324

enough by it to ignore its cause. "I'll expect you to be an impeccable example of British honor." He hesitated, and then added, "I think I ought to tell you something before I leave, since I won't be here to watch you as I have been. There was one night when you were quite sick and out of your head. I was waiting, and Stafford came into your room. I found a death threat in your room after he left."

"All the more reason to leave." Starlin carefully placed the violin down on the sofa again. "I'm not afraid of Stafford. I wish I could *do* something. Being holed up here all day is ghastly."

"If you like, I could take you to see Terry." Ben closed the notebook and stood up.

"Since you'll ride in the motorcar, you won't be exerting yourself much. It would help pass the time."

Starlin's eyes darted to his face and held there. "You bet. I don't think so."

"I think we will," Ben returned. "It would do you good."

"I don't want to get sick from the people at the hospital."

"You shouldn't. Your immunity is fine; you just need to gain your strength back. I'll have George give you an arm downstairs. It won't be a long visit, and I'd like to see you make things right with him before I go. You don't have any reason to be concerned—he's not a vindictive fellow."

"Bother."

Ben helped him into a light jacket and scarf and ordered George to help him to the automobile. It wouldn't hurt Starlin to face the results of his actions, and Terry wasn't likely to get reparation in any other way. Besides, it would offer Terry a much-needed distraction.

Starlin crossed his arms and sulked the whole way, while Ben enjoyed the speed and comfort of the motorcar. When they applied at the desk, the nurse told them Terry was able to see visitors.

As they reached the door of the men's ward, Starlin planted his feet and held back. "This is a waste of time."

Ben tugged at the boy's elbow. "You've nothing else to do, and this will speed your recovery. A clean conscience always—" He stopped, remembering that he, of all people, was ill-fit to speak to Starlin about conscience. "Never mind. Come along."

Starlin held back for a moment longer and then gave in. Terry turned his head as they approached, and his gaze locked with Starlin's for a long moment. Little impish twists quivered around his mouth in an attempt to hide ill-timed mirth, giving him a comical, elf-like appearance. Starlin was the first to speak.

"Well, I'm glad I'm not the only one."

Terry turned on his side the better to see his visitor, but he did not offer his hand in greeting. "It takes a real man to come and view his handiwork." He licked his dry lips and winked at Starlin.

Starlin took the chair Ben pointed to, and Ben saw him steal sideways glances at the patients in the adjoining beds.

"How are you, Terry?" Ben asked.

Terry gestured for him to take a seat on the end of his bed. "Well enough to be out of here."

"I give up." Ben laughed, but couldn't help thinking how much he was going to miss Terry. "If you were in your right mind, you would say otherwise. You do exactly as you're told; we don't want you breaking open your stitches like you did last time."

Terry grinned and ignored him. "Jaeryn came by and said you were leaving. I didn't know you weren't going to stick around for long."

He felt a twinge of annoyance at Jaeryn for telling Terry without asking leave. "That's right. I have things at home that need attending to, so I'm moving on for a bit."

Terry started inching up on the pillow until Ben gave him a stern look. He settled back down again. "Well, that's cause for rejoicing, isn't it? You're in need of a pleasure trip."

"I wouldn't call it a pleasure trip." He traced the calloused lines in his palm and along his fingernails.

"Oh, come now. A long face is all very well, but not all the time."

"I'm sorry." He allowed himself to smile.

"That's right. All better." Terry glanced at Starlin, who had his hands clenched in his lap, and a flicker of amusement crossed his face. Then he looked back at Ben. "I've been thinking about Erin with you going away. Do you think she'll move here soon? I don't want her to be without work, especially with no one to take care of her."

Ben nudged Starlin with his foot to keep him from staring at the nurse changing a patient's bandage across the way. "No, I don't think so. I wrote again and offered to help her find a place closer to you, but she needs time before she can trust a man again. She still hasn't found work yet. It might be wise to bring her to Folkestone when you're released from the hospital, but I doubt she'll come until you make her. Unless you write your parents about it. They might have influence with her."

Terry pulled himself up on one elbow. "That's up to her. She won't let me tell them. She made me promise."

And Terry, with his warm-hearted simplicity, would never think of breaking his word. "I wish I had time to write her before the steamer sails," said Ben. "I'm sure I'll be seeing your folks while I'm in Virginia." He would have ample time to do so if work was hard to find. If he hadn't found any two weeks after he arrived in Richmond, he would enlist as a private. He couldn't afford to wait any longer than that. "Do you want to send a message to them?"

"Sure. Give me a pencil and something to write on."

Ben gave him a scrap of paper and the pencil stub he always kept in his coat pocket. Laboriously, Terry traced out a message, taking one pause to catch his breath. Ben watched him in concern and once or twice urged him to dictate the message instead, but Terry shook his head. At length, he held it up in triumph.

"There you are."

Ben shoved it in his pocket. "I'll be sure to take it to them."

Terry talked for a few minutes of the home folks with a fondness that quieted his usual buoyancy. His siblings had hardly been out of childhood when he left. Though his mother wrote him often, he moved about so much that her letters were often misdirected. He didn't mention why he had given up a comfortable existence to come to England, but it didn't seem to be due to a strained relationship.

When he had exhausted that subject, Terry's eyes began roving around the room, looking anywhere but at his visitors. When he asked his next question, Ben realized that the chat had been leading to a different subject entirely.

"Are you taking Acushla with you?" Terry's voice was almost inaudible.

Ben sucked in an uneasy breath as a new complication rose before him. "No, she and Charlotte will be staying."

Terry nodded in satisfaction. "I'll take care of them for you when I'm back on my feet. Don't worry a bit about them."

"That's kind, but you'd best focus on getting your strength back before you start playing knight-errant."

"I'm better. I'm just humoring you folks." In spite of his words, Terry looked tired as he glanced at Starlin. "Your patient looks a bit wobbly. I don't think the air in here suits him."

Starlin's eyes shifted back and forth from Terry's face to his own lap. His body was so tense he was shaking, and he looked white around the mouth—probably from the antiseptic smell and the other sick people around him.

"Hold on, Starlin. We can leave now." Ben offered him a hand up, but Starlin leaned forward, and Ben waited.

The boy's lips were trembling. He had trouble forming the words clearly enough to be intelligible. "I wish I could take it back."

Terry watched him for a moment, and his eyes softened. "It takes a man to face up to what he's done and even more of a man to apologize." Then the imps came back, even amid the pain that tightened the lines in his face. "You have exceptional aim, King lad. But next time I suggest you try it on a German."

Terry was about to say more, but Ben forestalled him. "Don't encourage him."

Terry grinned. "He'll make a fine soldier as soon as he's old enough. Will you visit me again before you go?"

Ben helped Starlin up and grabbed his hat from the bed post. "I think not, my friend. I expect to see you on your feet when I return."

"You have yourself a deal, doc." Terry offered a strong hand whitened by confinement, and Ben gripped it heartily. "Maybe I'll even meet you at the station when you come back."

The act of shaking hands made Ben catch sight of the sapphire ring he kept on his finger, and he slipped it off. "I almost forgot. Here's the ring you gave me to show Erin."

Terry shook his head and dropped it back on Ben's palm. "Keep it until I ask you for it. It shouldn't be left unattended, and I don't have a place to put it."

Ben felt a surge of guilt for concealing the fact that he wasn't coming back, but there was nothing he could do for the time being. He was about to protest further when Starlin interrupted.

"Can we go, please?"

"Yes." Ben waved to Terry and gave Starlin an arm to the waiting car. The boy looked tired, but not overly so. It had been a good decision to make him come, breaking up the monotony and relieving his mind. Starlin looked more at peace than he had since Terry's accident.

Ben might never know the truth of what had brought those two incorrigibles together. Starlin was adept at keeping his own counsel, and Terry was supposed to be kept quiet until questions wouldn't upset his willingness to obey orders.

Someday soon he would know for sure what the coming months held, he thought, as he saw Starlin comfortably installed in his room and sleepy enough to lie down. Charlotte would go to Alisa's Sunday night so she and Pearl could settle in before he left. After that, he was on his own.

On the way home, he sent a telegram. His teeth clenched as he took the pencil and jabbed the words onto the paper along with the name "Matthew Dorroll."

Have given up the contract. Am coming to London Monday morning. If you wish to see me before I return to America, I will be on the first train. B.

If worse came to worst and his steamer encountered German resistance, he might not have a chance to see his father or any of others again. In his darkest moments, he almost hoped it would. He was accepting charity from a man who despised him, leaving his wife and sister in a country he detested, and cutting ties with everyone who had been a friend to him during his stay. Coming here had robbed him of his integrity, and now that he had lived a whole summer in Folkestone, he wasn't sure whether he owed his allegiance to England or to America.

Perhaps his return home would shed some light on the struggle that three months of espionage had only managed to further darken.

Chapter Nineteen
Implicit Trust

The cottage looked eerie with its empty cupboards and bare floors after the last arrangements had been made and he stood ready to go. It was the kind of eeriness that came from the ghosts of talk and tears and laughter, rooms full of life now emptied of their inhabitants. Ben was glad they were leaving this place. Ever since the night he'd fled to Jaeryn's, he had not felt secure sleeping there, nor easy leaving Charlotte alone. And strangely, his restlessness had only increased when the threat made no sign of resurfacing.

Mrs. Goodwin stood in the doorway, a thick gray shawl around her shoulders to ward off the early morning chill. Ben locked the door and handed her the key. "Thank you for allowing me the use of your cottage."

There was inscrutableness in every line of her pale, wrinkled face. "You're welcome, doctor. Safe journey. I'm pleased to have met you."

"And I you."

He held out his hand. She pressed it with a soft, cold touch; then he took a firm grip on his valise and set out for Alisa's, where he had left Charlotte and his trunk the night before.

As he walked down Tontine, he saw slim fingers appear at Jaeryn's consulting room window and ducked to the other side of the street. When he looked back, the curtain was pulled to the side, and the Irishman's steady gaze penetrated to where he stood. To his disappointment, Jaeryn made no attempt to signal him. That was the end of that. Tonight, he would take the steamer to America, and escaping from Jaeryn's prying clutches would be a great relief indeed.

Once Ben reached the end of Tontine, he signaled a cab and sat silently in the back, thinking over his decisions as they drove around the main gardens full of people. Jeremy had his steamer passage on file in London, and he would stop by later that morning to pick it up. But the appointment that lay heaviest on his mind was the long-awaited meeting with his father. Matthew Dorroll would meet him at the station and take him home for breakfast before he boarded the train for Liverpool. The prospect caused his stomach to tense, and his thoughts settled into a feverish mix of prayers and wondering and trying to imagine everything he would say and everything his father would say in return. He would almost sell his possessions to avoid it—and yet a tiny corner of his mind held onto the hope that it would turn out better than he expected.

"Here you are, sir." When they reached Alisa's door, the cabby raised a grizzled eyebrow at the fare. Ben tried to put a brave face on not giving a tip but ended with an apologetic shrug of the shoulders.

When he unlatched Alisa's kitchen door, he heard a sparkling, life-filled laugh that he hadn't heard for years. Alisa sat at the kitchen table, while Pearlie spooned out tea from a canister.

"After Ben's gone, we can take the baby for a morning walk," Pearlie was saying. "There's a place out beyond the best field that Terry said was beautiful. I haven't seen it yet. And then, if the shopping doesn't take too long and Matthew Benjamin has a good nap, we'll have a lovely quiet afternoon."

Ben tapped on the door just then, and Pearlie looked up, her mouth open. She closed it slowly and looked down at her shoes. "I didn't mean to sound—I am sorry that you're going away."

Ben shook his head. "You've found home. Don't be sorry."

Alisa murmured something about the baby and slipped into the parlor. Pearlie looked up and twisted her apron between her fingers. "After you left for college, I cried so much mother was angry." Her eyes grew large with wistfulness. "Why couldn't things have stayed the same with you and I?"

"Don't blame yourself. I've been gone for so long, we couldn't help growing apart." He tried to smile. "I miss you being small. You sat with me while I studied. I knew what to do with you, then."

"I've always been forgotten." A shadow fell across her brow. "I didn't even come to your wedding."

"I never forgot about you. Mother fought like a cat over the idea of you traveling. You stopped writing, and I thought perhaps you had grown out of caring so much…"

Pearl dashed at her eyes with the back of her hand. "I don't think I've ever loved anyone as much as I loved you. You were like some kind of hero in a storybook, always turning everything right and smoothing over my troubles and making me smile. I knew that whenever you came home, I would be safe and happy."

They heard Charlotte's step on the stairs. He reached out and clung fiercely to her fingers, whispering, "I'll come back, and we'll go back to the way things were. I'll make it up to you. I promise."

Pearl raised her head and mustered up a smile as Charlotte entered. Alisa tried to linger by herself in the dim light of the parlor, but Ben made her come in and be one of them. Alisa shook hands with him. It was hard to say good-bye to this little woman without knowing when he would see her again.

"You've been so kind to look after me," she said, holding his hand between her two tiny ones as if loath to let it go.

He returned the warm pressure. "And I wish I could look after you still. You've more than repaid us, opening your home to my wife and sister. But God's hands are far more capable than mine to take care of you, and Jaeryn Graham is a sensible man if you need medical advice."

When he took Charlotte in his arms and felt the shaking in her slender figure that she could not hide, his throat clenched. "You're safe here. It's all right."

She clenched the sleeve of his jacket. "I would rather share danger with you. I could be ready now, and we could go together."

"You are my one treasure," he murmured in her hair, "and I will never put you in peril if I can help it."

Charlotte's fingers glided through his hair one last time as she kissed him, and he wished—oh, how he wished—that he could do better for them.

Then he was alone, and the train to London hurtled through the countryside. The hard, third-class bench offered little comfort in the car. He was the only passenger to occupy it, and he was glad for the solitude. It gave him time to think, time to catch his breath after the tumult of arrangements he and Charlotte had talked through. They had finally decided to split the money between them, and if that didn't hold until he could send more, she and Pearl would look for work.

The creaks of the train car and the rhythmic whir of the wheels ground into his senses, turning the minutes into interminable agonies. He shifted, trying to find a more comfortable position, but his seat remained unyielding. Unstrapping his valise, he felt through his belongings until his fingers touched the book Starlin had given him the day he said goodbye. It was his to keep, which felt strange, for he had sold all his other books except his medical library, and his chances to read for leisure were few and far between. Ben untied the brown paper protecting the hardbound cover. It certainly was a thick little volume—a second edition, Starlin said. He rather doubted he would finish it all. But at least it would be a distraction. And between his nervousness at meeting his father and the humiliation of thinking through everything that had gone wrong, he wanted a distraction. The train wheels clacked quieter in his ears as he read; the car jostled in a pleasant way instead of an agony; and he lost himself in the strange, dimly-lit pages, drowning for a while the fear of the future.

"London!"

He tucked the book away and waited until the puff of brakes signaled that he could leave. Fog drifted past the windows, turning the lamps into yellow rims of haze, and crumpled trash tumbled along the pavement. A crowd of passengers in front of him blocked his view as he left the train. He slipped past them, scanning the crowd to pick out a man who might be a relation. He wondered what his father would look like. The only memory he had was a blurred face with a strange mixture of timidity and harshness in its angular lines. His father would not know him either, for a four-year-old child bore little resemblance to a man in his mid-twenties.

Slick businessmen, country farmers, and impeccable members of Parliament all hurried past, minding their own business and caring little for anyone else's. Questions crowded thick and fast upon his thoughts as he wandered through the men's waiting room and back out to the platform. Was his father rich? They didn't know; they had never known, but it seemed likely, for Edmond had posted letters from several places abroad before the war. Was he gray-haired and feeble or hale and active? The time he'd spent in Scotland Yard seemed to suggest a certain level of industry, but that did not mean he was vigorous still.

Deep down, however, all Ben wanted to know was whether they would like each other and why they'd had to separate in the first place.

"Doctor Benjamin Dorroll?"

He turned around and held out his hand to the white-haired stranger who had greeted him.

"Yes."

The man shifted and pretended not to see the hand. "You reminded me of your brother in your looks. I'm Matthew Dorroll. This way, if you please, to my car. I'll take you to my house before your appointment."

An odd flutter filled Ben's thoughts as he followed the man to a touring car and placed his trunk and valise in the back. He felt neither love nor hate. He was merely curious. The man claimed to be his father, and he took him at his word. Matthew Dorroll was about six feet tall, and had deep-set blue eyes, a determined chin, and thin lips, with well-developed shoulders that showed signs of losing their form after years of inactivity. A handsome profile, only marred by a look of insecurity deep in the black pupils. From the few words he uttered, his voice sounded smooth and well-cultured with a deep, even tone.

They drove in silence past rubble-filled streets and empty buildings. Few people were abroad this early, and no children were to be seen whatsoever. Matthew Dorroll took him to a comfortable brick house in London's Kensington borough and handed off the automobile to a man at the front door to be taken to the garage. He led the way straight to the dining room where a modest breakfast of toast, coffee, and broiled ham was set out in readiness for them. This meal looked altogether more in keeping with the times than did the food from the King or Emmerson estate.

His father spoke first.

"You wrote you were pleased with the practice in Folkestone."

It was awkward for both of them. Ben told himself nervously that he shouldn't expect his father to feel comfortable right away. After a few moments, they would be easier and say the things that needed to be said.

"Yes, sir. The medical end of things has been pleasant."

"Is it an involved occupation?"

"It can be, at times. I learned more about the war than I ever wished to."

Matthew Dorroll's mouth quirked grimly upward at the corner. "Ah, yes, the air raid. A most unfortunate business."

"It was." Ben handed his cup and saucer to the maid pouring coffee, and they waited for her to leave the room before they continued. "You said my mission was neither difficult nor dangerous, but I have found it to be both. I wonder what caused it to change?"

"No more danger than your brother saw in France," Matthew Dorroll countered, "or than many men have had to endure. Though perhaps you blame me for bringing you here just before the air raid."

Ben debated on whether to be diplomatic or truthful and settled for diplomatic. "No. How could you have known? Nothing like that was happening when you asked me to come."

"I was glad when you accepted, as was Ryson when I told him." Matthew reached for the butter dish and kept his eyes on the tablecloth as he spoke.

"Was he?" Ben tried in vain to attract his father's notice. "He never let on as much. I heard you had some connections to Folkestone that would have been helpful to my work. I'm surprised you never told me."

"I do not know of what you speak."

Ben looked at his father carefully, but he couldn't detect any sign of deceit in his face. No sign of anything, in fact: only the strain of doing a necessary duty by a guest that he knew from report to be his son. The surge of adrenaline he had felt since their meeting spiraled down. This man was no different than a stranger, and he knew how to talk to strangers. "One of your former acquaintances in Folkestone died recently, a Mr. Emmerson. Perhaps you heard of it."

Matthew's knife and fork stopped at the news. "I had not."

"Word has it you were his private investigator for many years."

He resumed eating again. "The reports are true, then. Perhaps best not turned into a subject of common gossip; but, of course, that is at your discretion."

"Sir," Ben continued, eyeing his father candidly, "I would have appreciated the help your knowledge of him could have given."

"Then you came to London to ask me for help?"

"No. I came to London to see you before I leave England. My work here has concluded unsuccessfully. I am going home."

He winced at the long sigh that swept through his father's frame. "I am sorry to hear it."

Ben laid down his silverware and placed his napkin on the table. "And I'm sorry to have failed your expectations. But I think you could help the man still working there if you were willing to tell me about your private affairs in Folkestone."

Matthew shook his head. "I'm interested in your success, not his."

"Why? Is it because you care about what happens to me?" Ben asked the question almost below his breath and did not dare to wait for the answer. "Why was my presence necessary? I was inexperienced and disliked the work and knew nothing of the people and their ways. The puzzle doesn't fit. What would I have been able to give them that they couldn't get on without?"

The stony blue eyes kept perfectly still, linking with his own as if testing his mettle for the answer he was about to receive. Ben raised his chin and met his father's gaze to tell him that he could bear it.

"You can give nothing. And it was not because I cared."

The words stung him. "Then why did you make me come? Am I some sort of foil to cover your purposes there?"

Matthew frowned in rebuke. "I have no object in Folkestone. Mr. Emmerson was strictly a political acquaintance."

Ben swallowed hard. "I haven't told Ryson about your connection with Emmerson yet, or Jaeryn, though he is beginning to suspect you have a part in this affair. Your foothold is precarious, sir, and in spite of your—indifference, I do not want to see you fall. You had a disagreement with Emmerson shortly after the war broke out. What is your purpose? I must ask it. It was not right to bring me here while refusing to tell me the whole truth."

His father hardly reacted, and with a great deal of trepidation, Ben persisted. "I would like an answer, sir. Did you bring me here to give me a start in life? Or to meet me, perhaps?"

"No, no." The small hope that he had harbored in his coming rankled, a bitter shard of pain, at Matthew Dorroll's words. "You are your mother's son; we made that agreement. I never brought you here to take you away from her. But I would like you to follow through on your commitment."

"I'm obliged to you, but I prefer the arrangements that have been made. If it were in my power, I would do anything to follow your wishes. But in this instance, I cannot."

Life was odd, he thought drearily. Here he was, torn between his loyalties to his father and his loyalties to Jaeryn. Two men who would use him and toss him aside without a qualm when he no longer served their interests. It would be more natural to side with his father and tell the truth about Jaeryn's disobedience. Matthew Dorroll would have the influence to smooth it over. But he stuck with Jaeryn—why? They had been constantly at odds with each other. They had parted ways forever. But for some reason that he could not put into words, he trusted Jaeryn more. In spite of the Irishman's wrongdoing, Ben felt that Jaeryn must have a good reason for his disobedience—a reason important enough to shield.

Matthew sighed again, and Ben felt the knot tighten in his throat. "Then you should do what you wish. But going to America seems rather foolhardy, as well as unnecessary. You could still serve your country by enlisting."

"I came to serve your interests, sir, not English ones. My loyalties lie with America."

"I had hoped that by coming here you might be persuaded to change your mind."

"Your country keeps too many secrets for my taste, I think." Ben searched until he found an angle that would take the focus off himself and make his refusal more palatable. "Edmond enlisted, and that will have to be enough for both of us. Have you heard anything of him? I haven't heard from him since he went to America."

"Neither have I."

"Then I shall hope to see him there." Ben wondered again if Edmond had ever told his father of his marriage. He decided not to chance it, for Alisa had never mentioned a personal connection to her father-in-law.

They were both ready to be done with the conversation, uncomfortable at best and not bettering either of them in the other's opinion. But they carried on, bound by duty, and Ben sensed that the subject they had both sidestepped was about to come to a head.

Matthew Dorroll rose and pushed in his chair. "If you are finished eating, we can talk in a more comfortable room." He led the way out of the dining room and down the hall, a mahogany-walled passage with one or two pieces of statuary and several old paintings. The living room was furnished in muted browns and reds, not sumptuously, but containing every possible article to gratify the owner's taste. There were curios from his travels ranged around shelves, articles of foreign make and little marble gods and goddesses, hangings of Indian manufacture, and books in several foreign languages. The only things lacking were any photographs or signs of family life. It was as comfortable as a club and equally as devoid of personality.

"You seem to manage a comfortable existence in spite of the war," Ben remarked, taking the seat his father offered.

Matthew crossed one leg over the other and leaned his head on languid fingers. "I am not physically affected by it. The only inconvenience is a slight monotony."

"Many of my acquaintance would envy that monotony."

"I think not."

They stared at each other for one suspended moment of good manners: father and son, together for the first time in almost two decades, the distance between them just as great as before.

"You are much changed, my—"

"You may say it, sir." Ben pressed his hands against the chair's arms. "After all, I am your son. No surprise that you see a change; I was a boy when we saw each other last. I don't even remember what you were like then."

Matthew Dorroll winced and nodded.

"I don't say it to blame you. You did what many men have done before." Ben forced a smile. "I trust you find the change an improvement."

A slight tremor went through the hand that was empty of its wedding band. "Certainly. You must have lived well yourself, with all the learning you managed to accomplish. You surpassed Edmond,

340

even though he had every opportunity I could give."

"I carved opportunities out for myself. School never gave me much trouble once I turned my mind to it."

"You had your intellect from me, at least. I'm pleased you took pains to better yourself. Did you—were you in much want all these years?" Matthew's eyes flicked once to meet his and then looked down again.

Ben twisted his fingers together and clenched them tight, but the tension inside him did not loosen. "My mother lacked for nothing, sir. She lived off her inheritance for a long time, and after that, she lived off of my means."

"And you?"

"My wants were provided for."

"Ah." His father looked far from convinced. "You must have worked hard. She couldn't have done much for you unless she is different than she used to be."

Ben's planning stood him in good stead, for he had thought out what he would say if he ever met his father face-to-face. Twenty years of imagining. "I fulfilled your promise to love and cherish your wife since you found yourself unable to."

"I don't see how you could stand to do it."

"It was an act of the will. Love is, I have heard. I have also heard the feeling follows after, but I have yet to experience it."

His father sniffed. "Do you expect to?"

"That hope has a cruel way of living even when I try to kill it. But even if I do not, I will follow the right way instead of my inclination." Ben raised his chin and then brought it down again lest it should be taken as defiance.

"Are you saying that to make me feel remorseful?"

He shook his head. "No, sir. I only refer to my own experience."

"I see." Matthew frowned. "I am surprised that a man as tenacious as you should be willing to leave your work here unfinished. If you have as much confidence in your abilities as you seem to, then you ought to be able—"

Ben interrupted. "I didn't come for the work. The money played a part in it—I needed the money. But defending England from infiltrators never factored into my decision."

"What did, then?"

"I just wanted to meet you—wanted to know if you wished to meet me. Or if you might think something I did was worthy of affirmation."

His words had a slight effect, if the hint of guilt on his father's face was any indication. In the end, however, there were many kinds of guilt, and this proved to be an ineffective one. Matthew Dorroll made no reply, and Ben took a deep breath.

"It was foolish of me. Now I see that I will never accomplish what I came for, so I go home with a clean conscience and free hands. Your choices have shaped much of my life thus far, but I do not think you regard me as your son, and since you gave me to my mother, my duty lies with her." He said it earnestly and promised himself that every word was true, but for all that, it would never be true.

"You blame me for what we did."

"That is not for me to say."

Matthew leaned forward with his hands on his knees, then on a sudden looked him straight in the eyes. "Go back to Folkestone and wait a week. I will clear your name."

"The tickets are bought."

"I want you to finish this."

Ben wavered. After a moment, he shook his head. "With all due respect, if you will not be honest with me, then I cannot change my decision."

He saw the anger flash across his father's face, and had he allowed himself, he doubtless would have been experiencing the same emotion. The chiming of the clock signaled an end to their interview. Matthew Dorroll pressed a buzzer to signal for the housemaid.

"My man will take you to your appointment. I trust you can find the station from there?"

"Yes, sir. Thank you for allowing me to meet you." Ben held out his hand, and his father took it hastily and dropped it again. "I had a favor to ask before I go. I am going to America, but my wife and sister are staying here until I am in a better position to send for them. Pearl is grown now, and she needs someone to look after her while I am gone. I had hoped you might. There are plenty of young men in Folkestone, and she has a pretty face."

A blank perplexity crossed his father's face. "Who is sh—? Oh. The girl will find better direction from her own common sense. My methods were far from successful."

Ben abandoned the attempt. He could only hope that Terry would be kept in bed long enough to allow their love to lessen to friendship. "My wife knows you are in London, and I have left her your address. If she ever comes to you in an extremity, please help her. She is a sensible woman, but we live in dangerous times."

"Such advice as I can give is at her disposal, but I think her own would serve her better."

He tried to think of anything to buy himself more time with this man he had wanted so much to meet, but he could think of nothing. "I suppose I should intrude no longer on your time."

Matthew Dorroll looked at him keenly. "I did not know what to expect when I agreed to meet you this morning."

Ben glanced up at his father's face, but neither of them could look each other in the face for long. "Neither did I. Thank-you for agreeing to see me."

A maid led him to the front door, where an automobile purred in readiness. The driver navigated with expert familiarity around blocked alleys and jammed streets, setting him down in record time before the door of Ryson's office building.

As he came through the door, Jeremy pulled his ticket out and gave it to him, looking a trifle ashamed. "Best of luck, sir."

"You too, Jeremy. And better success to both of us."

His father hardly knew him. The feeling was mutual and hardly surprising after all this time. But he did not want to feel contempt toward the man, and that troubled him most. Perhaps he had been hasty to hope that a personal meeting would smooth over years of indifference.

He felt like a little boy who had almost found his way and now was lost again.

* * *

That day it was Jaeryn's turn to find an intruder observing him. He came into his consulting room at lunchtime, balancing a full glass and plate, and saw Fenton sitting behind the desk. Fenton leaned back in the leather chair with an ease that sent Jaeryn into a slow burn of irritation.

"What do you want?" he snapped.

"Your undivided attention," Fenton returned, unperturbed.

He set down his plate. "You can go straight back to wherever it was you came from. I'm in no mood to discuss anything with you."

"Well, you'll do it all the same. It's about time you stopped acting like a fool, and since there's no one else to make you, I'll take the responsibility."

Jaeryn pointed to the door. "Out."

Fenton stood up and leaned toward him over the desk, so close that there were not six inches between them. "You'll sit, and you'll listen. Otherwise, I'll tell Ryson the truth, and he'll give your position to a man who deserves it."

Jaeryn looked down at him and drew his brows together. "I suppose you mean the American. If you brought him back, your source of income would be finished. He doesn't stoop to using leeches like I do. Besides, we've arranged matters between us, and I'll thank you not to interfere."

"Then you're a much smaller man than I took you for. The fact is, you've lost another decent assistant, and this time you could have prevented it."

He shifted impatiently. "I don't want to hear any of your

detestable conjectures. I'm running short on time, and I have a train to catch. Besides, I didn't forge the note that got him dismissed. That was Ann Meikle's fault."

Fenton rebuked him with feline delight. "Don't be rude, doctor. You're going to hear me whether you have the time or not. I wasn't referring to the position he lost. I'm referring to the fact that you lost *him*. A little tact on your part would have gone far to prevent all his animosity, but you can still get him back if you're willing to be reasonable."

Jaeryn struggled for a moment to overcome his inclination send the man away. He resented the fact that he had failed to win Dailey's respect, barely acknowledging it even to himself. The thought of someone he considered scum coming to rub it in sickened him. It was not to be borne. Fenton didn't even have the claim of loyalty to lend credence to his words.

But despite his ire, he began to see the benefit of hearing Fenton out, if only to learn why the mercenary wanted to heal the breach. If his breaking ties with Dorroll wasn't irrevocable, then this was the first time in a long series of similar escapades that he would have a second chance.

Jaeryn wasn't completely averse to that, now that he was cool enough to admit it. Granted, Dorroll wasn't likely to threaten him at any point in the future—but it was still an unsecured danger point. It was always better to close a door in friendship.

"Go on, then," he heard himself saying.

Fenton cleared his throat with infuriating condescension. "You might have been more circumspect about your dislike for him at the beginning. I don't know where all your training went, but it wasn't in your head. You couldn't have done worse if you were trying to turn him against you."

"I had good reasons to look into his affairs further than he liked. At first it may have been for reasons of self-interest, but later there was legitimate suspicion surrounding him." Jaeryn's jaw tightened with a return of his stubbornness.

Fenton's dark eyes twinkled and he smiled maliciously. "If you don't enjoy unjust accusation, then why did you expect him to?"

Jaeryn looked at the cold tea and abandoned lunch and grimaced. "You've had your say, and I've listened to you. Now, if you don't object, I have other things to do this afternoon."

"No, you haven't listened. One thing more, and then I've done with the unpleasant side of what I have to say. Charity is degrading to the likes of Dailey. But he can't refuse an appeal for help, and that's how you can twist him around your finger again."

Hot wrath rose in his throat. "I don't need his help."

"Don't you?" Fenton made a little sound of doubt in his throat. "That's your risk to take. You're a fool if you pass up an opportunity that could be to your advantage."

Jaeryn crossed his arms. "What benefit could his services be to me?"

"Very good benefit, considering the people he can put you in touch with. He's going back to his mother's place. While I was there, I found inklings that her—friend—was not what he ought to have been. I suspect he wants more from their acquaintance than the mere pleasure of her society." Fenton held his gaze to see if he understood, and Jaeryn's arms fell to his sides again.

"Such as?"

"It seemed odd that all her son's letters should be kept at his office rather than her house. They were addressed in Dailey's hand, or I miss my guess."

"Well, what of that?"

Fenton shrugged. "My steamer sailed before I was able to continue my investigations. But I told Dailey before he left to keep a sharp lookout. There's more there for him to find. After all, Richmond was marked on Emmerson's map."

Jaeryn caught his breath. "I didn't tell you that."

"No. You didn't."

He dropped the lesser issue for the greater one. "What did Dailey say to you when you told him he could help me?"

"He didn't say much. Seemed to share your opinion of me. But I know more about him than you do, and he'll come around in the end, even if it has to be for your benefit."

Jaeryn narrowed his eyes. "That's complimentary. Is the idea of helping me so awful?"

"Positively repulsive," Fenton countered swiftly. Before Jaeryn could respond, he continued, "Dailey has the power to look further into what I saw, which is to your advantage. And an apology is your ticket back into his favor. That's the only way around it. You were a fool to close the door on him in the first place, and if you're wise, you'll reopen it. It would be a detriment not to make up with him when you could be the gainer by his services." Fenton's lips twisted into a smirk. "The apology doesn't have to be genuine, you know."

Jaeryn watched him with keen attention, and the anger drained from his soul in the reawakening of hope. Nonetheless, he played the part of dubiousness to save his dignity. "It's rather late for that. I think he's more likely to leave me behind for good and consider himself lucky to escape. He had the talent to make a go of his position here, and I never understood why he seemed so set against it."

Fenton shrugged. "Neither you nor I are respectable men anymore; we've learned how to survive without our innocence. But he had to choose between his integrity and his father's request. He couldn't overcome his dislike of backstabbing and deceit long enough to do what it took. And I think he truly hated England."

Jaeryn rolled his eyes. "He could do with a bit less virtue; it won't hurt him in the long run. Besides, helping England isn't so bad. I'm Irish, and I manage quite well."

"You have your own private loyalties to make it worth your while. Benjamin Dailey will never give up his precious conscience without a fight, and you're going to have to figure out how to work around that. If you're committed to succeeding like I think you are, you'd better seal his friendship and keep it alive and well." Fenton slid down in the leather chair until his head rested against the back of it. "In future, his father is likely to be involved in your little investigations. If you pave the way now, you'll be able to put the son to good use when the truth of Matthew Dorroll's involvement comes to light."

Jaeryn frowned. "You're talking as if Dailey's still involved. He's going to America, he'll tell me what he finds there, and that's an end of it."

"Is it? I can give you better advice than I've given you thus far, now that you're listening."

Jaeryn shrugged in defeat. "I don't appear to have much choice."

"You need to bring him back, and that means you'll have to erase the shame he took for your sake. He's one key to your success, and for that alone, you should protect your assets. Ann Meikle didn't get him out of the way just for the amusement of it."

"That's a great deal of speculation on your part," Jaeryn remarked, with a less offensive tone than he had previously employed. "But it's possible, and I'm not so unreasonable as to ignore the sense of what you're saying." He reached into his drawer and pulled out the agreed-upon rate for occasions when his ferret brought something especially important.

Fenton held up his hand and shook his head. "None of that."

Jaeryn pushed the notes closer to him. "It's what you always take."

"I didn't come for money."

"Then why did you?"

Fenton tilted his head and fixed his gaze on the dark wooden floorboards. "Even a man such as myself can suffer the effects of—conscience."

Jaeryn stared at him in amazement. "I was going to Liverpool to get something from Dailey before he sailed. But not with the intention of making up with him."

"Before this is over, you may thank your luck that he crossed your path. Perhaps he'll be the one to offer you lasting service in the end." Fenton picked up the key ring lying on the desk and spun it around his fingers. "You're cutting it close if you mean to catch the train. I'll lock up for you if you wish so you can get there on time."

"I'm not as gullible as that." Jaeryn held out his hand, and Fenton surrendered the keys to him.

After Fenton left, Jaeryn flipped through the timetable to re-check the train routes. In the quiet that fell over the study, he was almost afraid to think for fear of the guilt that would crash down on him if he did. But it crashed down all the same, and a wave of remorse made him hunch his shoulders under the weight of it. He had been a poor mentor in everything that mattered, and a fool on all accounts. That was what the man he despised saw in him. The ignominy of it made him sick and speechless all in one.

But he had no time to waste. After scribbling a note to tack on the door for patients, Jaeryn left his lunch sitting on the desk and dashed off to reach the last train for Liverpool. He hated leaving things in abandoned chaos, but he didn't have another option. Charlotte Dailey wasn't there to tidy up for him.

Fenton was wrong, of course. Letting his assistant stay at the risk of giving up his own position wasn't a viable option. He had never done so in other assignments, and it seemed too late to try this time. He was much better equipped to succeed than Dorroll was. The train ride would give him several hours to plan his course of action, and he would need every single one of them.

* * *

It took Ben a little time to find London's Paddington Station in the maze of streets, but once he was there, he didn't have any great difficulty getting to the right platform. Securing a ticket was a quick matter, and once in a seat with his luggage in the overhead rack, he was content to watch the people scurrying back and forth. Men, women, and children; military and private citizens; rich and poor alike. A few of them were returning soldiers. In spite of their civilian clothing, the lack of one or more limbs marked them out. One man had a face so scarred and disfigured by burns that he tried in vain to conceal them with a heavy wool scarf. He was broad-shouldered, his hair brown and wavy, his blue eyes stern and piercing.

A cloud hung over Ben's horizon after seeing the man, for it reminded him of Edmond.

Through towns and cities, stopping and starting, across scenic and dull country alike, the train whirled on and Ben with it, surrounded by women busy at their knitting and men passing the time with a pipe. The train pulled into Liverpool at 2:25 in the afternoon under an overcast sky, and he left his trunk at the station to be collected later. He had until six o' clock to kill time without getting lost and losing his steamer.

Time dragged as he wandered up and down the streets, looking at window displays. More often than not he couldn't understand the talk of the people around him, and he suspected that the strange accent grating in his ears was Welsh. He walked his beat as faithfully as a policeman until a bobby stopped and asked him his business, prompting him to find another place to spend his afternoon. After a little exploration, an empty bench in a public park presented itself. Ben sat down and pulled out his wallet to count again the eight pounds he needed to change to American currency. All there, and whatever he had left when he reached Richmond went to his mother. She wouldn't be happy to learn of his plan to stay with her, but the shock of his coming might give him the upper hand, and he had every intention of taking advantage of it.

The clouds unleashed a spitting rain between two and three, and Ben took refuge in an Anglican church on a side street. The door creaked as he entered the welcome hush of empty pews. White cloud-light filtered through the stained glass, dust particles dancing through the gleam. The dark woodwork from floor to ceiling settled a sleepy aura over the place.

A gray-haired sexton wielding a broom observed him as he chose a place to sit. Ben folded his hands over his knees. All the need for talk and pretense was over. Now there was nothing left to do but wait for the time to pass as it had never failed to pass before.

After a while, the sexton moved on. Ben's eyes grew heavy from the culminating effect of an early start and all the preceding sleepless nights. It seemed a long time to him that he sat thus, though whenever he checked his watch, he found that time was moving slower than he thought. He leaned his arms on the smooth, amber-polished pew in front of him and closed his eyes.

Somehow, after a while, he knew that he had closed his eyes for a long time without realizing it. He straightened and found it was a touch from the sexton that had awakened him. The old man chuckled and drew his heavy hand away. "A church is a grand place for a wee nap in the rain."

Ben jerked up and shook off the last remnants of sleep. "I'm so sorry."

"You're all right." The sexton's deep, throaty voice tangled around remnants of Welsh in his talk. "You look respectable, and I had a guarantee about you."

Ben took up his coat and valise. "I'm waiting for the steamer bound for New York. I hope I haven't missed it. The rain came on, and your church being handy—"

"No, you have plenty of time left," the man reassured him. "But you do have a visitor if you're ready to see him. That's why I woke you. He came about ten minutes ago, and he told me you were a good lad."

Ben glanced up the empty aisle to see a man with a bowed head sitting in a pew. "Indeed."

"Yes, he's waiting for you over there."

With a guess that was an almost certainty, Ben stood up and made his way up the aisle. The man didn't shift his attitude of reverence, but Ben's suspicions were confirmed when he came alongside and saw the familiar dark hair and green eyes. Jaeryn looked sideways at him with anything but a solemn expression. Ben's mouth tightened.

"Hello," Jaeryn whispered.

"Hello."

"Would you let me talk to you for a few minutes? Perhaps a cafe?

351

I know it's raining, but the place isn't far from here."

He said nothing, stepping back to allow Jaeryn space to go before him. Jaeryn picked up his overcoat, nodding to the sexton as they stepped out in the rain. Ben followed with squared shoulders. They walked beside each other, neither of them offering to speak, though Jaeryn's lips moved incessantly as if he were running over something in his memory. Jaeryn didn't have an umbrella, and even though they had hats, they were both plastered from the wet before they reached the street he wanted. When they arrived at the cafe, an elegant establishment with glass-topped tables and metal chairs, their coats were soaked. Other customers had crowded the tables to wait until the rain passed over. Jaeryn chose a corner in the back and ordered coffee for two. They waited in awkward silence until the waiter deposited the tray and left them alone together.

"Help yourself; I never paid attention to what you took before." Jaeryn smiled and pushed the silver pot toward him. "What do you like?"

"Sugar." He dumped double rations into the steaming china cup and drank it down in haste from habit.

Jaeryn's eyes twinkled with merriment. "The fates are against us. No sooner do we agree never to see each other again then I must come post-haste after you to get something I forgot."

"What was that?"

"You left your forged medical certificate, but I drove you off so quickly you took your false passport. It has to be burned. I've done it plenty of times on my own account—it's an odd feeling to see all record of your present life perish in flames. Almost makes you feel like you've killed someone. Anyway, if you've no objection—or even if you have, I'm afraid—I'll have to confiscate your fraud identification."

He set down his empty coffee cup. "It's in my trunk back at the station. I'll have to get it for you when I pick it up."

"Not a problem." That was the end of Jaeryn's cheery words, and at length he said quietly, "I fear I didn't express my appreciation of your services in our last conversation."

Ben looked away. "It doesn't matter. They weren't anything worth mentioning."

"Oh, but they were. It was a kind deed, you saving my position for me, and more than generous, for I deserved the consequences you took."

The comforting aroma of coffee beans sent up a gentle steam from the pot to warm his face. "I didn't mind it much. You'll find it easier to work alone, no doubt."

Jaeryn looked taken aback. "I didn't really mean that."

"You say many things you don't mean, I think." It didn't matter now whether Jaeryn was offended by his insinuations or not; they were parting ways, and their relation to each other made no difference anymore. Yet Ben almost wished they weren't finished with their acquaintance. He was beginning to find his original annoyance shifting to—he hardly dared call it liking; that would be too warm a feeling after what had occurred—but a better appreciation of Jaeryn's abilities. Jaeryn had shown moral callousness every now and then, but he was so committed to his cause that perhaps he knew no difference between his truth and his lies anymore.

Jaeryn sighed. "You don't trust me now; I can see that. And you probably never will, after the things I said to you. I know you well enough to know that. But I hope you can a little, someday. The truth is, I would have tried to see you even if there was no passport to be gotten. I've never been so ashamed in all my life after what I said to you."

Perhaps, if he would admit it, the comforting warmth wasn't only from the coffee steam. "What caused that about-face?"

Jaeryn grimaced. "Fenton came this afternoon and told me what he thought of my methods. I never expected to get a dressing-down from such a rascal of a man. He told me what was in my best interest without my asking and took no money in return. I'm still not sure why. But the upshot of it is, we have been at odds, you and I; and if I

353

could do it over again, I'd do it differently."

A pointed silence fell between them. Jaeryn glanced at him over the polished silver cups. The chatter of fellow customers buzzed around them, wrapping them up in a small pocket of noiseless space. Every minute or so, a crack of thunder could be heard, followed by the answering shimmer of glass shaking from the noise. Ben waited for a long moment before responding. He returned Jaeryn's gaze unblinkingly, trying to measure how he should answer the appeal. Jaeryn probably wouldn't have made were it not for his henchman's suggestion. But as he gazed into that pair of green eyes, he realized that whether or not Jaeryn was sincere, he at least thought he was. An expression was hidden in their depths—the "priest look," Terry called it—a seasoned compassion that was rare to find in someone only twenty-eight years old. Surely even Jaeryn couldn't feign a look like that.

Ben shrugged and wrapped both hands around his coffee cup. "You weren't so bad that you should torment yourself in dust and ashes. I was at fault, too, and I would do things differently now. You were very hospitable on my first coming here. I should have made a better return of it."

"Yes, you should have." It was spoken under his breath, but judging by Jaeryn's candor, it was a sore point with him. "I'm not so unworthy of your confidence as you think. I wanted your implicit trust, and you made a fine botch of that."

"Well, I'm sorry. I trusted who you thought you were, at any rate."

"What?" Jaeryn stared at him.

"Never mind." Ben looked at his watch and stood up. "Thank you for the coffee. It's almost five, and I must be going, but I'm glad we met again before I left."

Jaeryn held up his hand. "Please don't go. I'm not finished. You still have an hour before you have to be on board; I'll make sure you're there in plenty of time. Besides, I planned out this confounded awkward speech on the way here, and if I don't say it now I'll have to write to you."

Ben chuckled softly at the distaste in his tone. Evidently, the shortness of Jaeryn's letter about the steamer passage hadn't been solely due to their disagreement. "That would be a tragedy."

"Yes. I mean, no. Of course, I shouldn't mind if it came down to it. Stay a moment, will you? Just for one more thing, and then we can go." Jaeryn looked almost nervous for once. "I wanted to say that you're more capable of making your way without me than I thought. And I apologize for what I said during both our disagreements." He said the words hastily as if eager to get it over with.

A strange, undefined feeling welled up within Ben—hope, perhaps, or gladness—or simply a sense of relief that they were settling their differences after weeks of standing at odds. "Apology accepted."

A smile spread across Jaeryn's face, easing the lines of tension away. "You're a close-mouthed fellow and too secretive for your own good," he teased, "but you're not half bad for all that."

Ben watched Jaeryn with a secret pleasure that he had not had to leave without seeing him once more. "I ought to be making my way to the dock now. I want to be there early. You can come with me, if you like, while I pick up my trunk from the station. But we won't be able to take a cab if you're going to say anything confidential."

"I'll come. I haven't finished with you yet." Jaeryn made quick work of settling the bill and left a sovereign on the table for a tip. "You'll have to tell me where you want to go; I've never been to Liverpool before. I saw this cafe as I was tracking you down this afternoon." He stepped aside and motioned for Ben to go first. "You were hard to find, you know. Which landing is your steamer docked at?"

Ben braced himself for the misting wet and ducked into the rain. "We're going to Pier Head, Prince's Landing Stage."

* * *

355

Now that they had managed to talk without spiraling into an argument, Jaeryn felt on a more solid footing. He had no idea where they were, but Ben seemed to be taking a confident lead, so he fell into step beside him and plunged into talk again. "Well, first of all, I'm going to London to tell Ryson the truth and clear your name."

Ben seemed less keen on the idea than he expected. "You're better off getting someone who can be of real help to you. I don't think he'll appreciate the truth."

"Make no protest. Go to America and do your work there. Even after I do tell him, I can't promise that he'll take you back. But I will not be satisfied until you receive justice."

Ben shoved his hands in his coat pockets, and his jaw had a more relaxed look about it, though he kept his eyes fixed ahead. "You haven't learned a thing, you know, for all your carefully planned speeches."

The words were so distant from what he was expecting that Jaeryn didn't hear them immediately. Ben glanced at him out of the corner of his eye, and Jaeryn suspected by the twitching of his mouth that the American was more amused than impressed by his offers of championship. He watched him, uncertain of what to say.

"I think you were born with it," Ben said, laughing quietly. "You're just as keen on managing my affairs as ever. Even now you can't let me go without your permission."

"Now, just a minute," Jaeryn protested. "I wouldn't—"

Ben interrupted him. "Yes, you would; there's no use denying it. If I came back tomorrow, you would set Fenton to watching me again and never see the problem in it. Capable of doing without you, indeed. That's the biggest falsehood you've tried to pass off thus far. I think we'd get on better all the same, though."

Jaeryn made a strangled noise of protest that died before it reached his lips.

"You're a prying fellow and too controlling for your own good. But if you once got over that, you would be fairly likeable." A hint of mockery edged Ben's voice and almost took Jaeryn's breath away.

Jaeryn scrambled to find his bearings again, and though he felt the pinch of truth, he didn't mind the pleasure at his expense. "*Touché*."

They paused their conversation while Ben retrieved his trunk at the station and tipped the porter who had kept it for him. It took him a while to find his real passport, but at length he dug it out and found Pearl's and Charlotte's alongside it. Ben looked regretfully at them before handing them back. "I can't give you my wife and sister's false ones; they're in Folkestone. But I would be obliged if you took their real ones back to them—if it's not too much trouble."

"None in the least." Jaeryn put the papers in his derby, taking care not to crumple them. He had no intention of burning the false ones, but it would be just as well to have them in his own hands for safekeeping.

The trunk wasn't too heavy, but rather unwieldy for one person to carry, so Jaeryn took one side of it and Ben took the other, and they set off. The rain fell lighter now, swirling over the street in little eddies of wind, diminishing as it blew.

"Would you like to come back if you could?" Jaeryn asked.

Ben shook his head. "I'm going home."

Jaeryn tried to read what Ben was thinking. He had a tight control on himself despite his pleasant expression, and evidently, he didn't care to reveal anything. "You don't sound too thrilled."

"It doesn't matter." Ben shrugged and stepped aside for two women who wanted to pass them. "I'm better off returning to my own people. The truth is, I can't imagine any greater misery than you telling Ryson the truth and bringing me back. But at the same time—" He broke off and pressed his lips tight together.

"Go on," Jaeryn prompted.

Ben hesitated. Regret shone in his calm blue eyes. "You said you looked into my face when I first came and you knew I had never lied before. You were right. I'm quite good at telling the truth. I always have been. And I was successful because of it, and that gave me the opportunity to earn money to enter medical school, though not enough to pay for it yet. Until I came here, I never had a clash between success and honesty. I don't like who I am here, Jaeryn. I've done things I never thought I would do and stopped doing things I never thought I would neglect. At the same time—well, it may sound odd to you, but I think I would give anything on this earth to have another chance and do it the way God intended, and try again to get my father's good opinion. But all that setting the stakes and gambling with morals—"

It was the first time Dorroll had called him by his first name, and also the first time he had made any voluntary admissions about himself. Jaeryn saw the embarrassment it cost him and made an effort to ease his mind. "It's rot, isn't it. Perhaps that's a mindset I've picked up to justify the darker side of my work. I didn't mean to pass the corruption on. It's just something we have to do."

Ben still looked troubled. "Success is poorly bought at the expense of truth. But I'm beginning to think you would do anything for success."

Jaeryn smiled, and his voice lilted with pleasure. "And you would do anything for truth. A fine pair we make, don't we? I'm going to keep your position open for you. I like your help, and I've grown used to it."

"No," Ben protested. "We've arranged it. If you want me to stay, then it doesn't make sense for me to take the next steamer. You're to stay. I'd much rather go."

"I have made up my mind, and no amount of protest on your part is going to change it." Jaeryn wiped away the drops trickling down his neck. "Even if I can't get you back at all, it's my duty to give you an honorable release so you can move on with your life. And if I am able to bring you back, sending you to America won't be a waste of time, according to what Fenton told me. That is, if you're willing to look into what he found there."

"Of course. I'm happy to try."

"Good man. You look into what he suspects and take some time to find your bearings. I'll write as soon as I have any news for you. Promise me you won't do anything rash like enlist in the meantime.

There's no room for advancement in the medical corps."

The rain was gone. Ben walked with his hair plastered to his forehead and his coat shoulders dark from dampness. "I may be driven to it. I don't have much time to wait, and that's a sure option of income."

Jaeryn felt a tremor of worry at his stolid resignation. "But once enlisted, that's a commitment I can't get you out of. If you can't manage, then let me give some money to your wife until I can tell you for sure what Ryson says."

"No," Ben said firmly. "Thank you," he added as an afterthought.

He persisted. "Just a loan. You could pay me back whenever you wanted. Promise me you'll consider it, at least."

"I'll think on it."

"Good, then. If you don't object, I'd like to have Mrs. Dorroll's help in the clinic while you're gone. I'll need it with both practices to keep up."

Ben smiled with weary acquiescence. "You're clever. I won't try to argue with you anymore. I find I can't do it with any success today. Tell her I said she could, but she may choose not to if she dislikes it."

They arrived at the harbor, the bustle of loading and unloading, the smell of salt, and a myriad of masts and sails filling the water before them. It was more than time to part ways, for the last of the passengers were going up the gangway. Jaeryn released his end of the trunk. "I'm sorry you had to come. But I'm glad for our sakes that you did. You're the first American I've met, you know."

Ben offered his hand. "Don't judge us too harshly. There are better ones than I am. Thank you for the passage, Jaeryn. You've been good to us here, and I'm glad we're parting on good terms. *Nous serons amis,* what? To quote a friend of ours."

Jaeryn shook the hand with a hearty grip and watched Ben shoulder his way through the crowd of onlookers. Then he was up the gangway and below deck, and Jaeryn lost sight of him. He had no idea what the French phrase meant. Languages had never been his forte. He could claim the Irish, but knowing something from childhood was far different than learning a foreign tongue like Dorroll had done more than once.

Jaeryn turned around and made his way in a southeasterly direction, not waiting for the steamer to sail. He walked sunk in thought, neither knowing nor caring where his wanderings took him, only making sure they carried him in the general direction of the train station. He had said everything he came to say and said it well. Come what might, they were on better footing, and he was satisfied with Dorroll's response.

He kept walking until he reached St. George's Hall, its Grecian pillars rising high above the equestrian statue of Prince Albert. Cheap-jacks called out hot tea and chips in the bustling whirl of street traffic, and numerous vehicles clattered to-and-fro over the stony avenue. Jaeryn took in the activity in amazement and realized just how sheltered a soul he was. He was more competent by far than Dorroll in dealing with people, and he always would be; in the narrow confines of his craft, he would always excel beyond Dorroll. But in matters of travel and knowledge and intellectualism, Jaeryn had to admit that this reticent American was miles ahead of him. Dorroll had seen all this before. He had faced not only learning a new assignment, but a new culture. Jaeryn only knew England and Ireland, and though they were as familiar to him as his own face, that wasn't much to boast of. Perhaps, because of the familiarity, he had expected too much from someone to whom it was all new and distasteful.

Well, there was still time. If Ryson would see reason, if Dorroll would hold out long enough without caving in and enlisting—if he, Jaeryn, could keep the practices together while he was arranging all the details—there were many variables, but he would succeed this time. He would not fail again.

Jaeryn raised a hand for a cab and ordered the driver to take him to the station so he could catch the return train to Folkestone. It had been a downright pleasant way to spend an afternoon. He took out Dorroll's passport and studied the photograph attached to it. There was no need to burn it just yet. He could always burn it later, when all hope was gone. But even then, he might keep it just for old time's sake.

He could look forward to one more letter from America, at least, if Fenton's theories proved correct. And he might even make an effort to write back.

END OF PART ONE

Part Two

Chapter Twenty
Welcome Home

Dear Charlotte,

Of all the men I have ever met, I think Jaeryn Graham is the strangest. When I loaded my things on shipboard, I found out he had paid for first class. Either he is a rich man with odd whims or he had to do something to try to even the scales between us.

Ben heard a knock at the door and set down the fountain pen Charlotte had given him to write to her while he was away. An assistant steward in a crisp uniform stood outside holding a stack of white towels and French soap. "I brought these for you, sir." His hazel eyes looked large in his thin face.

"Have you sailed before?" Ben asked as he took the towels.

"Never outside of England. This is my first time abroad, and now it's during a war, too."

Ben smiled reassuringly. "It's not so bad."

"Have you done it?" the young man asked.

"I came over from America in April. We're travelling in a convoy this time. I've heard it's much safer."

"I tried to enlist, but they caught me out for being too young, so

I'm helping another way. Couldn't live with myself if I didn't do something for the war effort." He bobbed a cheery goodbye. "I'm sure you'll be glad to go home, sir."

Ben frowned at that as he shut the cabin door again.

He spent most of the first days on deck, watching the coast of Ireland as it passed. Dublin, Arklow, the Old Head of Kinsale—he couldn't name many of them, but he saw them all. The captain stood near him during the late morning the day after they sailed, keeping a close watch as they crossed St. George's Channel. His gray beard moved up and down as his jaws reduced a toothpick to wood pulp.

"Here's to a safe journey, eh, doctor?" he remarked in grim tones.

Ben looked up from the volume in his hands. "Yes. I hope the Germans stay away this time."

"Aye. That's why we're sticking closer to the coast of Ireland than I ordinarily prefer. If trouble breaks out, at least we can choose the lesser of two evils."

Ben squinted into the sun to see the captain's expression. "Sir?"

The captain looked down at him and smirked. "Ireland's the other evil, doctor. You'll never find an Irishman that wouldn't knock the teeth out of the Englishman who drafted him. They're not fond of fighting our battles."

"But if we were in distress, they would give us shelter, wouldn't they?"

"From the Germans, yes. But I'm not so sure it would be to our benefit. Anyway, you being an American would save you from any discomfort; and a good thing, too, for I've orders to bring you safely to New York."

"From whom?" He asked the question involuntarily, though he thought he knew the answer.

"An Irishman who pays well enough to get what he wants. If anything happens, you're to go first into the lifeboats." The captain switched the toothpick from one side of his mouth to the other with one deft roll of the tongue.

"I hardly like the thought—"

"Never mind if you like it. You can go willingly or unwillingly, but go you must if the occasion arises. Once you set foot on the dock, someone can murder you for all I care. Until then, I'm responsible for your safety. The first time I've ever obeyed one of the rebel lot, and the last."

"Not all Irish are rebels," Ben protested.

The captain bit down on his toothpick until it snapped in two, then tossed the pieces into the waves. "All of them. Without exception. We've had enough trouble from the Rebellion, and the Irish will cause more grief than they're worth before they've finished with us."

* * *

They docked without incident on the evening of the twenty-first. Ben looked back as soon as he reached the end of the gangplank; the captain had turned away already, his duty done. The New York harbor was frantic with activity, crews loading and unloading, ships inbound and outbound. He pushed his way through the crowd, signaling for a taxi whenever he saw one, with a crew member carrying his trunk behind him. The first three were full, but the fourth took him to a hotel, cheap but accommodating, where he spent the night in a dimly-lit upstairs room.

The next morning, he tried to write a letter to Charlotte to post before he left so she could learn of his arrival as soon as possible. But he couldn't find the right words and looked at his neat penmanship in discontent. The letter was too stiff and awkward to send. He liked writing letters; he had always liked them and had sent quite a few to Mrs. O'Sean while growing up. But this was the first time he had written to Charlotte; he had never been away from her long enough to make it necessary.

Ben noticed the time and threw away the sheet of notepaper he had filled. He packed the things he had taken out, checked out of the hotel, and hailed a cab for the station.

The day was a blur of tickets and waiting and catching trains just in time, with all the tedium that travel afforded and nothing but his thoughts to occupy him. After reaching Richmond at five, he hired another cabby to take him to Mrs. O'Sean's before he continued on to meet his mother. He had never met the rest of the O'Sean family growing up or visited their home, for it wasn't near his own. But he had her address, and thankfully the cabby knew his way around quite well. As they drove further from the station, the houses became smaller, the lawns more worn and sparse; and the flower beds shrank to homey window boxes as they neared the southern side of the city. An eager thrill of pleasure ran through him when they stopped, and he gazed up at a two-story structure clad in white clapboard siding.

The door opened on Mrs. O'Sean's small figure and familiar blue eyes. Terry had gotten his eyes from his mother, if not his red hair. Her hair, formerly dark, had turned a light gray.

Ben gave her a broad grin. "Hello. I'm home from my travels, and I wanted to see you as soon as I could."

Her face lit up with delight. "You're home, lad! Well, of all the people I never expected to see today you were the last on my list. Come right in. I missed your letter this month and wondered why, but now that I see you in person, it's much better than any letter could be." She pulled him in amidst her eager talk and closed the door behind him. "It was gracious of you to go out of your way to see us."

He held her close and let the warmth of home seep into him. "It's not out of my way. Besides, I wanted to see you."

"And I'm glad you did, but Virginia Beach is a far drive from here."

Ben took off his hat and hung it on the bottom post of their painted wooden stairway. "I don't understand. Is my mother not here in Richmond?"

Mrs. O'Sean shook her head. "One day in June she moved off to a big, fancy place at Virginia Beach, and never have we heard from her since, except to pay for the washing bill."

A house. Unpaid for, and certainly not rented. Mortgaged, most likely. "I see."

She raised her eyebrows. "Didn't she tell you, being your mother and all?"

He sighed in resignation. "No such luck."

Mrs. O'Sean clucked her tongue in sympathy. "Ah, well, times haven't changed, I see. You poor dear. I'm going to give you a good hot supper before you go traipsing off to find her again. Come sit at the table and talk while I make it. The children will be home from work soon, and my man too."

Ben followed her into the kitchen and watched her contentedly while she asked him how he was and how he liked his work in England. He told her a little about the people and their customs and made mention of Jaeryn in passing, though not by name. After a shrewd question or two on her part, it all came tumbling out—all that he was free to tell at least: his perplexities, the problems with his father, and the utter inadequacy with which he had handled it all.

"Did you see your father?" she asked when he had finished.

"I did. And once was enough for both of us, I daresay."

She patted his shoulder. "Well, you did what you could, and that's all that's to be expected of you. Even if it wasn't what everyone else wanted of you, it's enough. You put too much stock in the opinions of others, lad. No one said you were going to be successful at it. And you're back now, so you can put it behind you."

He hoped he was back for good. "It wasn't all bad. I liked the son of yours I found while I was away. Turlough's in Folkestone. We knew each other by name and struck up an acquaintance."

Mrs. O'Sean stopped cutting out the dough and brushed back a loose strand of hair. "I heard that. Terry sent a letter early in August and told us he'd met you, but he doesn't write often."

"I have a note from him in my luggage. He gave it to me when he found out I was coming. You're Erin's mother, too." Ben winced at the thought of the news he had of them. He hoped she already knew, though from what Terry had said, he doubted it.

"Yes." Mrs. O'Sean smiled cheerily. "Have you met her? I haven't heard from Erin for even longer than Terry. She was teaching school in Dover last we heard."

He mustered up a smile. "Yes, I have met her. I was surprised to find them in England."

"We couldn't hang on to either of them forever. Terry was always a different lad. Born to be a drifter, I think, and he only finished school because we wanted him to. He wouldn't go to college. He left when you were only six, and Erin joined him as soon as she was of age." She folded the scraps of dough over on themselves and cut them out again. "She and Terry made their way quite well together, him with his government job and all. Terry loved us, even if he could never settle down, and wrote when he thought of it; but Erin stopped writing, and we only heard bits of news about her once in a while. Is she still teaching history?"

"No."

"She isn't? Terry never mentioned that. Why did she give it up?"

Ben worded his response with care to avoid an outright lie. "She couldn't keep doing it."

"Oh?" Mrs. O'Sean stopped placing the biscuits on the pan, and a flash of fear crept into her eyes.

Ben sighed. "I shouldn't be the one to tell you."

She patted his hand with her floury one. "I won't ask you now if you prefer to tell my man and me together. But I'll only ask—she hasn't—died?"

"Oh—no, no," he reassured. "She is alive and healthy in body. Struggling in mind, just a bit, right now."

"I see." Mrs. O'Sean put the pan of biscuits in the oven and took up a dish rag to scour the table. "My Erin doesn't know the Lord Jesus, doctor. She's bound to experience heartache without knowing that he's loving and caring for her. I pray for her every day."

"I believe your prayers have helped even more than you know."

She smiled at him. "Now, you're a visitor, so I'll get out the company things. You like fine dishes, don't you? If you'll move your elbow, I'll put the cloth on."

She arranged it to her liking while she told him about her other children. Patrick worked as a manager at a munitions factory and held a mechanic job on the side. He had signed up for the war, but they had turned him away for flat feet, much to his dismay. "He's a good boy," his mother said, "and he was sorely disappointed at losing the chance to go abroad." Emmie had work as a nursery maid, the only job she could find at her age. Terry had come back once or twice over the years and was acquainted with Patrick a little, but he had only met Emmie when she was quite young, and she hardly knew him.

"What does America think about the war?" Ben asked.

"Oh, there's grand excitement for it. We're helping out any way we can. I think we've all bought bonds with the egg and baby-sitting money, and Patrick's bought more of them than I thought wise. Half of his friends are gone—it makes him feel anxious to be doing something. Nobody's died, so it's all a game to him yet."

Patrick and Emmie arrived home between six and quarter after. Mr. O'Sean came in last, a kind, short, gray-haired man, more than willing to welcome guests to his table. They kept the chatter to happy themes, merry jests, and even scraps of war tunes from Emmie until her mother told her to hush. In his quiet way, Ben reveled in their family company. They didn't make much of him, but it was because they accepted him so completely as one of their own that the idea of company manners never occurred to them.

After dinner Ben told them about Terry and his gunshot wound, assuring them that he was making a steady recovery. Mrs. O'Sean cried a little, though her tears were mixed with laughter at her son's escapades since he was out of danger.

"Aye." She wiped her eyes. "I'll pray for my boy every day now, that he'll gain his strength back and be out of the hospital on your return. Poor lad, what an unfortunate accident. The boy who did it must have been beside himself."

"He certainly regretted it." Ben pushed aside his fork and plate and looked reluctantly at his watch. "I fear I must be going soon. Thank you very much for your hospitality; it was good to see you all again." He looked to Mr. O'Sean. "I must request a private word with you, sir, and with your wife before I leave."

"Right." Mr. O'Sean nodded and crossed his knife and fork on his plate.

Mrs. O'Sean cleared away the dishes and shooed Patrick and Emmie out of the room, though they were both taller than her and not children anymore. Her husband must have had a premonition of the nature of the news, for he sat in grave silence until his wife cleared the table and came to sit down beside him. They each took the other's hand in a good, firm grip, and after a deep breath and no doubt a silent prayer, Mr. O'Sean said, "Tell us what it is, doctor."

Ben was used to giving hard diagnoses in his work. No ill news, however, had been as hard to give as this. As he told them about Erin and her marriage, he saw the varied emotions cross their faces that he had seen many times in his patients: shock, concern, and the helplessness of being unable to do anything to change what their daughter had done. After he was finished, he sat a moment in silence while they let the news sink in.

"Erin's made some mistakes, but she's still ours." Mr. O'Sean let go of his wife's hand to shake Ben's.

"Yes, she is." Mrs. O'Sean gently rubbed her husband's shoulder and tried in vain to steady her voice. "And even though we wouldn't have had this happen, we still love her. To think I had a grandbaby and didn't even know it."

Ben looked down when he saw her beginning to cry. "I'm so sorry."

"It's no fault of yours." Mr. O'Sean stood up. "We'll think about what's best for us to do. Maybe Patrick should go out there to look after her until Terry's back on his feet again."

He frowned. "But, sir, you wouldn't send him just like that, would you? Not with the war."

Patrick interjected. "Family does what it takes to help each other out. And of course I can handle travelling during a war."

"We'll think about what's best to be done. Maybe you can help us get passage if we decide to send him." Mrs. O'Sean came around the table. "I've got to give you a big hug, lad, before I find your mother's address for you. You've not had an easy time either, I can see that." She proceeded to do so and then copied from a slip of paper before handing it to him.

"Thank you." Ben rose from the table. "I must be on my way, but I'm sure I'll be back." He smiled. "Maybe even more than you'd like."

Mrs. O'Sean gave him a warm smile. "You're as welcome as one of our own, Ben. Come soon." She walked with him to the front door and was about to open it when she paused. "But wait—I have something of yours I had forgotten about. Your mother asked me to return it to you if you ever came back. They're letters of yours, I think, that got misdirected." She opened a desk drawer and handed him three envelopes, all in his handwriting. They were the letters he had written to Edmond.

He wasn't surprised Edmond hadn't come to claim them. Nor was he surprised that his mother didn't want to keep them. "Thank you."

"God bless you, lad. It's been nice to see you again."

As Ben walked down the front drive, he saw her through the window hiding her face on her husband's shoulder. Mr. O'Sean wrapped his arms around her.

It was seven-thirty with the sun on the horizon when he set out for Virginia Beach. By eight it had grown so dark that he could only make out the outlines of objects they passed. He amused himself by thinking over the evening with the family he had left—Patrick, red-haired just like Terry; and Emmie a dark-haired miniature of her mother. Both of them had Terry's eyes, but neither of them exuded quite his spunk and vigor.

Their parents had taken the news about Erin with surprising strength, all things considered. He hadn't expected such a level of acceptance. Doubtless, they had saved some of their reaction for after his departure, and he felt grief for them. Yet for all he was glad not to be facing Erin's situation himself, he would have given worlds to have the family she did. Charlotte gave him a wife's loving adoration and Pearlie had always been sweet, but two right relationships didn't fix all the wrong ones. Erin had been foolish to throw so much love away.

* * *

Ben was tired as they entered the outskirts of Virginia Beach. No other cabs passed them now. As they drew closer to the ocean the air blew cool through his open window, but with a comfortable kind of coolness. The cabby dropped him off according to agreement, and he laid the money on the seat and collected his luggage. A dull irritation entered his soul at the prospect in front of him: a high, two-story house close enough to the ocean to hear the waves and smell the sea air tang, but not close enough to see the water, unless perhaps from an upper window. For all his nervousness at coming, he was glad the place was near the shore. He could endure it here, now that he had seen the waves—they were a tangible link to the people he had left behind. Walking up the stone path between cultivated lawn and garden borders, Ben noticed that a room on the second floor was well-lit, as well as a back room on the ground level. He took a deep breath, lifted up a silent plea for help, and knocked.

Listening in the dead pause that followed, he heard a door slam and a hurried scuffle. The entrance lit up, and the door flew open to reveal a young maid in a starched white apron. She stopped upon seeing him and said, "Oh." Then she squared her tiny figure in the doorway as if to keep him out. "Who are you, and what do you want?"

"I've come to see my mother, and I'd like to give her a surprise." He slipped past her and entered the oak-paneled hall. Scarcely pausing to glance at it, he passed through the first door on the right. It was the drawing-room, and he saw at a glance that his mother was sitting before the fire and she was not alone. She looked up from the man beside her with a lingering smile that changed to a look of surprise as she recognized her son.

"Hello, Mother." The greeting hung in the air between them, tentatively, awaiting her response.

Lisette Dorroll was almost as tall as her son when she was standing, with soft, manicured hands; a smooth skin well concealing her real age; and blonde hair that had not lost any of its color, whether by natural beauty or by artifice only she could say. Her eyes were a steel blue, and the dusky smell of her perfume hung about the skirts of her blue evening gown.

"You didn't tell me you were coming here," she said at last.

"I had no time to write. But I trust the surprise isn't unwelcome. I landed in New York yesterday and would have been here sooner, but I expected to find you in Richmond." He slung down his bag and coat on a table near the door. "I am glad to find you so comfortable, though I would have liked to receive your new address."

A choked sound escaped her throat, but she remained speechless.

"Pleased to meet you," Ben said, turning to her visitor. "I'm Benjamin Dorroll, Mrs. Dorroll's son." He emphasized her title ever so slightly.

The man before him would doubtless be a formidable adversary if they ever found themselves at odds with each other. He had the polish of a banker, from the shining ring of black and gold on his finger to the tip of his polished shoes. He wore a black suit, well-cut to conceal a stout figure, and his straight gray hair was slicked back from his forehead. As he took Ben's hand, the young doctor swallowed the metallic taste of soft benevolence. It took a dogged determination to keep from hating the man for his advantage, for wealth weighed far more with Lisette than a son's concern. This stranger was leagues ahead of him.

"Ah." The man's tone was as polished as his appearance. "Lisette mentioned you, I believe. A pleasure to meet you, Mr. Dorroll. I am Mr. Creswick."

"It's 'doctor,' actually."

Creswick inclined his head. "Excuse me, Doctor Dorroll. Of course. Your mother must be pleased to have you back for a holiday. How long do you stay?"

"I haven't solidified my plans, but I felt I had been too long away from her. She is a woman, after all, and whatever my duties to my country, I must not neglect to protect her."

"Very filial of you." Creswick fingered the gold watch gleaming on his waistcoat.

Ben gritted his teeth.

"You must be tired," Creswick said with smooth urbanity. "Please, don't allow us to keep you up. It's a long way from New York."

Lisette moved toward the door. "I'll show you to the guest room."

"No, no." Ben held up his hand. "I couldn't think of running away early."

There was such a thing, he reflected afterward, as waiting too long to rest. Perhaps, by losing this battle, he could have won his war sooner. As it was, he sat in an easy chair doing his best to enter into the conversation while they parried his efforts as though he were a ten-year-old child. He knew how he looked without needing a mirror:

travel-stained and tired from his journey; and though they couldn't know he was almost out of money, he felt the sting of it in their presence nonetheless. His answers to their questions about his work were necessarily scant, turning into clumsy evasions that weren't helped by his slow thinking.

At a quarter after eleven, his torture ended. Creswick took an affectionate leave of Lisette and a benevolent one of Ben, remarking that he had so enjoyed meeting him and looked forward to future chats. "But," he finished, "I will leave somewhat earlier than is my habit tonight, and allow you two some privacy."

After his mother had said her goodbyes and shut the outer door, she returned to put out the fire. Ben closed the door upon the maid standing in the hallway and commenced to do battle. "I'm here to stay for a while. Do you have room to put up a beloved son for about a month?"

The color drained from her face, except for a light spot of pink on either cheek. "You must be joking."

"I didn't know that the money I sent you could support the upkeep of such an existence." He looked over the pictures, the rosewood furnishings, the carpet and bric-a-brac, and engaged in the delicate dance of putting the verbal knife to the throat without drawing blood. "By all appearances, you have found a better source of income. But if you can't find room for me, I could always withdraw my meager pecuniary assistance. I'm sure with your talent for making influential friends you wouldn't miss it."

Lisette's lip curled. "I don't think you will find that necessary."

"Excellent." Ben kept his tone light to fend off the looming confrontation. "It's late, and I won't keep you up any longer. Do you have a guest room I can use while I'm here?"

"You may have either of the two you wish. For a price."

He should have expected it, but it still took him aback. He didn't have any money to give her, but it wouldn't help his situation for her to know that. If she knew, she could turn him out very easily, and his threat wasn't convincing enough to prevent her taking that measure. He would have to bluff as best he could.

"Mother mine, I'm afraid that will never do."

"Oh, yes—"

Had she not given off such a forbidding chill, he would have touched her to try to soften her feeling. But a wave of repulsion surrounded her, and he dared not cross the barrier. "We are family, and you are living on my means. It is right that I receive a return on my investment. It is the privilege of the investor."

Lisette picked up the poker and jabbed at the ashes. "I could call the police and have you arrested for trespassing."

"You could, but I wouldn't advise it if you want to keep receiving my money." He bit his lip. It was almost a lie, that. He wondered how many he had told and to whom he had told them. He couldn't remember now.

"I'm sure you would think better of it. You always have, you know," she said, biting off the words.

She left him to attend to the locking up. He did so, then climbed the stairs and found the guest room at the end of the hall. His eyes refused to close, and his thoughts ground on themselves like a mortar and pestle with all he could have said, every polite jab he was capable of making. If only he hadn't been too tired to remember them at the time.

* * *

The following morning at quarter after seven he pulled on his clothes from the day before and descended to the kitchen to find breakfast. It felt strange having nothing to do. In England, he had patients to treat and people to visit, so he would force himself to get to work no matter how tired he was. But now he could take the day at his leisure. His mother wasn't up—nor was the girl. He breathed a sigh of relief, made his own breakfast, and ate with relish, leaving his dishes in the sink when he was done. Then he spent a good twenty minutes familiarizing himself with the house.

His mother had as good a taste as his father; that he had to admit as he wandered the ground floor. Living room, dining room, sun porch, kitchen, and library: everything was furnished in natural wood tones and pale, ferny green, with hints of yellow and darker green accompanied by white accents. There was one locked room off the kitchen, which, from the sound of light breathing, he suspected was the maid's bedroom. Upstairs were two guest rooms, a guest bath, and three locked doors which he assumed led to his mother's suite.

It must have been a shock to her for him to appear in such an unexpected manner. He regretted it now; in retrospect, it seemed unfair to begin their visit that way. At the very least, if she had no one else to look out for her, he must try to be a creditable son. The poor woman hadn't had a husband for twenty years and lacked the cherishing and support she ought to have had. She had deprived herself of it by mutual consent with his father, but it couldn't have been completely without regret on her side.

Now, while the house was quiet, Ben had as good an opportunity as any to contact the man Fenton had mentioned. He pulled out the card that he had kept with him since leaving Great Britain and looked at the name on the pasteboard. Alex York.

He didn't know the right number, but he gave the operator the name and city and waited for the connection. After a few moments, he heard a man's baritone at the other end.

"Alex York speaking."

"This is Benjamin Dorroll. I'm calling on behalf of a man named Fenton. He promised he would send a letter to recommend me."

The baritone voice held a note of surprise. "I did receive it. He said you were an agent in His Majesty's secret service until something went wrong."

"I didn't make a go of it. I'm back in America and almost off the case, but not quite. I wondered if I could count on you to give me some help."

"What can I do for you?"

Ben paused a moment to make sure no one was stirring in the house. "I've been told to look for some information about a banker in Richmond. The information is meant to help one of my colleagues in Folkestone. I'd like to consult with you if I run into difficulty."

"Certainly. I'm here to look after our interests."

He glanced at the door again and cradled the phone closer to his ear. "I'm not sure that I'm within the jurisdiction of British authority. Nor are my activities here officially sanctioned."

Alex York spoke in measured tones as if weighing his words. "All help is sanctioned, whether you were ordered to do it or not. I don't catch your drift entirely, but if you need my help in finding anything or passing on information, I'm stationed here for that purpose."

"Good. I won't keep you longer; I know it's early, but I wanted to establish a connection. I'm in Richmond, Virginia, and that's where I intend to stay."

Ben clicked down the phone and the hint of a smile crossed his face. A couple of days' observation should set him on the right track, once he found out what sort of activities his mother—or perhaps her man of choice—had involved themselves in.

Chapter Twenty-One
Hazardous Ventures

A heady thrum of excitement rang in Jaeryn's ears as he closed up the clinic. He slipped a sweater over his head and gathered up a pistol and torch. Then he locked the door, leaving the lights on to deter any possible intruders. Ann Meikle would be at home now by his calculations—half past nine was late enough—and he had no intention of crossing paths with her during his errand.

A few people still meandered here and there in the streets, observing him with curious glances as he walked briskly past. Those who knew him better—or thought they did—called out a slow, cheerful greeting, asking him how he did. He returned their banter just as good-naturedly, and the steady serenity of a midweek September evening eased away some of the tension from the busyness of the day. But still, the excitement hummed in his veins, and his step took on a spring at the prospect of doing what he loved most.

Jaeryn walked nonchalantly down the alley behind the post office and slipped on a pair of leather gloves. Testing the knob of the rusty green door, he found it was locked. No matter. Fenton always came through with delicate commissions, and Jaeryn took a little silver key out of his pocket and inserted it into the lock. As he did so, a crack of light around the window shade caught his attention. Only a spark and it was gone, but the spark was enough to set him on his guard.

The door hinges were wet, and when he touched the substance he felt the slick of oil. Jaeryn turned the key as quietly as he could and twisted the knob with bated breath, hoping for silence. Then he peered through the gap.

A man was standing there—a man with a mass of cropped brown hair, shorter than him but more agile, turning something over in his hand. Jaeryn pushed the door open another inch and slipped through, then took one leap and struck the man's head with the butt end of his revolver. A sickening crack answered the blow. The man crumpled unconscious to the floor, and the handle of Jaeryn's gun was stained with blood when he drew it away. Jaeryn made haste to close the door so the light would not show out into the alleyway. Kneeling down, he felt for a pulse and found life still there. Then he reached into the man's pockets and up his shirt. An envelope met his touch at the waistband.

Jaeryn opened it and found a heavy sheet of cream letter paper inside, commencing with: *I have word that I am not long for this world. The new doctor who gave me the verdict tells me that my end will be an unexpected one, perhaps days, perhaps weeks, perhaps months away.*

It was the note Dorroll had tried to copy from memory the night before he went to London. Jaeryn's teeth flashed out in a grin of delight as he tucked it away in his own waistband, pulling his sweater well down over it.

Against one wall stood large bins for sorting the mail and a sink for washing up coffee cups. A little table in one corner served as a desk; there was a stove for coffee and a great safe along the opposite wall. The safe door was open and a mass of papers in it drifted out onto the floor. Other than that, the room was bare.

Jaeryn picked up the papers and turned them over in the dim light. After a fruitless attempt at reading them, he sighed and reached for his glasses. There was a telegram from 1915, which he opened and found to be a notice of death for Ann Meikle's son. A photo was taped to the back of it, and Jaeryn placed it aside with care. But in spite of a meticulous search, he could not find the little strip of paper he was looking for or any records of outgoing soldier lists. It would be just his luck if Ann kept the evidence of her more clandestine activities at her home. He gathered up the sheaf of papers and began shoving them back into the safe. There was no way he could return them as they were before; the other intruder had taken care of that. Jaeryn glanced down at him and saw the blood still oozing through his hair. It was a nasty crack and would turn him dizzy when he woke up.

He had the last of the papers in hand when he heard a rattling at the door. He stood for a brief second in suspended shock, then pushed the safe door closed and looked about for a place to hide. There wasn't one. Not a closet or a cupboard that he could use. He snatched off his glasses and flicked off the torch, then braced himself and pointed his Webley toward the door.

The door opened and a light flipped on. Mrs. Meikle gasped at the sight him, but she had enough presence of mind to keep her voice low and close the door. "Heavens above, where did ye come from?"

Jaeryn laid a finger on his lips to prevent any further noise. "Be quiet, woman. I'm not here to harm you."

Ann's sharp little eyes peered up at him. "Yer face is all peaky. Are ye afraid of me?" A chortle sounded in the back of her throat. Then she saw the body of the man on the floor, and her face, too, turned sallow.

"He's not dead. I caught him breaking in. We'll lock up and leave him in the back alleyway."

Mrs. Meikle shook her head. "Ye can't do that. I stopped in to pick up a wee item, and Mrs. Goodwin is outside waiting for me."

Jaeryn groaned. "Blast. I didn't know she was in the habit of fraternizing with you lot."

Her voice raised in ire. "It's not a secret. Mrs. Goodwin drops in some evenings for tea, and we have a bit of a chat together. I let her use my typewriter in the back room to write to her son while I take care of the post business." She glowered at him. "What are ye doing here?"

He sank his voice to a whisper. "Since you're here, I'm looking for the original of the note you forged Dailey's handwriting to."

She didn't bother to match his civility, though she took care to match his whisper. "You needn't worry; I burned it."

"But I wanted it." He looked at her in dismay. "You didn't actually burn it, did you?"

"Of course, I did. It wouldn't be safe to keep around a thing like that. You didn't need it falling into the wrong hands, and I certainly didn't want it to be seen."

He clenched a hand and thumped it against the wall. "I wish you hadn't destroyed it. Were you trying to get Dailey dismissed on purpose?"

Her expression turned to a most injured one. "You assume I was the one that did it."

"It's the truth of the matter, so you may as well admit it. Now that Dailey's gone, I'm out of reliable people, and I could use a good, strong ally at the moment. You *were* one of my best until the soldier lists." Slowly, he pulled his revolver out of his pocket, though he had no intention of actually using it. "Are you still with me, or not?"

Her eyes sparked with hate. "For the present. And if ye don't stop believing I never made those soldier lists, I just might kill ye."

Jaeryn slipped the Webley back in his pocket, but kept his hand near it to keep her in a compliant frame of mind.

"What did ye steal from me?" Mrs. Meikle asked, turning over the papers on her desk and swinging open the door of the safe.

"Only something that was mine. Now, my dear, since you've promised to be agreeable, I want you to get what you came for and go out and take Mrs. Goodwin away."

She disappeared into the other room and then returned, shoving an envelope in her apron pocket. "I have a hold on ye now, doctor."

"Do you?" Jaeryn put the Webley back in his shoulder holster. "If you have a finger hold on me, I have a chokehold on you. So keep quiet and you may just keep *your* place. Now, be off with you before Mrs. Goodwin wonders where you are."

She gaped at him for a moment, and Jaeryn chuckled to himself as she walked away. It was rather wicked to take enjoyment at turning the tables so neatly, but if she had served him a trick by forging his note, it was only fair to serve her one in return.

As soon as the two women were well away, Jaeryn hoisted the man under his shoulders and dragged him through the door. Leaving him in a crumpled heap in the street, he flicked off the torch and locked the door behind him. Everyone would be quiet over this, thank goodness. They all had too much at stake to go to the constables over the matter. And he had Emmerson's letter, whether Ann Meikle liked it or not. He hid his face in his shoulder to conceal the white teeth that flashed out in exultation.

* * *

Jaeryn was pleased with the arrangement of Charlotte working at

381

the clinic. They didn't know each other except through Ben, and the more Jaeryn probed, the more he suspected that Ben kept his town affairs firmly separate from his home life. It was awkward at first, but after the first two days, they found themselves on firmer footing and settled into a regular routine. He picked her up every morning at half past seven, and by eight his mug of tea waited on the desk with the appointment cards for the day sitting next to it in neat, legible writing.

The only thing he would have dispensed with had he the choice was her skill at reading him. She could see straight through him emotionally, and he didn't like that. She gave him the false passports without comment, but he knew she guessed at the truth. By the end of the third morning, he wondered uneasily how far she had managed to penetrate him and his affairs.

Four days after Ben left for Liverpool, Jaeryn replaced the phone on its hook and realized that Charlotte's humming in the kitchen had stopped. He heard a light conversation and walked stealthily down the hall with a sense of misgiving. Pushing open the kitchen door, he saw Fenton standing in the middle of the room. A bright spot of color was in either of Charlotte's cheeks, and she stood frozen by the stove, a silver fork still in her hand, and her attention fixed on the ferret.

Jaeryn took one stride and gripped him by the shoulder. "Sick?" he inquired.

"I am in perfect health, thank you," Fenton replied calmly. "You look rather overworked yourself."

"Do I, indeed? Well, you're not paid to comment on my state of health, are you? What have you said to Mrs. Dailey?"

Fenton tried to shake off his hand, but Jaeryn kept a tight hold. "A little civility wouldn't be amiss. I told her that I called upon Mrs. Alisa Dorroll today and revealed the truth of their relationship."

The words choked Jaeryn so that he could not speak. An extreme tension rolled over Charlotte's face in waves, and she struggled to hold herself as poised and tall as she could manage. Jaeryn's hands balled up into fists so tight that his knuckles began to turn white, but he controlled himself and began to release them. "So then. What was the purpose of such a drastic measure? I doubt she believed you."

"On the contrary, the proofs were irrefutable." Fenton presented Benjamin Dorroll's false passport with a flourish. "You've forgotten to lock your desk drawers, doctor, so I took the liberty of helping myself."

"Good heavens." Jaeryn snatched the passport back and stared at him as a flush spread upward from his collar.

"You've been forgetting things for about six weeks now, if my guess is correct. Rather careless, don't you think?"

Hot wrath swept over Jaeryn and he lunged toward Fenton. Fenton reached out quickly and grabbed Jaeryn's bicep, digging in his fingers as Jaeryn shoved him back against the table. Jaeryn caught the quick dive for his revolver with his other wrist, but not before Fenton had drawn the weapon out.

"Let go of my hand, doctor." A slow smile curved the edges of Fenton's lips.

"Not for a moment." Jaeryn twisted his fingers to make him drop the gun. A loud crack sounded, and when the ringing cleared, he heard a shivering sob behind him. He wrenched the gun from Fenton's hands and whirled around to Charlotte. "Are you all right? Are you hurt?"

"I'm all right." She pressed a shaking hand to her mouth and kept her eyes on Fenton. One of the cabinet doors was splintered around a tiny hole.

The whine of an air raid siren broke the stillness, and sounds of distress came from the waiting room. Jaeryn laid a hand on Charlotte's shoulder to reassure her. "Pull yourself together. Come out and we'll tell the patients to stay inside until we know what's happening."

A mother held her two children close to her in one of the chairs. An old man had risen from his seat, and another middle-aged couple sat in the corner, looking around in worry.

"Stay here," Jaeryn said as the older man fled towards the door. "Wait. You're safer under shelter."

"The Germans are coming." The mother pressed a trembling hand to her mouth. "We heard them."

"That was an accident. A gun went off. No one was hurt, it's quite all right. Listen for the planes."

They listened, and the afternoon air was as still as it had been before. For long moments of silence, they listened, until the siren died away again. The little boy under his mother's arm looked around her sheltering embrace with wide eyes.

"There," Jaeryn said soothingly. "You see? It was another false alarm. You're quite safe. Charlotte, perhaps they could use some tea. Would you bring some? I'll be ready for the next patient in just a moment."

He returned to the kitchen where Fenton was still waiting. "By heaven, I'll make you hate yourself for this. Why did you give Dorroll away?"

Fenton edged round to the other side of the table and eyed the revolver that Jaeryn made no move to offer back. "His brother's in town."

Jaeryn half-choked on his tirade. "Is he? Where?"

"My sources wouldn't tell me. But he's made no move to come to her, and it's only fair that she knows who she can look to for help. She now has the address of her father-in-law and knows exactly who her true relations are."

"This was the last thing we needed right now. How dare you jeopardize my interests like that?"

"If your affairs are jeopardized by one woman who comes barely up to your shoulder, I think they're on very shaky footing," Fenton retorted.

Jaeryn thought for a moment, watching Fenton out of the corner of his eye. "You were paid to tell, weren't you?"

"Not by you I wasn't." Fenton's eyes never shifted, but Jaeryn felt sure of the truth.

"Perhaps your services aren't as necessary as you deem them." His hand clenched around the revolver at his side, and Fenton paled around the mouth. "I will dispense with them for good if I don't have your undivided attention."

Fenton's fingers twitched nervously at his side. "I don't conduct all my investigations simply at your pleasure and for your money. Ryson will have something to say if you dismiss me."

Jaeryn laughed in scorn. "You have no help there. He trusts my judgment, and I'm the one running this business."

"Don't be too sure, doctor. He doesn't trust you any more than the next one."

Jaeryn opened the door and gestured for him to go out. "You stay away from Mrs. Dailey or I'll have you locked up in a stinking London jail, understand?"

Fenton settled his bowler back on his head and dusted off his coat sleeves. "Really, doctor, your high-handed ways would be amusing if they weren't so incredibly tedious. Leave off with them, won't you?" He stepped through the door and closed it after himself with the merest hint of a slam.

Jaeryn laid the Webley down as soon as Fenton disappeared and sank down on the corner of the table. He had never seen Alisa Dorroll, though he often wondered how Ben had managed their relationship. Evidently, he had told her nothing whatsoever. From Terry's description, she was a tiny woman, slight of figure and considerably below average height, with brown hair and a shy manner. He had kept a watch on the market for anyone matching that description, but after three months of fruitless observation, he assumed that she never went there to pick up her supplies. Thus far, he hadn't been able to bring himself to set Fenton spying on an unprotected woman. Evidently, Fenton didn't care to wait for his permission.

Charlotte returned just as Jaeryn heard the front door close. He pulled out a chair for her, but she waved a hand in refusal. Jaeryn plunged straight into the news. "Fenton said Alisa Dorroll's husband is in town. I don't know where."

Her eyes grew larger. "He hasn't contacted us."

"You need to go home. I'll call a cab." Jaeryn left her for a moment, went into his examining room to phone for one, and then returned. "I'm sorry that man talked to you."

Charlotte looked down and crossed her arms. "I'm not. It's a relief when someone talks."

He suspected it wasn't of much use to deceive her and decided to risk an open course. She had several heavy sources of worry, and if he could ease a part, it would be to his advantage to make her indebted to him.

"Mrs. Dailey, I think it would be wise if I met Alisa Dorroll soon—in case you need some help dealing with her husband. Shell shock is an ugly thing, and she may require a man to help."

Her blue-eyed gaze cut deep, and he shivered in spite of himself. "If you wish, I have no objection."

"I merely want to be of assistance if he doesn't choose to return to his family," he said defensively.

Charlotte's gaze remained steady as if studying him. "Ben said assistance is your strong point. I would be obliged to you if you would."

Jaeryn looked at her sharply to see if she was mocking him, but he couldn't detect any sign of it. "Your husband says that too." He gritted his teeth. "I doubt either of you mean it. The cab will be here any moment, and you are free to go as soon as it arrives."

She looked troubled and offered her hand. "I am sorry, I—would not wish to add to your burden. I am truly grateful for your help."

"I am not angry." Jaeryn forced a smile that convinced neither of them. "Don't hesitate to call if you need anything. I'm always available." The tension in the air repelled them from each other, and he made no attempt to bridge the gap. "Your husband and I have had private dealings together of which I'm sure you are aware."

"Certainly." She nodded. "I am aware of part of them."

He felt his face settle into rigid lines of resentment. "Why don't you trust me?"

She hesitated a moment. There was a yearning regret in her eyes that carried through into her voice. "When I was a little girl, my parents made sure I never had a moment's pain, and I was never afraid of anything. I gave that up to marry because I saw that a broken person needed me. I thought I could bring some healing there and ease the fear. And I have. At least, I know I did until we came here." Jaeryn stood quite still as her voice sank to a whisper. "You break him down faster than I can build him up again. Why should I trust you?"

He opened his lips to protest his innocence, but he could not force out the words. "I'll come by on Saturday if that's agreeable. Until tomorrow, Mrs. Dailey."

* * *

Fenton had stolen a march on him, but he would put it to good use. Oh, yes, he would.

He didn't like that. In every previous mission, he had partnered with people who cared less about the ultimate outcome, or at least had no individual problems tied up in the conflict. This time everyone had an agenda they wanted to advance. It was no longer a question of British and German loyalties, but a question of who would come out ahead with the least loss in the end. Everyone was top-notch in their individual responsibilities: trained to forge, trained to observe, trained to kill if necessary—the only training they lacked was the skill of working as a group. The team didn't work. After this was over, he would be a loner on every mission he undertook. Extra people meant more vulnerability, more responsibility, and a much greater chance of failure. He couldn't abide any of those things.

Starlin King was on his list of house calls the evening of Fenton's revelation. Jaeryn made that his first stop, and after arriving, he requested that the maid show him into the study so he could speak to Colonel King regarding his son's medical care. Dorroll had left lengthy, meticulously detailed reports, but when a case changed hands Jaeryn preferred to establish a new connection to make people feel at ease.

Colonel King wasn't in his study, so the maid left Jaeryn alone while she went to find her employer. He waited patiently until he heard a curious shifting noise and decided to investigate it. When he looked over the desk, a stifled gasp sounded, and a dismayed face met his gaze. A young man knelt on the carpet with the contents of a drawer laid out in neat piles around him. Jaeryn well remembered the slight dusting of freckles and blond hair worn too long to be in fashion. He raised an eyebrow.

"Hello," Starlin said in wary greeting, putting down the papers he held and rising to greet him. "Did you come to see us? My father's gone for the evening."

Jaeryn tried to catch a glimpse of the papers, but he couldn't read the tiny print from that distance and cursed the glasses in his pocket. "Is he indeed. I came to see how you were feeling. Any pain in your ribs? It's been five weeks now, but you were so sick, that probably slowed you down a little."

"I'm better. Just tired. And it still hurts like the dickens. I manage to get around though. It's not awful."

"Taking the painkillers?"

"No." Starlin knelt again and collected the papers, putting them back where he had found them.

"Well, you can tough it out, but they will give you some relief. And don't drink alcohol if you do decide to take them. Though I'm not sure why I'm telling you that, as you wouldn't anyway."

"Much obliged for the advice." Starlin shoved the drawer back in and locked it.

Jaeryn tried valiantly, but he couldn't resist a passing comment. "I take it you weren't supposed to be here."

"It's my house."

"That's your desk, is it?" Jaeryn returned.

Starlin scrambled up from the floor and thrust his hands in his sweater pockets. "It isn't yours."

The boy had quite overcome his initial panic. They watched each other, both unwilling to be the first to give in. Jaeryn, being the older and more assured, as well as taller, knew he had the advantage.

"Don't tell my father," Starlin breathed at last.

Jaeryn opened his bag and pulled out a stethoscope. He allowed a long moment to pass as Starlin unbuttoned his shirt and he listened to his breathing. "You can tell him if you'd rather."

"I won't." The thin fingers clutched the shirt together again.

"Then I will."

Starlin looked almost afraid as he glanced back at the drawer. "He doesn't need to know. What concern is it of yours?"

Jaeryn shrugged. "None particularly. But I can't sit by and watch you get into something that you shouldn't."

"Much you care."

"Cough once and let me hear you." His cough was lessened now, more spasmodic than anything, and Jaeryn noted it on the record. "I'm not completely heartless, you know. Come, what's he going to do to you? Just a scolding, I should think."

"You have no idea." Starlin clenched his hands together and the nails looked blue around the base as if they were cold from fear.

"Then suppose you tell me. If it's so important, I'll lay off. But I have to know why before I can do that." Jaeryn mustered up an inviting smile and wondered if bringing Charlotte with him would have been more productive.

Starlin resisted his efforts. "If it's something important, then he'll know. But it isn't—it isn't—"

"Important. Right." Jaeryn raised his eyebrow. "Don't ask me to believe that."

"You wouldn't," Starlin huffed. "Just like the Irish," he muttered under his breath. "I like the other doctor better."

"Well, I'm afraid you'll have to make do with me for the present."

Jaeryn continued looking him over, satisfied on the whole with his improvement. After finishing the examination, Jaeryn stood up and waited, but Starlin didn't offer to lead the way from the room.

"If you think I'm going to leave you here alone, the Irish are more backwards than I thought," he said.

Jaeryn drew his brows together. "You might pay me for your medical care, but I am not paid to take your insults. I'm happy to tell your father why I refuse to come anymore."

"If you don't come, then you can't pry into what doesn't concern you, and I don't have to deal with you." A smile curled the edges of Starlin's lips. "I'd say that's entirely your misfortune."

Jaeryn took a long, slow breath and clenched his hand over the handle of his bag. "Then I suggest you at least stand aside from the telephone so I can call a cab."

* * *

On Friday evening, while he had a spare moment, Jaeryn decided to see how Terry was getting on. He really owed Terry some company by now, and he wouldn't have another chance over the weekend, for he planned to go to London on Saturday evening to see Ryson.

Rather to his surprise, he found Starlin there before him, and Terry sitting on the edge of the bed talking. A little color showed in his face now and then, and he looked quite pleased with his visitor. It was mid-September, and if he hadn't precipitated himself into an infection, he might have been out by now. Even as it was, he wouldn't stay in the men's ward for long with his determination.

"Your ribs back to normal, kid?"

Jaeryn paused in the doorway to hear Starlin's response.

"I'm not a kid."

Terry raised an eyebrow. "Eh—what?"

"I'm not a kid. I'm seventeen next month."

"No offense. What would you rather have me call you?"

"I have a name," Starlin said contemplatively without a hint of disrespect.

"Well, if that's the tag you like best to wear, then your word is my deed—Starlin."

Even from where he watched, Jaeryn could see a rare hint of a smile on Starlin's face. "What makes you so—jolly?"

Terry cocked his head to one side. "I don't know. I guess I never had anything to complain of, really."

"Oh."

"You're not very talkative, are you?" Terry looked amused. "I believe I've been holding up both our ends of the conversation since you started coming here."

"No."

"Why've you come so much? I mean, I like your music and all, but you shouldn't be overdoing it too soon after you're up again."

Jaeryn chuckled to himself. Terry would ignore any like statements applied to himself, but he felt no compunction at saying

389

them to others.

Starlin sat still for a moment, looking at the floor. Then he shrugged his shoulders. Terry's eyes gentled as they rested on the boy's face. "You don't have to do acts of penance. It was an accident, and you atoned for it as such. Only come when you want to."

Starlin's eyes held stern duty. "Are you going to get out soon?"

"I've been holding my own, and if I obey all those confounded nurses, they promise I'll be better in no time. No need to worry." Then he caught sight of Jaeryn and tipped a wink to him. "I think you've stayed long enough for today, kid."

The boy rose mechanically. "Come back soon, won't you?" Terry asked.

It was like Terry not to hold a grudge against the person who had shot him, though Jaeryn wondered how Starlin could be an agreeable person to spend an afternoon with.

A shiver ran through the tense frame. "I'll come every day."

"That might not be healthy for either of us. Come Sunday afternoon, I'd like to see you then. And bring your fiddle with you. I missed it today."

Starlin straightened and shook back his hair. He gave Jaeryn a terse greeting as he passed, which Jaeryn returned in kind. Terry watched their exchange with amusement and nodded to him as he came up.

"Don't like him?" he queried.

Jaeryn smiled. "Not particularly. You look improved, and no mistake. Have they given you hope of getting out soon?"

Terry fidgeted with delight. "One more week, if I promise to be an angel of goodness after I go home."

Jaeryn took the chair Starlin had vacated. "Well, I've been waiting to tell you until now, but I have a room open for you when you get out of here. You're not going home to the rascal you room with yet. The atmosphere is less than conducive to getting your strength back."

"Oh, now, I think I'll do very well," Terry protested. "He's not that bad."

"No, you won't. Otherwise, I'll make the nurses keep you here longer. I want you where I can keep an eye on you."

"Well." Terry didn't seem put out by his insistence. "I'll stay with you for a few days, just to keep you company." He glanced at Jaeryn's jacket pocket. "You don't happen to have a cigarette, do you?"

"No."

"I wish you had. I haven't had one in ages. As soon as I get out of here I'm laying in a fresh supply."

"Trust you for that," Jaeryn muttered.

"Don't worry." Terry grinned. "For all my vices, I've been getting lots of culture lately. Hanging out with the upper crust, and no mistake. That boy came every day this week, and one time I made him bring his violin and play for me. Ran through enough classical jigs to give you the weeps."

Jaeryn laughed. "Terry, for shame. He's played in company with renowned performers at his father's dinners. He could make a career in music if his father didn't already have him marked out for politics."

Terry smirked. "I'm going to teach him some real music as soon as I can carry a tune. No wonder he's a morbid wreck. All those notes run together in one long wail of misery."

"Or perhaps he'll teach you an appreciation of the classical," Jaeryn teased. "You may be presentable in polite society after all."

"Much chance of that. Anyway, enough of him. How have you made out since Dorroll left?"

"Quite well. Busy." He sighed and rubbed his forehead to ease the tired lines away. "It's no joke holding down two practices. I'm off to London tomorrow on business."

"Did you two docs make up?"

Jaeryn nodded. "I believe we're on better terms at present. Not so keen to knife each other, at any rate."

"Good boy." Terry sighed in satisfaction. "It's about time."

"Have you." He stood up. "I can't stay long today, but I'll call in next week to find out when they're ready to release you. You've been out of things too long. We're looking forward to having you back."

Terry's eyes gleamed at the mention of his release. He shook hands with Jaeryn and would have walked with him to the door, but Jaeryn refused to let him come. After a good-natured threat or two, Terry obeyed. It would be hard work to restrain him once he got home. Punctured lungs took a long time to recover from, even after all the tissue was restored.

Terry had reassured Starlin the whole incident was an accident. Somehow, though, Jaeryn didn't quite believe that. He would have to ask when they were away from listening ears. Terry had never kept a secret from him up until this point, so he felt quite sure of clearing up the mystery soon. Perhaps Starlin King would provide a clue as to who in Folkestone wanted to break into the British Secret Service.

Chapter Twenty-Two
Well-Kept Secrets

Ben wasted no time in pressing the surprise of his arrival to his advantage. He kept out of the maid's way as she set the dining room to rights, and when he heard his mother's tread on the stair, he was ready. As soon as she appeared in the doorway, he pulled out a chair and gestured for her to take a seat. She hesitated a moment, then accepted the offer and made no protest as he took one opposite her. The maid brought in coffee for both of them and set a tray of hot rolls on the table just as the clock on the sideboard chimed nine.

When Ben didn't eat anything, Lisette opened her lips as if to question him, but she closed them again and reached for the cream jug. He passed across the sugar, but she waved her hand in refusal.

"I forgot to mention something last night. Pearlie wanted me to tell you she missed you." He had promised to carry the message when his sister whispered it to him. He hadn't had the heart to tell her that Lisette might not even care.

Lisette did not respond and commenced eating in silence. Ben thought he saw a smile ghosting about her lips, though he wasn't sure.

He tried broaching another subject. "I saw the O'Seans when I came, and they gave me the letters I sent to Edmond. Did you hear from him this summer, by any chance?"

A slight flush crept over her face, and her eyelashes flicked down. "No." She brushed a strand of hair from her cheek and picked up her coffee cup with both hands. The wedding ring that she had worn as a bare acknowledgment of her unavailability was gone. A tremor of tension laced through him at the sight.

"He told me he was in the States this summer. I just wondered."

Lisette set down her teacup with an angry clink. "Are you eating breakfast with me out of a desire for my company, or do you have another object in mind?"

Ben shrugged guiltily and abandoned the roundabout method. "Mother, I know you won't want to tell me, but I need to know who's giving you your money."

"You have no business knowing that."

"It isn't for my own amusement that I want to know. Is it Creswick?"

A red flush crept over her neck.

"How long have you known him? Certainly not long, for you didn't know him before I left. He seems a most—eager acquaintance. Is he something more—than a friend?" He could feel his face turn hot as he asked the question.

"If he is, I don't see anything wrong in it." She dabbed at her lips with her napkin. "Don't tell me your father hasn't found different interests after all these years."

"I saw him before I left, and I detected no evidence of another woman in his life."

"I'm sure you didn't see any evidence that I had once been in his life, either."

"No."

"You should know that I am considering filing for divorce, and possibly remarrying."

He tried to keep the anger from showing in his face, but he knew by the defensiveness sparking in her eyes that he had done a poor job of concealing it. "I don't think you're being honest with me. Is divorce really one of your intentions right now?"

Lisette pushed her teacup away so hard it rattled in the saucer. "I have lived twenty years looking out for myself. I am tired of it."

Ben kept his gaze fixed on her pale, impassive face. "I've always tried to look out for you."

"Oh, you've always been dutiful. I don't deny that." She looked at her empty ring finger and lifted her chin. "But in this instance, you cannot give me what I want. I prefer to seek it out myself."

He knew he had to ask, though he dreaded the answer. "Has Creswick actually talked to you about marriage?"

"We've discussed it on occasion."

"You're violating everything that a home is supposed to be," he said angrily. "It's a degradation to you and everyone connected to you."

"No one has to know, do they? You'll be going back, and you can forget all about it. I'm not going to discuss it with you any further."

So it was true, what Mrs. O'Sean had said. Home, as well as Folkestone, had its dragons. He drew a deep breath. "Well, that being the case, I wish to get the address of Creswick's office from you."

"Why?" She frowned at him with icy hostility.

"I want to talk to him. It's only natural we should meet if I am to know more of him."

"It's only natural that you shouldn't," Lisette retorted. "What possible interest could you have in a man you haven't even talked to properly?"

"My interest is my own." Ben resorted to the tactic he had used many times in his adolescence. "I'll buy the address off you."

"That's insulting."

He pulled out his wallet and, setting aside what he needed for train fare, laid the last of his money down on the table, placing two fingers securely over it. "Write it out and lay it on the table, and then you can have the money."

Her hands played nervously in her lap. He waited until he saw wavering in her face before pulling out the notebook and pencil he kept in his pocket and pushing it across to her. Her hand hovered over it for an instant. Then she seized the pencil and wrote down Creswick's personal residence and the bank where he was a director. When she finished, he released the notes, and she did not refuse to take them. Then she rose and looked down at him contemptuously.

"You're a fool, you know. Just like all the other Dorrolls."

Ben clenched his hand in his lap to keep away the sting. "I like to think that there are some Dorrolls who value personal integrity."

He hadn't gotten what he really wanted. But the address was enough for now.

* * *

He wasted no time taking advantage of the knowledge, for he didn't want to give his mother any opportunity to scheme with Creswick about protecting their privacy. She would have time while he took the train, but not much, and he took the first available one to Richmond. She did not inquire where he was going, nor did he tell her. Their business was their own, and evidently any maternal yearning that she might have felt during his growing-up years was completely spent.

The tall limestone and granite building of the Richmond bank was a familiar sight. During his residency year, his business had only been enough to deal with the lesser clerks as he cashed his paychecks, and he had never met Creswick or even taken notice of him. Now things were different. He briskly passed between the marble columns to an unoccupied clerk, and the man looked up with a pleasant smile as he drew near.

"How can I help you, sir?"

Ben handed the man his card. "I would like to see one of your directors—Mr. Creswick."

The man looked hesitant but still maintained his pleasant demeanor. "He's in a meeting now, sir, but he'll be free in a few minutes. His office is on the third floor. If you'll be so good as to wait in the outer waiting room there, I'll give him the message that you're here."

The clerk pointed out the brass elevator doors, and Ben followed his directions up to the third floor. He found an office with a gold name plate signifying James Creswick, and he opened the door. He found he was in an outer waiting room with another door leading to the private office. The room was furnished in sage and walnut, with a stack of newspapers on an end table and electric lamps in each corner. A tray of mail sat on a table just outside the private door. There was no one else in the room. Ben listened in the silence, and a low chat from the office told him that Creswick was still in conference.

He turned over the envelopes with the tips of his fingers, every muscle tensed for the sound of the conversation breaking up. One from his mother was in the pile. He frowned and picked it up to investigate it further, but approaching steps caused him to toss the envelopes back and choose a seat. The door opened on a gray-haired gentleman in a dark pinstriped suit who left by the outer door. Mr.

Creswick, following, caught sight of Ben.

"Ah, doctor. A pleasure to see you. What can I do for you today?" He beckoned him into his private office and gestured to a seat.

Ben saw an envelope on the desk in his own handwriting, and curiously he picked it up to see what was underneath. Every letter he had written his mother since leaving for England was there, and at the bottom was one with Fenton's name on the return address.

Creswick gripped his wrist with a strong hand. "You are not entitled to look through my papers."

Ben drew his hand away and raised an eyebrow. "I was merely wondering why some of mine had gotten mixed up with some of yours. These are my letters, I think."

"They are your mother's, are they not? She merely wished me to have some knowledge of her youngest son." Creswick feigned a concerned look. "Is that something to be afraid of?"

Ben gathered himself and pitted his vigorous determination against Creswick's malicious sagacity. "I don't think either of us likes the other, sir, and therefore keeping up appearances in private is rather pointless. I came to have a discussion with you about your visits to my mother."

"Ah." Mr. Creswick unbuttoned his suit coat and took a seat in the large leather office chair behind his desk. "I see you are a man of business, and I will do my best to serve you. But I hope that you have no objection to my remaining polite, however you may choose to conduct yourself."

"No objection whatsoever. My mother informed me this morning that you take a particular interest in her."

"Why should I not? Lisette is beautiful, charming, intelligent—in short, everything a man could wish for in a friend."

Ben set his jaw. "And everything a man could wish for in more than a friend."

Mr. Creswick took off his horn-rimmed reading glasses and laid them aside. "Why do you say that?"

"She also told me you both have spoken of marriage. She may be accepting your attentions, but she is still legally bound to another man. Until that changes, I object to them."

The banker inclined his head, but no sign of relenting showed in his professional demeanor. Ben wound his fingers in and out of one another until he noticed the ceaseless motion and forced them to

396

keep quiet in his lap. "You will not gain by this acquaintance," he went on, "either in money or happiness or intellectual companionship. My mother can give you none of those things. And I doubt that you both are doing it simply to make each other miserable. Why do you want her?"

Creswick frowned. "Your candor is more to be admired than your civility."

Ben pushed back his chair and stood up to gain the advantage of height. "I didn't come to be civil. I've met a good number of civil people in the last few months, and I should like for a change to meet some honest ones."

His eyes darted to Creswick's face, but still he could not manage to ruffle the man's composure. "My dear sir," Creswick said soothingly, tapping a paper for emphasis. "I believe I see your problem. You are disturbed by your parents' impending divorce. But you must look at such matters with the eyes of experience. Lisette may wish to take up new circles of society, and you can hardly wish her to do otherwise."

He felt his composure slipping through his grasp. "If she divorced my father that would be one thing, but a sham marriage is another matter entirely, and I will do everything in my power to prevent it. You will receive no money from her. The only money she gets besides what you give her is what I send every month. She is not a rich woman."

Mr. Creswick's face darkened. "I have never given her a penny of my money, and even if I had, neither of us is accountable to you. If I wish to cultivate a friendship with your mother, that should be sufficient for you. We both ought to desire and respect her happiness, and I think we must agree to leave it at that."

"I know what respect is, sir, and since you are trying to take advantage of a vulnerable woman, I do not think you are capable of it."

"You have made your point," Creswick said at length. "This is a place of business. I think you should find someone else to take your grievances to, as I have neither the time nor the inclination to listen to them."

Creswick rose from his chair and turned his back to him, and Ben turned to go. He looked over his shoulder once, just in time to see a slight expression of horror on the banker's face. Ben drew in his breath, for at the back of the cabinet that stood behind the banker hung a small map of the United States with thumbtacks scattered across it. Creswick flung shut the cabinet doors. To think he had almost missed it.

* * *

When he returned to his mother's house, the maid informed him that Lisette was out. Seizing the opportunity for privacy, Ben went into the library and left the door open so he could be sure no one was eavesdropping. He found the card for Alex York that Fenton had given him and gave the operator the Boston number.

The peremptory baritone clipped out a greeting after the first ring. "York."

"Benjamin Dorroll here. If I asked you to track down some information for me, would you do it?"

There was a short pause at the other end of the line before York responded. "Officially or unofficially?"

"Both."

"Tell me what you need, and I'll see what I can do."

Ben cradled the ear piece against his shoulder. "Would you have the connections to trace my mother's bank account? Someone's paying her money, and anything connected to her may also have a connection to our work."

"Not legally, we couldn't." The refusal was disappointing, but he hadn't really expected the request to be realistic. York continued. "At least, not in secret. We'd have to get a search warrant. Will she give you the information herself, or is secrecy necessary?"

"I doubt she would tell me if she could help it. Never mind, I might be able to get it another way."

"If you have evidence of something untoward, you can stop her account transactions while the bank investigates them."

"I might do that." He thought for a moment. "All right—if I asked you to dig up some dirt on someone, would you do it?"

"That's easier than tracing a bank account, as long as you give me a good reason for it." York gave a low chuckle. "Who do you want to know about?"

"The last name's Creswick. He's on the board of directors at the First National Bank in Richmond. He has a map that's similar to another one I saw connected with undercover German sympathizers, and he takes an uncommon interest in my mother. I want to know how long he's been a director at the bank and any information you can give me about his life and career. Anything you could find would be helpful, but questionable financial dealings abroad with Germany or her allies would be especially interesting."

"Hold while I get something to write with." A brief silence ensued before York spoke again. "Proceed."

Ben racked his brain for more specifics. "If you see anything connected to the name Dorroll, I can use that, no matter how trivial. The names Emmerson or King, as well."

"I can do that. I'll set some inquiries in motion and be in touch with what I find. Anything else?"

Ben pulled out his notebook and looked at the list of things he needed to investigate. "I wish I could track his letters. He has a letter from Fenton in his office, and I want to know why."

"You'd need a search warrant for that, too. I suggest using less drastic measures first. If you find more concrete proof that he's a subversive, then I'll set a watch on his correspondence."

Ben saw the maid pass through the hall. The outside door opened and he heard his mother's low alto giving the girl an order. "I have to go. You can find me by inquiring for Lisette Dorroll in Virginia Beach. Many thanks for your help."

He hung up the ear piece and slipped out of the room by another door before Lisette could discover he was there.

* * *

Ben spent the next three days in Richmond inquiring about job openings at the hospitals. He wasn't sure how easy it would be to find work after the inevitable economic changes caused by the war. He would take anything, as long as it was in the medical field. As he inquired, he was pleasantly surprised to discover that it was altogether hopeful that he would not only find an opening, but a lucrative one. With so many medical practitioners heading to the front, there was a shortage of good doctors. Now that he was free from England, he could start on work that he could be proud of and begin to establish a home.

The thought of the unpaid loans made him more pliable than he might have been otherwise. Charlotte would be getting payment notices in the mail soon, and he must find something so he wouldn't be late sending her money for October. Besides, his mother wasn't happy with his presence. He had a limited amount of time to get on his own two feet and persuade her to change her mind about Creswick. There would be time later to set up his own practice; for now, he would be content to be an employee once again.

By the time he returned to Virginia Beach on September twenty-sixth, he had left his qualifications in several places and called at the post office to set up a box for his mail. There was no use going to the bank yet; he had nothing to put in it, and when he got his first paycheck it would be going straight to England. But Virginia was beginning to feel a little like home again, and the progress lifted his spirits.

When he entered the living room, he found Lisette sitting on the sofa, toying with her fan and staring into the empty grate. Ben paused in the doorway.

"Hello. You look lovely this evening."

He spoke the truth. If his mother had one talent, it was dressing herself to advantage. Tonight she wore a straight-lined cream creation, ruffled here and there, with ivory tints in the shadows. In her ears and around her neck were jewels the shade of the Atlantic on a sunny day.

The doorbell rang before she could reply. "Expecting company?" he asked lightly.

"Just the usual." She smiled a victorious smile.

"Ah, Mr. Creswick. Perhaps I should dress more formally."

"Oh, no," she replied. "You look perfect."

He and Creswick exchanged greetings with veiled animosity, and Ben offered an arm to Lisette to take her to the dining room. She hesitated a moment before accepting his courtesy, then rested her hand at his elbow. He seated her at the foot of the table and took the head himself, while Creswick took the chair at his mother's right.

"So what gives us the pleasure of your company this evening?" Ben asked as the girl served the soup and filled the glasses with pale gold Chardonnay. "It's a long way from Richmond, you know."

"Ah, well," Mr. Creswick replied, picking up his spoon, "a very particular reason, actually. Lisette's invitations are special enough, but we met for the first time exactly three months ago, and I wanted to mark the occasion."

The smile that followed the statement chilled Ben to numb silence.

When they settled with a tray of coffee in the living room,

Creswick pulled a small white object from his pocket. It was a jewel box, and Ben shuddered as Creswick opened it and slipped a delicate gold-and-ruby ring on Lisette's finger. He took her hand and kissed the palm of it. "A token of affection. And I thought perhaps you might like to accompany me on a pleasure trip. I've secured tickets for a small yacht cruise in a couple of weeks—a pleasant little jaunt which I think you'll find enjoyable."

Lisette twined her jeweled hand around his arm and smiled. "With pleasure."

"You can't go with him."

The protest caused them all to start, even Ben himself. Creswick kept a benevolent set to his mouth, but his brown eyes glowered. "Just a casual token of friendship. No need to worry, I assure you."

Ben shook his head. "I'm not blind. I know what you're doing, and it is wrong."

Lisette laughed and toyed with the handle of her fan. "What a mature young man you are to hold your own opinions. But you can hardly object to innocent gifts, and even if you did, I have no objection to accepting them. So, you see, your attempted chivalry is all for naught."

"I do not think you ought."

She looked uncertain at his protest. He had come back neither so conciliatory nor so docile as he had been before he went to England, and he knew she could not tell how to interpret the change. But at length, she brushed it off and turned away from him. "I think you should leave us to ourselves."

"Mother—"

"Or I *will* call the police."

He broke off and complied. Lisette had just enough spite to do it if he stayed.

* * *

His room stifled him, and he soon descended the back stairs to find relief in the shoreline. Pacing the sand as he had in England, he set out the present difficulty and tried to make sense of it. He realized how much a foolish hope had entwined itself around his life—or perhaps not a hope: merely a security in the knowledge that his parents had neither divorced nor desired to do so. It was the only security he had ever received from them. Now his mother was determined to make it happen. He had a duty to save her from herself if he could, but she did not want to be saved, and that made everything more difficult.

It was still early, and the idea occurred to him that he could be in Richmond by ten-thirty and ask the O'Seans to put him up for the night. The thought of going back into the house was beyond him, and asking Terry's family for help didn't stick in his throat as it did with Jaeryn.

He left a message for his mother with the maid, collected his things, and slipped out to catch the next train. The journey took less time than he expected, and a taxi dropped him off at his destination about ten that evening. He saw with satisfaction that the lights were still on in the O'Sean house—all over it, in fact. A freckled, snub-nosed Emmie peered out the front window as he came up the front walk. He waved, and she flung open the door for him.

"You're a guardian angel, I do believe," she said happily. "Mum and Daddy are just talking over whether or not Patrick should go to England. You'll be able to tell us all about what it's like."

"Is someone there, Emmie?" came from the kitchen.

"It's Doctor Dorroll," she called back. "Come right in." She beckoned him to follow her. "They'll want to see you."

"Hello, dearie." Mrs. O'Sean smiled a warm welcome for him. "You need a place to spend the night, don't you?"

He sank gratefully into the chair next to her husband's and leaned his chin on his hand. "You said I could come, and I took you at your word. I wouldn't like to trouble you, though, if it isn't convenient."

"It's no trouble at all. You're looking a bit peaked. Have you eaten?" She poured a mug of coffee and pushed it toward him, and he inhaled the fragrant steam.

"Yes, I did before I came."

"Well, I bought some apples today and made them into a pie. You always liked that when you were younger. Have you come from your mother?"

"Yes." He watched contentedly while she moved about pulling a plate and utensils out of cupboards.

She came over and laid the plate before him. Then she placed her hands on his shoulders and whispered, "I see a few worry lines where there weren't any before."

He patted her hand. "It happens to all of us eventually."

"And some by age, and some by hardship. I'll not press you,

402

doctor, but you have people ready and willing to lend assistance. Perhaps you should think about getting some help."

He nodded, and she let go of him, coming around to sit and keep him company. Ben turned to Mr. O'Sean. "Emmie said you were talking about sending Patrick to Folkestone. As you probably know, it's very hazardous to cross the Atlantic just now, and if he were to leave the work he has now, there's no guarantee of finding equal opportunities in England. To be honest, I'm not sure Erin would even accept his help. It would be a pity to send him for nothing."

Patrick cut in. "I think I can handle Erin quite well. Besides, last time he visited, Terry said he could find me work if I ever came out."

Ben raised an eyebrow. "I doubt Erin would be more receptive of a younger brother, especially with the age gap between you."

"We got along fine when she lived here—for the most part."

"If Pat goes, he'll get to see the old country," Emmie said, her face lighting up with eagerness.

Patrick rolled his eyes. "I'm just going to take a steamer that lands in Dublin so I can get a glimpse of it, and then I'm going by ferry straight to Folkestone. England isn't the same as Ireland. Not half as nice, either."

"Well, it's closer than America." Emmie turned up her nose at him.

"We're not sure that he's going, but he's eager to, aren't you Pat?" Mrs. O'Sean smiled at her boy rather sadly. It must be hard, Ben thought, to lose yet another child to wanderlust. Somehow, though the parents had stayed in the same place all their lives, their children had an unquenchable thirst to see the world outside their little town limits.

"Not to leave you," Patrick reassured her. He patted her gray hair with his strong young hand, and she tried to look satisfied for his sake.

"What's England like right now, doctor?" Mr. O'Sean asked. "We're too far away to know the feel of war."

"You know as much as I do from the papers. I think if Patrick wanted to enlist, they'd love him. They're trying to push through at Ypres, and they've lost thousands since August. But if you ask me, I think he'd be one more body in the grist of war, and I wouldn't offer his help until Britain can come up with better results than what they've been offering. It would be a shame to waste him."

Patrick looked decided at that. "I'm not going to war for the

British. When I go, it will be as an American with American men. Until then, I'm a free man."

Emmie left at her mother's direction to make up an extra bed in Patrick's room. It was nearing eleven, and Ben thought he should follow her to keep them from staying up for his sake. But Mr. O'Sean's low, gravelly voice forestalled him with a question.

"What brought you to us tonight, doctor?"

Ben scrambled for words. "Several things. I'm looking for work, and I'd like to settle in Richmond if I can." Mr. O'Sean's steady blue gaze made him feel ashamed of his evasions. "My mother is trying to marry again," he admitted, "without a divorce."

"Well, I'm glad you thought well enough of us to tell us about it. We won't keep you, then."

After going up to the bed Emmie offered, which he found out later was Patrick's, he lay awake in the darkness thinking of many things. He would have lain awake at home, too, but at least here his thoughts were more tranquil. Patrick was asleep in a makeshift bed on the floor, and the household lay still and silent. He wanted to oblige the O'Seans by telling them his problems, but he wasn't ready to do that yet. He would try another meeting with Creswick at his office first and wait to hear from York. He had called York again with his post box number, and the man had promised to send him something. If neither of those efforts succeeded, perhaps he would explain the matter and see what they suggested.

The next morning, Ben woke in time to see Patrick scrambling up from his bed. Patrick saw he was awake and waved. "It's early, and I'm off to work," he whispered. "You don't have to get up yet. Not unless you like." He looked like a much younger version of Terry, except for the smile. Terry never smiled; he grinned. Patrick pawed through the bureau drawers for clothes and tiptoed out into the hall. Ben took the opportunity to slip on his suit from the day before, then changed places with Patrick to shave and wash up.

When he came out, Patrick met him in the hallway. "Mum and Dad's bedroom is the next door down," he murmured. "They're probably still asleep. I'll make you breakfast."

"You don't have to trouble yourself."

Patrick forgot to lower his voice. "Why?"

Ben shrugged. "I'll probably be on my way soon, and I've given you trouble enough."

"Well, there isn't much point to you going hungry." Patrick

padded softly down the stairs and Ben followed behind. "Mum always said you had an independent streak in you, and I can see that's the truth."

"Sizing me up, are you?"

Patrick winked. "Don't worry; you'll grow out of it eventually."

They entered the kitchen to find Mrs. O'Sean there before them and the table set and ready. Patrick dropped a kiss on her cheek and peeked over her shoulder to see what she was making. "Mum, I swear you were in bed when I got up ten minutes ago."

"Then you do wrong to swear." Mrs. O'Sean gently slapped his cheek and motioned Ben to a chair. "Sit down and dig in. Where are you off to this morning, doctor?"

"I'm going to check for mail and arrange a couple of interviews if I can." He filled his plate with griddle cakes and poured syrup over them.

"Patrick can go with you to ask for ours." Mrs. O'Sean poured a glass of milk and set it next to his plate. "Sure you can't stay longer, lad? We haven't gotten much of a chance to talk to you, and I'm sure you'll be busy with work soon."

"Thank you, but I can't this time. If you could tell your husband that I'll call and try to get a steamer berth for Patrick, I'd be obliged. He'll need a deposit ready in advance, and if he doesn't have a passport he'll have to get that process started as soon as possible."

She brought a hot pan of eggs over and joined them. "I'll tell him. You're very kind to help us that way. We can only try, after all. He might not be allowed room with all the soldiers going over."

Ben licked the syrup off his spoon and shoved the jar over to Patrick. "I'll pull what strings I can to hurry up the process, but I can't make any promises. When do you want him to go?"

"Let's try for the beginning of November, and see what you can find. That will give us some time to change our minds if we need to, and we'll write Terry and ask his opinion." Mrs. O'Sean put a motherly arm around him. "Doctor, we can't help feel worried about what's amiss with you and your mother. We won't ask for more than you want to tell, but you're always welcome here for a rest. And if you ever need a bit of experience behind you such as Mr. O'Sean and I might have, you can come just like Emmie and Patrick do. We love you like one of our own."

He returned the hug. "Your acceptance means a great deal to me."

* * *

At the post office, he inquired and found there were two things for him. The postmaster slipped a thin, perfumed envelope over the counter, and when Ben saw the girlish handwriting he snatched it up, expecting it to be from Charlotte. But it was from Alisa, addressed to his real name, and the expectation turned to dread.

The day after arriving in America he had written to her, telling her who he was and why he had kept it concealed. It wasn't fair to Charlotte to conceal it any longer, and he hoped Alisa would forgive him for not owning up to it in the first place. But the letter wouldn't have had time to get to her, and he was chagrined that he had not been the first one to tell her the truth.

"You'll need to sign for the package, sir." Ben took the receipt the postmaster gave him and wrote down his signature. Then a hard rectangle wrapped in brown paper was pushed across the counter.

"Who's it from?" Patrick asked, as they left together.

Ben looked at the corner of the box and saw no return address. "Nothing of consequence."

"I wanted to know who, not what." Patrick slapped him on the shoulder. "I'm off help make ammunition to kill the Huns. See you later."

As soon as Patrick left, Ben tore open Alisa's letter and raced through words. They breathed neither anger nor betrayal, only the trusting friendliness that he had come to love.

My dear brother-in-law:

I will not deny that when I heard of your relationship to me, I felt quite shocked. It was a stranger who told me, and I didn't believe him at first. But Charlotte said it was true, and I knew she would not lie to me.

A hot flush of shame burned his cheeks. She could not have written a sharper rebuke if she had tried.

She said you had promised to write to me, and I felt a little better after that, for I would rather have heard it from you. You must have had a good reason for not telling me, though I would have kept your secret faithfully. I promise I will do so now. In private, I must insist that you no longer call me "Mrs. Dorroll", but something more familiar.

406

Matthew Benjamin and I are both well, and he is growing finely. You left me in good hands while you are away. I pray for you daily—along with Terry and Edmond and everyone else I know. Terry is out of hospital, and he seems to be as well as ever; we are glad to have him with us again.

I miss my doctor sadly, and no one shall ever take his place. I do hope you will return soon. It seems as if all those I know and lean upon have left me for a time. I love Pearlie, and I am glad she is here me, for I would be quite forlorn if you had taken her and your wife with you. You didn't tell me when you were coming home, and I can't find that Charlotte knows either, from what she says of you. Please tell me when you are coming back; I want to see you again very much.

Your loving sister-in-law,
Alisa Dorroll

A sigh of relief swept over him as he closed it up. The package he didn't know what to do with; he couldn't open it in the street in case he was observed, so he signaled a cabby and ordered him to drive anywhere he liked until he told him to stop. Inside the package was a book and a note; the book was a manual of law, the middle volume in a collection. The note, unsigned and written in a firm, copperplate hand, confirmed his suspicions. It contained a series of words strung together which York had left him to decipher for himself.

Met G.E. on holiday in Italy, October, 1884. One connection so far to D.

The book wasn't hard to figure out. He flipped through the gritty, fragile pages looking for a sign. Some of the pages were ripped and dog-eared, and here and there he found a light dot under a word. He would have to go through it when he reached home.

When he had finished scanning the pages, Ben closed the book and looked up. What he saw out the cab window was a sight so familiar he had forgotten how much he loved it. The lawns on the street were well-trimmed and green, and most of the houses had window boxes on them. Outside one house—a particularly familiar white clapboard house with brown shingles—he asked the cabby to let him out. There were children in the backyard, shrieking in happy play, and a chocolate Labrador puppy regarded him through the white picket fence with a curious expression. He knelt down and held out a hand, and it wrapped a rough, wet tongue around his fingers.

It was the home that he and Charlotte had left six months before. For a split second, it seemed as if it were filled with visions of all the things he wanted, and he took fresh courage. It was a good omen for the future.

* * *

When he got back to his mother's home, Ben made himself a cup of coffee with plenty of milk and sugar, and when he saw the plate of jam tarts covered on the counter, he took them with him up to his room. He would be there for a while, judging by the thickness of the book York had sent him, and something nice to eat would make for good company. He took care to lock the door. Then he turned on the desk lamp and settled in.

Wherever York had underlined a word, Ben wrote it down on the paper. York had left a dot under each pertinent letter, spaced at intervals, until he had spelled the word he wanted. Ben went through the book three times before he found all the marks. When he was done, the clock read four in the morning, and his eyes burned with weariness. He rubbed them to keep them open and picked up the scratched-out, ink-blotted piece of stationery he had borrowed from his mother's downstairs desk.

Became director of Richmond bank in 1902. Opened a joint bank account in France with Gilbert Emmerson in 1913. His co-holder withdrew 15,000 pounds at the end of January and dissolved the account. An equal amount was left to Creswick, who opened up a new one in Germany. The affair was arranged by a private agent named Dorroll. I'm in contact with the British consulate to find out more. Y.

A little, nameless ache sharpened in his chest at the name Dorroll. This must be what his father wanted to hide from him—the thing that had separated him and Emmerson at the beginning of the war. Matthew Dorroll had started on the German side and had either resigned or been forced out. But he hadn't breathed a word to indict Emmerson, so he must sympathize with it.

The coffee mug had only a stained brown outline in the bottom, and the plate of jam tarts was reduced to flaky crumbs. His head ached from the lateness of the hour, and when he came back to the present the light seemed unbearably bright. He shut it off and sat in the darkness, thinking.

So Creswick was not who he seemed. He had seen proof of

408

Creswick's involvement before, somewhere with Jaeryn. It was a signature, something he had only seen once. Neither of them had known what it meant, so he had forgotten about it until now.

Emmerson's library—that was it. He remembered kneeling on the thick Persian carpet, looking over the receipt for the dissolution of a bank account. It had been signed "C." It must have been for the same account, for it had been written during the exact same year.

One tiny handle on the man's well-kept secrets. For one moment, he forgot about his father's involvement, and a smile crept over his face in the darkness.

Chapter Twenty-Three
Love and War

Perhaps, Jaeryn thought uneasily, he was losing his touch. Secret intelligence was more than a career; it was an art. Getting the appropriate information required a delicate finesse in probing people's limits as well as a subtle manipulation that took years to perfect.

He sat on the edge of his bed in the dark, his arms tensing as Ryson's tongue-lashing still rang in his ears.

"You blasted, idiotic Irishman. Seven years, and then this. You've almost died more than once from your carelessness, and now you've decided to jeopardize not merely your own life, but my long-laid plans as well."

Jaeryn had remained standing in front of Ryson's desk, looking down on his supervisor. "Frankly, I wasn't sure that I could trust you. Dailey was threatened, and London has wasted more men than I care to count at the front. I didn't want you to make a mistake putting lives in danger uselessly. I had every right to look into Speyer."

Ryson, too, had slowly risen to his feet, his eyes cold granite. "I do not make mistakes. I've given you months, and you've probed man after man for that June leak in Secret Service communications without coming up with concrete results." His mouth quivered with anger. "I need hardly remind you that any leak, at any time, can result in unimaginable damage. We are blind, and they could strike us any moment unless we find and secure the people who infiltrated our communication."

"Emmerson sent the letter, and Emmerson is dead. Christopher brought the letter, and Christopher is dead. I have secured the threats."

"You know as well as I that Emmerson wouldn't be foolish enough to carry his secrets to the grave without sharing them with at least one person. Perhaps you're not as indispensable as we thought."

Jaeryn got out of bed and slid aside the curtain, looking out on the dark silence of Tontine. He desperately needed to be indispensable. If he lost his footing now, the work of years could come crumbling down without a means of building it up again.

Ryson's voice had been clipped and hard. "There's a hospital in Nottingham needing a doctor soon. I may consider having you work strictly in your medical capacity for the duration of the war if you can't be of better service to us."

"No!" The involuntary protest had escaped him before he could bite it back.

Now, in the silence of his own home, he shivered in the darkness. If Ryson followed through on his threat, Dorroll would stay in America, and someone else would get the credit both of them deserved.

He hadn't dared keep his promise to try to get Dorroll back in favor. The only tendril of hope Jaeryn had at the moment was the possibility that he could invent a reason on Matthew Dorroll's account, or perhaps through Edmond, to cement Ben's importance to the assignment. Edmond's presence in town might prove helpful if they could form a connection with him. The older Dorroll son had apparently concealed his arrival, for Charlotte made no mention of seeing him. Jaeryn offered Fenton every reasonable bribe he could think of to find out Edmond's hiding place, but the ferret remained firm in his refusal. He was in someone else's pay now, and his conflict of interests made him worse than useless.

In spite of Ryson's anger, Jaeryn didn't regret his interference with Speyer in the following days. On the seventeenth of September, Ann Meikle brought a letter to his clinic after hours, when the Tontine street traffic had sunk to little more than an occasional passerby. The letter was just a small sheet of paper, unsigned and

411

written in capitals to disguise the handwriting. No postmark or stamp identified the sender, and Ann believed it had been passed from person to person to get to its destination. The date on the top of the letter showed it had been a long time in the coming. He couldn't be sure, but Jaeryn suspected the contents had been written by Speyer himself.

They tell me many things are not my concern: only success, at any cost. There are some costs I do not want to pay, and seeing evil done where I could prevent it is a price too high. I am told that Folkestone is no concern of mine, but I have not been able to get you out of my mind, and so I will risk it. I think if you were to need help, King's son might be of service to you once you had won his confidence. I cannot tell you what he knows without compromising my own mission. I am risking it with this letter as it is. But if you could persuade him, he might be able to investigate one angle of your work for you. I spent a good deal of time with him, and he sees more than he lets on. He may be young, but he's a force to be reckoned with, and worth having on your side.

At least keep him safe. He's in more trouble than he knows right now, and too sheltered to discern his own limitations. The best thing for him would be enlisting—if he was old enough. As it is, he's trapped until then. If I have left him to harm, I will never forgive myself, but I trust it will turn out all right for him.

This probably makes little sense. It is as clear as I dare to be in my present circumstances, and I hope this letter gets to you without being intercepted by any prying eyes.

The letter was most definitely from Speyer. Jaeryn put the note in his jacket pocket for safekeeping, not daring to trust it to his drawer. So Speyer, too, was one more suspect crossed off the list.

Jaeryn glanced to see that the curtains were pulled together, unlocked the drawer that held all his evidence, and laid it out on the desk. It was early in the morning, which seemed the best time to look at it uninterrupted, and he needed to start piecing things together before Terry came to stay with him. Once in the house, there was no predicting whether or not he would have time to concentrate.

He had a fine collection of items. There were the death threats, which didn't offer any light in themselves but might in the future. One never knew exactly what would prove to be important. The threats had tapered off after Dorroll left for America, but the day after his trip to London, another one had been pushed through the mail slot. If it was because the Folkestone opposition didn't want Dorroll involved, that was all the more reason to make Ryson bring him back. He would try again as soon as he could think up a reason that Ryson could not refute. He would even offer to pay for the return passage himself so that no complaint could be raised as to the expense of it.

Then there was, of course, the evidence taken from Emmerson's house. The letter about the bank account, the map, the photographs, and the identification numbers. Those were the best things he could have gotten his hands on; the bank account he wasn't quite sure about, though it was suspicious enough, so he kept the letter for future reference. But the cards—to have the identification numbers of each agent so clearly laid out—that had been the find of a lifetime, and entirely too lucky. Matching up the numbers with the correct people would be hard, but if they could, it would be the most condemning evidence when the guilty came to court.

And then there were the photographs of Emmerson's private room. These were also excellent if the room proved to be important, and there was no doubt it would. He had gone Sunday morning to see if any marks had been made on the new maps, but they were smooth and unblemished. Peters said he hadn't replaced them, and he didn't think anyone among the household staff had either, but he had promised to keep a careful watch.

As thoroughly as Jaeryn had studied the new ones, he couldn't get any new information out of them. He pulled out the photograph Ben had taken of the world map and looked curiously at the mark on Dublin. He had never been able to figure out what that meant, for he had no agent from Dublin on his side and no Irishman except himself. Which meant—

A flash of white teeth revealed his satisfaction. The marking was for him. It must be. They couldn't trace him back to his real location and had chosen a generic one.

Well, perhaps he had kept his identity a better secret than he thought. Only Ryson knew that the school, as well as the name on his medical certificate, was a forgery, and that on the genuine certificate he had used his middle name as a surname instead of his real one. There was no conceivable way Emmerson's hirelings would find him—no way anyone would find him. He was quite content to hail from Dublin if his opposition chose to put him there.

At the very bottom of the pile of evidence lay the letter he had stolen from Ann Meikle. A wheel started turning in his mind. The letter was written by Emmerson to someone who could carry on after his death. That would give them all the link they needed.

Jaeryn picked up the phone and called Ann Meikle's home. "It's Jaeryn. I wondered if you could use your talents to write a letter for me."

A defiant click on the other end was his only answer. He gave the number to the operator a second time, but the phone rang without cessation until he gave up.

Jaeryn looked at the other private drawer opposite the Folkestone one and reached down to unlock it. Then he shook his head and left it undisturbed. Playing with the key for the private drawers, he withdrew it from the ring and looked about for a safe place to hide it. But he could not find one that he thought would be any safer, so he returned it to the ring. Perhaps the safest place to hide a secret key was between two normal ones. One could only hope so.

* * *

Terry was ecstatic when Jaeryn came to pick him up on the twentieth of September and promptly decided that he was ready to go home for good. But Jaeryn was worth two for that, and though Terry tried to force his point, he installed him under protest in the guest room. He felt quite sure that Terry would stay, in spite of all his threats, for he had an open temperament. He might leave in defiance, but he would never leave by stealth, and Jaeryn had every intention of keeping him as long as possible.

"I don't have any of your things, Terry," he said, while they climbed the stairs to the room. "Ben never told me where they were, but I suspect his wife knows. You can make do with my things for tonight, and I'll get your belongings when I bring her to the clinic tomorrow."

Jaeryn persuaded him to go to bed early, and when he looked into the guest room the next morning, Terry was sound asleep in happy abandon. Jaeryn smiled as he closed the door and crept down the stairs to pick up Charlotte. He would have to prepare himself to withstand all sorts of persuasions. When Terry woke up, he was sure to anticipate his recovery and try things too fast. He could be a very eloquent fellow when he wanted something.

On the second morning, Terry came out with a brand-new pack

of cigarettes and no indication of how he had managed to lay his hands on them.

Jaeryn cleared his throat. "I don't recall taking you to get those."

Terry waved the little box in the air as he sat in Ben's chair and put his feet on the desk. "I was up early this morning. Didn't want to wake you, you looked so comfortable, so I went out and picked them up by myself."

"You would have been better off sleeping. Those aren't good after all your lungs have been through."

"Yeah." Terry looked down at them thoughtfully. "Well, I won't have them too often, to oblige you."

Jaeryn covered his mouth with his hand in order to hide a smile. "If you really wanted to oblige me, you'd lay them off altogether. For goodness' sake, take them outside and out back. I don't need patients seeing you in front of the clinic; you'd scare them away for good."

Terry tossed the box over. "I'll wait until I go home. You can keep them until I leave and make sure I don't take them."

"You don't have to do that," Jaeryn protested, clutching the box all the same and making no move to offer it back.

"Well, just to oblige you. If I've waited this long, I can wait another week."

He wasn't quite sure what to do with Terry, and Terry wasn't sure what to do with himself either. He agreed to come to church on Sunday, and though Jaeryn was surprised at his eagerness, the sight of honey-blonde curls three pews behind speedily enlightened him. But Monday there was no church to go to, Jaeryn and Charlotte had work to keep them busy, and Terry was bored out of his mind. He didn't read, and even if he had liked reading, Jaeryn had no leisure books to offer him. For two successive mornings Terry disappeared for hours, and when Charlotte questioned him upon his return, he only grinned, giving no explanation of where he had been. Jaeryn tried to appease her when she beckoned him aside in between patient visits and asked him rather sharply to keep Terry out of mischief. Her annoyance made him suspect a clandestine visit to Alisa Dorroll's back door for a chat with Pearl.

On making the polite suggestion that Terry stay close to town, Jaeryn found himself in a new quandary, for Terry was eager to oblige him, but instead of going out, he stayed in, spent the evening in Jaeryn's study, and talked to his heart's content. Jaeryn nearly pressed his fingers into his ears by bedtime. Terry didn't seem to notice his

415

increasingly shortened replies and wandered in happy oblivion from one subject to the next.

Friday morning a light broke on their difficulties when Terry said, "Jaeryn, I'd like to see that kid again."

"Who's that?"

"Starlin. Starlin King. I never told him where I went, and he's got to be knocking about bored stiff. I'll bet my copper pennies he's scraping away at his fiddle with a scowl on his face."

Jaeryn poured out antiseptic to get the examining chair ready for the day. "He doesn't make very good company."

"He's not company. More like a nuisance, so you can't object on that score." Terry opened the medicine cabinet and pawed through the labels until Jaeryn shook his head and pointed to a chair.

He thought swiftly. Asking Starlin and Terry a few questions in private about what had happened in August might be beneficial. Besides, Terry needed a distraction, and if an indolent boy toting a Guarnerius brought him comfort, then the nuisance was well worth enduring.

"Call him tomorrow," he conceded. "I'd like to talk to him."

Starlin appeared in short order the next morning. Terry's assertion about the boy's boredom must have been correct, for he looked eager to have something to do. Bearing Speyer's letter in mind, Jaeryn decided to be polite and put out some feelers for the future.

"Hello, King. Going to college soon?" he asked.

"Not this year." Starlin frowned as if forbidding further inquiry, but Jaeryn paid him no heed.

"Oh? I thought you were."

"I'm not."

"Why?" He had banked on Starlin being out of the area by the end of September. At college, he would be safe from whatever Speyer thought was threatening him, and if he didn't go, he would have to be looked after. Jaeryn groaned inwardly.

"My father didn't want me to."

The boy was too smart to stagnate in Folkestone, idling around and getting into trouble. Jaeryn wondered why King had chosen to hold him back for another term. He was better off with his books and a good, disciplined schedule.

Terry hurried down the stairs and slapped Starlin on the back, breaking up the growing tension.

"Hello, kid. I'm sure glad to see you. Did you bring your violin?"

Jaeryn interrupted before Starlin could reply. "Before you two get absorbed in that—and I would be grateful if you took it upstairs, so it doesn't disturb the patients—I have a question for you."

Terry grinned. "Got a bribe for us?"

"No." Jaeryn chuckled in spite of himself. "But we've been waiting a long time for the two of you to get better, and now that you are, we all want to know what really happened the night of your accident. So, before you go off and amuse yourselves, why don't you tell me?"

Terry hesitated. Starlin's gaze went from face to face. The boy said nothing, and no indication of what he thought crossed his countenance.

"Well?" Jaeryn prompted.

Terry jerked a thumb at Starlin. "One of my mates, Hugh, invited him to hang around my house where he didn't belong, and I told the kid to scram for good. When I left for work, the kid tried to follow me, and when I tried to scare him away, we mixed up a little too hard."

"A little? You very nearly died, both of you. Was it necessary to crack his ribs to warn him off?"

"He's stubborn." Terry's eyes twinkled. "I think he's going to have a lot more than cracked ribs in life; I let him off easy."

"Well, you never told me what it was that I wasn't supposed to see," Starlin muttered.

"You never told me why you carry a pistol around. That's a dangerous toy, and if I were a father of yours, I'd take it away from you."

"My father gave it to me," Starlin flashed back.

"Hey, kid, no need to get offended. It was just a joke." Terry turned back to Jaeryn. "He was trying out some stalking, and I don't like to be stalked. But if it makes you feel any better, he didn't mean to shoot me, and I didn't mean to crack his ribs. That was all an accident, and it's over and done with."

Jaeryn looked at Starlin. "Why were you hanging around?"

"I don't see what concern it is of yours." Starlin crossed his arms.

"Well, you'll just have to trust that my involvement is necessary."

Starlin's chin jutted out. "I'm not telling you."

"I could speak to your father about it."

For a long moment, he held Starlin's gaze in his and saw the faintest twitch of the mouth and a slight shiver that could not be hidden. But Starlin kept his lips pressed shut. Jaeryn frowned. "I'll speak to you about it later, Terry. I won't keep you two any longer."

Terry led Starlin upstairs, and Starlin looked glad to get away. Very shortly Jaeryn heard a gentle testing of notes on the violin, and he paused his work to hear what would follow. Fellow guests who condescended to talk to him at King's dinners told stories of the boy's talent, but King hadn't offered to exhibit them in a long time.

There was no sound from the violin at first. Though he couldn't make out the words, Terry was singing. Jaeryn thought with amusement that the poor fellow must have had enough classical compositions to last him for months and wanted to change things up. Immediately upon Terry's finishing, Starlin took up the melody on his instrument. A sinister wail poured from the strings, sending chills of dread up Jaeryn's spine. Starlin repeated it again and again until he had it fixed in his memory, slowly adding the embellishments he fancied. It sounded wistful once, and hateful once, then switched to noble, determined, sick with longing, one after another, until Jaeryn wondered exactly what it was Terry had sung to him. He didn't know how Terry could stand the sheer volume of the music, played so intensely, or why his happy nature could stand morbid songs like that. The performance stopped after a climax of ascending notes, and he sighed with relief. It was superb. Starlin was no child in his music, but no boy of sixteen should be able to play an arrangement so haunted with revenge and mad with anger.

The violin continued as Charlotte arrived and patients came and went, but fortunately for Jaeryn's work, it wasn't as forceful as before. Perhaps Terry realized what a mood he had unlocked and was working to bring Starlin down to a reasonable level again. The two were fairly unobtrusive on the whole; Terry knocked on the door once to ask for his bicycle, which was better than coming in uninvited, so Jaeryn counted himself well off. He saw them ride out, and they returned just before lunch, but the violin didn't start up again. Jaeryn finished his last patient visit and closed the consulting room door for a short break.

Charlotte brought him bread, cheese, and cold ham for sandwiches and then settled down with her own plate at Ben's desk. He had only just begun eating when the phone interrupted him. Charlotte moved to answer it, but Jaeryn shook his head and picked it up. "Graham."

"Hello, sir. This is Peters from the Emmerson estate. I am calling to tell you that my new employer, Edmond Dorroll, would like to schedule an appointment with you at your earliest convenience."

Jaeryn swallowed hastily. "Your—Ed—are you sure?" Of all the people he had expected to inherit Emmerson's estate, Edmond Dorroll hadn't been one of them. If anything, he thought the father might have a claim to bring forward once Ben left for America. But the other son—

If ever he could get Benjamin Dorroll back, this would do it. Ryson could be persuaded, and Ben could be persuaded as well, now that the incentive was strong enough.

"Yes, sir." Jaeryn returned to the sound of Peters' measured voice answering his question. "Mr. Dorroll requested me to call you after I informed him that his brother was out of town. He came home with his lawyer and expects to be occupied for the next week going through the workings of the estate, but if you could schedule him after that, he would be appreciative."

Jaeryn's excitement dimmed at the prospect of delay. "Of course. I'll be sure to drop in. Does Tuesday work?"

"He'll expect you next Tuesday, whenever it is convenient."

"Are you sure it wouldn't be better for me to examine him sooner?" Jaeryn asked hopefully.

"I suggested that, sir, but Mr. Dorroll was adamant in his refusal. He's been quite occupied going through documents since his arrival and does not wish to be disturbed. He said he looked forward to making your acquaintance."

"Very well, then. Thank you, Peters."

Jaeryn put down the phone and moved his plate from his lap to the desk. "Mrs. Dailey, I have news of Edmond. Emmerson has left his estate to him, and that is where he is currently residing."

"Who is Mr. Emmerson?" Charlotte arched an eyebrow and paused in eating her sandwich.

"A rich old member of Parliament who died to no one's regret and knew your husband's father. Emmerson was known for political indiscretions around the time the war broke out."

"Ah." The word fell from her lips with clipped understanding.

"He hasn't called Alisa, has he?"

She shook her head. "Not unless something happened this morning while I've been here."

Jaeryn pushed the phone toward her. "Call and find out, please."

Charlotte dialed the number and exchanged a few words with someone that Jaeryn could only assume was Ben's sister. She replaced the earpiece on its hook. "No. He hasn't."

The knowledge made him grit his teeth. He had seen Alisa once now, and if ever anyone deserved to be happy, it was a fragile little woman like that. She had elicited a brotherly affection in him from her first greeting, and he had sworn to make things right for her. But he would have to wait a week to persuade Edmond Dorroll to consent to a reunion.

Terry was in Edmond's pay now, too, he thought with amusement. Perhaps something good could be gotten from the small link between them. But Ben Dorroll would have far better access to the house if they could get him back to England.

Jaeryn went up to Terry's room only to hear them talking of the same subject he and Charlotte had been discussing. The room was trashed with Terry's belongings, and clothes lay on the floor wherever he had happened to drop them. Jaeryn sighed at the mess. Terry held a small knife in his hand, evidently about to show it to Starlin, but he looked up in eager welcome as Jaeryn came in.

"Hey, doc. This kid was just telling me that Emmerson's inheritor showed up yesterday."

Jaeryn shot a look at Starlin. "Edmond Dorroll. Do you know anything about him?"

Starlin shook his head, but Terry nodded, and Jaeryn felt a pulse of misgiving. "He's a good fellow to have a drink with."

"Is he? How would you know that?"

"I've done it. We're old pals, him and I. Well, not pals exactly. I met him a few times in France." Terry turned back to Starlin and held out the knife. "See, ki—Starlin, I could have done a lot worse than crack your ribs that night. I had this." He looked up at Jaeryn eagerly. "Want a look, doc?"

"I've seen it." Jaeryn glanced at the thin knife with the Celtic cross between the blade and the handle. Terry looked disappointed, and Jaeryn took it up to humor him. "It's a very nice blade. I'm glad you didn't use it." He tossed it back, and Terry sheathed it and shoved it in his pocket. "What's Edmond Dorroll like?"

Terry cocked his head. "I don't know. Told me he had a sweetheart. That's Alisa. We talked about the war. He was a crazy young soldier, eager to kill the Kaiser and all that. Always had a bit of swagger to him, but I think he had a couple of soft spots. He

420

mentioned his brother a lo—" Terry glanced at Starlin and changed his sentence. "I didn't know him long. Seemed nice enough when we met at the pub, but I lost sight of him after a couple of weeks. I didn't want to get drafted, so I kept on moving."

"I'm going to run an errand on my lunch break, Terry. You can find whatever you want in the kitchen." Jaeryn hurried down the stairs, full of what Terry had told him, and wrote a note to Ryson. Now, at last, he had a good excuse to ask for Edmond's brother back. He looked down at his attempt in satisfaction.

Edmond Dorroll inherited the Emmerson estate. His brother is indispensable to me. I need him back as soon as possible. Will pay for passage when you send me your agreement. J.

If Ryson proved to be reasonable, he would have a second chance with Dorroll after all. It was fortunate he hadn't burned the false passports. Jaeryn left to put his note in the St. Eanswythe drop before opening the clinic for afternoon appointments.

* * *

He was up late Saturday night balancing records and preparing a report of his practice's country patients. Half of his route was his only until the end of the war; the doctor who owned it had to be given a part of every bill, and whenever Winfield returned, he would have the immediate right of possession. The earnings report had to go out Monday in the mail, and even if it took half the night to finish it, he couldn't risk compromising himself legally. Besides, after the latest disasters, he couldn't take any chances of losing Ryson's favor through imbecilic mistakes.

It was quiet in the streets and even more quiet in the house, with no patients and Terry's ready stream of chat strangely absent from the chair next to his. Terry had gone out to take Starlin home and wasn't back yet. Jaeryn pulled the shades down and drew the curtains for security. Terry was nice, he thought fondly, even though he did talk all day and make a fearful mess of his things. He wasn't a particularly steady man, but good or bad, he was always kind and didn't get offended easily.

He finished his report sometime after eleven and left the addressed letter on his desk to mail in the morning. In two days' time, it would be the first of October. He hoped Ryson would give in soon. It would be the middle of October before a letter could get to Virginia, and the longer they took, the more chance Ben Dorroll would have of finding work he liked. He hadn't promised to come back, even if a chance opened for him to return.

Jaeryn felt the lock on his bottom drawer to make sure it was secure and flipped off the lights prefatory to going to bed. Someone knocked on the door. Sighing, he turned the hall light on again. Terry shouldn't be coming back at such a time of night; it wasn't safe to be on the streets that late with only a knife to defend himself with.

"I'm coming." He fumbled impatiently with the lock until it gave way, and he opened the door on the blackness. A moment of peering yielded nothing. He turned to close it again, fearful without knowing exactly why, when two strong hands covered his eyes. He had one last good breath before a thin cord cut off his oxygen.

He must break free, he told himself fiercely. He reached up to dig his thumbs into the eye sockets of the person holding him, but his fingers encountered glasses. By the time he pulled them off, a second pair of hands grabbed his and forced them down. All he caught in the split second of sight was a blur, featureless and unidentifiable.

Panic rose in him as the pressure built in his head. He couldn't think straight. All he could hear was the sound of his own choking. Jaeryn tugged at the strong arms and kicked his ankles without avail. A pitiful last try at the cord around his throat was all the resistance he could muster. In spite of his efforts, his hands gradually stopped their clawing and dropped limp at his sides. His knees buckled, and he felt the hard wood floor beneath him. It was so wrong to give in without trying, but he couldn't try anymore.

A roaring in his ears cut off all sound, and the dizzy blur gave way to blackness.

* * *

Green everywhere. The grass was so rich and thick that he suspected it was Ireland's green. With a rush of relief, he knew he was in heaven, far out of reach of strangling hands. A long stretch of river ran with mad abandon through the peaceful countryside, bubbling and twisting wherever it took the fancy. Jagged boulders wrapped in moss broke up the flow of the water. It was so *clear*. Aside from a gentle froth over the rocks, the water showed an icy transparency, without a speck of algae or mud to ruin its purity. He knew he was wandering along the river's length, but his feet were not touching the ground. When he passed a dark-haired girl placidly absorbed in playing a penny whistle, the girl took no notice of him. Nor could he call out a greeting. He could only watch, and drink in the sight, and wonder at it.

A weir stretched from one bank to the other, creating a little dam in the river's flow, and a gleeful exhilaration gushed through him as he passed from one rock to the next. But when he reached the meadow on the other side, the little girl with the pennywhistle—whom he so much wanted to talk to—faded to blackness, and a pang of grief swept over him.

"Are you all right? Please wake up. I'm going to call the hospital." Jaeryn was vaguely conscious of a buzz far away slowly growing into intelligible words, though he couldn't string any meaning to them. All he knew was that he could struggle again. With a fierce yell, he closed his hands around the throat of the face looking down at him. But there was no strength in his grip, and they were easily pushed away.

"It's all right. I won't hurt you. You're safe."

Jaeryn held his head and took a couple of ragged breaths. His muscles twitched uncontrollably, and he couldn't see straight no matter how many times he tried to blink the spots away.

"Where am I?" he gasped out.

"You're in your own house. Do I need to call the hospital? Are you all right?"

He looked up into the bright blue eyes with the smile wrinkles all around them, creased in concern instead of laughter.

"Who are you?" He couldn't put a name to them. He couldn't even put a name to himself. The only thing he knew was that he needed to be alert, always, and that something serious depended on his remembering his surroundings. This wasn't how it was supposed to be—though what was wrong and how anything was supposed to be, he wasn't sure.

"I'm Terry. You're not all right; drink this."

Jaeryn felt a smooth liquid turning the pain in his throat to torture. It tasted horrible, but it cleared his wits, and he remembered what had happened and where he was.

"It's all right. I'm all right." He pushed himself to a sitting position and felt Terry's strong hand at his back. "How long was I out?"

"A couple of minutes. Your nose is bleeding. Do you know what to do, or do you need me to take you in?"

Jaeryn took the offered handkerchief and cleared away the blood. "Just give me a hand up." Terry helped him to his chair in the study, where he sank down with a sigh of relief. "What happened?"

"As soon as I opened the door someone left like a shot down the back hall. Your eyes were rolled back in your head, and I thought you might be dead. You still aren't looking too good." Terry hovered over him in concern.

Jaeryn chuckled grimly. "I'm sure I'm not. Did you see who they were?"

"No. I'll get you settled and file a report with the police. Can you make it up the stairs if I help you?"

"I'll try." Jaeryn looked at his shaking hands and noticed blood on the thumbnails, but he couldn't remember why it was there. "Just—just don't let go of me."

"Have another swig of this." Terry offered him the brandy flask, and Jaeryn shook his head.

"No thanks. Give me some water, and I'll be fine. You shouldn't drink that stuff, Terry. It's not—never mind."

Terry helped him upstairs, and he leaned on the sink in the washroom, looking into the mirror. His eyes were red and bloodshot, and around his neck was a thin, bloody line. Ten black bruises stood out stark and cruel, clear marks from each finger that had almost squeezed the life out of him. A few scratches around them showed where his own hands tried to break the cord away. Why they wanted to finish the job with their hands when the cord would kill him quicker, he had no idea. But judging from how soon he had passed out, they had very likely cut off the blood flow and not just the oxygen.

He felt dizzy and sank down to the floor, leaning his head against the cabinet. It would be all right. It had always been all right before. Thank goodness Terry had come in time. He would write to Ryson and ask for an extra man as a bodyguard. That should take care of it. He must have done something to cause an attack to happen now. But he was too tired and too sore to figure out what it was, and it would have to wait until morning.

He heard Terry calling up the stairs. Pulling himself up, Jaeryn walked to the bedroom door and leaned against it. "What?"

"The police want your account; you can use the phone in your room. I couldn't give them enough to go on, but they're taking it down, and they'll send someone out tonight."

Jaeryn picked up the earpiece, trying to collect his thoughts in answer to the questions given him. They wanted a medical analysis, and that was simple enough.

He finished the conversation and hung up the phone, gingerly feeling his aching throat. Terry ran up the stairs and appeared in the doorway. "I'll let them in and talk to them. You can get some rest; if they need anything from you, I'll come up and get you. Are you sure you're all right?"

"I'm sure, Terry. Don't let me sleep in tomorrow; I have some work to do. Thanks for your help."

Sleep was a long time in coming. His head and neck ached too badly to rest, and whenever he did drop off, he started awake shortly after. Jaeryn tried to remember what had happened after he had blacked out. There was a blank there, and he felt an irrational sadness that he didn't know what it was. He had a vague suspicion that it was something pleasant and that he would never get it back again.

Sometime after two, he fell asleep to nightmares that left a cold sweat in their wake. Gasping, he pulled himself up in the darkness and ran a hand over his forehead to wipe away the sweat. After that, he was exhausted enough to fall asleep for good.

Terry had paid no heed to his request, he found when he woke up and the clock showed ten. Mortified, Jaeryn hurried on some fresh clothes, gingerly buttoning down his collar to avoid irritating his neck. He found Terry downstairs with his feet on the desk and a notepad beside him. A long list of messages was written on it in a large and clumsy hand. Starlin sat at Ben's desk drawing his bow over the strings, but softly so as not to disturb a sleeper.

Jaeryn had to try twice before his throat would make any sound. "What's been going on?"

"Hey, good morning," Terry said cheerfully. "You were out—I mean, you were sleeping well. People call, and I write down the messages they give me for you. Folkestone's been doing without you just fine."

"Terry, you should have—"

"No, I shouldn't. Want some breakfast? There's cereal left in the box."

"I don't think I could swallow it." He looked at the chaos the two had made of his room with a sinking heart. There were files mixed in with violin music, and Terry must have used every available pencil before finding one that was satisfactory.

"I told Charlotte about you, and she's skipping church and coming over. I'll make you some tea."

He couldn't stand the thought of what the kitchen would look like when Terry was finished with it. "Don't trouble yourself. I'll catch up on some work first."

"You know, the world will keep on turning without you being there to spin it." Terry raised his eyebrows pointedly.

"Well, perhaps so, but it might spin in the wrong direction. I'll be all right."

"You sound like you're talking over gravel, and you look like you have a headache. Sit down, and I'll bring you some breakfast."

Jaeryn quit protesting and obeyed. "Just bring me some tea."

"You'd be better off going back to bed," Terry grumbled, disappearing into the kitchen and leaving him alone with Starlin. Neither of them introduced a subject of conversation, and they sat in silence, Starlin pausing his music for once and staring into space. Jaeryn picked up the files and shuffled through them. A shiny piece of wrinkled paper caught his attention among the others: a photo paper with a long rip across its center, mended with a piece of yellowed tape. He looked down and saw his private drawers open.

"Where did you get this?"

Starlin froze where he sat as Jaeryn jerked a nod at the unlocked desk drawer. "We were just looking around."

"You had *no* business. You blasted whelp." A stab of pain made him hold his breath. Jaeryn shoved the photo in the drawer and locked it again.

Terry came back with a full mug and set it on the desk. "What's the matter, doc?"

Jaeryn pointed to the drawer he had just closed. "Why?" It was the only word he could force out from his tortured throat.

"I was seeing where you kept stuff. Is that picture yours? It's a cute little girl."

Jaeryn shot him a look of still fury as the outer door opened and Charlotte's voice sounded in greeting from the hall. Starlin had enough sense to make his farewells and leave while she came in and pulled off her gloves and hat.

"Terry told me about last night." Charlotte knelt down beside him and gently unbuttoned his collar so she could see the bruises.

"Wouldn't you like to go to the Royal Victoria?"

"Absolutely not." He would never have admitted it to a soul, but her soft, jasmine-scented hand felt good under his chin, and he didn't mind the cool silk of her dress skirt as it brushed against his hand.

"Stubborn man." She left the collar unbuttoned and stood up. "Then you'll have to spend a quiet day here and do exactly as we tell you."

Charlotte took messages for him; it hurt too badly to talk on his own. An hour after she arrived he found they had locked the front door, effectively cutting off stray Sunday patients. Terry went to Alisa's for lunch, and Jaeryn spent the afternoon on the living room sofa until he heard Charlotte moving about the kitchen making supper. Then he slipped back into the consulting room.

He was busy setting up appointments over the phone when Charlotte left for the night, but Terry made him stop when he got back. Something grave in Terry's face made Jaeryn more pliable than he would otherwise have been under the circumstances.

When Terry had finished the soup which Jaeryn was still too sore to eat, he tipped his chair back and locked his fingers together behind his head. "I have something I want to say."

"What is it?" Jaeryn wasn't paying much attention at first. Terry said a lot of things, and no doubt he was about to crack another one of his jokes. But when the actual words registered, he sat up and listened more carefully.

"I want to thank you for helping me back on my feet. It's meant the world to me. But I've been here for a week now, and I don't need a doctor to tell me when I'm feeling well enough to move on. I would have left this morning if you hadn't run into that spot of trouble last night. As it is, I've stayed an extra day, and I think that's enough."

"Terry—"

Terry held up his hand. "I have work to do just like the next man, which you very well know, and I'm better now. Tomorrow I go back to where my belongings and my housemates are."

Jaeryn waited until the furious throbbing dulled in his head before he tried to reason. He hated croaking; it was so undignified. Terry remained stubborn, his jaw set, but a compassionate gleam shone in his eyes. "I knew it would be hard for you, doc, but you've held on to me long enough. The boys in France are working hard in Passchendaele, and I need to find out who's collecting numbers on the outgoing soldiers so the Secret Service can keep them safe. I'd hate it if they lost because information leaked from Folkestone."

He and Jaeryn locked eyes for a long moment until Jaeryn's shoulders sagged in defeat. "You can go, Terry."

Terry nodded cheerfully. "I'm leaving tonight."

"For heaven's sake, wait until daylight at least."

He conceded the point. "Well, I'll be gone before you're up in the morning."

"Your judgment has returned to its normal state, I see." Jaeryn clenched his mug and drank the sweetened tea, willing it to soothe his throat.

Terry grinned.

"Just take care," said Jaeryn. "And I expect you to stop by often to let me know you haven't killed yourself through any lapse of judgment."

"Sure thing. What do you want me to do next, doc? We're at a dead end."

Jaeryn unlocked the drawer and pulled out the stolen letter of Emmerson's. "I think I know. I need you to take this to Ann Meikle and have her forge another note. I want to drop the bait and see where it will end up. The note needs to have a request supposedly from Emmerson asking the recipient to come to Dover to meet with one of his agents. We want the recipient of the letter to send an affirmative telegram to your work address. We'll sign off with one of the agent numbers we found on the cards in Emmerson's room."

Terry scratched the back of his head. "It's a risk, but I guess it's all we've got to go on. Which number do you want?"

Jaeryn rifled through the cards in his desk and turned them over thoughtfully. "I don't know. I don't know who they belong to."

Terry closed his eyes and reached out, picking one of the cards up. "00192. We'll sign it off with that one. Who are we going to give the note to?"

"I think you know who to give the note to." Jaeryn gave him a meaning glance. "He was trying to burgle Ann Meikle's place. He almost got the note from Emmerson before I did."

Terry sighed. "My housemate has a knack for being in the right place at the wrong time. Do you think we ought to get rid of him?"

"No. He's not the heart of the solution, but he might be a ray of sunlight on the solution. He's more useful where he is. I'll get you a photo of Emmerson's writing to give to Ann tomorrow."

And then they realized there was nothing left to say except

goodbye. Terry was determined to leave quietly the next morning to avoid any fuss.

Jaeryn clapped him on the shoulder. "Don't go back to your smoking immediately. I want you to keep what you've gained. And try to stick to regular hours."

Terry chuckled. "Can't promise about bedtime, but I'll stay away from the smoke for a day or two, just to oblige you. Don't forget to lock your doors, and I'd have the revolver out next time I answered the door at night if I were you."

Jaeryn laughed. Then his face sobered. "I'm worried about you, Terry."

"Don't worry. The luck of the Irish." Terry grinned. "You're not the only one who keeps the world spinning, you know." He proudly displayed the Celtic cross tattooed on his wrist, and the sight of it caused Jaeryn's protests to die on his lips.

* * *

Jaeryn had the photograph ready for Terry the next day. He was glad for the excuse to check on him. Terry was sure to be working too hard, sure to be smoking more than ever—sure to be hanging around at Alisa's with the smile that could melt a heart much harder than Pearl Dorroll's. And Jaeryn knew Ben well enough to feel sure that he would have put a stop to things on Terry's end if he had stayed long enough.

Jaeryn brought out his bicycle and pedaled over to the white farmhouse. As he leaned his bicycle against the porch railing, he saw Terry in a pair of worn-out leather boots leading the horse to pasture. The sight gladdened him. Only Dorroll knew how close Terry had come to death before they were able to get him in surgery. Now he looked none the worse, except for a wince of pain now and then, which should be quite gone in a few months. There was always the threat of the lung collapsing a second time, but that in itself wasn't a life-threatening ailment, and he might live his whole life without it occurring again.

Alisa answered the door, and Jaeryn put on his most engaging air of gallantry. Then he remembered the angry red line around his neck and ducked his chin to try to hide it.

"Hello." He tipped his hat to her. "Doctor Graham, just stopping by to see how you ladies were managing. Is there anything I can do for you?"

"We're well, thank you." She nodded back. "Won't you come in?"

"I won't trouble you. I see Terry's back at his normal work today; you must be glad to have him returned safe and sound."

A smile hovered around her lips, and she tilted her head as a fond softness glowed in her eyes. "We like having him come. He loves life so much."

"And more than life." Jaeryn let the shaft fly out at random and saw it hit home. Pearl might be reserved with her brother, but Alisa was a sympathetic girl around her own age. "If he bothers Miss Dailey," Jaeryn continued, "I'd be happy to speak to him."

The fondness gave way to cornered worry. "I don't think he's bothering her."

Judging by the way she spoke of the Dorrolls, Jaeryn suspected Fenton's meddling hadn't made any difference in her friendship. "I'd like to speak to her if that is possible. Is she in?"

"Terry asked her to come with him to the barn just before you came. I think she's still there. He sent the other man away this morning and told me he could look after things himself now."

"Did he? Maybe I'll go out and see both of them together, if you'll excuse me."

Terry was coming back from putting the horse out to pasture, rolling up his sleeves in readiness to muck out the stall. He whistled a bright tune and disappeared into the stone barn, and Jaeryn could hear him before he was close enough to see either of them.

"What would you do if I kissed you, Pearlie?" It was a casual question, and Jaeryn winced. If that was the sort of thing Terry said when they were alone together, no wonder Pearl Dorroll couldn't get him out of her head.

A very small voice replied, "I suppose I would slap you."

Terry's hearty laughter rang out. "A dozen slaps from your tiny hand would be worth one of them. Besides, you wouldn't do it to a man who almost died, would you?"

"No," the voice replied again, faintly.

"Want to try it, then?"

"No…"

Jaeryn sped up his pace, calling out, "Terry, I want to talk to you." But as he arrived in the doorway, he saw Terry stoop down to kiss her. Pearl held back stiffly, but Terry wrapped both arms around her and kissed her again as longing and guilt flickered across her face.

"Terry, don't," Jaeryn said breathlessly.

"That was nice, wasn't it, Acushla? You're interrupting, you know," Terry called back over his shoulder.

"Terry," Pearl gasped. "It wasn't—it wasn't—"

"Sure, it was. I'm going to give you my little sapphire as soon as your brother comes back and I ask him for you. What will you say when I do? Don't cry." He wiped at her tears gently with his rough fingers. "There's nothing to cry about. Say yes now, and—"

Jaeryn laid a hand on his arm. "Terry, you need to let go."

Terry looked from Jaeryn's serious face to Pearl's distressed one, and a flicker of concern entered his eyes. "Did I do something wrong, Pearlie? I thought you would like it. I know you liked it."

"I liked it, Terry," she said, the words almost unintelligible as she tried to steady herself. "I liked it very much, there's no need to feel badly."

Jaeryn took her cold hand and led her away. Terry stared after them, sweat-stained and remorseful, unsure of what he had done, like a little boy caught taking something forbidden.

"I'm haven't seen you for months, Miss Dailey." He was about to drop her hand, but Pearl snatched it away from him as soon as they distanced themselves from the barn. "You mustn't mind Terry too much," he said. "He didn't mean any harm, and I think he genuinely thought you would like it."

She flushed and did not meet his gaze.

"I can send him away if it would be easier for you," Jaeryn offered. She was beautiful, and he didn't wonder that Terry loved her. The way she looked up out of the corners of her eyes so hungrily, however uncalculated, had probably captured his simple heart the moment her gaze was directed at him.

"No," she said hastily. "Ben never said I wasn't to see him. He only told me I was to wait."

"You might be waiting a long time, Miss Dailey. You're only at the beginning of your life, and you might be wise to consider a different course. A man of thirty-five who traveled the world before meeting you is bound to have more to his past than you might wish to face. Terry's not a saint. He's a loveable sinner, but a sinner nonetheless, I do assure you."

She glanced at him, and the shy hunger turned to a harder spark. "Ben said I didn't have to marry a saint. He doesn't expect me to."

"Well, I think he expects someone better than Terry. But I'm not

431

here to antagonize you, and I'll do all I can to clean him up a bit to give you a better chance." Jaeryn gave her a reassuring smile. "You keep on hoping, Miss Dailey, and we'll see what comes of it. I wouldn't give him another chance in the barn, though, if I were you. I think he enjoyed it."

"He loves me," she said, so low that he almost couldn't hear her. "And I want to love him and help him, if he needs me."

Jaeryn reached for her fingers and pressed them gently. "I won't ask you to stop, but will you give me your word that you will listen to me if it is ever necessary to warn you about him?"

She gave one small, stern nod. Then she flushed again and darted away, but not before he caught a look of fear on her face. Jaeryn narrowed his eyes as he watched her go. Kissing Pearl had been an unfortunate rashness on Terry's part, but loving him had been a deliberate choice on hers. And what had she meant by helping Terry? He frowned as Terry's cheery whistle started up from the barn, and he turned back.

Inside the barn, Terry looked up and his whistle died away on his lips.

Jaeryn crossed his arms. "You told her about us, didn't you?"

There was a moment of silence, and the only sound was the shuffle and scrape of Terry's boots on the floor.

Terry's voice wavered. "I didn't mean to, doc."

"When did you tell her? Terry, you know the hazard it is to have outside people know who we are. You don't make slips like that."

"I don't know why. She never asked me, but her brother was involved, and I think she knew before I let it slip out. It was one afternoon in July. She was holding Alisa's little one while I ate lunch, and Alisa was asleep." Terry scraped his boot back and forth on the wooden floor. "I just—I knew she liked me, and I wanted her to know. Didn't want that little girl to ever think I had lied to her."

The ire drained from Jaeryn's voice. "What did she say?"

"She asked if I was going to leave her when I was done."

"And what did you say?" Jaeryn asked softly.

Terry shrugged. "I said I'd be hacked to pieces before I left her."

Jaeryn let out a long, deep breath. "Dorroll ought to know."

Terry's voice perked up as he disappeared in the stall. "Oh, he knows. He's got my ring, and I guess that means he doesn't mind."

Somehow Jaeryn doubted that. "Is she on our side?"

Terry's head popped up over the edge of the stall so fast that

Jaeryn took an involuntary step back. "Don't say that again, doc. If you do, I'll crack your jaw so hard you'll wish you'd never talked."

Jaeryn held up his hands in apology. "All right, all right. But our main priority is tracking down Emmerson's replacement. I just think you could be more efficient with your spying and your wooing."

Terry picked up his shovel again. "The boys in France are fighting back the Germans one yard at a time, and we have to, too. You can't rush these things. Now if you'll excuse me, I have work to do."

"I came to give you the photograph for Ann Meikle, and then I'll go."

Jaeryn held it out, and Terry took it without a word, shoving it his trouser pocket.

* * *

Jaeryn woke early the next morning after tumbling into bed dead tired. This work was almost beyond him, and he hadn't been running at full capacity since Saturday night. Today he would see Edmond Dorroll. He wondered how much one brother was like the other, and hoped fervently that Edmond would be easier to penetrate on first acquaintance than Ben had been.

After starting up a kettle for tea, Jaeryn left the kitchen to put his consulting room in order. He noticed a white scrap of paper on the hall floor. Picking it up, he unfolded it and saw Terry's laborious script, along with a second note inside.

Sorry about yesterday. Gave the order to A.M. Didn't tell her it was from you. She said she'd see what she could do. Off to see Erin and try to bring her back where I can keep an eye on her. Best if I leave town for a couple of days, let things blow over. Back Friday, if all goes well. Give Acushla a note for me and make sure she knows I didn't mean anything bad towards her. Terry.

Jaeryn smiled and fingered the enclosed note labeled "Acushla." Poor Terry felt badly about it. Perhaps he was more perceptive than they had given him credit for. Love had a wisdom of its own, after all, and a couple of days would smooth things over.

He shoved the letter in his pocket. Later that afternoon he would take it over, and perhaps he would have some good news about Edmond to deliver along with it.

Chapter Twenty-Four
Finis Coronat Opus

Ben woke up by late morning, feeling as if he had been drugged after his exertions the night before. Fortunately, Creswick appeared to be nowhere near the house, but that absence would doubtless be remedied sometime during the day.

After breakfast, he marked the whereabouts of the maid—she was dusting in the living room—and he found the telephone in the library. He could not legally prevent his mother's acquaintance with the banker, but he might not have to resort to legal methods once Alex York had given him solid proof of questionable activities. After that, he could produce enough incentive for Creswick to leave his mother alone.

Ben gave the operator the number he had now committed to memory. York answered the phone. "Yes?"

"Ben Dorroll here." He began by asking York to secure a steamer passage to Dublin in November and gave him Patrick's name and information. York promised to telegraph information about where to send the deposit when he found an available berth and to put in a good word with the British embassy for Patrick's approval.

Lisette appeared in the library doorway and stopped to listen to their conversation.

434

"Anything else?" York asked.

Ben looked at his mother and hesitated. "I have something, but I'll call you later."

"Don't hesitate. I have the authority to give you almost anything you need."

"Soon. Goodbye." He hung up and turned to face his mother.

"You may not like my guests, but you had no call to be uncivil last night." She frowned and put her hands on her hips.

"It's not like that, I promise. I'm simply trying to protect you." He had to admit that her soft seafoam dress and crimson lips made her a lovely goddess of wrath, albeit an unmerciful one. Small wonder Creswick pursued her. "You can't blame me if I try to keep you from an illegal marriage. I've kept you from all kinds of other harm over the years."

"I hardly think," she said coldly, "that you should have greater concern for my safety than I do."

He excused himself and escaped the house for a walk on the shore.

* * *

On October seventh, he started a part-time position at the hospital as a fill-in physician. Knowing that he would need money to tide him over until his first paycheck, Ben took the book Starlin had given him and searched Virginia Beach until he found a pawn shop. It didn't fetch an exorbitant price, but it was enough for train tickets back and forth to work.

As he passed it across the counter, the thought crossed his mind that perhaps Starlin had intended him to sell it all along. Such an offhand gesture came in handy. But Starlin being capable of doing something tactful seemed unlikely, and Ben doubted that he even knew their financial situation.

He had been working as an assistant at the hospital for one week and enjoyed having something he loved doing to occupy his time— and making decent money to send home. He wanted to find an apartment in Richmond but didn't dare relocate, for once he left he did not know if his mother would let him come back. He could not give up his hold quite yet. Every day he inquired for a letter from Charlotte at the post office, but aside from Alisa's note, no one had written him from Folkestone.

One day, the postman pulled out a telegraph form and shoved it across the counter towards him. "Send a telegram. Can't say much, but it'll get a message to her without having to wait for the mail ships."

But the telegram, too, elicited no response. And he began to wonder if London wouldn't allow her letters through for security reasons.

Creswick and Lisette left together for their weekend sail on Saturday afternoon, October thirteenth. Ben helped his mother stow her trunk and bandboxes in the back of the cab and wished her a safe trip, though he could not force out a wish for a pleasant one.

"Thank you, darling." She pushed back the brim of her ivory picture hat and blew a light kiss on his cheek. He drew away and handed her into the cab without a word.

After the cab drove away, he turned back to the house, feeling defeated on every front. There was no taste of victory in coming home. Only a terrible, unfinished feeling that he tried unsuccessfully to ignore. Even the glimpse of happiness from seeing the little white house hadn't lasted long. He resented the feeling that there was something he was supposed to be doing that he was avoiding. Hadn't he done enough?

The empty house mocked him with its soft comfort and sweetness. How could such an angry soul collect so much beauty around her? From the rosewood wainscoting to the sticks of sweetgrass incense on the hall table, his mother had surrounded herself with all that was pleasing. She'd had that knack all her life. He could resign himself to the injustice, but try as he would, he couldn't understand it.

That evening he rang up York again. "Hello, Dorroll calling. I received the messages you sent me. You'd better tell my English contacts; they'll need to know, especially about the connection to my family. We have proofs of the bank account in England."

"Do you? That's excellent. Did it say why they wanted the account in the first place?"

"No. Just a notice of the dissolution." Ben fingered the stationary with his deciphered lines written on it. "I'm not sure if it has a connection or not, but I want to know if Creswick is giving my mother money."

"Based on what we've found, anything connected with him is worth looking into. You should search her papers one day when she's absent. You might find something."

He shuddered. "I was afraid you would say that. But I will do it."

"Don't blanch from your duty, doctor. *Finis coronat opus*, and all that."

"Right."

Well, that at least he could do now before the maid came to tell him dinner was ready. Ben listened on the landing to make sure she was on the lower level and tried the doorknob of his mother's room. She hadn't locked it. It seemed wrong to violate her privacy so deliberately, and he debated whether or not he wanted to go that far. But she had no idea what he was involved in, or what Creswick might be involved in, and since she had refused to cooperate, she was placing herself in a compromised position. It was for her own protection. He slipped on a pair of gloves and opened the door.

It opened on a sitting room, blue-tinted and peaceful. There were two bookcases filled mostly with china figurines and pictures, with very few books. Ben took a closer look at the pictures and recognized them as old family portraits—some of her parents, one or two of him as a child, and one he thought must be Edmond, though he wasn't quite sure. Pearlie had the most. She had lived the longest at home and had had the most opportunity, though he never knew Lisette had taken her to have her likeness taken. There were none of Matthew Dorroll, but there were none of Creswick either, and that was a small satisfaction. Ben replaced the frames exactly as he found them and took a key on the shelf to try the maple chiffonier. It fit the locks on the drawers, and he opened one and pulled out a pile of papers.

Under the stamps and envelopes, he found an envelope addressed to himself. He recognized Edmond's large, sprawling penmanship, but there was no stamp in the corner, and somehow it had been forgotten in Lisette's desk.

"Curious," he whispered. But he didn't dare take the time to read it now.

He found an old packet of letters from his father. They must have been written before their marriage by the dates on the postmarks. There were one or two from Creswick which he laid aside for further consideration. Beyond those, there was nothing: none of friendship, a few from him during his time away at college, and one from Charlotte, written after their engagement. It was a lonely drawer, and he closed it with more sympathy for his mother than he had begun with.

437

The next drawer held a house deed in Lisette's name, as well as the mortgage papers. On his income, she would be paying for it for a long time, but the agreed payment was higher than the monthly allowance he sent her. He had never seen evidence of work that she had taken up to supplement her allowance from him, and her inheritance money had dwindled away years ago. Underneath the papers, he found a beautifully bound book in champagne leather. Inside were her financial transactions. They were not in her hand; they were in a man's hand, and when Ben compared the writing with Creswick's on the envelopes, he found they were the same. There were accounts for dresses and household expenses and a monthly subscription to several magazines. Ben frowned at that. He had never seen his mother look at magazines during his time home.

On the tenth page, he found the secret. The monthly deposits were from Edmond Dorroll. Six receipts, all in Edmond's hand, for four hundred dollars apiece.

A sudden sense of violated honor fell over him. Ben picked up the letters from Creswick and looked at them irresolutely, then put them in his pocket. A cream-tinted bedroom through another door beckoned him to explore further. Jaeryn would search it if he were there. But he wasn't Jaeryn, and he didn't do things Jaeryn's way. At least—he didn't used to.

* * *

August 20, 1917

Little Brother,

I told you in my last letter that I had stumbled upon a piece of luck. It turns out I've inherited property in Folkestone: the Emmerson place. Doubtless you've heard of it by now. He named me as his sole heir, for he never married. I think I was a kind of son to him when I was younger. It's a beautiful old place, and I went often there with Father as a boy. Emmerson always said he would make my fortune, but in the last few years he never mentioned it, and I thought he had forgotten. He was the only one to know about Alisa, you know. I always liked him.

There's a little piece of lake at the southeast corner of the house. I'm going to expand it and cut down some of the trees to open up a view to the front entrance. I can hardly believe it's mine. I'll be going home soon to claim my estate, and especially to see you. Just as soon as I can get up enough energy to think of crossing the Atlantic again.

We'll have to have those old times we were always planning to have as soon as I get back. I'll make your fortune, little brother. Couldn't enjoy my luck unless it helped you out as well. You never told me: did you come to Folkestone because Father asked you to take that job? I just remembered it the other day.

Ever Yours,
Edmond

Ben laid it down and rubbed his forehead. Why did his mother have this letter in her sitting room? She had never seen Edmond while he was in America. Why hadn't it gone to England? Why had she *kept* it, for heaven's sake?

He picked up his after-dinner coffee and swallowed the hot brew. There was no address to find Edmond at, as usual. He could be in America, or England, or even in France for all they knew.

He unlocked his trunk and took out the only letter Edmond had sent him from America. The postmark was from Virginia Beach, and the date showed he had been there in early August. Lisette had moved to Virginia Beach by then. Why would Edmond have come to Virginia Beach if not to see her?

But if Edmond had come, why hadn't he taken the letters from England instead of letting Lisette send them to Mrs. O'Sean? Ben rifled further down and pulled out the letters she had given him. He had never looked at them. The letters were all there, just as they should be, and he had had no reason to suspect anything untoward. The envelopes were the same ones he used; the writing was his own. But when he turned them around and looked at the backs, there were rips in more than one place along the tops. A thin sheen of glue shone around the edges of the flaps, showing where they had been resealed. Someone had seen them after all.

The maid came into the room and laid the day's mail on his mother's desk. He waited until she had left, then turned over the pile. None of it was personal. A newspaper, a dress advertisement, something that looked like a bill, and underneath, a magazine called *The Masses.*

He rang for the maid and resumed his seat, putting on a casual air as she entered the room. "Does my mother subscribe to any magazines, Jane? I have a free evening, and I'd like to read something."

"She does, sir, but I boxed them up this morning. They're to be mailed out tomorrow."

"If you give them to me tonight, I'll take them to the mail tomorrow for you."

She hesitated. He reached in his pocket for a bill and slipped it into her hands. She softened and threw a smile over her shoulder at him as she left the room. In a few minutes she returned with a box.

"Thank you very much." Ben took the box from her and set it down on his mother's desk. As soon as the maid left, he slit the box open with a knife and lifted the lid. Stacks of the October edition of *The Masses* and pacifist posters filled the box to the brim. He ran his fingers over the stack of posters, then took up the box and looked at the address. It was in a hand he could only assume was the maid's, and it was addressed to Mr. James Creswick.

Reaching in his pocket, he pulled out the letters from Creswick to his mother. Inside, once he had gotten past all the terms of endearment, he seized on the words in a paragraph towards the middle of one letter.

If you would be so good as to allow some of my mail to be directed to you, I would be indebted to your kindness, sweet. There are some things I cannot be seen to openly support, but I too have political convictions that I must stand by. If you will allow me to direct it to your home and store it there, I will make it well worth your while.

Ben closed his eyes in exultation. This—this was what he had needed all along.

* * *

He left Lisette alone when she came back Sunday evening and went to work Monday without seeing her. When he returned Monday night, he knocked on her bedroom door and asked to speak to her. She called for him to come in, and he found her at her dressing table slipping hairpins into the waved coiffure above her neck.

"Did you have a good time yesterday?"

"I did." She took up a mother-of-pearl comb and bit her lip as she positioned it into the golden coil of hair.

"I'm glad. You haven't had many good times."

Lisette's eyes darted up to his face, and he saw the stiffness of her figure softening. Her voice, when she spoke, was gentler than ordinary. "Did you want to speak to me about something?"

Ben hesitated. "I just wondered if Edmond has written to you lately. Or if Mr. Creswick has ever asked you to influence the war effort."

The light made her crimson lips shine as she turned her head away from him. Ben persisted. "I looked at my letters and noticed they had been resealed. Since you had them, I thought you might—"

"Your washerwoman friend had them after I did. I should think you would ask her."

"I will if you will assure me that you had no part in it."

Her lashes quivered as if at a private joke. "None."

He ignored her attempt to turn him away. "I don't believe you."

"Come, come." She touched both cheeks with the rouge brush and rubbed it in with her fingers. "It's not gallant of you to contradict a lady."

"Very well," he said simply. "Since you have not chosen to be honest with me, I must speak. If you intend to keep living off the resources and encouraging the company of Mr. Creswick, I will turn all the responsibility of your financial support over to him."

Her face whitened under the rouge, and she laid down her brush to look at him. "You will do no such thing."

"I supported you because it was my duty as a son to provide for you after my father left. But if you wish to enjoy a relationship that is not rightfully yours, it will no longer be my place to support you, especially as I have my own family to provide for."

"Your duty to me—"

"I assure you that if you fall again into unfortunate circumstances, I will supplement your income as much as I can. You can choose to live on Creswick's money or on mine, but you cannot live on both. I have every reason to suspect that he's a pacifist with ties to Germany, and I think he is using you."

"How dare you—"

His tone maintained its normal gravity as he interrupted her. "The second matter is that if you do choose to end your relationship with him, I cannot help to pay the mortgage on this house. I am sorry that this is the case, but with these hard times and the number of people I have to support, I cannot sit in the lap of luxury. I am happy to send you money, and if I could I would send you enough to allow you to live this richly, but I cannot. You will have to discuss with Mr. Creswick whether he would like to buy this house for you or not. One way or the other, you must keep or sell it on his money."

She watched him out of glittering eyes. "Are you going to let me speak?"

"Of course."

"I wondered when you would take after your father. He was an undutiful wretch. You're just like him, you know."

Her words took him aback. "I am not."

"Oh yes, you are. He was always quiet like you. Not as good perhaps, but you're more like him than you know. I see it in all your little habits. You memorize a man after you've been married to him for six years, and heaven knows I lived with you longer than that. You'll probably end up leaving me like he did before you're through."

Ben put a hand against the doorpost and felt himself shaking in the aftershock. If there was one person in the world he didn't want to be like, it was the bitter, discontented man in London who had given up trying to fix what was wrong with his life.

"I would never leave you. I might disagree with you, but you're my mother."

She shrugged, and one lip turned up at the corner as she turned back to her mirror. "We'll see, won't we?"

* * *

By late morning, Ben was at the door of the Richmond bank, just in time to meet Patrick coming out. Patrick didn't see him until Ben pulled open the door. He greeted him in pleased surprise.

"Why, hello, doctor. I didn't know you were coming to Richmond early today."

"You can call me by my name if you like," Ben returned. "I had some other business to take care of before I went to work. What are you doing here?"

Patrick held up a paper bag. "Just withdrew all my money from my account."

"I wouldn't broadcast the fact if I were you." Ben looked around cautiously to see if anyone was nearby. "Someone might overhear and want a share of the profits."

Patrick laughed. "Never try to steal an Irishman's pot of gold. Are you coming over to the house?"

"Not today. But I'll be sure to stop by before you sail to Dublin. Say hello to your folks for me."

"Mum likes to see you when you come. I think she likes you

better than us." Patrick winked at him exactly as Terry did and made his way out, swinging the paper bag at his fingertips.

Ben shook his head and handed his card to the same clerk he had talked to on his previous visit.

"I would like to see Mr. Creswick."

"I'm sorry, sir." The clerk smiled apologetically. "He's not available at present."

"He'll see me."

The clerk handed him back his card. "Mr. Creswick gave me instructions not to admit you after the last time you came."

"You will," Ben said grimly, "or I'll bring someone in and make it much more unpleasant for both of you."

He saw the words put a chink in the man's confidence. "Is Mr. Creswick in trouble with the law?"

"Not yet. But he will be if you don't let me in. I'll clear it with him; you don't have to worry about your position."

"Yes, sir." The clerk's eyes widened. "Two floors up, the same door on your right."

"Good man."

Ben rode up the elevator and pushed open the office door. He could see as soon as he entered that his sudden appearance caught Creswick off his guard, but he knew the coming power struggle would depend more on force of will than sudden shock.

"What is it?" Creswick asked, making no attempt at civility.

"I won't take up much of your time, sir." Ben clasped his hands behind his back. "I merely came to ask if you have an interest in reclaiming a letter of yours to my mother that hints at connections with the pacifist movement."

Creswick shoved his glasses higher up on his nose and shuffled the papers on his desk. "You make unfounded accusations, doctor. I hardly think that is wise in your position. Blind guesses are double-edged tools."

"If they're blind. Very well, then, perhaps you can help me with something else. I am looking for information about my brother Edmond, and you seem to have connections with him. Do you know his whereabouts?"

"I have never met the gentleman." Creswick shook his head.

Ben dealt the blow he had given up his conscience to make ready. "But you have written to him. He gives money to my mother every month, and you help her keep track of it."

Creswick's hazel eyes snapped. "His personal activities are of no concern to me. This establishment exists merely for financial transactions."

He had been prepared for this. During his journey by train, he had turned over the possible responses he could make in the face of a refusal. In spite of York's caution, he had settled upon a veiled hint as the best option. Ben sat down in the leather seat uninvited and crossed his hands over his knees.

"Oh, but I think they should be. Or do you wish to tell me about some personal activities of your own instead?"

"And what would those be?" Creswick watched him closely, letting not a single breath escape his notice.

Ben shrugged. "I would accept some alternate information I need. About financial investments in Germany, which could be frowned upon if known publicly."

Creswick shifted in his seat. "I had investments abroad before the war. There was nothing criminal in that at the time."

"I have learned much about your interests, sir, and I think you should be concerned."

The banker's face reddened. "You seem to think you are free of concern yourself. I, too, have connections to find out—information."

Ben smiled and raised his chin. "I have nothing to hide."

"A very good bluff, doctor, but not quite good enough."

"Be careful, Mr. Creswick. I know enough to place you on very fragile footing."

Creswick was not deceived. "I am not afraid of what you can do. You're too small a man to do any lasting damage to my affairs."

Ben held steady, letting not a tremor betray the truth. "I have no doubt of that. But I know people who can do more damage than I can. I suggest you end your acquaintance with my mother."

Creswick rubbed his chin with his fingers and closed his eyes in thought. Then he opened them and leaned forward. "I will only assure you that any letters you may possess do no harm to your mother. I warn you for your own safety, do not attempt to find out any more. I have nothing against you, but judging by your letters, I can see that someone does. There, sir; I have said all I am going to say to you. If you do not leave, I will phone the police."

Neither offered the other a hand of acknowledgment as Ben rose to go. He decided as he went down the stairs that if he had it to do all over again, he would have kept his cards closer to his chest.

October 17, 1917

Ma Chérie,

You haven't written, and I am worried about you. Perhaps I will hear from you even before this letter reaches England. I hope you aren't as lonely as you thought you would be—though I don't mind if you miss me a little bit. I miss you most of the day, but I think the time I most wish you were here is when I come home from work and there is no one to kiss me hello and ask how my day has been. I do not know what you are doing or facing right now, but I do know that whatever it is, you are handling it with grace and courage. You always have, and that gives me courage too. Keep trusting and praying, sweetheart, and we shall find a way to be together again.

How is Pearlie? I'm sure she is happy at Alisa's. Are you still working at the clinic? Jaeryn said he was going to offer you your position again, but I haven't heard from any of you to know if you have taken it or not. I hope you have. He and I are better friends than we used to be, and I think he would be kind to you for my sake. I want you to be well taken care of.

Work was easier to find here than I expected. With all the young doctors offering their services to the war effort, my skills are at a premium, and there are several positions at the Richmond hospital that will eventually open up. At first I was relieved, but this morning I read news reports and found that the fighting in France has taken another dark turn. British soldiers my age are drowning in the mud and rain in France. I cannot not help feeling like a coward. Why is it, now that I have lived in Folkestone and met the wives of men at the front, that it feels like a betrayal of them to be in safety? I never had reason to feel that way before.

I have one wish, and that is that you are safe and untouched by the war. I promise I will come back sooner than we planned if things continue to look grim in France. Richmond isn't the same without you, and there is nothing I look forward to more than seeing you again.

Your loving husband,
Benjamin Dorroll

The next morning Ben slipped across some of the precious book money for postage, and the postmaster handed him a letter in return. He looked at the near-illegible script on the envelope and swallowed hard. No one else on earth wrote like that. It was from London, England, but he knew the sender by its very illegibility.

Jaeryn Graham wanted him back.

Chapter Twenty-Five
A Problem of Ethnicity

Jaeryn thought he might have been better off taking a holiday after his ordeal. The line around his neck was too high to cover adequately, and he looked like one of the victims from the bar fights he patched up every few weeks. He wouldn't trust anyone looking like that to give him medical attention. He shook his head wryly as he took one last glance at himself in the mirror. Edmond Dorroll could hardly help knowing what he was involved in once he saw him. Thinking through the pain was hard enough, much less playing at cross-purposes. But today he would have to do both.

As he pedaled through town, he realized with surprise that the seasons were changing. The leaves were turning chestnut and crimson, and the wind blew its chilly breath around and under his open collar. It would be winter soon, and he would have to find a better means of getting around for the colder weather. He couldn't recall a summer that had flown by faster in his twenty-eight years. How had it vanished so quickly? The last time he had gone to the Emmerson estate was just before his argument with Ben in August. He winced—whether it was from the remembrance or from his headache, only he could have said.

Peters opened the door, as dignified as ever, and Jaeryn caught sight of another man standing further back in the hall. The butler took his hat and made introductions. "Doctor Jaeryn Graham, sir. Doctor, this is Mr. Edmond Dorroll."

As soon as he was inside, Jaeryn postponed his ulterior motives and looked Edmond over from a medical perspective. Below the dark brown hair, the skin was badly scarred, and any resemblance to his brother had completely disappeared. The shrapnel must have hit him straight in the face. No wonder he hadn't wanted to meet his family so changed. Jaeryn controlled his shock by a great effort and bowed in greeting.

Edmond held out his hand. "Doctor, I'm obliged to you for coming. I hope I'm not too hideous a sight to you."

"Not at all." Jaeryn smiled. "Anything I can do would be an honor, captain, after your hard work for us in France."

"You look like you've been through the wars yourself."

Instinctively, Jaeryn's hand went up toward his neck, but he stopped before touching it. "You could say that."

Edmond's lips quirked up at one corner. "I am not unaware of your work here. If I can be of service in any way, you needn't hesitate to tell me. But I understand, of course, that it is confidential."

Edmond led the way upstairs to the master suite. The gray-tinted chamber was little changed since Emmerson had lain in state before his burial, but now it housed shoes and a shaving kit, and a folding table held a deck of cards laid out in mid-game.

"Playing against yourself?" Jaeryn asked as he pulled out his watch.

Edmond unfastened his shirt cuff and pulled up his sleeve. "No. Peters obliges me when I'm bored."

"I imagine you would be now and then. Are you acquainted with many people here?" He gripped Edmond's wrist between his fingers to take the pulse—strong and steady. No doubt very little shook him after all he had seen in Europe.

"Only Emmerson, and he's dead." Jaeryn took his hand away, and Edmond pulled his sleeve down again. "And I met Colonel King once or twice at his home before the war."

Jaeryn hid his interest by sorting through the medical supplies in his bag. "You must miss Emmerson, then."

"Oh, yes. My father and I knew him all my childhood, and on up until the war. After that, they dissolved their friendship for some reason or other, but I kept up the acquaintance. I never wished him

447

dead." Edmond reached into the drawer and pulled out a box of cigarettes. "Want one?"

Jaeryn shook his head.

He shoved them back again and closed the drawer. "My brother was in Folkestone earlier this summer, but I hear from Peters that he left some time ago. The two of you had a partnership, didn't you?"

He held the stethoscope to Edmond's chest. "We did. Of sorts."

"Why did he leave?"

"He was finished with his obligations here, and the medical work didn't pay enough to support a family. He didn't wish to stay in England." Jaeryn winced at the rough exhalation of Edmond's lungs. "How did this happen? Did you inhale the gas?"

"Some of it. We were caught back on the first of March. I got a face full of it from the Germans when we charged."

Jaeryn dropped the stethoscope hastily and eyed him, but Edmond continued on.

"I was the lucky one. Three of my men died after weeks of agony." He looked down and pressed his lips. "When you're in that much pain, you'll pretty much thank anyone to take a pistol to you."

Jaeryn nodded sympathetically. "That's enough to put any man over the edge. Has traveling made it worse?"

"Traveling?" Edmond frowned in confusion. "Oh, you mean in America. I've had a week to recover, but I was exhausted when I first got back. Doctor"—he laid a hand on Jaeryn's sleeve, and his eyes darkened. "I didn't bring you here for my lungs. Every night I have to live those few weeks over again, and I can't take it much longer. I want anything you can give me to make me forget."

Jaeryn sighed and took a seat beside him on the bed. "I can give you chloral hydrate. But you should realize the danger of becoming addicted to it if you use it often."

"If you had to endure what I go through daily, you wouldn't blame my wanting relief from it."

Jaeryn pulled out the jar he kept for his visits and poured out two of the white rounds into his palm. "I don't blame anyone for that; it's natural, and I'm here to give you the help you need. But I'm also here to make sure the cure doesn't destroy you." He gave the pills to Edmond, who swallowed them down with a glass of water from the nightstand. "I'll give it to you in limited quantities so you can't abuse it. If you use more than I give you permission for, you'll have to endure the dreams until I can give you another prescription. It may

448

sound harsh, but you could very well poison yourself if you aren't cautious with it. You need to get back on your own two feet, not become a drug addict."

Edmond nodded. "Fair enough."

"Would you like me to be quite honest with you?"

"That's what I brought you here for." Edmond's eyes were blue like his younger brother's. But the blue was clearer and lighter, and their seriousness was more from willfulness than reserve, Jaeryn thought. He had a harsher edge than his brother, even if his polish was more civil. Unquestionably, he was used to having his own way and must be guided discreetly.

"I think you need someone close to you to give you a reason to come back." He didn't mention Alisa's name, but he saw Edmond knew what he meant.

Edmond shuddered. "I don't think so. My wife is happier without me."

Jaeryn shook his head. "The added guilt won't be beneficial to your recovery. She's eighteen years old, and it's your responsibility to look out for her. Let her help you as she wishes to. From what I've seen, she is strong enough to bear the change in you without breaking, and you need her just as much as she needs you."

"It was a foolish thing to marry her in the first place. I should have waited."

Jaeryn countered forcefully. "It's too late for that. Abandoning her with a baby son won't help either of you."

"You were honest." Edmond looked thoughtful. "I'm not ready for Alisa yet, and I doubt she's ready for me. But I'm not a brute, and I'll see that she's well provided for while she waits. Now, tell me your diagnosis, doctor."

Jaeryn gave his verdict with as kind and straightforward a manner as he could. "I've taken a good look at you, and I agree that the poison from the gas has left your lungs permanently impaired. You bear a greater risk of infection from now on, and it is highly likely that you will die by some respiratory illness. It is hard news to give, but you will live a shorter life than you might otherwise have done, and I would advise you to make your choices accordingly."

"Very good." Edmond stood up, erect and unshaken. "I've faced death more than once, and I can face it again."

Jaeryn collected his things to leave. "If you send someone down for the medication, I'll have it ready by this afternoon. I trust you'll find my services adequate in future, though of course I would understand if you ever wanted to seek a second opinion."

Edmond followed him down the stairs to see him out. "I don't see any need to do that. You're a straight speaker, and I expect you'll tell me if I'm beyond your abilities. A pleasure to meet you, doctor. I'll have you up for dinner in your unprofessional capacity sometime."

"I should like that." That was the truth. He needed another chance to observe him.

Jaeryn pedaled with all his might to reach home quickly. As soon as he reached the clinic, he dropped the bicycle at the steps and bounded through the door. Reaching for pencil and paper, he jotted down a note.

Want more information about March 1st gas attacks in France. Advise as soon as possible. J.G.

Sealing it up, he darted back out again and set off on his bicycle. He would put it in the drop for Fenton's private eyes. And then he had a visit to make. The kind of visit that made him want to march right back to Edmond Dorroll and drive a fist into his scarred face.

* * *

Alisa's side door was propped open to let in the cool breezes, and Jaeryn peeped in after a light knock. She sat at the kitchen table, cuddling her baby and sometimes receiving a chuckle from him in return for her efforts. Her hair was braided and pinned up, and she looked quite content—just as if she were waiting for her husband to come in from the fields instead of bearing the uncertainty of his return.

He took a deep breath. It seemed a shame to break her serenity, yet there would never be a good time to tell her what he had to say. There was no comfort to offer to a woman whose husband was a mental wreck as well as a physical one.

"Mrs. Dorroll?"

Alisa looked up from Matthew and smiled when she recognized him. "Hello, doctor. Would you like some lunch? We've already eaten, but I can make you something."

"No, thank-you. I want to talk to you about your husband."

Jaeryn came in and slipped into the chair opposite her.

Her eyes brightened. "Charlotte said he was coming back. Have you heard from him?"

"I have. I saw him this morning. Mr. Emmerson willed his estate to your husband, and he has been living there for some days now."

The smile faded from her face and gave way to an anxious expression. "Why hasn't he come here? Is he ill?"

Jaeryn clenched his hands behind his back. "Do you want the truth?"

"Yes, please."

"He's well in body, and I am afraid—"

"He should be here now?" Her face looked pinched and drawn.

"Yes, Mrs. Dorroll. I'm sorry. He has no intention of seeing you at present."

She shivered as if he had stung her with a whip. Matthew sobbed in protest, no doubt at a squeeze too tight for comfort.

Jaeryn came over to her side of the table. "I'll take the baby."

She shook her head and tightened her hold on the child, her other hand lying open on the table, telling more than words how much the news had emptied her. Jaeryn laid his hand on hers.

"He may come back, Mrs. Dorroll. You must keep praying. Your husband has been through unimaginable pain, and he's lost his grip for the present. I am hopeful that he'll remember the treasures he has here."

She closed her eyes, and he felt her fingers tighten around his. "Ben said he could be scarred for life if he recovered. Was he much hurt?"

"The shrapnel left its mark. I think you wouldn't know him for the same person he was before." Jaeryn remembered the crooked smile in the midst of the wreckage and grasped at a ray of comfort. "But some of the real man is still down there. I don't know him well, but I could tell."

She nodded. Her eyes were quite dry.

Jaeryn averted his eyes from her grieved face. "I'm so sorry."

Her voice quivered. "I wish—Ben were here. It isn't—it isn't supposed to be this way."

He had been thinking the same thing.

He felt a touch on his shoulder and glanced up to see Pearl. She slipped her arms around Alisa and leaned her head on her shoulder, and Jaeryn left them alone. It was better to leave her to those she knew best. Time would heal the rawness of her grief, he had no doubt. And in time, too, perhaps Edmond Dorroll would come to rights and see the help he was holding at arm's length.

* * *

When he got back to the clinic, Charlotte met him at the office door and asked how he was feeling. He shrugged off her question and scrubbed his hands at the consulting room sink. "No matter. I'm good as ever."

He reached for the mug of tea on the counter, but she gave a soft laugh and intercepted him. "That, sir, is mine. Yours is in the kitchen to keep hot. It will be at your service in a moment."

She slipped out with a rustle of her tan skirt, and Jaeryn smiled and shook his head. The tension that had been between them the week before had dissipated somewhat. As long as he kept away from mention of trust, she was cheery enough during work hours, and he capitalized as much as possible on the improvement. He even had an invitation to come to lunch after church on Sunday, which, considering that it was from the Dorrolls, he took as a very high mark of esteem.

When Charlotte came back and handed him the mug, he gave her the note Terry had written to Pearl. "I called at Alisa's this morning, but I forgot to give this to Miss Dorroll."

She turned it over disapprovingly and looked at the sprawling *Acushla* on the front. "I heard about what happened."

"I hope Miss Dorroll wasn't too upset by it. Terry didn't mean to harm her."

"Well, it was still wrong. But I don't think she's as unhappy about it as the rest of us. He's brought her steadiness during this time, which is strange, considering how unsteady he is."

It wasn't until lunchtime that Jaeryn suspected her happiness was a facade for something else. He saw the worry lines deepen around her mouth as she doled out aspirin and soothed small children coming in for examinations. Once, while he was looking over a baby with a bad case of croup, Charlotte closed her eyes as if to blink back tears. But he pretended not to see and continued giving directions as if nothing had happened.

After Pearlie dropped off a dish of hot baked apples and they started lunch, Jaeryn broke the silence. "You look troubled. Is there

452

any way I can be of service to you?"

"Do I?" She reached up and tried in vain to smooth away the crease between her eyebrows. "It's nothing."

"I'll be impertinent and pry. There is something, and your husband would want you to get help if you needed it."

"Would he want me to get it from you, do you think?"

Jaeryn kept his tone light and even, so as not to shut her off. "I think he would."

She looked down at the baked apples, wafting up an aroma of raisins and cinnamon, and pushed her plate away. "I got our loan notices in the mail yesterday. It's too early to expect money from him yet, but it worries me."

Charlotte Dorroll wouldn't borrow money from him easily, he knew. That would make persuading her all the more a triumph. "Will you give me the letters?"

"So you can pay them?"

He tried to brush it off. "Your husband can pay me back later."

Charlotte shook her head. "I don't think he would like that arrangement. I had thought of sending them to his father in London and asking him for help."

"Then let me take the letters for you. I'm going to London on Sunday, and I'll speak to him about them. Otherwise, I promise I won't touch them until your husband sends the money or you give me permission."

"You are kind to offer, but I would prefer to manage it myself. But I wonder—I wonder if I could work longer hours here. You have so much to do, and I could do more of it for you. It would bring in more income, and—I need it." Her voice trembled. He half-rose from his chair, but she held out her hand to prevent him. "Don't worry. I am just—tired of being Mrs. Dailey, that's all. I want to be Mrs. Dorroll again."

She pulled out a handkerchief, dabbed at her tears, and laughed. He shifted uncomfortably and hoped to high heaven no one was listening. Either they would take it as a highly inappropriate conversation, or they would know that Charlotte knew more than she should and set a watch on her. She folded her handkerchief again and continued. "I think when he comes back for us, I'll never let him go again."

Jaeryn clenched his teeth. "I sit and watch you all breaking—"

She sniffed back her tears, and a smile flashed out that grew and gathered confidence. "We do not break. While God is with us, we may crack and wear thin, but we do not break."

"Please, let me do something for you. Give me those letters to take to your father-in-law, at least."

She gave him one probing look, and Jaeryn kept every muscle still until she drew her gaze away. "I will give them to you." Charlotte reached into Ben's desk and pulled out three envelopes, which she placed slowly on his desk. "You must promise me that you will take them to London and not pay them yourself."

"I give you my word."

She brushed back a stray wisp of hair from her face and picked up her fork to commence eating again. "As a gentleman?"

His whole soul exulted. "As an Irishman. And that is the only word that I consider worth keeping."

* * *

Mrs. Goodwin came to drop off his clean laundry once a week. Normally, Jaeryn left the back door unlocked and she put the clothes in his bedroom, taking the envelope of money he left for her on the dresser. But on this Friday afternoon, he found her sitting in the waiting room with the rest of the patients.

"You can come back, Mrs. Goodwin." He beckoned her into the hallway. "Are you not feeling well today?"

She stood on tiptoe to whisper, and he bent his head down until she could reach his ear. "I would have left you a note, but I didn't bring any paper with me. I'm giving up my cottages, doctor, and wondered if you would put in a good word with your patients if any of them are in need of lodgings."

"Is Colonel King selling, then?" he asked in surprise.

"Yes." Not a muscle moved in her face to disturb its pale serenity. "He says he doesn't need them anymore."

"I wonder why he wanted them before," Jaeryn muttered. Then he spoke aloud. "What will you do?"

"Oh, he says he'll find me other lodgings, and I can still help with the washing and ironing. I'll keep working here as usual if you still want me. But, doctor," she tugged at his gray jacket sleeve, "I don't think King's a man to be trusted."

"Don't you?" Jaeryn's words were nearly inaudible, and he felt as if his breath had deserted him. "Why?"

"His son is so unhappy. I go three times a week, and that lad wanders around the house like a caged animal."

"That lad," he muttered, "is a caged scamp."

Mrs. Goodwin's faded eyes held a hint of rebuke. "Maybe. But even scamps deserve some dignity."

She left, and he turned the matter over in his mind all afternoon. Lodgings. Lodgings were a source of power, especially those particular cottages. If he could get his hands on them—but why did King want to sell now? And was there a particular reason why the colonel wanted him to know? Mrs. Goodwin's request was natural enough, for he saw many people in the course of a day's work. But still, something troubled him about it that he could not put his finger on.

Terry turned up at the clinic later that night, not quite as cheery as usual, with a little dark-haired boy clinging to his hand. He lifted the child to the desk, and Jaeryn lifted an eyebrow inquiringly.

"Brogan." Terry jerked a thumb at his nephew. "Erin asked me to keep him while she bought some things. We just got back; it took me until the afternoon train to persuade her to come."

Jaeryn couldn't imagine Terry pushing anyone to do anything they disliked. "Where is she now?"

"At Stoke's place." Terry reached into his pocket and tossed an object onto the desk. It flashed gold through the air, and Jaeryn picked it up. It was a wedding band, with three diamonds arranged in its center, two small ones girding a larger one.

"She wouldn't wear it." Terry looked at it unhappily.

Jaeryn laid it on an empty tray. "Don't worry, we'll figure something out. Where will you keep her?"

Terry brightened up a little. "I put her in the place the other doc used to live in. She'll like it there. But I'll have to find something else soon because Mrs. Goodwin said she was selling the place."

"I know. She told me this afternoon." Jaeryn frowned in disapproval. "Terry, that place isn't safe. Why did you put her there?"

"Well, it would have to be a pretty desperate fellow to mess with her like she is now. Besides, she can't come where I am, and that was the only place I could think of. I told her I knew of a place for her— she wouldn't have come otherwise."

Brogan held tight to Terry's hand and looked about him without talking. Terry ruffled his hair. "Poor tyke. He must not have a terribly happy go of it when they're alone together. I took him around to the post office to ask Ann about the letter. She gave it to me, so I paid her, and I'll make sure it gets to someone who can send it to the right person."

Jaeryn glanced out the window. "Hush. I see Erin coming."

A firm knock sounded at the door, and Jaeryn opened it on a lighter-haired, feminine version of his friend, with the same blue eyes but a more sensible expression—if unhappiness could be called more sensible. Terry looked from one to the other. "Erin, this is my friend I've told you about."

Jaeryn debated whether or not to offer his hand, but she didn't look as if she wanted it, so he passed over the civility. "Jaeryn Graham, at your service."

Erin nodded. "Hello. Terry, I bought what I needed, and the cab's waiting. We shouldn't inconvenience this man any longer."

Terry picked up Brogan.

"A pleasure to meet you," Jaeryn offered. "I hope you'll find your stay in Folkestone a pleasant one."

She glanced at him impatiently. "I am only here because I couldn't find work in Dover and Terry wouldn't help me unless I came with him."

"Well, your only other option at present is to go back to your own people or your husband's, and that's a perilous undertaking as well as a costly one."

Erin's eyes blazed. "Go to Germany? I would die first."

Jaeryn caught Terry wincing and decided to risk a bolder hand. "I can tell you that it takes a good deal more than that to kill someone. Someday, provided your husband lives through the war, he will want to go home. And he will want to take his wife and child with him."

"I'll get a divorce before I live with a German—in Germany or anywhere else," Erin retorted.

"Give me your hand." Jaeryn held out his own, and after a slight hesitation, she placed hers in it. He slipped the ring on her finger, ignoring her forbidding expression.

"I don't want to wear it." She took hold of it to wrench it off, but Jaeryn clasped his hand over hers.

"Leave it on. Doctor's orders. There is no need for you to bear people's misunderstanding."

She jerked her hand away. "I want nothing to do with a German."

"Oh, for heaven's sake." Jaeryn rolled his eyes. "If you want good work, it will be much easier for you if people know you're the respectable woman you are."

"He's fighting for the Kaiser, and I refuse to be identified with that."

"Is that an unforgivable sin?"

Erin's blue eyes held a contempt that sent tingles down his spine. "You'd better be careful, doctor. You sound like you have some interest in the German cause yourself."

He bowed gallantly. "But you know my real meaning."

"Thankfully for you. I'd take care how I talked if I were you."

Erin turned on her heel and left. Terry looked back and grimaced on his way out, mouthing a few words that Jaeryn could not make out.

Jaeryn tried to shrug off a feeling of uneasiness as he ate a cold supper before retiring to bed. Perhaps he had been too free with his words. It would never do to dig a pit for himself in an attempt to soothe a woman.

He lay awake for a long time wishing he could take his words back.

* * *

What was Matthew Dorroll thinking of, leaving his children in such straits? The bills Charlotte had given him lay on the hall table, and after lunch on Sunday, he snatched them up and headed out to catch the train to London.

The weather, cloudy when he set out, turned to biting rain as he neared the capitol. Fitting, Jaeryn thought, as he hurried through the crowded walkway of Paddington station. Newsboys called out the latest British scuffle near Ypres, and he tossed one boy a threepenny piece for a paper and glanced over the account as he walked. Still a stalemate—just like Folkestone. Perhaps the fate of one mirrored the fate of the other. If that was the case, he hoped the victory would go to the right side. He drew his cap further over his eyes and hailed a waiting cab.

The cabby took the folded telegram that Jaeryn had brought with him and set off, peering through the thick rain that spattered the windshield. The telegram was from Matthew Dorroll—an affirmative response to his request for an audience, along with an address and a specified meeting time. He didn't feel particularly nervous. He was quite sure of his ability to handle the Dorroll patriarch.

457

Upon reaching the brick house, he paid the cabby and confidently walked past the gardener raking the gravel drive. A maid opened the door just as he reached for the bell, and after taking his coat and hat, led him down a hall to the parlor. A tall, distinguished-looking man stood waiting for him.

"Doctor Jaeryn Graham, sir." The maid curtsied and withdrew.

Jaeryn removed his glove and held out his hand. "Mr. Matthew Dorroll?"

Matthew Dorroll's lips twitched, perhaps in an attempt at a smile. "It is. Please be seated." He gestured to an embroidered chair. "You said that you wanted to see me about my son. To which son do you refer?"

Jaeryn had forgotten about Edmond. Technically both sons had problems, but Edmond's was better saved for later. "Your younger son, sir."

The father raised his eyebrows. "Proceed."

"I'm not aware of how close you are," Jaeryn said, "nor do I need to be. I simply came on behalf of his wife to tell you of some difficulties she faces right now. I've been prevented from helping them myself, and I hope you will be able to." Jaeryn held out the letters Charlotte had given him, which, in spite of his promise, he had read on the train to London. "Your son left in some financial difficulty, sir, and will continue to be for some time yet. I wondered if you would care to open these letters and see if they require immediate attention."

Matthew Dorroll made no move to take the envelopes. "The point you are trying to make is?"

Jaeryn hesitated and wished the man would take his cue. Here he was treading on delicate ground. "What you choose to do with them is a decision for you to make, sir."

"You wish me to bail him out with my own money, I presume." Matthew Dorroll leaned back in his chair and put his fingers together. "Why did you bring them to me?"

"His brother has other matters to attend to. And I don't think Edmond is quite the person to deal with your younger son's best interests."

Matthew's firm-cut mouth opened in questioning surprise. "Edmond is not here to deal with them in any case."

"Oh, yes he is. He arrived in Folkestone recently, and I spoke to him this week."

Matthew put his hand over his mouth to cover a cough and crossed one leg over his knee. "I have no objection to your opening those letters, doctor, and dealing with them as you desire. I prefer to have nothing to do with them."

"Very well, sir." Jaeryn returned them to his pocket and pressed his lips together.

The man fixed him with his blue-eyed gaze, cool and defiant. "You disapprove of my actions?"

He replied with icy displeasure. "I wouldn't wish to express an opinion, sir."

"That means you do." Matthew sighed and picked at a minute speck on his black coat. "My life has not been such that it meets with the approval of my children and their associates."

"Neither son has spoken ill of you. Nor shall I do so." Jaeryn lifted his chin proudly.

"Out loud, I imagine."

He remained silent.

"Come, come, Doctor Graham. You were brave enough to call on me in the first place; now finish what you have begun, and tell me your opinion of me."

"Well, I think it's more financially convenient to give generously. You can always get a return on your investment from the person you give the money to."

Matthew Dorroll laughed heartily, albeit a bit gruffly. "You have a swindler's way of putting things. Is that all you have to say to me?"

Jaeryn stood up. "I know your son did not come here because he liked it. Why he came is between the two of you. But I don't think he can give much more without receiving something in return. That, sir, concludes my business."

From there, he went straight to Ryson's office, undaunted by his failure, and all in all quite satisfied. Now there was only the matter of one blonde-haired nurse standing between him and paying the bills, and Charlotte couldn't hold out forever. It was too bad the father wouldn't help, but there were others to step in if he refused.

Jeremy looked downright apprehensive when he saw Jaeryn. He crossed his fingers fervently. Jaeryn crossed his fingers back and grinned, but Jeremy didn't return the smile.

"Ryson dictated a letter this morning to fire you. It's in the mail."

Jaeryn halted on his way through to the back hall. "He did?"

"We haven't heard from you in days. Anything would have tipped

459

him off, and that was it. He's been building up a case against you ever since you meddled with Speyer."

"I did report," Jaeryn protested. "We've been making progress. I wrote him just as usual and put the letter in the North drop."

Jeremy shrugged. "Well, we haven't gotten it, and he's convinced it was negligence on your part. There's no talking to him."

"I'll go straighten him out. Head up, Jeremy; I've worked for him too long to be kicked down now. After seven years, I think I'm entitled to one mistake—if Speyer was a mistake."

"It was." Jeremy eyed him solemnly. "You overshot your luck this time."

Jaeryn pushed open the door into Ryson's little, windowless office. "Sir, I've come to straighten a few things out."

Ryson, standing before the bookshelf with an open book in his hands, did not turn around to greet him. "That won't be necessary, doctor. Jeremy put a letter in the mail for you this morning. It will inform you that your services are no longer required."

"I think you owe me more justice than that." Jaeryn closed the door behind him, but not before he heard a muffled gasp down the hall from Jeremy. "I wrote you notes as usual, detailing my next plan. We're currently using a letter from Emmerson to set a trap, and we expect to wrap up the leak in communications as soon as we receive a reply. Besides, someone nearly choked me to death a week ago, and if my services were dispensable, I doubt they would take the trouble of trying."

Ryson sniffed. "Unfortunate, indeed."

"Listen to me now. Benjamin Dorroll's brother is back in town and the heir to the Emmerson estate. I don't know which way his loyalties tend, and I told you, though you never received my note, that Ben's services are highly useful to me. I am willing to pay for his passage back if you will agree to take him."

"I am well aware that Edmond Dorroll is in Folkestone," Ryson said coldly. "That does not change the fact that I have dispensed with your services."

Jaeryn glowered at the back of Ryson's gray suit jacket. "I heard you, sir, but I think—"

Ryson turned around. "Is it true that you traveled to Dublin in September, where your movements were lost track of?"

Hot wrath swept over Jaeryn. "If it is, I hardly consider that a sin."

"And is it true that you kept photos of Speyer's German dog tags in your desk drawer after you gave them to me?"

Blast Fenton. If this was revenge for their tussle in September, then it was sweet and taken to the full. "I did."

Ryson's eyes kindled with pale retribution. "You've grown too independent. You always showed signs of it, but now it has become unmanageable. I want someone that will be more tractable to my orders."

Jaeryn shoved his hands into his pockets to hide the clenched fists. "That would be a waste of time after all the groundwork I've laid. Besides, who are you going to get? The Meikle woman? I doubt you'll find her more reliable. Peters is out of the question, and our undercover workers aren't exactly the stuff leaders are made of. You would have a massive amount of work to redo if you took me out of this now."

His supervisor replaced the book on the shelf and picked up a pile of envelopes, which he proceeded to stamp. "I intend to request that Dorroll come back."

Jaeryn stared at him. "In charge of all those people?"

"Certainly not. Having agents working together under you doesn't seem to be gaining us much progress. They can work individually under me, and I will oversee them."

Jaeryn ran a hand around his collar and drew his breath. Ryson was serious this time. He tried to think what was best to be done. Appeasement was out of the question; besides, he wasn't about to demean himself before the man. If only he had a trump card to force Ryson's cooperation, but he could not think of any.

"Are you serious about taking Dorroll back?" he asked at length.

Twelve envelopes stamped now with a steady indifference to his presence in the room. "I think he would be a useful asset at present. Fortunately for you, or perhaps unfortunately, Peters wrote to me upon Edmond Dorroll's coming to Folkestone and suggested that very thing."

The thought of all his hard work being thrown in the dust rankled. At length, Jaeryn could contain himself no longer. "This the most unjust usage I've ever had from you, and it isn't the first time you've mistreated me."

Ryson glanced up over the rims of his glasses. "Don't lose your temper, doctor. It won't be beneficial to either of us. You'll finish out the month that we've paid you for, and then we'll transfer you

461

elsewhere. I suggest you write to Dorroll immediately; if he agrees to come I want him as soon as possible, or the position will go to someone else."

"You can't transfer me." He brought his fist down and barely stopped himself before it crashed onto the desk. "I legally own one practice and legally hold the other, and I have every intention of staying. Nor will I finish out the month under such circumstances."

Ryson's hands stopped. He laid the envelope he was holding on the desk. Stern lines crisscrossed his forehead, and he spoke in measured tones. "Doctor, I could transfer you to some backwater hospital if you don't obey my request."

"I'll not be treated as Irish scum by you lot." Jaeryn tried to get a grip on himself, but the words lilted out before he could prevent them.

"We haven't forgotten your nationality. It would not be in your favor if you chose to cross us. I suggest you proceed with caution."

Jaeryn's eyes narrowed, and he set his jaw. "I think seven years of hard work deserves some consideration."

"You can give us many more than that if you choose to be reasonable. We will move you to a different position and make monetary compensation similar to what you have been receiving, as well as buying out your practice."

"I don't think so."

"You would be ill-advised to stay in your current position."

"I'll give you until the end of the month, as I'm obligated to. And then I think we're better off parting ways."

Ryson picked up his envelopes and proceeded to finish stamping them. "You have very little open to you if you choose to leave our English protection."

"I'll cross that bridge when I come to it." His voice went hoarse, and he had to swallow once to avoid betraying his consternation. "Why did you lose your confidence in me?"

"You showed me that you were playing this game for your own interests. In most cases I would ignore the fact; all of my agents have their own interests."

"Why didn't you in my case?"

"Fenton told me what he thought your interests are. And they are quite at odds with mine."

They looked at each other, and Jaeryn knew that he could not deny it.

Jaeryn sat for a long time upon his return to Folkestone on Sunday evening, holding his head in his hands and staring down at the blank sheet of paper in front of him. He would have to be persuasive to get Dorroll to return. It had been too long now; Ben was sure to have work, and if he had work, he wouldn't come back to something he had never liked in the first place. But Fenton said the American would do anything to help, even if he hated the work itself. He could only hope that was the case.

Jaeryn scribbled a few words on the paper and crossed them out again. Truthfully, he didn't need help. He wasn't on the case anymore. If Dorroll came, it would help Ryson and all the other London politicians who had a purpose Ben probably wasn't particularly interested in assisting. He himself certainly wasn't. There was, of course, the angle of Edmond Dorroll. Ben would come back if he suspected his brother needed assistance. Or would he? Perhaps it was better not to write him in the first place. Others could take on the work quite as successfully—better, even. Others who had a vested interest and wouldn't have to sacrifice so much to get it done. Surely it was more ethical to give the work to someone to whom it really was just work.

But that didn't satisfy him. If Ben came back then he, Jaeryn, would have a firmer hold to finish the work he had begun, in spite of Ryson's dismissal. The thought of failing after years of waiting for the opportunity set him to writing in mad haste, and for once he found an eloquence he didn't know he possessed. One letter would have to do it, and the reason must be strong enough. Ryson wouldn't allow weeks of coaxing. He left out the fact that he was fired and approached it from the angle of Edmond's inheritance, saying that no one else could make a connection with Edmond like his own brother. And though Jaeryn felt merciless for doing it, he gave a full account of Edmond's mental condition and told Ben that Edmond needed the help if he could see his way clear to come.

Before he could think better of it, he drove the letter to Ramsgate to prevent it from falling into Ann's clutches. A guilty shudder swept over him as it slipped into the mail bag. If he was responsible for making Dorroll lose a good position in America, he would make it up somehow—on his word as an Irishman.

The next week passed with interminable slowness as Jaeryn tried to make sense of what he was to do next. He wandered aimlessly through his duties, hearing nothing of Terry beyond the fact that Erin wasn't being too agreeable, and nothing of the Dorrolls, for Charlotte didn't offer much news when she came to work. Two days after his meeting with Ryson he went to Ramsgate again and purchased a motorcar to make his work easier. He couldn't keep up on the bicycle, and if he was to hold out through the winter, the investment was well worth the price.

On the morning of the sixteenth of October, he drove to the King estate one last time to look at Starlin. He hadn't been making weekly visits for a long time, and this visit was merely a formality. But even formalities paid money, and now that part of his income was gone, Jaeryn wasn't averse to picking up a little extra from the King estate.

A Stutz Bearcat, the best and newest to be found, sat in the drive, and he remembered that it was Starlin's birthday. It would have taken almost six months of his wages to buy an automobile of that caliber, not to mention the cost of fuel nowadays. What a waste, showering gifts on a boy who wasn't even planning to continue his education. Jaeryn shook his head and shivered from the nip in the air. It would be winter soon, and Starlin would probably end up in a ditch somewhere after the ice set in.

The maid opened the door and led him to the study at his request. Upon arriving, they heard heated voices coming from behind the door, and she led him to the opposite parlor and asked him to wait. Jaeryn obliged most agreeably. After she left, he looked about the hall to make sure he was alone, then crept softly to the door from which the voices were coming. Neither of them were difficult to overhear; it was King having an angry audience with his son. For once Starlin had been provoked out of his usual sullenness. He sounded downright demanding as Jaeryn distinguished the words being spoken.

"I want someone to teach me how to drive the Cat. And I want work to do."

King's impatient baritone sounded in response. "You have work to do if you wish."

"I don't want that work. I want to choose my own work. You never asked me what I wanted; I'm just a tool to you. But I refuse to be one."

"Remember, if you will, that you are a minor, and I am your

464

guardian until such a time as the law releases you. You will do as you are told. And until you do, the automobile is not yours to drive."

Starlin's voice rose in protest. "You promised it to me on my seventeenth birthday."

"A promise I fulfilled. I will hold it in trust until I deem you ready to handle it. You may go, sir."

Jaeryn slipped across the hall again as the door slammed open and Starlin appeared, dressed in clothes less trim than his usual attire. Starlin didn't look pleased when he recognized his visitor, and for once, Jaeryn felt sympathetic.

"Hello, King. I've come one last time, and then I'll be out of your way for good."

Starlin huffed, and his thin shoulders rose and fell in resignation. "Make it quick, then. I'm going to call a cab and see if Terry's at Mrs. Dorroll's."

"I'll take you there if you like," Jaeryn offered. "I'm heading that way."

Starlin eyed him suspiciously, doubtless wondering where the sudden friendliness had come from. "All right. But I'm not in the mood to be lectured, so you can forget whatever it was you wanted to pitch into me about."

* * *

Jaeryn held his peace with an effort, conducting his examination and driving to Alisa's in silence. Terry was sure to be there this time of day. Perhaps after a few minutes he could coax Starlin at least into a state of general civility, if not into good-natured conversation.

Terry was in the kitchen eating lunch, so Jaeryn didn't bother to knock. Pearl brought two more plates, and Starlin accepted the invitation somewhat graciously, though Jaeryn declined it, as he couldn't stay for long.

"Hey, Starlin. Many happy returns." Terry slapped him on the shoulder. "Did you land the automobile?"

"Yes." Starlin frowned at the mention of it, and Jaeryn gave a slight shake of the head, but Terry didn't see him.

"Have you driven it yet?" Terry popped the last bite of broiled chicken in his mouth and licked his fingers.

Starlin poked at his own plateful with his fork. "No, I haven't."

Terry sighed in satisfaction and pushed back his chair from the table. "Kid, as clear as your choice of words is, it's not getting through to my brain. Pull one of your Parliament speeches and tell me all about it."

Starlin unwound enough to put more than one sentence together, though the words ground out unwillingly. "It's a red Bearcat, and it's new this year and the finest thing I've ever seen. I can drive it on one condition. And I won't do it, so I can't drive it."

"Ah." Terry jerked his head toward the door. Pearl understood and slipped out. "So, what's the condition?"

"It's a private affair."

"Come on, kid. I'll try to help you out. Just a case of stubbornness, or what?"

Starlin glowered at the blue china jug of cream sauce. "It is a case of honor."

Terry smiled at the boy's solemnity. "You and the King's. Come on now, give."

"I can't, I tell you," Starlin said, between clenched teeth. "It is a matter that I won't back down on. Not to anyone," he added under his breath.

"Have it your way." Terry dropped the subject good-naturedly.

Starlin slumped in his chair and crossed his arms. "It doesn't matter anyway. Someday I'll be dead and everyone can ignore me."

Jaeryn rolled his eye. Terry's forehead had a faint line of concern through it. "What makes you say that, kid?"

Starlin pushed the vegetables around his plate with his fork, not eating any of them. "Doctor Dailey said Stafford left a death threat for me once," he muttered.

"Did you tell your father about it?" Jaeryn asked.

"There wasn't any point. I don't think he'd care."

The line deepened on Terry's forehead. "Of course your father cares, kid. I'll talk to him about it, and he'll make sure you're safe. Quit being a morbid loner and play Pearlie some music. She'd like that."

"I forgot to bring my violin."

Jaeryn left as soon as he could to avoid exploding with rage. He wasn't paid to put up with Starlin King's ill humor, and he wasn't about to do it as an act of charity. Perhaps King had seen the irresponsibility in his son and curtailed adult responsibilities like college and driving as a measure of caution. A part of him, somewhere deep down where he didn't like to admit it, almost wished something would happen so he wouldn't have to deal with the boy anymore.

* * *

He wasn't destined to stay away from Starlin long, however. The next day, Jaeryn picked up a letter from Ben. Enclosed was a letter to Terry, with a request that Jaeryn forward it to the right address.

When he arrived at Alisa's, he found Terry and Starlin there, playing chess in the parlor. Pearlie sat next to Terry, watching over his shoulder as he moved the pieces about on the board, her cheeks pink with excitement. Pearl was better for both of them than anything else could be; their faces looked gentler and cleaner in her presence, and Starlin looked almost happy.

Terry held a black piece in his hand as Alisa beckoned for Jaeryn to come in. "Got your queen, lad."

Starlin shrugged. "So, I'll win without it."

A stifled chuckle was his only response. In less than three minutes Terry gave the ominous "Check." Then came a long silence while Starlin studied the board. At length, Terry crowed, "Give it up like a gentleman, Starlin."

"It's not checkmate yet." He moved one of his men and took out the offending piece.

Two minutes later, "I believe it's checkmate." Starlin's tone was underlain with giddy excitement.

"I'll not believe it." Terry stared at the board in consternation. "I swear vengeance."

Jaeryn held back a smile. "You'll have to keep your vow another day, Terry. I have a letter for you from Ben."

A hum of excitement went round the circle. Charlotte started up from her chair, and Alisa dropped her work in delight. Jaeryn handed Terry the note and passed off his own letter for Charlotte to read.

Terry's whole face glowed with excitement when he had finished the letter and handed it off to Jaeryn. "That'll be nice." He sighed contentedly. "Doc says the folks want to send Patrick out to visit. To think I'll see him again. I can't remember how old he was the last time I went back. I wish they could all come."

Jaeryn looked over his shoulder at Ben's neat script. "The letter was written last month; he must have sent it just after he arrived. I'm surprised they're letting your brother take the risk."

Terry chuckled. "They probably don't know the risk. They're a quiet set, and I doubt they've followed the war much. How old is Patrick? Twenty-two? Well, he'd know all right, but I doubt he would tell them."

Jaeryn looked at Starlin, who hadn't spoken since his entrance. "Good evening, King. Tried out your automobile yet?"

"No." Starlin glanced up at him from under his shock of blond hair. "Not since your kindly meant inquiry yesterday afternoon."

Jaeryn lowered his eyebrows. "I do not tolerate disrespect."

Pearlie looked uncomfortable, and Terry, who kept her under his special observation, looked at them both reprovingly. "Leave off. I've seen cats that can put up a better fight than that. The kid isn't going to drive it yet, doc. He'll tell you when he does. And Starlin, this is my particular friend and your senior by almost ten years. He's not your equal in the House."

Neither Jaeryn nor Starlin offered a reply. Starlin subsided with an injured expression, and Jaeryn wondered uneasily if he had appeared to less than advantage in the interchange. He couldn't afford to lose the Dorroll clan's good opinion at present, especially Charlotte's. Besides, however exasperating the boy was, he was the weakest link in the King household and the key to infiltration, and therefore deserved a measure of decent treatment. He wasn't entirely sure why Starlin disliked him, unless—no, his secrets were safe. The only possible reason he could see for Starlin's despising him was his ethnicity.

Charlotte held out the letter for him to take back. "It says he applied for work at the hospital, but he doesn't mention his mother. I hope we'll hear more from him soon. I wonder why I haven't received a letter yet."

Jaeryn waved his hand. "Keep the letter. I'm sure you want to."

Her eyes kindled with pleasure, and she tucked it into the basket of mending at her feet. "Thank you very much, doctor."

Alisa stepped out into the kitchen to wash up a sink full of empty mugs, and Jaeryn followed after to speak to her before he left.

"I only came by for a moment, and now I'm heading home," he said. "Is there anything I can do for you?"

Alisa smiled up at him. "That's always what Ben used to say. We have everything we need here."

"Excellent. Don't let Terry and Starlin take advantage of you. If you're tired of them, they can find another place to make themselves at home."

"Why don't you like Starlin King?" she asked softly, as a frown gathered between his brows.

"The doc thinks he's indolent," Terry explained, appearing in the kitchen doorway.

Jaeryn started. "Shh. Don't speak so loud. He might hear you."

"In fact," Terry continued, ignoring him, "did you know, Alisa, that this man once asked the kid if he had an aim in life? The kid said no. And Jaeryn Graham, who has always had an aim in life, has never thought well of him since."

"That's not true," Jaeryn protested.

"Deny it if you dare." Terry grinned wickedly. "You know, in all the time I've known you, you've had only one fault."

Jaeryn rolled his eyes. "And that is, Mr. O'Sean?"

"You take life way too seriously. Cut the kid some slack; he's not as experienced as you are. Good night, folks. I'm off to work, and I sent the kid out by the front door. We've stayed long enough."

Jaeryn and Alisa exchanged glances of amusement as Terry left, and then Jaeryn, too, bid her goodnight. As soon as he reached the bottom of the steps, he heard Terry whisper, "Hey, doc. I told King about the kid and the butler today."

"What did he say?" Jaeryn whispered back.

"Absolute towering rage. I left and hung around in the hall to listen. King sacked Stafford on the spot. Stafford was in a towering rage, too. Said he'd served with respectability for two decades and had done no such thing and oughtn't be dismissed without evidence. King wouldn't hear any more and told him to leave before he was prosecuted. I saw Stafford at the Star Inn this afternoon and told him he could come live at my place."

"Turlough O'Sean, you didn't!"

"Well, if there's something deeper to it, we can't just let him roam free, can we? I'll see what I can find. I think he's the sort of man safer to keep in front of you than behind your back. By the way, I got our forged letter to Fenton, and he said he could give it to the right channel. I think we'll be in shape soon. Good night, doc."

Jaeryn shook his head as Terry whistled his way into the darkness.

Chapter Twenty-Six
Getting Advice

Ben turned over the envelope and savagely ripped it open. If Jaeryn wanted him to come back, he would wring his neck the next time he saw him. In spite of his regret at leaving Folkestone, the thought of seeing it again turned him sick with dread.

There were two sheets of paper, breathing all the persuasiveness that a man who hated writing letters could muster. Curiously absent from it was any reference to Jaeryn's progress in the assignment; it was only the news that Edmond had returned. He probably wasn't able to put down everything that he wanted to say. Wound through it all was a continuous mention of the fact that Ryson had agreed to take Ben back.

The letter ended by saying: *I've sent money to York to purchase a steamer ticket. You must not delay in your decision, or your position will be given to someone else. I have need of you if you can see your way clear to come. Either your father or your brother might know something important, and you're the best one to find that out.*

Edmond was back in Folkestone. That must mean Alisa was with him. Ben was glad for her, though it sounded as if Edmond was in a despondent state of mind at present. He didn't want Edmond getting inveigled into any treason as a side effect of his inheritance. Besides, his father's involvement with Gilbert Emmerson's affairs bore looking into, though he wanted nothing to do with apprehending him.

Today was the eighteenth of October. It didn't leave him much time to decide. He would take a few days to think it over, and then he would either book his ticket or write a letter for Patrick to take to Jaeryn explaining his refusal. Jaeryn must have been sure of carrying his point to send the money. But the knowledge didn't irk him as much as it had before; Jaeryn's way was Jaeryn's way, and the length of the letter and the confidence it expressed did much to turn his mind away from any resentment.

He tried to set the matter aside as he made his hospital visits that afternoon, giving directions to the nurses and examining patients with the grave gentleness that was his habit. But the words wound uneasily through his thoughts nonetheless, and he could not shake them off.

He gazed into the crackling fire that evening, and moments he wanted to forget flashed across his mind. Terry, bleeding on the moors—the bombing of Tontine—Jaeryn's green eyes when he looked up in the church—Stafford standing over Starlin's wallet—Creswick's veiled anger at the office. It was all a hazy swirl of events, only the mission connecting them together. Why couldn't Jaeryn have left him in peace? Because Jaeryn was the sort of person meant to turn the world on its ear and conquer great obstacles and lead men to the accomplishment of his goals. Like Haig with his grand plans for conquest, Jaeryn stormed through life in blissful ignorance of how much he required men to give up to follow him. Perhaps it didn't matter if he knew. In the end, it was for the men following him to decide how much they wanted to give, whether Jaeryn knew the cost or not.

The third evening of his wrestling with it, Lisette noticed his abstraction. She shifted about impatiently while Ben sat curled up on the sofa with his chin in his hand. Finally, she broke into his reverie. "What are you thinking about? You barely spoke at dinner."

"I was thinking about Great Britain."

"I thought you hated Great Britain," she remarked, abstractedly smoothing down the edge of her collar.

"I thought so, too. I almost wish I still did." Ben stood up, and she stared after him in astonishment as he left the room.

He went up to his bedroom and opened the window. Then he knelt down in front of it and leaned his elbows on the sill, listening to the haunting wash of waves upon the shore. The headlines in the papers from the last few days rang in his ears. France. Torrents of rain. A shuttlecock of wins and losses tossed back and forth between British and Germans while the lifeblood of Britain's army drained away in the muddy fields of Passchendaele.

If he could have anything he wanted, he would forget that Jaeryn and his problems had ever existed and stay to build up his career in Richmond. But what he wanted would turn to ashes in his hands if he didn't go back. It would only be delaying the inevitable. If the light didn't shine out in England, the darkness would come next to America. Perhaps the light in Folkestone wasn't robust enough to overcome the darkness without him.

"I have help to offer, Charlotte," he whispered, pressing his forehead against the windowsill. "And I would be a coward to stay behind in safety."

There were men in France dying tonight. Even if he did not have as much to give as they did, he still wanted to give everything he could.

* * *

When Ben called on the morning of October twenty-second, he found that York had the money safe and sound and had even booked a passage on the November third steamer.

"Before you confirmed it with me?" Ben asked in surprise.

"Graham told me to go ahead and book one on the soonest available steamer. It's leaving from Baltimore. Is the date all right, or do you need a different one? You asked me not too long ago to book passage for Patrick O'Sean, and I thought you might like to cross with him."

Ben shook his head wryly. The Irishman was still as controlling as ever. "No, the date's correct. Was the passage the only money he sent?"

"That's all I received. I can lend you more if you need it. Graham told me to make sure you had what you needed."

"Not necessary, thanks. I've borrowed all I intend to for the present."

York grunted in agreement. "I have some more news for you before you go: you'll need to come to Boston before the steamer sails. Graham sent me a packet with your name on it. It came separately from his letter about you, and it doesn't look to be connected."

"Did he? I wonder what it could be."

"You'll have to come here to find out. Have you found any new information the last few days?"

Ben cleared his throat. "A little. I paid a call on Creswick, and he told me the German investments were dissolved as soon as America entered the war. But before I visited him, I found a stack of anti-war propaganda that was sent on to my mother's house. She ordered them to be mailed out to him. That strikes me as inconsistent, dissolving a German bank account and protesting the war at the same time."

"What was in the box?"

"Mostly pacifist posters, and a magazine called *The Masses*. He's using her as a front to receive them, and then he's taking them for his own use. She doesn't strike me as wily enough to be involved in undercover propaganda herself."

There was a pause on York's end before he spoke again. "The government doesn't look kindly on the editors of *The Masses*. We could possibly work out an angle on that, but if the overhead has kept clear of penalties, I doubt we could pin anything on Creswick. It's good collective evidence, though, if we can trap him with something more incriminating. We'll keep up our surveillance. People who do that sort of thing can't cover all their tracks."

"Keep looking into Creswick, and see if you can find any more details about the agent who helped him set up the bank accounts," Ben said. "I'll take care of Fenton's end of things when I return to England."

"You said Creswick may have tampered with your letters. Why do you think your correspondence is still of interest?"

"I would assume it's because he doesn't want me to tell Jaeryn about him. But I think my letters are being censored from both the United States and England. I haven't received a letter or a telegram from home since I came here."

"Perhaps I should send a telegram. It's not good to leave a broken chain of communication. Whom do you want me to try to contact?"

Ben thought for a moment. He wanted most to make sure Charlotte had a letter, but if it was Ann Meikle who was diverting his correspondence, which seemed most likely, she might hesitate more before tampering with Jaeryn's mail. "Jaeryn Graham would be the best."

"Very well. But be careful you're not letting a family problem twist your perceptions. The letters may have nothing to do with your other work."

"It has a connection, I have no doubt. My mother and I aren't particularly interesting people in ourselves."

"Oh, trust me, doctor." York's baritone held a small hint of satire. "You may not believe it, but you and your family have all the makings of a melodrama."

* * *

The morning after he gave notice at the hospital, he searched the house until he found his mother in the library. She sat at a table writing a note on her white stationary. "Mother?"

"Yes?"

"I just received a letter asking me to come back to Folkestone, and I'll be leaving again. I have a passage for November third."

Lisette's pen kept steady pace over the paper. "I see."

"I'm sorry to leave you alone again."

The fountain pen stopped, and she looked up. "Very kind of you, but you needn't trouble yourself."

Ben turned away and ran his finger along the clothbound books lining one of the walls. They were unworn. Unread, unloved—merely there for the show of things, just like his mother. A stab of pity went through him that she had never known what it was to be loved, and now would never allow it even if someone wanted to. "Mother." He spoke low and calmly, so she would not feel threatened. "Did Edmond start sending you money before you met Creswick, or after?"

A higher note registered in her voice. "How did you find out?"

"I—made inquiries." Ben turned around and held out his hands entreatingly. "Please tell me."

"It was after," she replied unwillingly.

"And he came first to tell you about this source of income before he began soliciting your friendship?"

"That is correct."

He could see by the impatient lift of her shoulders that she was ready to end their conversation and quickly drew out the letter from Edmond she had kept. Lisette looked at it in dismay and tried to take it from him, but he eluded her grasp.

"Where did you get that?" she asked.

"Never mind where I got it. I'd like to know where you got it, though, if you never saw Edmond this summer. You don't know it, for I haven't told you, but I am involved in some less than safe activities at present. Who gave this to you?" She opened her lips, but he did not wait for her to refuse him. "Please be open with me. I don't want that danger to spread to you. Was it Creswick? You must tell me," he added forcefully.

"Yes."

"Did he give this letter to you?"

"Yes."

"Did he tell you where he got it?"

Lisette crossed her arms. "No."

"Mother, I shall be in England for an indefinite amount of time, and I would like to know you aren't putting my life in jeopardy by agreeing to do things you don't know the reason for. When someone gives you a letter for me, I want to receive the letter and know who you got it from."

"Your letters are your own concern if no one comes to collect them," she retorted.

"If you ever want to see another penny of my money, I shall insist upon it, for your own good as well as mine. And I think you would be safer telling Creswick that you will no longer agree to keep his war propaganda without knowing what it is for."

A red flush crept over her face. "That's a lie. Where did you hear of it?"

"I read his letter asking you to do it."

The outcome would not have been any different had she been prepared for his insistence. Time stretched out as she stood still in speechless fury. Then she caught up a letter opener and threw it straight at him before he had time to react. It grazed the side of his face, and he felt the sting as the blood trickled down his cheek.

"Everything. Pack up everything," she ordered. "I won't have you in my house another night."

"For heaven's sake, be reasonable." Ben stopped at the sight of the cold stillness in her face, a wave of anger so concentrated no words would appease it. "Very well, if you insist. I'll write when I return to England."

Within ten minutes, he had collected all of his belongings, called a

475

cab, and left for Richmond. He saw nothing of her from the time he left her in the library until he closed the front door behind him. He was not a penny the richer nor the poorer since his coming, but he left in possession of a little more information than he had arrived with. Fenton was right. There was something here to piece together as soon as all the information could be found.

* * *

More than one stray idler glanced at him curiously, as he sat on the bench in the car with his trunk beside him, pressing gauze against his jaw to stop the bleeding. As the train rumbled its way forward and the minutes ticked away, he relived the scene with his mother again and again, trying to think of what he could have said differently. But in the end, it did little good to think over what couldn't be changed.

He left his trunk at the station—the O'Seans could help him pick it up later—and walked through the busy streets. The O'Sean house looked peaceful in the afternoon sunshine. Climbing the porch steps and knocking on the door, Ben remembered that the family would be gone at work, except for Mrs. O'Sean. He was glad he could explain himself to her before the rest returned.

But instead of Mrs. O'Sean, Patrick was the one who opened the door. He raised an inquisitive eyebrow at the sight of Ben's face.

"Well, well, the prodigal returned, and from a back-alley brawl by the look of you. Come in."

"It's just a scratch," Ben protested.

"How'd you come by it?"

"Never mind. I thought you would be at work today."

"Quit last week to get ready to leave. My managers were sad to see me go and all that, but I think they liked the work they got from me more than my own charming company. It's not much of a loss. I have almost all my money put by, and that should last me for a good while yet."

Patrick beckoned for him to hand over his medical bag and hat, and Ben obeyed. "Did you get your passport?" Ben asked.

"In excellent time, thanks to you." As soon as he laid aside Ben's things, Patrick took a seat on the sofa with his legs crossed under him and leaned his chin on his hand. "I think you must have friends. So why did you come to Richmond today?"

"My plans have taken a turn, and I'm going to back to England."

A note of surprise crept into Patrick's voice. "I thought you were in Virginia to make sure your mum didn't marry."

Ben didn't try to explain. "I tried to scare Creswick off. We'll see if it holds. I hope you don't mind the company."

"Not a bit." Patrick grinned. "Are you coming third-class with me?"

He mustered up a return smile. "I doubt it, unfortunately. The man who bought my tickets pays first-class."

Mrs. O'Sean came through the living room with a basket full of laundry from the clothesline. "Hello, lads. Are you all right, doctor?"

Ben shook his head, trying to suppress his tired reaction to the events of the last twenty-four hours. "My mother turned me out."

"Why did she do that?" Patrick's blue eyes were bright with curiosity.

"That's prying where you don't belong, Pat," Mrs. O'Sean rebuked. "No need to understand it all now if he doesn't offer to tell you. Oh, dear, I'm so sorry." She set down her laundry and turned his head to see the cut, but Ben drew away.

"It's really nothing."

Patrick bit his lip, and Ben gave in after a moment's uncomfortable silence. "It's no secret. I needed some information from her. We've never been on very close terms, and we had a disagreement over some of my—affairs. She threw a penknife. I should have ducked."

Patrick snorted and crossed his arms. "When we were little, we got our backsides spanked for that."

Mrs. O'Sean frowned sternly. "Patrick Donal, I'll not hear another word from you."

"Yes, Mum." Patrick subsided, but the imps dancing in his eyes were anything but penitent.

"You can stay with us, of course. Why don't you take his things up to your room, Pat? Show him where he can sleep." She touched the cut gently and seemed to satisfy herself that it was nothing serious.

"All right." Patrick unfolded himself and picked up the medical bag. "Come along, my friend. Same place as last time."

* * *

The floorboards did not creak as he softly descended the stairs

477

after a fruitless attempt at sleep. When he reached the first floor, he saw a light in the kitchen and found Mr. and Mrs. O'Sean sitting at the table with steaming mugs of coffee, whispering quietly. He flushed in embarrassment as he met their searching looks.

"What can I get for you, doctor?" Mrs. O'Sean asked kindly.

Ben stood in the doorway, unwilling to join them. "I couldn't sleep. I was going to take a walk."

Mr. O'Sean raised his eyebrows. "The neighborhood's not safe this time of night."

"Do you want to talk to us, lad?" Mrs. O'Sean invited. "That would be a good deal safer than getting yourself lost in some back alley."

"If I did, it would save several people some annoyance." He laughed mirthlessly. "There's no need to worry," he added hastily, in response to their concerned looks. "I don't expect any trouble until I'm on English soil again. I won't burden you with our family's griefs; you've shown me enough kindness already, and I can't thank you enough for it."

"Lad." Mrs. O'Sean pushed aside her coffee mug and folded her hands one over the other. "You became our son when you knocked on our door last month. You had no family, and the good Lord knew we had family to give you." Her husband nodded in agreement. "So let's hear no more of thanks. But if you like, I'll brew a third cup of coffee, and you can talk to us."

Ben laid a hand on the chair nearest him, then changed his mind and shook his head.

"Lad—"

"Please. Let me have my way tonight." He held her gaze, and she returned it with one just as firm of her own. He broke the deadlock before his resolution could waver. "Can I have a key? There's no need for you to wait up for me."

She sighed, and Mr. O'Sean drew one from his trousers pocket, put it in his hand, and gripped the hand for a moment, warm and strong. Patrick pushed open the kitchen door and saw what was happening with one decisive glance of his blue eyes.

"Hey." He turned a chair backward and straddled it with his arms resting on the top. "You like the taste of your own counsel, hmm?"

"I don't—I can't—" He paused and tried to collect his words. "I'm not sure I know what to tell you."

"Start from the beginning, and we'll listen," Mrs. O'Sean said calmly. "Tell us what you've been doing here in Richmond during your stay. Pat's seen you at the bank twice now. We'll keep your secrets, Ben, but it's time you gave them to someone who didn't have such a vested interest as everyone else seems to. A little clear counsel never hurt anybody, did it now?"

Patrick gave him a full coffee mug, and he took a deep breath and plunged in. He talked slowly at first and gathered speed the more he told. He spared only the details that put his mother in a poor light, and for her sake said little of what had occurred between them. They listened in silent understanding, neither showing the indifference of curiosity nor smothering him in pity. He liked that, for he could not afford to begin looking at his own side of the affair if he wanted to keep a clear perspective. When he had finished, the coffee mugs were empty, and Mrs. O'Sean rose to collect them.

"What a mess." Patrick shook his head in disbelief.

Mr. O'Sean crossed one leg over the other and shoved his hands in his vest pockets. "If things are as precarious with the fighting in France as you say, and you have a way of helping them close one threat on the home front, I think you're right to go."

"What happens if we lose to the Germans in France?" Patrick asked.

"It means we've lost hundreds of thousands of men," Ben said, "and we'll need more to take their place. You and I might end up at the front after all."

Mrs. O'Sean patted his shoulder. "Did you sleep at all last night?"

"Not much."

"Well, here you stay until you and Pat leave; that's one less detail you'll have to decide. We've heard all you've had to tell us, and we'll think it over. But the night's getting shorter, and a little sleep never hurt anybody. It'll keep until morning."

He exhaled slowly, and the burden of the last few weeks lessened its weight on his shoulders. "I'm glad I told you."

"Thought you might be," Patrick said. He dodged his mother's hand of justice and escaped out the kitchen door with a laugh.

Chapter Twenty-Seven
A Promise Unfulfilled

"Well, Doctor Jaeryn Graham, it's been a long time since I've seen ye. Come to honor my humble establishment with yer mighty presence?"

Jaeryn ignored Ann Meikle as he looked at a short, gray-haired man going out the post office door. "Isn't that King's old butler?"

Mrs. Meikle hid a sheet of paper in one of the counter drawers as she watched the man disappear down the street. "Stafford? Aye, it's him."

"His friendship isn't to your advantage."

"Still looking to make me out a German spy, doctor?" She gave a throaty chuckle. "He's just picking up a letter, as he has a right to. This is a post office, after all."

Jaeryn narrowed his eyes at her and frowned. "I didn't come to listen to your jibes. I came to pick up my mail and ask you a question."

"As ye wish. Ye have one letter, from an Alex York in America." She reached into a slot behind her and pulled out a long white envelope.

Jaeryn turned it over and examined the envelope flap to see if it showed signs of tampering. "I trust you didn't open it."

"And what if I did? I'm paid to look through people's mail, ye know."

"My affairs are confidential and not to be trifled with." He tore open the letter and scanned its contents. When he was finished, he tucked it well inside his medical bag to keep safe. "Now, I want to know something. Mrs. Goodwin told me the cottages at Copt Point are for sale, the both of them together. Do you know when I can find her at home so I can make inquiries?"

"She's off work after six each evening. Ye can go down to Copt Point any time then and speak to her, except for Fridays, when she comes to visit me."

Jaeryn took out his notebook and scrawled down the time. "If I were her, I'd keep better company."

Mrs. Meikle snorted. "Than a skellum of an Irishman? I think she's right enough."

"Watch your tongue, woman. You can't afford to lose my good opinion at present."

"Can't I?" She peered up at him with her bright little eyes. "London seems to think differently. I've had a letter in the drop, and ye're not as important as ye once used to be. In fact, ye're not important at all now, are ye?"

He still felt raw over the conversation with Ryson, and her thrust was the last straw needed to make his patience snap. "Are you satisfied now? You got Dailey out of the way, and I'm no longer officially able to trouble you. It looks like you've cleared the playing field."

"You were a large obstacle to clear off. Ye might respect yer elders, ye know, young man. Ye're not yet thirty. Some folk have the priority when putting their foot in the door, and ye cut in line. I don't like folk who cut in line."

His voice rose to a bitter lilt in spite of himself. "I work hard enough to make your grandmother weep, and I have the duty to try and better myself by whatever means I can."

She tilted her head and raised an eyebrow at him. "Well, ye chose the wrong way to go about it. Ye've been given the sack, doctor. We have orders that ye aren't involved at present, and therefore, all the drops are terminated. And that letter ye stole belongs back to us now as evidence, so ye'd best drop it off here where I can keep an eye on it."

He vowed inwardly that he would stake his life before giving anything into her treacherous hands. "Oh, you're very clever, but I don't think I would trust you with something like that. I may be moving on, but I have the responsibility to leave my information in safe hands. Has a telegram come in for Terry yet?"

Mrs. Meikle shook her head. "Not for ye to know, laddie. It's time to give the letter back now. Yer grace is expired. Be a good loser and let the next person have a crack at things."

His eyes dueled with hers as he paused to choose his words. "They'll have a crack at it, but I'm going to choose who that next person is."

"I'll write to Ryson and tell him ye're keeping it."

Jaeryn shrugged. "I doubt he would pay much attention to you. The letter I took goes to Dailey as soon as he returns, along with any other evidence I have."

Her mouth took on a dour expression. "Dailey's coming back?"

"He is." A smile spread over Jaeryn's face.

She jabbed her long, bony finger into the counter. "Ye're going to use him to keep yerself in the game, aren't ye? Ye two were thick together, and ye're going to play him to yer own advantage. Mind, I'm watching what ye do, and if I see ye staying involved, I'll turn ye in. I'm sure we could pin enough on ye to get ye locked up."

A shiver ran over Jaeryn as he wondered what would happen to his evidence if Dailey didn't come back. But he raised his chin and fired another shaft. "Thank you very much for that vote of confidence. It's always refreshing to have honesty in one's workers."

"Former workers," she corrected.

Jaeryn clenched his teeth and stepped out into the golden afternoon haze to make his way back to the clinic.

* * *

At seven that evening, Jaeryn reluctantly glanced at the unorganized files strewn over his desk. He would have to get back to them later. Picking up a pencil, he crossed out the day on his desk calendar. His pencil slid to a stop when he realized that it was the twenty-fifth and the month of October was almost over. Where had the time gone? And when could he expect a telegram back from the recipient of his letter? Surely, wherever it had gone, he would hear soon.

482

Before he left for one last patient visit, Jaeryn picked up the phone and gave Alisa's number to the operator. When the call connected, he heard Terry's voice on the other end.

"Hey, doc! What's up?"

"Just checking in. You were supposed to stop by once in a while and tell me you were still alive."

"Oh, I'm alive."

Jaeryn smiled and held the phone away from his ear. "Grand. I'm thinking of becoming your sister's new landlord. Copt Point is for sale, and if Dorroll comes back, I want to make sure he has a place to stay. I think it would be too conspicuous for him to stay with me right now."

"You're owning houses all over the place. Say, you want to come here tonight and hang out with us?"

"I wouldn't want to intrude."

"Alisa doesn't care. Besides, the kid's got something to show you."

"Starlin King? To show me? Is that what he said?"

"Well, he didn't exactly say it, but I'm sure he wants you to know."

Jaeryn glanced down at his appointment book with the two slots still waiting to be crossed out. "I don't think so, Terry. I'll catch you around somewhere. That boy isn't particularly interested in my good opinion."

"Well, you ain't offering it to him, either. Come on, I want you to come. A few minutes won't hurt, will they, now that you've got your shiny new automobile?"

Jaeryn threw down his notebook in surrender. "All right, I'm coming. Give me a half hour to finish a call, and then I'll be there." He hung up the earpiece and grabbed his hat. Terry rarely insisted on anything.

From what Jaeryn had been able to find out from Charlotte, Starlin King had come every day since his first visit. His only absence was for a couple of hours on Sunday morning, which Alisa said was to attend Reverend Carlisle's church with his father. Terry seemed to do Starlin some good, but Jaeryn wasn't convinced that it was mutual. They played endless games of chess, bantered incessantly, and never called the limit until someone came and put an end to it. Perhaps the music was good—not the bloodthirsty vengeance song Terry taught him, but the endless classical pieces he had memorized, not to mention his own arrangements. Were the war not wreaking havoc in Europe, the lad would probably be studying music abroad. If only he were. It would be far less of a nuisance.

The only thing Jaeryn did not understand was regarding Starlin's Stutz Bearcat. Every day King's chauffeur dropped him off, and every day Starlin used Alisa's telephone to call home with a request to be picked up. It had been almost two weeks now, certainly enough time for him to begin driving it. But when Jaeryn asked him if he had used it yet, Starlin stared coolly out of those weird blue eyes and shook his head.

When he reached Alisa's, he saw a little knot of people standing on the front porch. A slight breeze lifted and ruffled Pearlie's curls, and Terry had one arm around her waist while he used the other to gesture in his talk to Starlin. Starlin leaned against the side of the house with his arms crossed, replying with a word or two when Terry coaxed it out of him.

When Jaeryn's tires crunched on the stones in the drive, Terry looked up and waved. Jaeryn nodded back and parked the car. "What's up, Terry? Hello, Miss Dorroll. Starlin."

Pearlie drew back slightly, and Jaeryn decided not to offer his hand, as she was still shy from their conversation after Terry's last escapade. Starlin didn't look like he wanted a greeting either, but Terry clapped Jaeryn on the shoulder with his free arm.

"You didn't ask the kid if he's learned the workings of his motorcar today." Terry winked at Starlin. Starlin stiffened against the house siding and looked down at his boots.

Jaeryn said dryly, "I thought you were the one who put an end to that subject, Terry. You shouldn't be teasing him."

Terry grinned. "I'm not. Ask him how he came to Alisa's this afternoon. You were late, or you could have joined in the fun."

Jaeryn glanced at the drive, empty of any car but his own, and then looked at Starlin again. "Very well. How did you come to Mrs. Dorroll's, Mr. King?"

Starlin kept his gaze on his boots. "I drove."

"Good for you. I don't see the Bearcat anywhere."

"I made him park it behind the barn." Terry's grin turned into a laugh of sheer delight. "He's been practicing for days with the chauffer since we saw you last, and he came by himself today. I haven't been for a spin in it yet. You and Acushla can take turns since we only have two seats."

Jaeryn shook his head. "Much obliged, but I'm afraid I can't. I have another call to make before it gets too late."

"It won't take long. We'll take you where you need to go. Where were you off to?"

He gave up. "I was going out to see Mrs. Goodwin this evening. I'm off to look at the cottages and talk to her about purchasing them."

"Let's go out now." Terry looked down at Pearlie. "Do you like Copt Point, Acushla?"

"Yes." Pearlie's soft blue eyes shone, and Terry's expression settled into irrevocable determination.

"We'll go now, then. Can Starlin can drive your car, doc? His Bearcat doesn't have enough seats for all of us."

Jaeryn's whole soul rose in sick revulsion. "I-I-don't—"

"Oh, let him drive. He won't wreck it."

He swallowed hard and turned to Starlin. "Would you like to?"

Starlin sighed. "It doesn't matter," he said in a low voice.

"Sure, he wants to," Terry urged.

Terry put Pearlie in the back and climbed in beside her, leaving the front seat to Jaeryn. Starlin turned the hand crank to start the car and gingerly settled into the front seat. His knuckles showed white as he gripped the wheel. He seemed capable as he guided the car onto the road. Even so, Jaeryn felt a strong urge more than once to put out his hand and take the wheel as they clipped a corner or swerved from the left side of the road. The only thing keeping him silent was the sensation of Terry's amused eyes gazing at the back of his neck.

Their drive took them along country lanes full of muddy ruts and flanked by brown fields. Dead leaves rustled under the tires, and the sky was a smooth, gray agate, fast turning to darkness. Starlin sat in silence, unwinding now and then when Terry asked him a question. When the whine of the air raid sirens started up, Jaeryn said, "Perhaps we'd better stop and take shelter now."

"No one pays attention to the air raid sirens," Starlin said. "You wouldn't either if you were the one driving."

After that, Jaeryn directed most of his chat to Pearl, who gave soft replies supplemented heavily by Terry's commentary. Once, when Jaeryn managed to tear his gaze from Starlin, he looked back and caught Terry squeezing Pearlie's hand in one of his big, rough ones. He cleared his throat pointedly. "Terry."

Terry winked. "You should be looking at the road to help the kid out, doc."

"I think I'm quite capable of both, thank you." Jaeryn tried to conjure up a frown, but failed dismally and shook his head instead.

It didn't take them long to reach the curve of the road closest to Copt Point. Jaeryn let out his breath in a long sigh when Starlin slowed to a halt. Terry jumped out first, and Jaeryn quickly followed, but Starlin made no move to get up.

"Coming, lad?" Terry asked as he helped Pearl to her feet.

Starlin shook his head. "I'll wait here."

"Suit yourself, then. Come on, Acushla."

Both cottages were brightly lit, but Terry made no move to go to Erin's or Mrs. Goodwin's. He set off toward the brush-bound cliff edge with Pearlie following. Jaeryn stopped him.

"Terry, where are you going?"

"Just for a walk with Acushla." Terry flung the reply over his shoulder. "You get the rundown and fill me in, will you?"

"Why don't you come with me and see your sister, if you don't want to talk business? Introduce Miss Dorroll to Brogan."

Terry looked back, a serious expression replacing the jesting lift of his eyebrows. "We'll stay in sight, but there's something I want to say to her alone. You needn't be afraid that I'll take advantage of her."

Pearlie's face was all aflame, and she tried to slip her hand out of Terry's grip, but he held her fast and guided her away. Jaeryn bit back a protest as he watched them. But surely they couldn't do much harm in sight of all the windows.

A furious growling sounded at the door when he knocked, followed by a calm, scolding voice. Mrs. Goodwin welcomed him in. When he entered, he found a short, brown-haired man sitting at the table with the remains of a plate of supper, while a large gray dog stood with the man's hand on his head. "That's Nimrod," Mrs. Goodwin said. "He hates men in general."

Jaeryn gave the man a thin smile. "He doesn't seem to hate you. Hugh, isn't it?"

Hugh rubbed Nimrod's ears and gave a stiff nod. "Any dog responds to a bit of kindness. You're Turlough O'Sean's friend, isn't that right?"

"We're acquainted."

Hugh rose from the table, giving Nimrod a last scratch. "I haven't seen you since my housemate disappeared. Last I heard, rumor had it that Christopher was a German spy and escaped to the continent. I never would have thought it of him."

"His disappearance certainly was strange."

"Your friend might be a German spy, too. He gets strange telegrams."

Jaeryn gave a thin-lipped smile, and Hugh disappeared into the night. Mrs. Goodwin picked up a sheaf of papers with neat columns of figures on them. "You caught me at my accounting, doctor." She offered him tea, which he accepted, and took a seat opposite him while the kettle boiled. "I suppose you'll be wondering about price first. Colonel King wants four hundred pounds for them. They have a good view, and they're built strong."

"That's sounds fair enough. I'll take them."

"You're not going to try to bargain, doctor?" she asked in surprise, as the kettle began to rattle and she got up to attend to it.

Jaeryn gave an easy smile. "I'm satisfied. I want them to rent, and I don't like delays."

"Fair enough. You can install telephones if you like." Evidently, she remembered their previous meeting when he had tried to bribe her to circumvent her employer.

Jaeryn watched as she set the tea things on the table. "Ah, yes. I shall be making some improvements, of course. When is Colonel King interested in signing papers?"

"That's at your and his convenience. I'm just here to show the cottages to people who are interested."

A sudden gust of wind picked up around the house, blowing hard against the shingles. Nimrod lifted his head from where he was lying on the sofa and gave a whine. Her clock ticked comfortably on the stone mantle, and a warm fire crackled in the grate. Jaeryn leaned his elbows on the table. "I'm surprised he's so eager to sell. He seemed content to keep them a while ago."

"He kept them for a reason." Mrs. Goodwin rose and took the lid off a crock. The sweet tang of peppermint wafted into the room. "He only kept them in May because you mentioned your new assistant was coming."

"Did I? I don't remember that. Why was King interested in Dailey?"

"He never said." The kettle whistled, and she brought it over and filled his mug. "I noticed your assistant seemed to be targeted by undercover activity in Folkestone while he lived here. Colonel King knew as well. But he regretted involving himself when the break-in

487

happened. He said he didn't want to be suspected of using the cottage for a trap for that young man and his womenfolk."

Jaeryn wrapped his hands around the warm mug. "I'm glad he kept his own counsel if he knew so much."

"He isn't one to damage another man's affairs by telling private matters, as long as they don't affect his own."

He decided not to mention the fact that Ben might be returning. All things considered, it was best to take Colonel King unawares. "And now that Dailey's left, he told you to put them up for sale."

"Surely." Mrs. Goodwin nodded. "He doesn't need them anymore."

"Mrs. Goodwin, if I were you, I would find a more reputable employer." Jaeryn noted the darkness through the open curtains and thought of the others waiting for him. "Very well, then. How do I open negotiations with him?"

"I'll set up a time with him and send word through the postmistress. After you do purchase them, I'll vacate this cottage as soon as you like."

"Good. I'll be going, then, and wait to hear from you."

Mrs. Goodwin made no comment on his mug, which was still almost full. "Wouldn't you like to look them over before you buy them?"

Making the purchase without seeming to care what they were like would draw unwanted attention. He accepted her offer and took a tour of the cottage's kitchen and three bedrooms. When they were finished, Mrs. Goodwin paused in the hall.

"The woman renting next door wants to have this cottage if you're willing to trade. Hers has smaller bedrooms, and she likes the space of this one."

"I don't mind." Jaeryn didn't think Ben would object to taking the same place he had used before. "Is Mrs. Reinhardt willing to let me look at hers?"

"Yes. I told her you might be coming by, and she's prepared to let you in." Mrs. Goodwin handed him an electric torch to light the path. "Would you like me to come with you?"

"Not necessary." He stepped out into the darkness and flipped on the torch. The cottages were built far enough apart to give each a feeling of isolation. In the night, when the lights were off, it would be impossible for either to see its neighbor. Jaeryn saw Terry and Pearl some distance off, standing and talking together. It wouldn't do to risk Charlotte's ire while they were under his care. He knocked on Erin's door, and when she opened it, he saw in satisfaction that the wedding ring still gleamed on her hand.

"Doctor Graham. How unexpected." Erin stepped aside to let him in. "You were the person who wanted to buy this place?"

Jaeryn shook hands with her. "The offer came my way, and I thought I would look into it."

"But why?"

"Well, partly because I wish to rent them out." He felt an old ghost of panic as Erin shut the door behind them. He still couldn't manage to like closed doors. "Mrs. Goodwin said you liked her place better. You can change as soon as she moves out if you wish. I'm going to have a telephone installed in both cottages so you won't be completely alone out here."

He heard the patter of a child's feet along the hall and saw Brogan peeking at him around the bedroom door. Erin, intent on what he had told her, hardly glanced at the little fellow. "This means I should draw up a contract with you. How much do I owe for my stay here? Terry insisted on paying my first rent himself, but I'm sure I'll be capable of taking care of it as soon as I hear back on my applications for employment."

"No money just yet," Jaeryn reassured her. "We'll come to that in a week or two after I've closed on the papers and gotten my bearings."

Erin reached up and brushed back a strand of red-gold hair from her cheek. "Are you being honest with me, or trying to be charitable?"

Jaeryn shrugged. "If your husband wishes to settle with me, he may do so. Beyond that, I will not speak of rent. And that's all I intend to say about it. You won't find lodgings elsewhere in Folkestone, so I suggest you settle here."

"Then you shall never see your money again, I am afraid," Erin replied coolly.

"I don't despair of it." He smiled. "Now let me look around for a moment, and then I won't disturb you any further."

Jaeryn glanced into the rooms that Ben and Charlotte had used and made note of several improvements he could make before they returned. He wondered if Ben would object to renting from him. He would have a fight on his hands to keep the price low enough without rousing the doctor's pride. But he felt confident of carrying the point with a little tact, and it would put one more aspect of Ben's life under his control, which he could use to his advantage.

After saying goodbye to Erin, Jaeryn told Mrs. Goodwin that she could set up an appointment for him with King. Then he took stock of the others. Starlin sat in the car, slouched behind the wheel, waiting for them to be finished. Jaeryn could barely distinguish his outline in the glow of the torch. Terry and Pearl stood a little distance from the cliff's edge, listening to the spray shooting up over the rocks. Jaeryn heard Terry talking as he drew near and could not help listening in before he disturbed them.

"You look worried about something. What is it?" he heard Pearlie asking.

"Oh, I just don't want a telegram to come while I'm gone," Terry replied. "Wouldn't do to have the other fellows learn about it. I might have to be scarce for a few days, but don't you worry. I won't forget about you."

"I know you would never forget about me. I love you so much." Pearlie leaned her head on Terry's shoulder, and he looked down at her in happy content.

"When's your brother coming back, little one? I've waited a good long time."

"I don't know. He hasn't said. We haven't gotten a letter from him since he left, except one for Alisa."

"He is coming back, isn't he?"

A feeling of unease crept over Jaeryn as he saw where Terry's conversation was tending.

"I don't know if he is," Pearl said hesitantly. "When he left, he didn't know if he would be able to come back for a long time, perhaps until the war was over. He went home to find work."

Terry stood rigid in protest. "What? He has my ring for you. I gave it to him, and I was going to ask for it back when he agreed to let me have you. He never told me he wasn't coming back. I've been waiting—"

Jaeryn broke in. "Terry, I've finished talking to Mrs. Goodwin. We need to go home."

"Sure thing. We'll be right there."

"Why don't you come now?"

Terry swung around to face him, and a flash of annoyance sounded in his voice. "We'll follow in a minute."

Jaeryn turned the torch directly on them. "I think you should come now."

Terry looked away and refused to acknowledge him. Jaeryn came forward and stood on the other side of Pearl. "Please come back with me, Miss Dailey. You promised, if I ever thought it best." He held out his hand. Her face crumpled silently and she placed hers in it. Jaeryn gave Terry a moment to collect himself as they walked away, but when he looked back, Terry stood with his shirtsleeves rippling in the wind, making no move to follow.

"Coming?" Jaeryn asked.

Terry shook his head, and Pearlie looked in dismay from one to the other. "I think I'll be off to work now. I'm going to stop by home first."

Jaeryn took a step back. "No need to be angry, Terry. Come home with us."

Terry made no sign of relenting. "You can take her home yourself since you don't trust me. But I mean to have her, and you can't keep us apart forever." He caught sight of Pearlie's distressed face, and his resentment gentled. "You wait for me until I see you again, Acushla." Terry set off along the cliff's edge away from the direction of town, toward a wild, empty space that held no reasonable occupation for that time of night. Jaeryn cringed at what he had so unwittingly started.

"Terry, we need to straighten this out. I don't know what you're up to, but I don't think it's wise, and I want to talk to you first."

Terry kept on his way. Jaeryn dropped Pearlie's hand to follow after him, then looked irresolutely at her and picked it up again. Pearlie followed him to the car, shaking from suppressed tears and glancing back once or twice at the strong figure eating up the ground in rapid strides.

Jaeryn was the first to break the heavy silence. "I'm sorry. It was unfortunate, and I didn't mean for it to happen. Give me a day or two to straighten things out, and I'll see if I can bring him round again."

Pearl made no response. Jaeryn opened the door for her and took a seat beside her in the back. None of the Bearcat's occupants offered to make conversation on the way home.

* * *

Jaeryn stopped by Terry's house twice during the next two days and asked for him at the door, but Terry wasn't in, and Hugh didn't

491

know where he was. On Saturday, he called at Colonel King's to close the deal on the cottages, and Erin promptly moved into Mrs. Goodwin's as soon as they were finished. But for all that, he was not able to discover anything more about them, and he dared not ask King to his face.

Monday evening, Jaeryn parked his car and waited on the road Terry used to travel to work. If he hadn't done so, he didn't know when they would have met again.

What began as a cautious attempt at reproof turned into a sharp disagreement that ended with Terry trying to pedal off. Jaeryn took a firm grip of the handlebars and stepped in front of him to prevent him from leaving.

"You let go. I'll not be dictated to any further." Terry looked angry, but his hands were gentle as he tried to pry Jaeryn's grip off the bike, and his eyes held a shame that belied his sharpness.

"How can I do otherwise when you put all of us in jeopardy, telling her our private business in the open air? I was appalled when I heard you the other night. It's for your safety, and hers as well, that you should leave off with your wooing."

"Let go, or I'll lay you out on the road. You aren't the only one who can manage things."

Jaeryn blocked Terry's attempt to shake loose from him. "It wasn't pleasant to say, but it was no more than you needed to hear."

Terry reached into his pocket, and when Jaeryn saw the etchings of the Celtic cross sliding out, he hastily let go of the handlebars. Terry slid the knife back in and went on his way without a backward glance.

"Recklessness will kill you, Terry O'Sean. I swear it will," Jaeryn called after him. He drove home faster than he would have approved of under normal circumstances and barely avoided hitting a pedestrian in front of his own clinic. An hour later the phone rang. He recognized Charlotte's voice on the other end. He had given her the day off, for she hadn't taken one since she started working with him. By the tension in her voice, it had been less than relaxing.

"I'm calling to ask if you know why Terry stopped coming," she said. "He sent another man to look after the horse on Friday, and when I asked Pearl about it, she wouldn't tell me why."

Jaeryn sighed. "He's being stubborn, and he's determined not to come around for a while. I'll try to bring him to reason as soon as I can. I don't know what he took into his head."

"Did something happen that night when you were out driving? Pearl seems out of spirits, and I found her crying in her room this morning."

He took up a pencil and jabbed it into the wood trim of his desk. "He almost proposed to Miss Dailey again, and he was upset with me for preventing him. And some other things."

"What other things?"

"It doesn't matter. Tell her I'll bring Terry back as soon as I can. How are things with you otherwise?"

Charlotte gave a wry laugh. "Not very well, between Pearlie's situation and Alisa calling Edmond this morning. She rang him up but he wouldn't talk to her personally, and she's been rather dejected since."

"I'm sorry. I will be going to see him again next week; perhaps I can do something then."

"Doctor Graham, you are very kind to want to help, but I don't expect you to take on all our problems. I know you are busy with other duties, and you have no obligation to look after everybody's worries."

"I don't mind," he reassured her. "It's nothing. Give me a couple of days to straighten things out with Terry, and then we'll see what we can do with your brother-in-law."

But one day slipped into another, and he had no time to waylay Terry to talk to him again. Influenza and colds were going around, and with no assistant to help, his workload was enormous. Each evening he tumbled into bed, his work half done, until a patient called him out again into the bitter chill of a November night.

Nothing was seen or heard of Terry for over a week. Though Jaeryn drove past his house more than once, Terry didn't come out to see him, and none of his housemates did either. Alisa had no news of him when Jaeryn stopped in one afternoon on his way through the country calls. When he asked Pearl, she told him Terry hadn't come to see her for several days. She looked worried, and he tried to comfort her, but he didn't have much to offer. It wasn't like Terry to hide from everyone he knew. It went beyond the disagreement at Copt Point—something deeper was happening, and Terry wasn't talking about it. That, more than anything, terrified Jaeryn. Terry had never stopped talking before.

The night of November sixth, therefore, he was relieved when Terry looked in at his window. It was dark, and at first, the face pressed against the glass startled him. But when he recognized his friend, he threw down his work and gestured for Terry to come inside.

"It's good to see you again." Jaeryn closed the front door and beckoned him into the living room. Terry wasn't wearing a coat, and he shivered from the cold. "Here, sit down. Are you all right?"

Terry obeyed, his face strained with worry. "Mind if I stay awhile?"

"Not at all. What's up?"

"I was by myself and wanted to make sure you were all right. Can't have anything happen to you, you know."

Jaeryn noticed Terry's hands playing nervously and pulling at each other. "I'm all right. Do you expect anything to happen?"

Terry shook his head. "Not particularly. Just wanted to be sure."

"Want something to drink?" Jaeryn knelt and put a heap of paper scraps in his fireplace, then struck a match to light it and slowly added little twigs to feed the blaze.

"No, I already stopped by the Fisherman's Bethel. I think."

Terry didn't speak further, and Jaeryn watched him covertly as the shadows flickered over his face. A frown crossed it every now and then. Tendrils of flame curled around the logs, catching them up into a gentle blaze, and the smell of wood smoke filled the room. Terry pulled out a cigarette, and for once Jaeryn made no protest. A second followed the first, and a third followed the second. At length, Terry sighed in tranquility and laid the box away. Jaeryn shook his head. Something must be up.

"Terry," he said casually, "I think Pearlie's missed you lately. Why haven't you been to see her?"

"I'm not good company." Terry pressed the back of his fist against his mouth and ducked his head. "I'm sorry about what happened. I don't know why. We've never had a disagreement before, you and I, and I can't think why we did now. No one should fight over such a pretty little thing, or anything else for that matter. But I don't mean to go back until I can ask her brother if he minds me seeing her, so you don't have to worry anymore."

"Oh, now, there's no need for that. We weren't trying to drive you away from her. Maybe don't propose to her just yet, but I think she's been missing you, and you're all right to see her—"

Terry shook his head. "It isn't just that. I know she likes me, and I like her, and I mean to have her. But hearing what Stafford tried to do to that kid worried me, and I don't want to hang around and put either of them in the way of trouble if he gets wind of what I'm up to."

Jaeryn nodded sympathetically. "Hang in there, Terry. I think she's safe enough, and you'll see her before you know it. I haven't told any of the Daileys yet, but her brother might be back soon. I wrote and asked him to come, and I think there's a good chance he'll accept. Then you won't have to watch out for me as much, and you can look out for her more." Terry moved to interrupt him, but Jaeryn pushed him back reassuringly. "I know you want to look after me, so I won't try to persuade you otherwise. I'll talk to Dailey about his sister after he returns, if you like, and put in a good word for you. Is that all that's bothering you?"

He got up and stepped across the hall to get some cocoa, and Terry raised his voice in reply. "No. I was in the house by myself tonight, and I guess it got to me. Haven't been alone for months now. It makes you think, and I don't like to think."

Jaeryn came back and put a warm mug in his hands. "Do you want to stay here for a while? You're more than welcome. I thought you went home too soon, you know."

"No." He gulped down the offered drink. "I'll stick it out. But you know what else?"

"What?" Jaeryn sat down on the sofa beside him, and the hot chocolate slipped down his throat and eased some of the ache in his own heart.

"I lost my knife. It was always a piece of good luck, that knife, but now I don't know where it is. The day after we had our fight I must have mislaid it somewhere. I've turned my room upside down, but I haven't found it yet."

"I'm sorry. Do you have anything else?"

Terry shrugged. "I picked up a revolver, and I've got other knives stashed away. But they're not the same."

They sat together in weary companionship, not needing many words to be glad in the fact that they were reconciled. At eight o' clock, Jaeryn got up and poked the glowing ashes in the grate. "The evening's getting on, my friend. You should go home before too long. I'd hate for you to be out late on the road where you live, and even now you should keep a sharp lookout."

Terry sighed wistfully and put his mug down on the floor. "I wish I could stay longer, but I have to go to work."

"Then all the more reason to be gone. I'll be all right, Terry. I'm on guard if anything should happen, and I'll be sure to lock up well tonight. But if you thought something was up, I could leave town and come back in the morning."

"Probably not. Sorry to bother you."

"It's not a bother. You come whenever you like. The house is always open to you."

Jaeryn followed him to the doorstep and watched him walk down the street. It was the first time he had seen Terry afraid before, and it disturbed him. Even the knife had shaken him, though it was such a little thing. He had always been fond of it.

He turned the matter over in his mind as he worked quietly at updating patient records. A quarter of an hour later, the ringing of the phone broke into his contemplations. Jaeryn cringed at the prospect of another late night house call.

"Graham."

"Hello, doctor. This is Charlotte Dailey calling. Have you seen Pearl by any chance?"

The unexpectedness of the question coming so closely on Terry's visit took him aback. "No. I'm sorry, I haven't. Should I have seen her?"

"I don't know where she is. I found a note in her room saying she had gone out for a walk. I don't know when she left, and I didn't find it until just a moment ago. I hoped you might know where she was."

A prick of worry started in the back of his mind. "Terry was with me until a few minutes ago, but neither of us had seen any sign of Miss Dailey. I'll come straight out."

"I'm very worried; it isn't like her not to tell me when she's going somewhere. Alisa and I will see if she's somewhere on the property. Could you look around town and see if you can find her?"

"I can, but I don't know where she's likely to go, and it's dark. I'll look for a half hour and then stop by your house for an update. If she doesn't turn up by then, we'll call the constables. She shouldn't be out alone this late at night."

Jaeryn drove to the Leas, keeping a sharp lookout for a woman with dainty boots and a cloud of honey-colored curls. But Pearl did not appear anywhere on the walk or on the beach. After leaving her description at the various hotels as he passed, he turned his search to the Warren and along the harbor, with a quick detour through the Promenade and the Madeira walk. He looked everywhere he thought

Pearl might be, but found no sign of her.

A little tremor tugged at the corner of his mind, but he pushed back the possibilities into some horizon of darkness that he did not want to face yet. It was too early to worry; this was ridiculous. Perhaps Terry had met her on his way to work. But Terry hadn't talked as if he had any intention of seeing Pearl that evening, and Jaeryn knew that he would not be able to throw any light on the matter. It was too early to worry him yet. Pearl was probably home by now, safe and sound, with a rational explanation of the matter.

When he pulled into Alisa's drive, Charlotte came quickly out the door to meet him and searched the back seat for signs of another passenger. Jaeryn shook his head, and in the light of the open shutters, he saw a pallor spread over her face.

"It's hardly time to be concerned yet, Mrs. Dailey," he began, but she interrupted him sharply.

"It is time. She would have come back by now unless Terry took her somewhere. Even then I don't think she would have gone of her own accord without telling us first."

"I saw Terry tonight, and he didn't mention going to see her afterwards. She wouldn't lie to you, would she, about her real reason for going out?"

"No, of course not. She's always been truthful with us."

Jaeryn gripped the steering wheel. "And always open?"

Charlotte shook her head unwillingly. "Not always. She hardly knew us when we brought her here, and I think—I think she was more distressed than we knew when her father refused to see her. She keeps her own counsel in spite of my efforts. Even Alisa remarked on her silence this week, and Pearlie is more open with Alisa than the rest of us."

"Has she ever shown signs of emotional instability?"

"What do you mean?" He saw she was refusing to take his hint, and he couldn't blame her. The hurt of it was too great to face without a struggle.

"Do you think she might have gone to end her life, Mrs. Dailey? That's what I mean. I'm sorry I have to bring it up, but it must be considered. That's not the only option, certainly; but if she has been keeping to herself, then it is one we must look into. Terry hasn't come to visit her this week, and they parted under less than pleasant circumstances. He meant more to her than she showed any of you, I think. Especially if her father didn't want to see her, Terry's love might have been a lifeline."

Charlotte's lips parted, her eyes a fragile tempest of fear and possibilities. He reached out to put a hand on her shoulder, but something in her gaze made him stop and look down awkwardly at his fingers. "If she did intend to do that—and mind, I do not say she did—it might take her a while to work up her courage. We could still have time. If that is not the case, someone may have taken her against her will, or perhaps she traveled somewhere further away. But considering the first option, where do you think she would have gone?"

"I—I think perhaps Copt Point." Charlotte gripped her skirt with both hands to still their shaking. "You don't really think she went there, doctor, do you?"

"I'm going to go see," Jaeryn said. "Erin Reinhardt lives there, and perhaps she saw her if Pearl went that direction. If I can't find a trace of her at Copt Point, I'll go straight to the constables and get help, and Terry too. Sometimes love can see clearer where law cannot find a way. He may know a place she likes that none of us are aware of."

He pressed the pedal to reverse the car, but Charlotte laid a hand on the door to detain him. "Do you think she is—gone?"

He knew she could not bring herself to say what she really meant. "I doubt it. It's only been, what? Perhaps a little over an hour?"

"No, it's been longer than that. I thought she was with Alisa, but we haven't seen her since seven o' clock."

"Then it's been two hours, and all the more reason to hurry. Let me go, Mrs. Dailey. I must be off to Copt Point as soon as possible."

He felt a cold drop on the back of his hand as he reversed out of the drive. Surely it wouldn't rain; that was the last thing they needed. He had been wrong to frighten Charlotte needlessly. But in his soul, he knew it was far from needless. Terry would never have kept Pearl out so long, and if he had, he would certainly have made sure she was safely home again. Besides, he had been at the clinic when Pearl disappeared. He had been sitting, looking at the fire and smoking. He wouldn't have kept her waiting if he had asked her to meet him.

The drops grew in number little by little, first on his hands, then on his shoulders, and Jaeryn felt them trickle down through his hair as they gathered thickness and speed. One curve, taken too fast, made him draw his breath between his teeth, but he picked up speed again as soon as he had safely rounded it. There was no time to waste.

When the road made the sharp turn closest to the cottages, he turned off the car and ran over the grass toward the tiny twinkle of Erin's lights. Pounding on the door, he watched the shadows shift on the curtains and waited for her to answer. When she opened it, the golden light streamed out to meet him, keeping the darkness at bay.

"It's an emergency," he said, to secure her utmost cooperation from the beginning. "Did you know Terry has a woman he's in love with?"

Erin stared at him wonderingly. "No. Why?"

"She's gone missing. I hoped you might have seen her. You haven't heard any activity around your cottage tonight, have you? We're worried she might have drowned herself."

"How horrible." Erin shuddered. "No, I haven't. I was gone until eight o'clock in town, ironing for someone. The kitchen has a view of the other cottage, but I haven't looked out that window tonight."

"No, I don't mean the cottage. She would have gone straight—I think I'll check it anyway, though, just to be on the safe side. You said you came back at eight?"

"Of course. I put Brogan to bed right away after we got back, and I saw the clock at quarter past when I came back out."

Jaeryn felt in his pockets, but the search yielded no key for the other cottage. "Let me have your key, will you, Mrs. Reinhardt? I'm sure it's the same; these are identically built."

She gave it to him and hurried after him out the side door and across the grass. Fitting the key into the lock, he found it worked and swung the door open. He felt for the switch and flipped on the light.

"*Déan trócaire.* Don't look, Erin."

"It's too late. I've seen it." Erin looked over his shoulder at the pool of blood staining the floor. A thin trail of red led to the doorway. "What happened?"

Jaeryn ran from room to room, stepping over the spot so as not to disturb it. He found nothing until Erin stooped and pointed to a thin silver knife with a Celtic cross handle, pinning a piece of folded paper to the wall. It was red to the hilt, and Jaeryn stooped beside her, horrified.

"They must have meant it to be found, or they wouldn't have left it in plain sight," Erin said. "You'd best call the constables, doctor. If there's a murderer abroad, your little woman friend isn't safe, especially in the rain. She'll be ill before you find her if she isn't in shelter already."

Jaeryn looked at her without replying and followed the trail of blood until he reached the doorstep and the darkness obliterated it. "Stay in out of the rain," he ordered Erin, "and look for any other evidence that might tell us who did it."

"That knife ought to be indication enough," she called after him, but he paid no attention to her. The rain ran down his face, and he heard the faint rumble of thunder—or was it perhaps the surf? Time stood still as he searched frantically in the darkness for what he knew he would find.

She was there, lying crumpled on the grass, drops of rain quickly turning her into a wet heap. She had been dropped in haste, and he fell to his knees beside her, ignoring the dampness.

"*Cuir in iúl dó nach mbeadh*," he whispered. "Miss Dorroll? Can you hear me?"

Her eyes were open and staring, with no sign of life in them, and when he took up her hand, it was limp and clammy with cold. He turned her over and saw in an instant what had been done. The back of her head was a matted mass of dried blood and hair. It must have been mercifully short after the shot was fired, perhaps even instantaneous. Dried blood stiffened the collar of her shirtwaist. She must have been left on the grass before it started raining, for the ground underneath her was quite dry. That meant sometime before nine o' clock when the rain had really picked up.

Jaeryn lifted the small girl to take her inside, and his heart tore in two as her head rolled forward on his shoulder. He gently bore her to the cottage where Erin stood waiting in the doorway. He laid her on one of the beds—his now, but formerly her brother's—and crossed her hands over her chest.

As soon as he could control his voice he said, "I'm going to look things over one last time, and then I'll have to drive to the constables."

Erin frowned. "You aren't thinking of leaving me and the child here, are you, when murder has been done? It isn't safe."

Jaeryn took her elbow and guided her toward the door. "If the murderer had wanted to kill you, you would be dead by now. There was nothing to prevent him from coming to you as well. Go back to your cottage and lock the door. You'll probably be questioned as soon as the constables are here, but there's no need for you to stay with the body while I'm gone."

"Do you think I should stay here for her sake? Brogan is asleep and wouldn't mind my absence." He saw a kind of moisture rise in her eyes as she looked over her shoulder at the still figure on the bed.

"It is a kind thought, but I think not. She will be taken to her own people, and they will perform any offices they consider necessary. She was used to a lonely life. I don't think she's starved for companionship now."

Erin obeyed and left him alone to look over things for himself. As soon as she was gone, he knelt beside Pearlie's still form and slipped on a pair of gloves, feeling almost as if he were about to commit a sacrilege with his examination. But it must be done, and he must do it. He found the gash from Terry's knife in her side. That and the bullet wound were the only marks on her. Why had the knife been used? It was too small to do lethal damage, and the gunshot had obviously committed the deed. He drew the covers over her and felt as if, after the death of such innocence, he were a man much older than his twenty-eight years. The tears silently gathered and ran down his face, as he murmured a low prayer in Irish over her body.

At the door, he caught sight of Terry's knife, and the sudden shock that had driven it from his mind cleared away. Jaeryn knelt and pulled it from the piece of paper. It was yellow telegram paper, and with a sudden premonition, he looked at the recipient and saw it had been sent to Terry.

Unusual request. Travel denied. Location confirmation required from 000192.

He did not know how long he sat with a swirl of questions turning his mind dizzy. When at length he staggered to his feet, he had just enough wits to hide the knife and the telegram in the cushions of the back seats and put the top up. Then he slowly reversed the car and made his way back toward town. Terry would be desperate if the constables traced the knife to him. They couldn't afford that. It would be hard enough to keep him alive as it was when he found out his sweetheart had been murdered.

And the rest of them. Jaeryn groaned aloud. He would have to tell all the rest of them.

If he had not known the route so well, he would have been hard pressed to drive it safely. From the time he left Copt Point until the time he pulled up at the police station, Jaeryn could not have told where he went, or if there was anyone else on the road, or how he managed to see with the rain pounding against the windshield. When he became mindful of his surroundings again, the glass in front of him was a mass of water droplets and he was idling in front of the station.

He started at a tap on the glass. A constable squinted through the rain that poured down his face, and Jaeryn opened the door. "Something wrong, sir? You've been sitting there awhile, and I waited for you to come in, but you never did. You look pale, if you don't mind my saying so."

"Yes, something's wrong." Jaeryn got out and slammed the car door shut. "I've come to report a murder."

Chapter Twenty-Eight
Don't Go Back

Ben's fingers shook as he laid down the letter his mother had forwarded to him. It was a death threat—two of them in the same envelope. She must have taken him seriously when he left, for she had forwarded it the day after she received it, and it had not been tampered with.

Don't go back. What did it mean? He was spent with anxiety, and there were still two days left of his stay. Every time a door slammed, he started up in dread expectation, and more than once his mind created sounds that weren't really there. Stealthy footsteps, rustlings, soft noises of someone creeping up behind him—he imagined them all and shook himself each time for being paranoid.

The revolver, which he had been glad to empty and leave at the bottom of his trunk, was back in a shoulder holster, fully prepared for action. In spite of his fear, he was going back. Terry's parents thought he was right in his decision. After hearing that his communication had been cut off and that his father might be involved, they knew as well as he that it was his duty.

All the same, it wasn't easy taking up the burden of darkness and danger again. The closer he got to leaving, the more the prospect set him on edge. He said nothing to the rest of the family of the threats, but it didn't take them long to catch the tension in his demeanor. The evening of November first, Emmie brought his jacket down to clean it before he left for Boston. Ben caught his breath as she paused at the foot of the stairs and pulled out the Webley.

"Why do you have this?" she asked curiously.

"No reason," he evaded, carefully taking it from her. "I keep it with me when I go places. You needn't trouble your pretty head about it."

His eyes met Mr. O'Sean's, and he knew that her father, if not Emmie herself, guessed at his real reason. Patrick looked sternly grim.

"I don't think they want me coming back," Ben said as soon as Emmie left the room.

Mrs. O'Sean's knitting needles continued slipping her yarn in and out. "Well then, you'll need an extra guardian angel or two, won't you, doctor?"

He smiled. "Do you know where to find me one?"

"No, but the Lord Jesus has a few in storage, and I know where to find him."

One day later he stood on the porch steps, ready to say goodbye. Mist blanketed the street in a damp haze, and he could truly sense the autumn in the air that had only begun on his arrival. He would be traveling overnight to Boston and arriving by seven the next morning. He didn't tell the O'Seans that he was booking a ticket for a seat instead of a sleeper car.

Patrick picked up his trunk and shoved it in the back of the cab. "I wish you would let me go with you."

"Meet you in Baltimore." Ben watched Emmie, who was apparently trying to decide the most proper way to say good-bye, and shook his head at her with a grin.

Mr. O'Sean clapped him on the shoulder. "Can we pray for you before you go, lad?"

He nodded readily. "I would be grateful."

Afterward, Mrs. O'Sean reached up and held his face in both hands, and he breathed in the last bit of her clean soap smell that he would have for a long time. "Now make sure you pray for yourself when you go back, lad, and we'll be lifting you up every day ourselves. Are you sure you're ready to go?"

Ben shifted the strap of his medical bag higher on his shoulder. "I'm ready. Please, don't worry."

"I don't know if I'll see you again." He looked down in surprise at her worried face. She had been encouraging him to go for so long that he hadn't expected her to fear for him. He laid a gentle hand on her shoulder.

"You'll see me again."

"But the Atlantic's so dangerous, and there are more than Germans that want rid of you—and—I'm sorry."

"It's all right. You'll see me again, I'm sure of it." Ben smiled to bolster her courage, though he was no surer of his safety than she was. It must be hard for her to let him and Patrick leave just as she had let Terry go so many years before. He didn't want her to worry after all she had done for him.

At length, he tore himself away. It was as hard for him to leave as it was for them to let him go, but he had a train to catch, and he couldn't afford to miss it.

Other than an occasional river crossing and two switch-overs, the day passed in a blur of boring stretches of field. Ben stared unseeingly out of the window, his thoughts with the people he had left behind. Though the time with his mother hadn't been terribly happy, he missed the normality her presence afforded. He had grown up with her, and the familiarity, if nothing else, was a form of happiness. And the O'Sean's. A smile flickered across his face as they came to mind. Mrs. O'Sean had tucked a letter for Terry in his bag and given him many loving messages besides, the half of which he couldn't remember. He couldn't wait to see Terry again.

In contrast to his lack of attention to the scenery, he kept a sharp watch on the passengers around him. The threats had probably come from Creswick, but there was no time to look into it further. He would have to keep a sharp watch until he was on the steamer, and then he would have a brief respite before the threat picked up again in England. Unless it traveled on the steamer with him. But he didn't like to think about that.

As early as it was, York met him at the station with a cab. As soon as they pulled up in front of the brown bungalow and the lock was safely fastened behind them, York spoke decisively and straight to the point.

"Sorry I couldn't make it more convenient for you by meeting in Baltimore. I'm planted here, and here I must stay."

Ben knew he shouldn't ask, but he did anyway. "Why are you looking out for British interests in America?"

"Trust no ally." York threw his house keys on the dining table and disappeared into what looked like a bedroom. He returned holding a locked box and put it on the table. "I'm not the only operative keeping an eye on our affairs abroad. We have them in many countries. So do the Germans. So does your government, for that matter."

"I never knew you had people here." He was rather surprised York had offered that much information.

"Well, you needn't talk about it, but it's fairly common knowledge. One of those unspoken things. Now, here's that package for you. I left it unopened." York unlocked the box and took out a thin parcel. "You'd best look at it now. That way if you have any directions, you can give them in person."

Ben did so. Though he recognized the smudged numbers in the address as Jaeryn's, he found letters inside that were decidedly not in Jaeryn's handwriting. A whole pile of them, and he recognized them as Charlotte's. He took up an unsealed sheet of paper on top and saw in chagrin that it was from Fenton.

I did not think you would come for a letter from me, so I paid Ann to address this in Graham's writing. A neat job of it, too, as you obviously came to get it if you're reading this now. You've been a wronged man in your absence, and I got your wife's letters back for you. I can't tell you who kept them, but it shouldn't occur again.

I'm sending you something else for safekeeping: a paper that will be of use to you in Virginia Beach. I could only send you part of the paper I found, for it was too perilous for me to take all of it. Use it well, and you'll be rewarded. Don't let it out of your hands, for this is likely the best evidence you'll have to indict C. in a court of law. I don't dare send more since you are so dangerous to communicate with. For heaven's sake, don't let Graham know anything about it. I say that in the interests of the British Empire, and I swear it upon any honor I once possessed.

I've heard reports that Graham is trying to get you back. You're much better off where you are. I wouldn't return if I were you. It would do none of us any good, you least of all. He's not safe, you know. F.

Fenton had folded the square of paper that he deemed so important inside his note. It contained a few sentences written in French, but it made no sense when Ben translated it to English. He held it out to York.

"Want me to run it through some ciphers?" York asked, taking it up and reading it.

"If you please. But wait one moment; let me look at it again." Ben took it back and ran a sharp eye over the paper's details. It was on a thick piece, written in pen in a spiky hand. He suspected by the ragged edges that it was a rectangular strip torn off the bottom of a larger page.

He returned it to York, who put on a pair of glasses and worked over it while he examined Charlotte's letters. There were almost twenty of them. He was relieved that she had kept writing, even though he hadn't received them until now. It didn't seem like Fenton to care about a husband and wife staying connected. He wished he could read them, but until he had a spare moment, he was content to finger the girlish writing and try to catch a hint of jasmine through the envelope.

"There you are." Ben looked up from the letters and took the notebook paper York held out to him.

He's useful for the small jobs and a worthwhile American contact if you need someone from the States. Hard-headed advice, and makes the necessary financial transactions almost impossible to trace. He'll put you in touch with the French contacts when you're ready.

"What was the cipher?" Ben asked, looking curiously at the message.

"It's a difficult one, even for my capabilities. I doubt even Jaeryn Graham has seen it used. It's lucky you opened it here, or you would have had to wait until you got to London."

"I don't believe in luck."

"Call it what you like." York tossed the pencil on the table and stretched. "What do you think it means?"

Ben looked at the writing. He had only seen it once before, but he remembered the spiky twists and turns of the cursive. "Gilbert Emmerson wrote this. I think it was torn from something, a notebook most likely. I don't know what notebook, or who he wrote it to, but it sounds like the rest of the message is in Folkestone."

York raised an eyebrow. "Graham didn't say anything about what it meant?"

Ben shook his head. "It wasn't Jaeryn that sent the box. Someone else used him for a cover."

"On to the meaning, then. How does it fit with the rest of the

507

puzzle?"

"I think it's talking about Creswick. It tells us he's still involved, even though they dissolved their bank account. But I have no idea what the French connections mean." Ben looked to York, but York gave him no sign of commendation or disapproval.

"It's your case and yours to judge. I don't know enough about it. What do you want me to research for you?"

"I want more specifics on my father's involvement with the German bank account and anything else he did for Creswick or Emmerson. Find it by whatever means you must, but I need to know as soon as possible. Send anything to Folkestone, care of Charlotte Dailey, and don't use your real name. Use a woman's name; we can't take the chance of it going astray again."

"I can do that for you." York pointed to the sheet of notebook paper. "Are you taking that, or am I? It makes reference to an American contact."

Ben looked at it undecidedly and then threw it back in the box it had come in. "I'll need to match the paper to its source when I find the original. Besides, I think Creswick is a link to the main man. If I find any information that's helpful to you, I'll be sure to write and let you know. I should be going now if I'm going to catch my steamer in time."

York picked up the locked box to put it back. "You'll find a train timetable in the sitting room. I'll call a cab. Do you have enough money for train fare?"

"Yes, thank you. I have everything I need until I get to England." Ben went into the sitting room and found a dusty train schedule on the coffee table.

"Good luck, then. A pleasure seeing you again, doctor. I'm sure you'll do us credit back in England, and I'll be keeping track of your progress. Don't write unless absolutely necessary; I have other means of getting the information I need."

* * *

Ben waited on the station bench for his train, processing everything he had just learned. He tucked the box from Fenton into his luggage while he waited, deciding to leave the letters from Charlotte until the bustle of boarding and finding a seat was over. It would be a long eight hours in third class, but he had traveled that

508

way before, and he didn't mind it terribly. He would rest later, in the comfort of the steamer's cabin.

Reading Charlotte's letters, he wished they had been able to reach him before. They were full of love and encouragement, though he could read insecurity between the lines. Perhaps he wasn't the only one facing things he was unfamiliar with. Again and again she had written that she was not hearing from him and asked if he was all right. There was even one letter in which she asked why he had not written to her when he had written to Alisa. He winced as the enormity of what she was going through hit him. If only he had gotten her letters. He would have written something to be of help instead of telling her the troubles he had found in Virginia. The passage to England, which had seemed all too short when he thought of leaving America behind, now seemed entirely too long before he could give her a proper explanation.

Jaeryn had troubles, too, by all accounts. He had almost been strangled, Charlotte said, though he had never disclosed the details. The thought of the Irishman in rough shape presented a picture that he couldn't quite wrap his mind around. Jaeryn was always so invincibly put-together—bloodshot eyes and bruised face were worlds apart from his catlike tidiness. Thank God he was safe. That was another good thing about returning: Jaeryn was still in charge.

The train traveled on through the morning and into the afternoon. He spent the time sleeping and waking alternately when he thought he was safe or he was too tired to keep his eyes open. At twenty to six, they braked to a halt in Baltimore.

It was November third by the calendar. In a few hours, the steamer for England sailed. Ben took time to send telegrams to both Jaeryn and Charlotte, informing them of his departure. He wondered if either of the telegrams would get through, and he added a third to Ryson just to be on the safe side. Then he dug in his pockets for enough change to hire a cab. When he arrived at the docks, the mingled smell of salt water and smoke, along with gasoline, coffee, and other cargo scents, swirled together, overwhelming and exhilarating him. The shrill cries of seagulls filled his ears, along with the bustle of boarding and incoming ships. It was bitter cold in the wind, and his nails turned blue before he ducked into a coffee shop and bought a drink to warm up with.

He came back to the thought of his return to England while he waited, and his heart leaped at the thought of leaving Virginia Beach behind. He was going home at last. Was it home now? In September, he had rejoiced at leaving his British exile. Somehow, after coming to America, what he had left behind then didn't look quite as dark as it had, and what he had come to didn't look quite as bright as before. He didn't know which country was home now. He was lost between two worlds and could not find his place in either one. If only he knew.

Come departure time, a uniformed seaman carried his trunk up the gangplank to his cabin. It was the same steamer as last time, with the same captain commanding. That was one more factor to his advantage, with threats against his safety on one side and a man assigned to protect him on the other.

The captain knocked on his door a few moments after he settled in. "You see I have charge of you again, doctor," he greeted.

Ben shook hands with him. "You got me here safely; I'm sure you'll do just as well getting me back. Are you under the same orders this time?"

"I've received a letter and compensation accordingly. But don't draw breath until you're back on British shore. We have a perilous way in front of us, and I only promise to do all that's humanly possible. Beyond that, you'll have to tell this doctor fellow that what happens to you is no fault of mine."

"I wouldn't think of blaming you if something were to happen," Ben reassured. "By the way, I have a friend traveling in third class, and he's under my protection until he gets to England. If it's not too inconvenient, I want permission for him to use the first-class deck."

The captain drew together his heavy brows. "You know that's not customary."

"I do."

"It's a privilege I give to few." He cocked his head and considered. "Very well. I have my orders, Doctor Dorroll. He can go on the first deck, but the other facilities are out of bounds for him."

"Thank you, sir."

After the captain left, Ben descended to the lowest level and found Patrick making himself at home. He shared a cabin with five other passengers, but he didn't seem to mind, and he had already selected one of the top bunks.

Patrick looked up from his scattered belongings and smiled. "Well, look who just arrived. Come down from your classy stateroom to have a chat with your pauper friend?"

Ben looked around the room, adequate yet so different from his own, and wished there wasn't such a distinction. "I'm sorry I can't do better for you."

"Don't take life so seriously." Patrick's eyes twinkled. "I have everything I want. The dining room is nice. We have a good bit of deck and almost everything you have. You'll make good use of your own luxuries. Did you find your cabin to your liking?"

"It was quite sufficient."

"That's it? If you're paying for first class, I would hate for it to be just sufficient. Over the top should be more like it."

Ben smiled.

"I forgot; there's a smoking room down here too. Don't be jealous." Patrick shoved the rest of his belongings under the pillow and beckoned for Ben to follow him. "We're going to leave port soon. Let's watch, shall we?"

Patrick shoved a way boldly through to the rail for both of them. A mix of sailors and soldiers clad in blue or brown lined the rail, and friends seeing them off waved handkerchiefs from the shore. The sun drew near to the horizon as the harbor drifted away, and the waves turned from gray to navy and silver in the fading light.

"Miss home?" Ben asked, watching the play of the water against the vessel and the knots of people moving to and fro on the docks.

"A little. The home folks are nice. But I'm glad I'm going to England. I was too stagnant where I was, working the same job day in and day out. Now I have a chance to reset and start fresh."

"Your ancestors started fresh by coming to America in the first place. It hasn't been that long."

Patrick leaned his arms on the railing to the chagrin of the small man next to him. "Upheaval only lasts for two generations; then the third one wants to go back to what it was like before things changed. I want change. I want new and better and progress. You can't have progress when you don't try things and take risks. You know that, or you wouldn't be coming to England yourself, would you now?"

Ben frowned in thought. "I think stability can be a kind of progress just as much as change."

"Well, then. You for one and I for the other, and here's to success for both of us." Patrick winked at him. "Too bad you weren't ours. Mum would like you—a good, steady fellow who would stay in Richmond all his life if he had the choice. Poor woman got two boys who like to wander instead. But you have to let go eventually. At least we can find out a bit more about Terry now. What does he do for work, do you know?"

He debated about hazarding a guess but decided to keep his secret to himself. "Terry never told me."

"Never told us either." The wind ruffled Patrick's hair, and he breathed in the salty air luxuriously.

"Terry never told you what he does for a living?"

"No. We asked him a couple of times, but he never answered us. We didn't like to mention it every time we wrote, and he's not much for writing himself. If we heard from him twice a quarter, we thought he must be all right. Erin wrote every month until the war began, but after she stopped, Terry always said she was well and thought of us all."

"Weren't you worried?"

Patrick shrugged. "We couldn't get there very fast to help if they got into trouble. Terry always seemed capable of looking after himself, and he said he was taking care of her. I don't know why he let her get married and all, but——"

"He didn't. She eloped, and afterward, she made him promise to let her tell. From month to month he kept pressuring her, but she couldn't bring herself to do it."

"Do you think he was right?"

He had never thought about the question before until Patrick's keen blue eyes searched his for the answer—eyes so like Terry's, but with a calm steadiness Terry didn't have.

"No," Ben said at length, "I don't think so. But he likes people to be happy with him, and you can't have people happy with you when you go against their will. You won't find your brother particularly steady, but he's warm-hearted. He doesn't have your moral compass, so I don't think he knows better."

"I remember that. Mum said he was always a little on the rough side. Well, never too late to change, eh?"

Ben waited until the ocean ran black beyond the glow of the vessel's lights and the first of the stars began to peep out before he suggested turning in for the night.

Patrick paused at the top of the steps that led down to third class. "Ben?"

Ben stopped at the door to his own block of cabins. "Yes?"

"I just wondered if you're keeping your revolver handy during our trip or if you're safe until Folkestone. I think I should know."

"I'm not sure. It's too early to tell yet."

"Well, I hope not. Tell me when you know so I can keep an eye out. Mum said to keep you safe."

Ben left his luggage to be unpacked in the morning and dove under the covers to find some sleep. But Patrick's question drove rest from his mind. He reached into his jacket, which hung over the chair back, and pulled out the death threats. Was he safe here, he wondered as he looked them over for the hundredth time? There was nothing to indicate who had written them. If only he recognized the writing. He got out of bed to make sure his cabin door was locked and checked his revolver to make sure it was loaded, then turned the light off again. For now, the threat was beyond his power to predict. He had taken all the precautions he could.

* * *

The next morning, when he returned from breakfast, there was an envelope lying on his bed with a message from the captain. Scrawled on the envelope was a note saying that a letter for Ben had been forgotten among the captain's other affairs before the ship sailed, but he had found it on his desk and sent it promptly by one of the stewards.

Dread rose up in Ben's throat. Tearing it open, he found it was another threat, warning him that if he returned to England, it would go ill not only with him but also with those he had left behind in Folkestone. He caught his breath. That was more than he could stand. He could endure any level of danger for himself, but the thought of another few days of travel without any way of warning the others unstrung him. He ripped the paper into pieces, crushing them in his hand.

The doorknob rattled, and he gave an exclamation of annoyance. "Come in."

"Ben?" Patrick entered, smelling of fresh air and bursting with good nature.

Ben turned and dropped the scraps of paper in the trash so Patrick wouldn't ask about them. Patrick tried to peer over his shoulder. "What are you doing?"

"I must speak to the captain. Stay here until I come back."

Ben hurried down the hushed, carpeted hallways until he found a uniformed steward. "Excuse me. Where are the captain's quarters?"

513

The young man stared at him coolly. "Why?"

"I need to speak to him on a matter of great importance. Government importance. It has to do with the war."

"You must be Doctor Dorroll, then?" he asked.

"Yes."

"We've had orders about you. Right this way, sir, if you please."

He followed the steward up a flight of steps, and the young man opened a door for him. "This is his office, doctor. Step right in. I'll go and inform him you are here."

It wasn't long before the doorknob rattled, and the captain came in answer to his summons. "What can I do for you, doctor?"

Ben spoke in a tight, worried way that betrayed his anxiety. "You left a message in my room. Who gave it to you?"

The captain chuckled gruffly. "I received a letter just before we sailed. It's a common enough occurrence, trying to reach people before they start the Atlantic crossing. Was there anything wrong with it?"

"It was—unexpected. Can I see the letter they gave you?"

"I didn't keep it. It went out with the other waste papers."

His heart sank as the only trail he had disappeared for good. "And might I ask if there are to be any more deliveries of this sort?"

"There are none."

"I want to see the passenger list, please."

The captain unlocked his desk and pulled it out of a drawer. "There you are. Do you have a problem, doctor?"

"I don't know." Ben took it and scrutinized it. He saw no name he recognized. "I'd like a copy of this if you don't mind."

"Do you think one of my passengers is a threat to you?" The captain re-locked his desk and laid a hand on the doorknob. "If you are in danger of your life, Doctor Dorroll, I expect to hear of it."

Ben straightened his shoulders and met the captain's gaze with some appearance, at least, of bravery. "I begin to think I am always in danger of my life, sir."

"If you are in more danger than usual, I wish to know. I have the responsibility to see that you arrive safely in Dublin."

"And once I set foot on the docks, I can be murdered for all you care," he said, with more heat than he intended.

"Quite so," the captain returned. "Well then, if that's all you had to say, I have many things to attend to."

The captain showed him out. Ben returned to Patrick and found him occupied in trying to piece the paper together, with very little success. Patrick looked up with a slight expression of guilt, but it disappeared as he gestured toward his fruitless attempt.

"Hullo. You destroyed it well. What was it?"

"Just a letter. It was sent to the captain before we sailed." Ben searched through his drawers and pulled out his shoulder holster.

"I thought so." Patrick said, handing him his revolver. "Any threat for the present, do you think?"

"Not to me. Perhaps to the home folks."

"What home folks? In America?"

"No. In Folkestone. The note hinted at it, I think. I can't do anything for the present, so I'll have to wait until I get back. Soon we'll be in Dublin, and then you can stay to look around and I won't stop until I get home. I can't do any more than that." He pulled out the box of ammunition from his trunk and busied his fingers with the familiar process of loading the chambers.

"So what's next?"

"I believe we should part ways for a while."

"But you can't be left alone like this," Patrick protested.

Ben shrugged. "I have a few days before I really have to watch my back."

"From the person who's giving these threats. There could be someone else."

He shook his head. "You can't stay with me all the time, Patrick. The captain would never allow it."

"Well, I needn't go yet, at least," Patrick said grimly.

"Since you force me to be candid, I should like to be alone. I have some things I need to think over."

"I thought you said we couldn't do anything about it. How is thinking going to help?"

When he returned no answer, Patrick was forced to yield to his wish to be alone.

Ben smoothed out the other two death threats and laid them on the table next to the heap of paper scraps. He saw that the clock hands pointed to ten and decided to wander on deck. It was empty; no one else was out in the cold except the uniformed sailors. A brisk wind blew about his neck and forehead, and he wondered what the last weeks of autumn would be like in England. He had the awful feeling that he would be better off never arriving at all. However much Jaeryn wanted him back, someone else was doing everything in their power to persuade him to stay.

But England was home now. That was it. The picture cleared in his mind, and he could see it all as he had never been able to before. All the people he held dear, and who held him dear in return, were there. It would be the same if they were in America; the country didn't matter, really. They made the place what it was, and he hoped desperately that nothing would happen to change that. As soon as returned to Folkestone, he would do whatever he could to see it safe and whole and clean again.

* * *

The night of November sixth, when they were walking the deck about half past eight, a sense of dread that had been with him all afternoon increased to a black horror that he could not shake off. He said nothing of it, hoping Patrick would make no comment, and fought to keep his mind on the conversation at hand. But at length, his attention slipped away, and Patrick noticed.

"What's the matter?"

"It's nothing." Ben tried to shrug off the worry, but Patrick would not be put aside. "It's foolish, Patrick. It was just a feeling, that's all. I wish—I wish we were there tonight. I have a feeling that something's wrong, and there's nothing I can do to stop it."

"It's probably just a feeling," Patrick comforted.

The worry only grew keener in his mind as the minutes passed. "It's no use. I know something's wrong."

Patrick opened his mouth with a protesting look, but before he spoke, it shifted to sympathy. "I'm sorry. I wish I could do something to help you. All we can do is pray that they'll be safe, and the good Lord will see to the rest. He's there, you know, even when you aren't."

"I know. Goodnight, Patrick. I'm not good company tonight, but I'll be over it by morning."

Slowly, the night crept on. One by one the passenger lights flickered and died out as third class went to sleep and Patrick with it. Ben stayed outside for a long time in the silence, watching the stars.

Chapter Twenty-Nine
Jaeryn Takes a Risk

Jaeryn did his duty by the constables and answered a myriad of questions. Then he sat by and waited while they did the same to Erin. She had no alibi to prove her innocence, but Jaeryn did his best to satisfy the man taking down evidence that she was clear. When he told them he was employed by Ryson in London for private investigations, they took his comments and observations into more serious consideration, thought they didn't promise to rule Erin out.

Once the rain stopped, they let Erin go and went to look at the muddy ground where Jaeryn had found Pearl's body. The traces were gone; not even blood remained to mark the spot, and it was only with great difficulty that Jaeryn was able to point out the place in the light of a torch. They would have to come back in the morning and look it over again when it was easier to see. Inside the house was a far different matter. Erin had mentioned the knife, and though the constables searched both cottages high and low, they could find no trace of it.

"Someone could have come back for it while I drove to town," Jaeryn said. "It looked like some kind of message to me, but perhaps they thought better of leaving any evidence."

All the same, the knowledge that the knife was hidden in his car made him nervous. It set his teeth on edge to see the four men gathered around the slight figure of Dorroll's sister, discussing the matter as if she were a mere object in the course of their work. He offered to bring the coroner, and they accepted his offer, sending a constable along with him. Jaeryn had a hard time keeping a calm demeanor with the evidence hidden in the back seat. The bobby sitting beside him conversed about mundane matters, little dreaming that he ought to arrest the man next to him for tampering with evidence.

Chadwick, the man from the morgue, came right away with his kit. He never suspected that the blonde girl was the same one another young doctor had frantically searched for in the aftermath of the bomb drop. Jaeryn wrote out the death certificate and drafted a medical report with all the evidence he could find. When he was done, he leaned against the bedroom wall, feeling dizzy from the loss of sleep and the scene before him.

Chadwick nodded comfortingly. "I'll get her cleaned up for the family, sir, as soon as they want to come for her."

"Obliged," Jaeryn muttered, pressing his hand against his mouth to keep from turning sick.

"Bad business that," the man continued.

He took in a shivering breath. "What can I do?"

"You'd best not help, sir. Doctors are doctors, but this isn't in your line, I think. The family can come to the morgue later today to see her."

Jaeryn made his escape gladly and turned northwest in the direction of Alisa's, relieved that he was no longer contending with the rain. When he pulled into the drive, he saw that all the lights in the lower level were still on. He closed the car door softly so as not to give away his presence. But they were watching for him, and the door hinges whined as Charlotte came hastily out.

"You've been gone so long. Did you find her?"

Jaeryn swallowed hard, and he could feel, if not see, that Charlotte was trying to read his face in the darkness. "I think we'd better go inside, Mrs. Dailey. I'll tell you about it."

She tried to resist him, but he took her by the arm and refused to answer her questions until she was sitting at the kitchen table. Her hair was mussed from sitting up late, and the blue eyes fixed on his face were wide from lack of sleep. A moment of silence fell between them as Jaeryn collected his words.

"She's still missing?" Charlotte asked, with a note of hope in her voice.

Jaeryn pulled himself together. "I'm afraid not. Miss Dailey was found at Copt Point. We think someone tricked her and met her unawares. She was murdered, and due to the rain, we have no trace of who it was that killed her."

"Oh." Charlotte's voice went flat as the hope died out of her face. Her eyes grew even bigger. "I'm—thank—I'll go and tell Alisa. She's waiting to hear." She did not want to give way in front of him, he could see that. Sharing the first moment of grief with a man she didn't trust was distasteful enough to keep her immediate reaction at bay.

"You don't have any idea who did it?" she asked abruptly.

"They don't know. I'm sure they'll try their best to find out."

She brushed aside his reassurance. "But you? Do you know?"

"It wasn't Terry if that's what you mean." He said it too strongly and bit his lip as the words left his mouth.

"I didn't think it was Terry." Her lips trembled, and the tears she had held back resisted her efforts. "I would never, ever have thought it was him. How could you say that?"

"I'm sorry. I didn't mean—I shouldn't have said it like that."

She continued on without stopping to hear him. "I only knew that you know more about what goes on here than most, and you might know who to suspect."

Jaeryn gave her a level look. "I swear to you on my honor that I will see justice done. I don't know what happened. I may be able to piece it together, but it will take some time, and I cannot tell you more."

Her words were just as keen as her eyes. "I should like to think you have honor. But I think it is dispensable to you. And I also know that you would hold your tongue so as not to jeopardize your work. I want justice done, and when I write my husband, he will want it as well. If I suspect you are withholding information, then I will go to the authorities myself and tell them."

He felt the sweat breaking out under his collar as he defended himself. "Listen, Mrs. Dailey. My relationship with the authorities is precarious at present, and you casting suspicions on me would do more damage than you have any idea of. I don't know who killed your sister-in-law, but as soon as I do, I promise they will hang for it."

They heard a timid knock and saw Alisa's concerned face peeping through a crack in the door. When she saw Charlotte's angry face, she hastily shut the door again.

"I should go to her. She's waited long enough." Charlotte rubbed her forehead wearily. "I don't know what to do. When can we see Pearl?"

"Leave everything to me. I'll be by in a few hours to help you through the process; I've seen it enough times. Miss Dailey is at the mortician's right now, and the coroner has to come to collect evidence, but you'll be able to see her later today."

"I don't know what Ben will do when he finds out." Charlotte started crying again. "She wouldn't have died if she hadn't come here, and he's going to feel so guilty about it."

Jaeryn came forward and took her hands in his, and though she tried to pull them away, he would not let her. "You must tell him that she would not have lived, either, if he had not brought her with him. It was the best thing that could have happened to her. Not the dying, but the living. She was as happy here as she could have been anywhere else. I'm sure of it."

He pulled out his handkerchief and offered it to her. Charlotte wiped her eyes. "You've been so kind to us. I can't imagine what it was like to find her. I'm so sorry; I don't know why I was so hard on you after all you've done."

"Please, don't distress yourself; it's not worth thinking about." Jaeryn was glad to get out of it so easily. "It's nearly four o' clock. As soon as you've told Alisa and you've both had some time to talk, try and get some sleep. You'll need all your strength. Do you want me to stay? I'm available as long as you need me, but I don't want to intrude."

"No. No, you should tell Terry as soon as you can. He has a right to know. And I should send a telegram to Ben."

"I'll take care of Terry for you. Don't you want your brother-in-law to know first? I can tell him if you like."

She sniffed back her tears and returned the handkerchief to him. "No. Edmond never even met her, and Terry loved her more. He should know first."

"Very well, then." He nodded. "Please call me if you need the slightest thing."

"You look so tired," she said. "Can I get you anything before you go?"

Her eyelids were red and swollen. She probably looked worse than he did, though he hadn't had the opportunity to see himself. As he looked down at his hands, he caught sight of the blood under his nails and hid them hastily behind his back. "No. No, thank you. I'll leave you now. But I'll be back later. I need to have a word with you about something else, but it will keep."

* * *

The cool wind felt good on his face as he put the car top down and started the vehicle. He wished it would blow away the grief he felt at the things that he had seen and the tension of playing desperately for the saving of his own position and for justice for the Dorrolls at the same time.

Charlotte was beginning to piece things together. He shouldn't have told that lie to the constables about still being under Ryson. It was foolish. If word got to London, or even to Ann Meikle, he would be locked up in some jail cell and stripped of his good reputation. But if he hadn't lied, they would have discovered things that he did not want them disturbing yet. He desperately needed to find out how Pearlie Dorroll had gotten possession of that telegram and who had found her with it.

And if he failed? Jaeryn shuddered.

Ben needed to come home. The work would be greatly eased with Dorroll to screen his movements. No word had come from America, and if Ben didn't write soon, a stranger would come to upset things and Jaeryn would have to make a quick escape to avoid the conclusion to this mess. He only had a little longer before his choices caught up with him.

His thoughts trailed off into incoherent exhaustion as he pulled up automatically before the clinic. Terry would still be at work, so Jaeryn had a couple of hours to try to catch some rest before he was up and running again. He would have to open the clinic today as usual, and he hoped wryly that he would be in good enough shape to make the judgments he needed to.

Taking out his key ring, Jaeryn looked at it doubtfully. Then he glanced down at the two desk drawers that he always kept locked. Opening the right one, he pulled out the battered photo Starlin had found and traced his finger over the image.

"If someone had murdered you, I would have killed them." His breath caught in his throat, and he tasted salt on his lips. Blasted tears.

He crawled into bed and set his clock so he would be sure to wake in time. He was too tired to put it back on the nightstand before he fell asleep.

* * *

Jaeryn drove the car as slowly as he could, dreading his disagreeable task. It was more than disagreeable. It would be devastating. He had already prepared himself to be stern if Terry needed it; Terry had never dealt with sorrow before, and the thought of the reeling blow his news would deliver to that cheery face made the windshield mist over again. He did not even try to pretend it away.

A golden glow of dawn flickered above the drenched trees, and he could hear the gentle twitter of sparrows in the hedgerows. If anyone should be alive on such a morning, it was Pearlie Dorroll. But that thought wouldn't do anyone any good, and he shook his head, the car swerving slightly as he did so.

He had timed his arrival perfectly. Ahead of him, Terry cycled along without a jacket, his shirt sleeves rolled up to his elbows and a cheery whistle sounding out on the frosty air. Evidently, he had recovered his spirits and was back to his normal self again. He never stayed down for long.

Jaeryn pulled up alongside, and Terry turned to see who it was. "Hey, doc!" He looked absolutely delighted at the surprise of seeing Jaeryn so early. "It's a grand morning out. Did you come to find me?"

Jaeryn gave a small smile. "I did. Can you take me to your place?"

"Sure thing. The other fellows won't be up yet, and we'll have it all to ourselves. I'll make you breakfast."

"No need. I only stopped by to tell you something."

Terry led the way at a brisk pace, and Jaeryn pulled up on the grass beside the old house Terry called his own. Technically, Terry wasn't supposed to be there. They should have fixed that sooner. It would be a pity to have him get in trouble over it.

When they were inside, Jaeryn silently handed over the knife. The constables had never dreamed of searching his car, and it had been well hidden there.

Terry laughed and tossed it up in the air, catching it deftly as it came down. "Sure, and you found my blade! Where was it?"

Jaeryn winced at the recollection of what had been on it only a few hours before. "It was—ah—I have something to tell you, Terry."

Terry stowed the knife in his pocket and gave it a fond pat. "What've you got, doc? I'm ready to face the world again since I have this back."

"It's bad, what I have to tell you." Jaeryn's voice cracked, and he ran a hand nervously through his hair.

An expression of concern spread over Terry's face, but the concern was all for him, he knew, and not for what he was saying. "Aw, come on. Life's never that bad. Tell me what it is, and we'll fix it up." He grinned.

There was no preliminary left to say. "I was out near Copt Point last night. Someone's been murdered." He saw that his words were not registering. "It was Miss Dorroll. I'm very sorry, Terry. She's dead."

The grin stayed frozen on Terry's face for one long moment and then faded to a look of terrified incomprehension that was burned into Jaeryn's memory for several weeks to come. That too disappeared, like a receding tide, into a blank expression. "Did you say Acushla's—what?"

"She's dead, Terry. I'm sorry."

Terry shivered, and a gasp loosed his tongue as Jaeryn's words hit him. "I don't believe it. I don't—she's *dead*? Not Pearlie Dorroll. Not *my* Pearlie." He grabbed Jaeryn's jacket in both hands. "You don't mean her, do you?"

Jaeryn put his hands on Terry's shoulders and held his gaze until he saw that Terry was listening and comprehending. "I mean her. Miss Dorroll is dead."

The spark drained out of Terry's face, and the impish twist at the corners of his mouth disappeared as his body accepted what his mind was still fighting to hold back. His hands dropped limp at his sides. The rest of him might have followed, but Jaeryn took a firm grip on him and cleared a chair of clothes and crumpled newspaper. Terry talked dazedly the whole time, and Jaeryn could hardly bear to hear him.

"I think you must have made a mistake. Acushla wouldn't die, not such a tiny, golden little thing. She was made to live, and I was going to give her my ring, and we were going to love each other. Are you sure she's dead?"

Jaeryn nodded, not trusting himself to speak.

The color drained from Terry's face until he was so pale that Jaeryn was afraid he would lose him too. "Where'd you put your brandy flask, Terry? Stay with me. I'll help you through, I promise I will, but you can't give up now."

"I ca—I can't breathe," Terry gasped. The veins stood out on his hands as he clenched them together, and Jaeryn took them and pried them apart. As they loosened, a great sigh swept over his frame.

"I don't understand. How did it happen? She wasn't even sick. Did she hurt herself?" Fear dawned in his eyes as he remembered the rest of Jaeryn's words. "You said she was murdered?"

"Last night. I found her sometime after nine at Copt Point. She told Charlotte she was out for a walk, and someone killed her there. She had the telegram we were waiting for. It was addressed to you. I have no idea how she got it." He left out the details of the brutality; no point in telling until Terry asked for them.

The part about the telegram didn't register either. Terry only had ears for Pearlie. "And she was by herself without anyone to help her," he breathed.

Jaeryn saw the Celtic cross sliding out of his pocket and gritted his teeth for what he knew was coming next. Terry looked at him with every muscle stretched taut. "I will hunt down the fiend who did it and squeeze the life out of his soul. I swear, Jaeryn"—pointing to the knife—"I'll kill him with this, and I don't care if I hang for it." Then a new level of realization came over his face. "Where did you find my blade?"

Jaeryn looked reluctantly at it, and Terry was not so lost in shock that he couldn't read his meaning. "You don't mean they used it on her?"

"They did. That's not what killed her, though," Jaeryn added hastily. "It was a gun that did it. The knife was just to take revenge, I think. It was pinning the telegram to the wall. Someone must have found her with the telegram and thought she had something to do with us."

Terry's face furrowed with grief again, but he managed to keep himself in check enough to get his words out. "Then I won't use it to kill the wretch. It touched her, and it would be sacrilege to use it for that. I'll never use it again." He touched the blade to his lips and sheathed it. "Where is she now?"

"She's at the morgue, in town. You're going to have to hide the knife, especially from your sister. If anyone sees it, they'll connect you to the murder. That's the only piece of evidence they have."

"Can I see her?"

Jaeryn shook his head. "Not yet. She belongs to her family first. But you can go sometime today, I'm sure."

Terry kept silent for a long time. His eyes had a hollow vacancy, and Jaeryn tried to read which direction his mind would take next. This was too calm for his liking. It couldn't last for long.

"Jaeryn," Terry whispered, "why would anyone want to be that evil? I don't think I could do something like that."

"I don't know."

Terry laid a trembling hand on the chair arm and stood up. "I'm sorry you had to tell. I won't be keeping you any longer."

Jaeryn stood up as well. He ran his fingers softly along the barrel of his revolver, though he could not have told why. "What are you going to do now? We have to talk. We have to figure out who might have done this and how on earth she got ahold of that telegram."

Terry stood resolute. Not a trace of happiness was left on his face, and an angry expression was stealing in to replace it. "I'm going to see Acushla and tell her goodbye. And then I'm going to find the man who killed her and riddle him with bullet holes for what he did to my little one."

Jaeryn groaned. "Terry, don't try to execute justice yourself. There will be time enough for that later after we've had a chance to regain some clear thinking."

Terry shrugged. "I haven't got much to lose if I fail. And if I succeed, then I reckon that's all I'll need to be doing in this life anyway."

"Yes, you do have a lot to lose. There is still much left to live for." He saw Terry's jaw tighten. "You must promise me that you will not try to take your own life, and I forbid you to take anyone else's."

He saw something sliding out of Terry's other pocket, and knew it was the revolver he had gotten when his knife turned up missing. "Do you know what you're asking, Jaeryn Graham?"

Jaeryn lifted his chin and braced himself. "No, but I'm going to ask it anyway."

"I could pull the trigger now, you know, and then I would see Acushla faster." Terry made a threatening gesture, and Jaeryn backed up to the wall. "You're asking me to live my whole life without Pearlie?"

"Yes."

Terry's eyes took on a look of uncertainty as he glanced at the revolver. He began to shake again, then burst into tears. It was heart wrenching to see a strong man give way to such an extent. But Jaeryn understood and waited patiently for it to run its course. It would help him to realize the finality of what had happened more than any words.

He cried on so long that at length Jaeryn grew alarmed again. He had never seen anyone with that many tears, not even a woman. The poor fellow seemed to be draining his very life away until he choked trying to draw breath. Jaeryn looked awkwardly down at his hands, then shrugged and rubbed Terry's shoulder. The human touch seemed to calm him. He swiped at his eyes with both hands and shivered.

Jaeryn took the revolver out of Terry's lap and laid it aside. Terry didn't look at him, but he was calm enough to listen again. "Come home with me, Terry. Please," Jaeryn pleaded. "You can stay for a while."

"Go away." Terry's eyes were dull and glassy, and Jaeryn knew that it was nothing personal, only a mighty effort to keep from cracking under his resentment at what Jaeryn had asked of him.

Jaeryn did not dare obey. He heard footsteps on the stairs and saw Hugh look curiously into the room. Jaeryn gestured him away, and he withdrew as silently and inscrutably as he had come. Then Terry gave a hasty exclamation and hurried out.

Jaeryn reached the door in time to see Terry's bicycle shooting down the road at a furious pace. But the revolver was still where he had put it, and in some relief, he decided that Terry would be safe for the present. Perhaps he was better left alone to face his sorrow.

* * *

Jaeryn operated the clinic as usual in the morning, but early that afternoon he closed it, went to Alisa's, and had a long talk with her and Charlotte over what was best to be done. They couldn't wait too long to inform the rest of the family. There was Matthew Dorroll to be told, and Edmond, though neither of them had ever seen Pearl.

"We need to make other living arrangements now. Neither of you can live here alone any longer. You have to be in a place where you will be protected and surrounded by people who can watch out for you. You could go to your father in London, perhaps. I'm sure he would take you under the circumstances."

Alisa shook her head. "I would like to go to my husband. And I would like to tell him what has happened myself."

"I think I will have to reserve that task for myself, Mrs. Dorroll. I would agree, but if you wish to live with him, I'll need some leverage to persuade him to take you. As it is, I'm not sure staying in Folkestone, and especially with him, is the wisest arrangement. We don't know very much about him."

Charlotte frowned in thought. "Ben said Peters was dependable, and we could go to him if we have any difficulties. I would like to stay in Folkestone if possible. After all, Matthew Dorroll is as little known to us as Edmond."

"That is true," Jaeryn admitted. "I would feel easier if Peters looked after you."

"I'll come with you, then," Alisa said. "We can talk to Edmond together." She went up for her hat and coat, leaving him alone with Charlotte.

"Is she all right?" Jaeryn asked, as soon as she was out of earshot. "She looks ill."

Charlotte stirred her cup of tea, and the bittersweet scent of honey and English Breakfast drifted out. "She's taking it very hard. They were together so often that they were like sisters. I hope—I don't want her to suffer more with another rejection."

"I know. But after something as shocking as a death, Edmond can hardly hold out much longer. From what I've seen of him, he isn't callous, and I think he won't be closed to persuasion."

Ten minutes later, Alisa's little hand rested on his arm as he led her up the broad walk to the house of which she should rightfully be mistress. She kept a firm and steady step, but her shining eyes betrayed the greatness of her hope. Jaeryn knew the direction her thoughts tended and tried to prepare her for the changes she would see in the man she had said goodbye to.

Peters met them in the hall. Jaeryn whispered a muffled stream of directions in his ear, handing Alisa into his care.

"When you're done, sir, I'd like a word with you," Peters requested.

"Of course. I shouldn't be long. Wait for me, Alisa, until I come back for you. Will you tell Mr. Dorroll I'm here, Peters?"

"Yes, sir. If you'll wait in the library, I'm sure he'll only be a

527

moment."

Jaeryn looked wryly at the desk he had rifled only a few months before. He took a secret satisfaction in the fact that he knew just as much about its contents as the owner, and the owner was completely unaware of it. When he heard the sound of heavy breathing, Jaeryn knew that Edmond was coming and turned to meet him.

"Good morning, doctor. This isn't your usual day—can I do something for you?" Edmond looked like he had dressed in haste, but he was as polished and polite as usual.

Jaeryn straightened his shoulders. "I've come to ask you to help your wife. Last night her closest friend was horribly murdered. It was a young girl, around her age, and she had been staying with Alisa for some time. It has been quite a shock to all of us."

"I am very sorry to hear it. What a horrible thing to happen."

"You also have a claim upon the young woman who died. She's your younger sister whom Ben brought over in May."

Edmond's breathing sounded even more agitated than before. "Then I am sorrier than words can say. When did this happen?"

Jaeryn went briefly through the whole story and told him all that had occurred during the police investigation. When he was finished, Edmond looked genuinely sorry. "I wish for Alisa's sake that she hadn't lost someone she thought so highly of. I'll have Peters see to it that all the expenses are taken care of. They needn't worry about that. You will excuse me, however, if I am not overcome with grief." He looked regretfully at Jaeryn, almost as if he was afraid the doctor would think ill of him. "But I have never seen her in my life, nor even a picture of her. I only knew of her from what others told me. I would have wished her a long and happy life, and I am very sorry that it was ended so cruelly."

Jaeryn could not find it in his heart to blame him. "I understand your family situation, sir. I don't think ill of you for being unaffected by the misfortune. But you know as well as I that money is not the only thing needed right now."

Edmond's brows contracted. "Are you asking me to go to Alisa?"

"No. I am asking you to let her come to you. She is stricken with grief right now, and I think you would be the greatest comfort that she could possibly have. She and Charlotte need a safe place to stay where they will be watched over, and you are in a position to take them both."

Edmond took a turn about the library, his fingers on his lips, frowning in thought. When he reached the standing globe, he stopped and turned around. "Seeing me would only be a burden to her, and I would be loath to add to her troubles. I don't think I have the ability to take care of her."

"She's not demanding," Jaeryn said bluntly. "You have the ability to feed her and put a roof over her head. She's easy to love, and you have the finest son that a man could wish for. You have a very happy existence in front of you if you choose to reach out and claim it. Besides, taking care of someone else will keep your mind off your own misfortunes."

"I still think she would be happier as she is."

Jaeryn drew his brows together. "She is not safe there. Someone has been murdered, and until the murderer is caught, they need extra protection. You promised to love and care for her, and it's high time you did. I think you could love her again if you saw her."

"I never stopped—" Edmond broke out into a coughing fit that left him panting from exhaustion. "You're not married yourself, so I doubt you know much about it."

"So?" Jaeryn prompted.

His shoulders sagged, and he pressed his eyes tight shut as if trying to hold back a nightmare. "I would not see her in harm's way if there was anything I could do to protect her. She always was a clinging little thing. Very well. I will invite her to come here if you think it best. I'll go over as soon as I get ready."

"There's no need. She's here, waiting to see you."

Edmond looked almost afraid at the fulfillment of his promise staring him in the face. "That's rather sudden. I haven't had much time to think about seeing her yet. I don't know what to say."

"I don't think you'll have much trouble with that."

Before Edmond could change his mind, Jaeryn rang the bell to signal Peters. Edmond drew himself more erect as he watched the door. It opened, and Alisa's tiny form stood in the doorway, her sweet eyes searching his face with a faint sparkle of happiness in them. Edmond fastened his gaze on her, and Jaeryn saw him catch his breath. She walked up to him without hesitation and stood on her tiptoes to kiss him. Jaeryn detected a moment of resistance on Edmond's part, but before Alisa noticed it, he returned her embrace, and Jaeryn slipped out to leave them alone. That would heal him more than any chloral hydrate if he gave it time.

Peters stood waiting in the hall. "All satisfactory, sir?"

"Indeed." Jaeryn flashed his white teeth—the first smile he had given that day, or indeed for a couple of days past. "Now that he's agreed to see her, the progress should be swift. What was it you wanted to see me about?"

"Well, I had expected to hear from you sooner, sir, but I just received word from London about your last meeting with Ryson."

"Oh." Jaeryn felt the smile disappear from his face. "And?"

"I'm very sorry about that, sir. But if you still want me to tell you about our work here, then I'm prepared to do so, of course."

"That's kind of you, Peters. I'll think it over." He studied Peter's face for any sign of discomfort. It might be a trap, and he couldn't afford risk that at present.

Peters clasped his hands over his brown tweed jacket. "Very good, sir. Did you know Dailey sailed by the November third steamer?"

"Thank heaven," Jaeryn whispered. A great sense of relief swept over him. "He should be here any day, then. He might be back before his sister's funeral if all goes well."

"I trust you've read the papers as well, sir."

"I haven't had the time. What's happened?"

Peters looked grave. "It's the Russians, sir. Utter chaos at the capitol. The government has been completely taken over."

"No," Jaeryn whispered.

"It's looking very likely that we'll lose them, sir. If we can't detect who is trying to compromise the British Secret Service, we will sustain a grave loss on two fronts."

"Give me a paper to take back to the clinic, will you, Peters?"

Peters selected one from a walnut table which had the mail laid out on it and presented it to him. "Anything else I can do for you, sir?"

"Just keep a close watch on the two young women, and make sure they stay quite safe. I'm on my way to Charlotte Dorroll."

"Should I expect to hear from you soon?"

Jaeryn looked up sharply. "No. Why?"

The slightest hint of suspicion appeared in the set of Peters' mouth. "With you no longer part of our operations, sir, I'm afraid you'll have to return what I sent to you."

"I don't understand. What did you send me?"

"Through Fenton?" Peters asked.

Jaeryn shook his head. "I haven't seen him in a long time. I don't know what you're talking about. What did you give him?"

He saw that Peters did not believe him, and that brought back his uneasiness. "Never mind, sir." Peters rubbed his hand along his chin. "Perhaps it's best if we take care of it ourselves. But if I may take the liberty of saying, perhaps the security of the Secret Service would be increased if, under the present circumstances, you were willing to step aside."

Jaeryn raised an eyebrow, and Peters looked discomfited as he held the door open. Shrugging off the Russians for the present, he rode away, relieved at the break in bad news. Dorroll was on his way back, and altogether this had been a good day's work. If he was running out of time to regain favor with London, at least the cards were starting to line up in his favor for the final draw.

Jaeryn only stopped to pick up his mail before continuing on his way. He opened it with one hand as he drove. One of the letters further brightened his mood, and the darkness of the previous night did not seem quite as black as it had before.

Charlotte was waiting for him at Alisa's, and he assured her that the reunion had gone better than he had expected. She was glad to hear it. There were dark circles under her eyes, and she couldn't muster up much of a smile in spite of his encouraging words.

"I have something that I think will ease your mind, Mrs. Dorroll." He handed her the letter he had received, and she took it, glancing from it to him as she saw the postmark. "Why, it's from America." She drew the paper from the envelope. "Is it from Ben?"

"No, I'm afraid not. But it has news of him all the same," Jaeryn added hastily, as her face fell. "It's from a contact of mine, Alex York, and he explains why you haven't been hearing from your husband. Apparently, Ben hasn't gotten any news of you either, and he's been writing to you every week. So, you see, he didn't forget about you after all."

She read through the letter and returned it to him. "I'm glad."

Jaeryn opened his mouth to tell her the good news about her husband's return, but something held him back, and the words did not cross his lips. Better to make sure he was back safe first and not add concern for his travel to her burdens. Besides, she didn't know Ben had accepted the position again, and she was too overwrought for more news.

"I saw Pearlie before you came this morning," Charlotte said, breaking in on his thoughts. "And I took Alisa with me."

Jaeryn frowned. "You should have let me come with you, to help."

"It was hard," she continued, not heeding him. "Terry was waiting across the street when we came out, and he asked permission to go in and look at her. I told him he could. I even told him he could kiss her goodbye if he liked. It only seemed right when he loved her so much. But he wouldn't do it. He looked so broken." She shook off the remembrance and returned to the present. "At least it's over now."

Jaeryn sighed. "I wish that were true."

He drove by Alisa's house again that evening, but instead of the glow of lights he had grown used to, he saw two men boarding up the windows and a woman loading a car with household items. It was best for them to live with Edmond. They would be safer, and better taken care of, and more comfortable. Alisa would be happier. Charlotte might be lonely, but with Dorroll coming back that couldn't last for long.

The dark house gave him rather a sad feeling as he turned around in the drive and headed home. Less than two weeks before, a very different Terry had been standing with Starlin and Pearlie on the front step, spreading his joy to two people who very much needed his happiness. Terry had been there so many times, making the nights ring with his laughter. Hopefully, there would be some left in him after he had time to heal from his loss.

The constables called late and gave him a report of the murder investigation. They had sent Pearl's bloodstained clothes to the forensic lab, along with everything on her, but released her body for burial. The detective was unhappy that Jaeryn had carried her inside and damaged the evidence. Jaeryn pointed out that the rain would have washed away all traces anyway. They would have to do the best they could with what he had managed to salvage. The investigators had gone back to Copt Point, but though they searched far and wide, there was nothing left to find.

As soon as they were gone, he pulled out the telegram and laid it out before him. The attempt to contact one of Emmerson's partners hadn't worked. He had no way to confirm the location, and he had no idea who 000192 was. But it had served a tragic kind of purpose. Someone from Emmerson's side had responded in rage at the idea of Pearlie Dorroll having the telegram. But how, in heaven's name, had she gotten possession of a telegram for Terry? And how had she ended up at Copt Point with it? And who had met or followed her there?

The telegram would have been delivered to Terry's house. Ann Meikle would have seen it. Terry's housemates, Hugh and Stafford, might have seen it as well.

Stafford was known to have dropped a death threat in the past. He knew of nothing against Hugh except the high esteem of Mrs. Goodwin's guard dog, which certainly wasn't in his favor. And Ann Meikle—

Jaeryn gathered up the telegram with a determined look. Perhaps she would be the best place to start.

Five minutes later, he knocked at her front door for the first time in his life. A lace curtain lifted to the side and then dropped again. Jaeryn smiled grimly to himself and pounded again. Then he waited. Still no answer. He pounded without stopping until the lock rattled and the door wrenched open.

"What is it?" Ann Meikle asked. She had a shawl wrapped around her shoulders, and her feet were clad in a pair of bedroom slippers. "I don't like my evenings interrupted."

"Pearlie Dorroll is dead," Jaeryn said. "She died last night at eight o'clock, and I need some information from you for the investigation."

"I'll wait to talk to the bobbies, thank-you." Ann shoved the door almost closed. Jaeryn thrust his arm in and with a great effort, kept it open enough to see her face.

"I only need to know if you saw her at the post office the day she died. Did you give her anything that day?"

"Her mail isn't yer concern. Find what ye can find, doctor, but I'll not tell you what I gave her or didn't."

Jaeryn raised his voice in ire. "You exasperating woman. At least tell me if you saw her at the post office. That's all I need to know."

"If ye stay, ye're trespassing on private property. I only answer to official police. Now take yer arm out, or I'll scream to the neighbors."

Jaeryn stood outside the closed wooden door for a long moment, clenching and unclenching his fists. Then he returned home. He hoped Ann wouldn't give the constables a reason to suspect that he knew more about it than he was letting on. Terry's knife still weighed heavily on his mind. The bobbies would be around to question Erin again, and there was no telling what she would say to them. The fear of discovery, along with everything else that had happened that day, made it difficult for him to fall asleep that night.

* * *

On Thursday, the temperature dropped and the rain turned to spitting snow, though it didn't stick to the roadways. Jaeryn hoped impatiently for word of Ben. He even called at the post office to ask for telegrams, but there were none. As the day passed in silence, he grew worried at the delay.

He had called Charlotte one last time after closing the clinic to make sure she had everything she needed. She wasn't upset with him now, at least. She was quiet, not openly confiding like Alisa, but he could sense more reliance than she had given before. According to Charlotte's news, Edmond had offered Terry a new position working on the grounds now that he was no longer needed to help Alisa. Reportedly, Terry had accepted, but she herself had not seen any sign of him. They had no way to tell him about the burial service, for none of them had seen him since Wednesday morning, and they could only hope he would see the notice in the paper. She had not considered it necessary to tell Edmond of Terry's interest in Pearlie. They had also informed Matthew Dorroll of the goings-on, but they had not seen him yet, and he had given no word as to whether or not he was coming down from London.

At seven-thirty, Jaeryn went up to his room and pulled out a sweater, then went down to the kitchen and put the kettle on. He only had to go down to his private drop to leave a message for Fenton, and then he was done with work for the day. It had been entirely too long since their last meeting. Fenton wasn't safe left to his own devices for any length of time.

Jaeryn was going into his consulting room with a steaming mug in one hand and a sandwich in the other when he heard a knock on the door. After ducking back into the kitchen to set down his impromptu meal, he opened it and saw Starlin King standing on his front step.

"Come in. Please." He put on as polite an air as he could muster. Starlin didn't look the least bit deceived by it, though he was civil in return.

"I came to bring a message from Terry." Starlin looked about the hall, at his boots, at Jaeryn's hands—anywhere but at his face.

"You've seen him? Tell me what's been happening. I haven't been able to get any word with him today to make sure he's all right."

Starlin's gaze came up at last to meet his eyes. "He's not all right.

534

He won't be all right for a long time, if ever. When I heard the news about Miss Dailey yesterday morning—which you didn't bother to send me, by the way, even though I've known her just as long as you have—I went straight over, and he was almost ready to do away with himself. He had the gun out. He told me he had promised you he wouldn't pull the trigger, but he wasn't sure he could keep that promise anymore."

"Oh, no."

"He's still alive. Not alive, really, but still breathing at any rate."

Jaeryn tried to keep a grip on his self-control. "What happened after that?"

Starlin scraped one boot against the back of the other. "He'd been drinking, I think. He didn't always make sense when he talked, and I could smell it on his breath. I asked him if he wanted company, and he said he didn't know, so I said I would stay. I brought my violin with me, and I played. His housemates didn't like it. They came down and swore at the both of us and told us to take our music somewhere else. But Terry got up and pushed them out and locked the door after them. I played every piece I knew until I couldn't play anymore, and he looked a little quieter after that. I knew if I could play long enough he might fall asleep, so I kept on until he did. Then I left."

Jaeryn looked at the lad's face in wonderment. It had a soft expression, and his eyes were not as dark and sullen as they normally were. "That was kind of you, Starlin. I think it was the best thing anyone could have done for him."

Starlin shrugged off the words. "I dropped by today, but he told me not to come back anymore. He said he would see me when he could, but it wasn't right for me to visit his place. I stayed away since he seemed so worried. Terry said to tell you that you shouldn't come around either. He said to be very particular that you knew. That's all."

"Well, that's one thing I can ignore," Jaeryn muttered. "Thank you, King. If you see Terry again, I would take it as a kindness if you sent me word."

"I'll think about it." Starlin was back to his normal surly self again, and Jaeryn had a strong urge to smack him in the face. He restrained himself and closed the door after the boy in pointed silence.

As soon as Starlin left, Jaeryn walked out to the shopping district to leave the note for Fenton. When he unlocked his private drop, he found that Fenton had been there before him. According to the time in the corner, the note was a couple of hours old. *Friday night,* it read. *St. Eanswythe church, 10 pm. Don't be seen. F.*

Jaeryn crumpled up the note he had written and re-locked the box. That would save him the trouble of arranging something. The ferret must have something important to tell him.

* * *

It was a quiet service in the Tontine Congregational Church Friday afternoon. There was no sign of Matthew Dorroll, and Colonel King was in London for the day, though he sent a massive wreath of roses. Alisa sat by Edmond and held his hand. Jaeryn could tell that it cost him some effort to be seen in public, but he seemed determined not to mind the discomfort. Charlotte sat beside Alisa as well, and Jaeryn took an empty pew on the other side of the aisle. His hair was combed back, as neat as a wet brush could make it, and his hands were clasped over his knees. He looked behind him more than once, but he saw no sign of Terry, and when the service began he had to turn his attention toward the front. It was hard—an unsolved murder case with an innocent girl. He didn't envy the clergyman officiating. Edmond slipped his hand out of Alisa's and put his arm around her shoulder halfway through.

Jaeryn could not help looking behind him as the service neared its end. He saw Terry's stricken face in the back pew, Starlin sitting erect and uncomfortable beside him. He had hoped that Terry would come, but he had never expected Starlin. At least the lad had some compassion, though whether by good breeding or by accident Jaeryn could hardly say.

Terry got up as soon as Jaeryn caught his gaze and beckoned sternly to Starlin to follow him. Starlin shot a glance over his shoulder before they disappeared through the church door. He looked as if he was afraid of what would happen if he refused. As much as Jaeryn wanted to follow them, he could not.

When the service was concluded, he met Charlotte at the door and offered her his arm. "Are you sure you and Alisa want to stay? I can take you home now if you like," he offered.

"I should like to stay." She pulled on her thin black gloves and gave a small nod in thanks for his concern. "It is so hard to let her go. I would like to know that I stayed as long as I could, for Ben's sake."

Jaeryn did not try to dissuade her and stayed by her side until the last shovelful of dirt was cast into place. Then he handed her into the car and watched it drive away.

When he reached home, there was a telegram on the hall floor. He snatched it up and tore it open.

IN DUBLIN. COMING ON SOON. DAILEY.

* * *

Jaeryn was at his station that evening fifteen minutes before the appointed time, standing near the St. Eanswythe graves. He kept a sharp lookout for Fenton, revolver in hand. This meeting made him uneasy; it was after dark, and Fenton never asked him to meet in deserted places so late. The spy liked dingy pub corners where he could leech a glass of beer off his employer. In fact, for a man who'd never drunk a beer in his life, Jaeryn had bought quite a lot of it, and the peculiarity of the fact struck him as he waited.

It was three minutes past the hour. A movement caught his eye farther down in the graveyard. He saw a dark figure moving toward the steps where the drop box was hidden. Straining to see who it was, Jaeryn noticed the outline of a smaller, slighter figure following in the first one's shadow. He crept closer. If he crouched near the corner of the church, he could be hidden by the wall and still overhear their conversation.

He thought he recognized the first figure, with the strong shoulders and the casual gait. As he caught the man in profile, he blinked and looked again. It was Terry. The little fellow behind him— he couldn't make out who the little fellow was. Terry reached behind the gravestone of Rebecca Rogers, and Jaeryn clenched his teeth as he came back up with the box.

"This is the main drop," he heard Terry whisper. "They have another one at Radnor Park, but they stopped using that after we found it. I'll show you the doctor's personal one later. I haven't been around lately, and I don't know the safest time to look at it."

Terry did not act nervous or under constraint, and there was no sign that he was giving information against his will. Jaeryn looked down at the Webley in his hands and clenched it tightly. A sick feeling grew in the pit of his stomach as Terry and the other man turned to go. The little man looked about him, and as he turned his head,

537

Jaeryn recognized Hugh.

They disappeared, and Jaeryn remained crouched at the corner of the church, sore at heart. He must get word to Fenton before the man put something into the drop that no one else should see. Scrambling up, he kept his gun at the ready and he looked over his shoulder more than once on his way home. He couldn't remove the drops; it would give away the fact that he had overheard them. But in the morning, he would get the truth of the matter, whether Terry wanted to see him or not.

At dawn, when Jaeryn parked his car at the side of the road and waited, no Terry cycled by. After waiting long past the usual time, he drove up to the house. He pounded long on the front door. When no one answered, he peeked into the dusty windows. The trashed belongings were gone. There was no trace that anyone had ever lived there.

* * *

As Saturday progressed, Jaeryn wondered uneasily at the absence of any message from Ben. Dorroll would have to make some kind of report to Ryson, but after that, it seemed reasonable to expect a phone call telling which train he was on. Jaeryn secured a timetable in the course of the morning and looked up the possible trains from London that Ben might take. The earliest would have him in town around five and the latest by one in the morning. He rearranged his schedule to make sure he would be home at the various arrival times, in case Ben called when he reached Folkestone. The first train came and went with no word.

Fortunately, a phone conversation with Charlotte gave him something else to think about. She asked when the evidence would come forward, and Jaeryn told her the coroner's report was scheduled for Monday. He and Erin would both have to be there.

It felt odd exchanging commonplace chat with her after all they had been through, but Charlotte was pleasant to talk to, and Jaeryn knew how to put on the extra polish when it was most beneficial. He asked her how they were all managing, and Charlotte said Edmond had been a polite host thus far. He seemed quite affectionate toward Alisa, and though he was shy and often disappeared to be alone, he did not refuse to keep them company.

"Did you know I saw Terry this morning?" Charlotte asked.

"You did?" Jaeryn sat up, alert. "What was he doing?"

"He called at the house to talk to me. He said he had borrowed Alisa's house Wednesday night for Starlin because he had been drinking and needed a place to sleep it off. He would have told me sooner, but he didn't think it was right to disturb me yesterday. He didn't say a thing about why, but he seemed nervous and wanted to make sure we wouldn't mind."

"That's odd." What had he been doing with Starlin only a few hours after he heard about Pearl? Starlin said he had gone Thursday to see Terry, but the boy had made no mention of Wednesday.

"He didn't say a thing about Pearlie when we talked, and he seemed unlike himself."

"That's hardly unexpected. I don't think he's up to cracking jokes at present."

"No, I mean, he looked—I had never seen him like that before. He looked resentful, somehow, and angry. There wasn't a trace of the Terry I knew in his face. I asked him to come inside, but he wouldn't, and when I asked him if he was coming back, he didn't give me a straight answer."

"He's left the place where he was living," said Jaeryn, "and he won't talk to me. If you see him again, please tell him to call me. Or better yet, keep him there and give me a call so I can come down."

"I'll try. I hope you'll find him; he looked like he wasn't fit to take care of himself."

Jaeryn looked over his evening calls after he said goodbye. He hurried through them as swiftly as decency allowed to make it home in time for the next train from London. It came and went without a word from Ben. He decided that it might be prudent to catch some sleep before the one o' clock and stretched out on the couch with his pocket watch clasped in one hand.

He woke with a vague sense that much time had passed. Gray dawn flooded through the uncurtained window. Wonderingly, he opened the watch cover and saw the clock hands pointing to half past six. What had happened? Had he slept through the ringing of the phone—or had Ben not come? No doubt the poor fellow had tried to call and then put up in a hotel for the night. Confound it all. That hadn't been the arrival he had hoped to give him. But when he inquired, the operator had no messages for him, and Jaeryn was forced to conclude that none had come.

Impatiently, he washed, dressed, and ate a cold breakfast. In an hour or so the skies turned an ominous black, and the rain poured down in torrents. In spite of the weather, he made an effort and went to church. None of the Dorrolls were there, but there was evidence of a visit from Terry by way of a flower placed on Pearlie's grave, rapidly turning into a sodden heap. Goodness knew where he had laid his hands on a flower in this downpour.

The whole service was lost on Jaeryn, and he ducked out in embarrassment when he realized he hadn't even stood for the singing or the prayers. As he opened his front door, he heard the end of a telephone ring. Not bothering to close the door, he ran to the consulting room and leaped over the remaining space to his desk. Breathlessly, he picked up the ear piece.

"Graham."

"Hello." His heart sank when he did not recognize the voice. It was weary and hesitant.

"I'm in London, and I need some help. I thought you might be out of church by this time."

Jaeryn breathed a sigh of relief. It *was* Ben, and at long last, he was home again.

Chapter Thirty
Allies Turn to Adversaries

Saturday morning turned to afternoon as Ben left Patrick in Dublin, crossed the Irish Sea, and landed in Liverpool. He had secured a train ticket to London and was now sitting on a third-class bench, listening to freezing sleet crackle against the glass.

The moment he set foot on British soil, the anticipation of the threat against him returned in full force. But because he had kept the exact time of his return uncertain, he had a good chance of warning Jaeryn before anything happened. Until he got to Folkestone, he would focus on relating his news to Ryson and try to keep his mind off fears that might not be realized.

He was glad to be back. He could see Alisa as her brother-in-law with no pretense to keep up. He and Jaeryn were on friendlier terms now, which would make life a deal easier. Terry was out of the hospital, and Starlin would be driving his automobile. Soon he would be home with the people he loved, and that was all that mattered.

The train slowed down, and he was off as soon as it braked to a halt. He wanted to confront his father with what Alex York had found, and he could not stand to wait any longer. At the telegraph office, he asked to look at a street map. The man obligingly provided him with one, and he studied the streets until he had a fair idea how to get to his father, and then to Ryson. Back in the street, the wind nipped him mercilessly, playing about his chapped face and hands. The sky looked ominous, but fortunately, the rain held off for a brief while. Soon his task in London would be over, and then—then only a few miles of rail to be got over before Folkestone and home.

At length, he reached his father's door, but the maid informed him that Mr. Matthew Dorroll was not at home.

Ben felt a stab of disappointment. "When is he returning?"

"Day after tomorrow. He's in Ramsgate right now." The maid barely finished her response before she shut the door with a shiver because of the cold. He resigned himself to the delay and continued on his way.

Nothing had changed in the neighborhood of Ryson's office. In spite of everything that had happened, Ben felt as if no time had passed since his leaving. When he opened the door to the glass warehouse, he found Jeremy engaged in perusing a dog-eared stack of magazines as if he had nothing in the world to worry about except waiting for customers.

"Well, look who's here." Jeremy brought his chair legs down to the floor with a bang. "Glad you made it back all right. Did you come for Ryson? He nearly had a nervous conniption when you didn't telegraph your exact plans."

"I had a good reason. Is he available?" Ben asked quietly.

Jeremy nodded. "Always for you, doctor. Same door as usual." This time, however, Jeremy followed him down the hall and opened the door for him. Jeremy's gaze met Ryson's, and he shook his head ever so slightly. Ryson nodded in return. Ben wondered why.

Ryson also acted out of the ordinary. After looking up, his gaze remained fixed on Ben's face for a long moment, and he offered his hand. "I'm glad you agreed to come. We won't forget your services to us."

Evidently, he was more important than he had been before, though he couldn't imagine why. Ben shook Ryson's hand. "I'm glad you let me return, sir."

Ryson motioned him to a seat. "You deceived me when you didn't tell me about Graham's involvement with the note. I've decided to overlook it since I think you were being used without knowing it. You aren't supposed to cover for other people's mistakes. I need your word that you won't do so from this time forward."

A flicker of doubt ran through him. "Do you mean mistakes

against the law, sir, or all mistakes?"

"I mean against the law or against my orders."

There was no earthly reason to deny him his request. "Yes, sir."

"Good, then." Ryson continued a sharp inspection of his face. "You'll have a lot of work to do. It's a risk to have you back again after you've been gone for two months, but I'm willing to take it. I hope you'll keep a level head and attend to your responsibilities after all that's happened."

There it was again—the hint that something was not quite right and they were keeping it from him. The fears that had nagged at his mind since the threat a few days before sharpened to a fever pitch. "Are you trying to tell me something?"

"Nothing at all," Ryson said hastily. "I merely wondered if you knew—never mind. We'll hear about your affairs first, and then we'll fill you in on ours. York told me you found some things while you were in America concerning our work here."

"I made the acquaintance of a man that Fenton told me about. His name is Creswick, and he's a bank director in Richmond. He's involved in distributing anti-war propaganda, and he recently dissolved a joint bank account with Gilbert Emmerson. Jaeryn and I have a letter saying as much in our possession."

Ben took the note he had decoded from York's book and handed it over. Ryson put on his glasses and read it carefully through. "York mentions a Dorroll here," he remarked.

"My father. I have yet to speak to him about it; he's in Ramsgate on business."

"Do it soon. It would be disastrous if this is true, considering Matthew Dorroll's current involvement in our international war relations. What else did you discover?"

"Creswick tampered with my correspondence to my mother. He also writes to Fenton, and somehow, he had an unmailed letter from my brother to me in his possession."

Ryson looked thoughtful. "That's singular. And all this means what?"

Ben doubted that he should pass along theories. Ryson hated theories without ample substantiation, but that was all he had to offer at present. "Perhaps—"

"Perhaps what?" Ryson never picked up on half-sentences.

"It is only conjecture, but it seems likely that Creswick supports German interests."

"You jump forward too fast, Doctor Dorroll. I've never heard of the man, and I could think of an infinite number of possibilities, none of which include him being a German subversive. You need to look into this more before we make any conclusions."

It was about the response he had expected, and Ben quickly moved on. "I think perhaps I have more proof, sir. Fenton sent this to me while I was away." He pulled out the thin box and handed over the scrap of paper that Fenton had deemed so essential. Ryson scrutinized it carefully, along with the translation York had written down. His pale eyes kindled with pleasure, like a hawk scenting its prey.

"Why does he not want Jaeryn to know about it?" Ben asked.

Ryson frowned in concentration. "He told you. In the interests of the British Empire, and for once he speaks the truth. You're to keep this to yourself. It sounds as if Creswick is an American front for Emmerson's financial transactions. I like rooting out middle men. Where did Fenton get this?"

"Somewhere in Folkestone, I think."

"Well, if he set you on the track, then he holds the answers. You'll be able to ask him in person later. Don't let him keep his knowledge from you. He's rather wearing with his penchant for secrecy and power. Were he a different kind of man, I would have him put away, but he doesn't want the sort of power that will damage my interests, so I let him be useful."

"If you have trouble getting information from him, sir, then I doubt he will give it to me. I have even less influence with him than you do."

"That's your concern, isn't it?" Ryson handed the papers back with unruffled composure. "At any rate, you must try."

Ben sighed and acquiesced. "I'll try to get something out of him, but if I can't, perhaps York will find what we need. He told me he would look into it."

"One way or the other, so long as you get your information soon. The point is, doctor, we're running out of time." For one moment the aloof mask slipped, and Ben saw the ardent passion that consumed the man in front of him. "With Russia in turmoil, we can no longer depend on the invincibility of the Allied cause. We're weakening from without, and we cannot stand by and allow treachery from within. Your task is a pressing one, and we need results soon."

"I think our interest in finishing is mutual. I doubt I have much time to work with, either."

Ryson glanced at him sharply. "What do you mean by that?"

Ben dug up the threats from his jacket pocket where he had put them to be ready at hand in their conversation. The gray-haired government official glanced over them, hesitated, and frowned.

"I wish I had known this sooner; I might have looked for someone else after all. But it can't be helped, and I can't think of any one of you that isn't dispensable if worse comes to worst." Then understanding dawned in his eyes, and he handed them back. "Perhaps it is a personal threat to you and yours and not to our work at all. I've known family members done away with before in the hopes of hampering an agent. Tell me, are you afraid?"

He had thought about the question so many times, and every time, there was an emptiness where he was concerned, but a stabbing fear when he thought of the people for whom he was responsible. "I am afraid that I will bring danger to others. But I am not afraid of dying for myself."

"Fair enough. Be sure that your concern for others doesn't cause you to pull back. Whatever happens, we want your fullest attention and commitment."

Ben clenched his hands. "I won't pull back on my own account. But I will look out for those who belong to me."

Ryson did not grow angry with him, and he wondered at it. "Doctor, I have some things to tell you before I send you back home. To begin, I assume Jaeryn Graham informed you he is no longer involved with us."

The unexpected blow snatched away the last vestige of relief he had clung to. "You're not serious. I thought—he wrote and asked me to come and paid for my passage back."

Ryson gave a short, sharp laugh. "Oh, he's still in Folkestone, but he isn't there under our sanction. After I learned that he had persisted in communicating with Speyer, I told him he was finished. It proved to be a wise decision. We've been tipped off by a reliable source that he is turning to his own interests."

"I'm sure he's loyal. He never showed himself otherwise when I—" Ben trailed off, and Ryson pounced on his hesitation.

"Never showed himself otherwise? Not once?"

"Ann Meikle did tell me to beware of him when I first came to Folkestone. Jaeryn said it was a grudge, but in the same breath he practically told me not to trust him. I forgot it even happened."

545

The cold gray eyes kindled with triumph. "I'm glad to find you aren't completely oblivious. When I told Jaeryn Graham not to meddle with Speyer this summer, he wasn't loyal enough to obey orders. I've already received news that he's been hindering a police investigation for his own ends, and he expressly disobeyed my recommendation to leave the area, though I warned him he would be outside our protection if he stayed."

Ben swallowed back the annoyance that rankled in him. "In the name of justice and common sense, sir, what was wrong with looking into Speyer? Surely Jaeryn had to see if he was doing damage to our concerns here, especially with Speyer's connections to King. He didn't want us to be put in danger needlessly by ignoring him."

"I told you to leave him alone, and I expected you to obey that order. Graham drew attention to him, and in so doing, placed Speyer in severe jeopardy of his mission as well as his life." Ryson clenched his fingers as dark warning shadowed his face. "What I am about tell you, you are not to repeat—to *anyone*. Do you understand?"

"Yes, sir." Ben kept his eyes fixed on Ryson's face, wondering what was coming next.

"Nathan Speyer's father lived in England as one of our spies leading up to the war until the Germans tapped him to corrupt our agents in Dover. They used him for several years without our knowledge, but when the war broke out, he was compromised and returned to the court of the Kaiser. We haven't been able to track down the man who replaced him. He had to leave his family behind, and his son is part English and loyal to our cause. King and I trained Nathan and sent him off to his father to take up a position in the German court. He will be able to get more inside information than anyone else we have there, and no one was to know of it."

"You mean you're turning him against his own father?"

So indifferent, those gray eyes in front of him—like a reptile. "He's a double agent. He'll be feeding both sides information, and he'll have to be skillful at it. But his father sent for him and offered a position. We couldn't pass up on the opportunity. Before he left, Nathan told us that King had offered him an incentive to feed us false information. King claims he was only testing the young man's loyalties. We have no evidence against his claim, and for all we know, he may be sincere. Nathan refused his offer, and he went to Germany."

So that was Nathan's secret and his connection to King. "He

must be capable for you to place him so high."

"He is, but only just. We've prepared him well, but he'll be lied to from all sides. I told him I expected and demanded success by whatever means necessary, and he was prepared to follow through, wherever his commission took him. I hope you'll take a lesson from him and do the same."

"I will certainly try my hardest, sir," Ben returned quietly. "But I still don't understand what damage Jaeryn did him."

"After Ann Meikle spread her rumors, none of our agents would trust Speyer. That damaged his usefulness in Germany—we hope only temporarily. We've only heard from him once since he went to the continent, and that was in September. He told us it wouldn't be safe for him to send messages for a while yet to come. And it was all Jaeryn Graham's fault that this happened."

"He said he was trying to keep the people underneath him safe. Was he lying? Do you suspect him of turning to the German side?"

"Not quite. We're working up another line of investigation on him that will explain matters. It has nothing to do with you, but it will prove his disloyalty if we find our suspicions are correct. You are not to place any trust in him at present."

Ben closed his eyes, trying to shut out the inevitable. "Are you saying I can't work with him at all?"

"Absolutely. All tangible evidence he has must be confiscated as soon as you arrive, and you are to keep him at arm's length in all of your affairs. If he gives you trouble, I expect you to tell us, and we'll see he's gotten out of your way. Keep a sharp eye out for anything untoward in his behavior. Make sure he isn't meddling in your affairs and taking advantage of your inexperience."

Ben gripped the edge of Ryson's desk to steady himself. Surely this could not be happening. He had relied on the assurance that he would have Jaeryn's advice, and now that too was being taken from him. Why hadn't the Irishman written the truth? "I can't turn against him."

Ryson showed no sign of softening. "Do not let personal feelings hold you back from your duty. If he is subversive to the government, then he must be taken in."

He did not know how to respond. Everything in him rose up against Ryson's command. Ryson saw his reluctance and did not wait for his response. "The choice is not yours to make, doctor. You are under authority, please remember, and while you are instrumental in solving this case, you are not in charge of it."

Ben flushed. "I'm an independent agent."

"We chose you because we know you can deliver. You'll be getting an increase in your pay for what we're asking; in fact, you'll be getting paid the same as Graham was when he first came here. You're not in charge of anyone, so you don't have any responsibilities other than what you had before. You have the connections we need both to your father and to Graham, so we're prepared to use you if you're willing to cooperate with us."

He sat dumbly, shaking his head. Ryson's eyes snapped. "We have not invested in you for six months to receive nothing in return. Come, doctor, we have full confidence in you. That's why I let you come back in the first place."

The clock hands ticked on. Ben argued as long as he dared, long enough to miss the first evening train, until he sensed Ryson's patience wearing thin. But he could neither persuade him to take Jaeryn back nor get out of the command to confiscate the evidence Jaeryn had worked so hard to gather. He didn't dare press too far. Stubbornness would merely put him in a worse place than before. Now, if he committed an irretrievable blunder, Jaeryn could not get him out of it. No one could.

At length, Ryson told him the conversation was finished. "I have nothing more to say to you. I've told you what you must do, and if you persist in disliking it, you'll do more damage to both yourself and Graham. I've waited a long time for you to come back and delayed my own deadlines in doing so. I suggest you start doing the work I hired you for."

Ben rose from his chair and walked out, steadily ignoring Jeremy's attempts to attract his attention. Once out of Ryson's hearing, he muttered, "I will not take part in turning him in."

Jeremy heard him. But it was none of Jeremy's business, so he didn't bother to concern himself with it.

The next train left at quarter after eight, and Ben set out for the station. There was no need to go until it was closer to the time, but he had nothing better to do. The chill November air bit a frosty red into his cheeks, and his knuckles dried and cracked from the keen wind. He was too dazed to care.

A tug at his sleeve interrupted his thoughts, and Ben looked down to see a small boy offering him a grimy news sheet. "You want a paper, mister?"

"No, thank you."

"Please, mister. It's my last one." The boy shoved it closer and tried to force it into his hand.

"I'm sorry. I can't buy it from you." He gave it back and pushed his way through the crowd. There was a long line before him when he went up to get his ticket, and even more gathered to catch the best train out. When he came up to the window, the man gave him the ticket and told him the price. But when he reached for his wallet, it was not in his pocket, and though he made a frantic search under the man's skeptical eyes, it did not turn up.

"Blast," he whispered. A pickpocket in the crush of the crowd. Of all the awful, awful luck. He had saved plenty to get him to Folkestone before it was all stolen. Patrick had even offered him a loan, and he hadn't taken it because he hadn't needed it. And now he didn't even have enough for a train ticket.

He gave the ticket back and stood uncertainly, trying to decide what to do. An evil twinkle from Terry's sapphire, which he had kept on his finger during his travels, attracted his attention. For one moment he indulged the temptation. It would fetch a good price at a pawn shop. Ben took it off and twisted it round in his fingers. It was then that he saw again the engraving on the inside. *Always Remember.* He had forgotten it was there. No, he couldn't pawn it. It wasn't his to sell, and it meant something important to Terry that he didn't know about yet.

He would get a loan from Ryson for the train home. As awful as the option was, his father was out of town, and he didn't know anyone else in London. But when he reached the glass warehouse, the doors were locked, and he pounded on them to no avail. Surely eight wasn't too late—it couldn't be too late. But the shades were pulled down, and no one came to answer. There were hours scrawled on a scrap of paper on the door, and he saw with dismay that it didn't open until eleven on Monday. With one last, futile effort he tried the door and then resigned himself to the inevitable.

As soon as he reached his father's and persuaded the maid to let him use the telephone, he put in a call to Alisa's house to try to tell Charlotte what was happening. He let it ring for a long time, but there was no answer, and he was forced to hang up. A quarter of an hour later he tried again with the same result, and then he called Jaeryn. The operator told him Jaeryn was out and asked to take a message for him. He did not give one. Jaeryn could not do anything to help him over the phone. By the time he got money, the last train back would reach home after one o'clock. He didn't want midnight explanations and confrontations. Trying for Charlotte one more time, he finally gave it up and asked the maid if she would let him stay the night. She took pity on his plight and went to prepare the room for him. Within an hour he had eaten what he could, and by ten he was under the sheets in a spare room.

He woke again as the hall clock chimed seven. Lying there idly, he schemed how to bridge the remaining distance between London and home. He could not ask his father for a loan even if he wanted to, nor could he wait for Patrick. There was only one option. He must call Jaeryn again. The thought of asking Jaeryn for a favor after Ryson's orders the previous day sickened him to the teeth. But there was nothing else to do, and as soon as Jaeryn was out of church, he would talk to him.

When the time came for the service to end, he gave the number to the operator. It kept on ringing with no response. He counted up to the seventh ring before he wondered if Jaeryn wasn't in. Perhaps he was—

"Graham."

"Hello?" His voice sounded dreadful. Jaeryn would never recognize it. "Jaeryn, I'm in London and I need some help. I thought you might be out of church by this time. My father is away, and I'm dead broke." He jammed the telephone tightly against his ear to steady it "I don't know how to get home."

The familiar laugh sent shivers down his spine. "Is that all? I thought I had missed your train. I fell asleep before the late one came in last night. Listen, old fellow, I'll come and pick you up. I've bought myself a shiny new auto, and I'd enjoy a run with it."

"You don't have to do that. There must be an easier way."

"It's no trouble. I don't have anything else to do today, and I'd like it. I'm on my way. I only have one errand to run, and then it's straight to London."

"Jaeryn, I have something to tell you."

"Save it until I see you. It'll keep, whatever it is. Your check from Ryson will probably arrive tomorrow, so you'll be in business again soon. Where shall I meet you?"

"Make it the train station. I'm in Kensington."

"Very good. Don't do anything desperate; I'll be there as soon as I can."

Ben heard the click of the other phone and replaced the ear piece in the holder. It would take Jaeryn a couple of hours to drive to London. That was just as well, for he needed time to think about what he would say when they met.

* * *

The sun was on its downward spiral at four when Jaeryn pulled into the train station and looked for a place to park. He scanned up and down the waiting figures, and it didn't take him long to pick out the one he was looking for—brown hair, not too tall, and slightly lost in the crowd. He pulled the car to the curb and turned it off, then got out and waved to attract Ben's attention. He could tell by Ben's expression as he wove his way through the people that Ryson had given him the full particulars of the situation.

Jaeryn put on an air of nonchalance and grinned widely when Ben came up and shook hands with him. "Benjamin Dorroll, you've been gone entirely too long. Come, my car is waiting. I hope you haven't had to wait out here the entire time."

Their breath drifted away in frosty clouds from the cold. Ben shrugged. "It's only been for the last half hour. It wasn't too bad."

"It's starting to snow," Jaeryn protested. "I could have found you just as easily inside. How did Ryson greet you? I hope he didn't bite your head off. In my experience of him, he doesn't like lies directed his way."

"About as pleasant as you would expect." Jaeryn braced himself for what he knew Ben was about to say. "For pity's sake, why didn't you tell me the truth?"

Jaeryn looked away. He hadn't been able to think of any excuse to soften the blatancy of the deceit. "I wanted you back. I didn't think you would come if I told you I wasn't officially part of things anymore."

"This wasn't exactly what I wanted, you know." Ben looked anxious and not a little disappointed, but he did not sound angry. Jaeryn's fears of a disagreement eased into a return of confidence.

"Never mind," he answered cheerfully. "I'll make it up to you, I promise, and you'll do just fine without me technically in charge. I've worked it all out. Even though I'm not officially sanctioned, I can still pursue my own investigations, and we'll use you to cover our working together. We'll have to be cautious so the others don't catch on, but

551

I'm sure we can manage."

Ben slipped into the passenger seat. "If you shouldn't be involved, then I think I'll have to keep you out of it. I'm very sorry, but it's more grave this time if I go against Ryson's orders. You don't have a family to think about if something goes wrong, but I do."

"You won't get in trouble." Jaeryn started the car and pulled out into the meager stream of traffic. "I'll make sure you don't."

Ben looked out the side window. "Ryson told me to make sure you give up all the evidence. If you don't, I am to turn you in. I don't think he's being fair or just to turn you away, but I'll have to think it through, and that's all I can promise you. Until then, I can't even tell you what we talked about. I hope you won't think ill of me for it."

"I don't," Jaeryn returned quietly, deciding to be candid now that Ryson had done more damage than he thought. If only he knew what the man had said to turn Dorroll so firmly against him. "But while you're thinking, consider this: it would be wise to have me on your side and not working against you. You're going to be under intense pressure from fellow agents, London, and the other side. I can hold you steady and help you see clearly. I would not like to be at odds with you after we've worked so closely together."

"Is that—is that a threat?"

It wouldn't do to put him off his ease, or he would never be persuaded. "No. I wouldn't threaten you. I want to move up, and this case will mean a lot of prestige if I solve it myself. It's a risk for me to take it on against Ryson's authority, but if I succeed, they won't care that I went against him. I'm experienced enough to pit myself against the whole lot of you if necessary." Ben remained silent, and Jaeryn softened his tactics. "You're free to choose whichever side you think best, and I won't fault you for it. But decide soon, because we're crumbling even worse than we were before. If you want to salvage anything of the British Secret Service in Folkestone, you'll have to move quickly. We need any evidence we can get. As soon as we have the least proof of your father's involvement and King's, I think we should take it to court."

"Finding evidence will be hard."

"But not impossible. Did you find anything in Virginia that we can use? Fenton thought you would."

"Perhaps. York's looking into it for me to confirm our suspicions."

"Excellent. What did you find?"

Ben shot him a glance, and Jaeryn realized that with their present standing, he wouldn't be able to say.

"Never mind. Of all the infernal luck," he muttered. He had never questioned the fact that Ben would come back and things would be as they were before. He had neglected to factor in Ryson's authoritativeness. Ryson was taking no chances. Ben wouldn't dream of going against the law, and if he were to be persuaded to go against orders, he must be persuaded that it was the moral thing to do.

"I don't think I want to do this," Ben said. "I'm going to tell Ryson to send me somewhere else."

The jerk of the brake was Jaeryn's only indication of dismay. He quickly picked up speed again. "Don't give up yet. You've only just learned about the situation, and you haven't had time to get your bearings. A lot has happened in your absence, and I think you'll want to at least give it a chance."

"I had no idea when I came back that it would be like this, and I don't know what's right. Ryson's giving me your pay now, and I wish I didn't have to take it, but I need it."

Jaeryn clapped a hand on his shoulder. "Think nothing of it. I'm not suffering for cash. Besides, there will be time enough to figure things out after you've gotten all the news. Shall I tell you what we've been doing while you were away?"

"If you wish. Are the others all well? I've been afraid for them; I wasn't sure if they were safe."

Charlotte had not allowed Jaeryn to send a telegram about Pearlie. She told him with firm decision that she intended to tell Ben herself, and she had sent a telegram the same day, unaware that he wasn't in America anymore. Jaeryn debated between preparing him for what was coming and saying nothing about it. He decided against it. Ben was quick to take a hint, and if he thought something was wrong, he would not rest until he knew. Best to say nothing about it and let Charlotte break it to him how she liked.

"All well. They'll be happy to see you when you come."

"I'm glad," Ben said, and some of the tension in his face eased. "We'll have to watch. I got a threat just before I sailed saying that if I came back, the people here wouldn't be safe. I was so afraid."

Jaeryn repented of the lie when he saw the keen relief and tried to bring back a little of the doubt. "That's hardly surprising. They'll do their dead-level best to intimidate you, and the threat may be well founded."

"I'm sure it is. They already showed they meant it when they tried to strangle you."

"Who told you about that?"

"Charlotte. And I can still see the bruises on your neck."

Jaeryn laughed. "I didn't think you'd notice. Meddling woman, she shouldn't have mentioned it. I have people looking out for me, and you should, too. Did Ryson offer official protection?"

"No. He's too upset to do that at present. But he didn't mention it even when I told him of the renewed threats, and that was before we disagreed. We'll look after everybody between us now that we both know."

"We will indeed." But it was too late for one of them. "Was Charlotte worried that I'm late getting home?"

"Not particularly, as I didn't tell her you were coming. I didn't know for sure myself until Wednesday. I'll take you over as soon as we're home."

Ben frowned in confusion. "I told you both I was coming. I telegraphed from Baltimore and again in London, and I tried to call Alisa's last night, but the phone wouldn't go through."

"Well, we never got them. Ann Meikle's probably at the bottom of that, being in charge of the post. And you wouldn't have gotten through by phone because they aren't at Alisa's any longer. Your brother came back, and he took them in at his place."

More of the tension drained away, and a real smile crept over Ben's face this time. "Did he? I'm glad. What do you know of his involvement? Does he seem to be on our side or theirs?"

"Neither, that we've been able to find. There's a rift between Peters and I at present, which is why we need you. For one thing, you're Edmond's brother, and for another, Peters won't mind talking to you. But you must be tired, and we won't go into all that now. Tell me about your trip. I've been waiting to hear."

Jaeryn used his tact to the utmost in distracting Ben from current difficulties while they drove. There would be time later to force his hand, and Ben wouldn't be difficult to manage once he felt secure in their friendship. Ben acted differently than he had in the spring—the dogged self-concealment that had characterized him before his trip to America was gone, replaced by a worried insecurity. Jaeryn wasn't surprised at the difference. Ben was the sort who wanted to hold both law and friendship inviolable, and he had come to a crossroads between the two.

Minute by minute they ate up the distance between London and Folkestone. It was dark when they entered Tontine Street. Jaeryn pulled into his driveway and stretched his shoulders luxuriously. "I'll call Charlotte to tell her you're here. Can't show up with you in tow and give the poor lady no warning."

Ben grabbed his medical bag from the back seat and followed him to the house. "Thank you, Jaeryn, for picking me up. It's good to be back."

Jaeryn inserted the key in the lock and opened the door. "It was no trouble; I enjoyed it immensely. I'll drive you over in five minutes if you can bear to wait that long."

A smile played around the corners of Ben's mouth. "I suppose I'll have to."

"It's been a long time since I've seen you here," Jaeryn remarked as he flipped on the lights and opened up the consulting room.

"When was the last time?"

"End of August." Jaeryn looked sideways at him to see if he recalled it.

Ben chuckled. "That doesn't bring back particularly good memories."

"A self-sufficient little demigod, I called you. Anyway, no need to remember all that. I know you better now." Jaeryn picked up the phone and told the operator to ring up the Emmerson estate. While he talked, he could see Ben listening eagerly to catch what Charlotte was saying.

"Mrs. Dailey? I hope you don't object if I stop by this evening. I have someone for you, and I think you'll like him. Yes, he came into London last night. Don't fault him for not telling you; he tried several times, but it didn't get through. No, don't talk to him now. I'll bring him straight over."

"There." He dropped the phone back and picked up the messages in the hall that had been pushed through the door slot. There was nothing urgent, so he left them all on the desk to attend to later. "I'll take you over to say hello. I'm sure Edmond will offer you a room when he meets you, but under present circumstances, and especially with your name change, it wouldn't be a good idea for you to live with him. You're welcome to put up with me while you're here. You and Charlotte can have the guest room."

"It's very kind of you, but I'd rather rent Copt Point if it's still open. Or has someone taken it?"

He had forgotten that Ben didn't know what had happened there. It wouldn't be long before he found out, and Jaeryn wondered how he would take it. "They're still open. In fact, telephones are going in now, which is much better for the lodgers than before."

"Oh? What caused that change?"

"A lot has happened this month. I'll tell you about it later."

Jaeryn decided to be kind and drive faster than he normally approved of after dark. When they reached the Emmerson estate, he debated whether or not to leave them alone. Ben was already out and hurrying up the steps before he stopped the car. In the end, his curiosity got the better of him, and he followed behind. The heavy oak doors opened as Charlotte ran out, and Ben caught her up and kissed her until her cheeks turned pink.

"Don't," she gasped, as soon as she could get a breath in edgewise. "Doctor Graham is here."

"And what if he is?" Ben teased, snatching another one. "He isn't the one who had to miss you for two months."

"I'm so happy you're back safely. He didn't tell me you were coming. He keeps too many secrets." She threw a reproachful glance at Jaeryn, but Jaeryn knew she didn't really mean it. He stood back, pleased to see them together again, and just a little envious of the spot she had in Ben's confidence.

"Never mind. We'll get them out of him between us. He can't keep them forever." Ben laughed and kissed her again, then took her hand and led her up to the house. "I thought I would never get home. I didn't hear from you, and I was worried something had happened to you while I was away. But here you are, safe and sound, and no reason to have worried after all. I am glad of it."

Charlotte glanced back with a questioning look, and Jaeryn shook his head in the negative. She pulled back and tried to keep Ben from going in, but Alisa appeared on the steps, and they could see Edmond waiting further back in the hall.

Jaeryn hadn't seen much of Alisa since she'd left her house. He could tell the difference between the simple country girl and the mistress of an English estate. She was just as quiet and timid as before, but now she had a maid to pin her hair up for her, and the skirt and shirtwaist she wore were unquestionably made by a dressmaker. Evidently, her husband was providing well for her comfort, and though her happiness was on fragile ground, Jaeryn hoped it would turn out well in the end.

Alisa looked shyly up at Ben from under her soft lashes, and he started to offer his hand, then leaned in and hugged her. He wasn't ready for Edmond, though, and Jaeryn berated himself for not preparing him better. Ben couldn't disguise the look of shock when he saw his brother's face and the purple scars that covered it.

"Behold the handiwork of the Germans," Edmond said grimly, coming forward and offering his hand.

"I'm so sorry."

"Everybody is. Unfortunately, that's not a remedy for the situation. But you weren't made for such misfortunes, thank goodness. What brought you back to England, little brother? I thought Doctor Graham said you had gone away for good."

Ben's shoulders tensed with nervousness. "Not for good. Just for a visit home."

"Really? I thought you had gone back to find work in Richmond. I must have gotten that wrong."

Ben glanced at Jaeryn, who gave the best evasion he could think of. "I must have given the wrong impression when we talked the first time."

"Well, it's good to see you." Edmond's eyes glittered as he looked from Ben to Jaeryn. "We'll have to talk about your plans later; I should like to hear more of them. Charlotte's been staying here, and until you have another place lined up, you're welcome to as well."

"Thank you. I'm much obliged, but I won't trouble you for long. Jaeryn tells me Copt Point is still empty." Even as he spoke, Ben was hardly paying attention. He looked around as if he couldn't find something that he wanted. Jaeryn and Charlotte both knew what it was.

"Come away with me," Charlotte said, tugging at his elbow.

"Where's Pearlie?"

"I'll tell you. Please come."

"Why? What's wrong?" He pulled out of Charlotte's arm and looked at each face in turn.

Charlotte tried once more to lead him away, and then when he would not come, she attempted to satisfy him with part of it. "We couldn't find her on Monday night. She was gone for a very long time, and—I wish you would come away with me."

"No." He cupped her chin in his hand and lifted her face until she would look at him. In spite of his calm tone, Jaeryn detected fear underneath. "You can tell me where she is. It's all right. Jaeryn told me you were all right."

Charlotte threw a nervous glance to Jaeryn. "I'm afraid it isn't, darling," she said. "I asked him to let me be the first to tell you. Pearlie isn't coming back. Doctor Graham looked so long for her, but when he found her, she was dead—murdered. We buried her Friday morning. I'm so, so sorry." Her voice broke, and she swallowed and finished with a great effort. "I wish you could have come back—in time."

Jaeryn found his hands were clenched without exactly knowing why. Only a rapid flicker of Ben's eyes showed how hard he was trying to accept Charlotte's news. In the silence, a quiver crossed Alisa's face, and Edmond looked apprehensive. Jaeryn felt guilt so intense that it physically hurt. Was it really worth it, what he was going to ask Ben to do, in the face of such injustice? They deserved resolution, and Ben needed it most of all, and here he was going to ask him to delay the investigation by any means he could. There was no other option. He had hidden evidence, and he didn't want to go to jail for it. Besides, the murderer, once they found out who it was, needed to go to trial for something much larger than murder, and they could only prove the other thing if they had more time.

"I wish I could have been there too," Ben said at length. Jaeryn could hardly hear the words when they were spoken.

"Please come away, darling. I'll tell you all about it." Charlotte pulled him toward the double doors, and this time he did not resist her. He did not look back when the servant closed the doors behind them.

Edmond drew a sigh of relief. "He took the news better than I thought he would. We'll see that he's all right, doctor. Thank you for bringing him from London. I would have been happy to send someone if it had been too inconvenient for you."

Jaeryn unclenched his hands as the tension drained away. "It wasn't. I knew you wouldn't mind, but I wanted to see him myself before he came back. The inquest is tomorrow at two if he asks, but I hope he won't try to come. I'm sure it would be better if he stayed away. I won't trespass on you any longer; send me word if you need anything."

"We will. Alisa tells me he's the steady sort, though, so I'm sure he'll be all right. Good night, doctor."

Later that evening, Jaeryn sat alone in the living room with his hands clasped over his knees. He would have to be on the alert in the morning. After all, the bobbies thought the tampered evidence had been stolen by the murderer, and he didn't want them to suspect otherwise. No matter what happened, he had been justified in taking the knife. Terry was innocent.

Still, it would be hard for Ben to swallow if he thought his former associate was thwarting justice, and Charlotte wasn't likely to hide her suspicions. The way of the transgressor was hard indeed, he thought dully.

But he wasn't a transgressor. He would stand on that, let all the agents of Folkestone say otherwise. He had been fair, and he had given much, and he would stick to his story. Jaeryn hoped to his very soul that Ben would not join the others in turning against him.

* * *

"Dorroll, I'm sorry it happened." Jaeryn sat, his fingers tapping in an absent-minded frenzy on his desk.

"I wish I hadn't neglected her so much."

Jaeryn drew his eyebrows together. "She was not neglected."

"Do you really believe that?" Ben stood up and paced the floor of the consulting room to keep down the rising anguish. "I don't."

"She's happy now, and she was happy while she was here. I saw her pretty often; she was good friends with Alisa, and most times Terry was there too. She was content."

Ben gestured angrily. "She should have been happier than that. You don't understand, Jaeryn. I was the only one she had to love her, but I made a fine job of ignoring her, and this is what came of it. Well, there was Terry, I suppose. And that only made it worse when I wouldn't let her have him. Now she's gone, and he must be beside himself."

"He is," Jaeryn admitted.

"How did he take it when he found out?"

"Badly. I haven't seen him to talk to since last Wednesday. He's come around once or twice to a couple of us and acted very strangely. I'm worried for him."

Four steps to the window, four steps back. One step at a time to hold back despair. "If I had taken her with me, then she might be safe now. Or if I had never brought her here, she wouldn't have met Terry, and neither of them would have had to go through this."

He saw Jaeryn wince. "Stop, for the love of heaven. You did the best you could, and you can't fault yourself for anything beyond that. None of us knew she would be a target."

Ben stopped at the window, and his eyes glazed over with his own private pain. "Pearlie is dead," he whispered again as if hearing the words might convince him of their reality.

He started when Jaeryn touched his shoulder. "I have to go to the inquest now. I'm closing up, but you can stay here as long as you like. Make sure to lock up when you leave. Don't answer any calls; just let the operator take messages."

Ben heard the words from far away. When Jaeryn went out and closed the door, he stood still for a long time. He had promised Charlotte that he would not be gone long, but it penetrated his mind that this was Pearlie's inquest he was missing, and he ought to go to it. He didn't know where it was, so he set out and asked a passerby if they knew anything about it. Apparently, the business had created a mild stir—when he had come seven months ago, he little knew his sister's murder would be common gossip—and they directed him to the building where it was held.

Jaeryn was there to give evidence, as was Erin Reinhardt. Ben had participated in one or two inquests in America, but this was like nothing he had seen before. The authorities merely established who Pearl was and the cause of her death. He saw relief spreading across Jaeryn's face as the cross-questioning progressed.

When it was over, with nothing said that he had not known before, he went back to the clinic to confiscate Jaeryn's pile of evidence. Now he understood what Ryson had meant when he urged him to keep on working no matter what happened. Ryson had known about Pearlie's death, and Jeremy had known, and Jaeryn too, and none of them had been willing to tell him. In spite of the conflicts between them, they all had one thing in common: they wanted him to push through the grief so they wouldn't lose any time. It stung him, but he hoped it wouldn't overcome him.

Someone was in the waiting room when he opened the front door. He had forgotten to lock up. There was no reason why he shouldn't offer to help, he decided, though technically he wasn't Jaeryn's assistant at present. He had always assumed they would resume their former relations once they were back together, but that was when he had assumed everything would be as it was before.

It was Fenton, sitting erect in one of the wooden chairs. Ben hadn't seen him since the end of August, but he possessed the same meticulous care for his appearance, the same reticent expression in the eyes, the same quiet slipping in when he wanted to see people.

"Hello, doctor. I'm glad you're back again." Fenton offered his hand. Ben took it hesitantly, but there was only an honest handshake—nothing to be afraid of.

"Why did you come to see me?" he asked.

"Just to tell you that I'm available if you need my services for anything. I hear we're done with Jaeryn Graham, so I can devote my entire attention to your interests if you like."

At least he knew that wasn't the truth. Ryson said Fenton had many interests, so he couldn't possibly offer his full attention. "No, thank you. I don't think I need anything at present."

"Oh, you will, I'm sure. And besides, I've come to tell you something."

"I don't have any money."

"I'll tell you anyway. Since you're not working with Jaeryn Graham anymore, you might be interested to know that I've found out his real name. You can pay me later."

Ben drew in his breath. That was what Ryson wanted him to look out for. He hadn't expected an opportunity to find out so soon. And he wasn't ready yet. Charlotte had told him everything Jaeryn had done for them after Pearlie's death. He had been kind to look out for them, and Ben hadn't yet decided which direction he was going to take in all this.

"Thank you, but I'd rather have you take your information straight to London if you need to tell someone. I don't think I want to find out through you."

Fenton's eyes turned into slits of thwarted malice. "You're making a mistake."

Ben spoke with firm decision. "I've made mistakes with you before. I'll come to you later if I want the information."

"I'll only offer once."

He thought he heard the click of the latch, but when he glanced out at the hall, no one was there. His hand reached out and gripped his revolver, and one of his fingers softly rested near the trigger. "I don't want it. He's treated me fairly thus far, and I'll do the same for him."

Fenton crushed his hope. "He hasn't treated you fairly enough for you to feel compunction over exposing him. A few smooth words come easily to him. Everything he's done is within his own interests.

You would do well to accept my help. You're going to need it."

"I don't like the way you do things."

"Well then, I'll tell you something else and see how you like it."
Fenton was still just as smooth, just as collected, but a keen barb lay
under his words this time. "Your sister, the one that was murdered. If
you hadn't come back, it wouldn't have happened. She was already in
danger, but your sailing from Baltimore tipped the scales completely
against her."

His mouth went dry. "I don't believe you."

"It's not every man who would watch his sister be murdered so
he can pick up his work again. Since you were willing to go so far, you
would do well not to refuse crucial information."

The words shook him, but he held fast to his resolution. "I won't
do it until I am clear about the right path to choose in all of this."

Fenton's lip curled. "Then you're a fool. You're going to lose on
all counts before this is over, and I can only pity what you'll—"

Jaeryn shoved Ben aside and landed a crushing blow to his ferret's
face. "Get out of this house."

Jaeryn hadn't managed to draw blood, but his blow must have
had some force, for Fenton staggered back against the wall. "I see
you've lost your head too," he said grimly. "I've only spoken the
honest truth."

"You do shame to truth, then," Jaeryn growled. "Some of it
doesn't need to be spoken. If I see your face again, I'll drive more
than my fist into it."

Fenton tried in vain to smooth down his crumpled cuffs. "I take
it that I am dismissed from your services."

"You are correct. You'll never get another penny from me."

"Well, then." He dusted off his sleeves and collected himself. "I'll
take my abilities to those who need them. Good afternoon,
gentlemen."

Ben made a move to follow him, but Jaeryn held him back until
the front door closed. "You don't want to get entangled with him,
trust me."

He pulled away. "Why did you antagonize him? He has
information Ryson told me to look for."

"Not anything you can't find a different way," Jaeryn reassured.
"Fenton only wants to use your own needs to twist you to his ends.
Be wary, and don't let trusting too far be your first mistake. A high
hand is the best way to deal with him."

"I thought implicit trust was vital between allies." Not that he was about to trust Fenton, but the thought of having no one sunk him into utter loneliness.

"That was between us," Jaeryn said grimly. "And we aren't working together at present, are we?"

Ben ignored the question. "What did you hear us say?"

"Only what he said about your sister. It was sheer ignorance on his part. That's not why she died. Terry and I managed to penetrate Emmerson's communications enough to get a telegram back. I don't know how it happened, but Miss Dorroll was the first to see the telegram. She was found with it and killed."

Ben looked at him in wonder. "How did she know about it?"

"I have no idea. But we need to know how she got it. If you want to do something to bring her justice, you might try getting Ann Meikle to tell you if Pearlie stopped by the post office the night she died. That would give us some kind of clue as to what happened. She won't talk to me, and I suspect she's involved in the matter somehow."

"Who can I trust in all of this?"

Jaeryn gave a grim smile. "You can't trust anyone right now. We're all of us playing at cross-purposes, and if you know what's good for you, you'll do the same. Trust Charlotte, trust Alisa, but there's not a person on this earth beside them right now that you can put faith in. Unless," Jaeryn added, raising an eyebrow, "you want to trust me as well."

He wanted to. Oh, how he wanted to. And Jaeryn's green eyes piercing through him understood the struggle, though he did nothing to alleviate it, nothing to swear his loyalty, nothing to try to clear his name. If he would, it would all be easier. But it was as if once brought under suspicion he had given into a reckless urge to win through on his own merit and cunning.

"I don't know what to do with you, Jaeryn. I must go now, and I need to collect any evidence that you have before I leave. That means the camera and the photographs and the letters and any notes you've made."

Jaeryn's eyes glinted sharply. "Rather ironic that you should be confiscating it now when you were reluctant to steal it in the first place." He took a key and unlocked one of his drawers. "I pity you. You're trying to be honest in a very dishonest business, and I think it will go ill for you. But I'm not angry with you. I know you wouldn't do it unless you thought you had to, and you'll keep these things safe." He pulled the things out slowly, glancing through them as he talked. "I can lay my hands on them again if I need to." Jaeryn dumped all the papers and the Brownie on the desk and motioned for Ben to take them.

Ben picked them up one by one. "I wish you wouldn't talk like that. If you do, I'll have to take you at your word and turn you in."

Jaeryn watched him with blank indifference. "I looked after your interests while you were gone. I trust you'll return the favor whenever it's in your power."

"I will. But my power does not extend to breaking the law to further your interests."

"Ryson isn't the law. He's a narrow-minded British bureaucrat. Mind your back taking those things home. I would take a cab if I were you."

He didn't have money for a cab. Edmond had offered him the use of the car, but he didn't know how to drive, and he couldn't bring himself to admit it. Jaeryn read his thought and reached for his wallet, but Ben shook his head. Jaeryn extracted the money anyway and forced it into his hand.

"There's no need to be rash. Take the money and keep these things safe. Don't let your brother know you have them. He'll have to know about your name switch so he doesn't try to introduce you as his brother. If he's involved on your side, he'll be glad to help you, and if he isn't, he still might be shrewd enough to keep your affairs secret. You'll have to do some playing off him, you know, to find out where he stands. It can't be helped."

Ben's voice shook in spite of his efforts to steady it. "It used to be our side and *our* affairs."

"Well, it isn't now. Not yet, anyway." Jaeryn shrugged. "I hope you'll try your hardest to get me back in good standing. Until then we'll have to wait unless you change your mind and let me help you sooner. Oh, I have something else for you." He unlocked another drawer and pulled out more papers. "Here are your passports. I never burned them. Fenton got hold of one when he told Alisa who you were. I wasn't able to learn if he did anything else with it, but at least he gave it back."

"Jaeryn—"

"It's all right," Jaeryn said tightly, looking down at his desk. Ben looked over at his own desk. Jaeryn hadn't changed a thing since the afternoon they argued, as if he had kept hope alive that they would be working together again.

"You've been through a lot," Jaeryn said, sighing heavily as he stood up. "You didn't know what you were coming back to. Take tomorrow to get your affairs in order and reestablish connections. Your responsibility is to see that right prevails. You'll be better off if you decide what that right is to you."

Ben took up his things and left without saying more. He did not want to be at odds with Jaeryn. Neither of them wanted it, nor did he believe Jaeryn was as bad as Ryson suspected. Odd, yes, and secretive, with aims very much for his own advancement; but never treacherous, surely. Otherwise, the hurt would not show so sorely in his face when he talked about them being adversaries.

* * *

As soon as Ben left, Jaeryn closed the empty drawer and sat with his head in his hands. It had been degrading to be stripped of all the things he had worked for. Ryson had done a thorough job turning Ben against him. It was a simple task with his sort, and Jaeryn burned with indignation at the advantage Ryson had taken of dutiful inexperience.

Perhaps his friendship could be played on. Friendship and loyalty meant a lot to Ben. Jaeryn had tried breaking the bonds of conscience before, and though Ben had followed, it had not made him more trusting. Yes, friendship was the best way to play him. And help, Fenton had said—ask him for help, and he would never refuse.

Or perhaps there was another way: the stack of bills that Charlotte had given him to take to Matthew Dorroll. His promise not to touch them was null and void now that her husband was back, and they couldn't be terribly expensive. He would send them on, paid in full, and keep quiet about it until he saw an opportunity to use it to his advantage. Fenton could be hired again to blackmail. Or perhaps being under obligation would be pressure enough for Dailey.

Jaeryn got them out and looked through them, scrawling out checks one by one. Even though it wouldn't yield any immediate benefits, the fact that he was accomplishing something was a small relief. He addressed all of them and gathered them up to take to Ann Meikle's.

A lean, strong figure came out of the post office as Jaeryn made his way up the street. Even from that distance, Jaeryn thought he recognized the bicycle that wove its way through the crowd.

"What can I do for ye, doctor?" Mrs. Meikle asked, when he came up to the counter.

"I came by for my mail. And to mail these, as long as you promise not to meddle with them." He pushed the envelopes toward her.

She threw them into a wooden box behind her counter that contained other letters. "You've got the weight of the world on ye, from all appearances."

"Not quite. Who was it that just came in? I thought I recognized him."

"It was a man from the Emmerson estate, come to collect the Dorrolls' mail."

"Which man?" Jaeryn said sharply.

"Redheaded fellow. I've seen him once or twice. He works there, ye ken."

So it *had* been Terry. They would be able to catch him now; Ben could surely find him. But why had Terry come for the mail? That wasn't on his list of duties that Charlotte had mentioned.

Mrs. Meikle handed over a thick stack of envelopes addressed to him. "Sorry to put an end to yer chat, but I can't stand around all day." Smiling brightly, she waited, hands on the counter. He nodded in cold silence and the shop bell tinkled as he closed the door.

He had to find Terry soon, and he had to figure out a way to persuade Ben to let him stay involved. What a ghastly mess. If he couldn't find someone to give him information soon, he would be working blind. And in his experience, working blind had never turned out well.

Chapter Thirty-One
Not One Gray Among Them

Late Tuesday morning, Ben found Peters overseeing the table preparations for breakfast. When Ben beckoned to him, the butler promptly came out of the dining room and met him in the entrance hall.

"Peters," Ben began, "I assume London has told you of our present circumstances."

"Of course, sir." Peters maintained the same distant and dignified poise as ever. "A pleasure to be working with you again, if I may say so."

"Thank you. I wondered if you could tell me anything I've missed since my going away, especially about my brother."

"Yes, sir. But first, if you have no objection—"

"What?" Ben lowered his voice.

Peters looked cautiously at the servants to see that they were out of earshot. "Well, I stopped communicating anything of a delicate nature to Jaeryn Graham as soon as I heard of his dismissal, but I am concerned that he may have hidden some evidence I gave him."

That was the last thing he needed to hear. He had sent a message to London the night before, asking if Ryson would allow them to work together a little, but if this was true, he couldn't even justify that much contact. "Jaeryn gave everything to me yesterday. I wasn't under the impression he kept anything back."

"Did he give you a slip of notebook paper, sir? I sent it care of Fenton several weeks ago; we often send consequential things to each other that way. It was heavy, like book paper, with writing on it. Doctor Graham pretended not to know anything about it when I asked him, but I'm not sure he was telling the truth."

"What did it say?" Ben asked.

"It looked like French, sir. It had Mr. Emmerson's writing on it. I found the notebook in the upstairs room after your brother came back. I still go there occasionally, though it's harder than it used to be. Doctor Graham gave me a key, and one day I saw the journal on a chair, so I tore off one of the corners and sent it to Fenton. When I asked him about it, he claimed he had delivered it to the proper person."

The box from Fenton. Thank goodness that in this, at least, Jaeryn was in the clear. "Is that what he said? The proper person?"

Peters gave a mechanical nod. "Yes, sir. Those were his exact words."

"As a matter of fact, Fenton sent it off to me. I have it safe in my possession, so you needn't be worried. But I wonder why he gave it to me and not to Jaeryn."

Peters looked gravely surprised. "How strange. I expressly directed him otherwise."

"I was going to ask him about it, but Jaeryn sent him packing, and he may not come back." Ben grimaced at the memory.

"Do you think that was intentional on the doctor's part, sir?" Peters asked.

There they were again, the tendrils of suspicion clinging to Jaeryn that he could not seem to avoid. "I don't know. He's smart enough to do that if he likes, and he certainly had no qualms about giving offense during their conversation. I'll bear it in mind. Have you seen the journal since, Peters?"

"No, sir. Nowhere. I assume your brother has it locked away."

"Any indication of which side he's on? He had to be fairly close to Emmerson to inherit his estate. He must know something."

"He doesn't correspond with anyone suspicious. I've looked through the mail before it goes out, and Ann Meikle reads it as well, but neither of us has found anything thus far." Peters tilted his head and clasped his hands behind his back. "His actions have been very quiet and respectable, nothing to give rise to concern. He lives alone for the most part and doesn't go out if he can help it."

In the two days since his arrival, Ben had found that to be true. "How long has my sister-in-law been reconciled with him?"

The butler paused a moment, casting back the days in his mind. "Only a week, or a little less. He gave her a room in the west wing and a nurse to help with the child."

"And how does he treat her?"

"He seems to be kind, sir. Rather distant, but that's understandable under the circumstances. He told me he doesn't want her to get hurt when he's not himself, so he keeps her away at night. He's been taken more than once with nightmares, and it requires a lot of talking to calm him down again. Some days he'll be angry with everyone, while others he's completely tranquil. It's hard to read exactly which direction he'll take."

Ben nodded. "From the shell shock."

"Yes, sir, but I wouldn't call it shock if I were you. Our government doesn't look too kindly on that diagnosis at present. I only wish they could see the people who have it, and then they might not think it's a mere lack of courage. I was able to observe your brother many times while he was growing up, and he was as brave as they come."

"Was he?" Peters would have seen Edmond before—somehow he had never thought of that. To think that all this time he could have asked him, and he had never taken advantage of it.

A hint of pleasure crossed Peters' face. "Oh, yes, sir. Not steady, but warm-hearted and open-handed. I always liked it when he came. He livened up the old place, and my employer liked him too. I didn't know he was your brother until last night. You had a different name, and I would never have known what it was until you came back and it couldn't be helped."

No, it couldn't be helped. Too many people knew who he was. Before he had been able to keep his identities quietly separated, but there was extra risk as more and more found out, and that shortened the time he had before he must move on from Folkestone.

"Thank you, Peters. Is my brother up yet?" he inquired.

"Yes, sir. I think you'll find him in the library. He likes to be there a good deal, and today he got up earlier than usual."

"I'll go find him, then. Keep me informed about anything else you find. I'm glad you took the paper when you did. It gave us a line on Emmerson's financial transactions for his German work."

"Very good, sir."

Peters went back to his duties, and Ben found the library. He had only been in it twice, but both of the occasions were such memorable ones that he remembered quite well where it was. The door stood ajar, and he pushed it open and saw his brother pacing the floor with a thoughtful frown. Edmond looked up when he entered, and the blue eyes amidst the wrecked face shone clear and bright in greeting.

"Good morning. Not keeping very early hours, are you?"

"Just this morning." Ben slipped in and shut the door behind him. "You aren't either."

A box of cigars sat on the coffee table, and Edmond offered it, but Ben declined. "I'm glad to see you again, little brother. I always wanted the leisure to cross over to America, and behold, when I did have the leisure, you had already come to England. Strange, isn't it, what's happened since we last saw each other? I own a whole library now, for one." He gestured to the rows of books. "Did you know I've read most of these? Peters used to let me in here while our father had long conferences with Emmerson. I grew tired of kicking my feet against the chairs and took to study."

Ben looked up at the tall shelves, with the rolling ladder to reach the highest ones. "I was surprised when I heard Emmerson had left everything to you."

"Oh, I think he always meant to. We saw each other quite often, and he took a fancy to me. My father didn't like me to be far away from him, so he brought me along when I wasn't in school. He must not like you to be far away either."

"Apparently not."

Edmond broke into a fit of coughing and covered his mouth with his hand. When he found his breath again, he said, "What tipped the scales to make you to come here? Mercenary concerns or patriotic?"

"Neither. Both. I thought it was right to come." Ben saw a pitcher on the desk and poured his brother a glass of water. "Why did you pretend you didn't know my reason for being here on Sunday?"

Edmond laughed, and for a moment the quirk showed at the corner of his mouth and made his scars invisible. "Thought I would keep it between us two until I found out exactly what was up. Besides, I didn't know what Charlotte and Alisa knew."

"I see."

A thin gold light filtered through the clerestory windows, and

Edmond glanced out on the quiet landscape. "I love this place. I'm glad you could see where I grew up and fight to keep it clean while I was gone. A little less glorious than fighting on the front, but fewer scars to show for it. A much safer form of patriotism, and a wise choice."

Edmond's frankness brought out his own in return. "Maybe your scars show more than mine, but I think this work comes with scars of its own. We lost Pearl. I would hardly call that a small thing."

"No, that's true." Edmond's face sobered. "I'm sorry about that, little brother. I tried to do right by her afterward, even though you weren't here to oversee it. I wish I could have known her. She was a pretty girl, and she looked almost like Alisa, only with lighter hair."

The only sound was Edmond's heavy breathing while Ben steadied himself enough to speak. "Thank you. I'm glad you were here to look after them."

Edmond shrugged and waved it away. "I've stirred up the police to try to get some results, but they don't have much evidence to go on. There weren't any fingerprints, except from the two people who found her. They found a couple of dark hairs on her dress, and there was a man's shoeprint in a larger size than your doctor friend's. The evidence didn't fit the young woman who lives out at Copt Point, so that helped to clear her. There's some question about a knife or something that disappeared, but I don't know the exact details of it. They were talking about bringing up your doctor friend for questioning, but they haven't yet, or if they have, I haven't heard about it."

A fresh stab of grief twisted his heart. "I hadn't heard that. What happened when you told our father?"

"Nothing at all." Edmond's mouth held a twist of disgust. "Did you tell Lisette?"

"I sent out a letter last night."

"Good. I would have, but I thought it might come better from you, since you grew up with her. You'll have to tell me what name you want on the gravestone. Charlotte told me you were here under a different name, and I didn't know if you wanted Pearl's real name or the one you've been using."

Everyone in town knew her by the alias, and it would probably be best to keep it that way. Perhaps when the war was over they could change it. For now, she would have to be remembered by the name that wasn't truly hers. "I think we'll have to use the name we've been

571

using. I assume you don't know why she was murdered."

Edmond shrugged. "I can put two and two together. My brother shows up with a different name, and my sister is done away with. It's evident she trampled somebody's interests."

"Perhaps I should ask how fully you are aware of our work here." It was better to come straight out. They could skirt the subject for hours, but in the end, unless he wanted to start making assumptions, he would have to ask for the truth.

Edmond reached for a cigar and pulled a lighter from his dressing-gown pocket. "Just that Emmerson was suspected of being a German sympathizer. That's it. I knew he was involved with something—Peters asked a bunch of queer questions after I came back, and I came to suspect that this house wasn't just an inheritance from a kindly old gentleman. But to be honest, I don't know much of your work. I've been going through the house to see what information I could find. I don't exactly want to be connected to a house that was a front for German spy work, and I'd like to get it cleared up as soon as possible."

He had hidden the collection of evidence in the room he and Charlotte were sharing, but it couldn't stay there long if Edmond was looking about. "Have you found anything?"

Edmond held the lighter to the cigar and turned it until the end glowed red. "Not yet. There was only one thing I saw to be of consequence. Peters told me that Emmerson kept one of his upstairs rooms locked all the time. I asked him where the key was, and he told me Emmerson had never given him one, so I had one copied from the lock. Remind me and I'll show it to you sometime. It might be important."

Ben saw nothing in Edmond's frankness to give rise to suspicion, so he thought it safe to risk another question. "What exactly was the connection between Emmerson and our father? I think Emmerson isn't the only one who has had interests here."

Edmond raised his eyebrows in amusement. "I wouldn't put it past Father to be involved in this kind of thing. He's always been involved with international concerns. He and Emmerson went to school together when they were quite young—until our father went into the navy. And when he retired from that, they took up connections again. I was about ten, I think. You had been in America several years at that point. They always had private conferences together, and I was never invited to be involved. Sometimes I asked

572

Peters what it was about, but he said it wasn't any of his business. This was before the war, so he wasn't concerned about subterfuge. And after the war started, I never saw Emmerson alive again."

Ben gave him a skeptical look. "Not even when you married Alisa?"

"Oh—well, yes, I did then. No one knew about it except him. It was all a private affair. It wasn't the wisest thing to do, but Emmerson didn't mind my liking her. I always valued his opinion over Father's, in any case."

A discreet knock came at the door, interrupting his reply. "Come in," Edmond called.

Peters looked in. "Apologies for interrupting, but there's someone on the phone for Doctor Dailey."

Edmond turned to him. "There's a phone in here if you want to pick up. Do you want some privacy?"

Ben suspected it would be Jaeryn and didn't dare take the chance of Edmond overhearing something. "Yes, please, if you don't mind."

Edmond went out, and Peters closed the door. Ben picked up the phone on the desk that Jaeryn had rifled through so thoroughly in June. It looked like someone had gone through it again. Probably Edmond.

"Hello?"

It was Patrick. "Hey, I just got off at the train station and asked the operator for Dailey. Do you want to come meet me, or shall I come out to you?"

Ben was glad to hear his voice again. "I'll get you and take you somewhere. I'm not sure where. A lot of things have happened that I wasn't expecting, and I don't have a place to lodge you yet."

"Oh?" Patrick sounded curious. "Would it be better if Terry picked me up instead?"

"I don't know where Terry is. Wait until I come to get you; it will be better to tell you in person."

"Okay. I'll stay put here."

Ben clicked down the phone and looked down the hall for Edmond, but he had disappeared. The conversation with his brother had been an interesting one; between Edmond and Peters, he was now enlightened on several points. He would have to tell Jaeryn—or rather, he would have to think about it later and see what he could figure out by himself.

"You're going to have to come here," Jaeryn said, closing a drawer precisely so as not to jostle any of its contents. "There are no other lodgings you can take. I assume you've had a conversation with your brother."

Ben took up the instruments Jaeryn was cleaning and began working on them himself. Jaeryn took them from him and shook his head.

Ben responded, "Of sorts. Why can't I have Copt Point? I'd rather have Copt Point, and there are telephones out there now, so we would be quite safe."

"You want to rent from me?" Jaeryn almost laughed, but he remembered that his assistant was still suffering from fresh grief and not ready for laughter yet. "I'd be willing to put you there, I assure you, but I'm surprised Charlotte hasn't told you."

"Told me what?" Ben's eyes took on a cornered expression. He had probably been told more than he ever wanted to hear in the last couple of days.

"Copt Point. Your sister—well, it was done there."

"She wasn't murdered in the house, was she?"

Jaeryn finished cleaning the instruments and laid them away. "She was."

"I hate this place," Ben said with a frown.

Jaeryn looked up, but in spite of the words, he did not see hate. He exchanged a glance with the redheaded man hovering in the doorway. Patrick O'Sean had said very little after the initial introductions. A bright face, calm and steady. Since Jaeryn and Ben were getting on rather tenuously at present, it was a relief to have a third party to break up the tension.

"I'll take it if no one else wants it," Patrick offered. "It's close to Erin, and it won't be so hard for me."

"Never thought I would be renting to Terry's younger brother." Jaeryn paused his work and ran his fingers through his hair. "You can look it over and tell me what you think. What are you going to do with yourself? I'm sorry I can't tell you where your brother is, but unless he hears that you're here and wants to see you, I don't think we'll see any signs of him soon. And I don't have any work to give you."

"I intend to find work for myself." Patrick flashed a smile behind

Ben's back. "A couple of older siblings of mine are requiring a deal of straightening out, as far as I can hear. That ought to keep me busy enough."

Ben turned to look at Patrick. Jaeryn was concerned as well. "You can deal with Erin, if you like," Jaeryn said. "None of us know what to do with her, and I haven't seen her to speak to in the last little while, except—well, you know. But Terry is a different matter."

"I already told you, Patrick, that you can't get mixed up in this," Ben added.

Patrick feigned innocence. "I'm not getting mixed up in anything. I only came out to see my brother, and since I've traveled all this way, it's only fair to let me look for him, isn't it? He doesn't sound like he's in good shape right now."

"Who told you anything about him?" Jaeryn glanced at Ben, but he shook his head.

"Just a guess." Patrick leaned a shoulder against the doorframe. "I can see a problem when I want to. So, tell me about it."

"I think you'll understand that we aren't able to do that," Jaeryn said coolly. "You'll have to let us handle him for the present. Now, Doctor Dailey and I have a lot to discuss, if you wouldn't mind finding something else to occupy yourself for a few minutes."

"I'm not going off like that." Patrick remained settled against the doorjamb. "Seems to me I have a right to hear more of this conversation if it concerns me and mine."

Ben looked at Jaeryn, almost amused. "He is persistent."

"And I am more so." Jaeryn leveled a stern gaze at Terry's younger brother.

A sparkling light leaped into Patrick's eyes. "Or perhaps I am. We'll have to see, won't we?"

"I don't think that's a challenge you want to try, Mr. O'Sean. I suggest you take a cab to Copt Point and look around. By the time you're finished we should be finished too, and I can talk with you again."

"Oh, very well. I'll dig something out of Erin. And then I'll get the rest out of Ben later; I can see he's easier to crack than you are." Patrick looked from one disapproving face to the other and evidently deemed it prudent to leave before he damaged his position further. As soon as he was gone, Ben reached for a pair of rubber gloves, but again Jaeryn circumvented him.

"I don't think that's a good idea at present. Leave the work to me."

"Jaeryn, I have to do something. I have to have a reason to be here."

"Right now, you're the fellow whose sister was murdered while you were away. It would look odd for you to pick up business as usual just after hearing about it. Besides, I can see that your mind isn't completely on your work, is it?"

"Not exactly."

Jaeryn threw a sharp glance at Ben's face and shook his head. Ben appeared lost in thought, but the duty he had to go on was stamped all over his face, so ingrained that even in sorrow it continued automatically. But it was best restrained. "You know as well as I that medical work requires close attention. Besides, I have a responsibility to Doctor Winfield to keep a strict watch over the patients he's entrusted to me. Give it a week, maybe two, and we'll see what the general feeling about the case is then. We have to take that into consideration before you come back."

"What else do you expect me to do?" Ben twisted his fingers together and glanced at the desk that Jaeryn had kept empty and waiting for him.

"You have work that the general public doesn't know about, and you can continue on with that. And you promised to try to get me back in good standing with Ryson."

"I tried already. I wrote to him last night."

Jaeryn nearly dropped a tray of instruments he was looking over in his eagerness. "What did he say?"

Ben's face didn't give off any hopefulness, and Jaeryn's eagerness died away. "I heard from him this morning, by the new drop I told him to use. We can work together in a limited way."

"What does that mean?"

"Ryson told me that he thought your loyalties were not ours. He has no proof, of course, or he would arrest you now. But until he does, I am instructed to allow you some free rein to try to find out where your interests lie. I probably wasn't supposed to tell you that."

Jaeryn glanced sideways at him. "And are you going to do it?"

"I haven't decided."

He thought for a moment, and then managed to throw out some words of reassurance. "You can do it; don't hold back on my account. I've set my stakes, and I'll not draw back."

Ben winced. "I don't like this."

"Nonsense. We'll do our best to beat the London fellows, and while we're at it we may as well be good friends, eh? I don't see why his orders should force us to work separately from each other. I haven't done anything wrong, and there's no reason for you to take Ryson's word above mine."

"When you're known for tampering with evidence?" Ben's voice sounded tight with frustration.

Jaeryn shook his head. "That wasn't for me, I give you my word. I only did it for Terry, and I'll keep the secret, whatever the police unearth. A detective came from London to question me today, and I revealed nothing. But I'm called in for more questioning tomorrow, and I'll have to watch my steps. Which ties into something I wanted to ask you. I wondered if you would be willing to write to Ryson and ask him to see if he can delay the investigation." He continued on rapidly before Ben could reply, afraid that the hard-set face before him would turn to utter refusal. "I don't want anyone to influence the outcome of it. I wouldn't expect that. But I need a short delay to figure out how to get Terry out of the way, and I have to find him first. I've looked and looked for him, and he's made no move to contact me."

Ben looked puzzled. "Why did you hide his knife? Why not just prove he was with you and you're both innocent? Charlotte told me he was at the clinic all evening."

"He was. But it's not as simple as that. If they find the knife, they'll find him, and if they find him...they'll find one of the men they're hunting from the Irish revolt last year. Even if they determine he is innocent of your sister's death, they won't overlook his other activities."

"How involved was he in the revolt? Is it serious?"

Dorroll didn't know the full truth. Jaeryn drew in a breath of hope and seized the chance to win his help. "He would probably be hung once they found out who he was. He didn't escape to France for no reason, and it wasn't wise for him to return. That's why I ask you to do what you can. If I can find him and get him out of the way, then I would be grateful to you." Jaeryn overcame his reluctance and gave the final thrust. "I think your Pearlie would ask it of you if she were here."

"You ask too much." A grieved expression settled on Ben's face, and Jaeryn saw one of his hands clench at his side. "But I will try."

"Thank you, Dorroll," Jaeryn breathed. He had carried his point, and he was glad, but he wished he had not had to take such advantage. "It's for Terry and him alone, I swear it."

"Better in the end to help the living; that's what you mean. But it won't help all the living, as I think you should realize. I will only agree to this if you tell me who you think might have done it and which people are working for our side. I can understand why I wasn't privy to that information when I first came to Folkestone, but I have the right to it now."

"Ann and Peters have been here for years. They never knew about each other until I came. We thought we had the perfect positions to find out everything we needed: a doctor, a postmistress, and a butler. But it wasn't perfect, because Ann hated the idea of an Irish supervisor so much that she preferred to become a German spy," Jaeryn said bitterly.

"We don't have proof of that. What about Fenton?"

"Oh, he helps everyone. He travels up and down England, I think."

"And on the other side?"

"Emmerson was a given. Stafford might be a spy, or he might be a butler who wants to take advantage of a rich man's son. Colonel King has nothing but neglect of his son to cause us to suspect him. If I were to guess who killed your sister, I suspect it might have been Ann and Stafford working together. If we could get her to admit Pearl came to the post office, we would have something to go on."

Ben drew a long breath and traced his finger along the wood grain of the desk. "Thank you. All of this is very helpful. I'm curious what would happen if I asked Peters and Mrs. Meikle where they thought your loyalties tended."

Jaeryn could not think of a response, and so gave it up and changed the subject. "Are you staying here with me or not? I don't think you have any other option, to be honest."

"Let me see. Shall I stay in the house where my sister was murdered, or with the man who doesn't want her murder investigation to proceed? What a pleasant choice to have to make."

"Well, I can't make it for you."

Ben's mouth settled into grim lines. "I don't want to have another falling out with you, Jaeryn, but I won't take much more. I'm going to ask Edmond for Alisa's old place. I think that would be wiser than here under present circumstances."

They did not argue then. There was uneasiness between them the following day, and Jaeryn knew he had only himself to blame. He had told the truth about Terry, but Ben wasn't satisfied with partial admissions, and somehow his smooth generosity was not generating the trusting response he had hoped. Ben wanted to trust him, but he also wanted honesty with the friendliness. Their current standing was further strained when Ben called that evening and asked him if he knew anything about some bills that had been paid. Jaeryn pretended innocence in spite of a sharp question or two, but he could tell that Ben was not convinced. He lay awake that night trying to figure out how far he could go without jeopardizing his own interests.

Ben and Charlotte moved into Alisa's old house the next afternoon. Jaeryn learned it though an offhand comment from Charlotte when she came to help at the clinic for a few hours. But even Charlotte he only saw once in the following three days. Patrick he never saw; he must be spending his time entirely with the Dorrolls. Patrick must not have found Terry yet, or they would have sent word. Surely it couldn't be too hard to find a man like that. Edmond ought to be able to lay hands on his own employees.

Jaeryn's desk was showing tiny dents where he ground pencils into it as he sat and thought. It couldn't be that things were happening after all and Ben had chosen not to tell him. A limited way, Ryson had said about them working together. Surely that meant Ben could confide in him a little. Perhaps he should bring Ben back to the clinic after all. He couldn't bear this silence.

If Ben wouldn't trust him, he would see what he could find out on his own. He had kept back one piece of evidence in his drawer, and he would put it to use the next morning, early, before he opened the clinic for the day.

* * *

The evening after Ben's conversation with Jaeryn, Edmond invited him to his den after dinner. Ben, glad for a chance to talk to him, eagerly accepted, and Peters installed them in cozy comfort with a tray of hot cocoa and shortbread. He left them with a fire too, which was rather warm in spite of the time of year. It was a cloistered room with a green sofa and leather chairs and a soft fleur-de-lis rug that made Ben think of the carpet in Emmerson's private room.

Edmond took one of the leather chairs and shuffled a deck of cards between his tanned fingers. "Want to play at cards? I'll teach

579

you how."

Ben, in the chair opposite, shook his head. Cards seemed too frivolous in the face of what he was enduring.

"Chess, then. You know chess, surely."

He relented at Edmond's eager effort to be hospitable. "I know it."

Edmond brought out a black and white painted box and laid an enamel chessboard on a little round table between them. They set up the pieces in silence, one white side, one dark side, with the warm sweetness of the chocolate lending an air of lost childhood to the occasion.

"Don't mind being without the ladies, do you?" Edmond asked, studying the empty squares between the opposing forces.

"No." Ben set the final pawn into place, with a dry inner laugh of sympathy for it. Of little use and easily sacrificed, yet the game could not be played without it. "I wanted to ask you, does our father know about Alisa?"

"Father? I should hope not. I never told him, and I didn't give her his address. I suppose it will have to come out soon. He would have met her if he had come down for the funeral, but he didn't." Edmond picked up his white knight and advanced it three squares on the board.

White—black—so simple. What color was Jaeryn? What color was Ann Meikle or Peters—or Ryson himself, for that matter?

"Edmond, you left her here alone, and when I found her, she only had one of your servants to take care of her. Turlough O'Sean was reliable, but hardly the most fitting person to look after your wife."

Edmond grinned. "Oh, him? He was one of Emmerson's men; I never chose him. Emmerson promised to look after her, and I trusted his word. Speaking of Turlough, I kept him on after Alisa came here since she asked me to. He's respectful and a strong worker, and he does what he's told. I like what I've seen of him. He is a somber fellow, though, isn't he?"

"He and Alisa were good friends. I'm glad you kept him on." A month ago, Edmond would never have thought of his hired man as somber. Terry must have changed since Pearlie died and changed considerably. Ben hoped they could bring his happiness back again. "I would like to see him sometime. He probably doesn't know I'm back yet, and I have a letter for him from his family in Virginia."

"I'll have him come up to the house so you can give it to him. Speaking of Virginia, what sent you there? I assume it wasn't a pleasure trip."

"No. It was for business. I found something odd while I was there. It was something concerning you." Ben watched Edmond as he threw out the hint, but Edmond's sole focus was on moving his queen. "I found it interesting."

Edmond drew his attention away from the game for a split second. "Oh? What was that?"

"My mother said you had never been to see her while you were in America, but you mailed a letter from Virginia Beach." He captured one of the white pawns and sent it to the side of the board.

Edmond nodded with approval at his move. "Well, one can be in Virginia Beach without seeing Lisette, I'm sure you'll admit. I did attempt to look her up in Richmond and got her new address, but when I reached as far as her street, I decided she wasn't worth it. Father had told me enough about her to make even the bravest man question the necessity. Sorry I didn't pick up the letters you sent me. Beastly selfish, I know. But I mailed one for you at least, while I was there."

"Why was one of your letters to me in her desk, then? It didn't have a stamp on it, so I'm assuming she got it from someone in person."

"Oh, that." Edmond picked up his cocoa and drank deep before responding. "I wrote to her and told her I was discharged from the war. And I wrote you at the same time, and I mistakenly put your letter in her envelope. By the time I realized it, it had been posted and it was too late to get it back."

He could feel the skepticism spreading across his face and tried to hide it before Edmond noticed. "My letter was in an envelope addressed to me, and the address was in your handwriting."

"I must have shoved the whole thing in when I mailed it. I was in a rush. After I found out, I assumed she would mail it to you. I sent her the letter I wrote to her in the next post. Didn't she send it to you?"

Ben shook his head. "No, she didn't. I'm not sure if you're telling the truth."

"I'm not suspected in this, am I?" The scarred face remained the same as it always did, but alarm grew in Edmond's eyes. "I know you don't have much reason to trust people, but I swear I'm not as deep

581

as all that. It was an honest mistake. If she didn't send it to you, then maybe there's something from her end, but there's nothing from mine."

He was so hard to read. A light conversationalist, always ready with a glib answer. Everything he said seemed to tie together, but there was still something he was hiding. It might not be for himself; it could be for someone he wanted to protect. But it was a secret all the same.

Edmond tilted his head as if he could read Ben's thoughts. "Listen, little brother. I know you don't think I'm too steady. But I'm better than I undoubtedly seem sometimes. It was desperately dull for both of us growing up, and I know we don't know each other very well, but I'm more worthy of your trust than you think."

Ben tried to smooth over his suspicions. "I didn't say I doubted you. I just wanted to know. It was my responsibility to find out what it meant, and there were some things that made us suspect something was amiss with you. My mother was getting money from you, and she wouldn't tell me—"

Edmond chuckled. "Strange woman. It wasn't meant to be a secret. I only wanted to take some of the burden off your shoulders."

"—and then we weren't sure you were going to come back, and when you did, Jaeryn told me you wouldn't see Alisa right away. None of us knew why you wanted to keep away from her."

"You're going to be angry with me if I tell you."

"I won't."

Edmond set down his cocoa mug, and his breathing came heavier in his agitation. "I just don't feel the same way toward her as I did before, and I don't want her to know it. She always was a clever little thing, for all her soft ways. I knew I couldn't keep it a secret if I brought her here. I've seen and done things that she has no part of. I lost a piece of myself over in France, and I haven't been able to get it back again."

The words were callous, but the confession was one that Ben could only pity him for having to make. "She still loves you the same as before."

"I know. There's no one else I would rather have married, but—it's different now. I'm doing my best to keep her from finding out, but it won't be long before she starts to suspect." Edmond dropped his gaze. "I told you, you wouldn't like it."

He could not find it in himself to be angry. "I understand. And

I'm sorry. She was so looking forward to your return."

"Oh, I don't hate her. She just seems like a stranger, and I never was fond of strangers. Maybe it will change once I get my bearings back. But that doctor fellow of yours forced the point, and I wish I could have waited a little longer."

Jaeryn was the type to force a point prematurely, Ben thought in annoyance. "Do you feel the same way about your son?"

Edmond's blue eyes sparkled, and his face creased into a smile. "Oh, no, he's a fine little fellow. I wasn't sure about him, but I've grown used to him. I'm sure he'll be nice enough. It's pleasant to watch Alisa with him; mothering comes so naturally to her."

"I'm glad. Alisa's waited for you and been faithful to you, and I hope you'll do the same for her. I think you should tell her the truth and let her help you through it. It would be better than having her suspect and not be sure."

"That sounds awful." Edmond shivered. "I don't want to tell her. It would hurt her, and I don't mean to do that. No, I'll find a better way. But enough of my concerns. You've looked after Alisa and our son, and I'll see that it's returned to you." He sat in silence, and not until he remembered the chessboard did his face brighten. "Your move, little brother. Enough of deep subjects for tonight."

"All right." Ben turned back to study the board and the rows of chessmen before him. White and black—and not one gray among them.

* * *

Early on Friday morning, Ben felt a soft hand on his shoulder and opened his eyes to a phone ringing downstairs. Charlotte sat up in the bed beside him. "Telephone, my dear," she said. "Shall I answer it?"

"No, no, I'll get it."

He hurried down the stairs and caught the phone before the caller gave up. "Hello."

"Doctor, it's Alisa. I'm sorry to call so early."

"Not a problem. What can I do for you?"

"Doctor Graham just came by a few minutes ago, and he dropped off another prescription for Edmond's chloral hydrate. Peters sent a maid down to the chemist's to pick it up, and when she got back, I looked at it first. I think there's something wrong with it."

Ben looked at the clock and saw the hands pointing to almost seven. "Oh? What's wrong?"

"It looks like too much. The directions still say it's only for a week. Do you think I should ask him about it? Edmond said he didn't trust Doctor Graham completely, so I thought I would ask you. I don't want him to have it if it's too much for him."

"I'll come and look at it. Leave it with Peters for me. If it looks all right, I'll have him bring it back to you, and if not, I'll see that it's straightened out. How long has Edmond been taking it?"

"Ever since he came back, as far as I'm aware. He's tied very closely to it."

Ben took a bicycle Jaeryn had loaned him and set off in the cold gray morning. As his mind grew more alert, the stirring suspicions about his former mentor started up again. They had never fully left him since Tuesday, and Alisa's news certainly added to them. Jaeryn had been stirring early this morning. That in itself was odd. It was odd, too, that he had let Edmond take chloral hydrate to the point of being unable to go without it. That didn't seem in keeping with his normal practices—unless he had a reason for wanting Edmond to become addicted.

He didn't understand. Sunday night Jaeryn had acted as if nothing was wrong. It had been comforting to see the Irishman in his usual cheerful control, and even Monday he put everything down to just an odd conversation. Sometimes Jaeryn did say things that didn't make sense. But on Tuesday—on Tuesday the fact could not be ignored that Jaeryn was hiding something and all was not as it should be.

Ben cycled into the Emmerson estate by the back way to avoid being seen and asked for Peters at the kitchen door. He had a double motive for telling Alisa to give it to Peters. For one, it would be easy to discuss the matter with Peters directly if he found something wasn't right. For another, he intended to take advantage of the opportunity to examine the upstairs room again. Edmond wouldn't be awake yet, and it would give him an opportunity to look around without Alisa's knowledge, as long as she didn't come to meet him.

She didn't, and Peters handed him the bottle of chloral hydrate at the door. Ben read the label and looked inside. There was enough for a lethal dose if Edmond took it all at once. He asked Peters what the directions had said before and compared them to the new bottle. The dosage on the front had been increased, enough so that if Edmond lost his head, he could go on taking it with less and less ability to resist the urge.

Had Jaeryn done it on purpose? It made no sense for him to try to murder Edmond now. Even if Jaeryn was with the Germans and Edmond wasn't, Jaeryn was already in trouble with the law. He couldn't afford any more suspicions.

But Ben couldn't keep ignoring the warning signals forever. It was time to admit a small level of possibility. Jaeryn had been acting unlike himself—almost as if he was panicking. He had already tampered with the evidence for one murder, and now it looked as if he were party, whether witting or unwitting, to another attempt. Thank heaven Alisa had caught it in time.

Ben climbed softly up the servants' stair and scouted out the hall before entering it. The servants had already been through to dust the other bedrooms, and the hall was clear of people. Rather odd that Edmond had kept it undisturbed so long—but he might not have had time to attend to it yet.

He took out the key that Jaeryn had given him with the other pieces of evidence. A faint rustle sounded from within the room, and with a feeling of foreboding, Ben unlocked the door and glanced inside. There was a figure already there, bent over the table. One hand rested on a Webley, and the other ran slim fingers through dark hair.

"Jaeryn?"

Jaeryn jerked up, but his alarm dissipated when he saw Ben in the doorway. Ben wasn't sure that was a good thing. Evidently, Jaeryn didn't think him threatening enough to be concerned about.

"Dorroll," Jaeryn said smoothly, an uneasy smile resting on his face. "I didn't know you were here. Came to look at something?"

"Yes. How long have you been here?" A suspicion flashed across his mind as he felt the cold glass bottle of chloral hydrate in his pocket.

"A little while now. Since seven, I think. What brings you here?"

"Alisa asked me to come." Ben drew the chloral hydrate from his pocket and held it out to Jaeryn. "Did you drop off a prescription for this?"

Jaeryn took it up and turned it over. "Just a few minutes ago. Why?" Ben pointed silently to the directions, and Jaeryn frowned and took a closer look at it. He raised an eyebrow. "I think I'll take it back and get it corrected. That isn't really a safe amount to use."

Ben's voice registered at a higher note. "Safe? Potentially lethal, I suppose you mean."

Jaeryn's eyes widened as he looked from the label to Ben. "Don't look at me that way. I didn't intend that. I didn't."

Ben locked the door to make sure he wouldn't escape. "I don't deny that you might not have done it. But I have to suspect you. You've already tampered with evidence, and you were here, and you are out of favor with the men above us. It's in your writing, and you've been a doctor too long to make mistakes with a thing like that."

"Dorroll," Jaeryn began persuasively, but Ben cut him off.

"I don't want to believe that you've done it. You've shown yourself friendly to me and mine, and there's nothing I dread more than finding out that you are not who you say. But you're not making my position an easy one. You try to be friendly, but then you do things that I can neither overlook nor understand."

Jaeryn held out a peremptory hand. "If you would listen for just one moment. I gave him a prescription to take to the chemist, and I put the correct amount on it. How it got altered, or if it was a mistake at the chemist's, I don't know, but I think you ought to give me the benefit of the doubt."

Ben's eyes narrowed as he looked at him. "It's easily proved, isn't it?"

"Yes, it is. Haven't I shown myself to be trustworthy?" Jaeryn asked. His shoulders tensed as he glanced at the door lock. Ben moved between him and the door.

"I don't know. I thought you were pro-British and just manipulative, but now that I think of everything you've done, I could see them serving the British or the German interests equally well. The balance is starting to tip, Jaeryn, and it is not tipping in your favor."

"Trust me for a little longer. Please."

"I would be happy to. Tell me the truth about your object with Speyer, and I'll tell Ryson how you've been misunderstood."

Jaeryn's mouth clenched. "There isn't anything I wish to tell."

"Very well, then." His throat tightened at Jaeryn's refusal to be open. "Tell me the truth about who you are. We're all wondering. I've suspected for a long time that you aren't who you say, though you've taken great care to avoid bringing up the subject."

Jaeryn's lips opened, and he hesitated. Then giving a shrug, he said, "If you find out who I am, I'll have to take measures to make sure you don't tell anyone. I'd rather not have to do that."

"But Ryson knows your name, and you haven't threatened to kill him."

"Did I say I would kill you?"

"You implied it." Ben waited for a reply, and when none came, he said quietly, "Give me something, Jaeryn."

Jaeryn laughed—with a hint of nervousness, a hint of pain, it was impossible to tell which. "You've handled this case better than I thought you would. I didn't know how you'd take it when you got back and things were different. But you're tenacious, and perhaps you'll make a go of it after all. Carry on. I have work to be doing now, if you'll let me out the door, please. In fact, if you walked downstairs with me that would be even better, in case anyone notices us."

Ben made no move to obey him.

"Please let me out, Dorroll," Jaeryn whispered. "I'm not about to run away; I'm only going to the clinic. I wasn't going to take anything. I only wanted to have another look. That's all I came for, I swear, along with giving your brother the prescription. And I didn't try to kill him with it. Will you believe me?"

Ben shook his head, though it went against everything in him to do it. "I don't have anything to believe yet, much as I would like to. If you give me the key you have, I'll let you go until I can speak to the chemist."

An innocent wondering stole into Jaeryn's eyes, but Ben cut it off swiftly. "I know you have a key. Peters says this door is kept locked all the time."

Jaeryn surrendered and tossed the copied key over to him. It fell short and dropped to the carpet, but Ben didn't take his eyes off Jaeryn to pick it up. "I'm sure you'll understand that I have to relieve you of my brother's medical care. You can explain it to him however you like, but you can't continue overseeing him under present circumstances. I'll be coming to the clinic to start work again and keep an eye on you."

The Irishman's face tightened with defiance. "I could keep you from starting again, you know. You can't practice legally unless I hire you."

"No, you can't. It's too late for that unless you want Ryson to hear what you've been doing. I am your assistant again starting this afternoon."

Jaeryn looked down at his boots. "You could trust me."

"I trust you. I'm not turning you in for breaking in today, or on suspicion of attempted murder, or for hiding evidence that might shed light on my own sister's death. If I didn't trust you, I would be alerting authorities to all those things. But, Jaeryn, you would do the same thing if faced with my circumstances, and I have no choice but to take necessary safeguards."

Ben stepped away from the door and pushed it open. Jaeryn looked uncertainly from him to the door. "Are you coming with me?"

"No." He shook his head. "You'll have to get out on your own. I'm staying behind to look at these things, and I'll lock the door after me. Are you going straight to the clinic?"

A flash of anger sparked in Jaeryn's eyes, but he restrained himself from giving it speech. "Yes, I'm going straight there. You needn't worry that I'll do anything I shouldn't."

"Very good. I suggest you go then, as I don't have much time."

After Jaeryn left, Ben retrieved the duplicate key from where it had dropped and locked the door from the inside. He approached the table and looked at the pile of papers that Jaeryn had been examining. They were all of Emmerson's Parliament cases. But it was not the papers that drew Ben's ultimate attention. It was a little leather-bound notebook, just like the one Peters had described. It was the notebook Peters had torn part of a page from; it had to be.

He couldn't take the whole thing. A missing notebook would be sure to tip Edmond off to his suspicions. Quickly, he turned the pages one by one. If they were encoded, he wouldn't be able to read them now. But he could take a couple of them. There were enough that they wouldn't be noticed right away, and he could send them to Ryson to be deciphered.

Drawing out his pocket knife, Ben cut a page along the spine somewhere in the middle, then one further toward the end. He would have to chance it and see what came of them. He could read French, but if it was the same cipher as the one he had shown to York, the key was no common one.

He was out of time. He couldn't stay any longer, or Edmond might find him. Taking up the chloral hydrate, Ben made doubly sure that he had both keys and locked the door from the outside. He had to put the pages in the London drop as soon as possible, and then he would go to the clinic and take up his old position. It was high time he kept Jaeryn Graham under constant observation.

* * *

He had been caught. Of all the amateur blunders, he had been caught. Of course, it had been a risk in the first place, but anything was a risk in that house. With Alisa and Edmond there now he could hardly hope to find it empty, and Peters was always hovering where he wasn't wanted. But he could have gotten away, he really could have, if only Dorroll hadn't taken a notion to go up to the room at the same time.

Perhaps it just went to show that even Jaeryn Graham was capable of making mistakes. But he didn't make mistakes. He wasn't supposed to make mistakes.

It was just at that thought that Jaeryn's bad day suddenly became worse. He had cut through the grass and into Emmerson's woods to get to the place where he had hidden his bicycle. It was a good distance from the house, and he was almost there when he stopped. A tremor of shock ran through him. Terry stood by the bike with a revolver in his hands, absorbed in attaching a silencer to the end of it. Jaeryn stood frozen, unsure of what Terry meant to do. But he did not have time to decide, for just then Terry looked up. When he saw Jaeryn, he jerked up the gun.

Jaeryn's eyes widened. "No. Don't—"

It discharged, so close that he could feel the slight rush of air as it splintered past him into the tree. Jaeryn crouched, ready to spring as Terry aimed again.

"Don't kill me," he gasped. "You wouldn't do it, would you?"

Terry hesitated. Jaeryn made a dive for the revolver in his pocket, but before he could reach it, he felt the cold muzzle of the revolver against his head.

"Keep your hands out where I can see them." Terry's eyes did not meet his, but they kept a stern watch on his movements. "And then you get on your bike, and you head back toward town, and don't stop until you get home. You're not welcome here."

"Terry?" Jaeryn asked, his voice shaking. He tried to look up, but the revolver pressed in harder, and he did not dare. "What are you doing?"

"None of your concern. I didn't come here today to finish you off. If you hadn't come so soon, you wouldn't have seen me at all. But I'll come for you one day, so don't say I didn't give you fair warning. Now be gone, and when you've started, don't look behind you. This is loaded. I could shoot you before you got the chance to try anything."

"Where have you been, Terry? I don't understand what you're doing, but I don't think it's wise, and—"

Terry hesitated and then lowered the gun. "You said that before. If I recall, what happened after wasn't my fault. Be moving on. If you turn me in for this, I'll give the police everything I know about you."

Jaeryn gingerly got to his feet and picked up his bike. "If you would just talk to me—"

"No." Terry backed away and brought up the gun again. "I don't want to talk to you. Now will you go, or shall I send you off sooner than later?"

Terry kept the gun trained on him as he wheeled the bike to the road and set off. Though he tried to turn his head once to look back, Terry's voice ordered him to keep straight ahead. When he was far enough away so that he could look, Terry had disappeared. Jaeryn stopped and leaned against the handlebars. He shivered as he listened for indications of anyone following him. He could not detect a sound.

Chapter Thirty-Two
Double Blackmail

Ben took the appointment book Jaeryn handed him and tried to decipher the black scrawl. He passed it back. "What does this say?"

Jaeryn squinted as he tried to read it. "I don't know. Never mind, I'll write it again."

After collecting the pages from Edmond's book, Ben had placed them in the London drop and come straight to the clinic. Jaeryn seemed on edge, and at first, he put it down to their confrontation an hour earlier. But as the morning went on and Jaeryn's tight smile during consultations faded away completely, he knew it was due to something else. When the Irishman's writing deteriorated so badly he couldn't read it anymore, he determined to have it out.

"This is completely illegible. Tell me what's wrong."

"I don't know." Jaeryn's accent twined thickly through his words. "He only came back because I asked him to. If it was too much for him, I'll never forgive myself."

Ben frowned. "Who?"

"Some people crack, you know. You might before this is over, and Terry's been through more than you have."

So he was talking about Terry. "Did something happen I don't know about?"

Jaeryn picked up his pencil and made a futile effort to regain his composure. "I saw him this morning. I thought he was going to make an end of me. He said he was. He shot a gun, and he wasn't in a state to take chances with."

"Terry shot at you?"

"As soon as I left you. I ran into something he was doing on my way home, and he wouldn't let me stay."

Ben watched him meticulously trace out the addresses for the morning's calls. "Then I assume he was doing something that isn't of benefit to our side."

Jaeryn groaned. "I never should have brought him here. Some people aren't made for this work." A card slipped through the slot, and they heard the gentle murmur of people in the waiting room. Jaeryn rose to call the next person, but Ben held him back.

"You say you shouldn't have brought him here. Why did you ask him to come if you knew it was dangerous?"

"He was a friend of mine, and loyal to a fault. That was before you came. I needed someone who would be committed to me."

Here he was at the truth of it if Jaeryn would not refuse to tell him more. "And what did you ask him to do?"

Jaeryn's gaze swept over him as if wondering how he would take what he was about to hear. Ben let the silence lengthen to increase the pressure. But even he did not expect the disclosure that followed.

"He was the only person I had to directly infiltrate the German sympathizers here."

Jaeryn refused to tell him more, saying that it was too complicated and they must have time to go over it all at once. Ben had to content himself to wait. The day stretched into a long morning, picking up house calls again and waiting for Jaeryn to finish at the clinic. Most of the patients were glad to see him back. He would be a nine days' wonder for a time, and then they would forget that he had ever left and he would be one of them again. But what Jaeryn had said about Terry, and the knowledge that there was more, much more, that he had not told, kept Ben's thoughts busy until late afternoon. At five he returned, determined to make Jaeryn reveal more.

Jaeryn had regained some of his composure, looking ashamed for having broken down in the first place. But once it was out, there was no going back, and he quietly acquiesced when Ben introduced the subject again.

"We worked together once before," Jaeryn said after Ben told him to continue. A golden glimmer of defeat shimmered in his eyes. "I couldn't choose my own people then. It was dangerous, and my supervisors assigned Terry as my bodyguard. We worked well together, but we split ways after he joined the Irish rebels. After the death threats came to Folkestone, I offered him the same position on this assignment without Ryson's knowledge."

Ben leaned his elbows on the desk and frowned in concentration. "How could he be your bodyguard? I never saw him around here."

"There's more than one way to do it. Sometimes you're just as useful keeping a watch on the killers as staying with the intended victim."

"You mean—"

"He's lived in the same house with my enemies for months now. He was so efficient and dedicated I never worried much about their threats. But I don't have his protection anymore, and now I don't know where to turn. I don't know if they were the ones who killed your sister, but I'm sure they were the ones who tried to strangle me in September."

"Hugh and Stafford?" Ben sat quite still. "Tell me what you know about them."

Jaeryn shook his head. "Well, them now, but at first it was Hugh and Christopher. They met Terry after Mrs. Goodwin drove him out of her cottage. They knew about Terry's... Irish business. They agreed to keep it to themselves if we gave them a place to live. We thought they were common enough thieves until the business with Christopher in June. After that, I was afraid Hugh would find out what had really happened and try to take revenge."

"Why didn't you tell Ryson? I'm sure something could have been done."

"I knew Hugh didn't know if I was involved or not. It was all a sheer, blind attempt to intimidate. All the threats were about being Irish, and I thought it had to be some kind of prejudice on his part. Sometimes I even wondered if I had misjudged Christopher, and they were both British spies sent to find out if we were Irish rebels. What kind of sympathy would Ryson give for something like that?"

And Terry had laughed, and been as carefree as if he had come to Folkestone on holiday. "Is Terry only a bodyguard?" Ben asked.

Jaeryn toyed with a scalpel lying on his desk. "No. When he helped me with the whole business with Christopher in June, I knew I could use him for more delicate work. He's the sort of fellow everybody overlooks, and nobody dislikes. I told Peters to hire him into Emmerson's staff, and he's been trying to track information about Hugh's connections to the Germans ever since. If Hugh and Stafford find out what he knows, they'll kill him. It was such a horrible risk, letting Terry do it. But I knew if anyone could convince Hugh to trust him, it would be him. Who would suspect Terry of lying? He's as honest as the sunlight."

"How much did he find out?" Ben drew the record book toward him to file the morning appointments, but he didn't write anything in it.

"He didn't have enough time to get past Hugh. We think Hugh is a messenger who takes things from person to person, but we've never been fast enough to catch him at it. Hugh came to trust him, but he wouldn't let Terry deeper into what was going on, and then that nuisance of a boy shot him and put us all back. We were delayed for two months, and I was without a bodyguard. I never had a peaceful moment until they released him from the hospital."

"I remember you were worried."

Now that the secrets were out, he could see how much the pressure had borne down on Jaeryn, and he wished Jaeryn had confided more so he could have offered more support.

"You and I were at odds," Jaeryn continued, "and then the whole downward spiral with Ryson began." He rubbed at the worry lines on his forehead. "It's been a dreadful summer. I hope I never see another like it."

"I hope I don't either."

"I'm sure." The old empathy surfaced, as distraught as he was. "You've had it far worse than I have. Don't think I haven't blamed myself for that, either."

"It wasn't your fault." It wasn't often either of them confessed things, he thought amusedly. They were alike in more ways than they knew. Neither wanting to show they were unsure of themselves, both taking responsibility for the misfortunes of their subordinates. "If Terry collected information for you during the day, then what did he do at night when he said he was going to work?"

"That, I'm afraid, is something I'm not about to divulge to you or anyone else. It has no bearing on our present conversation. It was a separate responsibility in addition to the other ones."

"That's a lot for one man to carry."

Jaeryn straightened his shoulders, and the pride of his work glowed in his face. "We carry what we must." Then he sobered again. "I'm afraid I gave him more than he could handle, and we lost him because of it. The worst thing is, he knows all my habits and ways of thought, and he can find me when I'm most unprotected."

Ben opened his medical bag and took out the used tools that needed cleaning. "I don't understand why he would try to kill you now."

"Stafford and Hugh must have forced him to turn. Two days before you came, he gave Hugh all the drop locations without consulting me. This morning he didn't give me the slightest indication that he was on my side. He wasn't Terry like I've ever known him. Even if I haven't lost him to the Germans, I may have lost him to me."

"He may not intend to kill you. I doubt he'd have the heart to kill anyone."

Jaeryn smashed his hand on the desk until he winced from the sting of it. "And that proves how little you know. I've seen him. I've seen him when we were all like rats in a trap, and he got me past every single adversary, even if I did break my fingers." His words trailed off in guilty anguish, and with a gesture he refused to continue.

"Tell me the rest," Ben insisted. "What do you mean, he knows how to kill? Has he killed before?"

"Yes."

Ben tried to fit the picture of Terry in such an occupation as guarding secret agents—tried to imagine the strong hands doing anything but clearing the rubble from the bomb damage, feeding Alisa's horse, and offering hearty service to those around him. Somehow, it fit. The first time they met, there was a slight edge to Terry's good nature. It had quickly melted away, but doubtless it was after Terry learned that he was no threat to Jaeryn. The night Starlin shot him, too, his other side had shown through. But he still could not picture Terry turning from a jolly soul into a cold and calculating betrayer.

"I still don't think Terry would do it."

"It's a possibility that we have to entertain, no matter how little we like to think about it." Jaeryn rushed on in the skeptical silence. "That's the thing about Terry—you never really know how deeply he takes things. He always seemed to wear his heart on his sleeve. I thought he was guaranteed forever. After what happened this morning, I think he must have felt things deeper than I realized. I should never have trusted him so much after working with him only once."

Ben eyed him as he got up and began pacing the floor. "Was it during the Irish revolt that you worked together?"

Jaeryn stopped pacing. "If I was fleeing the law, I would hardly be in quiet possession of my own practice."

"That doesn't answer my question," he persisted. "Where did you meet Terry?"

"Listen, Dorroll." The gold sparks in Jaeryn's eyes snapped with anger. "You may be wrenching out everything concerning Turlough O'Sean, but that doesn't mean you're entitled to all my concerns. The question is not where we met. The question is how we are ever to get through this alive now that he's broken off contact. He knows everything from our side. Do you understand that? He knows every single thing. He could give away the whole lot of us if he wanted to."

"Well, then." Ben did not know what to say. He looked down at the appointment book and fingered the empty page, searching for a light through all the murky insecurity.

"And not that I care particularly," Jaeryn went on, "but there's another person I haven't seen any sign of since your sister's funeral, and I suspect Terry's at the bottom of it."

"Who is that?"

"Starlin King. The day of Miss Dorroll's funeral he came with Terry. They both left early, but Starlin didn't look too keen on going with him. He's not important to me. I could never see any earthly use in him. But I am concerned by his absence."

"He's still our only connection to the King estate," Ben pointed out. "If Terry's keeping him from talking to us, then Starlin may know something we need. It would be foolish to overlook him just because he's young and stubborn."

"Try to see him, then." Jaeryn shrugged. "He hates me. If Terry's compromised, then we're running out of time. My cards are being wrested from me. London doesn't like me, you aren't telling me anything, and I have lost the only person who was looking out for my personal safety. If I tell the police what I know of Hugh, they'll question him, and then I know he'll tell about Terry's Irish business. We have to get Terry to safety before trying that."

Ben sighed. "What do we do now? There's no way we can be on our guard every waking minute."

Jaeryn took a deep breath. "We have a small thread, and that's it.

They can threaten us, but they can't actually kill us yet. It would create too much of a stir after what's just happened. If they hesitate a little longer, we may have enough time. We have to find out who took over after Emmerson died, which means you'll have to dig up everyone in this town who we know is involved and get them to give up their information to you. Even that won't be enough, but we have to try."

In the last few minutes, Jaeryn had managed to get a grip on the shreds of defeated panic. Now a steely resolve was stealing in to replace it, and Ben could tell he had gathered his resources together again. "We will win. If I have to kill every one of them and bring myself down at the same time, we will get to the bottom of this. I want to know who turned my allies and bring them to justice."

"Are you willing to bring Terry to justice too?"

Jaeryn's face creased with indecision. "If I went by my oath, I would be obligated to do so. But in spite of it, I'll do whatever I can to get him out. I asked much of him, and he has suffered much for my sake. But we're going to have to find a new bodyguard to replace him."

"I don't know of any likely candidates."

"What about that friend you brought back with you?"

Ben held his breath. "You don't mean Patrick, do you?"

Jaeryn looked at him pointedly, and Ben shook his head. "No. I told him he wasn't getting involved. I kept everything from him."

"He's young, and he's strong, and he knows Terry. He might be our only option."

"Of course, he knows Terry—they're brothers. But he doesn't even know what we've been doing, Jaeryn. If we can't handle it, I doubt he'll be able to either. Besides, he doesn't know how to use weapons. I'm sure he doesn't."

Jaeryn stood over Ben's desk and leaned toward him in his eagerness. "Patrick seems willing to help. He's shrewd, and he may be just the right sort for this work."

"Expecting him to be an infiltrator is a bit much," Ben said dryly.

"That is not what I mean," Jaeryn snapped. "Just to watch our backs, that's all. Surely that wouldn't be too hard. It's either that or getting security from London. If Terry can be persuaded to trust his own brother, then he may tell him something we need. Please, Dorroll. What harm could it do us?"

Ben frowned. "I wasn't thinking of us. I was thinking of him. He could very easily get himself killed."

"Many a man has died for a worse cause," Jaeryn argued.

"No. You can get someone from London, but you can't have Patrick."

Jaeryn threw up his hands in despair. "Very well. Get killed if you like, and bring us all down with you. I still think it's worth a try."

He refused to give way. "I'm sorry, but I don't. If we hang on for another day or two, I'm expecting help from London on some evidence I sent them. I'll write and tell them of our difficulty. In the meantime, I'll see if I can catch sight of Starlin King."

Jaeryn looked at the clock, as the hands drew near to chiming the hour. "I think you'll have to leave me to my own devices if you take that route." His eyes hardened, and whether wittingly or unwittingly, he began rubbing a crooked finger along the edge of the desk. "How strange that every one of my tools, even you, has now turned double-edged in my hands."

A sudden thought occurred to Ben. "You don't suppose Terry's been making those lists of soldiers, do you? He goes everywhere, and he never says what he does. Does he ever travel?"

Jaeryn's eyes grew wide in the silence, and he slowly dropped his head into his hands. "Maybe Turlough O'Sean was the leak in the British Secret Service this whole time."

* * *

The scent of ink and paper greeted him as Ben entered Ann Meikle's post office on Saturday, the seventeenth of November. It seemed a logical place to start after his conversation with Jaeryn. He certainly had enough explanations to demand of her. Charlotte had never gotten his letters, in spite of Fenton's intervention, and Mrs. Meikle was the only one who could have kept them. He hated the thought of her shrewish eyes glancing over their words of affection, or laughing, perhaps, when she read their fears over each other's silence.

There were other people waiting to collect their mail, and since he wasn't the tallest by far and she hadn't seen him, he ducked into the line and counted on giving her a surprise. She couldn't have been the only one looking through his mail now that he thought about it. When he questioned Charlotte about the bills that had come in his absence, she told him that Jaeryn had persuaded her to give them up to him. Apparently, the prying fellow had even gone to London to talk to his father about them, neither of which items of information Jaeryn had offered when he asked about the payments. He would be glad when he could read his mail again without wondering how many people had read it before him.

When the line grew short enough, Ann Meikle caught sight of him. Her sharp eyes did not look the least disconcerted, and she even smiled at him when she caught his attention. He did not return it.

Someone had paid Terry's bills, too. Perhaps it was the same person, watching over all of them and smoothing the way. Only Jaeryn had the money for it, or possibly his father—or even Edmond. But Edmond didn't seem the type to pay attention to those things.

When his turn came, Mrs. Meikle greeted him with cheery unconcern. "Well, laddie, it's a pleasure to see you again. I never thought you would be back."

"I'm back." But he was not the gullible newcomer he had been the first time, and he made sure she knew it. "I've come to see if I have any letters."

"One, I think. Can I sell ye some stamps? I'd buy some if I were ye."

He took the hint and put down a spare coin on the counter. She took it up with her blunt fingers and tossed it in the cashbox, then reached back for his letter. "There you are, doctor. I have that payment on our wager for ye laid aside in the back."

Ben frowned and opened his mouth to question, but she gave him a meaning glance. He took up the letter, hardly glancing at it. "You have some explaining to do," he said in a low voice.

"Do I now? I think you'll find all the explanations you need from other folk. That doctor fellow, for one." She looked past him to the next customer. "And all I have to say comes through Fenton."

Fenton. And Jaeryn had scared him off. In fact, Jaeryn had cut off communication with everyone Ben wanted to talk to. Fenton first, and then apparently Terry as well, and Terry had cut off Starlin. Was this all a setup to keep him from discovering anything? He could only get his information through Jaeryn now, and Jaeryn had an unmistakable bias in all of this.

"When can I talk to you?"

"I'm not available to ye, laddie. All booked up, I'm afraid. Say hello to yer pretty wife for me, and I hope ye find what ye're looking for. Now, I have some others to attend to."

599

Ben stood firm and raised his voice so the people surrounding him could hear. "I wondered if you could tell me the last time you saw my sister? I was gone for so long, it's a comfort to hear anything people remember about her."

Mrs. Meikle glared at him, but she kept her voice sweet in the silence that settled over the room. "I saw her that evening walking down Tontine. I had stayed late to balance up the accounts. But I never spoke to her. I wish I had, poor girl. Was that all ye wanted to know, laddie, or is there anything else I can help ye with?"

"Thank you. That's all. I'm so obliged to you."

Mrs. Meikle gave him a motherly nod. "Good day to ye, laddie, and don't forget that wager money."

He hesitated, then walked behind the counter and through to the back. The room was not empty as he expected. Mrs. Goodwin sat at a typewriter with a paper of names and figures, and she looked up as he entered.

"I hope I'm not disturbing you." He glanced uncertainly at the desk and saw a packet with his name on it bound up beside the typewriter. "I've just come to collect something."

"Oh, you're not disturbing me, doctor. I'm making up the accounts for my laundry clients, that's all."

She shifted her chair to the side, and he took up the little package just as Mrs. Meikle looked into the room. "Did ye find it, doctor? I was going to tell ye to use the back door as ye go out, if ye like."

"I found it." He gave a nod to both of them. The rattle of coin met his ear as he exited the post office, and when he tumbled open the package, three cool sovereigns pressed into his hand.

Ben looked at his letter while he walked. He didn't dare open the sovereigns until he was in a more private place. It was a dinner invitation for December first. Evidently, King knew he was back. He cast up the date in his mind. Two weeks from now, on a Saturday night. Was it nearly December already? He had seen most of three seasons in Folkestone, and he had never expected to stay so long.

Later on, when he located the pin prick in the side of the sovereigns and twisted them open, he found something that further surprised him. Each of the three squares of paper, less than an inch across, had the number one written on it. The first square was signed with a minute *F* on the back. The second said to be ready. The third came with no personal message. Ben took out the invitation and looked it over again. It could be no mistake that the two coincided—

on someone's part, at least, whether or not King had planned it. He decided not to show the messages to Jaeryn yet.

If he wanted to be ready by the first, he had a lot of work to do.

* * *

When Jaeryn heard a knock on the door Monday evening, sometime after Ben left to go home, he debated over whether or not he should answer it. The last time he had opened the door to an unknown caller he'd nearly been strangled, and the bruises had only faded completely in the last few days. It was very cautiously and not without some trepidation that he cracked the door to see who it was. Even then, he wasn't too keen on letting his caller inside.

"I thought I told you not to come back."

Fenton held up a telegram. "Ann Meikle had this for you. She thought you might want it sooner than later. And I have something important that you should hear as well."

Jaeryn lifted his chin. "Since when did I ask you to start delivering my mail? That's illegal, anyway, for her to give it to you."

"Mrs. Meikle is not always law-abiding, but in this instance, she had only your best interests in mind. She knew I wouldn't tamper with it."

"That's a ridiculous lie. You've tampered with more mail than any of us." Jaeryn peeked in the envelope, but he did not recognize the sender. It was from France by the postmark. "Is that all you wanted?"

"No." Fenton tried to slip in through the door, but Jaeryn held it against him. He shrugged resignedly. "If you will have it that way, doctor; but I think you should let me inside for this conversation."

Jaeryn stepped aside slightly to allow him into the entrance hall. "This far, and no farther. What do you have to say?"

Fenton gave a complacent bow. "Just that I'm a forgiving man, in spite of what happened the other day. I don't think you want to get rid of me yet. You would regret your rashness later on."

"On the contrary, I think I would find it exceedingly pleasant."

"It wouldn't be safe to let me go completely when I know who you are and where you come from."

"Empty threat," Jaeryn replied coolly, trying to detect some crack that would tell him whether or not he should be concerned.

"Threats are never empty when I give them." Fenton smiled. "You're telling me you don't have anything to hide?"

"No more than the next man. And nothing that you know of."

"On the contrary. One of your people let something drop. Just an odd little sentence that didn't fit what I knew about you. I didn't hear it myself, but it was reported to me, and I took the liberty of a trip to Hull do some digging. Since then, I've found people more than willing to give me the information I needed."

Jaeryn kept up a bold front, though inside he was far from happy at the news. "You're a sly ferret, I'll grant you that."

Fenton bowed in acceptance of the compliment. "Not especially. But if ever I'm not heard of for twenty-four hours, my contacts know who to give the information to. Now, what I would like to know is how much my silence is worth to you. Because if it isn't worth anything, then there's hardly a point in my keeping silent, is there?"

Jaeryn drew his dark brows over his eyes. "Are you blackmailing me?"

"Well, since you don't want my other services, I have to find a different way to keep up my income. I think you would rather have me keep what I know to myself."

"I'm not afraid of you," Jaeryn said contemptuously. "Besides, if you give away my affairs, then I'll give away yours, and I don't think you would like that."

Fenton smirked. "I would come out of the fire unharmed, while you—well, let's just say a man with your political interests would find it hard to explain his way out of them. When I reveal that you're a subversive agent for the sake of—"

"Stop." Jaeryn drew in his breath. "I don't want to hear any more."

"Excellent. I was hoping you would take that line of thought. Well then, I'm sure we can make arrangements for your protection. But mind, I don't promise to keep it secret forever."

"Get on with it. How much do you want?"

"A hundred pounds will be sufficient."

Jaeryn weighed the options in his mind and reached for his checkbook. "You're a fiend."

Fenton took the check and looked it over to make sure it was satisfactory. He smiled with pleasure. "I'm glad you were persuaded to see reason. After the other day, I was concerned. In return for your cooperation, you might like to know that you have two weak points, and both of them are dangerous to you."

Jaeryn swallowed down his wrath. He was in no position to take a high hand, but he would bide his time and exact full payment later. If he ever got to later. "What are they?"

"Dorroll and yourself. Everything else you've proved you can overcome, but you two are the strongest jeopardy to your success."

"I think Dorroll may be my strongest ally before this is over," Jaeryn retorted.

"He won't be on your side by the end if I have anything to say about it."

"You can't have him. He's mine, and nothing will change that. You have your money, and you've done what you came for. Leave now."

Fenton turned toward the door, but before he went out, he stopped to give one parting shot. "I think he's better off with me than with you. Our side would be more to his taste if only he knew it."

As soon as Fenton closed the door, Jaeryn picked up the telegraph, tore it open, and scanned over the contents. Then he snatched up his hat and went out, locking the door behind him.

* * *

It was dark when Ben made his way home Monday evening. As he rode Jaeryn's bicycle, he kept a sharp lookout for trouble. He didn't like the sun setting earlier and earlier now. What Jaeryn had told him, added to the knowledge that he was hardly in a safe position, set his teeth on edge. He wondered if Terry was watching him—or someone else even less likely to let him go by unharmed. His watch hands pointed to seven, about the hour when Pearlie had disappeared. Much as he tried to ignore the thought, it kept surfacing without permission. He would never find help as good as Terry, but there must be someone he could trust who would ease this burden of apprehension.

However much the sunset seemed to forebode trouble, he reached the white farmhouse without incident. The front of the house was dark according to regulation, but inside he found that supper was almost ready and Patrick had dropped in for a visit. He liked Patrick, and Charlotte appeared to like him too, though she had only seen him once or twice since his arrival.

"Been looking all around Folkestone for Terry," Patrick offered, as Ben kissed Charlotte hello and handed her his coat. "I got his old

603

address from Jaeryn and broke in to look around the place, but I didn't take anything."

Ben smiled. "You're more conscientious than some. Most of us have been taking things where we like." He felt a peaceful contentment now that he was back safe in the homey kitchen. The house still had Alisa's presence in it, and he missed her shy smile and bits of conversation. Staying at her house since his return, even without her, was the closest he would ever get to feeling normal again.

"Have you?" Patrick said. "Guess I'm not so bad after all. Mum wouldn't be happy if she knew you were turning my morals so badly."

"I didn't do it," he protested. "It's your own responsibility if you break the law. I wouldn't recommend it."

"Well, I have to do something besides wait around for you to do it. By the way, I stopped in this morning to sign rent papers with your doctor friend. I've never gotten rent so low, and he gave me a heap of advice I didn't want while I was at it. And then he asked me if I knew what Terry did for work, and I said no, but that I'd like to do whatever Terry did and I was willing to give it a shot if I could find out what it was. Jaeryn said he didn't mind, but that you didn't seem too sure that I would be capable of it." Patrick looked aggrieved. "I'm able to take care of myself just as well as my brother."

"In most cases, I would agree with you, but when you find out what Terry has been doing, you may understand our hesitation."

"So you know what he does for work?"

"I found out. Last week Jaeryn told me. He's known all this time, but he wouldn't tell me until Terry started down the wrong path. We may have to bring him in for turning sides, Patrick."

"Oh, dear. I'd better keep looking for him, then."

"I give up, I really do. When you—"

He left off his sentence when Charlotte came in again. She pulled a pan of baked pork and beans from the oven and during the lull in the conversation relayed her own piece of news. "Darling, I think Doctor Graham wants to know something about you. He asked me all sorts of questions today, and I couldn't understand what he meant by them. They were very disconnected. For being so precise and organized, he doesn't seem to keep his thoughts in good order."

Ben pulled a stack of plates from the cupboard and placed them around the table. "What sort of questions?"

"What you thought of your brother, and how you had been

handling things since coming back. He kept coming back to you, and if I didn't answer, he would repeat the question until I said something that satisfied him. And that wasn't all, either. With every patient I called in, he tensed up as if he expected something bad to happen until he saw who they were. It may be nothing, but he seems concerned for his own welfare."

"He has reason to be." Ben pushed in her chair and took one himself.

"If questions are any indication, he was concerned for yours as well."

"I hope you didn't—" They heard the click of the front door latch on the other side of the house, and when he asked Charlotte if it was locked, she shook her head. Patrick stiffened and half-rose from his chair when a voice came from the intruder.

"Who do you think you—oh." A shock circled through them. Charlotte and Patrick settled down as soon as they saw the reddish-brown hair and lean figure, but Ben did not. His pulse quickened as he noticed how different Terry looked from September.

"Terry. What are you doing here?"

"Hello, doc. I thought someone had broken in. Do you live here now?" Terry hovered uncertainly in the kitchen doorway, ready to take flight, but he did not try to leave. There was a dark bruise down one side of his face, and as Ben scrutinized him, he saw more than one. It looked like there had been a fight, and evidently Terry hadn't come out on the better end of it.

"Since last Tuesday. Did you hurt yourself?"

Charlotte looked questioningly at him, as if wondering why he didn't offer a warmer reception.

"No, I'm all right." Terry saw his brother, and the dullness in his face was replaced by something more animated. "Are you Patrick?"

"As sure as you're Terry." Patrick grinned, not as wide or bright as Terry used to, but like him all the same.

"What did you come here for?"

"I came to see you. Where have you been? I've looked for you everywhere."

"I haven't gone anywhere." The big hands relaxed at his sides. "I didn't know you were here. No one told me the doc was back either. Well, I won't be troubling you any further now, if you'll excuse me for intruding."

"You're welcome to stay and eat with us if you like, Terry." Ben offered the innocent invitation, and it hung between them like a challenge. "We would all enjoy talking to you. I haven't seen you for a long time."

Terry shook his head and backed away. "I won't disturb you folks. You've seen enough of me already."

"Wait." Patrick toppled his chair and caught Terry by the shirt before he could leave. "Why are you going away? I thought you were friends with the Dorrolls. That's what Ben told me." He looked to Ben for affirmation, but Ben gave him no reassurance.

"Are we friends, Terry?"

Terry shifted nervously. "I don't wish you any harm. Unlike some folks."

"Jaeryn told me some things about you. Very interesting things."

The bruise showed even darker against Terry's pale face. For a moment, he looked like he was going to be sick. "Did he?" he managed at length, glancing at Charlotte. "Maybe we should talk about it sometime else."

"I'd be happy to, but you're harder to find than you used to be. We've never seen you at my brother's place, even though you work there. Tell me where to find you when I stop by, and we'll talk then."

At that Terry's words failed him altogether, and he stood with his mouth open, trying to form a response.

"Do you really work for Edmond?" Ben asked.

"Yeah," Terry said lamely. "But he's got a big place."

"And where exactly could I find you on it?"

"It varies. Nowhere in particular."

Terry's secrecy decided him. Charlotte knew half of what was going on anyway, and he couldn't risk losing track of Terry for the sake of keeping her out of it. "We'll talk here then. I know how you're involved now. I had suspected you were working for the spy ring, but yesterday Jaeryn confirmed it. The first day I met you, you gave it away. You came to see Jaeryn after he and I argued, and I listened to every word."

Terry's eyes widened. "But I never said anything."

"You lied to me, you know. You promised to keep my name a secret, and you didn't."

"The doc already knew who you were," Terry protested.

A frown appeared on Charlotte's forehead, and Patrick, who had been trying to fit a word in edgewise, jumped in as a pause on Terry's part gave him an opportunity. "Would you give him a chance to explain himself? I'm sure if he could get three seconds together he would tell us what's wrong."

"Terry," Charlotte put in softly, "can we help you with something? We haven't seen you in a long time, and we've all been worried."

Terry shook his head. "No, Mrs. Dorroll, you can't, and neither can my little brother. I wouldn't want either of you to get mixed up in this. You stay safe and out of the way."

Ben softened his tactics. "Is this what you really want, Terry? Because if it isn't, we can help you out of this between us all."

"This is what I want."

"I don't think you're sure of that."

"I'm sure." Terry's gaze broke from his. "This is what I want, and I don't need your help."

Ben tried the last persuasion he could think of. If he could break Terry down, then there was a good chance he would open up, and the only way was touching on a very sore spot for both of them. "No matter what you've done, I'll help you because of what you did for Pearlie. She loved you, and for her sake I'll overlook your actions, even threatening Jaeryn, if you tell me everything."

Terry wrenched away from Patrick. "Let me go. I've stayed long enough."

"No." Patrick seized him by the sleeve. "You stay right here."

Terry landed a stinging blow in Patrick's face, and when he clung firm, let loose one after another until Ben leaped up and pulled Patrick away. He pressed his revolver into Terry's side before Terry could get his own out. Charlotte pressed shaking hands to her mouth, and Patrick swiped at the blood on his face to try to see.

"You'll stay here until Jaeryn has a chance to talk to you," Ben said. "Charlotte, please call the clinic and tell him to come over as soon as possible."

Terry leaned against the wall, tense and sweating. "You said you would help me for Acushla's sake. If you really want to help me, then you'll have to let me go."

"I'm afraid I can't do that. You've threatened Jaeryn and stopped communicating with us, and you'll have to give some kind of explanation before I set you free. Charlotte, please call Jaeryn."

Charlotte went to the phone and asked the operator for the doctor. Ben hoped that Jaeryn was home.

"Do you want to leave a message?" she whispered over her

shoulder.

"No. No message."

Terry kept his hands up, but he was watching for a chance to get free, and he shifted against the gun. Ben pressed it in closer. "Would you let me *go*? I have that kid with me, and I have to get him out of here."

"Starlin King? You have Starlin with you?"

Terry tried to twist out of his grasp, but his attempt failed. "I do, and I can't leave him outside. You're going to have to let me get him, and you can't come with me. That's the only way."

Patrick went to the door. "I'll get him."

Terry swore under his breath so Charlotte couldn't hear. "He's going to get killed."

"Wait, Patrick." Ben searched in Terry's pockets until he found a revolver and tossed it over. "Take that with you."

As Patrick closed the door, Terry was still shaking, and Ben took a good look at him. "Are you all right?" The bruise on the side of his face had darkened, and it looked like it was swelling. "How long ago did that happen to you?"

"Just before I came here."

"Sit down and let me look at it." He took Terry's arm and kept a firm hold on him while he led him to the kitchen table.

Terry seemed to find his tongue again, for he suddenly began talking without it being dragged out of him. "I don't know what Jaeryn told you to make you distrust me, but you're making a mistake."

"Then tell me everything, and I'll correct the error. But only when I know and not before."

"Stafford's out there."

"With Starlin?"

"No, but he's always around. And he doesn't like Starlin too well, and he won't even give Patrick a chance if he sees him."

A knock came at the kitchen door, and Ben looked uncertainly from Terry to Charlotte. It wasn't safe to send her to answer it, and he couldn't leave Terry to his own devices, or he would bolt for freedom.

"Come here and hold this." Ben held out the revolver, and Charlotte took hold of it. "It will only be for a moment, and then I'll take it back. Got it?"

"I have it." She nodded and took a firm grip on the handle. Ben let go.

"She knows how to use it, Terry."

It was rather pointless, but even if Charlotte weren't strong enough to prevent his grappling her, Terry wouldn't offer to lay a hand on a woman. He hoped. Going to the door, he opened it and found Jaeryn on the step.

"Thank goodness you came. I tried to call, but you didn't answer."

Jaeryn slipped through the door and looked in surprise at the scene in the kitchen. "I didn't get it. I left ten minutes ago to come and tell you something."

"It's no matter. We weren't about to let him go until you came."

"You can take the revolver away, Mrs. Dailey." Jaeryn shut the door and locked it. "He's outnumbered now." Charlotte lowered it in relief, and Jaeryn took it from her. Terry didn't look at any of them, only stared down at his open palms.

"You have a few explanations to make," Jaeryn said.

Terry darted an angry glance at him. "If you don't let me out, then I'll go straight to the police and tell them who you are."

"No, you won't," Ben returned coolly. "We have you here, and here you'll stay, which makes going to the police impossible."

Terry didn't respond but looked straight at Jaeryn. "Then I'll tell *him*."

Ben, too, looked at Jaeryn, but Jaeryn did not return the glance. He gazed for a long moment at his former bodyguard, and a little more of the spark of life faded from his green eyes. "Would you really be so disloyal, Terry?"

"Without a second thought," Terry retorted, though he didn't look glad in the threatening of it.

Jaeryn stepped away from the door. "I'm sorry to hear it. If that's what you want, then you're free to make that choice."

"No." Ben grabbed Terry's shoulder. "Surely it isn't worth that much. Why does it matter if I know who you are?"

"Get out before I keep you here," Jaeryn said to Terry. "I'm the only one in this room who has a gun right now."

Terry turned faster than light and shoved Ben away from him as he fled toward the door. Jaeryn opened it as soon as he reached it, and Terry ran into the darkness.

Ben turned angrily to Jaeryn. "Why did you do that? He was here at our fingertips, and you let him go."

Jaeryn closed the door. "It was worth it to me."

"I shudder to think who you really are if it's that terrible. I'd rather know the truth now and have it over."

"But I would rather not." The Irishman drew out a telegram and handed it to him. "This came today from France, and it concerns you."

"What is it?" Ben pulled the telegram out and read it. "Why, it's from the other doctor—Winfield."

The door opened again and Patrick came in, his breath blowing frostily from the crisp night air. He laid Terry's revolver on the table. "There was no one out there that I could find. Why, where's Terry?"

"You can ask Jaeryn. He let him go." Ben scanned through the telegram again. "Winfield is in critical condition? What does that mean?"

"It means that if he gets a medical discharge, then I have to turn his practice back over to him." Ben looked at Jaeryn in dawning comprehension, and Jaeryn told him the rest. "If he dies, the practice will revert to his daughter. In either case, you'll be out of work, and you won't have a cover for being here."

Chapter Thirty-Three
The Price to Pay

Ben came home on Wednesday to find Charlotte there by herself. Patrick hadn't dropped by, and for the first time since his arrival, it was just the two of them. By the time they had moved into Alisa's, Ben was working again, and when he wasn't with Jaeryn, he made sure Charlotte was, so that Jaeryn would know he was being watched. But now they were alone, and as he came into the kitchen that still held so much of Alisa's presence, he was glad to have the prospect of a quiet evening in front of him.

"Package for you from the post office," Charlotte said as soon as he came through the door. "Two things, actually. Jaeryn dropped a letter by and said it came to him, but you would want it. And some lady I don't know sent me a very strange letter. It didn't make sense."

"Oh, no." He had forgotten about telling York to send information to Charlotte. "That letter wasn't for you."

"I didn't think so." She gestured to the kitchen table, where they were all spread out. "You can look at them whenever you like."

He smiled at her eagerness. "Which means now, doesn't it? All right. I'll look through them, and if I can, I'll let you read them too. I know you like letters."

Her eyes sparkled. "I do. And I didn't get any of yours. You're going to have to write them over, you know, so I can have them. You have all of mine."

"I enjoyed them, I assure you." He grinned and turned over the addresses, postmarked London and America—except the one from Jaeryn, which didn't have a postmark or return address on it. "You can have mine if that Meikle woman hasn't burned them. Or you can have me instead. But if you want new letters, then I'll have to go away again, and I'd rather be with you."

She tilted her head and thought for a moment. "I think I'll take the letters instead."

"I may just take you at your word."

He sat down at the kitchen table, and for a moment, there was nothing but the sound of a pan sizzling in preparation for dinner and Charlotte humming. Then, before he could pick up the first letter, she came up behind him and wrapped her arms around his shoulders.

"I have questions."

Ben gave a dry chuckle. "I'm sure you do. Which one do you want to start with?"

"What happened with Terry last night? I didn't understand any of it. At first I thought you were angry because he kissed Pearl."

Ben looked up at her and frowned. "He did? I wish he hadn't. He had no right to take advantage of her like that."

Charlotte hesitated. "I don't think he went unencouraged."

He reached up and squeezed her hand. "Whatever happened wasn't your fault."

She leaned closer and spoke soft and low in his ear. "We haven't talked about Pearlie much since you got back, either."

His chest tightened, and he drew a slow breath against the pressure. "I'm sorry. I'm sure you must be grieving so much. I should have asked you."

"Of course I'm hurting like anyone else. But I was thinking of you."

He looked down at his hands. "I'm all right."

"I don't believe you."

He didn't like talking about Pearl. Every time it came up, it wasn't long before he changed the subject. It hurt too badly. The only good thing about breaking with Terry and not living at Copt Point was that if he tried very hard, he could almost pretend it hadn't happened. If he was honest with himself, he knew it wasn't working. But when he kept quiet, at least he could keep control of it.

"I'm all right," Ben repeated. He kissed her and picked up one of the letters. Charlotte resumed making supper, but she watched him while he read, and he knew she wanted to learn from his expression what he was finding.

The one Jaeryn had dropped by was unsigned as well as unaddressed, but he recognized the writing as Speyer's.

I found something you'll need, so I am sending it to you. I'll start it a couple of hours after this letter, and it should get to you intact, as our chain of communication is reliable. Actually, I have two things you need, but I am only sending one. The other is not the sort of object that can be filtered through several messengers without great damage. Unless you send an agent to fetch it, I have no way to get it to you. I think you can finish your mission in Folkestone without it, but if you want to wipe out every trace of foreign activity and prevent it from cropping up again, you'll need to come and get it yourself. This is the last thing I can do for you. I won't be writing again. Best of luck.

Jaeryn had given him this letter when he would never have known about it otherwise, and surely that was a point toward his honesty. Ben folded up the note and put it back with more hope than when he had opened it.

When Charlotte looked at him inquiringly, he shook his head and turned to the thin package from London. It held the notebook pages and the typewritten sheets containing the translations. Whoever Ryson's little henchmen were, they had done their work in good time. Apparently, the cipher was known to others besides York.

I have cracked them at last. They're a fractured group, and easy enough to scatter once we begin. But my time is running out, and I only hope I have the strength to finish this. Since you aren't here in person, and I probably will not see you again, I intend to write this out. It is dangerous to commit everything to writing, but you know our way of communicating, and it is no common one. They are so inefficient and unprofessional, I think I shall be safe.

I have a butler who watches me closely. You must be careful when you come back. He respects you, and that will help you a long way towards deceiving him; but be wary all the same. I wish I had longer to show you how this is done. You are young, with little practical experience in the field, but I trust my choice will not be a detrimental one. I would rather have you, in all your inexperience, than King. He expects to control this himself as soon as I am gone, but I charge you: do not let him. I have worked without him all my life, and my work must continue without him after my death.

I have done all the preparation for you, and you really have very little left to arrange. We can turn most of their agents, I think, and silence the rest. The postwoman is hardly one to be concerned over, and the wanted man is already ours. The only person you should be wary of is Jaeryn Graham. He's the sort of man who wants to be in charge, and I have no use for that. Get him out of your way. Carefully done, that will only strengthen your position.

There is a new agent I am concerned about. They tell me he is coming from America, and I have not been able to find anything—

The page stopped there, and Ben took up the translation for the other page he had removed toward the end of the notebook.

—two volumes. The second I will not send to you directly. Even you I do not trust, and the only way you can secure it for your own is to prove you are one of us. You must go to Germany, and you must take the letter I gave you and enclose it with one from yourself. Use your number, not your name, in case it is ever discovered. I will not write the contact names you need here. After you have read the other notebook, leave it with its keeper. I want nothing from there traced to our work here, and my great object you must wait to touch until you have gained experience in this lesser territory. That way, even if this first notebook is found and you are taken, my other interests will be protected.

It really is child's play, what we're doing here in Folkestone—an amusement that I keep up for the sake of interest now that I have retired. I've turned more agents than they shall ever find, but these people are of no use to us if they have no leader to guide them, and it is you and I that London is after. They don't want the civilian informants; once those have no one to report to, they are useless. No, they want the core of the movement. I trust we have enough time for the division in their ranks to bring them crashing down upon themselves before they get too far.

Fortunately, our real German contacts are secure, and there is no breath of suspicion concerning them. Be careful not to jeopardize their position in any way. If we all fall together, we will be replaced, but they cannot be, and they must not be—

If only he had the rest of the notebook. Evidently, Emmerson had been part of something besides their interests here in Folkestone. What a chance the old man had taken to write the information out, and what a deep-seated animosity must exist between him and King that he was determined to jeopardize the whole mission rather than turn it over to his rival.

The "wanted man" was loyal to Emmerson's side. That obviously meant Terry. And Emmerson wanted Jaeryn out of the way. Did it mean Jaeryn was on Emmerson's side and ambitious to move up, or working against Emmerson and a threat to his interests? It was hard to read the exact meaning. Peters had been mentioned indirectly as well. There was doubtless more to be discovered when he read through it again. Even if they never got the rest of the notebook, these pages opened up several new avenues of thought and confirmed some old suspicions.

As Ben looked them over, so absorbed that he forgot Charlotte was watching him, he fitted the pieces together between Emmerson's instructions and Speyer's letter. Speyer had something that he could not give them, something so dangerous that he could not let it out of his hands. From all appearances, there was a second journal of instructions explaining the real work that Emmerson was covering by this so-called child's play. Could the two items be connected? How strange if the journal had fallen into the hands of a double agent not yet twenty. But Speyer would not be writing again to tell them more particulars, and after what Ryson had told him, Ben could only be glad. It would put too much risk on Nathan's assignment, and it would not be right to jeopardize that.

Child's play, he thought bitterly, as Emmerson's words rankled in his mind. It was not child's play when friendships and loves and careers and families were broken without remedy. It only went to show how heartless the old man was who had set this all in motion.

Before he had an opportunity to look at York's missive, the phone rang. Ben had a premonition that it would be Jaeryn and that it would be about the item Nathan had promised to send. Charlotte looked at him inquiringly in case he wanted her to answer it, but he shook his head and took it up himself.

"Hello?"

"Graham speaking. I have something I need to talk to you about. I'll bring it over after I get a bite to eat, but I wanted you to know that I had it and wasn't keeping it from you."

"It's all right. I wouldn't suspect you of holding back after you gave me the first letter. You can come over for dinner if you like. You don't mind, do you Charlotte?" he whispered over his shoulder.

She smiled and shook her head.

"Are you sure?" There was a hint of eagerness from Jaeryn at the prospect of a home-cooked meal.

He had been angry with Jaeryn on Saturday for letting Terry go, but the hurt in Jaeryn's eyes at Terry's betrayal was so strong that he had not dared to be harsh. So there was only friendly honesty in his tone when he said, "I'm sure."

"I'll be glad to come then." Jaeryn hesitated. "Actually—thank you for the offer, but I think I'll take a rain check. Now isn't the time for friendly visits, and I have a feeling this letter is something important that we shouldn't wait to look at. I'll grab a bite to eat on my way, and we'll save the dinner for another time."

"As you like. We'll see you when you get here."

They ate and cleared away in short order, and the kitchen was set to rights. When Jaeryn came in, Ben noticed that he looked hesitantly toward Charlotte, and when she was friendly toward him, he took his cue from her and stood at ease. Ben smiled to himself. Even Jaeryn liked to be on good terms with a woman. They made themselves comfortable in the parlor, and Charlotte offered Jaeryn tea, which he accepted.

"Seen Patrick about?" Jaeryn inquired when Charlotte disappeared to the kitchen to put the kettle on.

Ben shook his head. "No. I've been busy. He told me he's applying for work at the Shorncliffe camp."

"He isn't enlisting, is he?" Jaeryn asked in alarm. "What sort of work?"

"I doubt it." The kettle whistled in the kitchen, and a cupboard banged as Charlotte pulled down teacups. "Why?"

"I was just asking." Jaeryn smiled, but the smile did not deceive him.

"You haven't asked him to be part of our work here, have you?"

"I did." Jaeryn's expression held a mixture of defiance and guilt. "You'll thank me for it later."

"No wonder he hasn't come to see me. Very well, then, out with it. What did you ask him to do?"

Jaeryn shifted. "Nothing threatening. He'd be happy to explain it to you himself, but I forbade it. I gave him proper arms."

Ben frowned. "Proper arms—he hasn't shot a gun in his life."

"But you have, which I find curious, considering your background. He said he liked the knife better, so I found one for him. You can protest all you like, but I doubt you'll be able to change his mind." Jaeryn pointed to a paper lying on the coffee table. "Have you read the news from the front?"

"I was too busy talking to Charlotte."

"They're trying again in France. They're bringing the tanks out this time. It's already going well. After the madness this fall, I think they're finally advancing over at Cambrai. We're going to end the year with the taste of victory in our mouths."

Ben savored the word victory, and it tasted sweet. "I'll be glad of that."

Jaeryn picked up the letter from York lying next to the paper. "This is in French. What does it say?"

"I started to look at it before you came. Let me see it first." Jaeryn passed it over, and Ben scanned down the page. His father's name jumped out halfway down, and he quickly translated the line containing it: *Further results on former information. Matthew Dorroll not agent who set up bank account. Reliable source confirms he was in London at the time. Agent is person by name of Edmond Dorroll, army captain. Received medical discharge in May. Withdrew money for Emmerson in 1916 on half-day leave from his command.*

Edmond? Emmerson had mentioned a young replacement. A black pit of horror yawned in front of him, and he dared not look into it. Jaeryn was examining the translations from London, a stricken look in his green eyes. They held something like—compassion. Ben folded the paper, and Jaeryn held out his hand expectantly, but Ben kept it back. "I didn't tell you about my business in America, if you'll recall. I'm afraid I'll have to keep this to myself."

"Oh." Jaeryn subsided again, disappointed. He had gone to some effort to look nice just for dropping by, Ben thought. His hair was combed, and he had a new pair of boots on instead of his regular ones. It was like him to care how he looked. It was a little glimpse of the old Jaeryn, a side which had disappeared since the incident with Terry.

Jaeryn thanked Charlotte as she handed him a steaming cup, then looked to Ben. "If you have no objection, I think your wife would benefit from staying with us for the next few minutes. Or rather, you would benefit from having her stay. It doesn't make any difference to her personally. Do you mind?"

"Why should she? I don't mind, but I don't know what this is about." He watched Jaeryn reach inside his front pocket and braced himself for what he would pull out.

"It's a letter." Jaeryn found it, but he did not give it up right away. "I really am sorry, Dorroll."

"Why should you be sorry?" Ben asked, his voice taking on a cooler edge from worry.

"Because I suspect you're going to have to make a very hard decision, and it's partly my fault that you have to make it. Perhaps I should have left you in Virginia, and you would never have had to know about this. I don't know. At the time, I only wanted to succeed, but now I think there may be a higher price to success than even I am ready to pay. And if for me, then much more so for you."

There it was again—some price he was to pay as if all this were his fault. Ben prayed silently that he would have the strength to bear it. Charlotte sat down next to him on the sofa and held one of his hands, just like Terry's mother had with Mr. O'Sean when he told them about Erin. The O'Sean parents had paid a price in all this too. He had to bear his end, and bravely, just as they had done.

Ben took a deep breath and raised his head. "I'm ready."

Jaeryn handed him the letter. "It's from Fenton. Apparently he's been keeping something from me, and Ryson made him write to tell us."

Ben opened it and read.

Doctor Dorroll,

While I don't consider it necessary to write to someone who has dismissed my services, I am overridden. Ryson considers it important enough to pass on, and even though Jaeryn Graham was the one who paid for the information, he said it must be given to you. After considerable pains, I was able to confirm that Edmond Dorroll underwent gas injuries and a burst of shrapnel to the face at Vimy Ridge on the 1st of March. Men from his squadron were ordered to assist the initial charge of the Canadians after the gas attack failed. While details have not been confirmed, he and his men were found on the correct side of the line, and there is no reason to suspect treachery.

Ben frowned over the words and scanned through them a second time. "That letter was to me."

"It was. But I suspected what was inside it, and I thought I ought to read it first. Edmond's initial story struck me odd when we first met, and I thought since the British weren't involved in the attack that he might have been helping the wrong side."

The mental weight pressing on his shoulders eased off. "I'm glad you were wrong."

Jaeryn took another paper from his pocket and gave it to him, but this time, when Ben reached out to take it, Jaeryn held on to the paper. "Speyer sent this. You'll have to read it to us," he said. "I know whose writing it is, but I can't read German. Read it out loud, if you don't mind."

Ben tugged at it, and Jaeryn released it. It was a small envelope with no name or return address and no postmark. He knew the writing at a glance, though it was in German and not in English. Letting go of Charlotte's hand, he pulled out the letter. It wasn't long, and he started out briskly. As he got further down the page, his voice slowed, and Jaeryn had to prompt him once or twice to continue on.

August 12, 1917

The old man sent me. You'll find his letter of recommendation taped to the envelope. He's dead now, and I'm his successor. I want to meet you and get the information he intended me to have, but they won't let me see you unless I write and ask first. They said I must write so they could have concrete evidence of my commitment. Well, here is my commitment, and if it falls into the wrong hands, I'll have your soul for it. I'm influential in the cause, and if you do me a good turn, I won't see you go unrewarded. Now tell me when I can see you. I don't have much time, and this isn't the safest country I've ever been in. 00192

"I assume you know who wrote that," Jaeryn said when he had finished.

"I know." Ben stared down at the paper, unseeing, hardly hearing. There was nothing in the wide world except him and the letter, and what it meant he must do. "It's Edmond's writing."

"It's the same number from the telegram your sister had when she died. Agent 00192 was asked to confirm the location we picked to try to meet Emmerson's German correspondent. That confirms he must be in a position of authority."

Jaeryn's words triggered the memory of something Ben had not told him yet. "Ann Meikle admitted that Pearlie had passed the post office the evening she died. I asked her when there were witnesses by."

Jaeryn nodded approval. "That was keen of you. Did she say anything about the telegram?"

Ben shook his head. "She didn't indicate that Pearlie had come into the post office, just that she had walked by."

"I don't understand," Charlotte said quietly. "What does the letter we just read mean?"

"It means my brother traveled to Germany in August. Rather curious, isn't it, Charlotte? He wanted us to think he had gone to America, and he sent us letters to make us think so. But I think Creswick was the one who mailed those letters, even if Edmond did write them."

Jaeryn took the paper from Ben's hands and looked over it himself. "He gives us his number. That's going to help a lot. And he as good as admits what his role in all this is. I know it isn't good for you, Dorroll, but it's a relief to know, and it's best the damage stops where it does."

Ben nodded, and his throat tightened, but he held steady in front of Jaeryn. "Yes, I think you're right."

"That letter—the one that was sent from Virginia Beach—do you have it still?"

"I have it."

"Excellent. We can use it for the trial, and it will—" Jaeryn subsided at the sight of Ben's face. "I'm sorry. Never mind. I won't try to go through all the details yet. Forgive me for saying it, but it could be worse. If you had grown up with your brother, it would have been much harder. He may have been inveigled into it, and if he was, I think Emmerson would have done the same with you." Jaeryn waited for him to respond, but Ben didn't speak. "For heaven's sake, say something."

"I think we are cursed," Ben responded, gripping his hands together as if by that he could keep his world from falling apart. "Our whole family. I don't see any other explanation for it."

"That's ridiculous. You aren't cursed any more than your sister was. The choices others have made are theirs, and you do not share them."

"But I share the consequences for them. I wish I had never lived." He saw that Charlotte was close to crying and slipped his hand back into hers. "No, that isn't the case either. Not everything is bad; I didn't mean that." Charlotte leaned closer to him and squeezed his fingers, and there was a glimmer of comfort in that despite what he had just learned.

"You have a decision to make," Jaeryn said, looking at the papers that were in front him so as not to intrude on their grief. "He is your brother, and if you don't want to bring him down yourself, we won't make you. But I confess, I hope you won't back out now."

Ben shivered at the thought of what he had to do. "There's hardly a decision to be made. I knew that Edmond had come to Emmerson's estate and that my father's involvement was a possibility. Besides, if this is true, then Alisa is going to need someone to take care of her, and I carry that responsibility. I don't know how I'm ever going to tell her that her husband is a German sympathizer."

He leaned forward and hid his face in his hands.

* * *

Charlotte looked at Jaeryn when Ben fell silent. He took the hint and stood up to leave. "I'll show you to the door," she whispered.

They paused in the kitchen when they heard a strangled sob. Jaeryn asked, "Do you really think he's going to follow through?"

"I think he will. If this is all that he has to bear." Charlotte looked up at him keenly, and Jaeryn felt his face turning hot.

"I'm afraid I can't promise that."

Charlotte twisted her dress skirt between her fingers. "I've only seen him cry twice. Once when Pearlie died—he was so very sad about it—and I think he will again after you are gone. He doesn't show his feelings much, but when his sister died, he hoped for Edmond, because that was all he had left."

"He has you left. You'll help him, Mrs. Dorroll."

"I'll try. But that doesn't make the others easier. He counts on you, Doctor Graham. I think you should know that," she offered, not ungently.

Jaeryn straightened his shoulders. "I don't take it lightly, I assure you. I wish him all success."

"He wants to know that his success will be yours as well."

"I hope it will be. Good night, Mrs. Dorroll. You should go to him now. Tell him he doesn't have to come in tomorrow unless he likes." Jaeryn pressed her hand and picked up his coat to slip it on.

Charlotte touched his sleeve. For a moment, she let down her guard and spoke breathlessly, hurriedly. "I'm worried sick. He's so quiet. He isn't talking to me, and I'm sure he isn't talking to you either. There's no way he can be handling all this as tranquilly as he wants me to think. Something is wrong, and I don't want—I don't want him to face it all alone. I know that I can trust you where he is concerned. Perhaps together, we might—"

"I'll see if I can help him. I promise." Jaeryn laid a hand on her shoulder to assure her of his sincerity. Then he put on his coat and left her to face the troubles in the other room alone.

* * *

That night, when Ben joined Charlotte in bed, he reached out and ran his hand down her soft flaxen hair. "What are you thinking of, *ma chérie?*"

She smiled sadly. "You have lost all of them now. Pearl, and now Edmond. It must feel so strange to be the last."

"It makes me afraid sometimes," he admitted.

"Afraid of what?" She slid down under the quilt and laid her head on his shoulder.

"If they could not make it through this, then how can I?"

"You will, darling. No one can stand of themselves, but—to him who is able to keep you from falling, you know."

"I know."

Her cold little hand slipped into his. "What a strange way for it all to end."

"I only wish it was finished." Ben reached over and turned off the light.

* * *

Jaeryn wasn't surprised when Ben showed up the next day as usual. Even though he hadn't thought it wise, he said nothing and only suggested that Ben save house calls until the next day. By afternoon, they had discussed what they needed to, saying little about Edmond and keeping mainly to Terry and Starlin King. Ben could have one day to come to grips with it, Jaeryn decided, and then they would have no choice but to discuss when to take Edmond in. They had all the proofs they needed for him, but they still wanted the henchmen, and Jaeryn was reluctant to move prematurely lest the other German informants escape justice.

There was one good thing about the whole mess. Ben seemed so beaten that he didn't put up his guard as well as before, and though Jaeryn felt a twinge of guilt at taking advantage, he managed to get more information than he had ever thought possible before the morning was over, down to the three sovereigns with the messages inside them. In spite of that, he didn't inquire about the murder investigation. After the previous evening, it didn't seem wise to bring up the subject, and Ben didn't offer any information. He didn't talk much at all, and Jaeryn didn't know what comfort to offer. What could he say when a man's brother turned out to be a German subversive?

For all their careful avoidance of important subjects, they did manage to plan out one thing. They needed to locate Starlin King if they wanted to put all the pieces together. Ben insisted that the young man was the key to it all, and as reluctant as Jaeryn was to credit the notion, he was forced to agree. They needed the information he could give about Terry. At least, Jaeryn needed the information. Ben seemed more concerned for the boy's welfare. Jaeryn tried not to be heartless, but in spite of himself he couldn't dredge up any concern. Not that he wanted to see Starlin die—definitely not that—but a healthy fear for his safety might teach the boy a little responsibility. The end result was that Jaeryn set out in the cold, gray afternoon for the King estate.

He had set Patrick to watching Ben while he was gone—never mind if Patrick was untrained and Ben didn't want it. The choice wasn't Ben's to make, and since he thought it his duty to refuse, Jaeryn made the decision for him. It was a stopgap measure, designed to get them through the next few days until they could wrap up their work. Not to mention keeping Patrick out of Ben's way so the two of them couldn't talk to one another.

When he knocked on Colonel King's door, a maid took him straight to the study, and he looked up at the man, wondering how in the world he could ask him to borrow his son. He was given more grace than he had planned on, for as he entered the room, someone brushed past him. Jaeryn looked over in surprise and saw Starlin standing just inside the door, almost as if he had waited until that moment to come in. The thought suddenly crossed his mind that the wish to meet might be mutual.

Colonel King raised his eyebrows at his son's interruption. "Is something the matter, Starlin?"

"Yes," Starlin said. "I want my birth certificate."

It shocked them both, the words that came out of his mouth. Starlin was the only one who kept his cool. Colonel King's eyebrows went up even further, but his voice was smooth and quiet when he replied. "Your birth certificate? Why would you want to see that?"

"It's mine, isn't it?" Starlin shoved his hands in his pockets, and his eyes fixed everywhere but on his father's face, betraying his apprehension.

Jaeryn looked down at Starlin's hands, and it suddenly registered in his mind that the boy had white gloves on. How odd to wear dinner gloves during the day. Not only that, but they were unbuttoned, and one of them was wrong side out. As he watched, Starlin furtively slid the gloves off his hands and into his pockets without attracting his father's notice.

Colonel King sighed and glanced apologetically to Jaeryn. "Starlin, there is only one possible reason why you would want your birth certificate, and that is so you can fake a second one to enlist. You may not have it."

Starlin tilted his chin in defiance. "If you won't give me work, then I'll find some myself."

"I have the resources to track you down even if you change your name. You will not take such a foolish step for your own gratification. There is better and more legal work for you to do that will be just as useful to the war effort."

"I could just take off one day, you know."

"With not a penny to live on." Colonel King gave a gesture of dismissal. "I will see you at dinner."

Starlin's face smoldered with the sting of his failed object. "I'm not coming to dinner."

"Don't be a child. You may leave the room. Now, what was it you came for, doctor?"

Starlin shut the door as loudly as he dared, but Jaeryn opened it and called him back. "I actually came for your son, sir. Ben Dailey hasn't seen him since he came back and wanted to say hello. Would you be willing to lend him to me for an hour or two?"

Starlin returned in answer to his call, and though he gave no sign, Jaeryn felt hope coursing through the slim frame next to him.

Colonel King looked dubious. "He's not in a state to talk to people at present."

"It doesn't matter," Jaeryn returned cheerfully. "I doubt Dailey will mind."

King turned to his son. "Will you go, Starlin, and do as you are told?"

It might be an overactive imagination, Jaeryn told himself, but he suspected there was more to that question than appeared at first glance.

"Otherwise," King continued, "you'll stay here, and I will speak to you further about what you just asked of me."

"I'll go," Starlin said hastily. "And I'll do as I'm told."

"Then he's yours, doctor, for as long as you like."

Jaeryn didn't think a single person in the room was deceived by what had just been said, but he kept up his side of the charade and bowed politely as he returned his thanks. Then he and Starlin went out, and Jaeryn waited in the hall while a maid brought Starlin's coat.

When they were in the car, Jaeryn dropped his act immediately. "We've been concerned about you. After Saturday night we knew something was wrong. Am I correct in assuming you need some help?"

"I can handle it myself. My father's going to ask me what we talked about when I get back."

"I'll take that as an affirmative. Who will you talk to?"

"Anyone safe. Anyone I like," Starlin muttered.

"In other words, you're not about to bare your soul to me. Well, then, tell me who you like."

"I like Doctor Dailey."

"Excellent. I'll take you to him before you change your mind."

Jaeryn offered no more conversation while he drove back to the clinic, and Starlin said nothing himself. His mouth was clamped tightly. He leaned his chin on his hand and looked out the window to hide his face from Jaeryn.

When they got to the clinic, Jaeryn put a hand on his shoulder and led him upstairs to the guest room, telling him to wait there. Ben was still in the consulting room, thankfully, and Jaeryn made him drop his work to come upstairs. Ben looked glad to see Starlin when he followed Jaeryn to the upstairs hall.

"Did you come here to get away, Starlin?" he asked.

"No." Starlin sighed and looked for words to explain. "Doctor Graham got me out, but I've been trapped there for days. I just need to talk to someone. It's urgent, but it's not an emergency."

"You could have told me, you know," Jaeryn pressed, "if it was urgent."

Starlin turned his strange mix of penetration and childishness on Jaeryn, almost making him wish he hadn't said it. "I'll talk to someone who trusts my word."

Jaeryn frowned. "I would if it was trustw—"

Ben shot him a glance, and he subsided.

"Go on," Ben prompted. "What's wrong?"

Starlin took a deep breath. "My father is involved in German secret intelligence, and I'm not sure what to do. I found out in August."

Jaeryn exploded in hot wrath. "You found out this summer, and it's almost December, and you never said a word about it. Do you realize what's at stake? People have died over this, and you held your tongue for months when we could have cleaned up—"

"Jaeryn," Ben said sharply, "I think we'd be better off alone. If you'll leave us for a few minutes, I'm sure we can get this straightened out. I'll tell you what you need to know."

Jaeryn stopped and looked uncertainly at Ben. "Are you telling me to leave?"

"That about sums it up. You stir him up too much, and we need to know what he has to say."

Ben opened the door. Jaeryn stared at him in disbelief, but Ben was firm, for all that he was shorter, younger, and more inexperienced. Something in Jaeryn gave way. He went out, and Ben closed the door after. The Irishman growled under his breath and descended the stairs.

* * *

Ben turned back to Starlin as soon as Jaeryn was gone. "There, we won't be disturbed now."

"Thank you," Starlin breathed. "I hate him."

"There's no need to hate him. He's not always polite to people he dislikes, but that doesn't mean you should return it. You're not a child anymore, and it's a man's part to be polite to everyone. But I don't blame you. I haven't always liked him either. Now, tell me what makes you think your father is involved."

"I don't think. I know. The week after I shot Terry, my father made me give him an explanation. After I did, he told me about his work. He said I had stumbled upon something, and I had an opportunity to help him if I wanted. When he told me it meant getting information about Terry, I asked which side Terry was on, and he said Terry was loyal to the Germans. So I asked him who we were loyal to, and he said we were working for Germany as well. The week before I had told him I wanted some work to do instead of being bored at home, and he said if I was going to be involved in politics, I might as well begin if I liked. But I told him I didn't want that sort of work."

King must have been sure of his son's silence to reveal his work so freely. "And what did he say to that?"

"He said that was all the work I would get, and I would agree to it or he would find ways to silence me. So I kept quiet because it would be just my word against his. Perhaps you haven't noticed much, but no one believes when I say things."

"I've noticed," Ben sympathized. "I think you've been underestimated, and that's not entirely your fault. If your father thought you were valuable enough to offer you a part in his work, then we will consider you valuable to our side as well."

Starlin seemed to shrink into himself as the whole story came out. "I think he was bringing me up to it. He gave me the maps in my room and made me follow all the war effort. That wasn't so bad; I liked that part. But he was always asking me which side I thought was right. I've been doing what he wants all my life, and I'm tired of it."

Ben wondered why it should be that Starlin, such a sullen seventeen-year-old, stood resolute in his convictions and he had not, though older and more mature. "You're fortunate to be alive, Starlin. There was the death threat, and then you were drugged—I'm sure your father was trying to frighten you into compliance. He must have placed great stock in you to take the risk for this long."

Starlin shrugged. "Not especially. I'm his son, and I think that has counted for something. It couldn't have counted for much though, because when I wouldn't give him any information about you, he wouldn't give me my Bearcat, and he kept me out of college. He couldn't hit me because you came to the house so much."

At least his own father hadn't played such a ruthless game when he asked him to take part in intelligence work. It wasn't as bad as Starlin's situation. It couldn't be.

Or had two fathers done the exact same thing, only on opposites sides of the war? Ben shook the thought away.

"What caused your father to change his mind?"

"He heard I was making friends with Terry, and I told him little things when I could. So he gave me the automobile, but he couldn't let me go to college after that when I would have told so many people about him. This morning I found something he wouldn't want me to see."

"What was that?"

"There's a list of registration numbers for every agent you need in his study desk. I can lay my hands on it anytime I like. It has numbers for the people on your side, too. I'm not sure how he got them, but somehow he knows the whole truth of who's involved and on which side now. The good ones are mixed in with the bad, so I couldn't tell which was which. But you're there, and Doctor Graham, and a bunch of others. That's how I found out your real name was Dorroll."

Ben drew his breath in amazement, hardly believing what Starlin had told him. "Incredible," he whispered. "That's the last proof we need."

Starlin nodded. "It doesn't have the first name on the list. My father's name isn't on it, either."

"I already know the first name." Ben's lips tightened. "It's your brother, isn't it?"

"I don't believe I told you I had a brother."

"My father writes to him."

"Ah. If you can get those letters for me as well as the list, I'll make good use of them."

Starlin frowned. "I never said I would give it to you."

Ben gripped his shoulder. "You must. You are only seventeen years old, and the weight of many affairs is affected by your actions."

"You can't make me."

Ben stared down at the defiant face and realized how much Starlin had been pushed and pummeled as if he were a dispensable object in a very messy game of politics. All of them had discounted the fact that he was a real person with choices to make like everybody else. Ben removed his hand from Starlin's shoulder and let it fall to his side.

"No, I can't make you, nor will I try. You have interests in this just like the rest of us, and the decision is yours. Will you give them to me?"

He let Starlin think as long as he wished, and as he expected, the boy thought better of his secrecy. "I supposed if you're going to turn your brother in, I can turn in my father." Starlin stood almost as tall as he did now, and his eyes, on a level with his own, held a hint of wistfulness. "I'll do it for you. But I won't do it for that doctor."

"Do it for me, then, and I'll be grateful to you." Ben felt remorse for the troubled face. "I'm sorry you have to do this. I know it is no light thing you are offering, and I'll try to keep you out of it as much as possible. We can't take the list yet, or your father will find out and slip through our fingers. Jaeryn and I will be at his dinner on

Saturday, and we'll take it then, if you think you can manage it."

"I'm afraid he's going to kill me before then. He's never said so, but he might."

Ben pulled out his notebook and tore a piece of paper from it. "Watch your back. Try to stick it out through Saturday, but if you see any sign of danger to your life, then leave immediately. Go to London, to my father's house. His name is Matthew Dorroll, and I'll give you his address. He has connections to London officials who can keep you safe." Then another thought occurred to him, and he asked, "I'm sure you're all right, but do you have enough money in case you need some?"

Starlin shook his head. "I don't have any money. I used it all."

He took out two pounds from his wallet and gave it to Starlin, along with the address. "Did your father take it from you?"

"Not in that way. I asked him if he would let Turlough O'Sean's case go to court after I shot him, and he said no. I said it had been my fault, and I wanted to make it up to him, and I told him if we didn't pay the hospital bills I would take it to the police myself. So he said I would have to pay all my money and then he would take care of the rest, and he kept his word. But it didn't work. Terry found out about it afterward."

"How did he find out?"

"He asked, and he wasn't in a mood to be refused. But he never offered to pay me back."

A suspicion flashed across Ben's mind. "Was he the only one you helped?"

The toe of one black boot crushed against the heel of the other as Starlin deliberated his response. "I helped him mostly."

"Did you help me?"

Starlin's face turned red. He remained silent, and the black boot continued scraping against its fellow. Ben had mercy on him.

"I won't make you tell me right now. We only need to know one more thing, and then I think we'll have everything we need from you. Can you tell us, has Terry been threatening you?"

A quiver crossed Starlin's face as he nodded. "The night before your sister's funeral. I'm sorry about her. I wish it hadn't happened."

"You were kind to come to the service. Tell me why Terry threatened you."

"I paid him a visit where he and his friend and Stafford lived, and he was pretty unhappy about it. They almost wouldn't let me leave. I pretended to have something to offer them, but they didn't believe me much, so I had to tell them more than I meant to. I gave them your name and told them it wasn't your real one. Terry made me tell them, but I won't help you turn him in for all that. He was nice to me, and even though he's not on our side now, I won't do it."

"I won't make you," Ben reassured him.

"They want me to come back and tell them more," Starlin said, a weary shudder sweeping over him. "I've been staying home, but I know they'll make me tell them private information as soon as they catch me outside the house. They'll kill me if they find out I'm not as obedient as they think. What if they find me before Saturday?"

"If that happens, tell them everything you know about me except that I know the people involved. Don't drop a hint of the list, or that you know about my brother, not for the life or death of you. The rest you can give away. Pretty soon it won't matter."

"I wish Terry wasn't on their side."

"Are you quite sure he is?" Ben tried to ignore the fresh twist of pain at the confirmation.

"His name is on the list with the others, and he pulled a knife when I told him I knew he was involved."

"Write the names down for me."

Starlin complied. There were eight of them. Ben folded up the paper and placed it in his jacket pocket. He knew them all; that was hardly a surprise. But the numbers would be more than helpful. Starlin rose to go, and Ben shook hands with him. "Thank you for coming to me. I appreciate it, Starlin."

Starlin's hand was damp and didn't offer a very firm grip, but he couldn't be blamed for that after what he had been forced to tell. "What if my father decides to change the paper's hiding place?"

Ben pressed his lips together grimly. "We must pray to God that he does not, or we'll have lost what we need to finish this. Hold tight, Starlin. We're none of us safe, but we'll have to hold together somehow until December first."

* * *

After taking Starlin home, Ben found Jaeryn and told him what the boy had said. When Ben apologized for sending him out, Jaeryn didn't seem too upset about the matter—rather relieved, even, that he had not had to deal with Starlin himself. He took in everything Ben repeated with careful precision, his mind apparently putting together the new information with the facts they already knew.

"I wonder how he got the numbers," Jaeryn said.

"Who on our side knows the identification numbers?"

"I do, but I never wrote them down. Ann Meikle knew, and Terry as well."

"Terry could have given them up."

Jaeryn's shoulders slumped. "He could have. I'd rather believe the Meikle woman did it, but Terry had the opportunity."

"Didn't you say when King dismissed Stafford that Terry as good as invited him to stay with them?"

"He said it was to keep an eye on him." Jaeryn's voice sank to a defeated whisper. "To think I believed him so easily. And now the British Secret Service is compromised for sure. He knows London headquarters, past cases—he knows everything."

Ben felt as sick at heart as Jaeryn looked. "We'll stop the leak as quickly as we can."

"Even a brief one can be a disaster. I still don't know why young King didn't tell us sooner," Jaeryn said in disgust.

Ben frowned. "You don't just turn your father in like that without any hesitation. He sacrificed to tell us, Jaeryn, even if there was no love lost between them."

Jaeryn was a man without a past, without friends, without family, and Ben wondered how much an appeal to family relationships could mean to him. Evidently, not much. Jaeryn shrugged. "King wasn't much of a father that I ever saw, but I see your point. I suppose that's to the boy's credit. We'll arrest King along with the others as quietly as possible. According to the messages you got in the sovereigns, we should take them all on Saturday. There must be a reason three different people have alerted you to it. Any ideas?"

"I called Peters today. He said my brother had an invitation for Saturday as well but did not intend to come. He obviously has other plans, and I think that's what we're being asked to be ready for. Are you coming to the dinner?"

Jaeryn found the invitation with King's signature and held it up. "I wrote back and said I would. We might have to leave early, though, to finish this business. Are you bringing a guest?"

"I don't have one to bring." Ben narrowed his eyes at Jaeryn. "And if you think I'm going to bring Patrick, you can think again. He isn't presentable. He's horribly American, and he can't pull off a gathering like that."

"I didn't say anything," Jaeryn protested. His white teeth flashed out in a smile. "I'm rather surprised that you think being American is a detriment. You didn't used to. Are you going to involve him at all?"

"Certainly. I have something else for him to do."

"Care to confide?" Jaeryn asked lightly.

"No, thank you. But I have something else you'll like that I learned this morning."

"All right, then, let's have it."

"I wrote Ryson to ask him to delay the murder investigation as a personal favor. He's sending a man down to work with the local authorities and tell them what's going on. He'll make sure that nothing happens until we're ready."

"I'm surprised you did."

"I will not have the one person who loved my sister hung when I can do something to prevent it," Ben said sternly. "What happens to him afterwards is his business."

"We're free of obstacles to wrapping up the turncoats and German informants then." In spite of Jaeryn's seriousness, a sparkle of gleeful anticipation darted across his face.

"And then—it will be done." Ben sighed.

Jaeryn tilted his head and considered him. "Would you like to go back to Virginia after this is over?"

"Originally, I would have. I'm not sure now."

"Oh?" Jaeryn raised his eyebrows. "Like England better since you've come back, do you?"

"Not particularly. It's hasn't treated me better than before. But I couldn't leave Alisa alone, at least not right away. And Pearlie's here for good now. It would be hard to leave her just yet. I'm not sure what I'm going to do, but I think I'll have to stay for a while, at least."

Jaeryn's eyes twinkled. "We may be able to keep you in spite of yourself. We'll have to see about that, won't we?"

Ben wondered, as he went out to call in the next patient, if Jaeryn was right. He might not see Virginia again. But even if he didn't return to America, he hoped that it would be due to a long and peaceful life in England, and not because someone did away with him. There was a strong possibility that he might die before December first. The thought sent an odd shiver through him. After his conversation with Starlin and the letters about Edmond, he knew too much for his own safety.

Chapter Thirty-Four
Final Preparations

He hadn't expected to set foot on this corner of English soil again. Not after what had happened to his sister. Already the only remembrance he had of Pearlie were the images in his head and the tiny thumbnail portrait on her passport. They didn't have any other photos, and all her things were packed away out of sight. Coming to Copt Point brought up accusations recently abandoned and highly unwanted. Every memory that rose in his mind was of that dreadful night and what it might have been like. Imagining the moment of Pearlie's death, and how she must have felt, afraid and alone, was pure torture.

These thoughts occupied his mind as Ben wheeled Jaeryn's bicycle down the gentle slope to the cottages. At least he didn't have to enter the one where she had been killed. Erin Reinhardt occupied the other one, the one Mrs. Goodwin had lived in that spring, and Patrick was sure to be with her.

He knocked at Erin's door, trying his best not to imagine that he could still see bloodstains on the ground. Erin answered immediately. It was evident that something had happened to disturb her equilibrium before his knock. When he saw Patrick with a slightly annoyed expression on the sofa behind her, Ben realized he had interrupted an argument.

"Mrs. Reinhardt. Patrick." He nodded to both of them. "I'm sorry if this is a bad time to stop by."

Patrick let out a low growl. "You might as well. We weren't getting anywhere."

Erin's lips were pressed thin with anger. He didn't know what to say to Patrick's grumbling and decided to ignore it. "I've only come for a moment—to drop off something of Terry's. He gave me his ring to keep, but I can't stand to have it at the house anymore."

Patrick came over to see it, his curiosity getting the better of whatever he was displeased about. Erin untied the string fastening the box, but when it opened, she frowned in confusion. "There's nothing here."

She tilted the empty box towards him. Ben took it up and looked inside himself, but it was quite empty. "It had Terry's ring. I put it away in the attic, and I haven't touched it since."

"I'm sure you only lost it," Erin reassured him. "It will turn up."

"I didn't misplace it. Someone took it."

"I believe you," Patrick said. "Who do you think it was?"

"I don't know." Ben gritted his teeth. "I wish it was over and done with and I could have him out of my life for good. I'd like to knock him in the teeth for thinking he could marry my sister." He looked to Erin. "I'll leave now; apologies for intruding on you with no reason. Patrick, I'd like a word with you."

Patrick followed him outside, and Ben explained briefly that he was making his final move on Saturday and needed Alisa and Charlotte kept safely out of the way. Patrick nodded.

"Don't worry about anything on that score. I'll see they're kept safe. If they came here, they would be even safer."

Ben shook his head. "I doubt Erin would let you."

Patrick muttered something under his breath. "It's not her choice." He opened the door and poked his head in. "Erin, you have company coming Saturday. They'll be spending the night."

"Patrick—" Ben protested.

"Oh, it will be good for her. Besides, Brogan will like Alisa's baby. It can't do any harm, and then I can keep them under my eye together. Leave them to me and don't bother your head about them."

"All right. Wherever you think they'll be safest."

"You can count on me." Patrick looked exhilarated at the prospect of having something depending entirely on his shoulders.

634

One late night of thinking on his sitting room sofa, frowning heavily all the while, put all the facts in place in Jaeryn's mind. If he wanted any part in the final capture, he was going to have to force his way into it, whether his colleagues liked it or not. The following morning, therefore, while Ben was focused on opening up the clinic for the day, he launched his plan of attack.

"What's your plan for the first of December?" Jaeryn asked.

"I haven't told anyone. I'm not about to tell you, either."

"Well, you have to tell London at the very least. They expect to be informed of these things. Take it from someone who's done it before. If I were you, I'd run up to London to inform them what you're thinking and give them the evidence you've collected. It would be a disaster if someone found it this close to the end."

"All right."

"And I think you should take Patrick with you."

Ben glanced up from the mail he was sorting and looked him straight in the eye. "Absolutely not."

"Don't be foolish. You have to take him."

"He doesn't know where the London offices are. Ryson wouldn't want him to."

"All right, then," Jaeryn said, holding his breath as he spoke his next words. "I'll go with you."

Ben raised an eyebrow as he collected a stack of new magazines and took them to the waiting room across the hall. "I don't think so."

Very carefully, Jaeryn mixed an edge of forcefulness into his words, just enough to be persuasive without rousing Ben's suspicions. "It would be foolish to be murdered because you took a train ride alone. You can take Patrick or you can take me, but you can't go alone."

After a moment's silence, Ben's voice came from the other room with an edge of frustrated resignation. "Come along, then. I'll let Ryson deal with you."

Jaeryn hid a smile of satisfaction.

Thursday morning, Ben put a message in the drop to inform Ryson of their coming, and late Thursday evening they left by way of Jaeryn's back door for the train station. They were going at night so they could keep the clinic open the next day. They also took the train so no one would see Jaeryn's car gone from the drive. No one knew of the matter, not even Charlotte.

At Jaeryn's request, the cab dropped them two blocks from their destination. They could see through the window that Jeremy wasn't sitting in his usual place. When they entered and tried the door to the warehouse, it was unlocked and opened without resistance. The front room was empty. Jaeryn looked tentatively down the hall before gesturing Ben to go first. A light shone from under Ryson's door, and Jaeryn thought it wisest to follow behind Ben since he wasn't really supposed to be there. Ben knocked. A voice invited them to enter, and Ben turned the knob and shoved the door open.

"Well, Doctor Dorroll," Ryson greeted, "you told me in your note that this is where we plan for the finish line...why did you bring Jaeryn Graham with you?"

"For safety," Ben replied. He didn't seem afraid, but he was diplomatic enough to put on a deferential air. Jaeryn wondered if it was actually genuine. "I'm not safe at present, and two are better than one. He's the only other person who knows of this location, so I brought him with me. It couldn't be helped. He knows most of what we know anyway."

A surge of confidence rushed through Jaeryn when Ryson pointed to an extra chair against the wall.

"Now." Ryson leaned back and folded his hands together. "Tell us what you need."

First, Ben handed over the evidence: the letters and cards and photographs, the keys, the Brownie camera, and the death threats that he and Starlin had received. Jaeryn thought of his own, safely locked away at home. He was thankful that Ben hadn't asked for them. Not that they were anything that people couldn't see, but he should be able to keep something after all his hard work. Ryson scanned through the various pieces, pausing the longest over the German letter written by Edmond Dorroll. Jaeryn realized that Ben had withheld the letter from Nathan Speyer. He wondered in amusement if the young doctor was more calculating than he had thought.

His suspicion proved correct. Or at least, so he believed when Ben tried introducing his question as a rumor instead of giving a full explanation. "We heard that Nathan Speyer has something we need for our work in Folkestone."

Ryson looked up quickly. "How did you hear that?"

Ben hesitated and then handed over Speyer's letter. Jaeryn

groaned inwardly. He wasn't calculating after all. It might not get Ben into hot water, but Ryson would rake Jaeryn over the coals when he found out Speyer had sent it to him. He sat in agony as Ben explained it—the whole truth of it—and Ryson listened with keen displeasure. Ryson took up the letter when Ben had done, reading it in silence. Jaeryn gave Ben a freezing glance. Ben shrugged his shoulders as if to say that if Jaeryn had something to hide, he would have no part in the deception.

"I have heard nothing to substantiate this. I have no idea what is referred to here, and I am surprised that Speyer would write to Jaeryn Graham to begin with," Ryson said.

"I don't think Nathan Speyer is at fault if anything is the matter, sir."

Jaeryn gasped, but Ben did not look as if he enjoyed the admission. He was only trying to be truthful, and Jaeryn couldn't deny that he was right. If anyone was to blame, it was not Nathan Speyer.

"I have no doubt of that. Leave the matter to me; it has no bearing on your work, so you'll be better off putting it out of your head." Ryson searched through the papers and found the German letter again. "Who is this from?"

"My brother, sir. You'll notice that he admits to being heavily involved. Emmerson wanted Edmond to be the ringleader after his decease."

Ryson looked taken aback. "Are you sure?" he exclaimed, murmuring the translation to himself as he read through the letter a third time. Ben produced another sample of Edmond's handwriting, and Ryson compared the proofs. "Then I wonder why—" He broke off and looked at Jaeryn. Jaeryn shifted and bit his lip. He wanted nothing more than to put in a word, but he didn't dare. He couldn't afford to do anything that would cast more suspicion on him.

After that, Ben laid out their plan and what they needed, coolly, calculatedly, and with not a detail forgotten. He acted almost as if he was planning the arrest of complete strangers. He asked for nine men, fully armed and carrying proper warrants. Jaeryn couldn't help noticing that nine would be enough for each person involved, including him. He mustn't be afraid now, he told himself sternly. He wasn't taken yet, and if the worst came to the worst, Ben wasn't the inexorable sort that couldn't be persuaded.

Ryson wrote down the instructions, sometimes adding suggestions here and there, but allowing Ben to take the lead. "I'll have the reinforcements in town tomorrow morning. They'll be entirely at your disposal. You say you intend to take Edmond Dorroll first, before the henchmen?"

Ben nodded. "Right after the dinner. Edmond and King come first, and then we'll move on to the others while they're asleep. If it takes longer than we expect, we'll send your men ahead to the others. We don't want to leave anyone who might have killed my sister loose for long."

Ryson grunted in satisfaction. "Don't hesitate to kill them if they give you trouble. It's the only way, and you have official sanction." By the aversion on Ben's face, Jaeryn knew he was unlikely to follow that order. At least there were others who could do it for him.

"What will the penalty be for my brother once he is arrested, sir?"

For the first time, Jaeryn saw Ryson's typical indifference soften to concern. Both of them knew the answer, but Ben didn't, and for the first time that day, Ryson was at a loss for words. It was hard to know how Ben would take it, and it was a pity to give him more guilt to bear when he was weary and beaten. Yet bear he must, if he would insist upon an answer.

"I would prefer not to say, doctor." Ryson looked down and fiddled with the watch on his wrist. "I strongly advise we wait until the court verdict before making speculations."

Ben's face settled into stern lines. "He is my brother. I have the right to know."

"Oh, very well. If you must be obstinate. Most of the German sympathizers will get imprisonment of anywhere from five years to life."

"And is that what my brother will get?"

Ryson's expression was sympathetic, though his words were hard. "Edmond Dorroll, as a ringleader, will likely receive capital punishment."

"That is execution."

"It is."

"How could you do it?" Jaeryn cringed at the anguish in Ben's voice. "How could you hire me to destroy him? For the love of heaven, is life a—a game to you, your agents pawns with no feelings? We are *people*. He has a father I will have to tell, and a wife. Am I to be responsible for killing my own brother?"

"Calm yourself," Ryson said.

Jaeryn gritted his teeth. It was awkward to men like Ryson when they had to face the idea that they were trading in flesh and blood. He would try to hush the protests, but he would not offer any resolution. There was no comfort any of them could offer, in the end. "You will remember that we had no idea your brother was involved when we brought you here. I cannot alter the consequences for treason, and your brother went in with open eyes. But I will not force you to continue if you do not wish to do so."

Jaeryn reached out and laid a steadying hand on Ben's shoulder. He must not back down now. If he did, then every chance of getting Terry out—and making sure Jaeryn's own interests were protected—would be over. In that gentle grip he concentrated all the will power he could conjure, hoping fiercely that everything would not fall to pieces so close to the end. A flood of relief ran through him when he was not disappointed.

Ben recited the words without feeling, as though he had rehearsed them many times before. "I am committed to the end."

"Very good, then." Ryson continued briskly on. "A man named Allan Evesham will oversee your reinforcements and any matters you need extra authority to handle. That includes your sister's murder investigation. He is a man of high position, and you should treat him as such. Tall and dark-haired. He will come tomorrow afternoon to the Tontine clinic, and I expect a full report as soon as you are finished on Saturday. Nothing is to go wrong. Nothing at all."

Jaeryn saved Ben from having to reply. "Understood, sir. Is there any way we could get Edmond Dorroll off on a medical diagnosis? I don't think he's been right in his head since his return." That wasn't entirely truthful, but for Ben's sake, he had to try it.

"None at all. Now you, Doctor Graham, can wait in the other room while I have a private word with Dorroll here. Don't try to leave; I have people watching the entrance, and they will take you up if you do."

Rage boiled within him at the insinuation. He had felt that rage often in the past weeks, at bay against so many people, treated as a traitor without proof. He would show them, every one of them, that he was not a man to be meddled with. But he managed to keep his lips firmly pressed together and he held his tongue. "Of course, sir."

Jaeryn made his footsteps sound loud enough to make them think he had gone into the next room. Then he unlaced his boots and slipped them off so he could return without a sound. The door stood ajar, but he paused well beyond it so as not to cast a shadow. He heard Ryson's voice first.

"Do you intend to take Doctor Graham with you when you make the arrests?"

"I think he intends to be there, and I haven't tried to refuse him."

"Excellent. I hoped that would be the case. Let him come with you for the captures and keep him at your side the entire evening. We want him with you where he can be easily taken."

"Then he *is* being taken?"

"Absolutely. He will be the third person we arrest, right after Edmond Dorroll."

Jaeryn gritted his teeth. Ryson needn't worry. He had no plans to escape, and he wasn't such a coward as to take the easy way out.

"I will try, sir, as much as is in my power, but I'm hardly a match for Jaeryn Graham."

"You'll have others who are more than a match for him to help you. I believe that is all, doctor. You're ready, and this is almost finished."

Jaeryn slipped out to the other room and pulled on his boots. He didn't have time to lace them, but it didn't matter. Ben wouldn't notice anyway. Ben came out, and Jaeryn clapped a hand on his shoulder as they re-entered the street. "You did well, my friend. I noticed you didn't give him the telegram with Edmond's number. That was wise for the present."

Ben shrugged and said nothing.

"Come home with me. You can use the guest room until morning."

"I should be getting back to Charlotte."

Jaeryn held up his hand for a cab. "Patrick will make sure she's all right. Do you need to see your father before we go back?"

Ben shook his head. "I'll come back later. I don't know how to tell him yet."

"We'll go home, then."

It was as dark traveling back as when they had left. Jaeryn's eyes felt leaden from being up all night, and the prospect of being up all the next day did little to hearten him. He hoped nothing had happened in his absence, either with clinic business or with their other work.

Sliding down in his seat, he closed his eyes, opening them once or twice to look at Ben. Concern crept over him at the sight of the white face. Maybe this was too much. To see all this heartache the first time out—it couldn't be healthy. The raw hurt was quite evident, but doctor though he was, Jaeryn knew it would be cruelty to touch the wound there. Not yet.

* * *

There were only two days left that he would have another living sibling. Only two days left working with Jaeryn. Only two days until Terry, too, was taken, unless Jaeryn found a way to help him escape. The thought of that made Ben sick. He hadn't been trained for this situation. It was supposed to be strangers, people he didn't know or care about, that he was taking in for justice. Not his only older brother, who would be hung if they were successful.

But he didn't have long to dwell on what would occur. Almost before he dared to hope, Ryson sent concrete evidence that he was overseeing their success. He must have attended to their business in short order after they left, for Allan Evesham arrived too soon for the early trains. He must have come in his own car to make such good time.

Jaeryn called the tall, dark-haired figure into the consulting room around nine o' clock. He was sitting with the other patients in the waiting room, though he didn't look ill. Quite the contrary—hale and hearty and full of vigor. Probably in his late forties or early fifties, if the slightly weathered face and few gray hairs gave any indication. When Jaeryn stood by the door to let the man pass, Ben recognized him with a thrill of pleasure from the first dinner at King's.

"Allan Evesham," the man offered, pulling out his wallet and showing them his passport. "How do you gentlemen find yourselves today?"

Ben looked to Jaeryn. "We're pleased to see you here," Jaeryn said, glancing sideways at Ben and lifting his shoulders as if to indicate that he should take the lead.

Evesham's blue eyes were set deep, with smile wrinkles around them. They held a reserve that hinted at wisdom and secrecy in equal measure, and while not stern, there was a grave set to his mouth—an earnest expression. He looked as if he enjoyed life but didn't consider it a business to be taken lightly. "I've come to talk to Benjamin Dailey."

Jaeryn gestured for him to take the leather swivel chair. "This room should be private if you think it's satisfactory."

"I came to talk to Doctor Dailey alone, actually. Do you have him occupied here, or can you spare him for a half hour?" Evesham sauntered over to where Jaeryn's medical certificate hung and lightly underlined the name with his finger. "You're Jaeryn Graham, aren't you?"

For a split second, Jaeryn's eyes held the cold calculation of a cat's. "Does that mean something to you?"

Evesham turned away from the frame, and his smile was kindly toward Ben, but toward Jaeryn he looked like a parent warning a wayward child. "A pleasure to meet you, Doctor Graham. I look forward to making your better acquaintance."

"Ryson sent you to help us," Ben said before Jaeryn could get in the next word.

He did not know exactly what it was about the man that gave him confidence. It was as if Evesham had a full understanding of the workings of men and knew how to act accordingly. In this swirl of untrustworthy people, having someone reliable to help him through the final stretch was a great relief. He didn't have the mental detachment at present to arrange details as he ought.

"He did indeed," Evesham said. "And from what I see and hear, I think you need some help. I would like to transact our business in private."

Ben looked questioningly to Jaeryn, who nodded for him to go. He took up his coat and led the newcomer outside, but not before Jaeryn slipped a pocket revolver into his hand and he transferred it carefully to his coat. It wouldn't do to be reckless, even if the man was a London official.

He led Allan Evesham out toward the Leas. They would be sure of privacy there, and even if they were followed, they would be able to see anyone coming from a long distance away. There weren't many people out for a stroll with this wind blowing in from the Channel.

Evesham made small talk, asking him about his medical work in Folkestone. He hadn't had anyone take a personal interest in him for a long time without ulterior motives attached to their questions. After all that had occurred, he was cautious not to give away important details, but he chatted as easily as if he was at one of King's dinners, and his answers seemed to please the man. Once he looked back, and far away, at the end of the walk, he saw a redheaded figure in a tan coat. It must be Patrick. It was too small to be Terry, and Patrick was neither very tall nor very brawny. Evidently, Jaeryn had sent him to follow and make sure they were all right.

When they were sufficiently far enough from anyone who might overhear them, Evesham dropped the pleasantries. "I've come to supervise the reinforcements you asked for and to manage your sister's murder investigation. I'll speak to the detective this morning and alert him to what's going on. Technically I'm rather high up to attend to something like this, but your needs tied in nicely with mine. I'm willing to handle this angle of our work as it also serves my interests."

Allan Evesham made a careful distinction about being Ryson's equal. There must be something important to bring him out. "Would it be indiscreet to ask what your interests are?" Ben asked hesitantly.

Evesham pulled out a small envelope and took an engraved invitation card from it. "I have this connection to King, and my other interest is Jaeryn Graham. He's been causing headaches in more than one part of London, and I would like to see how he has handled the business we've entrusted to him. A man of his experience requires a man of even greater experience to detect if there's anything amiss."

"He has seven years in this business."

"And I have twenty," Evesham countered good-naturedly.

His questions didn't seem to offend the man, so Ben risked another one. "Why are you the one interested in Doctor Graham? He works for Ryson."

"His work in Folkestone is in Ryson's jurisdiction, but if he ever needed to be captured, he would come under mine." Evesham laughed at Ben's confused look. "I'm involved in foreign intelligence. We're part of two separate branches, but we cooperate on some cases, especially when the Irish are involved. It's hard to understand, I know."

"Oh."

"I'll explain later. Tell me, doctor, do you like this intelligence work?"

Ben was quite sure he didn't want anything more to do with the British Secret Service, but for some reason, this man was someone he wanted to please. He tried to soften his dislike as he answered. "Not particularly. I might if it were more reputable."

"Reputable?" Evesham looked surprised. "Why is it not reputable?"

"It's full of lies and deceit and back-stabbing and not knowing who your friends are. Not to mention all the moral gambling—setting the stakes and determining to win, rather than being honest."

"Who taught you that?"

"Jaeryn."

Evesham looked thoughtfully out to the Channel. "Ah, yes. Jaeryn Graham. I think your training may be lacking in some areas, and the fault is hardly yours. If I offered you better training, would you consider it? I am a man who prefers honesty, and if you would like to continue advancing the war effort, I can show you a better way. Your trial period will be up soon, and Ryson has agreed to transfer you to my department if you are interested."

Ben's lips parted in surprise. "What do you mean?"

"After this first round in Folkestone is over, the next phase will pass into my care. I've taken a close look at your work here, and Ryson recommended that I let you come to my branch and continue working in Folkestone. Another of my reasons for coming today was to make you the offer. How would you like to work with me in future?"

The offer took his breath away. He hadn't considered himself particularly skillful, and he didn't know he was even wanted, but this proved him wrong. To think Ryson had recommended him. "I didn't know there was more to be done."

"Much more. But I can only give you details if you agree to work with me."

"I'll consider it." He kept his words tranquil, but his mind still whirled with the surprise.

"We'll speak more on it later, then. For now, I'll attend to the business you asked of me. We shouldn't be seen together after this. Keep an eye out, and you'll see some new men filtering into town throughout the day; they'll be your extra hands tomorrow night. I'll connect with you at King's dinner and make sure everything is in place."

"Are you coming tomorrow to help us?"

"Perhaps. Tell me, do you think you can keep Jaeryn Graham occupied at King's dinner and out of my way?"

He glanced at the confident figure beside him. "Yes. Ryson specially requested that I keep him in sight."

"Excellent. Keep a close watch on him; we wouldn't want him to do away with you just as we're about to succeed."

"Do you think he'll be arrested tomorrow night?" Ben asked, hoping that Ryson had been harsh in his assessment and Jaeryn was not under as much suspicion as it seemed.

His hope died again. "I think it extremely likely. Ann Meikle, the postmistress, has been working with Fenton for some time to bring Jaeryn Graham down. We know she's under suspicion of being unreliable, so we aren't sure if her case against Graham is trustworthy. If it is, it will come out. And if not, then it was worth the time it took to be sure."

"I hope you're wrong."

Evesham gave a small nod. "Cases where associates turn traitors are always hard. Ryson tells me you've had a rough time of it, and what he does not tell me, I can see for myself. I know that you lost your sister recently, and also that you agreed to help us take in your brother. I won't see you go unrewarded. Ryson doesn't notice things like that, but I do. Not all of us take your sacrifice lightly."

"Thank you."

"You're just the sort of worker we want in our business— trustworthy, and willing, and even principled. You're one of few, let me assure you. Under the present circumstances, you probably wish you had not accepted this position, but not every case will be centered around your family. I think you could find more satisfaction in your work here than you have thus far. I am pleased what I have heard of you since our first meeting in June, and I would like to see you succeed."

Ben took in the words of praise hungrily. Even though they were few, he wasn't used to praise. At the moment, they made him feel that it had almost been worth it just to hear them. "I'll bear your offer in mind. You are very kind, sir."

"I want my men to know, in spite of how finite our abilities are to use them well in this war, that I am watching out for them. I'll be in town if you need me. Rest assured that everything is taken care of. All success to you, doctor."

Allan Evesham shook hands and then walked away. He looked like he knew quite well where he was going. His dark gray suit fitted as if it had been tailored to him, and Ben realized that it probably had been. A rich man, an authoritative official—and someone who looked at agents not just as pawns, but as real human beings. He might be able to work for a man like that.

Ben took one last look out over the Channel before he turned to go. It glowered under the sullen sky, and small, choppy waves broke up its surface. He shivered and turned away, waving to Patrick to wait for him. He was glad Evesham had agreed to help them. It was almost as if the man was Providence, assuring him there was still hope after tomorrow night instead of the blank despair that he had expected. And that was a mighty relief.

* * *

Just as Evesham had promised, Ben saw strange faces strolling about the Folkestone streets by mid-afternoon. There were only a handful of them, in ones and twos, but according to Ryson they were trained fighters, and they would be useful in twenty-four hours. Since Ben knew what he was looking for, he could pick them out from the other inhabitants as he rode through town on his way to Alisa's.

Jaeryn didn't want him to tell her until everything was over. If he told her now, she would have to hide her knowledge from Edmond, and that would be hard for her. But he was her brother-in-law, not just an agent obligated to see that nothing hindered their mission. It was not right to save such a crushing blow for the following night. Besides, he wanted her far out of danger if they could manage it, lest someone try to take a terrible form of vengeance while he and Jaeryn were occupied.

When he arrived, Peters let him into the kitchen where Alisa was already waiting and left them alone. Ben peeled off his wet gloves and rubbed his hands to warm them, but he declined her offer of tea. "No, thank you. I have something to tell you about Edmond."

"What is it?" Alisa looked frail and girlish in her light purple dress with her hair partway down, as if a physical blow would break her in two. Ben closed his eyes against the news he was about to deliver.

"I received a letter from someone last week," he said, choosing his words so as to tell her as quickly and gently as possible. "A letter which grieved me very much. It was about Edmond's present political involvement." He tried to judge the effect his words were having on her, but he could not tell. "My brother has been deceiving us. He is involved with German secret intelligence, and it will be my duty to apprehend him tomorrow night. I tell this to you, but you must breathe no word of it to anyone."

Alisa's eyes remained steadily on his as she took in the implication of his words. "Perhaps you mistake his true intentions."

Ben shook his head. "I fear that is impossible."

"But he may even be allied with the Germans and noble of heart.

Surely..." Alisa trailed off when he put a hand on her shoulder.

"Edmond is doing it for selfish reasons, Alisa, not for any patriotism. You must not allow yourself to hope in goodness that is not there. I am sorry."

She buried her face in her hands, and he waited for the sound of tears, but none came. Only a bitter little silence. He drew her close to comfort her.

"Do not hold back your pain. It will be better that way."

She burst into tears as if she were a child.

He held her until her grief calmed down and then let her go. She wiped her reddened eyes with the back of her hand. "What will happen to Edmond? When will you take him?"

Ben held out a handkerchief, and she took it. "Tomorrow. You must go to Charlotte as soon as you can in the morning. I have people to keep you safe. I would ask for your prayers for tomorrow night, but it is unfair even to mention it to you."

"It is not unfair. I shall pray for you"—her voice trembled—"I shall pray that God will work rightly and grant me the strength to bear it. Please"—she clasped his arm with both hands—"tell me what will happen to him."

He drew away. "Don't ask, Alisa. I know nothing for certain yet. I will tell you when I know for sure."

That was the truth. He wouldn't know for sure until the noose was drawn.

Ben stayed until he was sure that she was stable enough to be left alone, and then he hugged her and whispered all the words of hope that he could think of before telling her goodbye.

By prior arrangement, Peters met him outside on the cobblestone walk. Ben gave him a letter of instructions that he and Jaeryn had written out between them. There was one line at the bottom of the page that he had written without Jaeryn's knowledge, telling Peters that if he did not come with Jaeryn at the proper time, Peters must carry on and finish it himself. Jaeryn had never threatened him, but they must take the possibility into consideration. At least they hadn't received any death threats in the past few days. It was as if the whole ring of workers on both sides was in suspense, waiting for what was about to come. He and Jaeryn and Peters were the only ones who knew exactly when they would be making the arrests, though the others might suspect. Fenton and Ann Meikle were not in their confidence.

"We have some new help," Ben told Peters before he left. "The man's name is Allan Evesham, and he's here to capture Jaeryn Graham if he can find the proof he needs. He's over six feet tall, with dark hair and blue eyes. If he asks you to do anything, you may obey, and if he comes tomorrow night before Jaeryn and me, or even after, you're to let him in."

Peters opened his brown jacket and tucked the letter into an inside pocket. "Oh, of course, sir. I know Allan Evesham. He is an old political ally of King's, and he thought King might be disloyal to British interests long before you came. He was the one who started this case."

Ben raised an eyebrow. "So that's why he came. How strange that I've only seen him twice, then."

"Not very, sir. Evesham isn't one to broadcast his work; he likes to keep to himself. I'll see that everything he wants is taken care of."

"Very good." Ben wondered what other parts of their work Allan Evesham had orchestrated. He must be significant if he had kept himself a secret all this time. Perhaps Evesham had had something to do with smoothing over their difficulties and controlling Ryson's outbreaks. He evidently had the authority for it. It would bear investigating after this was over.

"Is Jaeryn Graham coming with you or working on his own tomorrow night?" Peters asked. "I wouldn't like to do anything he tells me if you aren't there."

"He'll come with me. We'll come as soon as we can get away from the dinner. We have someone getting a final piece of evidence for us at King's, and then we'll be ready to make the arrests."

"Do you know who to take in?"

Ben nodded. "Most of them, but we're not quite sure where all of them stand. There are a few agents who will only be taken for questioning unless we can find more concrete proof of their innocence or guilt beforehand."

"You might be interested to know, sir, that Edmond Dorroll has given most of the servants a free weekend starting tomorrow afternoon."

"Did he? Why would he do that?"

"Well, as he isn't attending King's dinner, I would imagine he is trying to clear the house of unwanted eyes." Peters gave him a sideways glance to see if he took the hint.

"Do you think King's dinner is a distraction so he and my brother can do something while no one is around?"

"I hardly think so, sir. Colonel King has never worked in collaboration with either of my employers, and they are unlikely to begin to do so at this late date."

Ben realized, when Peters referred to Emmerson and Edmond together, that the butler too had an interest in the people here. He wondered how it had affected the man to watch Edmond sink so low. "Are you very disappointed that my brother is one of the people we must arrest?"

"It is most certainly regrettable, sir. He was a fine lad."

"I'm sorry for it, Peters, indeed I am. I wish it didn't have to be the case."

Peters forgot his station and shook hands with him after Ben took up his bicycle. "You're quite honorable yourself, sir, and just like he should have turned out to be. A pleasure to have someone reliable to work with, if you'll excuse my saying so."

Ben gave a wry smile. "Reliable, perhaps, but not very knowledgeable, I'm afraid."

"Oh, that's no matter, sir. That comes in time, and reliability is more important than experience. I would rather have someone like you watching my back than someone like Jaeryn Graham, even though he is a better spy. At least if something went wrong, I wouldn't be stabbed from both sides." Peters looked down at their hands and stiffly withdrew his, a hint of mortification crossing his face. "Apologies, sir. I forgot for a moment that we were anything but agents."

Ben stifled a chuckle. "No matter, Peters. I'm just an American, that's all, so I think you can be excused the liberty."

Peters smiled and turned back to the house, his gray hair lightly misted over from the drizzle in the air. But Ben did not smile as he turned in the direction of home and Charlotte. He was thinking of the tiny woman in the vast mansion behind him and how much she must be grieving at this moment.

* * *

Saturday afternoon, Ben went to Pearlie's grave for the second time since his return to Folkestone. He had been once before with Charlotte and had stood stiff and miserable, looking down at the neat little plot, trying to remember everything he could about the early morning when he had said goodbye. It had been the last time he would ever see his sister alive, but neither of them had known it then.

His mother would have received the news by this time. He had written as sympathetically as possible, and he wondered how she had taken it. Pearl's photos were displayed in her room, so her daughter must mean something to her. That was another thing he hadn't been able to ask Pearlie—how she and his mother had gotten on together. He should have looked after her instead of letting her shift for herself while he handled other things.

Ben stood for a long time looking at the grave, too recently dug to be covered over with grass. Dusk crept over the churchyard and the shadows lengthened, reaching out as if to seize him in their darkened grasp. In a few minutes, he and Jaeryn would drive to Colonel King's and face whatever awaited them there. He had told Charlotte he was going to Pearl's grave first, and she thought it was a good idea. Even so, he didn't quite know why he was here. Perhaps, after trying to avoid it all this time, he had come to say goodbye. He had not had the service like the others, and through Allan Evesham's intervention, they were giving up their right to justice for her death. Oh, the murder would be one of the charges in the end. But the charge of being a German subversive would take the forefront, and the other, though receiving punishment indirectly, could never be fully spoken of. That would ache, to have the justice kept secret.

"It hurt dreadfully last night to dream and think and remember you," he said, hardly aware that he had begun talking out loud. "Maybe I'm feeling some of the pain you felt for so long and could never tell anyone about."

The letters on the gravestone were small, only giving her identification and the years of her birth and death. Edmond hadn't been elaborate in his arrangements. It seemed appropriate that an unknown girl should have such a simple marker.

"Would you be upset with me if you knew I was going to take down your oldest brother, and he—he would die for it? I don't think you would say anything against me, but you never criticized my decisions whether you liked them or not."

The wind rustled a dead leaf against the gravestone, and he cleared it away with his boot so it would not obstruct the words. "You were always helping people, and you wanted to be loved. That's all I know about you. I wish I knew more. It seems wrong that you died when there was so much good in you that I didn't find out, and

Edmond lived so I had to discover more evil about him than I wanted to know."

His eyes rested on the name etched in the stone. Pearl Dailey. She didn't even have her real name. Then he looked furtively over his shoulder to make sure no one was watching him. He didn't want to be overheard. But he was alone.

"I think," he said slowly, forgetting that she was not listening, absorbed in talking to her as he wished he would have when he could have seen the gentle glow coming into her timid eyes, "I think I am glad that you are happy now. God can keep you happier in heaven than I could keep you here, and I would rather that you were happy than that I had you."

The gray stone stood cold and unmoving, a grim affirmation of his words.

"It's going to be lonely when I'm the only one of us left. All three, never to know each other—and I'll be the only one in a few hours."

He shivered and ran unsteady fingers through his hair to straighten it where the wind had tossed it. He thought he heard the sound of someone a distance away trying to hold back tears, but when he looked around, there was no one.

* * *

When Ben returned to the clinic, he found Jaeryn tying his necktie in the consulting room mirror, his boots shined and his wavy hair tamed. He pointed to the newspaper lying open on the desk. "The news came from the front. We lost everything at Cambrai. The Germans were too much for us."

Ben picked it up and scanned through the column, clenching his brows. "I hope that's not an indication of the way tonight's going to go."

Their gloves lay on the table, along with something more ominous: two silencers, ready to be attached to their revolvers.

"Do you think we'll need those?" he asked, not daring to take up his.

Jaeryn didn't answer right away, he was so absorbed in making sure his tie was straight. When he was finished, he said, "Yes, most likely. I've always had to. They won't be happy, and they'll be putting up a fight."

"I put a medical kit in the car with things we might need."

The golden sparks appeared in Jaeryn's eyes, and a smile crossed his face—probably the anticipation of a game he had played many times before. "Are you thinking that's for us, or for them?"

"I don't know."

Jaeryn tossed one silencer to him and took up the other. "Then take one more piece of advice from me before this is over. It's always best to determine that nothing will go wrong, while still preparing for any emergency. So let's assume for now that you're saving it for the people you'll be arresting."

He had to ask it. Jaeryn wasn't likely to give him an honest answer, but Ben hoped madly that he would. "Will I be arresting you tonight?"

The smile was still there. The spark was still there. But neither was entirely friendly as the dark-haired Irishman looked at him. "That's not for me to say, is it? I think, in the end, the choice will be up to you. Ready to go?"

Here it was. His last chance to back out, say that he would not do it, abdicate responsibility for what was about to happen. If he refused, no one would blame him and he would not have to follow through. He didn't know what his father was going to say when he found out that his youngest son had been responsible for the execution of his eldest. Or what Alisa would think of him when this was finished—or what he would find out about Jaeryn.

"I hope that I am brave enough," Ben said breathlessly.

Jaeryn laid a gloved hand on his shoulder, and the dangerous glint faded away, just like it always did, to a casual friendliness. "Yes, you are. You are destined to finish this. If we're on the same side, I want you to be with me to taste the victory. And if we are not, then there is no one I would rather face off with than you."

Ben sensed that Jaeryn was preparing to gamble that evening and did not know which way the stakes would turn. "Why won't you tell me who you are and what side you're on?"

Jaeryn gazed thoughtfully at the consulting room floor. "I still may be able to keep my secrets after tonight, and if that is the case, I have every intention of doing so. Besides, when it comes down to it, I can't tell you whether I'm loyal or not. You'll have to decide that for yourself."

"What do you mean?"

Jaeryn gripped his shoulder and guided him toward the door.

"Come along. You're ready."

He did not feel ready, but he went through the door and then stepped aside for Jaeryn to lead the way. As the doctor passed in front of him, he prayed desperately that he would not have to find out what Jaeryn meant—that Jaeryn could go on keeping his secrets after the night was over and they could continue just as they had before. Somehow, he knew that petition was not going to be granted. As Jaeryn started the car, he changed it and pleaded instead that whatever his former mentor had done, he would have a chance to turn around before it was too late. He wasn't sure how that request would be answered either. As the car backed out of the drive, Ben wished the agent next to him would simply turn out to be Jaeryn Graham—that all this had been a mistake, and he wasn't so dangerous or enigmatic as he seemed.

Glancing over, he saw not one revolver but two secreted in Jaeryn's overcoat pockets. He wondered why the Irishman had not offered him two and what he intended to use the second one for.

Chapter Thirty-Five
A Series of Catastrophes

Jaeryn wondered again where Ben had picked up his social graces as they entered King's grand drawing-room. His natural conversation, pleasant laugh, and ready handshakes combined to give the impression of a man quite at his ease. Only those who knew otherwise would suspect that he was an ordinary man and unused to wealth. The room was filled with people, and a grand piano stood at the far end of the room, providing soft background music. Jaeryn chuckled as he pictured the musician breaking out into ragtime. Thank heavens he wouldn't dream of it. Starlin's violin would be infinitely more interesting to listen to, but it was just as well that Starlin wasn't the center of attention.

Waiters stood against the wall or wandered through the rooms, proffering trays of champagne and *hor d' oeuvres*. The pointed slippers and filmy, lacy evening gowns were something unusual for King's events. It must be quite a social gathering, unlike the purposeful events he was used to. King didn't seem to be the type to amuse himself for the pleasure of it, but a man with his connections had to entertain London acquaintances that they knew very little about. Jaeryn turned to Ben and raised his eyebrows.

Before he could speak, Colonel King came over in a breeze of smiling urbanity and greeted both of them. "A pleasure to see both of you, gentlemen."

Jaeryn dutifully shook hands. "A pleasure to be invited."

King made another remark and Jaeryn responded automatically, not paying attention again until his host walked away. For the life of him, he couldn't remember what he had said. Had he flung out something in Irish? He did sometimes when he was on edge.

He looked about for Evesham, but they were early, and no sign of him appeared in the entrance hall. There was no sign of King's son either. "Where do you suppose that young imp is?" he asked Ben when they were past the front of the room.

"If you mean Starlin King, then I have no idea. Perhaps he isn't around yet."

They looked among the MPs and their wives, but not a sign of the blond-haired lad could they find. Jaeryn glanced at the waiters carrying the alcohol, and Starlin was not there either.

"He probably backed out."

"He might be dead," Ben said sharply. "We haven't heard anything from him this week."

Jaeryn tugged at the wristbands of his gloves to loosen them. "You can't just kill a boy and have no one comment on it. King hasn't corrupted all his servants, and they would be sure to turn him in if the boy went missing."

"Unless he wai—" Ben broke off as they came face to face with Fenton, his French cuffs neatly pressed as if he were one of the guests. Ben's lips kept moving, but no sound came out of them. Fenton brushed past as if he didn't know them and went out the front door. King's dismissed butler, Stafford, met him at the door in full livery and spoke to him before he disappeared.

Jaeryn whistled under his breath. "I don't like the looks of that. Perhaps I should follow him."

"No. We'd better stay together."

He remembered then that Dorroll had been ordered to keep him in sight that evening. If he hadn't been so worried, he would have pressed further solely for the amusement of it. But he didn't want to attract attention with an argument, so he acquiesced.

Stafford caught King's eye as soon as Fenton slipped out, and after a few minutes, King left his guests and spoke a word in the butler's ear. Ben was looking at the two of them in utter, frozen stillness. His memory of the details would be perfect, but that would never do; he would give them away if anyone noticed him watching them so closely. Jaeryn nudged his side and looked back. King and Stafford conversed quietly for a moment, master and man, and Stafford concluded their conversation with a slight bow. King went back to his guests. Stafford signaled to a footman to take his place and departed by the front door just as Allan Evesham came up the steps. Evesham looked after him before handing his coat and hat to the footman.

Jaeryn glowered as Evesham greeted King with kindly confidence. Allan Evesham couldn't be as genuine as he liked people to think; that was too good to find in their business. There must be an ulterior motive beneath the man's apparent clean integrity.

Ben broke into his thoughts. "King and Evesham used to be political allies."

"Did he? I'm surprised London trusts Evesham if the two were so closely connected."

Ben didn't take the hint. "I saw no reason to distrust him."

"But don't you think—and don't be offended—that two heads are better than one, in this case, just to be on the safe side?"

"No, I don't think so."

Jaeryn rolled his eyes. Confound that doctor's tight-lipped secrecy.

He watched Evesham warily. The man was closer to King's height than the rest of them, but still slightly below it. Evesham was so tall and so—*expert*. Jaeryn felt misgiving in the pit of his stomach. He was used to London men who couldn't see a threat if it hit them between the eyes, but he recognized experience when he saw it. If there was one man he did not think he could cross with success, it was this new fellow. Evesham was twenty years older than him if he was a day, old enough to have seen many scenarios that Jaeryn hadn't. And worse, Ben already trusted him. He had said nothing of their conversation on Friday, even though Jaeryn had asked three times that afternoon. Jaeryn realized then, very quietly, that the last hold he had was slipping away for good. He was alone now. Dorroll liked to help people, but he had found an honest man to help, and that had won out.

"Look." Ben's voice shook him out of his worry. "I see Starlin coming over now."

Every blond hair in place, every crease where it should be, Starlin wove inconspicuously through the crowd. Once he reached them, he shook hands—a bit hastily with Jaeryn, but warmly enough with Ben. "I'm glad you came. If you'll please follow me, I have a safe place for us to talk." He kept them close to the edge of the room and opened a door which led into the long dining hall. There were servants making the table ready, but none took particular note of them. Past the dining room, they came to a second room, a music room that neither of them had been in before. It had a piano and stands and racks of music arranged from the floor almost to the ceiling.

"Is this a safe place to talk?" Jaeryn raised his eyebrow critically.

Starlin's blue eyes took on a sullen stare. "You won't have anyone listen or surprise you; this room is particularly my own, and my father wasn't watching when I took you here."

Ben laid a hand on his shoulder. "Relax, Starlin. It's all right. Do you have the list for us?"

"No. It's too early yet. My father's been in and out of his study all evening, and I don't want him to notice that anything's been disturbed."

Jaeryn protested at the delay. "We can't afford to have him move it before you take it. Besides, he can't make a scene while his guests are here, even if he does find it gone."

"Don't make him nervous," Ben reproved. "It won't help matters. Starlin, I think it would be best if you got it soon, but we leave it to your discretion."

Jaeryn sighed. Discretion was all very well, but he had never seen it in Starlin before.

He glanced again at the boy. In the eyes and the stiffness of the shoulders he caught a hint of frightened vulnerability. Poor fellow. It had to be a rotten go to turn his own father in. He hadn't even considered how to keep Starlin safe this evening. The boy would have to fend for himself as best he could.

Starlin steadily avoided looking at or speaking to him and addressed all his communications to Ben. "What's going to happen after tonight?"

"At the very least, all parties concerned will go to prison. An executor for your father's estate will handle things during his sentence. Do you have any idea who that person might be?"

Starlin shook his head. "I know my guardian, but I don't know the executor."

"Well, it doesn't matter at present," Ben said. "Don't worry, we'll see you well provided for. We shouldn't stay much longer here; we might attract attention. If all goes well, I'll come back tomorrow and find out what you need to know. Get that paper for us as soon as you think it's safe. Or you could tell us where it is, and we can find it if you'd rather."

"No. I'll get it myself. I said I would do it, and it's the safest way."

They separated from Starlin, and Jaeryn saw that his watch hands now pointed to eight. The front doors were closed, and the rest of the guests must have arrived while they were gone.

"I wish we hadn't come tonight," Ben murmured. "I haven't seen Stafford since King spoke with him."

Jaeryn looked around the room in dismay. He had been so focused on Starlin and Evesham that he had forgotten Stafford. "Perhaps they know something's up and they've sent him out to warn people."

"Should we make our move now?"

Jaeryn thought quickly. The chatter of people and the soft music wound its way through his thoughts, only serving to intensify them. "No. It's too soon. We'll have to stick it out. If we leave now, we'll have to take King first, and that could be disastrous. Besides, we don't have the list from that boy yet. I wish he would hurry up."

Ben lowered his voice even further, but Jaeryn could still hear annoyance at his insinuation of Starlin's inability. "He's doing the best he can. We must have a little more time. Evesham's over there talking to King, and he doesn't seem to be concerned. King won't try anything until he sees us go out. Until then, he'll feel safe."

They separated so as not to attract attention, and Jaeryn was left to watch from his customary position against the wall as others made conversation. He hated making conversation at large gatherings; it was easy to manipulate one person, but events like these always had three or four in a group together, and then it was impossible to have an edge. Besides, he never knew what to say. Politics didn't interest him, and he didn't pay enough heed to be knowledgeable in discussing them. As soon as people heard his Irish accent, he was politely ignored. And he wasn't going to stand for that tonight.

Jaeryn checked his watch again. An hour since they walked in the door, and still no sign of Starlin King. Forty minutes since Stafford had left. He sighed. He wanted to work, to act. This waiting was intolerable. It really was effrontery on Dorroll's part to look so smooth, as if he were enjoying himself, when Jaeryn knew he was devastated over all that had happened. How could he turn around so completely like that? It wasn't natural, and he was talking French to someone again, which wasn't natural either. He didn't look like someone who should know French.

A servant opened the great double doors and announced dinner. Jaeryn moved with the rest of the crowd. It was only the adults filing into the dining room. Starlin was nowhere to be seen, which was a good thing, as it might give him time to get the list. In the dining room, Jaeryn found he was sitting next to strangers while Ben sat next to Evesham on the opposite side of the table, further down. Jaeryn frowned. He was out of control when those two were together, but there was nothing he could do to separate them.

He didn't try to signal any messages, for he knew that their actions were likely being watched. Since he was near the foot of the table, he was content to eat his dinner in peace without worrying about immediate observation. He liked dinner here in spite of the present circumstances. It tasted better than the ones he made for himself, and though he struggled to keep up his side of the conversation, he took a wicked delight in how little his neighbors knew of his real purposes. A waiter proffering more water startled him from his train of thought. He declined, and the waiter worked his way around the table, coming at last to Ben. Jaeryn only saw it because he was watching, but he knew that as Ben turned to ask Evesham a question, the waiter passed them an envelope. It was foolish to deliver the message in front of everyone—but they might get away with it if no one else had seen. The waiter moved to the next guest, and Jaeryn was left alone with his impatience as the dinner ground on.

At nine, when the last course was placed, he glanced at Ben again. His face looked waxen in the brightness as if he was struggling to keep up; his smiles were strained, and his expression held a dogged concentration. He would give it all away if he weren't careful. Jaeryn felt a drowning sensation as the clock ticked second after ruthless second. This wasn't going to work. That boy should have managed to get them the list before this; then they could have left to set things in motion without saying goodbye. Who knew what damage had already been done. They would botch it somehow and likely end up with a bullet hole between their ribs.

He felt as if he couldn't breathe from panic and could keep his seat no longer. But at that moment he realized people were breaking up, and he eagerly followed suit, gasping a deep breath at the blessed release.

As soon as they found each other, Ben held up the envelope the waiter had given him. "Starlin got the list."

Jaeryn almost wept from sheer relief. "Thank goodness. He was slow enough about it."

Ben frowned. "Jaeryn, he probably gave away his last chance at any sort of normal happiness with this. He'll have to live with the knowledge that he was the one who gave up his father, and you blame him for not being more eager? You could have a little more understanding."

"Of course," Jaeryn said hastily. "Why were you so upset at dinner? I'm sure someone noticed."

The worry lines stole in again to replace the rebuke that Ben had just given. "Starlin wrote on the back. His valet told him that Terry was at the kitchen door earlier, trying to persuade the servants to let him in. They turned him away, but if Terry wants to find a way in, it's likely that he will or already has."

Jaeryn's relief drained away again. "Why would Terry be here?"

"I imagine he came for the same thing we did. He must have found out that Starlin had something of importance. I think Starlin should leave now before Terry finds him."

That would never do. Jaeryn shook his head. "He can't leave yet. If he does, his father will notice, and the whole game will be up."

"We're putting him at too much risk," Ben argued. "We can't take the chance of Terry doing something to him."

"Just until we come back to arrest King, and then we'll let him go."

"The danger will be over at that point. It might be too late before then."

Jaeryn sighed in frustration. "I can't help that. I'm not trying to be inhumane, but many people have their lives on the line for our success, and Starlin needs to be ready to make that sacrifice as well. At least make him wait until we're gone."

His earlier comments about Starlin didn't help his case now. Ben apparently didn't think he had Starlin's best interests at heart. But he carried his point in spite of that, for Ben gave in, though reluctantly. "If we must, then it's only fair to tell him. I'm going into the library to look at the list, and then we'll talk to him. Wait a minute after I go, and then follow me."

Jaeryn wasn't about to let slip this chance to see exactly how incriminating the proof would be. He wasn't about to let Ben hide the paper, either, without knowing where he put it. "No. I'll come with you."

"Two of us leaving at the same time might attract attention."

"It couldn't possibly; we'll be in the library before they even look up." Jaeryn pushed him through the door before he could protest and pointed out a quiet corner with two chairs, well out of the light in case they were surprised. Ben unfolded the paper. Jaeryn tried to look over his shoulder, but Ben refused to let him and held it so he could not read what was written there.

"It's only common sense to let me see it." Jaeryn snatched the paper from his hand and scanned down the list. "There's the Goodwin woman. She's not under me; she must be for them."

All the names were there: Stafford and Ann Meikle, Peters and Hugh and Terry; Ben had a number assigned to him too, probably for identifying him in messages without using his name. Even Fenton hadn't escaped detection. Jaeryn's own name was on the list, and he was tempted for one wild moment to try by any means he could to erase it. The others didn't matter. They deserved all the questioning they would get, but he didn't want to be mixed up in an interrogation. He handed the paper back. "Do you think you can remember which name goes with which number?"

"I shouldn't have to, as we have this," Ben said coolly, taking one of his boots off and shoving the paper down to the toe of it.

"Yes," Jaeryn persisted, "but if something happened to it, would you remember?"

"Absolutely."

Jaeryn didn't know if that was a reassurance or a warning, but he suspected the latter. He looked out the library door.

"We're clear to leave. Where are we going now?"

"I'm going to mingle with the other guests, and I want you to talk to Starlin King and tell him when he's safe to leave."

"But he doesn't like—"

Ben cut off his objection. "It doesn't matter; you're only delivering a message from me. I suspect he's up in his room. Second floor, down the hall to your right, and it will be the first door past the landing."

Jaeryn saw there was no use arguing. After forcing the list, he didn't want to further jeopardize his standing. So he slipped out of one of the library doors and into a long side hall. It wasn't lit very

661

brightly, doubtless because no company was expected to use it. Softly treading down the carpeted hall, Jaeryn listened to the low murmur of voices and debated in his mind which direction to take.

He didn't know his way around this part of the house; he had only been upstairs once, and that had been by the front staircase. Well, he would go up the front then, even if someone did see him. If he took the back stairs, he might open the wrong door and run into a servant.

He made his way up the grand staircase, keeping close to the wall, with the awful worry that someone would hail him from the bottom landing and ask him what he was doing. But he got up to the second story without incident, and from there he knew exactly where Starlin's room was. He knocked softly at the door.

The door opened slowly, a little at a time. Starlin's face appeared, a mask of blank terror. A silver pistol flashed in his hand, but when he saw Jaeryn, the terror slowly receded. "Oh. It's you."

"I doubt we'll see you again tonight," Jaeryn said quickly, "but I hope you make it through all right."

Starlin nodded.

"If you feel that you must leave, then you have your car available, don't you?"

"I hope so."

"But I can't have you leave until after we're gone. Can you wait that long?"

"Sure."

"No matter what happens?"

Starlin nodded. "Sure."

"Good lad."

"Don't call me that," he said indignantly. "You don't have any right."

Jaeryn drew back. "I'm sorry if it offends you."

"Go away and leave me alone. I hope you get locked up tonight with the rest of them."

Jaeryn held his tongue only by a supreme effort of the will and slipped out. Were he a different sort of man, he might have wrung that slender neck and taken care of Starlin's fate himself. Starlin would be fortunate to evade discovery even half an hour after they left. Perhaps he had been wrong to make him stay. If something happened, the boy's death would be his fault for forcing the point. But it was too late to change now.

When he returned to the drawing-room, he saw Ben conversing with Evesham near one of the large windows. Ben's face looked almost animated, the most off its guard that Jaeryn had ever seen it in all of their acquaintance. Perfect. Evesham had the monopoly, and he wasn't in the inner circle anymore. Well, after tonight, Dorroll could confide in whomever he liked.

Jaeryn didn't reach them in time to join their conversation, for he could tell they changed the subject as soon as they saw him coming. When he came up alongside, Ben offered no introduction, and Evesham left them to speak to each other alone.

"Twenty after ten," Ben said as soon as Evesham was out of earshot. "Our reinforcements will be in place by now. Two men at Edmond's place and the others posted in every crucial location."

"Excellent." Jaeryn shoved his hands in his pockets and leaned against one of the window pillars. "A little less than ten minutes," he said cheerily, "and then I think we've done our duty toward our host and we can leave."

"That will be a relief."

Jaeryn sighed at the continued coolness in Ben's tone. He shouldn't have forced the list.

But it wasn't even ten minutes they had to wait. One of the waiters advanced from the wall where he had been standing, and Jaeryn recognized him as the servant hired for Starlin's particular use.

"Message for you, sir," the young man whispered, handing a note to Ben. "The messenger came to the kitchen door and said I was to give this straight into your hands."

Ben took it eagerly. "Who gave it to you?"

"Peters himself, sir. He only stayed a moment. Said he was jeopardizing everything, but he had to do it, or it would all be too late. I'm not sure what he meant by it."

"Don't look so on guard. We don't want them to think anything has happened."

Jaeryn realized he was the one being spoken to and tried to assume an expression of ease. "Stand in front of me while I open this," Ben ordered softly. Ben nodded for George to go, and Jaeryn stood with his back to the room. He had never felt so vulnerable. Ben quickly scanned through the note, his lips forming the words as he read them.

"We need to leave now," he said, crushing it in his hand as small as he could make it. "They're all at Emmerson's estate, every one of them except Fenton. Peters waited until they all got there, and then he took a risk and came himself to tell us."

"We can't go straight there," Jaeryn protested, shifting so he could see the room again. Everything looked to be as it was before. "Our reinforcements are scattered around town, and we don't have any way to tell them."

Ben gestured for Starlin's valet to come back, and George crossed the polished parquet floor. "Take this note to that man over there." He nodded in Evesham's direction, and Jaeryn hoped that the note would go to the right person. "That's all you need to do. Don't talk to him. Just give it to him, and then you focus on keeping Starlin safe. Make sure his father doesn't take him anywhere. Understand?"

"Yes, sir."

"I'll see you well rewarded for it if he isn't harmed at all. You've done well looking after him. Be off, now."

Jaeryn shook his head in disgust. If everything had gone according to plan, he would have preferred less help, for it would have given him a better chance of escape. Now that the German agents were in one place, he welcomed the security of numbers. He had seen where this such a turn of events led once before, and he didn't want to ruin the rest of his fingers reliving it a second time.

"I wouldn't go in without the reinforcements if I were you," he said. "It's the most desperate move you can make in a capture scenario short of going in alone. We'll only have the two of us."

"What else can we do?"

"Nothing," Jaeryn admitted. "Except take the risk of losing all of them."

"Evesham will read the note and know where we've gone. We'll trust him to collect the men and bring them to us in time. Besides," Ben said, a recklessness sounding in his voice now that things had gone so wrong, "I am going in alone, as far as I'm aware."

"Not as much as you think," Jaeryn said reassuringly. "I don't want to see harm come to you."

"I hope not." Ben shrugged his shoulders to straighten his jacket. "Let's say our farewells and get this over with. If we're going to be at odds tonight, I'd rather be finished as quickly as possible."

Jaeryn glowered as he led the way to the door. Ben was too wise now for his own good. He shook hands with his host and said, "A splendid evening, sir," then waited, shivering outside while Ben finished talking at the door. He was almost numb with cold by the time Ben joined him.

"Did you have to take that long?"

"It will make him second-guess himself if he doesn't think we're in a hurry."

They made haste to where a valet had parked Jaeryn's car. As they got in, they saw another car coming up the drive, and Jaeryn recognized Stafford behind the wheel. He seemed to be in a hurry. They watched as he left the car idling and ran up the front steps.

"Something unexpected just upset their plans, or I miss my guess," Jaeryn whispered. "I suspect this conflict will be split three ways tonight. I'll be right back." He slipped out and wove his way through the parked cars until he reached Stafford's. Then he pulled out a pocket knife and slashed all four tires. When they were flat, he returned to his own car and started it up.

"What did you do?" Ben asked suspiciously.

"Nothing," Jaeryn evaded. He was done playing the game square. This was the end, and he would win, whatever it took.

* * *

It was dark when they left, but the night was clear of rain, and in the cold blackness, the stars came out one by one. A fitting, expectant stillness hung over the quiet trees.

"Take off your jacket. It won't do you any good when we get there, and you don't want it to get in the way." Jaeryn slipped off his own while he drove, and in his white vest and shirt, he looked like he was ready to go home and relax after an evening out. Ben followed suit, even though it was cold. The distance from King's to Edmond's wasn't long, and every second counted.

Jaeryn picked up speed until he was driving faster than he ever had before. Ben caught his breath once or twice, for there were cars on the road in spite of the hour, and they missed more than one by a hair's breadth. The empty fields flew past in a blur. Ben's watch hands showed twenty minutes after ten. They would be early by their former calculations, but perhaps too late considering the turn things had taken. Earlier he had been quite confident, but now he didn't dare hope things would go smoothly. The feeling of responsibility almost choked him. It was too late to draw back. He had committed for the last time, and the choice of refusal was out of his hands.

"*Cuirfidh mé de dhroim seoil iad,*" Jaeryn whispered. He had two shoulder holsters showing now that his jacket was off, each holding a Webley from his coat pocket.

"What does that mean?"

"It is my vow. It means I have sworn to bring them down. I swear it every time I prepare to end a mission, and in the last six times I have sworn it, I have never failed, though I came very close once. I think this will make a second."

"Who did you just swear to bring down?" Ben didn't like the sound of it. No other agents mentioned making vows at the end of an investigation. It sounded outlandish. It must be something from the Irish side.

Jaeryn took his concentration off the road briefly, and his green eyes smoldered with an inner fire. For a moment it made him look more like some fierce rebel from an older time than a twentieth-century doctor in shirtsleeves. "My enemies."

Ben didn't dare ask who those enemies were. He only hoped that he was not one of them.

At the entrance to the wet gravel drive, a figure stepped out from the shelter of the trees. It was one of Evesham's men.

"How many of you are here?" Ben whispered.

"One other and myself," the man returned.

His heart sank, but he endeavored to keep up a confident air. "You two split up and bring the others here as quickly as you can. Be quick about it. We're going in now."

"Yes, sir."

"Evesham has the warrants," Jaeryn protested. "We can't go in without those."

"Well, we don't have time to wait, do we?"

Ben ran up the steps, past the empty fountain, and on to the mansion itself. The whole house was dark. He was so focused on what he would find inside that he would have given away their presence if he hadn't noticed the man at the bottom of the steps and stopped short.

Jaeryn slipped out one of his revolvers. Ben knew when he saw the rolled-up shirtsleeves that it was Terry. Terry leaned his bicycle against the stone balustrade. Then he slipped around the house, and Jaeryn jerked a nod to follow him. Ben refused and ran up the rest of the steps to knock on the door. He heard Jaeryn give a soft hiss, doubtless at the audacity of it, and a second click followed from his other revolver.

The door opened. When the dim form of Peters appeared, three Webleys stared him in the face.

"Good evening, gentlemen," he said quietly. "How may I assist you?"

Ben lowered his revolver, and Jaeryn followed suit. They both slipped inside and let their eyes grow accustomed to the dimness. "Tell us where they are," Ben said swiftly.

"In Emmerson's private room, sir."

"Good. Wait here to let the others in. We have more following behind. Move Jaeryn's car somewhere safe and out of sight, Peters. I'm the only one you're to bring it out for."

Jaeryn looked disturbed at that. "But—"

"We can't take chances."

"I see you like to even the odds," Jaeryn said, a small lilt to his words.

"I do." Ben pointed out the bicycle to Peters. "Be sure to disable that. We don't want anyone using it to get away."

"I'll take care of it right now, sir." Peters left them to their own devices, and they heard three quiet snaps before they were too far to hear any more.

"That means we can't use it either," Jaeryn whispered, "but it's best to take precautions, I suppose."

Jaeryn took the lead; he had been in the house often due to Emmerson's health, and even in the darkness he knew where he was going. He opened the double doors opposite the entrance and led them up the polished spiral steps. Ben felt like a blind man and kept one hand running along the wall as they ascended. Upstairs, they reached the door to the third floor stairway without tumbling anything over and found it was locked. Ben stopped. "I forgot to get the key from Peters."

"Never mind." Jaeryn reached in his pocket and flourished another. "This should do it."

"I'll have to ask you later where you got that."

"Ask all you like, but I won't tell. Ready?"

They had a silent struggle over who should go last, but Jaeryn won the last spot and Ben led the way down the hall, trying to make no noise. A square of light came from the private room. They saw the door moving as if someone had just looked out. Ben exchanged an uncertain look with Jaeryn, but Jaeryn gestured for him to keep going. He stopped just before crossing into the patch of light. The door wasn't completely closed—doubtless a safety precaution. They could hear voices from inside the room. Ben stood against the wall and listened, and Jaeryn fell in place beside him. The voices were just a hushed murmur at first, but gradually, he sifted out the words. The first thing he understood was a question from his brother.

"Why is the postmistress here? I wasn't aware that Mrs. Meikle was one of us."

Mrs. Goodwin's voice answered him. "She's not, sir. I found the agent identification numbers in her safe, but you don't want her here. She's not loyal to us."

Jaeryn glanced back at him, his face a mass of confusion.

Mrs. Meikle gave a nervous chuckle. "Now, Mrs. Goodwin, I think ye're mistaken there. When ye came to me and asked me to tell the doctor that yer house was open, I never questioned otherwise."

"That proves nothing," Mrs. Goodwin replied.

"I told ye that Speyer was a double agent when I heard the news from the Irish doctor."

Hugh's voice cut in. "And took away our use for him. I'm going to exact full revenge for that. Besides, you can hardly claim credit for passing on a rumor."

"And why not?" Mrs. Meikle said indignantly.

"I want to know the truth of this," Edmond said. "We're here to change numbers, and if she's one of ours, she should have one. We're running out of time."

"Well, if I'm not yers, then I'll turn Mrs. Goodwin in as an accomplice to theft and treason. She sheltered Hugh when he tried to rob Dorroll—or kill him, for all I know—and she used my typewriter for her soldier lists." They heard a muffled protest from Mrs. Goodwin and Ann Meikle's shrill response. "I knew the instant ye told the doctor ye were making a list of yer clients. Ye'd told me ye were writing a letter not five minutes before. Ye with yer laundry, running all over town and keeping an eye on everyone. But who'd notice ye, all angel-like? Ye'll be better off to shut up yer protesting. If I can't work for ye, I'll work against ye, so I think ye should let me try."

So Mrs. Goodwin had lied when she said she had come back and found the break-in already committed. No doubt she had let Hugh in.

"I wasn't trying to kill Doctor Dorroll," Hugh said. "I was trying to kill Speyer."

Mrs. Goodwin spoke. "Mr. Dorroll, this woman isn't useful to us whether she's loyal or not. Neither Doctor Graham nor Doctor Dorroll trusts her. She would be more of a liability than a help."

In the silence that followed, Ben felt Jaeryn shift beside him very quietly.

He heard Edmond's voice again. "If the woman isn't fully ours, then she doesn't stay. We can't take any more chances."

"I was told to come," Ann protested. "Fenton told me I was supposed to be here." A low growl sounded, and Ben realized Nimrod, too, was in the room. Ann shrieked. "Keep that beast away from me."

"Well, I didn't tell him to invite you," Edmond said. "Someone silence the woman; she's of no use to us."

Ben spoke so low that his breath was barely a sigh. "We can't just let them kill her."

A look of dismay crossed Jaeryn's face. "Do you want to give up our plans? For her?"

"It would be cruel to leave her."

"We'll go in now, then. Take the top folks first." Jaeryn brushed past him and threw wide the door.

Ben would have followed immediately, but at that moment he saw a tall figure coming down the hall. For a moment, he hoped it was Allan Evesham. But as soon as he caught sight of the gray brows, he knew it was Colonel King.

Caught between facing King and letting Jaeryn confront the room of hostile people alone, Ben thought the latter more advisable. He plunged in on Jaeryn's heels just as a shot went off. One muffled yell sounded out in answer, but only one. Two hands seized him around the neck before he got off the first shot. Edmond's voice spoke right beside his ear.

"Don't shoot, little brother, or we'll kill your friend."

Edmond's hands applied pressure—not tightly, but enough to be a warning of what was to come. Ben turned his head enough to see Jaeryn gripped in the strong arms of Stafford. Stafford had two fingers pressed into his eyes to keep him incapacitated while Hugh emptied the holsters that he had prepared so carefully in advance. King slipped in and locked the door from the inside.

"Drop the gun," Edmond ordered.

They must have been waiting right inside the doorway. Ben tried to consider the best thing to do, but Edmond wouldn't give him time.

"Make your decision," he said sharply.

"Give it," Jaeryn gasped, trying desperately to pull Stafford's fingers away from his eyes.

Ben dropped the Webley to the floor. Hugh darted over and picked it up, looking fiendishly pleased with their speedy success.

Edmond kept a tight grip. "Hands behind your backs, both of you, and somebody put handcuffs on them."

Terry strolled over with his thumbs in his pockets and came around behind him. Stafford still had his fingers pressed in Jaeryn's eyes, and tears ran down his face from the pressure. Ben felt the cold bite of steel on his wrists. Terry had known Edmond in France. They hadn't taken that into account, Ben thought unhappily.

Terry kept winding the handcuffs until they cut into the skin and Ben gasped from the pain. Surely they couldn't go any further.

"Tight enough?" Terry asked, slapping him on the shoulder and giving them one more twist for good measure. Stafford and Edmond let go of both of them at the same time, and Terry held a revolver to Ben's head. Jaeryn made no move to resist, and Ben took his cue and stood quite still himself.

"Away from the windows, both of you. Over against the fireplace."

Ben obeyed and stood next to Jaeryn, who looked happy just to be free with both eyes intact. Terry handed off his gun to Stafford as soon as they were in place and put his thumbs in his pockets again. Mrs. Goodwin was too busy holding back a growling, snapping Nimrod to pay attention to them, but Ann Meikle looked happy to see Jaeryn at a disadvantage, and Hugh was delighted.

For the first time that evening, Ben got a good look at his brother. Edmond was unarmed, dressed casually in a blue sweater as if he were enjoying an evening out with good friends. He was tall and young, and were it not for the scars, he would have been handsome.

Edmond looked at King for the first time and gave a polite bow. "I know you have guests, King. Don't let us keep you."

King returned the nod. "I left them without a host for the first time in my long and varied career. I found I had a higher interest in your concerns here."

"I knew you'd try to meddle. Very well, if you want to see your involvement come to an end tonight, it's of no consequence to me."

"Just the two of you to try to take the six of us," Edmond said. "That's really too bad, you know. If I hadn't had people on the lookout and gathered everyone here, you might have been successful.

I never thought you would get this far. Here you are claiming to be such a good fellow, and it turns out you're a dirty spy."

The laugh that went around the circle made him wince. Glancing at Jaeryn, Ben was surprised to detect a sudden twinge of fear—the Irishman's face looked impassive above his white shirt, but his hands were shaking a little behind his back. His eyes flickered back and forth between the faces in the room and something else, and when Ben followed the direction of his glance, he saw the locked door. Was he afraid of it?

Whatever he was facing inwardly didn't stop Jaeryn's determination. The Irishman pressed an elbow into him in an attempt to be reassuring. Ben could almost feel the pulsating calculations going on in Jaeryn's head; if anything, the Irishman looked fiercer than ever.

"Change of plans," Edmond announced. "New numbers, and then scatter to the four winds. We'll have to regroup somewhere else. It's too late here. I'm sure they have people following them."

"Are we killing them?" Hugh asked eagerly. "We can't really keep them."

"After we change numbers, in case we need them for bargaining power. All right, Terry. Hand over the list you took from King, and we'll destroy it and get on with business." Edmond held out his hand expectantly, and the whole room waited.

Terry looked guilty. The heel of his shoe scraped back and forth across the floor. "I didn't get it. The kid had given it away by the time I got to him."

"You didn't think," Edmond said crossly, "that we could actually change numbers tonight if we didn't destroy that, did you?"

"I tried, but I wasn't there soon enough. I nearly had to wring his neck to find out what he'd done with it. He gave it to the two doctors."

Jaeryn groaned under his breath.

"Then it's good we have them safe here. Which one of you has it?" Edmond looked from one to the other. The piece of paper scratched where Ben had hidden it in the toe of his boot. It wouldn't take them long to find it. Their only hope was to hold out until Evesham arrived—unless Jaeryn came up with something in the meantime, and he didn't look like he'd had any revelations yet.

Edmond pushed Terry toward them. "If you didn't get it from Starlin, then you can redeem yourself and get it from them."

"All right. Which one of you has it?" For a long time, Terry looked thoughtfully at Jaeryn, and then he let him go and turned to Ben. Ben shook his head in a silent plea with Terry not to do it, but it didn't seem to have any effect.

"We can search you," Edmond said. "I'm being kind. We could just as easily search your dead bodies."

"I think we should do that," Hugh muttered.

"That's what I'd expect you to think." Edmond looked from Ben to Jaeryn. "Give it up. You're not in a position to take the upper hand, so you might as well save us the inconvenience."

"We don't have it," Jaeryn said.

Ben sucked his breath between his teeth, and a smile spread across Edmond's face. "A good thing my little brother couldn't lie to save his life. I know you have it."

Jaeryn shot him a furious glance. "You could have been more loyal than that. You promised you wouldn't give me away."

He wasn't sure what Jaeryn meant until he realized that Jaeryn had countered the truth with another lie. Fortunately for him, he did not have to decide what to do with it. Terry looked quite satisfied. "Ben Dorroll has it."

"Hurry up. I don't want Peters finding out that we're here." Edmond double-checked the lock on the door to make sure it was secure.

"Peters knows you're here, and we sent him out for men to arrest you," Ben said quietly.

"Get that wretched list," Edmond snapped.

Terry went through his pockets and turned up nothing but his wallet, which they went through without finding anything. He hoped in desperation that Terry would not think of his shoes, but it was no different from everything else that had gone wrong that night. Terry pointed to the shoes next.

Ben wondered why their unlucky streak had to surface now. There was nothing for it but to slip them off. He heard a slight breath from Jaeryn as Terry crouched down and pulled out the list. Edmond took it with a sigh of relief.

"The notebook is burned, and I'll keep this with me." He tucked it in his pocket. "That's all the proof they have."

Jaeryn's shoulders slumped in defeat. "Terry, why are you doing this? If you keep going, there's nothing I can do to get you out."

Terry grinned at Ben. "You can have your shoes back."

Then Hugh spoke up again. "You were supposed to succeed the first time so they didn't see it at all. If you would quit grieving over that wraith, you might actually be of some use to us."

The words were so cruel that Ben almost gasped, and even Jaeryn looked taken aback.

The grin disappeared from Terry's face. "What are you talking about?" he said, a keen warning sharpening his voice.

"Spirit, corpse, the dead. That girl."

Terry ate up the floor in one long stride and struck Hugh in the face. "I've waited. I've waited for days and days to kill you for that. You took my—her, and I don't know what her last minutes were like, but I think they were more torment than anything she should have to bear. You were a fiend to kill her."

Hugh tried to wriggle away from Terry's grasp. "She didn't know. I did it when her back was turned. Let go of me."

"Why? Why did you kill her? She was innocent."

"What did that matter?" Hugh's voice was cool—almost wondering, as if he couldn't fathom why that should be a problem. "It wasn't my fault. She intercepted one of your telegrams at the door, and I knew she had to be working against us. King had already told me I could do away with her and shake everybody up. After all, that's what you did to Christopher. It was all fair play, and it brought you to our side in the end."

"I'm sick of you," Terry burst out as if a torrent had finally let loose in him and now there was no holding back. "I haven't had a minute alone for two weeks. You took away my Acushla and then acted like I did it myself. I hate you. I hate your dirty soul, and you might as well say anything you have left because I'm going to kill you. You made them all think I wasn't one of them, and there wasn't a thing I could do to tell them otherwise."

A quiver ran through Jaeryn as if he had been stung. Ben listened wonderingly.

"They're going to arrest me with the lying, dirty lot of you, and I'm going to get hung for it. But I never came back to *you* for a moment, so stick that down your throat and swallow it."

"If that man isn't one of ours, will someone disarm him, please?" It was a calm voice—Edmond, Ben was quite sure—that gave the order. "We really can't leave him like that."

Terry gave one half-yell before Hugh began a muffled rain of blows and Mrs. Goodwin slipped Nimrod loose from the collar, holding him at the ready. Stafford gave his gun to Edmond and slipped into the fray. King took no part in it. It was odd to watch a fight with no sound except the muffled smack of fists. They were too afraid of being overheard to make it an out-and-out brawl. Terry was always in the middle, trying to give as good as he got, but sadly hampered when Nimrod's teeth sank into his leg. Still, they might not have overpowered him if Hugh hadn't given him a hard crack over the head, turning him dizzy while he was fending off the others. His revolver was raised aloft and flung as far as Hugh's arm could throw it. King stooped down to retrieve it.

It didn't take long for them to pin him down once the revolver was out of the way. Stafford would have killed him on the spot if Edmond had not called out to keep him alive. It was strange to see Terry's strong arms restrained by the people he had warded off for months on end—especially small, dark-eyed Hugh, whom Terry could have snapped and flung in the corner under ordinary circumstances. As it was, his eyes clenched tight shut for a moment as he let the pain wash over his bruised face. Then he opened them and stood firm, and his gaze went straight to Jaeryn.

They couldn't say anything aloud, but a look of understanding passed between them, and a little of the wildness softened from Jaeryn's eyes. Not much—just the devil-may-care edge that had characterized him since Terry's leaving. It was odd to think that perhaps unsteady Terry had been a source of steadiness to him. They had faced death together, after all.

And now it was the three of them, all restrained, but all together. And three were stronger than two, and Ben began to hope again.

Terry looked down and spit in Hugh's face, as he could do nothing else. Hugh cursed, but Terry only looked deeply satisfied. Stafford made Terry kneel on the floor, and Hugh fastened a pair of handcuffs on him.

"Here, Nimrod." Mrs. Goodwin called to him and slipped the collar over his head again. She and Mrs. Meikle sat next to each other on the cushioned, gilded chairs. Both ladies had their gloved hands neatly folded together, and not another sound escaped them.

"Two minutes by the clock, and then I expect everyone to be out of here," Edmond said. He turned to Colonel King, who stood near the door with his arms crossed, watching everything with his brown eyes. "We've enjoyed your company, but it's time for you to leave now. Your involvement with our side is concluded."

"Rather unneighborly of you to make this switch without including me," King said.

"We are going to save you the trouble of bothering with it."

"How kind of you."

"I'm not interested in being neighbors," Edmond said angrily. "You killed my sister and stole my assassin. I find it hard to forgive you for that."

Colonel King gave a dry laugh. "One little girl dead, and three men to mourn her loss. It was too good to pass up. Besides, once she had the telegram, we didn't have a choice."

"At least I haven't stooped to murder." Edmond looked almost ludicrous with his inexperienced youth facing off against King's calculating maturity. "I'm one better than you, and you killing a woman I never knew did nothing to change my designs."

"Perhaps I should have killed your wife instead of having Fenton tell her you were in town. You would be wise to combine forces with me, sir."

Edmond smiled in easy arrogance. "I have no intention of giving up what Emmerson started. If you're willing to be satisfied with a subordinate position, then I have no objection."

King frowned. "Absolutely not. It would be foolish to put you in charge."

"I think we'll have to part ways, then. There isn't room for both of us here."

"I concur."

Ben realized afterward that Jaeryn must have seen what was coming. The Irishman struggled to break his hands free and gave up all caution to voice his protest. "No! Don't do it!"

But the gun went off just the same, and the King and Emmerson rivalry ended for good in one well-aimed shot to the heart.

Chapter Thirty-Six
"I Will Thwart Them"

Before the words left Jaeryn's mouth, Edmond fired, and King fell without a sound. Ben looked down in horror at the crumpled body. "Oh God, have mercy. Why did you do it?"

Edmond bit his lip in the dead silence following his act. "I didn't mean it to go quite that far." Then he shook it off. "Well, if it hadn't been him, it would have been me. Someone see if he's dead."

Stafford knelt beside King and gently flipped him over. King's eyes were still open, and he struggled to draw breath. There was a kind of grief on the butler's face. He and King must have worked together for a long time, and Stafford probably knew the secrets that no other soul on earth had been privy to. Jaeryn was too stunned to say anything. He had stopped his useless struggling and stood stock still again, his shirt plastered to his back with sweat. Ben managed to find his tongue. "If you get him to the Royal Victoria in time, it might save you a murder charge."

"Let him lie there," Edmond said roughly. "He never did me any favors. Hugh, stand guard over Turlough O'Sean, and if he moves, you shoot him. I want the rest of you to write down your names and numbers as quickly as possible, and then out and down the back stairs. Hide wherever you like; just stay out of the public eye. I'll leave a note in the drop telling where to regroup."

There were pencils and paper lying on a chair. Mrs. Goodwin was the first to scrawl her name on one of the sheets. She did not stop to look at King lying on the floor, only quickening her steps and tugging Nimrod along with her as she passed him. Even Stafford's remorse was quickly overcome, for he stood up with the rest of them and put a new number by his name. Only Ann Meikle kept quiet in her corner.

"He's dead," Hugh said, peering down at King as the last signs of movement faded away. King's face was stern and still, his tall figure as imposing in death as it had been in life. An ugly red stain soaked into the white and gold carpet around him. "The old man tried to kill you once with an overdose of chloral hydrate," Hugh continued, jerking his head toward Edmond. "But you must not have gotten it. Wanted me to kill his son, too, but that didn't work either. The only one that worked was the girl because he let me handle it myself. You seem to have all the luck on your side."

Ben looked over to Jaeryn. He caught a hint of elation under the dark eyebrows at being proved innocent of the murder attempt. He was too relieved to care. Then Jaeryn and Terry exchanged glances. Ben saw Jaeryn jerk his head sideways as if to point to him and Terry nod in agreement.

Ben looked questioningly at Jaeryn, and the Irishman risked a low reply. "You're safe first."

"No. Jaeryn—" But he was cut off, for Edmond turned on his heel and posed a question.

"Do you want to join us, little brother? I'm afraid we can't keep the Irishman, and that bodyguard is no use either, but you are family, so I'll give you the option."

Edmond spoke lightly as if the whole thing was an innocent game to him. For a moment Ben wondered if it was. King's death might have been instinct, an adrenaline reaction left over from war scenes, the horror of which they could only imagine. The dull ache from the handcuffs echoed the ache in his mind as he tried to think through every angle that might persuade his brother to change his mind. But there was no alternative; Edmond could not be released or pardoned now.

He swallowed back the fear and asked the thing he had to know. "Is our father in with you too?"

Edmond's mouth drew up in its funny quirk. "Him? He's as

677

British as they come. No, I took Emmerson's side because he actually took an interest in me. Is that so terrible? Worth arresting me for?"

The grief tore at him. Was it wrong for Edmond to follow a man who loved him, even if it led to the German side? He was relieved to hear that his father was innocent, but Ben thought that Matthew Dorroll, in spite of his refusal to be personally involved, was not entirely guiltless in the matter.

Edmond's breath sounded heavier. "What were you going to tell our father when he learned that his eldest son was executed because of his youngest?"

A cold sweat broke out on his forehead. Jaeryn's eyes blazed green fire. "Leave off."

"Shut up, Irish rat."

Jaeryn's teeth showed through a little as his lips curled back in disgust. "I'm not a rat."

"We're done, sir," Stafford spoke up by the cream-cushioned row of chairs.

"Excellent." Edmond pocketed Jaeryn's revolvers and pointed Ben's straight at his heart. A bolt of fear shot through him, and his hands behind his back were clammy with anticipation.

"Goodbye, little brother."

Jaeryn tried to wrench his hands free. "For heaven's sake, he's your own kin."

"That made no difference to him. It's one or the other of us, and he's much more fit to die."

"You're a wretch," Terry muttered, starting to scramble up in spite of the gun against his head.

"Keep quiet," Hugh ordered, shoving him back to his knees.

It all happened in a moment. Ben only had time to see Jaeryn's face a dull white, and his breath coming faster and faster, building up for what he was about to do. Then the gun cracked out.

Something shoved against him at the same instant. Ben's eyes flew open to see Jaeryn stepping back, a spot of red, hardly bigger than his finger, appearing on his right shoulder. It grew and grew, and in his mind grew as well the realization that Jaeryn had been shot, and not him. The slim white fingers clenched and unclenched. Only the lines creasing Jaeryn's forehead and his teeth grinding together gave any indication of pain.

Then they heard a soft click at the doorknob.

Edmond stiffened and nodded at Hugh. Ben wanted to shut his

eyes again, but by a supreme effort of the will, he kept them open. Terry rolled out of the way just as Hugh's gun went off. The door smashed open. Peters landed a shot between Hugh's eyes before the doorway was filled with several more men behind him. There were only five, but that was enough to fill the room, bringing Stafford to his knees and a snarling, snapping Nimrod to heel.

Evesham brought up the rear, still in his dinner suit. Edmond backed against the window with a pistol in each hand, one pointing out at the room and one in his own mouth.

Evesham kept the Webley trained on his heart. "Edmond Dorroll, I arrest you for treason and call on you to surrender yourself."

Edmond shook his head. "I'll give everything I know if you let me go free."

"It's too late for that; you'll be giving us what you know anyway."

"You have no proof."

"We have abundant proof," Evesham said dryly. "Let's not make this more complicated than it has to be."

Jaeryn seemed occupied with keeping his pain under control and didn't look up when Mrs. Meikle whispered in Terry's ear. But Ben did. Terry whispered back, and she reached into one of his pockets. A moment later, his hands were free. He reached for the key, but she would not give it to him, and he looked frantically at Ben and Jaeryn as he scrambled up.

"If any of you make one move, I'll kill myself," Edmond yelled.

Evesham sighed impatiently. "You're wasting our time and what little you have left."

Ben was so afraid that Edmond would shoot himself that it was a shock to feel cold hands—a woman's hands—on his numb ones. There a painful tug to get the handcuffs off, and then his hands swung down to his sides, limp from the lack of circulation. He looked at his wrists, raw and bleeding from the tightness of their constraints, and tried to will feeling back into them.

"Get me out," Jaeryn pleaded.

"Not on yer life, ye Irish rebel," Mrs. Meikle spat.

"Give me the key." Ben tried to take it from her, but she gripped it tightly. Terry grabbed her by the shoulders and held her while Ben grabbed her hands by force.

"Ye'll regret it if ye let him go."

He pried back her fingers until she could not stand the pressure and was forced to give way. The stain on Jaeryn's shirt was growing fast. It was all down the back of his sleeve now in great blotches, and he was dripping with perspiration. There were too many people in the way to get a proper glimpse of Edmond now.

"Here, sit down while I take these off," he whispered.

Jaeryn shook his head. "I've borne more pain than this."

"I don't doubt it." He fitted the key into the tiny lock and twisted it, and the handcuffs fell free from Jaeryn's hands. As soon as the cuffs were off, Jaeryn whipped around and landed a square blow in his throat that knocked his breath away.

"*Fág láithreach*," Jaeryn threw the words over his shoulder to Terry and took to running.

It was only a moment before Ben recovered from his bewilderment and took off after Jaeryn. Evesham looked in their direction at his cry. But they weren't quick enough. Jaeryn reached for the light switch, and the room was thrown into complete blackness.

Nimrod broke into a deafening cacophony of barking. "The door, go for the door," Evesham ordered curtly. Ben slammed it shut and threw the lock on. Jaeryn used his left hand, the only one he could, to try to force his hands off the knob. Ben held firm and elbowed him away in spite of the long fingers trying desperately to get a hold.

"Let me go. Let me go," Jaeryn hissed.

"No." He clung to the handle. Jaeryn tugged at his arm in a desperate attempt to loosen his hold. A scuffle sounded from the other men; no doubt Stafford and Edmond were trying to take advantage of the diversion.

"You wouldn't actually keep me here. I've done no harm to you—I've kept you safe a dozen times."

"Absolutely," Ben said. The words came without thinking, along with a granite determination to stick by them. The window smashed behind them in a rain of tinkling glass. Ben almost let go in response to it, but he caught himself just in time. What did it mean? It was something to do with Edmond, and he would be on the other side of the room helping if it weren't for Jaeryn trying to escape too.

Jaeryn was still surprisingly strong for having been shot. He clamped down on Ben's wrist and twisted it until Ben was forced to let go. Someone slammed into them and shoved them away from the door. Jaeryn's grasp slipped down to his fingers. Ben threw his whole shoulder into freeing himself and managed to wrench all his fingers out of Jaeryn's grip except one. In the final twist, the last finger Jaeryn held gave off a dull snap, and he let go.

For the first time that night he felt pain—real pain, of bone scraping bone. It was so sharp he yelled out, but he managed to cling to Jaeryn's collar as the lights flashed on.

"Get the door. *Get the door*," Evesham shouted.

Out of the corner of his eye, Ben saw Edmond throw the lock off by a mighty effort and sprint down the hall. He let go of Jaeryn and darted after him with Peters at his heels. Edmond slammed the servant door in his face, but Ben yanked it open and kept going. Down the hall, over the thick red carpet, past the marble busts and mahogany side tables he kept up the pursuit, all the way to the spiral staircase. They were halfway to the first floor when the curve of the stairs slowed Edmond down, and Ben skipped the last few stairs to close the intervening space.

Edmond muttered a curse and tried to shake him off. When that did not avail, he grappled with him until Ben was pressed against the outer railing. Edmond landed a blow in his mouth before he had time to think. A feeling of panic rose within him as he felt himself tipping too far over the balusters. He loosed his hold. That was all Edmond needed. One kick sent him off-balance on the narrow tread, and Edmond pushed him back over the railing. Ben made a frantic grab for the rail. His fingers brushed Edmond's sweater, but it wasn't enough to hold on to. He felt a rush of air and slammed against the floor below.

He couldn't breathe. Edmond rushed past him, and then Peters. He lay for one dazed moment against the dark parquet wood; then he pushed himself up and caught his breath as pain spread from his finger down to his wrist.

"Get up," he muttered, hardly realizing he was talking to himself. There were a few drops of blood on the wood, and he swallowed the taste of salt and copper as he rose to his feet. But he was too late. The front door stood open, letting in the cold and black. Running feet sounded in the hall above. Evesham appeared at the top of the stairs.

"Ed—" He choked on a mouthful of blood and pointed to the door.

Evesham frowned at the sight of him, but he did not ask if he was all right. "Doctor Graham needs medical help. We'll take it from here." He ran down the stairs and out the door.

Ben swallowed the rest of the blood and grimaced. Merciful Heaven, if he had landed any differently—

The library door opened and he startled. But he relaxed again when he saw Fenton's familiar, drooping face, palms out to reassure him. Fenton flipped on the hall lights and offered a manicured hand. The diamond cufflinks winked in the light.

"You're late." Ben pulled himself to his feet and held to the stair railing as the pain flooded his shoulder and side. "You can still go help them."

"I think you could use it too." Fenton gave his small, cat-like smile and offered him a shoulder to lean on. Ben accepted it and slowly followed him out the front door and down the stone steps. They walked toward the garage so they could get the medical kit in Jaeryn's car.

"You're dripping blood on your shirt, doctor," Fenton said.

"It's nothing compared to upstairs. I don't have anything to stop it until we get to the car."

Fenton drew out a starched handkerchief and gravely presented it to him. Ben crammed it against his mouth and kept going. At least his wrist wasn't broken; he could move it a little, though it hurt terribly. But the finger was bent out of place, and he would need help getting Jaeryn's shoulder bandaged.

Jaeryn had given their scuffle his very best up to the end, but they were too many for him. He had lost his vow to conquer on the seventh time out. Though they could not have wished him the victory, it was an ugly thing to see him fall. Ben wondered if his part in the capture would damage their friendship for good. He would find out soon enough.

* * *

It took two men to hold Jaeryn after Ben ran out. They could only do it by getting a tight grip on his bad shoulder and bearing down so hard that his knees nearly buckled from the agony. He was forced to take a firm hold of the arms constraining him and put his head down to keep upright. His white shirt was completely red at the shoulder and streaked red and white down toward the cuff.

Terry stopped fighting the guard and held up his hands when Evesham pointed a gun at him. The guard brought over a pair of handcuffs to put on Jaeryn. Terry looked pleadingly to Evesham.

"He's hurt. Please leave them off."

When Jaeryn heard Terry's voice, he broke down completely.

"You were supposed to leave. You were supposed to leave, and now it's too late," he said, his voice catching at the last bit. He tried desperately to hold back the grief, but the pain was starting to get the best of him, and he didn't know how much longer he could control it.

"You hired me to look after you. I had to do that, now," Terry said soothingly. He crossed the intervening space and tried to give Jaeryn a sturdy shoulder to lean on. Evesham would not allow it.

"You can't touch him, Turlough. Guard, come here." Evesham changed places with the guard and gave terse directions to the rest of his men. "Two of you patch him up as best you can. Keep the others in this room until I get back."

"What about the postmistress?"

Evesham opened the door and flung the words over his shoulder. "She's one of ours—to a degree. Let her be."

As soon as Evesham was gone, a guard motioned for Terry to put his hands behind his back and handcuffed them together. Another trained a Webley on Jaeryn for the short walk down the hallway to a private room.

"Let me go with him. I won't do anything," Terry pleaded.

Jaeryn tried to steady his voice and raised his head proudly. "It's no use, Terry. We're finished."

Terry gave the guard an anxious look, but he kept his words calm for Jaeryn's sake. "Rest now, and we'll figure out what to do in a minute. We'll be all right, you'll see."

The guard hesitated. He must have seen something in Terry's face that eased his suspicions, for signs of relenting showed on his thin, angular face. "If you'll keep him quiet and not try to escape, you can come. Otherwise, I'll separate you again."

"I'll be good." Terry nodded resolutely. "I'm not going to leave without him."

"You can come with us, then."

They brought Jaeryn into the next room, and in spite of Evesham's earlier leniency, handcuffed him to the bedpost by his good arm. He winced when his hand went through the steel circle. They didn't tighten it down as far as Terry had, but he was well restricted nonetheless. He sat on the foot of the bed and waited, his shirt beginning to stick to his shoulder and dry there. That would sting coming off. But he couldn't have it come off. It was his last protection.

"Do you have my knife?" he whispered to Terry.

"No whispering," one of the guards ordered brusquely. "You keep your talk loud enough for me to hear. What did you just say?"

Jaeryn flashed him an angry look and held stubbornly silent. The man took a grip on his shoulder again, and he gasped and gave way. "I wanted my knife."

"You can't have it. From now on, you send your requests through me. Talk to him in English if you're going to talk." The man searched through their pockets and emptied them while his companion stood in the doorway to block anyone from entering or leaving. Jaeryn sat until he could no longer bear the silence and turned to Terry.

"Tell me why you lied to us," he snapped. "We could have used you all this time if we had known you were still ours. I don't think you'll ever know what you put us through."

Terry drew back at his harshness. "I know, doc, but you brought me here to protect you. I had to do what I could. Hugh always suspected I wasn't one of them, but he couldn't pin it on me until after he tried to strangle you. You said I couldn't kill them yet, and they were ready to kill you straight off. So I make them think that I got scared and decided to come back to them. It kept them off a little longer."

Jaeryn frowned. "You planned all that?"

"Yeah." Terry didn't take the disbelief as an insult. "And if I even talked to you for a moment, they'd have known I was lying, and you would be finished, and all this would go to smash. So I couldn't."

"But you threatened to kill me that morning. Not to mention hurting your own brother. And I'm not one to complain about the mistreatment of Starlin King, but you weren't entirely innocent on that score, either."

"Hugh was coming to meet me," Terry said with a funny mixture of guilt and innocence. "You wouldn't leave if I didn't threaten you. It was the only way I could think of to get you off safe. When you looked back, I thought you were going to die for sure. And that other night at Alisa's you nearly blew my cover again."

Jaeryn refused to soften his displeasure, in spite of Terry's efforts to appease him. "You threatened to give away my name."

A flash of annoyance crossed Terry's face. He spoke more sharply than Jaeryn had ever heard him before. "You're a stubborn man, and you wouldn't let me go otherwise. I only had a few seconds before Hugh found out I was inside talking to you." His blue eyes filled with wounded defensiveness. "You doubted me. How could you doubt me

684

after I proved myself to be true?"

He *had* proved himself true. On a dark night just like this, and worse in some ways, with only the two of them together instead of three. Jaeryn felt a tightness in the back of his throat. "I'm sorry, Terry. I didn't want to doubt you. But there were others acting just as true who proved false to us, and you did give away the drops."

"And told your little scamp to make sure you were there when I did it, so you would know."

Fenton hadn't told him that part. All this time, the man could have revealed Terry's need when Terry was unable to let them know himself. What callous cruelty, to withhold the truth of it. "He never told me. I'll break his neck for that."

Terry's eyes widened. "Don't do that," he said in concern.

They heard Ben's voice in the hall, and Jaeryn leaned forward. "Terry, you would help me with one more thing, wouldn't you?"

"Sure," Terry said eagerly. "If I can."

"I've thought about it, and if we could try to buy them off, then I think it would be the best way. I know you can't get any money right now, but if you could try—"

Terry drew away. "That's only going to get you into worse trouble. You hired me to keep you safe, not to help you get jailed for life."

"Terry, please—"

"No."

It was no use to argue further with the guard listening to every word, and Jaeryn subsided in sharp despair. It was too late. He would be implicated without question, and there was nothing he could do to prevent it.

* * *

Ben hurried, and it didn't take him long to get what he needed. Peters had moved the car to the garage in the back. They didn't drive it to the front door in case Edmond was still out there. But they saw no sign of him, and though it was tempting to search himself, Ben didn't want to disobey Evesham. Fenton went down the hall to see the results of the mayhem, and Ben went with him to inquire where Jaeryn was. He entered the bedroom just in time to hear Terry's refusal.

"Don't worry, Terry," Ben said, startling both of them. "He won't

685

be doing it."

The guard nodded to Terry. "Do you still want handcuffs on him, sir?"

"That won't be necessary. Unlock him, the two of you, and stand guard in the hall while I treat Doctor Graham."

"Are you sure that's wise?"

"As long as Terry promises not to help him try to escape."

Terry looked uncertainly to Jaeryn, who offered no words and stared down at his knees. He nodded unhappily. Ben jerked his head for the guard to go out, but he closed the door, for he wasn't about to take chances. He took a deep breath so Jaeryn wouldn't know how much he was hurting and swallowed hard.

Terry winced when he caught sight of the thin red lines around Ben's wrists. "I didn't know they would hurt you like that. I was going to unlock them as soon as I could, but it didn't work."

"It's no matter." He taped his index finger to the next one to stabilize it and then took out bandages and a pair of scissors to cut away Jaeryn's shirt. "Jaeryn, I wish it hadn't ended this way."

Jaeryn shut his eyes tightly. "Not over yet. You could still let me go."

"No, I couldn't."

Jaeryn looked up at him, and his mouth twisted with anger. "Is that what all I've done for you is worth to you?"

Ben winced. "Don't. You know it's not."

"Prove it, then."

He could barely keep a grip on himself after that, barely hold back the feelings that urged him to unlock the handcuffs and set Jaeryn free. It would be cruelty when he was so hurt, but Jaeryn wouldn't be able to see that. And words of thanks for saving his life would be empty insults at the moment. He would risk seeming ungrateful and wait until they were actually worth something.

Before he could think of anything to say, Mrs. Meikle peeked around the door frame. "One of the men came back for the bodies, so I'm free now. Can I help ye patch him up, doctor?"

Jaeryn jerked up, and the spark returned to his green eyes. "Don't you dare touch me."

"Be rude all ye like, but I still feel sorry for ye."

She might have worked for him once, but it would be an awful indignity for Jaeryn. Ben didn't feel too warmly toward her either after all that had happened. "Your sympathy is untimely, Mrs. Meikle.

I have things well in hand."

"Suit yerself, but two find an easier job of it than one." She looked straight to Jaeryn. "I never did write those soldier lists, did I?" She withdrew, and after she had left, Jaeryn broke into a fit of shivering.

Ben motioned for Terry to unbutton the white vest. "I'm going to take off your shirt. The wound will probably break open again, but we'll stop it as quickly as we can. The bullet went all the way through, so that's good news."

"You don't have any proof against me. Just Evesham's word, and that's it," Jaeryn protested. "I may have given Speyer away, but there's nothing to pin the other claim on me."

Ben ignored the protest. Jaeryn tried to bring his left hand around to prevent Terry from taking the vest off, but the handcuffs wouldn't allow him to reach that far. "No. Leave it on."

Terry stopped and looked at Jaeryn in surprise. "Someone has to look at it, doc. You can't do it yourself."

"I'll have you look at it."

The pressure must have turned his head for good. Ben motioned for Terry to finish unfastening the buttons and pull away the vest. "That's ridiculous. Why him?"

"He's helped me before. I'll tell him—what—to do." Jaeryn gritted his teeth against the pain and tried to struggle against them, but he couldn't do much with one hand locked up and the other lying useless on the bed. Ben took up the scissors and snipped off the shirt buttons relentlessly.

He cut the sleeve away from one shoulder so it could be removed without taking the whole shirt off. Then he took a firm grip and forced it away from the wound. Jaeryn gave a high, unsteady gasp, and Ben pressed gauze against it to staunch the blood. He held it there for a moment, then pulled it away and begin cleaning it. But it wouldn't clean properly. There was something there—dried blood, or an old scar perhaps. Ben looked closer, and then he saw why Jaeryn had put up a protest at the last minute. A Celtic cross showed under the blood. It was just like Terry's, only larger, and low enough on the shoulder blade to be covered by a shirt at all times.

Jaeryn knew as soon as he had discovered it. "Don't say anything. To think you were my downfall in the end. I thought I was cleverer than you, and I was, but you—" He shivered and sucked his breath between his teeth. "You're the sort that people can't find it in

687

themselves to stand by and see shortchanged. It wasn't in my best interests, but I couldn't stand to see that you were ill done by."

"I don't know how to thank you for it." A wave of grief swept over him. Even if Jaeryn had lied for months on end, he had taken Ben's shot for him, and they had seen too much together to part in resentment now. But the evidence against him was too damning to remedy, and there was nothing either of them could do. Escape was the one thing he couldn't give him. "Jaeryn, I wish—"

"You don't have to say anything. What I did, I did with my eyes open. I realized I was in a perfect position here, trusted by the British, knowing the very intelligence secrets that they would use against us later. We had—still have—a lot of preparation to do. I was a substantial financial backer for the uprising, and I helped smuggle a couple of people across to France after it failed."

"Was that where you broke your fingers? Fighting in the revolt?"

"No. It was for the British," Jaeryn said shortly.

Evesham looked in the room and offered a steady hand at Jaeryn's back while Ben and Terry bandaged his shoulder between them. "I've alerted the local authorities to your brother's escape, and they're sending out more people to help us. They'll alert the ports and train stations as well. With his face, he won't get through easily. We're taking the others to be locked up, and we'll take Graham off your hands from here."

Ben nodded. "I can manage now if you want to keep looking."

"I'm not concerned about him. Edmond Dorroll is Ryson's business. Jaeryn Graham is mine." Evesham held out his hand. "We lifted these from Doctor Graham's house while you two were away this evening."

Jaeryn looked like a fox, tensing under the hunter's aim. Ben glanced at what Evesham was holding. In his palm was a silver ring, much like Terry's, but with an emerald instead of a sapphire. It winked evilly under the light as if it delighted in divulging its owner's secrets. Underneath was a photograph of a little girl with curly dark hair. "There were telegrams to Calais as well. They revealed everything we needed to know."

Jaeryn stared at them with his mouth open, and the color came and went in his face. Ben knew instinctively that the objects were ones that he had kept concealed for months—years perhaps. Terry had waved his ring about in the light, showing everybody that would look, while Jaeryn kept his so hidden that no one ever dreamed of its existence.

"When he came to town in January, Ann recognized him from earlier the previous summer. He had sent telegrams to Irish revolutionaries in Calais. She suspected he was trying to start something up again, and she kept a watch on him. But Graham thought Ann was a traitor, so there was very little she could find out. We only knew for sure when Ryson fired him and Graham brought you back because he thought you were inexperienced enough to manipulate."

Ben waited for Jaeryn to deny it, but he did not. "Jaeryn?" he asked unsteadily.

"It's true." Jaeryn's face changed from quiet calculation to dark malice.

Now that he knew the truth, his whole soul revolted at it. "You said it was to help. I don't understand. You were genuinely determined to capture these people tonight, or you never would have come."

The room fell silent. Jaeryn opened his mouth. Finally, he spoke. "One does not have to love Britain to hate Germany. And I do not like to fail in something I have begun."

"Tell us the rest of it," Ben said insistently.

Jaeryn clenched his fist. "Folkestone was a convenient place. We were lying low, getting ready to try again once we had all our resources together. Is that so bad? That's everything I have to tell. The rest is mine to keep. I don't mind you winning out, but it's hard—to—know—that people I despise will see my downfall."

Jaeryn's blood ran dark red over his fingers, and Ben hurriedly applied gauze to keep him from losing more. "Mr. Evesham, please tell the guard to bring the car around. I need two of them to carry him downstairs. He'll never walk it on his own, and he should be taken to the Royal Victoria immediately."

"Gi-give me my things," Jaeryn panted. "You have—no right."

"They will be returned to you." Evesham unlocked the end of Jaeryn's handcuffs that was attached to the bed while he spoke to Ben. "Your part is done now, and you can get some rest. I'll meet you at Graham's clinic at six this morning. We'll discuss where to go from there."

"I want to go with him."

"I'm afraid not. You wouldn't understand everything we have to do, and you would only hinder us if you were there." Evesham put his jacket around Jaeryn's shoulders. Jaeryn didn't look too keen on accepting the favor, but he didn't have much choice.

Ben looked up at Evesham fearfully. "You're not going to hurt him further?"

"I hope not. How far we go depends entirely on his cooperation. Rest assured, we'll only go as far as we must."

The two guards picked up Jaeryn between them. Evesham beckoned for Terry to lead the way and called for Ann Meikle to come as well. Ben stood in the doorway and watched them down the hall. After all that had happened, Jaeryn didn't look like a battle-hard, dishonest agent. Just a bested revolutionary involved in stakes too high for him, with a zeal for Irish justice for which he could hardly be blamed. They disappeared through the servants' door, and Ben lost sight of them.

So this was the end of it all. He never would have guessed when he arrived at the Tontine clinic that morning in May that he would end up taking Jaeryn in the end, or that his brother would be involved, or that Edmond would get away due to Jaeryn's struggle to escape. What was it Jaeryn had said? Most agents weren't ready for what they would find, and if they knew the end, they would never attempt to follow through. Jaeryn had said that yesterday, but it felt like a lifetime ago.

"Sir?"

"Yes, Peters?" Ben held against the door frame as a hot wave of nausea ran over him. He could still smell the gauze and tape, and he wished he could get rid of the sensation. Not to mention how much he ached from the fall.

"You should look at yourself. There's a washroom down the hall if you'll come with me."

Ben followed mechanically, glad to have someone else tell him what to do for a little longer. He should have insisted on going and seeing that Jaeryn was properly done by. They would treat Jaeryn first before they questioned him—surely they would. But what were they going to do after that? Evesham didn't seem the sort to be unduly cruel.

Peters opened a door, and they entered a cool, quiet washroom. There were soap and towels laid out next to the sink. "I didn't bring any of my things with me, Peters. Will you go back and get them?"

"Of course." Peters left him, and Ben leaned against the gray and white marble counter top and looked in the mirror. There was blood on his lower lip, caked and smeared where it had dried. The rest of his face was hardly different in shade from his shirt.

He pressed his hot forehead against the white tile and waited for Peters. He had done it. He had taken Jaeryn in, an Irish rebel. A *tattooed* Irish rebel. The tea and tidy papers and precise ways had all been so real that he never would have imagined Jaeryn doing something as passionate as tattooing himself. And Jaeryn had betrayed Nathan Speyer to damage British interests but risked his life to bring the other spies down at the same time.

He didn't understand it. He only knew that with Jaeryn turned in for treason, and partly by his hand, something inside him was broken, and he doubted it would ever heal properly. This wasn't the way it should be. They were supposed to be friends, and now to end up like this— His mind raced ahead with all that might happen, but it only led to darkness, and he shook the thoughts away.

His hands were still stained. Ben looked down at them and shuddered. There was no getting away from it. The sink and mirror faded until he could only see red. A purple cross took shape in the center and grew larger every second. Jaeryn's vow echoed in his ears: *"Cuirfidh mé de dhroim seoil iad."* Then he thought he heard someone calling his name, and the cross turned black and swallowed up his vision completely.

* * *

Neither Fenton nor Peters would listen to him when he said he could take care of himself, and Peters pulled a car around to take him to the Royal Victoria. He didn't want to see Jaeryn there—he almost didn't want to see Jaeryn again, after all that had happened. To see him angry or defeated would be too much after all that had gone on between them. But Fenton and Peters couldn't be reasoned with, and at one in the morning, Ben found himself in the same building to which he had directed so many other people for help.

It wasn't terribly serious. They got the bleeding inside his mouth to stop, and all things considered, it was better than it might have been. The finger was broken and would take time to heal, but they let him go after putting it in a splint. It might heal straight, it might not. They didn't know for sure, and he didn't particularly care just then.

When they let him out, Peters asked him where he wanted to go. He could go to Alisa's place, but he would be alone there, and he did not want to be alone. Jaeryn's clinic was entirely out of the question. He wouldn't enter that house until he had to. Those were the only places he had.

He needed Charlotte's comfort, and she was at Copt Point—likely asleep by now, he tried to tell himself. But somehow, he knew she wouldn't be, and he wanted to see her most of all.

It was dark when they got there, but the stars were out. Ben heard the great wash of the waves and smelled the fresh coldness, and he knew that this had been the right place to come.

"I'll drop by the clinic tomorrow, doctor," Fenton said. "I have something to give you for the trial."

"All right."

"You don't have a coat, sir," Peters told him. "Borrow mine, and you can give it back to me later."

Ben accepted it. His heart leaped when he heard the door opening and saw Charlotte looking out.

She ran toward him. Her flaxen hair hung down over her shoulders, and the wind fluttered the white collar of her shirtwaist. Peters turned the car around and drove off. Ben hurried to meet her. It didn't take her long to catch sight of his bloodstained clothes.

"What happened?" she called softly. "Are you all right?"

"I'm all right." Ben held her tightly until she pulled away to look at his face. "It's nothing. See?" He held out the hand with the splinted finger. "This is all, I promise. I got off pretty lightly on the whole."

Alisa lifted the window curtain, but Ben did not meet her gaze. He could not satisfy her with a look, and he did not want to raise false hopes. A few hours ago, he had been in anguish at the thought of his brother's sentence and Jaeryn's secrets, but he had clung to the belief that it would be resolved quickly. Now the resolution was far from complete, and he did not know what would happen to either of them.

"Alisa and I waited up for you," Charlotte said. "Erin is asleep, so we'll have to be quiet." Ben put the coat Peters had given him around her shoulders. She tried to make him take it back, but he refused. "Were you successful?" she asked hesitantly.

"Partially. They're still searching for Edmond, but the rest were taken. Jaeryn and Terry were arrested as well."

"Oh." Her face fell, and she searched his eyes to see how he was bearing it. They were shrouded in darkness, but they could feel each other's souls well enough in spite of it.

"Jaeryn and I were never good friends, you know, even when we wanted to be. I think we lost our chance at that tonight." He shivered from the pain. "Walk with me, Charlotte. I want to clear my head."

Ben took her hand, and they walked closer to the edge of the cliff so he could feel the waves crashing against the rocks below. He hadn't seen these waves since leaving for America. Shoving away thoughts of Pearlie, he forced his mind to think only of the present, and listened. One wave after another. One crash after another. Life went on, and they would go on, he told himself. But as he listened, he could not get the picture out of his mind that each wave died on the rocks as it hit them. One gently lapped up to a peaceful end, and the next, like Jaeryn, erupted in a huge crash of thunder as it shattered to pieces. The sound he thought would soothe him only reminded him of all the hopes that were dashed and could never be gotten back again.

He thought of Terry then, loyal to Jaeryn against all odds. There was some goodness, some simple love and loyalty still left in the world, for all the convoluted lying swirling around it. Even Terry's change of face had simplicity underneath it: a steady purpose to keep Jaeryn alive all the way to the end. And that was a comfort, after all that had happened.

"Terry was true," he said softly. Charlotte didn't answer. Ben heard her crying as she gazed at the black emptiness before them.

Charlotte looked up and saw that he had noticed. "I'm sorry." She wiped her face with the back of her hand. Ben put his arm around her, and she leaned her head on his shoulder. Neither of them knew they were standing where Terry and Pearlie had stood together, for Jaeryn was not there to tell them.

"What will happen to him?" Charlotte asked.

"I don't know. He and Jaeryn were both taken for being Irish revolutionaries. I don't know what will happen to either of them." The cold penetrated his shirt, and he thought of going inside to warm up. Alisa needed to be told what had happened. It wouldn't be fair to keep her waiting much longer.

An overwhelming desire for sleep came over him, but he wanted to see Charlotte in some peace of mind first, so he waited a moment longer while he looked for words to ease her.

"We can pray that they will find mercy with their justice. And beyond that, it is out of our hands."

Ben ran his fingers through her hair as he always liked to do when they were alone together. The soft, clinging realness of it felt good after knives and death and impending sentences. This time she must have known it comforted him, for she did not laugh and push his hand away like she normally did.

At length, he softly told her that it was too cold to stay out longer. Charlotte lifted her head from his shoulder and they walked toward the cottage, hand in hand. Alisa stood in the doorway, waiting for them to tell her that her husband and his older brother was no longer a brave soldier nor an affluent gentleman of leisure. He was simply a German sympathizer, guilty of murder and on the run from his pursuers.

Chapter Thirty-Seven
Allan Evesham's Justice

Ben ended up leaving Copt Point shortly after he arrived. As soon as he entered the cottage, he remembered Starlin King, and that was something that he could not delay dealing with until morning. He only stayed long enough to tell Alisa and Patrick what had happened, and then he borrowed Erin's key to open up the other cottage and use the telephone that Jaeryn had put in. It would be private there and not disturb the others.

It took some time to get through to the King estate and coax a distraught maid to find George, but at length his efforts were successful and he heard the familiar, eager, absolutely British voice on the other end of the phone.

"We waited until Stafford got back," George said, "and then he left straight for London as fast as he could go. I haven't heard anything since. Is it true that Colonel King is dead, sir?"

"It's true. I wrote out the death certificate myself. Where did Starlin say he was going?" As Ben looked at the room he had not seen for months, he noticed that Jaeryn had refurnished the house. The Irishman must have been eager to have him back.

"Where you told him to go, sir. Your father's."

"I'm glad he got away safely. I'll put a call through and find out if

695

anyone from London has seen him."

He should have sent a note with Starlin. Something to tell his father that Starlin was speaking the truth when he asked for a place to stay. Hopefully his father took the boy at his word. It wasn't likely that he would turn away a young man purporting to be Colonel King's son, however late the hour. Ben rang through to London and waited for the connection. He did not recognize the voice that answered.

"I'm calling for Starlin King."

It must be one of the household help. "Yes, sir. He came in very early this morning, but he's still up. I'll get him."

Starlin sounded quite alert on the other end of the line. The drive to London had been such a risk, but he had managed to find the place and get there safely, which was a miracle in itself. Safe and unharmed, and Ben was glad.

"I'm not asleep. What happened?" No wonder Starlin hadn't slept. He sounded on edge from all that he had been through.

"We have a lot left to sort through, but we captured almost everyone, thanks to your help. I'm glad you reached London safely."

"Did you take my father?"

"He didn't get away. None of them got away except my brother, and the search is going on for him right now. He can't make it far with his face. I'll tell you more when I come to pick you up, but I have many details to arrange first. Can you stay in London until this afternoon? I'll call later and speak to my father about it."

"I can come back the same way I went."

"That was only out of desperation, Starlin. I wouldn't have risked you on such a drive if there was any other choice."

"I'm coming back now," Starlin insisted.

"Wait until daylight, at least. You must be tired, and you'll be much safer if you delay your start a few hours. Did my father mind you coming?"

"He was surprised to see me, but he didn't seem to mind. He's interesting to talk to."

"Is he?" Ben hadn't imagined his father finding much appeal in talking to Starlin King.

"I told him I wanted to stay up until you called, and he let me. I'll come soon. As soon as I can keep my eyes open, anyway."

"Don't hurry." Some good news occurred to him then, and he passed it on, for Starlin wouldn't have much later on. "Starlin, before you go—Terry never meant to harm you. He was working under constraints and couldn't tell you, but he was sorry he had to treat you so harshly. He wanted to keep you safe and foil other people's efforts at the same time."

"Did he?" Starlin didn't sound convinced. Terry must have done a good job of making him believe otherwise.

"I'm sure of it. He's not free to talk right now, but I know he'll want to speak with you when he gets the chance. Goodbye, Starlin. If you want to wait until the afternoon, I can come to London to get you, but otherwise, I'll see you when you get back."

Of all the people who had managed to get themselves into scrapes, Starlin had gotten off with the least amount of trouble. He was glad of it. The boy had had trouble enough in his life, and perhaps now they could repair some of the hurt in him. If it weren't for Nathan Speyer, they might have completely discounted his importance.

Ben wondered who would look after Starlin now. A guardian might not be as lenient with the boy as his father was. But they would be truer, and kinder, and better for him. He could move forward with college and a future, without political intrigue to jeopardize his brightness. And if some of the rough edges could be smoothed out, Starlin King would rise to be a great man indeed, in spite of an inauspicious childhood.

* * *

In the cold darkness of the early morning, Ben walked to Jaeryn's clinic. There was nothing to be afraid of this time—no one following him that he had to keep a lookout for. Hugh was dead, the rest were locked up, and he was free to come and go as he liked. But he took his revolver with him anyway. After all, Edmond was still on the loose, and it would not do to be foolhardy. Besides, the tense alertness had become so ingrained that he doubted he would ever be able to unwind from it.

The lights were on in the consulting room and the kitchen. Evesham was there before him, looking through Jaeryn's papers. He sat in the leather swivel chair, something about his figure giving off the same aura of neat preciseness that Jaeryn did, but holding a calmer, steadier air. Ben didn't even know it was missing from Jaeryn until he saw it in someone else. That was something about the

Irishman—he was never relaxed, even though he could give off an excellent imitation of it. Always on guard, controlling which way he wanted the conversation to go, never letting down his alertness for a moment. It must have been exhausting to keep that up non-stop. He had only lightened up once, during the early morning walk before his secret trip in August. Ben wondered where he had gone for those few days.

The leather chair was intact, but Jaeryn's desk lay torn to pieces. The bottom drawers were empty, and one was splintered irretrievably. The other bookshelves and cabinets were a mess as well. Jaeryn would hate Evesham even more for the invasion of his privacy when he heard of it.

Evesham looked tired. He probably hadn't slept at all, but he appeared to be content with their night's work and glad for the chance to stop and catch his breath. As trim as ever in his suit from the evening before, his dark hair was the only thing slightly out of place.

"Doctor Graham's in the Royal Victoria," Evesham replied, to Ben's question regarding Jaeryn's whereabouts. "Where he should be. He's out of surgery. It didn't hit the bone, but he'll be there for a week or so before he's released, and then he'll have a long recovery before he can use the arm again."

"What did you do to him?"

Evesham knelt down to turn over the remnants of the desk and motioned for him to do the same. "Nothing, as it turns out. I think he'd had all that he could take. I was prepared to give him a stiff questioning after he came out of surgery, but it was beyond him." Evesham picked up the box where Jaeryn kept all his threats like trophies and put them carefully on a shelf. "After a few moments, I let him rest. He has his own private room with a guard outside it, and I'll give him until early afternoon before I talk to him again."

Ben turned over the files that Jaeryn kept in his desk and began putting them back in order. He couldn't take in the words that he was reading, and he didn't think he was actually doing anything to straighten the mess. "When can I see him?"

"Whenever you like. He might be more willing to talk to you than me. I mentioned your name, and he wanted to see you, but I told him you wouldn't be in until later."

"Is he angry with me?"

Evesham paused in his search, and Ben felt as if he had asked a question that he ought to have known better than to voice, though he wasn't sure why. "Would you be?"

"Perhaps it wasn't right to take him."

Evesham smiled. "You cannot rethink your entire code of ethics in a moment of stress. He has enough against him to be legitimately arrested for, and it was right to take him. In answer to your question, I don't think he's angry with you. But he's unsure of where you stand in relation to him at present. There's one thing about the Irish, doctor: they always believe that Englishmen assume the worst of them, though that's far from the case. He isn't sure if what you heard last night made a difference in your opinion of him. Or at least, I'm assuming as much, though he didn't honor me with his confidence on the matter."

"He isn't going to be executed, is he?" Ben pleaded.

Evesham stared. "Good heavens, no. Who told you that?"

"He seemed terribly worried when he was caught. He thought he had lost out, and he was worried for his bodyguard too. That's why he turned the lights off; he wanted to give Terry a chance to get out."

"Rather counterproductive in the end. The British have given amnesty for the Easter Rising. If Jaeryn Graham told you otherwise, he was manipulating the truth. The only threat of hanging he and Terry are under is from their current activity, not their past scrapes." Ben saw Evesham's keen face filing the information away as if it were a piece of evidence that he did not want to forget. "Terry—that's Turlough O'Sean, I believe." At the mention of his name, Evesham's eyes twinkled. "I enjoyed our conversation early this morning. Tell me, who is this Acushla he speaks of? I gather it's a woman. She's so wound in and out of everything he says that she may be important to us."

"That's what he called my sister, Pearl." Ben didn't find it difficult to believe that Pearlie was what Terry came back to in the aftershock. What a man to love his sister. Impulsive and slightly reckless, but loyal to the core, and never a breath of premeditated evil in him for all his bad habits.

"I see," Evesham said. "That would explain things. I gathered he loved her very much. Well, at least the man who took her life is dead now, and we have one less spy to deal with. I'll clear it up with the authorities, but you'll probably have to be a witness to Hugh's confession, and Graham as well, since Hugh can't give it himself. Turlough told me the whole business about his knife. He said Doctor

Graham was trying to save him from getting caught up in it, but under the present circumstances Turlough didn't want that to do more damage to him, so he came clean."

Ben looked down at the papers in his hands, scrawled over in Jaeryn's inky black script. There was nothing here to help them, he felt sure, and all of a sudden, he knew that it was wrong to go through Jaeryn's work when Jaeryn was not with them to defend his secrets. He set the papers down. Evesham continued by himself, talking as he did so.

"Ryson is coming down to deal with his end of things as soon as he gets my telegram. I sent one to him just before I came here. I expect the conspirators will be transported to London shortly after that. You and Graham are two of the principal witnesses, so we'll have to wait until he's able to travel to get his testimony in court. Oh, and Ann Meikle was taken with the rest, which you ought to know."

"Why?" Ben asked, shocked. "I thought you said she was one of us."

Evesham's face held the same kind of disgust as Jaeryn's when her name was mentioned. "Not so much as we thought. She's not of the German persuasion, but she's an ambitious woman. I had an enlightening interview with her last night. It was evident she's been trying to oust Graham since he arrived, for no reason other than she didn't like him having preeminence over her. Then you came, and she determined to get rid of both of you. You were easy enough. She knew if she could implicate both of you at once, then Ryson might dismiss the two of you and leave the field clear for her. She confessed as much, and I took down the confession and had her sign it. Not that that is a crime in itself. Nor is withholding mail, I'm afraid, in our current way of working. But it's best to keep her confession all the same so she can't slither out of it later." The smile wrinkles around his eyes creased. "You see, I'm taking full advantage of Ryson's absence. They'll be questioned again later, but I knew you would want to know."

Ben tried to comprehend it. "I don't understand. You arrested her because she was in a rivalry with us?

"Well, forging notes for her own benefit would be reason enough. But she was frightened by the time we ended last night"—and small blame to her, Ben thought—"and she confessed something else that cast a more serious light on her activities. She'd taken commissions from more than one side for her talents. One of them was writing up the threats for Jaeryn Graham so no one would recognize Hugh's writing."

"Did she know the man was a murderer when she did it?" Ben asked.

"She suspected as much," Evesham replied. "However she said Graham didn't inform her of the German side of Hugh's work. She also gave Hugh enough of an idea of Graham's habits so he knew an opportune time to try the strangling attempt. She hates the Irish enough to see them murdered. Whether or not Ryson indicts her for being an accomplice, I will make sure she is prosecuted."

Evesham took up the papers he wanted and cast a quick glance over the rest of the room to make sure he hadn't missed anything. "I must be going soon. Are there any more questions I can answer for you first?"

He tried to think of something to ask. There was no one that he cared about except Jaeryn and Terry at this point, except—except, perhaps, his brother.

"What happens now that Edmond has escaped?"

"We have professional trackers after him. If he went to the north, then it's a toss-up if we find him or not. He hasn't attempted any of the public railway stations or crossings to France, but we'll use every resource in our power. His description is everywhere, and with his face, it will be hard to slip through. You can't do much at this point except carry on as normal unless you have a better idea where he might be than we do. There's an outside chance that he'll try to contact you, but I would very much doubt it. Search your house and his house for any clues we may have missed, but beyond that, I think your responsibility lies with me for now. Ryson will be angry with you for his escape though it wasn't your fault. I'll do my best to keep him away from Graham, but I'm afraid I can't save you from at least one tongue-lashing."

Ben shrugged. A tongue-lashing was the least of his worries at present. "What do you want me to do now?"

"My goal for the present is to settle business with you and Graham. He's entirely in my charge, and a good thing, too, for Ryson hates the Irish. The first thing we need to do is see him recover his strength, and then we'll attend to matters. Don't go see him just yet. I left him resting, and the stronger he is when we talk, the better."

"I'll go whenever you think he'll be ready." Ben didn't know if he wanted to see Jaeryn. Part of him wanted desperately to see him, to find out where things stood between them. The other part did not want to face Jaeryn's displeasure at being taken in.

"Why don't you see him just before two this afternoon, and I'll come shortly afterward. Don't mention the Irish business unless he brings it up. No matter what we do, he'll think we're taking advantage of his Irish nationality. If he mentions a concern on that score, try to reassure him that it will have no adverse bearing on the matter. The Irish subversion is a serious enough charge, but it's not enough in itself to take him down yet. It's that coupled with his disobedience to Ryson's orders that concerns us. He's been one of our best, and we want to know why he should turn now."

"What will you do if he has turned?"

"I will prosecute him," Evesham returned promptly.

Ben voiced the question he was dreading the answer to. "Do you think he has?"

"That remains to be seen. We'll see if we can straighten it out, the three of us, this afternoon."

It was just after seven by the clock, and the darkness was transitioning into a gray dawning visible through the parted curtains. Evesham took up the hat and coat lying on Ben's desk. "I'll leave you now. You won't be able to open the clinic today. We'll try to get Graham to turn it over to you, but for now you'll both be out of office. Don't stray too far, doctor. I'll need you again before the morning's over. There's a lot left to attend to."

* * *

The pews of the Tontine Congregational church would be missing a good number of Folkestone's occupants, Jaeryn thought idly when he woke up late that morning. All the German conspirators would be absent, and the entire lot of Dorrolls as well.

And him. He would have liked to go to church. Anything was better than this waiting and wondering and wishing he could know his sentence so he would know what he was up against. If only he could meet with Terry. They could arrange something between them, perhaps, and find a way to get out of this. If only his shoulder hadn't given out on him. He couldn't manage the care of it on his own if he escaped, not even with Terry to help him. To come so close to winning, and to spoil it all by doing such a fool thing. He wasn't paid to take other people's shots for them. He could have won if he hadn't. He could have won.

Jaeryn drifted in and out of pain as nurses came to check on him. He tried to draw his faculties together, but felt strangely lethargic. It was as if, after the previous night, all his ability to collect his thoughts was gone. He had poured everything into winning, and now that one last effort was needed, he could not get up enough concentration to do it. He could try to disappear without Terry's help, but then Terry would be left to fend for himself, and that wasn't an option. He could get out and try to set Terry free, if only he knew where he was. Probably in jail. But the possibilities never turned into energy for action, and his schemes drifted away, circling around later to torment him.

He wanted to see Ben. Wanted to know if their conflict the previous night had all been spur of the moment, or if being rebel Irish made a difference in the American's opinion of him. If it did, then good riddance. He could get on quite well by himself. He would wait to see if the man he had given so much for still looked upon him as a staunch friend, or an object to be pitied—or, worse yet, a thing to be despised. After that, he would leave. There was more than one way to win. He hadn't lost yet.

Jaeryn spent the morning waiting, trying to remind himself that he was only a small part in a large mess to be arranged. It would take time for Allan Evesham to get around to him. Eventually, he drifted off again, and he was only just awake when a nurse came in to tell him he had a visitor. His eyes were a little sleepy and out of focus, but he was alert enough to recognize Ben standing in the doorway. He was glad, after all the strange faces, to see someone familiar again. Then he remembered that he hadn't shaved and his hair wasn't combed, and he felt oddly ashamed, thought it wasn't his fault.

"I came to talk to you."

A red scab stretched angrily across the corner of Ben's lower lip, and his wrist and finger were wrapped up. His words were awkward, uncertain. Jaeryn knew with a flood of relief that the man standing before him knew nothing of Irish prejudices, and when it came down to it, nothing much of their work either. He was only struggling with a much more common conflict, that of whether or not he had done right to arrest a man who had done him a good turn. And that was something Jaeryn could overlook.

"You look like you've been to the wars yourself," he remarked, trying in vain to pull himself up on one elbow.

Ben came to his side and raised him to a sitting position. He looked as if he were the one coming to face trial instead of the other way around. "It doesn't matter; it was nothing."

"Will your hand heal all right?" He couldn't imagine Dorroll ending up with a crooked finger. It wouldn't suit his quiet ways and middle-class practicality.

"Possibly," Ben said stiffly.

Jaeryn felt a renewal of confidence. Evidently his role in taking the upper hand hadn't changed. "I didn't mean to hurt you. But it was a fair return; you did slam the door in my face."

The stiffness faded away. There was only regret in the man before him, and nothing of aloofness at all. "I'm sorry. I wish I hadn't—I wish I could get you out. There wasn't any time to wait, and you as much as warned me beforehand that you thought I would do it."

Jaeryn gave up thoughts of rebuking him further and offered his left hand. "It's all right. You chose what you thought best, and that was your duty. What's done is done."

Ben took the offered hand, trying not to hurt him. Jaeryn smiled to set him at his ease, but he did not return it. "I thought you might hate me after what I did," said Ben.

"I don't hate you. You did what I expected of you, even though I do wish you hadn't been so narrow-minded. Ireland's not bad, and fighting for her isn't ignoble."

"I wouldn't know."

Jaeryn chuckled softly. "I know. You're not a revolutionary. You're the sort that countries lean on, but they don't use you to get them started. Never mind. I'll never speak revolt to you, you needn't worry about that. Now, tell me what happened last night after I left."

"Ryson came by the first train this morning. He and Evesham are arranging things between them. I'm just a lowly agent, so I'm not in his confidences. I think he's quite unhappy with me."

Jaeryn suspected that was a good part of Ben's present dejection. Ryson knew how to lay the words on so they stung well, and he probably hadn't offered much recognition of what had gone well the previous night.

"Don't pay him any heed. He wasn't there, so he didn't know what you were up against. What did he say about your brother?"

"That was why he was angry. I told him that I had tried my best, but he wouldn't listen. I didn't say anything about you accidentally helping Edmond's escape."

"Thank you."

Another knock sounded, and Ben turned to see Allan Evesham's tall figure standing in the doorway. Jaeryn's smile faded, and he ran one hand through his hair to straighten it. Slowly and carefully, he collected his scattered plans as to what he would say. Ben stayed standing in the room, and he was glad that a third person would be there to witness the conflict.

"You don't have to sit up," Evesham said, as he took off his jacket.

"I would prefer it." Jaeryn winced as he settled in position, but he held every other sign of pain. He would show the man that he was made of sterner stuff than the evening before.

"I would offer to shake hands, but I doubt that would be an expression of goodwill in your present situation. Do you feel able to talk now?" Evesham took a chair Ben offered and gestured for him to take another.

"Yes, sir." Jaeryn felt tension running through him just from Evesham's presence. Here he would be rebel Irish, and here he would get his sentence. He looked over at Ben, and for once, the American didn't look to be hanging on Evesham's every word. More divided between them, trying to decide whom he would take sides with.

Evesham's keen blue eyes followed Jaeryn's glance, and a flash of warning passed through them. Jaeryn returned his gaze levelly. They both wanted control of the man there. Evesham would speak what he came to say, but he would not be the master; of that Jaeryn was determined.

"First of all," Evesham said calmly, as if he had thought over his words and intended every one to count, "this is the most tangled, twisted capture that I have ever seen as far as motives are concerned, and I've seen quite a few. Out of all the people involved, only two of them had disinterested motives. Yours were far from disinterested, but I think you were remarkable to get as far as you did with the resources you had. You have talent which I would like to see used for us and not against us."

Jaeryn eyed him warily. This was a strange beginning. He had never been in an interrogation before, but he knew this wasn't normal. Flattery was all very well until one discovered the shackles it was intended to conceal.

"Part of your incrimination is the result of Fenton's investigations. He worked with Ryson extensively to track down your identity and a number of your activities that we do not approve of. Your trips to Calais last year are not in your favor, nor are your unaccounted movements during the Easter revolt."

Jaeryn made his first defense. "It seems to me that Ryson should be suspected in all this as well. I may be on the losing end because I'm Irish, but I still maintain that he took unlawful means to investigate my activities. Perhaps he didn't like an Irishman working for England."

Evesham paid no heed to his accusation. "Ryson is honestly British and has never given a breath of suspicion otherwise. He detests the Germans as much as he detests the Irish. Anything that violates what he considers to be the proper system is distasteful to him. No, you yourself have given quite enough indication that all is not as it should be. You've been disobeying a lot of orders lately."

"That's no reason to treat me like a German ringleader." Jaeryn's voice took on a sterner tone, and Ben shifted in his chair. The creases around Evesham's eyes hardened in response to his words. "I'm just a rat, that's what you think, isn't it? To be pushed and pummeled and jailed for wanting freedom. You didn't seem all that keen on listening to my view of things last night. I've proved myself again and again to you, and all my service was thrown aside for one postwoman's insinuations. That's what is known as a grave error in judgment, Mr. Evesham, and hardly fair, even if I am Irish."

"I don't care if you're Irish," Evesham said, and his face was as graven and firm as if he was an offended god of justice. "I do care if you're planning a revolt, but beyond that your nationality makes no difference to me. Furthermore, I never base my accusations on insinuations. Be reasonable and stop thinking that everyone is out to hurt you."

"It's a natural thought when there was far more force used in my arrest than necessary."

"I was never present when you were abused, or I wouldn't have seen it done."

"I still maintain that you took me in and completely ignored my record of service."

"You can hardly call that foolhardy when you gave me such good reason. I am concerned with your part in the Irish revolt, certainly, and you imply that your part is not entirely in the past. Let me warn you, now is not the time to be resurrecting old grievances between your people and ours. We are in the middle of a war with a common enemy. Right now, you should be helping England win, not trying to strangle her from behind. There will be time to address the Irish complaint later, and there will be better ways to do it than out-and-out plotting. Parliament, appeals—all these are in place for a reason."

Jaeryn shook his head. "I think we've seen all the justice we're going to get from there."

"Like it or not, sir, it is the case. You would do well to consider it. Your present course will only give you grief, and I hope you will think better of it. But that was not the only reason we took you in, as I think you very well know. The Irish business only added to our concern."

"Then tell me what the charges are."

"I have lodged no official charges against you as yet. I have to determine how far you've gone to see what I should do to you. You were under suspicion of being a German sympathizer as well, and for that mainly I need you to answer my questions."

Jaeryn felt a surge of dread sweep over him. Irish and German—he wasn't likely to escape either of those accusations. "I'm not a German sympathizer. Of all the unfounded—"

Evesham cut off his argument. "Listen to me. I have four charges to bring against you. Now, will you answer me so I can sort this out, or must I call in someone to reason with you more strongly? I am prepared to do so, and you can deal with more pain than you have now, and less patience, if you prefer."

Jaeryn evaluated his draining strength. He hated the man beside him with a passion, but he could not despise his help. It might be hard questioning, but it would be clean, and he must not throw the opportunity away.

"I'm listening. And I'll answer all that I think right. More than that I can't promise," he said finally.

Evesham nodded. "I can ask no more than that. The first charge, and by far the least important, is your turning the lights off last night and helping a prospective prisoner escape."

"You can hardly blame me. I waited as long as I could to turn the lights off. You should have had him; I gave you every chance."

"We should have, and I'm not saying it was completely your fault that Edmond Dorroll escaped. It was the responsibility of my men to hold him, and they failed in that duty. I don't blame you for that. I only say that because your interests were split from ours, that made any capture scenario more difficult. A conflict with two sides is hard enough, but we had four last night, and that type of situation is never be likely to succeed. So, though I don't blame you entirely for what happened, you did contribute to our failure. If you are innocent as you claim, then why did you try to run?"

"I didn't turn the lights off for my own sake."

"For whose sake did you do so?" Evesham took out a leather-bound notebook and a pencil and prepared to take down what he was about to say. Jaeryn eyed it and deliberated well before answering. Evesham made no move to hurry him. As he thought, he glanced once or twice at Ben to see how he took the silence. Evidently their conversation before Evesham came hadn't set him at his ease, for he still frowned in thought, and he was playing with his wristwatch as he waited for Jaeryn to answer.

Jaeryn turned back to Evesham. "I didn't want you to hang Turlough O'Sean on suspicion of taking part in the Irish revolt. I knew you had a case built up against me, and I knew you would make a case against him as soon as you found out who he was. My work was finished as soon as your men arrived. I saw no reason why you should take the two of us when we had done much to help you."

Evesham listened until he was through and wrote down something. "We don't hang the Irish simply for being Irish, doctor, even though they seem to think so. What is O'Sean planning to do in the revolt that you should be so concerned about us catching him?"

Jaeryn did not answer. Evesham must have some kind of charge against Terry, but he wasn't about to add to it.

"I can only help him if I know the truth of the matter," Evesham said gravely, in response to his silence. He turned to Ben, and Jaeryn shook his head to warn him to hold his tongue. "We learned from your reports, Doctor Dailey, that Turlough was working as a double agent for the Germans. He, however, swears he didn't, and that was the one thing we got out of Graham last night—assuring us that Turlough was loyal the entire time. Is this the case?"

Jaeryn wondered what else he had said when he was under the influence of anesthesia. He let his breath out through his teeth in warning, but that did not prevent Ben from replying. "Yes. Jaeryn was afraid of that, but Terry said he wasn't, and we believe him."

Jaeryn relaxed again. There was nothing incriminating in that. If Dorroll threw his good opinion to their side, then it might help them.

Evesham looked thoughtfully at the pencil he was turning between his fingers. "Most of the 1916 rebels were pardoned in June.

If Turlough was involved in the Irish revolt, his past actions cannot incriminate him now. We took him as a German rebel, not as an Irish one, and now we find that it has no foundation."

"So, you are going to release him?" Ben asked hopefully.

"I don't think he poses a threat to us, but if he's planning another revolt, then I can't let him go yet. There is one thing I don't understand about this whole business. He doesn't sound completely Irish, and he doesn't sound English either. Was he born in Ireland?"

"No. He's technically of American citizenship, but he's been abroad for a long time."

"Does he have proof to substantiate this?" A hint of alarm showed in Evesham's face. Jaeryn saw an opportunity to twist his arm and grasped at it.

"Absolutely. If you touch him, then I'll make sure it comes out that you arrested an agent who's done good service to you, and an American one at that."

Evesham didn't look too keen to test his threat. "If he's American, then it doesn't matter if he's revolted from here to Galway. We can't touch them in the present political crisis. The only American who was captured after the Easter rising got his sentence transmitted to a lesser one, and we're not going to imprison another, especially right now. You can rest assured that he will receive his freedom as soon as we settle things here. But I make no promises for the future if he revolts again."

"Fair enough." Jaeryn felt a little surer of his ground. He had carried his first point, and the first charge was dropped—or at least, Evesham did not seem likely to pick it up again.

Evesham looked less than pleased, and Jaeryn knew he would have to tread carefully so as not to offend the man. He was still Irish, and that alone could tip the balances against him.

"I will not ask you about the imminence of an Irish revolt or the extent of your involvement in it, as I doubt you would care to answer me." Evesham paused and took his silence as an affirmative. "Therefore, I will only say that since Ann Meikle brought the Irish charges against you, the evidence is not substantial enough to bring to court, though I have no doubt it will be in future."

"I'm glad," Jaeryn said in satisfaction.

"However," Evesham continued, not relaxing his sternness, "the other three charges are all proved against you, and they are serious ones. First, you held back evidence in a murder investigation.

Turlough O'Sean—he told me it was to save him, but I think it was also to try to wrangle your position back again by stealing the glory of the solution. That was something you should not have meddled with, sir, under any circumstances. The law must have its way, and there are better ways to make sure truth prevails than taking evidence. Second, you disobeyed orders and compromised the security of one of our agents in Germany itself. And third, you persisted in staying here and staying involved though you were dismissed and acting as a rogue agent. It was for these causes, as well as the Irish charges, that I arrested you."

Jaeryn held himself straight and proud, ignoring the throbbing in his shoulder. "If my success has not outweighed these charges, then you may do what you like, and I will take whatever sentence you choose to give me."

"Your success does not excuse your method of reaching it," Evesham rebuked. "We are mindful of our debt to you, but we are also mindful that you took matters into your own hands. That is not something we can either encourage or condone. You nearly got yourself arrested in October when Ryson dismissed you, and he would not have been merciful. Even now, between the Irish charges and the German suspicions, I hardly know which course to take."

"Ryson may believe that I interfered with Speyer to ruin his plans, but I did not." Jaeryn's voice rose with passion. "I investigated him because I had men whose safety was under threat. Your government sent our men to useless slaughter in France again and again, and I refused to fall prey to the same short-sightedness. Put me in prison for it if you will, but by all that's fair and just, I maintain that I had every right to do what I did."

For a long time Evesham sat looking down at his notebook in silence. At last, he spoke in such a quiet way that both Ben and Jaeryn leaned forward to hear him. "I cannot deny that we deserve a double measure of fault. It seems wrong to imprison a man who was instrumental to our success, but I cannot excuse your defiance. I am inclined to issue a burn notice against you as an untrustworthy agent and leave it at that."

Jaeryn drew back in dismay. "But that's shutting down my entire career, sir; no one would trust me again. I'd rather go to jail if it comes to that. Giving me a burn notice is as unjust as executing me."

"I would be loath to be unjust. You were a brave man to risk your freedom for the sake of our success. For that alone, I don't think you are totally against us. But I must give you warning that you took one step too far this time. You are growing self-sufficient. Talented, yes, and capable, yes, but we have no room for self-sufficiency here. If you say that is unjust, then what do you propose as fair punishment?"

Jaeryn sized the man up and considered whether he could pit his strength against him. Evesham would know in a second if he was lying, so he would have to tell the truth. But if Allan Evesham issued a burn notice against him, it would mean his whole life over before he was thirty, and he could not bear that. The man had the power to do what he threatened, and once decided on a course of action, he would not change his mind. Jaeryn's only choice was to ask for pardon.

That stuck in his throat and choked him, for he had never asked for mercy before. Had it been for the Irish charges, he would have died before he did it. But this was fair on Evesham's part, and Jaeryn could not deny it. Nor could he defend himself in court. It was only right to admit the errors and see if he could salvage something. Jaeryn gritted his teeth, lifted his chin, and made his request.

"As you say, sir, it is my first time defying London's orders. I give you my word that I am not a German sympathizer, and I ask you for another opportunity to regain my former position of trust. If I fail, then burn me as an agent, and I will say that you have not only been just, but also merciful."

Allan Evesham closed his notebook. The grim lines around his eyes smoothed out, and a pleased expression stole in to replace them. "I never doubted that you were a shrewd man and a daring one. Today you have also proven yourself to be wise, and I commend you for it. You may try once more. If you fail your trust at any time, in any way, then I will burn you and you will be prosecuted. And I call that fair enough. Do you agree?"

Jaeryn nodded. "Only…I'd rather work under Ryson, if I can."

Evesham muffled a slight chuckle. "Because you can control him, no doubt. You can't control me, but I think we can find agreement just the same. Ryson will never take you back again, so you have no other choice."

Evesham stood up, and Ben followed his example. "If nothing else, this network is totally unsalvageable. But you two have taken down the German civilian spies in Folkestone, and Edmond Dorroll can't set up operations again here. In that you were successful. We would like to go further back and take not only the British informants, but the German contacts abroad as well. I think Ryson has made a poor job of his side of things thus far—though don't tell him I said so—and I should like to do better. With the two of you."

Jaeryn said nothing. Ben asked, "The two of us?"

"Yes. Doctor Graham has accepted my offer, and it still stands for you as well. Would you like to continue?"

It was Jaeryn's turn to wait while Ben deliberated on an answer. He hoped that Ben would make his own decision and not simply give the answer that Evesham wanted from him. But when the words came, they were neither a negative nor an affirmative.

"All of this was different from what I expected when I first came."

"I promise that I will give you a better way of working if you agree to stay," Evesham said.

Jaeryn interjected. "He only came for one assignment, and we've had him long enough. You shouldn't press him."

Ben held out his hand. "I will make this decision without help, thank you."

"I should like until Jaeryn is out of the Royal Victoria to think about it," Ben said at length. "If that is too long to wait, then I will say no."

"I can give you that long. We won't start anything until then. Very well, gentlemen. This is concluded more successfully than I had hoped. I have other matters to attend to, so I will leave you. Doctor Graham, you are not free to follow your own devices unless you check in with me first, but right now you are not in threat of prosecution."

Evesham shook hands with Ben, nodded to Jaeryn, and walked out. After he was gone, the rush of adrenaline from all that had happened made Jaeryn feel sick. He sank back and closed his eyes.

"I want to tell you," Ben said after a few minutes, "that last night, what happened couldn't have happened without you. Not many men would have had your determination, and I look up to you for it. And furthermore, you kept me out of harm's way at great cost to yourself, and I owe a debt to you which I will not forget."

Any remaining anger Jaeryn still possessed melted away. They had been through too much together. Besides, Ben was young and had only seen this work for six months. He had done what he thought best in a situation that men older and wiser than him often found confusing. Perhaps he was right not to have let past favors sway his sense of justice.

Jaeryn opened his eyes. "The past is the past, and I've gotten off with rather less than I deserve. You did well last night, Dorroll. I wouldn't change you for a thousand men as experienced as Allan Evesham."

Ben's tense face eased with release at his words. "Thank you. You must be tired. I won't keep you any longer."

"That am I." Jaeryn closed his eyes again, then opened them a crack to ask a question. "I was thinking something. I don't know what's going to happen next, but it will be at least a week until I get out of here. Do you have enough money to last that long, or do you need some? There's a stack under the mattress at the foot of my bed for emergencies."

Ben shook his head. "It's kind of you to offer, but I'm not taking your money after all that's happened."

"You use it if you need it. I'll know if you lie to me." He gathered the last of his strength. "One more thing. I want you to understand something about last night. Revolt is between a man and his conscience. You may not choose it, but I am free to do so and take the consequences if I desire. You fight for peace, I fight for freedom, two very good things. Allan Evesham is bound to look out for British interests, but he cannot keep me from doing what is right."

"I can see your point," Ben said, as he helped him slide down on the pillow. "But I know Evesham wants to see you done well by."

Jaeryn kept silent for a long time, concentrating on all that had been said. He heard the door handle and realized that Ben thought he was asleep. "I think I'd rather take my chances and keep my secrets than give them to him. Will you look after things until I come back?"

"Of course."

"If Evesham lets Terry out like he said he would, then he can stay at my place, if it's not inconvenient to your work."

"Not at all."

"Come again when you get the chance." Jaeryn lifted his head to watch him out of the room, and then let it fall back on the pillow.

He was free. Bound by his promise and treading on a knife's edge as far as keeping his interests alive without Evesham's interference was concerned. But free to work, and generously dealt with, and honorably acquitted. Perhaps he had lost a hands-off employer to an all too observant one, but it was a sensible trade. Compared with losing his career for life, it was a good alternative, and he was satisfied.

Chapter Thirty-Eight
To Go or Stay

The afternoon turned to rain and the rain to snow, and it was a miserable time for the searchers and their dogs tracking the vast empty fields beyond Folkestone for Edmond. The rain made it almost impossible to find traces. Though his scent around the house was potent, they searched it from cellar to roof without result. Ben spent the afternoon and early evening joining them, going through rooms that he had never seen in his visits to Emmerson's house— rooms that were wrapped in neglect, full of hushed memories and luxurious furnishings, but no Edmond.

At six, he ended his search and called Charlotte to give her an update. Then he set off for the Tontine clinic to try to organize some of the chaos that Evesham's search had created. He would have to clean it up before it could be used again. When he reached Jaeryn's house, he found that Evesham had been true to his word, for Terry opened the door before he found the key.

"Hey, doc," he said cheerily. The skin around one of his eyes was red and bruised, and the rest of his face didn't look much better. But the eyes were bright and blue and alive for all that, and his big smile shone out like it hadn't for weeks. He was as unshaven and relaxed as he used to be. "Is the other doc all right?"

"He's good, Terry. I left him earlier this afternoon, and Evesham seems favorable to giving him another chance. I think he'll be all right."

"I hope so. He's gotten knocked around enough. They always give him the hard ones because they know he can do them, but there are only so many you can succeed at before it goes wrong. I thought this time was the last for sure. He's been doing it since he was in college and never failed yet. Did you know that?"

"No, but I expect there's a lot more I don't know about Jaeryn." Ben stepped in and dried his boots on the doormat to keep water off the floors.

"Well, he got them all, even if he did get reckless with the Irish side of things. I told him we were going down, and we fought over it once, but he didn't agree with me. He won't give things up once he's started. Don't let him start anything else yet, now that he's just gotten free from this one."

Ben smiled. "I believe he already has."

Terry shrugged in resignation. "He'll run himself into the ground someday. At least he's in the Royal Victoria for a while; that's bound to give him some rest."

"It wasn't successful with you."

"I hate the Royal Victoria. I'll never thank that kid for laying me up there, that's certain." Terry grinned and pulled out his box of cigarettes.

Ben hung up his coat and opened the consulting room door. He couldn't manage with one hand, so Terry helped him pull his desk over into Jaeryn's space, drawing at the cigarette in between whiles. Ben took all the things that had been piled on the floor and began finding places for them. Jaeryn would want a new desk, no doubt, but until he got back, they wouldn't need two of them, and his own would do for the meantime.

"What did you do to Starlin last night after we left King's?" Ben asked curiously, once he had begun working. "We were terrified for him."

Terry leaned against the doorframe and watched him. "The kid's tough as old shoe leather. He wouldn't give me the paper. I wanted it for safekeeping."

"He gave it to me."

"You were probably the best one to have it. They might have found it on me and taken it."

Ben looked up from sorting the papers, wondering why he sounded so regretful. "Did you hurt him?"

Terry glanced sideways at the floor. "Not quite. I could have cracked him, but I wasn't going to take it that far, honest."

"You had us all convinced otherwise. We weren't sure what you were going to do."

"I didn't mean you to be. And I don't know how he's ever going to believe me when I try to explain it to him."

"You were brave, Terry."

Terry looked pleased with the compliment. "Hugh suspected me before the kid filled me up with lead. I wasn't rotten enough for his comfort, and I think King only agreed to fire Stafford so he could watch me along with Hugh. I figured that was why, so I invited him to stay. They watched me, and I watched them, and we mixed it up a couple of times, but we finally got all the way to the end. I knew they would never let me switch numbers when it came time, and I figured they'd try to kill me after we met Edmond."

Ben listened absently as he tried to remember where Jaeryn put everything. "I wish we could have helped you."

"We were all taking risks. Besides, I did tell you. I sent a message through Ann Meikle and said they were planning something for the first of December. I didn't know what, but I overheard Hugh talking with Stafford about it."

"You were a sight to behold last night. You looked like you'd seen it all before."

Terry raised an eyebrow. "Oh, I've been in that room three times. Once when you and the other doc were going through the library, and then again when you were taking pictures. Jaeryn told me to watch you and make sure you were all right. And then last night."

He had forgotten about the night in the library when they'd had other people helping them and Jaeryn had kept them confidential. That was before he had met Terry. Ben wondered if Jaeryn had been pleased with their acquaintance or if he would have kept Terry a complete secret if he could have managed it. It was likely, with the Irish charges, that he would have. He was glad that Jaeryn had failed in that objective, at least. A good deal of brightness would have been lacking in his time here if they had never met.

"I meant that sort of situation, actually—not the room."

"Oh, that. I've seen it once or twice. Picked up that sort of thing for a living, you know." Terry drew on his cigarette, and Ben held his tongue and ignored it.

"I'm glad this is finished." Terry looked down at the little white cylinder in his fingers. "I was up to a pack a day by the end." He glanced at Ben and waited for him to protest, grinning when he did not. "You look like you want to say something," he teased.

"I'd say it's not good for you, but I suspect you've already been told that."

"I know, but I had to do something to keep from going mad. I'll try to cut back." He stubbed out the cigarette on the bottom of his boot and sighed. "Acushla never liked them either. By the way, Evesham sent something for you. He said he needed it back, but he thought you and I would be interested." He dug a considerably mud stained, crumpled paper out of his coat pocket. Ben folded it open.

My dearest love, —

The writing slammed into him like ice. His hands shook slightly, and he folded it back up and held it out to Terry. "This is from—her. She wrote it to you before she died."

Terry stared at it. He reached out, but his hand shook so badly he couldn't take it. "Read it," he said in a strange voice.

There was nothing on earth he wanted to do less. Some deep, secret hurt was about to tear open inside. It would bleed beyond stopping if he did. "I can't do it."

"You've got to, doc."

Ben clenched his mouth and looked down at the folded paper. Very slowly, he opened it again.

My dearest love,
I was just passing by the post office twenty minutes ago and heard Mrs. Meikle giving a boy a telegram to deliver to you. I remembered you telling me that you had something coming and you did not want it to fall into the wrong hands. As soon as I heard her, I knew you would be gone this time of evening, so I took a cab to your house and reached it just as the boy was knocking at the door. I did not know what to say, but I thought just quickly enough to tell him that I had gotten home, and I would take it for you.
I am going to leave it with your sister. I saw a man looking out the door as I got back into the cab, and I don't want to put you at risk in case he recognizes me again. I think it will be safe at Copt Point.
With all my love,

717

Terry ran his thumb and finger across the corners of his eyes. "That little girl is the most courageous, precious thing I've ever been conceited enough to kiss."

"I didn't think she had it in her to be that brave," Ben said in awe.

"I wish I could have told her why I stopped coming around every day. She never knew that I didn't want to put her in danger, but even though I quit coming, I think they already suspected she might know about what was happening. I should have stopped sooner."

Ben had only seen Terry happy, and he had no idea how he would take to grief. He tried nervously to offer some kind of comfort. "You have nothing to blame yourself for. You kept them safe every day, and you were still trying to do that. It wasn't your leaving that did it in the end."

"Do you remember the first day we were properly introduced, and I sat by her, and she looked so scared?" Terry asked.

"I remember." He could still recall it, the way her eyes widened when Terry called her by their pet name, and how shocked he himself had been but how unwilling to dampen Terry's enthusiasm.

Terry made a gesture as if he imagined Pearlie sitting next to him and he was putting his arm around her. "She always was a timid little thing, but she looked almost happy when I talked to her and laughed sometimes. I wonder if she has anyone to make her happy now. She might be scared in heaven, you know, just her all alone."

It felt odd to have a smile and an ache tugging for mastery at the same time. Ben turned away to hide it. "I think she's happy. But I suspect she would be even happier if you were there with her."

"Yeah. Would you have said yes, if I had asked you for her?" Terry said wistfully.

He had been dreading that question, for he didn't know how he could honestly answer it without giving pain. "I would have done the right thing."

"Ah." Terry sounded crestfallen.

And then, in his soul, Ben knew that there was little point in holding out. It would only give pain when there had been pain enough. Terry had been kind to her, and even if he didn't think Terry was the kind of man Pearl ought to have, perhaps he was wrong. Terry had sacrificed and offered her love day in and day out while no one else paid attention. And though he had been denied the asking, it was unfair to deny him the hope of what might have been the answer. "Thank you for loving her, Terry," Ben said quietly. "I'm glad you did. She loved you much in return, and I think I would have said yes."

A warm glow spread in Terry's eyes, and at that moment, Ben caught the shine of gold and sapphire on his little finger. Terry saw what he was looking at and flashed him a wink. "Safe and sound. I wanted it, but I couldn't ask you for it, so I took it back."

He was too glad that it was found to mind that Terry had broken in to take it. "I thought someone had stolen it."

"Oh, I wouldn't call it anything as bad as that." Terry grinned. "You've taken it halfway across the world with you since I gave it to you last."

A tidal wave of overwhelming memories crashed over him. Ben leaned against the door of the consulting room, pressing his forehead against it and closing his eyes. A warm handgrip weighed heavy on his shoulder.

"Don't think too hard after last night. It isn't a good idea," Terry said. "It was right that Jaeryn should be brought up a little, and he won't hold it against you. There aren't many things he won't come around on. Only putting down the Irish and false accusations. That's what sets his temper blazing. Most of what was said last night was true, so he can't get too upset about it. You followed orders, and you'll have to be more experienced than you are now to disobey when someone higher up tells you to do something."

"Maybe."

Terry nodded and slapped him on the shoulder. "I'm going out now. I want to talk to that kid tonight, and I want to see Alisa. Will you come with me?"

Ben looked at the work that was left to be done. There was a great deal to put back in order, but he hadn't visited with Terry properly since September. He decided to let the work go and finish it later. "If you like."

Terry seemed pleased to have company, but when they reached the King house, he asked to go in alone and left Ben sitting in the cab. A maid opened the door and Terry disappeared, emerging a short time later with a serious expression.

"Well?" Ben asked when he was back and they were on their way.

"I told him I was sorry. I think he'd just heard about his dad, because the poor kid seemed glad to see me. He doesn't show he's glad often, you know. I told him he was brave and we could be good chums after this, and I said I would come tomorrow to hear his violin like old times."

"What did he say to that?"

"I don't think he trusts me yet, but he will. Just give him some time, and he will."

Alisa and Charlotte were back in the farmhouse together. Alisa didn't want to stay at the grand estate for the present. Ben was rather unsure of coming in case she wanted to be alone, but the thought of their visit being an intrusion didn't seem to cross Terry's mind. He opened the door before Alisa answered his knock, and a smile slipped over her face at the sight of him.

"I haven't seen you in ages." Terry wrapped her in a big hug and laid a kiss on her hair. "I've come to have a chat with you."

Charlotte offered her hand, but Terry gave her a hug too, and she exchanged an amused glance with Ben over Terry's shoulder.

Terry made himself comfortable on the sofa and kept up most of the conversation of his own accord. Ben took one of the chairs in the corner, half-hidden in the darkness, with Charlotte sitting on the arm of it beside him. Alisa sat on the other end of the sofa, alone with her thoughts. Terry must have forgotten his resolution about the cigarettes, for he pulled one out and lit it, and before it was finished, he had told Alisa all about the evening before, including a good deal that she shouldn't have known. Even so, he seemed to have an inadvertent tact that kept him from mentioning Edmond.

When his cigarette and his chat finished together, Terry put his arm around Alisa's tiny form and pulled her close to him. "You doing all right, Mrs. Dorroll?"

She smiled up at him and nodded, though Ben thought it might be more for Terry's sake than for the truthfulness of it. Terry drew her head down to his shoulder and patted it fondly with his large, strong hand. "It'll be all right, now. I can come by every day again, and they haven't found your husband yet, so that's good."

Alisa peeked out from under his arm to speak to Ben. "Do you think they'll find him?"

Ben shook his head. "They didn't find any traces of him on the grounds. It's the strangest thing. He disappeared into thin air, and even the dogs couldn't pick up his trail. I'm afraid I don't know whether they'll find him or not."

Terry smoothed her hair with his rough palm, and comfort stole into her face. He looked deeply contented at the thought of bringing relief to someone. They sat in the quietness until his chat lessened and the last twenty-four hours caught up with him and he fell asleep.

Alisa slipped out from under his arm and beckoned to Ben. He followed her to the kitchen.

"Are you going to leave soon now that this is over?" she asked wistfully.

Ben looked into the large blue eyes, as soft and bright and brave as when he first met her. He hadn't forgotten what his leaving would mean to her, and though he hadn't made his final decision yet, he wanted to make arrangements for her no matter which way he chose to go. "Not right away. I have a few days to think about it before I decide for good. Would you like me to stay?"

"I should like to be near you if you don't." She looked up at him pleadingly, and he nodded in reassurance.

"I think I can promise that. You'll always have a place with us, wherever we are, unless you wish otherwise."

She looked relieved, and a little, shy smile crept over her face as she let him out the door.

* * *

Terry came home and went to bed sometime after Ben and Charlotte returned to the clinic. Ben didn't pay attention to the time, and Terry only said a cheerful, if sleepy, goodnight before leaving them to their work. After a whole night without rest and a couple of rigorous questionings, he must be tired out.

Ben was glad. There were a lot of things that needed to be put to rights, and he could do the job more quickly with only Charlotte's quiet assistance.

They hauled the broken desk out to the backyard and left it against the side of the house. He didn't attempt to sort through Jaeryn's papers. It would be of no use when only Jaeryn could arrange them as he wanted them. He contented himself with putting the box of death threats in the desk drawer that corresponded most closely to the old location and returning the tools and trays to their proper places. A good many of the trays were broken along with the desk, as well as a few odd bottles of medication. He and Charlotte were searching for a pair of gloves to pick up some jagged shards when a smooth voice said,

"Hello."

Ben dropped the gloves and looked around. Behind him stood Fenton, his dark suit in impeccable order and a brown paper package under his arm.

"How did you get in?"

Fenton looked down at the wood floorboards and smiled in satisfaction to himself. "I can get into most places without asking first."

"So I've noticed." Ben stood up and felt the empty shoulder holster he was wearing under his jacket. He had laid the revolver on the windowsill while he worked. Not that he would need it, but he wished he had it all the same.

Fenton laid the parcel on the desk. "That's for you, doctor. Evidence for the trial, if you would like it and want to pay for it. I'm leaving by the early train tomorrow, so this is your last chance to talk to me. Ryson has work for me elsewhere."

Charlotte untied the string for him, and Ben lifted the pasteboard lid. Inside were the two maps, the ones that had been taken from Emmerson's room, with the gold tacks to mark the locations.

Ben looked from them to the man before him. "Where did you get these?"

Fenton seemed quite satisfied with the effect of his surprise. "From Emmerson's room, of course. I'm the one who replaced them."

"You replaced the maps?"

"Oh, yes. I took the evidence before we found out the heir's identity. There was no need to give unnecessary advantage to our adversaries. They've been in my care since August."

"Why didn't you tell us sooner?"

"Why would I? Ann told me why you were going to London then, so I knew it was fairly certain that Ryson would give you the sack. And I wasn't about to give them to Graham. Now that I'm finished with Folkestone, I'm offering them to you—for a price."

Fenton crossed his arms while Ben looked at the maps and considered. He had a very slender amount of cash, but probably enough to bribe the man. Fenton knew he wasn't affluent and wouldn't press for more than he had. But that would drain him dry again, and there was still most of December left to go, and he still did not know which direction he was going to take. He did have Jaeryn's money at his disposal, though he hated to take it. It didn't seem right to give the Irishman's money to someone he disliked. He had been stripped of enough already. Jaeryn would be more pleased lending it to him than giving it to Fenton.

"I'll give you six pounds. It's all I have."

Fenton held out his hand, and Ben turned it over to him. The man had the talent of giving his blackmail a kind of class—almost as if he were doing favors by accepting money for his services. Even so, it didn't feel pleasant to have his hand forced.

Fenton tucked it away. "Ann Meikle was honest when she warned you about Jaeryn the first day you came."

"I know."

"No matter now." He turned the maps over as if to say farewell to them. "Emmerson used these to keep a record of who was on each side so he could plot out his moves. He wanted all of you on his side in the end, but Edmond Dorroll knew that he couldn't get all of you, so he abandoned that idea."

"How did you know what my brother thought?"

Fenton paused, as if he didn't expect that statement to be taken up and wanted to take it back again. "I know what many people think."

"Jaeryn said you hinted at working for someone else. It wasn't him, wasn't it?" Ben pressed suspiciously.

Fenton's pale lids narrowed over his eyes. "I never give one client's concerns away to another. I'm afraid that's a confidential question, doctor."

"I suppose you want me to pay you again for the answer."

"Not at all. That information is not for sale. You asked why I didn't tell you sooner. The truth is, Ann Meikle and I between us were trying to get Graham dismissed, and we thwarted him as often as we could to slow him down while we dug up who he really was. She hated both of you, but she hated Graham most, so you were the lesser of two evils. I had hard work to contain her malice against you."

"Except when she forged threats against us for the German side. You didn't prevent her from that," Ben replied bitterly.

Fenton lost his words for a moment. His face held a hint of regret, but then he shrugged his shoulders. "I didn't know she was doing that until afterward. Even if I had known, I wouldn't have tried to stop her. If she wants to pick up money by that means, it's her business and not mine."

"And she's gone to jail, but there's no justice for you. That doesn't seem fair." Ben came out from behind the desk, and Fenton backed up to the doorway with a satisfied smirk.

"It's regrettable that Ann was so rash. She's young to retire from being an informant, but Jaeryn Graham was too much for her and she was too much for herself."

"I think you should go."

Fenton turned to obey, but stopped at the door. "One more thing, for free. I told Edmond Dorroll who Jaeryn Graham really is. You would be wise to have a knowledge equal to your brother's."

"Oh, I intend to. But I'll not stoop to leeches like you to get it. I'm going to ask Jaeryn himself."

Fenton looked amused by his naivety. "Suit yourself. I'll say goodbye then, and good luck for your future career."

"I can't say I'm sorry to be finished with you," Ben said.

"Never finish with anyone completely." Fenton bowed politely. "It might be worth your while to take up my acquaintance again. If you get lonely for me, just drop a hint in the right place, and I'll be sure to come back. Peters knows who to send a message by."

"I'll bear that in mind."

"It's been a pleasure to meet you, doctor. You're not in the common run of the people I have to deal with, and it was... refreshing."

Ben ignored the compliment. It wasn't likely to be genuine, and in any case, it wasn't disinterested. "Jaeryn Graham won out over you, you know. He's back in London's favor and free to follow his own devices again. I would take care if I were you."

Fenton raised an eyebrow, and his face took on a mournful cast. "I heard about that. You've tied your own noose to be hung with, and he'll be the rope that strangles you. Now, I have a train to catch, if you'll excuse me."

Ben opened the curtain and watched Fenton proceed down the street until the darkness swallowed him up. He was glad to see the back of Fenton. It was safer to be without his information than to have a double-edged tool like him jeopardizing their future interests. Allan Evesham had been right; there was no salvaging the Folkestone ring. A complicated mix of conflicting agendas and loyalties had brought it crashing down, and more from the people working for British interests than those working for Germany.

"You said you would bear him in mind," Charlotte remarked, kneeling down to pick the glass fragments into a saucer. "Does that mean you're thinking of staying?"

Ben couldn't wear a glove over his splinted finger, so he contented himself with sitting in Jaeryn's swivel chair and watching her. "I don't know. Would you like to stay, *ma chérie?*"

There was a long moment of silence. Only the chink of glass on saucer answered him. Her face was flushed from stooping, and she kept her head down so as not to meet his gaze.

"Charlotte?"

She gave a shrug and put the saucer on the desk. "Part of me wants to go back. I haven't seen my parents in almost eight months, and I miss them dreadfully. I miss working at the Richmond hospital. I miss the house we lived in. But wherever you are, I feel at home. And if you need to stay, then I would rather stay with you than have those things."

He reached out and grabbed her hand as she passed him with an armload of medicines. "I'm glad you came with me, darling."

She stooped down and snatched a kiss. "So am I. Only, Ben, if we are to stay, then I want to think about settling here. I want a baby."

"Good heavens. We'll talk about it."

"You promised when we were done."

"I did not."

A laugh bubbled up in her throat. "And I know you keep your word. You keep it even when all Ireland and Great Britain conspire against you."

"I'm not sure that's a virtue." A sudden thought occurred to him. "Was that why you volunteered at the maternity wards? Because you wanted a baby?"

She set the bottles with a soft thump on the shelf and pushed them one by one into place. "Yes. You weren't the only one who had to give up dreams, you know."

"I didn't know."

"Shh. It's all right. I thought seeing other peoples' babies would ease the ache, but it didn't, so I came to help you and Doctor Graham instead. It was part of the price of coming."

He leaned his chin on his hand and let the words sink in. So she too had kept secrets all this time. He wished she could have told him.

"Allan Evesham talked to me about a position here," he said at last. "He says it will be more dangerous, but he will be paying more accordingly. And he gave me a better proposition to help with the medical side of things as well. With that...I think we could afford a baby now. Perhaps. I'm not promising," he added hastily, as delight brought a faint blush of color into her cheeks.

She wrapped her arms around him and leaned her chin on his shoulder. "I love you very much, Doctor Dorroll."

* * *

On Monday morning, Ben called his father on the phone to tell him a part of their work's results. When he rang home, he found his father was in Paris for a week, discussing the implications of the peace Russia had offered to make with Germany. So he was forced to wait. In the meantime, there were a great many details regarding keeping up the practice that needed attending to, not to mention talking with Evesham about his future. He also was intent on turning over every last piece of evidence that could provide a clue about where to look for Edmond.

When no sign appeared to give them any indication of where Edmond had gone, the active manhunt was abandoned, and one man was commissioned to devote his energies to following up on any sightings. On Saturday afternoon, reports of a scarred man trying to book passage to France came in from Dover, and the detective went to see if it was indeed Edmond Dorroll.

Ben purchased a ticket for London that same afternoon after seeing Jaeryn and making sure he had everything he needed to make him comfortable. Jaeryn was full of prospects for the future and as open and confident as before. He seemed less distraught at the discovery of his Irish sympathies now that it had not proved detrimental, and he was glad to hear that they were finding a respite from their work after the initial hustle of wrapping things up. Terry had taken to working at night again, Ben told him, though he still wouldn't say what he did. Jaeryn only smiled and wished him a safe journey.

When he reached his father's house, their conversation was stilted at first, his father inquiring and he answering concerning what had happened. The one moment when Matthew Dorroll showed a little more feeling was when Ben told him that Edmond was the ringleader.

"You continued on with your work even after finding out that your brother was involved?"

"Yes, sir."

"And you were willing to do so solely because I asked you to?"

It wasn't much, in the end. Just a small indication that the extent of what he had asked had penetrated Matthew Dorroll's mind. But it gave Ben courage to tell the rest of Edmond's secrets since they were now his to tell.

"You have a daughter-in-law, sir, and a grandson anyone might be proud of. Edmond may not have made the best choices thus far, but in that instance he chose well, and you would be proud of Alisa. I would like to bring her to meet you, with your permission."

He was surprised when his father agreed and asked him to bring her up whenever he found it convenient.

When he left, the cab took him past the warehouse where Ryson sat brooding over his web of homeland security. As they drove by, a blond-headed man slipped inconspicuously out the door and locked it behind him. Ben thought of stopping, but Jeremy wouldn't want attention drawn to him, so he contented himself with watching him crunch through the dirty puddles of snow toward home. Now their paths were diverging, and he might never have cause to see him again. He had no desire to see Ryson, but Jeremy had done him a few good turns, and he wouldn't object to learning more about him if the opportunity came his way.

It was early evening when Ben returned to Folkestone. Twilight brooded over the shops on Tontine Street. Only seven months ago they had lain in shambles after the bomb drop, and now they were pristine and perfect, just like they had been the day he arrived. Just, perhaps, like the lives recovering after the wreckage of December first. The lights winked out one by one as shops closed for the evening. In another twenty minutes, the streets would fade to winter blackness, and Ben quickened his steps. He had an errand at the clinic before he went home for the night.

The door was unlocked when he tried it. Curious at this, Ben peeked noiselessly into Jaeryn's study. He was amazed to see the tall, slim figure standing absorbed in front of the shelves, turning over his precious documents with one hand and painstakingly putting them back in the order he craved. Were it not for his obvious handicap, it would look as if the events of a week ago had never occurred. Jaeryn seemed as tranquil as if he had never been under threat of his freedom. A thrill of delight ran through Ben as he watched, coupled with the nervousness that he had been unable to shake off since Jaeryn's arrest.

Jaeryn saw him standing in the doorway, and Ben advanced reluctantly into the room. "I'm sorry; I didn't mean to intrude. I didn't know they would release you today."

"No intrusion," Jaeryn said cheerily. "Come in, I want to talk to you. They let me out this afternoon, and after Evesham cleared me, I came straight here. I've been working ever since. I'll be glad to take a break."

"How is the shoulder today?" It was in a sling, and Jaeryn looked like he had been using his energy rather too freely. No doubt the thought of his possessions being out of place was more torment than his mind could take. Ben didn't scold him. It was a small indication of normality returning after the nightmare of distrust and darkness.

"Aches a bit." Jaeryn sat down in his leather chair and held on to the edge of the desk for a moment. "It probably needs the bandages changed, if you don't mind. I'd do it myself, but I can't manage it."

"I don't mind at all." Ben drew the curtains and Jaeryn slowly unfastened his shirt buttons. Ben made no move to offer help with the buttons, getting out the supplies he would need while he waited. It was better to let Jaeryn conquer it himself and feel the satisfaction of it.

"There." Jaeryn slipped out of one sleeve. A corner of the tattoo showed under the thick wrap of bandages, and Ben worked at peeling them away. Jaeryn shivered under his touch, but he kept talking and said nothing when it caused him discomfort.

"Whatever became of King's dinner guests?" Jaeryn asked.

"They went their way once the police came and took over his study. A lavish entertainment and a fresh subject of gossip. Not everyone can claim to be so fortunate." The last of the bandage came away, and he felt Jaeryn hold his breath until it slipped off.

"Well, it's over. And I'll admit, it was one of the hardest missions I've been on yet. You know, I was looking through the copies of the notebook pages that Ryson passed on to Evesham. Evesham gave them to me again for safekeeping, as long as I promised to tell you where I put them. There was one thing I didn't understand. In the first letter Ann found, Emmerson wrote that he had handed over something to 'R' for safekeeping. It doesn't seem to mean Ryson, so I wonder if it was that other item Speyer found."

"I'm sure I don't know. Speyer said he wasn't going to write again, so I suppose it'll have to be discovered another way." The angry red wound showed above the Celtic cross. Ben took a wet cloth and gently cleaned both sides of the shoulder. There was no sign of infection, and it seemed to be making steady progress toward mending.

"Well, we'll find out. Or I'll find out, anyway." Jaeryn looked up at him, and the green eyes so near his own gave Ben an odd sensation, almost as if he was too close to a source of power that he did not want to offend. But he returned the glance as if it was nothing and continued with his work.

"Did you give Evesham his answer?" Jaeryn asked.

Ben took away the cloth and waited for the moisture to dry from the wound before putting on a fresh bandage. He had thought his answer over every day, and he was pretty sure that he was right, but the finality of it still gave him a cold, unsettled feeling.

"I will tomorrow."

Jaeryn asked to see his shoulder, and Ben gave him a mirror. Jaeryn looked curiously at the place where the bullet had entered, then set the mirror down and returned to the question. "Mind if I know what your plan is?"

Ben folded up the gauze against both wounds, and Jaeryn shivered again between his cold fingers and the sting of it. "Evesham told me that if I stayed, he would try to buy out Winfield's practice. I could work off the debt to earn it for my own, as well as managing it at the same time."

A swift frown crept over Jaeryn's face. "That's outright, blatant bribery on his part. You'll be trapped."

Ben smiled and shook his head. "I told him I was obliged, but I didn't like the thought of being locked in like that. So he said he would buy it and pay me wages from it, and I could buy it from him later if I wished. That way I wouldn't be bound to him if I changed my mind. He wants me to stay until all of Emmerson's work is cleared up. It's damage that my family has been involved in, so it is only right and honorable to do so. Besides, I have a great many people here whom I can help. It would be wrong to leave them now."

He glanced at Jaeryn to see if he gave any indication of dislike at the idea of them continuing on together.

"I thought so. You always were one to oblige where you could. Dorroll, it's not my business to make your decision for you, but I've been in this work a long time, and I know what it takes. You shouldn't come just to oblige Evesham. This choice requires that you either love the country you're working for or you love the work itself, and I know you're not keen on either of those things."

"I'm not coming entirely for the work. I like the people here, and that would be enough to stay for." Ben finished layering the bandages and helped Jaeryn draw the sleeve up over his shoulder.

"If you intend to stay, then you should love the work as well as the people. Don't just put up with it. Make it yours." Jaeryn struggled with the buttons again. "You put your life on hold to come here, and if you stay longer, then you should decide that your life starts now, not after you're finished. You're twenty-four, or perhaps even twenty-five—?" He looked at Ben inquiringly.

"I'm twenty-five now."

"Then it's time to start doing what you've always intended to do. England can use skilled doctors if you really mean to stay. You could change your name to Dailey legally, you know, and settle here. Do your duty, if you feel that you must, and stay on. But you went to school for your practice, and I think you should not ignore that calling."

"I told Evesham about that, and he has every intention of helping me move it forward. He's training me to be a civilian informant, and that will leave me plenty of time to attend to a practice. Only until the war is over, and then I'll be done with the Secret Service. I'm sure you and Evesham will teach me to like this sort of thing in the meantime."

"Albeit with our different methods." Jaeryn finished the last button and held on to the desk while Ben fastened up the sling. The Irishman looked at him thoughtfully for a long moment and nodded finally. "I'm glad we'll be working together again." He smiled and stood up. "I appreciate your help with the shoulder. I'll be back; I'm going to make some tea. I don't know what food there is in the kitchen, but you're welcome to whatever I have if you haven't eaten yet."

Ben worked on updating the last patient records until he heard Jaeryn's returning step in the passage. Now that he knew Jaeryn was pleased with his decision, he decided to ask him something he wanted to know. They were between missions, and closer to each other than they had been in May. They knew each other's strengths and foibles, and there could be no threat in Jaeryn revealing more about himself now that the Irish secret was out.

"Do you mind if I ask you a question?" he said, when Jaeryn returned from the kitchen with a mug of tea in hand. The gentle steam rose up from it, giving off an air of comfort.

"Anything you like." Jaeryn set the mug down and gave him his full attention.

"I should like to know your real name if we're to work together more."

A smile tugged at the corner of the Irishman's mouth. "Strange question, that. It's Jaeryn. Haven't I told you before?"

"That's your real name?"

"Christened it, yes." Jaeryn's eyes were frank and open, and Ben saw no reason to doubt him.

"Then what is your real surname?"

Jaeryn hesitated and turned over the question in his mind. He sat on the desk, and while he thought, he rubbed his sore arm absentmindedly, as if he hardly knew that it was there. At length, a flicker of playful malice darted across his face. "Graham."

"That's not—"

"It's true. I am Jaeryn Graham, just as you are Benjamin Dailey. If you're to continue this work, you should take on your false identity to the exclusion of all others." Jaeryn drank from his mug and then turned back to organizing his files.

Ben decided to drop the questions that Jaeryn couldn't answer. But he was loath to let the conversation die away for good, now that Jaeryn was home. "Terry told me you paid the money I owed. I haven't thanked you for it yet, but I'm obliged to you."

A faint flush of red tinged Jaeryn's ears. "That wasn't entirely disinterested on my part. I was going to use it to force you to take my side in case the fates turned against me. But in the end, I decided that you must make your own choice, so I let them go."

"I'm obliged to you all the same."

He was constantly of two opinions regarding Jaeryn—seeing him as a genuinely caring man who liked doing a good turn, or as a ruthless agent that used a smooth, brittle generosity to trap those around him. He could not go any longer without finding out which one of them was the real man underneath. "How much of what you've been telling me all these months is true? About myself, and being friends, and saying you wanted me to succeed?"

Jaeryn turned around. "In that, I gave you the honest truth. I really did want to see you succeed—though not at my expense, and I think you can hardly blame me for that. I liked you, but I wasn't averse to lying to you when it served my turn. For one thing, I told you Terry and I had worked together once before, and the fact is, we've partnered twice. The first time was for British interests and the second for Irish ones, and I hope you never find out about either of them. But I truly was here to help you, as long as you didn't tread on my own objectives. You and Evesham came very close, but he was more generous than I expected."

Perhaps Jaeryn was both generous and ruthless without knowing it. He didn't know. "I never wanted to succeed at your expense. I'm glad you got off all right."

Jaeryn saw his discomfort and tried again to assuage it. "I know you have a hard time reconciling it in your mind. You're accustomed to being used, and I used you. I was in charge of this assignment, and I had to keep you here whether you liked the work or not to make sure we succeeded. I had too much depending on our mission not to. But I hope you realize that I only took advantage of you because I realized how valuable you were. We were successful, and I'm grateful to you for coming back in November. I needed you last week, even if you were the one to keep me from escaping. In the end, it turned to good, which I never expected. I have succeeded seven times, with a clean record and a rather tenuous favor with those above me. I am still free, and we can go on as we did before."

"Was that the only reason you came last week? To succeed at what you had started? It seems strange that you would risk your freedom simply for your reputation."

"That was a large part of it. I wanted to gain London's favor back if I could. The Irish causes were entirely separate from my work here, and though I'm sorry they came out, I was committed to seeing my British work finished too."

"But if you had left, the Irish accusations would never have been discovered. Was it worth so much risk, just to finish something you had undertaken?"

Jaeryn only smiled and shook his head.

Ben asked again, sensing that Jaeryn would tell him if he pressed for it. "Then why did you come?"

"I needed to see Terry safely out. And if I had promised to help him, then why should I do any less for the other agent under my care who was just as faithful?"

Ben frowned, taken aback. "You—you came for me?"

Jaeryn nodded. "You gave much, even when you did not want to come here in the first place. I could give no less to you in return for

732

what you had given me."

"But you didn't have to do that much. I could have died and it would have been all right, Jaeryn; honestly it would have. Or we might have been able to arrest them without you."

Jaeryn held his gaze seriously. "No, it wouldn't have been right. Few people would have stayed as long as you did, and it would not have been just for you to receive such a poor reward for your labors." He looked down at his sling. "I don't know what it is about you. You're not particularly remarkable, but you wrap others around you somehow. Look at Fenton—even he wanted to see you dealt a good hand in the end. When you first came, I thought you would only be an encumbrance, and you were. But now I want to see you live, and see the reward of your labors, and find some happiness after all this heartache. Whether you find it in a practice in America or in continued work here is up to you, so long as you find it."

It took his breath away. The simple words, not entirely complimentary, showed that Jaeryn was not indifferent to those beneath him after all. Even in the midst of the man's push to win and his near fall from grace—in all that, he had not been as callous as he appeared.

Jaeryn smiled, and his green eyes sparkled with a little golden shine in the lamplight. "I'm not surprised you're staying longer. You'll make a proper British gentleman."

Ben opened his mouth in protest. "I have no intention of being British."

Jaeryn laughed outright. "That's what you think. I'd rather have you stay American; I like their view of the Irish more. But I think you bid fair to settle the dispute in England's favor."

Ben grimaced. "I hope not."

"It's not a bad thing," Jaeryn returned seriously. "It will keep you with us longer, though I don't expect we'll have you here forever."

Jaeryn looked tired. Ben knew that he should leave and give him a chance to rest. "I should be going now unless you need me to stay the night. If you need help until Terry gets off work, I'd be happy to stay."

Jaeryn shook his head. "I've kept you long enough. We can discuss some arrangements for the clinic in the morning. I'll need you to carry the bulk of the load until I get this sling off. You won't mind, will you?"

"Not at all. Goodnight."

Ben closed the door and left Jaeryn with his mug of tea near at hand, determined to finish putting everything in its proper place.

It was dark in the streets now, and he was on foot again to save cab fare. He wondered where his brother was. This was a cold night to be on the run, away from comforts and luxuries, with no one to offer him shelter. But Edmond would welcome the darkness since it hid him better. And this time Ben didn't mind it either, though for far different reasons. For the present, there was no threat in it and no sadness. Only a deep kind of ache for the past—an ache he was used to and could live with.

He had been here six months. Long enough to lose a great deal and gain something in return. He had decided to stay, though Evesham warned him that his assignment would have less room for error now. They would be searching for the details of the larger work of which Emmerson had written to Edmond. Speyer would turn over the evidence that he was saving if someone came in person for it. Perhaps that would give them enough to start on.

The air-raid sirens went off, but Ben ignored them and continued his trek homeward. He reached the point where the shops ended and entered the dark stretch between the town and the cliffs. He would start a life here, like Jaeryn advised. He had been reluctant to come in the first place because it delayed his plans, but what he had come to had proved to be not so very different, and perhaps a little better, than what he had left behind. This place had given him grief and pain, but he had found Alisa and Terry and Jaeryn, and Pearlie had found some happiness in her love-starved existence. They had seen some of the evil subdued, and he had done what his father asked of him. Jaeryn didn't understand why that was so important. Perhaps no one else did. But he knew that Matthew Dorroll counted more on his presence than he would say, and as long as his father needed him, he should have him. There were many people here whom he could help, and that was more important, in the end, than his practice.

The town dwellings gave way to fields already harvested for winter. Lamplight winked from the open shutters of Alisa's house. Terry must not be at work yet, for through the window Ben could see that he had made himself comfortable in the kitchen, and Patrick sat opposite him at the table, talking eagerly. In the corner of the room, Alisa stood listening to them in contented serenity. Charlotte came to the window to close the shutters, and she waved as he came up the drive.

Yes, it was right to stay. Make the work his own, Jaeryn had said. Well, he would try. He wasn't the most capable man for the kind of thing he had agreed to do, but that mattered not. Men more capable than he would show him what to do. He was willing to try his best since Allan Evesham was looking out for his interests. Perhaps he would like the Secret Service in time, but even if he didn't, his part in it wouldn't last forever. Only until the end of the war. And if this was to be home for the present, then he would take the whole, and take the broken, and see if by staying he could bring some healing to those who were left.

And with that, Ben unlatched the door and went in to join the others.

THE END

With Heartfelt Thanks

While only one name appears on a book's cover, a host of names combine to make this book possible with one Name over them all. I am blessed to be loved by Jesus, who has listened to every desperate prayer for wisdom and given me every resource necessary to write, but most of all, who has saved my soul. Without that, *War of Loyalties* just wouldn't matter at all.

To my parents and family, who worked to lovingly instill in me a love for God, a love for reading, and provided so many resources to help me in this writing journey. Thank you for your tireless commitment to help your daughter become an author, and for your strong support as your children pursue their dreams. I love you!

To my Kickstarter family: thank you for backing this project with your wallets, your kind words, and your constant support. I will never forget the joy on the night when we reached 100% funding together. I am so grateful for you.

To the Council: Emily, Elisabeth, Lydia, and Scott (and your family!) for spending many golden years sacrificing your time and creativity to get this book out of first draft stage and into each successive draft. Emily, you taught me how to write in a much more vibrant way than I ever could have done on my own as I watched you write your own beautiful books. Elisabeth, I will always treasure the encouraging feedback you sent me. Lydia and Scott, your excitement for the story inspired me to keep going on all those late Saturday nights. I am floored by the love. Thank you for bringing this book baby into being along with me.

To the generous people who gave their time for beta reading: Kaleigh, Suzannah, Bob, Michael, Kyla, and Lizzy. Thank you for reading this book and giving invaluable input on how to make it even better.

Many thanks to my editor, Steve Mathisen, for working with a tight schedule and bringing this book to a high level in both plot and copyediting that I never could have achieved alone. I am greatly indebted to his expertise.

Elisabeth Hayse gave an incredible sacrifice of love and time for the final line-editing and proofreading. I love this book so much more for her beautiful polishing.

For help with Jaeryn's Irish, Aoibhinn McNamara gave me her generous assistance, and Renee Ann offered her assistance with the French. Thank you so much, ladies!

A huge shout-out and thank you to the folks at Damonza for designing this beautiful cover—I am so thrilled. It brought *War of Loyalties* to life in a whole new way, and I could not be more pleased with the result.

To all the people who prayed for me throughout this process, especially my grandparents: you held up my hands when I was weary, and I'm so grateful to be able to rejoice in this answer to prayer now.

And thank you to everyone, with a special shout-out to Joy and Annie, for loving and cheering for this crowd of extra "friends" that seems to follow me wherever I go. It is my profound joy to share their story with you at last.

Bibliography & Author's Note

While it's impossible to remember all the ins and outs of research after seven years of work, there are a few key sources that I'd like to acknowledge in the making of this book.

Carlile, J.C. *Folkestone During the War: A Record of the Town's Life and Work, 1914-1917*. Folkestone: Parsons, 1930.

Whitehead, Ian R. *Doctors in the Great War*. Yorkshire: Pen & Sword, 2013.

Easdown, Martin. *A Grand Old Lady: The History of the Royal Victoria Hospital, Folkestone, 1846-1996*. Folkestone: League of Friends of the Royal Victoria Hospital, Folkestone, 1996

Harris, Paul. *Francis Frith's Around Folkestone*. Wiltshire: Frith Book Company, 2002.

Gilbert, Martin. *The First World War: A Complete History*. New York: Holt, 1994.

Liddell Hart, B.H. *World War I in Outline*. Yardley: Westholme, 2012.

Berg, A. Scott. *World War I and America: Told by the Americans Who Lived It*. New York: Library of America, 2017.

Zieger, Robert H. *America's Great War: World War I and the American Experience*. Oxford: Rowman & Littlefield, 2000.

Seaman, L.C.B. *Post-Victorian Britain, 1902-1951*. New York: Methuen, 1968.

Taylor, A.J.P. *The First World War: An Illustrated History*. New York: Penguin, 2009.

I am especially grateful to Ian R. Whitehead's book for the life of doctors in England during World War One, the rules about holding someone else's medical practice during the war, and a peek into the amount of work Ben and Jaeryn might have had to shoulder.

Carlile's *Folkestone During the War* provided invaluable help recreating the bomb drop scene, the committee chairwomen, and the memorial service.

Berg's *World War I and America* provided the initial inspiration for Creswick's support of pacifist propaganda.

While some of the locations on Tontine and around Folkestone are real, including Radnor Park, the Leas, and the Royal Victoria Hospital, the cottages at Copt Point and most of the other houses in Folkestone are dearly loved products of my imagination.

About the Author

Schuyler McConkey is a writing teacher, book reviewer, and ministry leader living half of her life in happy fellowship with her family and the other half in angst-filled fictional worlds. She is passionate about classic Dickensian stories and characters who have deep struggles touched by grace. Irish music, British movies, and chai lattes are the fuel for her dreams.

Drop a Note on Social Media:

Twitter: @schuylermc1
Website: www.ladybibliophile.blogspot.com
Facebook: @authorschuylermcconkey

Help Spread the News

Did you enjoy *War of Loyalties*? Would you consider leaving a review on Amazon or Goodreads? I'd love to hear your impressions!

Made in the USA
Columbia, SC
20 April 2018